DEIRDRE PURCELL

Falling
For a Dancer
and
Love Like
Hate Adore

D1151582

PAN BOOKS

Falling for a Dancer first published 1993 by Macmillan
and first published in paperback 1994 by Pan Books
Love Like Hate Adore first published in 1997 by Macmillan
and first published in paperback 1998 by Pan Books

This omnibus edition published 2003 by Pan Books
an imprint of Pan Macmillan Ltd
Pan Macmillan, 20 New Wharf Road, London N1 9RR
Basingstoke and Oxford
Associated companies throughout the world
www.panmacmillan.com

ISBN 0 330 42097 6

1 3 5 7 9 8 6 4 2

A CIP catalogue record for this book is available from
the British Library.

Printed and bound in Great Britain by
Mackays of Chatham plc, Chatham, Kent

FALLING FOR A DANCER

For my father, Bill

Acknowledgements

Heartfelt thanks to the following:

On Béara: Jerry and June Harrington, Joe Kelly, Doctor Colin Gleeson, Sergeant Willie Gleeson, Dr Aidan McCarthy and John L. Sullivan.

In Dublin: Robert Carrickford, Christopher and Glynis Casson, Jim Cantwell, Pat Brennan and my parents, Maureen and Bill Purcell.

Thanks also to Jimmy O'Mahoney of the Eccles Hotel in Glengarriff; Ray Hennessy from Bantry; Archdeacon Cathal McCarthy from Rush.

To Fiona Murray and Shane Price from Computing Workshop in Lombard Street and to Adrian Weckler for his help with research when time ran out.

Thanks to my editor, Jane Wood, to Hazel, to Charles and Treasa – and most particularly to Felicity Rubinstein whose faith I hope I'll justify.

And thanks to Kevin, Adrian and Simon for helping to keep the show on the road.

Chapter One

'Sorry, ladies and gentlemen, there's a problem with the fuel pump, I'll have to contact Maryborough – I'll be as quick as I can.' The driver's worried face vanished from the door opening.

The passengers groaned. Most got off the bus for the second time and stood about on the footpath; a few went back into Sheeran's pub. The village of Durrow was a traditional rest stop for travellers on the main road between the cities of Dublin and Cork and there had seemed nothing wrong with the vehicle as they pulled up as usual.

But after the customary twenty minutes' break, nothing the driver could do would start the vehicle again.

'Will we bother? Do you feel like a lemonade or anything?' By the way she offered, Elizabeth Sullivan tried to show her friend that she was so tired she was reluctant to move from her seat.

But Ida jumped to her feet and retrieved her handbag from where she had stashed it under the seat in front. 'Let's stretch our legs anyway! It's a lovely day, let's walk down to the green and have a goo at the marquee.' Her voice was taking on that cast of determination Elizabeth had learned to dread. She and Ida had been friends since their school-days but this trip to the Dublin Horse Show – a nineteenth-birthday gift from her parents – was the first occasion they had been thrown together twenty-four hours a day for an appreciable time.

During their school years, she had known Ida was highly charged but they had been day pupils and she had not fully realized just how strong was her friend's constitution, nor how relentless her proclivity for action. From the moment they had set foot in the capital, Ida had dragged

1

the two of them through a schedule which would have taxed the stamina of a marathon runner. Elizabeth's parents had set them up in the Shelbourne Hotel around which swirled the social side of Horse Show week, but both families had friends in Dublin and the girls had been provided with lists of names and telephone numbers. Ida had worked her way through every person on both lists so that day blurred into following day in a permanent bedlam of lunches and teas, parties and balls.

The repetitive chitchat had bored Elizabeth and, after the novelty of being in Dublin without having her parents in tow had worn off, she had found she was enduring rather than enjoying the holiday. Now, gritting her teeth for one last effort, she forced her body out of her seat to follow Ida, who bounced down the aisle as though she was just starting the week's activities.

'Whew! It seems to have got even hotter in the last five minutes.' Having alighted into the sunlit street, Ida set a brisk pace, walking a few feet ahead of Elizabeth, whose feet felt like dinnerplates as she trudged along.

'Come on, slowcoach!' At the edge of the green, Ida waited for her to catch up and took her arm. 'Don't forget to tell your parents what a great time we had and how much I appreciate it . . .'

Elizabeth barely listened. She had developed a habit of confining Ida's chatter to a particular part of her brain while the rest of it took on more restful pursuits, like absorbing the sights and sounds of the surroundings. Although she had passed through Durrow many times, both in her parents' car and in the bus, she had never before appreciated what a pretty place it was. In a country where the village and small-town streetscapes were usually narrow and straggled like uneven teeth, Durrow's wide green, bounded by substantial houses, an old Bianconi inn and the high stone walls surrounding Castledurrow lent an air of serenity and space. The green was recently mown. The cuttings, already turning to hay, spiced the humid air and on this August Sunday afternoon the village drowsed in peace, suggesting to Elizabeth, an avid reader, a likeness to some of the places she had pictured from the words of Jane Austen.

She started as Ida gave her an accusing dig in the ribs: 'You're not *listening* again, Beth.'

Elizabeth's attention returned. 'Sorry, what was it you said?'

'I was asking had you ever heard of this company?'

They had reached the play tent. Dun-coloured, crowned with tattered pennants, it sagged heavily at the roof-line but the canopy over the entrance porch had been freshly decorated with the twin masks of tragedy and comedy and sported the red legend: *Vivian Mellors' Touring Company, England, Ireland and the Commonwealth*. The word 'Ireland' had been overpainted in emerald green.

'No, I'm afraid not, but there are a lot of English companies around this year.' Elizabeth had no idea whether or not this was accurate.

'What about this play, then?' Ida pointed at the poster tacked to the front of the tent.

Elizabeth peered at the hand lettering:

TONIGHT! AT 8.30!
Great Variety Show, Full Script Drama, and Sketch
Back by Public Demand!

Mr Dion Boucicault's hilarious comedy,
CONN THE SHAUGHRAUN
(a CONTEMPORARY, NEW production specially designed
FOR THIS YEAR of 1937 with SPECIAL EFFECTS
never before seen in Ireland)
with FULL Company
STARRING (as The Shaughraun himself)
Mr Vivian Mellors
(*repeating the role Which Thrilled The Whole of Ireland and Many
of The Crowned Heads of Europe!*)
with:
Mr George Gallaher as dashing Captain Molyneaux
Mrs Lydia Smythe-Mellors as the beauteous Arte O'Neal
and
Miss Claudette Latimer as her Comely Cousin, Claire Ffolliott

And Introducing Durrow's Very Own New Canine Star,
RODDY
Playing, 'Tatters The Little Dog'.

Then, on a separate piece of paper tacked on at the end:

This Show is Guaranteed to be Free of Vulgarity

'I've heard of *The Shaughraun*,' said Elizabeth, 'but I've never seen it.'

'What's it about?'

'I told you I haven't seen it!' She tried to keep her irritation from showing. 'Something to do with the British army in Ireland, I believe.'

'Hey!' Ida was off on another tack. 'Speaking of armies, what did you *really* think of *Mister* DeValera parading like that at the Horse Show? How many more years of him do we have to put up with?'

'Look, shouldn't we go back to the bus now?' Elizabeth, who cared nothing about politics, tried to avert a political discussion. 'The driver said he wouldn't be too long,' she continued, but without much hope. Ida's family, who hated everything about the re-elected Taoiseach, and her own, had supported opposite sides in the civil war which had ended fifteen years previously. DeValera's re-election had already been thrashed out between them several times during the week.

This time, however, she was lucky; Ida was still gazing at the playbill. 'Mmm, I suppose,' she said. 'I love plays. Pity we can't stay to see this one.'

'We might, by the looks of things.' The terrifying thought of another twenty-four hours with her ultra-active friend was enough to spark Elizabeth's spirit a little. 'If we do have to stay here,' she said firmly, 'I'm having an early night. All right?'

'Don't worry about it, Beth, we won't have to stay. The driver'll get it fixed, they always do . . . Let's see what's in here.' Ida attempted to pull open the doorflap of the tent.

Sighing, Elizabeth joined her.

They found their view obscured by a securely fastened inner sheet.

'May I help you?' The mellifluous voice made both girls jump.

Even Ida was dumbstruck as they wheeled round to see

4

the man who was standing behind them. Elizabeth, who was taller than the norm and whose shoes had two-inch heels, came up only as far as the middle of his chest. Dressed in a curiously cut pale suit, spats, high collar and wide green tie emblazoned with a palm tree, he stood easily six feet three or four. 'The show doesn't start until eight-thirty,' he continued, as though unaware of the effect he was having on them, 'but I'd be glad to give two such delightful young ladies an advance tour.'

'Th-thank you.' Ida had found her voice. 'But I'm afraid we're here only for a short while. We're on that bus, you see.'

'Mmm!' The actor placed a hand on his heart and raised his voice:

> '"Riddle of Destiny, who can show
> What thy short visit meant, or know
> What thy errand here below?"'

He smiled at their shocked expressions. 'Charles Lamb,' he explained. Then he inserted both thumbs into the waistband of his trousers – exposing a darn in the stuff of his waistcoat – and added in a normal tone of voice, 'Sure you won't change your minds and stay?'

'I don't think so, Mr – er –' surreptitiously, Ida glanced at the billboard, 'Mellors?'

'Unfortunately, no,' said the man. 'I'm not the boss just yet – have high hopes, though!' He bowed. 'George Gallaher,' he said gaily, 'at your service, girls.'

Elizabeth could see that the actor's physique, good looks and charm were having the same effect on Ida as they were on herself. She had never before seen so gorgeous a creature. She cleared her throat. 'You're playing the Captain in the play?'

'Yes. I'm great, too. What a pity you won't see me, Miss – ?'

'Sullivan,' Elizabeth supplied, 'Elizabeth Sullivan. And this is my friend,' she went on, 'Ida Healy. We're both from Cork city.'

'Ah yes, Cork,' he sighed, 'by the lovely Lee. Know it

5

well. I might have known the two of you were from there. Best-looking women in Ireland!' Utterly at ease, he smiled at each of them in turn.

Elizabeth, flustered, tried to guess at his age; his face was smooth but he was so self-assured she decided he had to be more than forty. And there was a peculiarity in his phrasing and accent she could not place. 'You're not Irish yourself?' she asked.

'Why? Do you not like Irishmen?' His eyes looked so frankly at her that she felt herself grow hot.

Then he relented. 'I'm Scottish, as a matter of fact. But this is my second season in Ireland. Great place. Love the porter,' his eyes, so blue as to be almost violet, creased, 'not to speak of the women.' This close, he smelled faintly of *eau-de-Cologne* and of old clothes, like a chemist's shop on a fair day; he also had a way of speaking that cut out all the surrounding material, the old tent, the green, even the sunshine. And to Elizabeth's consternation, he seemed to be cutting out Ida too.

On the other hand she felt absurdly glad that she had decided that morning to wear her 'good' dress of yellow crêpe-de-Chine.

She detected Ida's tug at her left arm. 'Very nice meeting you, Mr Gallaher,' her friend was saying, in a high, thin voice, 'but I'm afraid we must get back to our bus now.' It had not been her imagination, Elizabeth thought, her unsettled feeling growing: Ida had detected she was being left out and was nettled.

'Such a pity you have to go.' The actor grinned at Elizabeth. 'I would so have loved to have had you see me tonight.' He widened his eyes provocatively but before Elizabeth could respond, he had crooked both elbows and bent his blue gaze on Ida. 'At least let me escort you both back to the bus?'

Although she knew full well he was performing, Elizabeth, who had always thought of herself as forthright and quite sophisticated, felt as impressionable as a child. She had never in her life encountered such an extraordinary person with such a direct approach. She was about to take

6

his arm when she felt Ida pulling her away. 'Thank you, that won't be necessary.'

'Ida, Ida,' he chided, 'there be robbers about these here parts. And have you never heard of the Durrow Ripper?'

Ida was mollified. 'Oh, for goodness' sake, Mr Gallaher!'

But he was unabashed, smiling at the two of them like a schoolboy sure of indulgent parents. 'Well, come on, shall we?'

Ida was mesmerized into taking the proffered elbow. 'What part of Scotland are you from, Mr Gallaher?' she asked, and Elizabeth, who needed time to cover her own confusion, was glad to hear the unusual uncertainty in her friend's voice.

'Glasgow.' The actor adjusted his long stride to theirs.

'But you don't really have a Scottish accent.' Ida had recovered.

As they walked across the grass, Elizabeth became aware that while George Gallaher continued to maintain a bantering conversation with Ida, something was happening to herself that she could barely believe. Under the actor's arm, hers was gradually being squeezed harder and harder until she was forced into such close contact with him that her hip was grazing his and his forearm massaged her breast.

She glanced across at Ida but it was obvious from her friend's animated expression that the same thing was not happening to her.

With the bus less than forty yards away now, she felt she should do something to break free. The sensation, though, was anything but unpleasant.

The blood rose and fell several times in Elizabeth's face while she dithered as to how or whether to react.

The decision was taken out of her domain as they arrived at the bus. 'Here we are!' Although he did not let go of her arm, Gallaher released the pressure with such disturbing suddenness that she almost staggered. 'We seem to be the only ones here,' he went on calmly, surveying the empty vehicle as though the closeness of the physical contact between himself and this girl he had known for five minutes had been a normal part of a customary Sunday afternoon stroll.

He glanced over his shoulder towards Sheeran's. 'Your fellow travellers have clearly decided that this is a heaven-sent opportunity.' Then, decrying his casualness, he again looked directly at Elizabeth and fluttered one eyelid in a wink.

Reeling, the side of her breast tingling, Elizabeth went to mount the steps of the bus but he held her back: 'Hold on – surely you wouldn't prefer to sit all alone in that decrepit-looking thing on such a nice day and with such great company available out here?'

'Good idea,' Ida cried. 'Let's all have a drink.'

'Go into that pub? But we couldn't.' Elizabeth was totally taken aback. Ida well knew that segregation of the sexes, unofficial but unbending, was the practice in pubs. Women, if tolerated at all, were herded into snugs or, in the case of Sheeran's, into the ladies' 'parlour'.

'Come on.' The actor grinned his wickedest grin. 'Let's all three go in together for a drink. Scandalize the good burghers of Durrow. What harm could it be? The worst that can happen is they'll talk about us and won't the two of you be gone in a few minutes? So what do you care what anyone says?'

Elizabeth found her voice. 'But what about you? You have to stay here – your play tonight.'

'Actors are a lost cause, everyone knows that. And anyway,' he went on cheerfully, 'I've a special dispensation. Everyone loves me, lets me get away with murder.' He took her hand and bent his head over it, keeping his eyes fixed on hers. 'Don't *you* love me already, Elizabeth?'

'Oh, come on, Beth, don't be a spoilsport,' Ida cut in. 'Anyway, he's right, how much scandal can we cause? This is nineteen thirty-seven, for God's sake, not the Middle Ages. And even if they do talk about us, what difference does it make? He's right, we don't know any of these people and we'll probably never see any of them again.'

But as they went through the door of the pub, Ida

8

leading, Elizabeth's nerve failed. 'Sorry,' she whispered, pushing past George Gallaher and out into the street, 'you two go ahead. I'm – I'm very tired, I think I'll just go and sit on the bus after all.'

'You're so right, Elizabeth.' To her confusion, Gallaher promptly turned and followed her. 'It's much too glorious a day to spend it sitting in a stuffy saloon. What'll we do now?' Effortlessly, it seemed, George Gallaher had created a threesome.

Elizabeth spotted the bus driver and another man hurrying towards them and did not know whether to be relieved or disappointed. 'Let's wait and see what the driver has to say,' she offered.

The man accompanying the driver turned out to be the village blacksmith who peeled off the jacket of his Sunday suit. One or two at a time, the other passengers drifted out of the pub and joined Elizabeth, Ida and George in watching the blacksmith tinker with the exposed engine. When the number of bodies present was sufficient to be called a crowd, Gallaher, who up to then had seemed concerned only with the work going on in the bowels of the bus, pulled himself up to his full height. 'Good afternoon, ladies and gentlemen!' he intoned, so loudly that several members of the group stepped back in alarm.

'We are the Vivian Mellors company of actors,' George continued, his voice playing like bells across the startled faces, 'perhaps one day we will come to your town.' Out of his waistcoat pocket he took a handful of small, crudely printed playbills. 'Perhaps,' distributing them, 'happily, the good Lord has sent you to support us even tonight . . .

'I, madam,' he bent over the hand of an elderly woman in a black coat, 'play Captain Molyneaux in our play. I am honourable, I crave the hand of the maiden and I wear *uniform* . . .' He twinkled at the woman so outrageously that she burst into nervous laughter. 'And,' he stood back to encompass all of them, 'because it is Sunday, and our last night here, our raffle tonight is for a whole *ten pounds* . . . Ladies and gentlemen, your ship is coming in!'

Watching George Gallaher's performance with the

passengers, Elizabeth wanted very much for the bus to stay broken. Although, like most of her friends, she had flirted with boys in Cork – more particularly, when she and her parents went on holiday to the seaside resort of Crosshaven – this assault on her senses was a revelation. Since early childhood she had tended towards superstition and now searched the street for a suitable omen.

It came immediately as the driver approached the group. 'Bad news, I'm afraid,' he said. 'I thought we might be able to do a temporary repair but it seems we can't.' Behind him the blacksmith, Elizabeth saw, was wiping his hands on a rag and nodding agreement. 'I've been in touch with Maryborough,' the driver went on, 'but the spare bus there is out of action as well. They're trying to get a part for us but it looks like the only hope is to get on to Dublin and to get a replacement car from there. But this being Sunday, I'm afraid that with the best will in the world it'll be a few hours, at the very least, before we can go on.'

'What time does the train go through?' It was one of the male passengers.

'Ye've missed the one from Maryborough,' replied the blacksmith on the driver's behalf, 'but there's a slow train that stops at Attanah at around seven this evening.'

As the group turned to commiserate with one another, George Gallaher held up his hand. 'Ladies, gentlemen, please! Why not stay in one of Durrow's fine lodging houses and make your evening's entertainment complete with a visit to our show tonight?'

'Some of us have work in the morning,' said a young man.

'"When fate summons, monarchs must obey."' The sweep of Gallaher's arm was so wide he knocked the hat off the head of a woman immediately to his right.

But most of the group showed little interest in fate or in play-acting and began to discuss with the bus driver how best they could get home. George gave in, shrugging at Ida and Elizabeth as though they, being of finer feelings like himself, were the only two within the group who would understand the rare treat he was offering.

10

In the end it was decided that the local hackney should be summoned to take the passengers to Attanah station, making as many trips as would be necessary. The blacksmith went to fetch the vehicle and its driver, and while an argument began with the bus driver about who would pay for this service, George detached Elizabeth and Ida. 'You'll stay, surely? There's bound to be another bus tomorrow.'

'What do you think?' Reversing her wishes of only half an hour previously, Elizabeth hoped that Ida's enthusiasm for adventures had not waned.

But Ida made her wait. 'Oh, I don't know,' she said, looking off into the distance. 'For instance, how could we get word to Cork? They'll be worried if we don't show up tonight.'

'Surely everyone who travels on this route is well used to such delays, alarums and excursions. Are your families on the telephone?'

George Gallaher seemed to be taking charge of their lives so completely that Elizabeth felt a little like Alice in the grip of the White Rabbit. 'Both our parents have telephones,' she said faintly.

'Wonderful,' Gallaher chirped. 'I'll accompany you to the post office. It might be Sunday but I know the postmistress.' For the second time, he winked at Elizabeth.

'Just think, Ida,' Elizabeth said quickly, trying not to let her friend see just how important it had now become to stay in Durrow, 'another day off work.' She knew Ida detested her job as a clerk in one of Cork's retail stores. 'And we would have a perfectly good excuse,' she added. 'No one could blame us.'

'What's happened to your tiredness all of a sudden?' Ida was determined not to make it easy.

'I feel fine.' Elizabeth was surprised to find this was the truth. She felt energized, alert and overpoweringly aware of the sweet and sour smell of the huge man standing only a few inches away.

'It's settled, then.' George drew them away from the group which was still discussing the shortcomings of the Catherwood bus company.

11

'Only if we can find decent lodgings, mind,' Ida warned.

'Ida, hand on heart,' he splayed his fingers over the buttons of his waistcoat, 'you can trust me. I would never, *never* place two such beautiful girls in discomfort.'

'I said enough!' But a smile twitched at the corner of Ida's mouth.

As they were travelling light, retrieving their luggage was simply a matter of getting into the bus and taking the valises off the overhead rack.

The postmistress, on whom George's charms had clearly been worked before, co-operated fully in the making of the telephone calls but neither set of parents answered in Cork. 'It's a fine Sunday afternoon, naturally they'd be out taking the air.' Gallaher remained blithe. 'We can try later.'

He led them around the handful of village landladies, bringing them eventually to a solid, two-storey house, one of a terrace opposite the gates of the castle. This establishment enjoyed, in his opinion, the inestimable privilege of being within sight of his theatrical marquee. But the landlady seemed reluctant to take them. 'Will ye be wanting to wash yeer hair?'

'Mrs Cahill prefers male guests,' Gallaher explained. 'She has to fetch all her water from the pump, you see, so it's a bit awkward to take actresses. These ladies are not with our company, Mrs Cahill,' he bestowed on the woman his most incandescent smile, 'they find themselves here unexpectedly, stranded by the bus.'

'All right,' the woman said, standing aside in the tiny hallway of the house to let them pass.

'I'll reserve passes for you both for the performance. *A bientôt.*' Taking his leave, George Gallaher kissed each of them in the French manner, chastely on both cheeks. As he bussed Elizabeth, however, he contrived to slip his hand under her hair, brushing the skin at the back of her neck with his fingers in such a way that her scalp prickled. 'You're beautiful,' he whispered into her ear, so quickly and quietly that she might have thought she had imagined it, and when

12

she looked at his face, it was as mild and inscrutable as the one on the Child of Prague. 'I'll see you this evening.' He included both of them. 'Now don't run away after the show. Wait for me outside the tent.' With a final smile, he turned and walked away.

Elizabeth followed the landlady down the hall and into a ground-floor room. Smelling of lavender and beeswax and furnished with a brass featherbed, washstand and mahogany dressers, it shone with care and cleanliness and its shadowy coolness felt like a shower of rain on her hot cheeks. After the woman had closed the door and left them alone, Elizabeth dropped her bag and stepped out of her dress, draping it carefully across the back of a chair. She glanced at Ida, who was pacing the room, taking up and replacing objects – a porcelain oil lamp, a set of bagpipes on a sideboard, a pair of china dogs flanking the aspidistra in the window well – as though she were picking over a huckster's stall. For some reason she could not yet fathom, Elizabeth did not want Ida to mention George Gallaher. 'I'm so tired,' she said, 'I think I'll have a little rest.' Removing the brocade coverlet from the bed she sank into the feathers and turned her face to the wall.

'I'm not tired.' Ida restored a china dog to its niche on a bureau. 'I'm going out again for a walk, all right? I'll have another go at the telephone.'

'All right,' Elizabeth mumbled, trying to give the impression she was already half asleep.

But when she heard the door close behind Ida, she threw herself on her back. Images of the last hour paraded in quick succession across the low ceiling: George Gallaher's stance, those violet eyes, most of all the feel of his arm against her breast and of his fingers under her hair . . .

On the other hand, the actor's own hair, thick and worn longer than was fashionable, was suspiciously and uniformly reddish brown. Did he dye it? And those spats: she had noticed they were frayed around the buttons. The white old-fashioned suit, the palm tree on his tie, the darn on his waistcoat – he was not exactly the type of person a

13

girl could bring into her daddy's office on the South Mall. Elizabeth realized she was deliberately trying to dampen down her excitement.

But her aroused senses were operating independently of her brain.

The exterior sounds filtering through the sunlit lace curtains at the windows were muted and peaceful: from the pump directly in front of the house, neighbours' quiet conversation over the flood of water into buckets; from the backyard, a pig's intermittent grunt and the subdued chatter of hens. Elizabeth tried to calm down by letting herself slide into the peace of it all. Turning on her side, she attempted to sleep and pictured herself back at her desk, as a sober assistant-to-an-assistant in her father's office.

By the time Ida came back from her walk, however, Elizabeth was in a state of high excitement at the prospect of seeing George Gallaher again. Yet she could not let Ida see this and, stretching in the featherbed as though she had just woken, she smiled. 'Well, any more adventures out there?'

'Sunday afternoon. You know what Sunday's like in the hick towns of Ireland.' The outing had restored Ida's good humour. 'If it wasn't for those play-actors, this place'd be as dead as a doornail. I got through to my parents, though – Daddy said he'd ring yours. I thought the postmistress was a decent enough soul, didn't you?'

'Yeah, thanks for saving me the bother.'

'You're welcome.' Ida undid the clasp on her bag and rummaged around inside.

'Did you meet any more of them? The play-actors, I mean.' Elizabeth tried to keep her voice casual.

'No, but I saw two of them, another man and a woman.' Ida came over to sit on the bed. 'You wouldn't believe it, Beth. You know how hot and sticky it is out there?'

'Mmm . . .' Elizabeth pretended to yawn.

'Well, the woman was parading up and down the street with a fox fur around her neck!'

'Parading?'

'You know what I mean. *And* they went into the pub!'

'Good for them. What time is it? My watch has stopped.' Elizabeth's wristwatch, a present from her parents for her eighteenth birthday, had been keeping perfectly good time the last time she had checked but she did not trust herself with this conversation.

'It's nearly seven.' Ida kicked off her shoe and massaged her toes. 'Are you hungry?'

'Oh, no, it's much too hot to eat. But I think I'll have a wash and start getting ready. To go to the play, I mean.' Elizabeth rolled off the bed, went to the washstand and, in pouring water from the jug into the basin, made a great deal of noise.

Chapter Two

An hour later, as she and Ida stood on the footpath opposite the high wall of the castle, Elizabeth noticed immediately that the atmosphere in the village had quickened. Playing tig, children raced around the green; a small group of men lounged at the street corner nearest the boarding house and, across the road, a few more gossiped in front of the castle gates. The green was roughly bisected by the main Cork road and on the far side, two hundred yards from where the girls stood, a dozen men had stationed themselves where they would have a good view of anything that might happen around the marquee.

As yet, although the entrance porch gaped open, there was no sign of the players.

'I wonder did they manage to fix that bus?' The butterflies were beginning in Elizabeth's stomach and she was determined not to let them take control.

'Let's go and see.' Ida was being agreeable but as they strolled around the corner and saw the bus had not been moved, she sharpened. 'I wonder are we the only eejits to stay – hey! What's happening now?' All the children on the green had started to run in the same direction.

Elizabeth heard what had attracted the children's attention: tinny music, issuing from the street they had just vacated. She and Ida turned back and as they again rounded the corner, caught sight of the entrance march of the Vivian Mellors Touring Company.

Preceded by a girl playing a piano accordion, a lorry was being driven slowly down the hill; its bed carried a ship's piano, at which sat a woman with hair as vividly red as new paint on a fire tender. Her lips and cheeks were

16

almost as fiery and although her plump, bangled arms were bare, the head, feet and tail of a fox dangled around her neck and bosom. On a stool beside her sat a small, fat man in a white, full-sleeved blouse, tight trousers and a satin cummerbund of midnight blue. He appeared to be leaning on a crutch.

Two young men dressed like soldiers walked to attention behind the lorry and behind them strode a couple, who, Elizabeth presumed, were Mr Vivian Mellors and the leading lady of the company. Mr Mellors, dressed in a costume which might have been Shakespearean, or even clerical, kept in step with the march-time music. Although the street was sparsely populated, he waved an arm in continuous benediction, first to one side, then the other. The woman at his side had caught her hair in a snood; under the evening sun, her long, full-skirted dress flashed with jewels and sequins. She made no attempt to walk in time to the music but glided along as though on castors, the front of the dress bunched in both hands to keep it clear of the dust.

Next came Roddy, Durrow's New Canine Star. A happy, overweight little Pomeranian, he panted along at the end of his leash, borne to his last night of glory by his beaming owner.

Two girls were next, dressed more simply than the leading lady but their dresses, too, were long and sparkling; one was tall and pretty, the other, much younger, had a squint. But both smiled with great determination and jingled streamered tambourines from side to side in time to the march.

But Elizabeth's sight was riveted on the tailguard of the parade. A heavy velvet cloak flowed from George Gallaher's wide shoulders as he strode along in slow, booted glory. He had added a luxuriant moustache to his face; the scabbard at his side and the buttons on his redcoat uniform gleamed with brass and, completely out of period, ostrich plumes waved grandly above his Napoleonic hat. The only other occasion on which Elizabeth had seen a vision of such

17

splendid confidence had been among the massed bishops at the Eucharistic Congress held five years previously in Dublin.

'My God!' breathed Ida at her side. 'Would you take a look at that . . .'

Gallaher spotted the two of them as he came up to them, raised his plumed hat and grinned in their direction. Elizabeth was horrified that they had been singled out from the other parade-watchers. She did not dare look round to see what the reaction was; at the same time, he was so spectacularly attractive that, when Ida pulled her into the street to join the little bunch of people who were following the procession, even had she tried, she could not have summoned an ounce of resistance.

The tent was packed solid by the time the performance began forty minutes later. As act succeeded act during the variety show which preceded the play, the tension in Elizabeth's stomach grew – although she had to admit that the Vivian Mellors Touring Company was nothing if not versatile. The man with the crutch – he had only one leg – turned out to be a tenor of huge power if little subtlety; then the girl played popular tunes on her accordion.

At the end of the set, acknowledging the applause from the audience who evidently approved of effort, the little girl switched to a Scottish lilt and George Gallaher walked solemnly on to the pocket stage.

He had changed his splendid uniform for a kilt, complete with sporran. Placing a pair of swords across one another at his feet, he raised both arms to shoulder height and proceeded to dance around and through them with more energy than skill, possibly because he had to keep his head bent to avoid butting the low canvas ceiling. From her seat near the back, Elizabeth could see only his bobbing torso – but he was not wearing a jacket, and the sight reminded her of their physical contact of that afternoon. Her heart began to thud painfully against her ribcage.

The acts which followed the sword dance flowed through her brain like dreams: a juggling act by the young

18

accordion player, a Negro spiritual sung by the two younger actresses who had blackened their faces, another Neapolitan song from the tenor; then 'The Rose of Mooncoin' rendered by the leading lady and a sonorous recitation of 'Dangerous Dan McGrew' by Mr Vivian Mellors himself.

George Gallaher came out a second time for the finale, an ensemble version by the entire company of Percy French's 'Abdul A Bul Bul Emir'. Head and shoulders above everyone else, he stood at the back of the group but although Elizabeth could see his lips move, she could not distinguish his voice over the booming of the one-legged tenor.

During the short interval which followed the variety show, at Ida's urging – 'Ten *pounds*, Beth!' – she bought a handful of raffle tickets. Then the curtain parted on the play.

Conn The Shaughraun was well known to the audience. They cheered the patriot-hero, booed the villains, roared with knowing delight when the heroines ran idiomatic Irish rings around George, alias the very English Captain Molyneaux. And when Conn, carrying Tatters/Roddy sprang onto the stage from the wings, the applause went on for a full minute before he opened his mouth.

Even to Elizabeth's relatively inexperienced eye, George Gallaher, although magnificent as a peacock in full display, was a dreadful actor. To be fair, none of the others, particularly the tenor who played the traitor, Harvey Duff, would have won any awards, but they had a certain enthusiastic sincerity. Gallaher used his beautiful voice like an organ and struck the right poses but, as a performer, he was about as natural as a hen's tooth.

Elizabeth was greatly relieved. Half unwilling to admit it, she had been asking herself why someone who looked and seemed so extraordinary would be travelling the small towns of Ireland with a fit-up company and not be performing the stages of Dublin, or even London. She had even entertained the suspicion that he might have a criminal record and be hiding out in this country.

Now, seeing his graceful but inappropriate movements, it was evident that George Gallaher was merely a big, beautiful ham.

The play, abridged to fifty minutes, finished to wild clapping throughout the tent. 'What did you think?' Ida dug Elizabeth in the ribs while they were waiting for the final part of the show which was to be a 'sketch'.

'I thought it was very good.' Elizabeth hesitated. 'I thought Vivian Mellors was great as Conn and the woman who played Arte O'Neal —'

'Yes,' Ida interrupted, 'but what did you think of our friend, Gorgeous George?'

'Oh, he was all right.' Elizabeth studied the planking on the floor under her seat. 'He wasn't the best actor, by a long chalk.'

Half to her relief, George was not in the final sketch – a knockabout comedy routine peppered with local references which were greatly enjoyed by the audience. When it was over, Elizabeth, claiming she needed to get out of the stuffy tent to get some fresh air, did not wait for the raffle.

'Well, I'm staying, I could do with ten pounds. Here, give me your tickets.' Ida took them out of Elizabeth's hand and fanned them out with her own. 'I'll see you outside when this is over, all right?'

Outside, the green was deserted except for a few people unlucky enough not to have the sixpence it cost to get into the show. They hung around the entrance, however, being able to follow the show with their ears, if not their eyes.

Anyhow, it was not necessary to be inside to get the benefit of 'O Sole Mio', now being reprised by the tenor while the final pennies were being extracted from the audience for the 'last few' raffle tickets. The soaring voice followed Elizabeth as she walked slowly across the dark grass towards the far side of the green.

A cat slunk from under the moribund bus as Elizabeth came close; she watched it make a dash across the road and vanish through an opening in the rotting wood of a yardway gate, then she leaned against the cool metal, willing herself to calm down and to get sense.

20

You'll never see him again . . . How could someone like that be really interested in someone like you? . . . He's just passing the time with you . . . He probably does the same thing with someone in every town in Ireland . . .

As the song finished and the applause which followed died down, Elizabeth's ears adjusted and she began to hear other sounds coming from behind the façades and gateways of the quiet houses: a sharp, single bark from a dog, the guttural murmur of a hen settling more comfortably on her roost, a whicker from a horse.

There was no moon but the sky, heavily quilted with stars, glittered like an inverted chalice over the roofs and chimneys of the village. Etched against its brightness the crenellated gate lodge and high walls of the castle appeared to be as theatrical as any painted backdrop; so were the solid lines of the houses, broken only with a few squares and rectangles as light spilled through windows and open doors. But no artifice, Elizabeth thought, could have replicated the familiar smells.

Although she had been born and bred in Cork city, from where she was standing Elizabeth could identify the distinctive aroma of an Irish country town: grass, manure and hay, horses, lamp paraffin, turf-smoke, chicken droppings and the peculiar sharpness of the gravel with which the roads were dressed blended together in a sweetish cocktail. Even as she identified this, however, her eyes were fixed on the marquee, riding its dark moorings like a bright yacht, the hangers-on moving like shadows against its yellowy walls.

She recognized Gallaher just as the flaps of the entrance were thrown back to let out the audience. He had changed out of his uniform but she saw he was carrying it, complete with cloak and plumed hat.

He came from behind the tent, strolling around the side and into the centre of the green where he stopped and looked in her direction. Her heart thudded. Had he seen her?

Evidently he had because he began to walk directly towards her. 'Hello again,' he said as he loomed over her. 'I saw you and your friend. Did you enjoy the show?'

21

'Very – very much,' stammered Elizabeth. 'Thank you for the passes.'

'My pleasure,' he said, then looked over his shoulder. 'Where is Ida, by the way?'

'She waited for the raffle. I – I was too hot. So I came out. Yes, it was very hot in there.' She heard herself gabbling and could have kicked herself. 'You were very good in the play,' she said more firmly. 'I – we both enjoyed your performance very much.'

'So did half the crowned heads of Europe,' he said, the irony so clear she could only smile. 'Look,' he said then, 'it's a lovely evening, would you care to go for a walk?'

'Sure,' she said brightly. 'Just let me go and get Id–'

'Just the two of us.' He gathered both her hands into his and bent his head so his face was only inches from hers. 'Enough of the twin-sister act.' The uniform over his arm smelled even more musty than the suit of the afternoon but his breath was scented with mint. 'Don't misunderstand me,' he continued, 'Ida's very nice, I like her. But it's you I'm interested in.'

Joy and panic fought together in Elizabeth's breast. 'I – I don't know how–'

'–you're going to tell her? Leave that to me.'

'No, that's not what I was going to say.'

'Then what, Elizabeth?' Over his shoulder, Elizabeth could see the crowd spreading out over the green. It would be a matter of seconds before Ida joined them. What she had been about to say was something stupid and childish, an automatic query as to why someone like him was interested in someone like her.

'Elizabeth?' he asked again. 'What was it you were going to say?'

'I – I'd love to go for a walk.' For a split second, Ida's thunderous face hovered before Elizabeth's eyes. 'For a short walk!' she added desperately.

'Wonderful. It's such a warm evening we'll walk down by the river. Stay here. I'll find Ida and tell her.'

Giddy with trepidation, Elizabeth watched him weave

his way through the people in the green, pausing from time to time to accept congratulations.

She saw Ida before George did. Her friend was standing just in front of the lighted opening to the tent, looking right and left, obviously seeking her. Like a thief, Elizabeth shrank into the shadows behind the bus.

Then George Gallaher also spotted Ida and as Elizabeth continued to watch, he walked across and, for an agonizingly long time, engaged her in conversation.

Elizabeth's legs seemed to lose the power to support her as she saw Ida's head snap round in her own direction and just as quickly snap back. *Stop it!* she admonished herself. She wouldn't be thinking about you if things were the other way round . . .

She saw Gallaher's arm go around Ida's shoulder and the two of them walk a few steps in her direction; for a moment, she thought they were coming right over to her and took a step forward. But they stopped, he kissed Ida's cheek and, without looking in Elizabeth's direction, Ida walked away towards the lodging house.

'What did you say to her?' Elizabeth allowed Gallaher to take her arm and propel her along the periphery of the green.

'I said we were going to have an affair. Good evening!' Gallaher bowed to a wellwisher.

'You did not!'

'You're right. I told her I was in love with her and couldn't wait to see her and had to get rid of you first.'

'Mr Gallaher! Please – what did you really say to her?'

'Evening!' Serene as a yacht in full sail, George acknowledged the open stares of a small group of Durrow citizens as he escorted Elizabeth across the open space in front of the arched bridge at the bottom of the town. 'What's that you said?'

'Don't tease me, please. What did you say to her?'

The hump of the bridge was occupied by two youths who had turned from their contemplation of the river to gawk at them. 'Lovely evening, isn't it?' Gallaher, still imperturbable, raised his hat to them as he bore Elizabeth off the bridge and down on to the bank beside it.

A little towpath, beaten from the grass with much usage, meandered along the edge of the fields a few feet above the water. From where they stood, Elizabeth could see that two courting couples had already taken up residence on the riverbank just below it. Horrified, she pulled her arm out from under George Gallaher's. Was this what he had in mind for her – to make a public show of her?

'Easy.' He retrieved her arm and tucked it back under his. 'How horrible! Some people have no sense of decency.'

She looked sharply at him but could not detect whether he was making fun of her. 'I didn't mean—'

'Of course you did. And you are quite right. Come with me.'

As they walked along the little pathway away from the town, in Elizabeth's ears the subsequent silence between them, broken only by the shuffle of their feet against the dry earth, spread then sank like a rock into deep water. For the life of her she could not think of anything ordinary to say.

George Gallaher did not seem to mind. He led her off the pathway and into an open space beside a curious stone monument rearing like a blunted needle against the sparkling sky. 'I know it's round and doesn't look at all like one but that's the obelisk.' He turned her to face it and standing behind her, dropped his costume on the ground and put his arms around her from behind. 'Hello,' he whispered.

'I see.' Elizabeth, standing rigidly in the circle of his arms, felt she might explode with tension. 'What – what is it, do you know?'

'Apparently it's to commemorate the death of some girl in the hunting field.'

He picked up the heavy cloak and flung it in front of her, using it like a tie to bind her to him. 'They say she haunts the place where she died,' he breathed in a sepulchral whisper, 'they sa-ay when you see her she's all in white.'

'I – I see.' Imprisoned by the cloak, Elizabeth did not dare move a muscle. But she knew it was only a matter of

24

time before he kissed her. She tried to prevent herself from licking her lips.

Then he surprised her by scooping her off her feet and carrying her like a child across the grass towards a pair of entwined ash trees. Unsure of what to do, she lay stiffly in his arms, surprised at the coldness of the button which scraped against her cheek.

'Elizabeth,' he said when he put her down, 'look at me.' His face was in shadow but she caught the faint sheen of his eyes as he bent to kiss her mouth.

The kiss was gentle, his lips soft and quiet. He did not prolong it or force a response, pulling back to look at her, his eyes black in the darkness. 'You're very lovely, a lovely yellow flower.' His voice was serious and tender. He shook out the cloak and spread it over a flat place between the trunks of the twinned ash. 'Come, sit beside me, don't be alarmed.' Lowering himself, he patted the space beside him.

Elizabeth's body was tauter now than ever with nervousness – and anticipation; she knew there was no going back now without serious loss of face. He caught her to him as, doing what he asked, she sat down beside him. Slowly, he pulled her backwards with him until he was lying with his head pillowed against the tree and hers caught to his chest. 'Eliza-beth, Elizabeth.' His voice caressed the word like the bow of a cello on its strings as he raised the hair on the back of her neck with his fingers, combing it through and letting it fall back on her shoulders. 'Never cut that lovely hair,' he breathed into her ear. 'In this light it's as soft and bright as liquid silver.'

'It's – it's too thick.' Elizabeth's hair was strawberry blonde and defied all attempts to curl or wave it.

'That's sacrilege.' As he continued to play with it, she could feel the hair lift of its own accord off her scalp. Although she had kissed and been kissed before, any previous physical contact between herself and boys had been clumsy and rushed, producing nothing like this novel and exquisite set of sensations.

As George Gallaher maintained his combing action,

25

little by little, she began to relax. He took her face and kissed her again, longer than the first time and a little more insistently but still so sweetly that her own lips parted. He flicked his tongue briefly inside her mouth, just once, and came away. 'Eliza-beth, sweetest little thing . . .' He kissed the base of her neck and used his tongue like a butterfly's wing against the skin behind her ear. Reflexively, Elizabeth arched her back and wound her fingers into his thick hair; she did not want him to stop, ever.

But then he slid his head off the tree so he was flat on his back and looking up at her. 'Do you mind?' he whispered.

Dumb, half panicked, half excited, she shook her head.

'Are you sure?'

'No,' she whispered.

'In that case, it's your turn now, Elizabeth – you kiss me.'

As she lowered her lips to his he kept his hands away from her, responding only with his mouth, until, without any warning, he caught her and lifted her bodily on top of him, pinning her to him with one hand behind her shoulders, the other round her waist.

'Oh—' She reacted involuntarily.

Immediately, he slackened his grip. 'Don't worry, nothing will happen, nothing bad will happen to you.' He moved one hand so it was again stroking the back of her head. 'All I want is a kiss, kiss me again, Elizabeth . . .'

After a second or two, she fastened her lips to his again, and this time when he tightened his arms around her, she did not resist. Even through the stuff of his jacket and waistcoat, the warmth of his body seeped through her thin yellow dress. 'There,' he murmured between kisses, 'there now, isn't that all right? Nothing bad, everything quiet and calm.' The back of her dress, which was belted, had an inverted pleat running from neckline to hem. His fingers found the pleat and began describing slow sensuous passes inside it along her spine, stopping always at her waist. 'Is that nice? Do you like that?'

'Yes,' she whispered, her eyes closed.

26

'Let's loosen that belt, then, and I can do it properly.'

Knowing she probably shouldn't, she raised herself to allow him access to the buckle. He undid it and had removed it from its waist loops and discarded it on the ground beside them in a matter of seconds. 'There now, isn't that much nicer? Come back to me . . .' Again he settled her on his chest and began that slow, almost hypnotic run with his fingers, with each pass going lower and lower until every inch of her spine, from neck to base, was being massaged. 'We'll only do what you like, Elizabeth,' he said. 'Do you like this?'

'Yes,' she whispered, ashamed at how much she liked it.

He shifted them so they rolled to face one another and she was hammocked along his right arm. With his left hand, he kept up the spine massage for a little while and then, watching her face, gently raised the skirt of her dress and began to stroke her stockinged leg. 'Nothing you don't want, Elizabeth,' he whispered, 'remember that.'

She nodded and burrowed her head into the shoulder of his jacket. The touch of his hand on her thigh was even more pleasurable, if that were possible, than when it was on her spine.

Gently, ever so gently, he stroked her thigh, moving his hand gradually higher and higher until he encountered the bare island of flesh between the top of her stocking and her knickers. 'Oops! What have we here?' He grinned. 'Real skin!' Before she could say anything he had removed his hand and was again stroking the silk.

'It's all right.' The scandalous words were out before she realized they had even entered her mind.

'Are you sure?' Using only the tips of his fingers, he petted the few inches of skin as if it were the membrane of a particularly delicate egg. She nodded acquiescence again into his shoulder and then felt her suspender snap. 'Now, how did that happen?' His voice was playful. 'Shall I do it up again?'

'If you like . . .'

'What would *you* like?'

27

'You don't have to fasten it again, I don't mind.'

'Well, a bird never flew on one wing, did it? No point in having only one . . . Is this all right?' Elizabeth felt his fingers creep round to the other suspender and then it too snapped open, releasing her stocking half-way down her thigh. He pushed it down to her knee and resumed his stroking. 'That's better, isn't it? You have wonderful legs, Elizabeth, you shouldn't hide them, even in silk. Maybe we should take these old things off?'

She had to sit up to remove both stockings. Her fingers were shaking.

'Elizabeth,' he whispered, 'please, don't be nervous. All I want is to give you pleasure. That's all. Here—' Swiftly he, too, sat up and, unbuttoning his jacket, enfolded her in it, holding her firmly but gently as though she were a bird and her pinioned arms were wings. 'There now, there.' He rocked her a little. 'Is that all right? There now, my little yellow flower.' He kissed the top of her head.

Seemingly of their own accord, Elizabeth's arms crept round his neck and her lips sought his. They kissed, with more urgency than before, his tongue moving freely now inside her mouth.

He again shifted her so she was on her knees, one bare leg on either side of him and straddling his lap. His hands went behind her and under her dress and slip until he was cupping her buttocks. 'Is this all right? Is this comfortable for you?' She closed her eyes and kissed him and when she felt his hands grope for the waistband of her knickers and push them down, did nothing to prevent it.

His hands were so large she felt they covered her entirely as he used them firstly to knead her hips and bottom then travelled them in random patterns, lighting fires everywhere, sides and back, shoulders and breasts, until after a short while she felt she could not get enough breath and strained against him as thought he could supply her with oxygen.

When he pushed her off and spread her on her back, the parting from him was such a wrench she had to draw up her knees; gently, he pushed them straight again so he

28

could more easily undo the buttons of her dress. She helped him, shrugging her shoulders so he could ease the dress off them, herself lowering the straps of her slip and bra to give him greater access.

He pulled the bra cups down and delved with both hands for her breasts. 'Beautiful!' he whispered, holding them for a second before lowering his head to insert his tongue into the little canyon between them. Then he covered them with small licking kisses, his teeth tugging at her risen nipples so pleasurably that Elizabeth felt as though she were almost in pain.

Quickly, he raised himself from her, lifted her bottom like a mother does a baby's and with one swift movement, removed her knickers. Before Elizabeth had time to react, his mouth was again on one of her breasts but this time the shocks coursing through her flesh were augmented by the previously inconceivable sensation of his finger slithering in the creaminess of what her mother always referred to as 'down there'.

'Oh, God!' she cried out, from pain, pleasure or shame – she was past caring.

'Hush!' he soothed, but did not pause. 'Hush. We'll stop any time you want to.' Although she had her eyes closed, she felt him change position so he was directly over her; she heard too, that his breath was coming faster. 'Oh, God!' She flung one elbow over her eyes as though to blot out what was coming.

He oscillated the finger faster and faster and, at the same time, used his tongue like a snake's, flickering it up and down over her throat and breasts. 'Do you want me to stop, my darling? Tell me if you want me to stop.'

'No, no!' She sobbed the words.

'Open your legs a bit wider . . .'

Almost of their own accord, she felt her treacherous thighs part company from one another.

'That's my little darling,' he whispered hoarsely, 'wider again, wider . . .'

And she obeyed and the feelings engendered by what he was doing grew more and more heated. He kissed her

29

mouth for a second or two and then, while she was kissing him back, she felt his finger being replaced by something thicker, cool and dry. Again she cried out: 'Please!'

'I told you we won't do anything you don't want to—' His beautiful voice was cracked. He was panting now.

'No, it's all right. It's just that—'

'I know. I'll be gentle and very, very careful . . . You're so, so beautiful.' He knelt between her open thighs and lay on her, engulfing her mouth with kisses.

As she felt the pressure grow more insistent, she clung to him. 'I want to, I want to, but I'm afraid—'

'Don't be afraid, there's nothing to be afraid of, my little darling—' He used one hand to help push himself in. 'You're wonderful, it's perfectly natural to be nervous the first time, but you're wonderful, you're—' She whimpered as he broke through.

Instantly, he was still. 'Everything's fine now, don't worry, I won't hurt you, kiss me!'

As Elizabeth returned the kiss, her passion began again to build through the working of his tongue and lips. When he raised himself and kissed her breasts, she moaned.

'I'm not hurting you?' Again he was still.

'No! I'm fine.'

'Good, my darling, you're doing wonderfully.' He began to move a little and although it hurt, she went with him, faster and faster. Then his body became abruptly as stiff as a board.

Elizabeth's eyes flew open as he jerked himself out of her and convulsed. It was the first time he had allowed his full weight to fall on her and she could barely breathe; nevertheless, she held him tightly as the spasms racked through him and hot fluid spread over her belly, bare under her ruched-up dress and slip.

Her head was spinning; it had happened so suddenly, what was she supposed to do now? Faces, accusing faces – Ida's, her mother's, the faces of the nuns who had warned them all about this – paraded in front of her as she stared wide-eyed over the top of George Gallaher's head at the thick lacework of leaves stitched against the stars.

She stroked the back of his head as she felt him quietening; it seemed the right thing to do. He rolled off her and for a moment or two, lay beside her, breathing hard. She wanted desperately now to cover herself but felt it might be insulting to him.

'Are you all right, Elizabeth?' He was looking away from her.

'Yes,' but now she felt like crying.

He took a balled handkerchief out from his pocket and heaving himself on his side, tenderly wiped her stomach. 'I should ask you if it was good for you, but I know that would be stupid. I didn't hurt you at least? You're not hurting anywhere? Here?' Gently, he touched her between the legs.

'A little.' The tears threatened to spill over and she turned her head away. It was not even the soreness; it was the abruptness of it all and how fast it had ended. And the uncertainty. Elizabeth could not have defined the uncertainty but it invaded her and grew like seaweed.

'Hold on a second.' He got up and adjusting his trousers, moved out of her sight for a few moments. Elizabeth lay where she was without moving; she still felt as if to do so would somehow be rude.

When he came back, his handkerchief was sopping wet. 'I dipped it in the river,' he explained, lowering himself to his knees beside her. 'Here.' Delicately he placed it between her legs.

The shock of the water's coldness made her gasp but it felt clean and good. 'It'll be better the next time and better and better – I promise.' He finished cleaning her and then after throwing the handkerchief into the shrubs behind them, gently pulled down her dress to cover her. He touched her face with his lips. 'You're a natural for this, you'll love it. You just wait and see.'

She could hold on to the tears no longer. 'I'm sorry –' she gulped, humiliated at her lack of sophistication.

'Come here, come here.' He pulled her to him and folded her into his arms. 'Don't cry, what is it? Please don't cry. If you're worried about getting pregnant, you needn't. I was very careful.'

The possibility had not occurred to Elizabeth. Doubly shocked now, she gazed at him through eyes blurred with moisture. He misunderstood her reaction. 'I came out in time,' he explained, taking both her hands in his, 'it's called *coitus interruptus.*'

Elizabeth felt she had nothing to lose. 'It's not that,' she said, 'it's just that you're going away now – I've done this with you, I've let myself – and you're – you're going away.' The tears came again.

He fondled the side of her face with gentle fingers. 'There'll be wonderful times for you in the future, Elizabeth, and you won't give me a thought. I promise, not a thought. Old bastard like me. You're young and beautiful.' He rocked her while tears of loss and shame scalded her face.

After a while, she brought herself under control. 'I'm all right now,' she mumbled.

'That's my girl!' He kissed her. 'Come on, cheer up – try to look on the bright side.' He pushed her away from him a little and started to do up the buttons on her dress. 'Now's your chance to tell me what you *really* thought of me tonight. Take my dancing, for instance. You thought my sword dance was terrific, now, didn't you? Be honest.' His teasing good humour was infectious and he pulled such a funny face she actually laughed.

'Well . . .'

'Think I have a future in ballet?'

'Undoubtedly.' Elizabeth wiped her eyes.

'Come on, let's dance!' He sprang to his feet.

'What? Here?'

'Why not? God's own green auditorium.' He held out his arms.

Bemused, Elizabeth got to her feet and smoothed down her dress.

'Milady!' He clicked his heels as he took her in his arms. 'One-two-three, *one*-two-three,' and to the soft accompaniment of the river, waltzed her slowly from under the trees on to an open area of rough grass.

His performance that evening with the crossed swords had not done justice to George Gallaher's exquisite technique as a dancer. As, gravely, they glided in a wide circle, his propulsion of her was so subtle it anticipated her own movements, and the small adjustments he made with his arms and hands seemed to mould the small bones of her hand and the hollow of her back so that her body blended perfectly with his. And as the dance began to feel to her as natural as breathing, gradually, luxuriating in the sensations as her dress brushed like warm milk against her bare legs, Elizabeth forgot the incongruity of the setting. Always having loved dancing, she closed her eyes and allowed herself to be wafted like mist across the cool, moist grass; in George's arms she felt as light as one of the fairies illustrated in the Mabel Lucy Atwell books she had loved as a child.

Then Gallaher began softly to sing:

> "'In my sweet little Alice blue gown,
> When I first wandered down into town . . .'"

As he breathed the old tune above her, a fragment of Elizabeth's babyhood arose from the deepest recesses of her memory. Awakening in the darkness of the night, she had climbed out of her cot and toddled downstairs in search of comfort; trailing Thumper, her golliwog, she had crossed the vastness of the cold dim hallway of the house and hearing soft music, had opened the door of the drawing room. Seated at the piano, her mother, dressed in a powder blue dress, was playing softly for her father who was sitting on a pouffe at her feet. Seeing her coming in, they had both risen and crossed the floor with arms outstretched to take her up . . .

That single bittersweet image was all she could remember but, emotional as she was at present, she had to bury her head against George Gallaher's broad chest so the renewed tears would not show. He responded by lowering his tone even further until the song resonated against her ear in snatches, like stray notes from a distant organ; at the same time, he slowed the pace of the waltz and held her to him as though her body were made of bone china.

The song petered out but, folded in one another's arms, they stood still for a few seconds. Then George, detaching her, held her away from him and gazed down at her. 'My sweet little Elizabeth yellow gown,' he said, 'will you think of me?'

If Elizabeth had not known better, she would have thought George Gallaher was sad. But determined not to cry again, she broke away and pretended to be looking across the river at the big house, hulked blindly against the stars. He came and stood beside her, nestling her head against his side. 'Castledurrow's a convent school now,' he said in the jocular tone she now associated with him. 'I hope none of the good nuns is looking out at us and thinking that the lady in white has found herself a companion.'

'Will I ever see you again?' She did not want any more jokes and the words were out before she could stop them.

'*Malesh*,' he said quietly. 'That's Arabic. It means, if Allah means it to be it will be.'

'Do you want to?' Elizabeth heard herself as though she were someone else.

'I'm a nomad – and I'm no good. You mustn't pine for me.' There was no trace of the actor's mask or manners as he took her face in his hands. 'I'm also too old for you, and young women need young men.'

He kissed her with great tenderness and held her close. 'But I'm truly glad I was the one who was with you tonight. What we did tonight is beautiful. Don't ever let anyone in this country tell you otherwise. All I can hope is you'll remember that I was gentle and that you'll never be afraid again. Enjoyment is permissible. Love between a man and a woman is allowed, Elizabeth.'

Chapter Three

In the seven weeks since she had first met George Gallaher in Durrow, Elizabeth became word-familiar not only with *Conn The Shaughraun* but with *Murder in the Red Barn*, *East Lynne*, *Gaslight*, *The Lily of Killarney* and all the other plays and melodramas in the repertoire of the Vivian Mellors Touring Company.

She also became familiar with the schedules and vagaries of every bus route in Munster as, flying in the face of her parents' strong disapproval, she travelled every weekend to wherever the company was playing in Kilkenny, Waterford, Tipperary and latterly in Cork county itself. At Midleton, she even won second prize in that night's raffle and spent her £2 winnings on a present for Gallaher, a little travelling case containing a set of pewter-topped glass bottles to hold his pomades and colognes.

It was not only her parents who had objected: from the first, Ida, too, had tried to dissuade Elizabeth from her 'mad' passion. After that first night, it had taken days for Elizabeth to bring her friendship with Ida back on to an even keel. And it was weeks before Ida had admitted that she was jealous at having been discarded, albeit in the most charming way, by George Gallaher. Apparently, during that two-minute conversation he had had with her in front of the tent he had told her that he was not making a choice between herself and her friend, but was appealing to her as one sophisticate to another, and in doing so had flattered her so outrageously she could not have objected without seeming to be a curmudgeon.

To be fair to him, at the beginning even Gallaher himself did try – half-heartedly – to discourage her. Obviously taken aback when she turned up again at the tent

35

after the show the following Saturday night, he bore her off for a 'talk'. But during the talk, one thing led to another and the 'talk' ended up with George sneaking her into his digs. And so Elizabeth, bewitched, had embarked on the first love affair of her life.

During the magical seven weeks since she had met him, she had not needed sleep and had barely touched food. Yet, she seemed to burn with energy; even the other partners in her father's practice had noticed how much work she was able to pack into a day. She carried the glow with her, too, because outside the office males from seventeen to sixty, delivery boys, office clerks, shop assistants, even the postman, flirted openly with her and paid her compliments.

And each time she met Gallaher, she learned more about how to make and receive love.

Now, on the company's last night in Mallow, she sat in her seat in the back row of the tent, clutching her farewell gift to him, a pair of cufflinks engraved with the masks of comedy and tragedy. She was half ashamed to offer something so mundane but, having spent all her dinner hours of the previous weeks hunting, could not find anything original in the whole of Cork city. It hardly mattered now, she thought, as she fought back a wave of bitterness, it was all about to come crashing down. George Gallaher was going back to England and only God knew when she would see him again.

It was raining outside and the drumming on the tent roof contrived to insulate players and audience from the world outside as Elizabeth gazed round her, committing this night to memory. One by one she memorized the appurtenances of the marquee, its support poles, its pocket stage only inches above the bockety plank flooring, the coloured spotlights, the vivid dropcloths of the scenery, the revolving globe which, when activated, played a kaleidoscope of colours over all the heads and faces, the uncomfortable wooden forms for the general audience with, at the front, a single row of chairs for the clergy, professionals and local scions of commerce; the rouged cheeks and black eyes

36

of the actors – even the bulging patch in the canvas which drooped over her head.

She memorized the sounds: the thunder and lilt of the actors' voices, the piano, which had one key out of tune, the fruity cough of the elderly man sitting beside her. Smells, too: of the diesel which ran the generator, of sweat and feet, mothballs and musty canvas, of people jammed so tightly together that condensation from their body heat and damp clothing made it almost as wet inside as out.

Then Captain Molyneaux entered and feeling the communal quickening in every female breast throughout the tent, Elizabeth could concentrate no more. Ida had called him 'Gorgeous George' and Ida had not been exaggerating. Looking at him on stage for the last time, Elizabeth's own breast strove to harness triple horses of pride, jealousy and despair. These other women could look and fantasize all they liked but this man had been hers, he would be hers tonight. Her skin already tingled in anticipation of what they would do together but tomorrow she had to return him.

She reminded herself again that George had not made any false promises; in fact, in putting her off he had seemed bent on making himself as unattractive as possible. He had told her he was nearly fifty years of age, for instance; he had never mentioned the future, nor any existence he had outside the theatre. And fearful of what she might hear, she had not asked about it.

At the beginning, the easy-going ways of the rest of the Mellors company, all of whom seemed without comment to accept her as George Gallaher's weekend companion, had almost lulled her into believing that this was real life. But the most surprising discovery of all was how natural and right it felt to make love with a man; she was not at all ashamed of her grievously sinful behaviour with George Gallaher and when she examined her conscience, found that she was ashamed not of what she was doing but only of not caring that her soul was now in mortal sin. In fact, she found it quite easy to convince herself that what they were doing was not sinful at all.

On the other hand, although she continued to attend Mass on Sundays, she did give up the sacraments. There was no point in going to confession if you had no purpose of amendment and Elizabeth had no intention of giving up making love with George Gallaher until she had to. Her only sacrament now was loving him; when she was with George she blotted out all considerations except his physical presence. Now here it was, nearly time to pay. Elizabeth's fingers tightened around the little box containing the cufflinks and, afraid she would soil it, she put it in the pocket of her jacket.

She left her seat as soon as the play was over. George would not be in the comedy sketch and although he had to return to play his part in the final raffle, he had agreed to spend every possible minute with her.

Familiar with the company's work practices, Elizabeth now knew that going off with her that night in Durrow had got George into trouble with Vivian Mellors; all members of the company, no matter how lofty their billing, had to help with every facet of the work, with erecting the marquee, setting up and striking the sets, loading, unloading, selling tickets, publicity, even repairing the canvas and cleaning up after each show. She had been flattered that he would risk his job for her but accepted now that he could not do it again. She, too, was now in the habit of helping.

Outside, it was raining harder than ever and she put up her umbrella. Not wanting to attract too much attention, she stepped away from the steamy triangle of light which spilled out through the entrance and huddled into the lee of the tent, which had been pitched on a flat field across the road from a dense forest and about a mile outside the town. In counterpoint to the laughter and music inside, the black mass of the trees opposite seemed to rear across the road at her through the darkness and rain. She shivered and lowered her umbrella until all she could see were its ribs and taut fabric.

'Hello! Wet enough for you?' He was there, rain hopping off the suitcase in which he had packed his costume and make-up.

'Only for ducks,' she replied automatically, then, 'Oh, George!' Dropping the umbrella, she flung her arms around his neck.

'Whoa!' he protested into her neck. 'Let's get in somewhere out of this. Over there.' He indicated the company's vehicles, parked about thirty yards away across the field, then picked up the umbrella and held it over her. 'Come on.'

When they were half-way there, Elizabeth skidded on a cowpat but he managed to catch her before she fell and they continued on. 'In here, quick.' He pulled open the door of the lorry and lifted her into the cab. She scutted across the seat to make room for him beside her.

'There!' He slammed the door. 'That's better.'

They smiled at one another for a few seconds, then Elizabeth could no longer keep up appearances. Now he was beside her there was no escaping the sense of loss. Afraid he would see how upset she was, she lowered her eyes; if she had known she was going to feel like this, she thought, she would almost have preferred not to have met him at all.

'Are you all right?' Gently, he raised her chin.

She nodded, but still could not look at him.

'You're not – what's the matter?'

'Do you have to ask?' She was angry now, although she knew it was irrational.

'Look, you know the rules – I can't –'

'I know the rules all right!' she blazed at him and was instantly contrite. 'Oh, George, I'm sorry, I'm sorry. Please, I don't know what I'm saying.' Again she threw her arms round him. 'Of course I know the rules, I've known all along. It's just that I wish –' She stopped. What did she wish? That he would take her with him? Even marry her? That she should give up her job and be a camp follower as these itinerants moved around the British Isles? She didn't even know what George Gallaher did in the winter.

'What do you wish, Elizabeth?'

'I just wish it didn't have to be like this. You're my whole life.' She sobbed it against his lapels.

'Of course I'm not your whole life, my darling. I'm only the first part of a life that's going to be as exciting and lovely as you.'

'Stop it, stop the big talk!' She pulled away, angry again. 'For once in your life talk real talk, not this – this –'

'This what?' he asked, after a pause. 'This what, Elizabeth? Spit it out!'

She realized they were having their first row and gazed at him in horror.

'For the third time, this what?' he continued. 'Up to this, you seemed to like the way I talk.'

'I do.' Elizabeth became aware that the rain hummed two separate notes; one against the roof, the other against the windscreen. 'Sorry,' she whispered. 'George, I'm so sorry.'

'You're overwrought.' He smiled. 'Understandable, of course, in light of the tremendous performances you've just witnessed.'

She saw he was watching her carefully and raised her head high. 'Naturally,' she said in as light a tone as she could muster. 'Particularly in regard to the performance of the star.'

'Ah. You refer, I presume, to Mr Mellors?'

'I refer, sir, to one Mr Gallaher.'

'Ah, yes.' He bowed from the waist. 'As enjoyed by the –'

'Crowned heads of Europe,' she finished. She scrubbed at the windscreen as though to clear a space through the rain, now streaming in sheets. 'Did you know that St Patrick is supposed to have struck a bargain with God that Ireland would drown seven years before the rest of the world? This might be it.' She glanced at him. He was smiling: the danger had passed.

'And did you know,' he replied, continuing the game, 'that Vivian Mellors's real name is Sid Thornberry?'

'No, I didn't. But I'm not surprised.'

'C'mere, you!' he took her in his arms. 'Silly little thing!'

'I'm not silly!'

40

'And I'm not fifty.'

'What? You said you were.'

'That was to put you off, to protect you against me. You see, I do have finer feelings! I said, if you remember, that I was *nearly* fifty. It was you jumped to the conclusion that nearly was actually there.'

'Well, how old are you?' Elizabeth felt a flicker of hope. Maybe he was going to ask her to become a feature of his life after all.

'I'm forty-six.'

She nestled in his arms while she digested this information. 'Sure that's not old at all,' she said slowly. 'Why are you telling me now? What difference does it make?'

He doused the hope. 'It's more than twice what you are,' he whispered into her hair, 'a lot more. And I want to be honest with you.'

'It's not only that, is it?' Instinct warned her that there was something more to come.

'What do you mean?'

'No more games, George, we don't have time. It's not only your age. You're warning me off again.'

'Am I?'

'Yes, you are.' She waited.

'It's nothing, you're imagining things.' He tried to pull down her blouse to kiss her shoulder but she shrugged it away from his lips and put some distance between them on the lumpy seat. 'George, you said you were going to be honest.'

He stared at her for a moment then looked away. 'I under-estimated you.'

'Tell me, George, for God's sake, I deserve it.'

'If you think about it, you'll probably know.'

'I want to hear it from you.' The rain beat a tattoo on the silence between them but there was something else, a sort of hiss, as though the air around George Gallaher's head had uncoiled itself and was slithering across to the back of her own neck.

She waited, watching the struggle on his face. Finally he turned to her, almost defiantly. 'I'm going to America,

41

Elizabeth. For good. I'm going to Hollywood to try to get into moving pictures. And opportunities are opening up in England, too. You know the BBC is now broadcasting in sound as well as pictures on that new television service?'

She stared at him, knowing full well by the way he was speaking that he was improvising. Without doubt he had been going to say something else. The message was clear however: whether he was going away or not, George Gallaher was saying goodbye. The harmonies of the raindrops against the old lorry had become cacophonous and it was only when she became aware of the window and door handles digging into her back she realized that, without meaning to, she had shrunk away from him.

Dignity. She must maintain dignity. 'Well, congratulations!' she said. 'That's a splendid idea. I wish you all the luck in the world.'

'Elizabeth, please, I'm sorry.' He attempted to pull her towards him but she resisted.

'I'm sorry too,' she answered, looking over his shoulder. 'Look! The show's finished, they're coming out.'

'Let them, we've got to talk.' This time, limp as waterweed, she did not resist as he took her in his arms. 'This doesn't change what happened between us in the last few weeks,' he said, 'you've got to believe that, Elizabeth. What you and I had and did was something very special.'

'Oh, by the way.' Elizabeth pulled away and to her surprise, her voice sounded almost casual as she rummaged in her pocket for the cufflinks. 'These are for you . . .'

He took the small package but did not look at it. 'Elizabeth.'

'Yes?' Her anger was swelling so fast she had to strain to compact it.

'Can you try to see it from my point of view?'

'Certainly, of course I can. You're going away, you didn't tell me, I've no right to know, I didn't stop to think, I'm a fool. End of story.'

'No. That's not it. Give me your hand—'

'No!'

He was taken aback by the violence of her reaction but

recovered sufficiently to insist, prising her hand from where she had clamped it tightly over the steering wheel. 'What's changed? I'm still the same person, you're still the same person—'

'What's changed? You can't be serious.' She almost laughed at his audacity.

'Did you really think we might go on? Even get married?' He seemed undeterred. 'Think, Elizabeth. What kind of life would you have with me?'

'Oh, the same kind of life any theatrical wife has, I imagine.' Doubly mortified, she dashed away the moisture which threatened to spill out of her eyes. Now he had trapped her into admitting she had had expectations.

'Poorest form of wit, Elizabeth.' And when she glared at him he elaborated. 'Sarcasm. It doesn't become you.'

The anger boiled over and she snatched her hand out of his, scrabbling at the handle of the door beside her. 'I'm getting out of here.' With an apologetic 'plop' the handle came off in her hand.

She looked at it, big tears of humiliation now coursing freely down her cheeks. What had she expected, anyway? She had always known that he was leaving Ireland at the end of the season and she had tried always to be realistic. *Oh, no, you didn't.* A deadly little voice trickled its poison somewhere at the base of her skull. *You always hoped you could go on.*

'Thank God for old bangers,' said Gallaher, taking the door handle gently out of her hand. 'Now you're my prisoner. Come here to me, kiss me. Will you forgive me, Elizabeth? I wanted you so much I was afraid you would run away from me if you knew the truth. I wanted not to spoil this wonderful summer. Will you give me a kiss? I need you not to be angry.'

Then say you'll take me with you. Somehow, Elizabeth managed to halt the words before they leaped off her tongue. 'Leave me alone.' Not knowing whether she was more angry with herself or with him, savagely, she pushed him away.

He regarded her calmly for a moment, then looked

down at the door handle in his hand. 'I am just me, my darling. I made no bargain with you, if you remember.' He placed the handle carefully on the seat between them.

> '"Yet this inconstancy is such,
> As you too shall adore;
> I could not love thee, Dear, so much,
> Loved I not honour more!"'

His readiness with the quotation rekindled Elizabeth's anger until she was consumed with it. 'That's another thing. You're so trite, you've something for all occasions but it's all words, words, words. Where do you get it all? I suppose you sit up all night learning all this poetry and Shakespeare —'

'Richard Lovelace, actually —'

'I don't care who it is!' she shouted. 'It could be Attila the Hun for all I care. Shut up, shut up, shut up . . .'

He let her cry for several minutes then reached out and touched her shoulder.

She jerked it away from him but he persisted, touching her again. Stubbornly, she craned her head away from him, but then found herself responding as he started to stroke the back of her neck, lifting her hair and combing it through his fingers as he had done that first night in the grounds of Castledurrow.

'That's my girl,' he coaxed. He pushed back her hair and moving the flesh of her ear out of the way, worked with his tongue on the fine skin behind it. 'Let's not spoil the few hours we have left.'

Despite her best intentions, Elizabeth felt her anger subside and her desire for him ignite. 'Oh, George,' she whispered, 'what am I going to do?'

'That's tomorrow's problem,' he said. 'Tonight, now, is still ours. Live in the present, Elizabeth, it's all you'll ever own. I'll try tonight if you will.'

She raised her face to him for a kiss. 'It's so hard.'

'It's not that easy on me, either, you know.' He kissed her chastely. 'May I open my present now?'

'It's nothing. It's only cufflinks.'

He tore off the paper and examined the jewellery. 'They're gorgeous, really lovely.' Seconds later, they sprang apart as the driver's door was pulled open from the outside and the face of the piano player appeared in the opening. He made no sign of discomfiture at discovering them locked in each other's arms but squinted in at them. 'The raffle's startin'.'

'All right. Be right back, Elizabeth.' Gallaher opened the door on his side and pulling up the collar of his jacket, jumped down from the lorry and was instantly concealed by the black curtain of rain which seemed to have intensified now that Elizabeth was alone in the dimness of the humid cab. She tried to calm her mind, to think with logic and not emotion: she had had no right to behave like that towards George Gallaher; everything he had said was correct – they were ships in the night, this was a holiday romance, she must behave sensibly, like an adult.

In the next second, sense and reason flowed off her as fast as the rain off the lorry and she moved across to sit in the spot he had just vacated. She closed her eyes; it was still warm. The smell of him lingered there too, overlying the smell of metal, worn leatherette and oil. The better to feel his heat, she slid both her hands underneath her. Then, inhaling deeply, she drew in his smell, conscious of it passing through the top of her nose, down the back of her throat, into her lungs.

Her foot nudged something: the suitcase. Although she knew she shouldn't, she drew it up on to the seat beside her and snapped open the clasp. His costume had been stuffed in any old how; she lifted out the cloak and as best she could in the cramped conditions, shook it out and folded it neatly. She did the same for the jacket, the pants, the bandolier and belt on to which he fastened his scabbard.

Underneath the clothes were the little travelling case she had given him and a battered cigar box, long since bared of its labels. She opened it, releasing the pungent aromas from a jumble of make-up sticks, false hair, bootblack, spirit gum, toothbrushes, pipe cleaners and the carbon from spent matches. She opened a large round tin and dipped a finger into a white substance which creased up on itself like soft fat. Puzzled, she held her finger under her nostrils: it had a smell similar to lard, but sweeter.

'Caught red-handed, eh?' The door beside her was wrenched open and Gallaher leaped in. 'In case you're wondering, it's coconut oil,' he said cheerfully, pulling the door closed and showing no sign that he objected to her prying.

'I wasn't expecting you back for ages.'

'Obviously.' He continued to grin. 'They didn't need me – most of the tickets were already gone by the time I showed up. It's the last night, big prize – a whole twelve pounds!'

They had just finished repacking the suitcase when the driver's door was pulled open and the piano player rejoined them in the cab. 'Horrible night, isn't it? Shove over in the bed.' He had difficulty with the handleless door as Elizabeth and Gallaher made room for him, but eventually managed and started the engine. 'Are ye going to the pub?' he asked cheerfully as the lorry shook to life. 'We're all going.'

'I don't know.' Elizabeth looked at Gallaher.

'Please yeerselves.' The piano player shrugged. 'This bus's goin' to town anyroads.' Alone in the troupe, the piano player was Irish. He had been hired not only for his musicianship, which was shaky enough, but for his lorry, the company's original vehicle having died a week after it arrived in Ireland.

'Of course we'll go, won't we, Elizabeth?' Gallaher put his arm round her shoulders and although she settled into its curve, she was newly upset that he had agreed so readily. The boat the company was taking for Liverpool was not leaving Cork until late afternoon tomorrow so, for once, they were not striking immediately after the show but planning to pack up in the morning. Now, more than ever, surely he would want to take advantage of every single minute of this time?

She stared at the twin cones of light piercing the rain in front of the lorry as her emotions swung again. He didn't want to know. For him it was just a fling. She had no right

46

to assume possession even for one night. She had made this bed, now she had to lie in it and she might as well make the most of whatever he might deign to throw at her.

He sensed the turmoil and whispered, 'Are you all right?'

She was grateful that normal conversation was impossible over the screaking and roaring of the windscreen wipers and the old engine and simply nodded that she was, indeed, all right.

An hour later, as part of the sycophantic circle around Vivian Mellors, the muscles of her face sore from smiling, she tugged at Gallaher's sleeve, whispering, 'Could we go soon?'

'Sure, in a few minutes.' Gallaher patted her arm.

Pledged since Confirmation not to drink alcohol until she was twenty-one, Elizabeth sipped her lemonade and seethed as the precious minutes stretched into two hours and the bonhomie and banter around her grew ever more raucous. 'Shouldn't the pub be closing soon?' She took advantage of yet another of Mellors's interminable stories coming to an end. 'It's after midnight.'

'Ssh, darling,' Gallaher whispered back. 'We'll go in a few minutes, I promise.'

But it was nearly one by the time the proprietor, with many jokey protestations about losing his licence, finally let them out into the night. Almost miraculously, the rain had stopped and, although it was chilly, a half-moon rode high in a clear sky. Whereas most of the company were heading off towards boarding houses and digs, Gallaher had booked himself and Elizabeth into the local hotel for the night. Slightly drunk, he cuddled her to him as they walked along the empty street: '"How peaceful the heavens look now, with the moon in the middle . . ." Oops!' He beat his breast. 'Sorry – I forgot we don't like quotes.'

Now that at last she had him on her own, Elizabeth had relaxed a little and she was determined not to let anything – not the fact that he was going away, not their earlier rows – stand in the way of this night. 'Quote the Bible, Shakespeare, even Vivian Mellors!' she said, pulling

47

down his head and kissing him. 'Quote away, it's music to my ears.' In one of those rare moments where a person steps outside a scene, Elizabeth saw and heard herself as if she were a third party, saw how she had changed in seven weeks. This was not the Elizabeth Sullivan who, with her friend Ida Healy, had gone by bus to the Horse Show only seven weeks ago. That Elizabeth would never have dared to have taken the initiative in kissing a man, nor have made any demands on him, even by implication, much less ask him to leave a pub.

Gallaher returned the kiss. 'That's my girl,' he said, his breath smelling not unpleasantly of hops.

To make things easier for Elizabeth, whose first experience of posing as a married woman this was, he had checked them into the hotel earlier in the day. Even so, she had to take a deep breath to calm the butterflies as she saw the night porter come to open the locked front door to their knock. And although she managed to keep her head high as she marched past the man in the lobby, she was sure his eyes could see clear into her sinful soul as he watched her every step on the stairs to the marital bedroom.

She threw herself on the bed as soon as Gallaher closed the door. 'I never want to go through that again!' Then she realized she probably never would and turned on her back to look up at him. 'I'll miss you,' she whispered.

'And I'll miss you.' He was on the bed beside her in an instant, covering her face and neck with kisses. Then, 'It's cold in here.' He sat up. 'Let's get undressed and get in under the bedclothes.'

Elizabeth was disappointed. She had wanted this last night to be a sort of ceremony, a ritual she could remember all her life. Since this was the first time they had been together in a proper bedroom, she had imagined they would start with a slow mutual undressing, a feeding of one another's fantasies by offering bits of their bodies to one another for partial feasting.

But she held her tongue, slipped out of her clothes and a minute later had joined her body to Gallaher's warm one under the sheets. He held her, then raised himself on one

48

elbow and looked down at her, his violet eyes unreadable. 'You've changed.'

'How?' She had to be careful here. Given the circumstances, she had to protect herself a little and must resist the temptation to give him any more rope with which to hang her higher than she already swung.

'I don't know, in some way I can't define.' He nuzzled her bare shoulder. 'You seem a lot older, more confident somehow.'

'I know. A lot has happened in seven weeks.' Relieved, she licked her way into his mouth. 'Do you like the change?'

'I like everything about you.' He pushed down the blanket and engulfed one of her breasts with his mouth, sucking so hard on the nipple that she cried out with surprise and pain.

They started the preliminaries of lovemaking and Elizabeth closed out her mind, determined to live only within each second as it happened. In this bed she had no past, no future. She wound herself like a python round his massive body but he pulled away, puzzled. 'What's come over you?'

'What do you mean?'

'This is new, Elizabeth – I think the pupil is surpassing the master.'

'You sound almost disappointed.' She tried to challenge him, to incorporate his puzzlement into her game. 'You taught me well, master.'

She tightened her legs on his pelvis but he did not react, continuing to look at her as though trying to work out a very difficult crossword puzzle. Then: 'Have you been with someone else?'

'*What?*'

'Well, have you?'

'George! Of course not.'

'Well, you're different.'

'So you've already said.'

He stared at her and knowing she had little to lose, Elizabeth stared back. In this way, she seemed to win some sort of contest because after a second or two he kissed her. 'I'm sorry, I shouldn't have said that.'

'No, you shouldn't.' But for the first time since she had met him, Elizabeth found it difficult to respond. Again some part of her stood outside them while they made love, a hard, competitive love, where one vied with the other in giving and taking pleasure. When she saw he was coming towards his climax she stilled. 'George?'

'Yes?' He, too, stopped. Like a horse responding to the dandy brush, he was trembling inside his skin.

'Don't come out. I want you in me tonight.'

'Is it safe?'

'Yes.' Elizabeth did not know for sure whether or not it was safe. Information of that nature was hard to come by. But she had learned to hate the violent end to their lovemaking and wanted, just once, to experience its natural conclusion.

'Well, if you're sure—' He kissed her hard and she clung to him, assisting in his climb.

He stifled his cry as he came, pumping into her so strongly that for a few seconds, she too felt convulsed. She stroke him as he calmed, her fingers and palms sliding on the film of perspiration which covered his back; as she did so, she realized she felt slightly disappointed. The full act of sex had made very little difference to her own sense of pleasure, nevertheless, she was glad they had done it.

Still in her, he raised himself above her and looked down. 'What about you?'

'I'm fine.'

'It's your turn now, Elizabeth.'

'I'm fine, really.'

'Ssh. Trust me.' He slipped out of her. 'Now, open your legs and arms, don't touch me at all.' Gently he spread her out. 'Just close your eyes and leave everything to me.'

Her shell of a few moments before crumbled and she felt exposed and defenceless, but she did as he bid. As he began thoroughly to handle her, her vulnerability was overcome by a shaky excitement. She wanted him to do more, go faster. But each time she closed her legs over his fingers or reached instinctively for him with her hands, he returned her firmly to the position in which he had placed her: 'No, no, not yet, trust me, just feel me, feel me here . . . there . . . no, don't open your eyes . . .'

Through her skin, she could feel his own passion beginning again to build. And when he slipped into her, she resisted the temptation to look at him, to do anything to assist him; instead, she continued to rise on the little ridges of her own sensations as he thrust, gently first, then, as she built with him, harder and more urgently until without warning, high in her abdomen, missiles of flame and heat fired one after the other until, remembering just in time where she was, she had to restrain herself from screaming aloud with astonished pleasure.

Swiftly, his orgasm flooded in on top of hers and shuddering, they held one another until they had subsided.

To her horror, Elizabeth started to weep as happiness, misery, loss, love and hatred reared up together on a flood tide of confusion, breaking down all her natural dams. 'I'm sorry,' she sobbed, 'I'm sorry, I don't know what's wrong, it was wonderful, I don't know why I'm crying.'

'Of course you don't.' He pulled out and held her, smothering the storm with his warm bulk. 'There, there, hush . . .' For the second time in a few hours, he waited it out while she shook and cried.

'I've got pains in my shoulders.' Through her tears, she laughed at the absurdity of the statement. 'Oh, God!' She clutched at him. 'I don't know what that must have sounded like!'

'Ssh.' He did not laugh at her. 'That's natural, too. It's all the tension coming out of your muscles. There, there, my little pet.'

When at last she felt calmer, she pulled back from him and saw he was regarding her with an expression bordering on triumph. 'You look like the cat who got the cream,' she said, wiping her eyes and this time managing a laugh which sounded half-way normal.

'Well, I did, too, didn't I?' He caught between her legs with the full of his hand and despite what had just happened, she was overcome with a wave of shyness.

'I didn't know it was like that,' she whispered.

51

'How could you? You never met me until seven weeks ago.'

'Oh, shut up!' But she smiled at his crowing. She felt loose and free, hollow-boned as a bird.

While he made small lazy patterns on her stomach with his finger, she stretched, luxuriating in the elongation of her arm, leg and back muscles and, for the first time, took account of her surroundings. Everything in the room was in shades of brown – brown-patterned carpet with lighter brown squares, buff wallpaper with reddish-brown stripes, plain brown curtains at the single window, mahogany dressing-table and wardrobe, even the lumpy bed had not escaped brownness, being dressed with a brown-gold spread. 'A brown study!' she said, giggling, as though the witticism were as original as the way she felt. Because Elizabeth was convinced that no one in the world could ever have felt like this.

Gallaher yawned and then smiled. 'If only –' he said and then seemed to change his mind.

'If only,' she repeated, 'if-ff o-o-only,' sliding in the deliciousness, 'who cares?' This was not the time for if onlys. 'Supposin', supposin',' she nuzzled his neck, 'two men were frozen, one died how many were left?'

'Stop that! You're tickling – what was that?' He caught her but they were both slippery with sweat and she evaded him. ''Tis a riddle, boy!' She dug him in his large ribs. 'Supposin', supposin –'

'I give up!'

'You can't give up.' She laughed outright. 'Come on, come on, how many were left?'

'One?'

'None. 'Cos we're only supposin'!' All traces of her tears gone, she doubled up with giddiness. 'Oh, God! Do you think sex is making me lose my reason?' She sobered. 'Sorry, I interrupted you. What were you going to say, "If only . . ."?'

'Nothing, it doesn't matter.'

'Come on,' she coaxed, 'we don't have much time left.'

'I promise you, it was nothing, just a silly thought.

Let's go to sleep, I can't keep my eyes open. See what you do to me?' He attempted to kiss her, but suddenly she was wary.

'Tell me!' There was that curious hissing again as a column of air uncoiled away from him towards the back of her neck. Something crucial was about to happen.

'Elizabeth.' He hesitated. 'I've . . .'

Elizabeth lay very still. She wanted to shout at him to get to the point. But she felt if she spoke now she would ruin it, whatever it was.

The window curtains fluttered as someone downstairs in the hotel slammed a door. 'I wish I could take you with me,' he said, 'to Hollywood, I mean.'

Elizabeth's stomach turned. But she forced herself to wait. There was more, she knew it, but she could not read his expression. He flung an elbow over his face, covering his eyes and she felt him making some sort of decision. She could not bear it, she must not push. He uncovered his eyes again and against all that brownness, their violet depths seemed almost black as he stared straight up at the ceiling. To cover her panic, she kissed him on the neck. 'Let's go back to the beginning,' she cried. 'You said "if only", if only *what*?'

With brutal finality, he turned his back on her. 'I'm married.'

Chapter Four

Adultery, adulteress, adulter-ee, adulter-ess ... The words beat time with the swish of the windscreen wipers on the Cork-bound bus.

Elizabeth rejoiced blackly in the rain which, after the brief clarity of the night before, had poured incessantly since early morning. She wiped clear a crescent of glass in the condensation on the window-pane beside her seat; outside, the river Lee was in flood and the leaves, on the turn, hung miserably from suburban trees. They had reached the outskirts of the city.

What was she going to tell her parents? Certainly not the truth: *Hello, Mother. Well, you were right to warn me off him – he's married and I was a fool!*

The bus trundled into the bus station. Elizabeth alighted, put up her umbrella and trudged along the slick streets towards the South Mall and her father's office. The small bag she carried seemed to double in weight every ten steps and she felt old, about a hundred years old. The heavy rain had delayed the bus and she was even later than usual for a Monday morning after a weekend with Gallaher: the pack of work-going cyclists and pedestrians had already thinned out. Wonderful, she thought savagely, that's all I need ...

As she walked, each detail of the past eight hours ran in her head like a repetitive magic-lantern show. After Gallaher's awful revelation, she had jumped out of bed; her immediate instinct had been to run away, to get away as far as she could. But then common sense had overtaken her. Where could she run to at two o'clock in the morning in the town of Mallow?

So she had snatched her nightdress out of her valise,

54

put it on and curled herself into the bedroom's rickety brown armchair, making herself as small as possible.

She started to shake, with rage and fear and a *mélange* of feelings which she would rather not analyse. Despairing questions plunged round and round in her mind. Why hadn't he told her before? Why now?

Then, sneakily, who was his wife? What was her name? How old was she? Was she beautiful? But what came out of her mouth was, 'Are you bringing your wife to Hollywood?'

'No.' Avoiding her eyes, he remained in bed.

'Why not?' Elizabeth kept a tight grip; in the circumstances, she felt she was handling this quite well. At least she forced him to meet her eyes.

'She doesn't want to come.' He studied the weave of the brown bedspread. 'She wants to stay with the children.'

'Oh.' She did not trust herself to say any more. The trembling in her body spread in concentric waves around the room until the floor, the walls, the furniture seemed to shake too. Her gorge rose. 'I've got to go to the bathroom,' she gasped, bolting for the door.

The bathroom which served their room was at the end of a short corridor. Elizabeth succeeded in making it as far as the sink before vomiting. Again and again she had retched until there was nothing left and her throat was dry. Then, shuddering, she sank in a heap on to the cold linoleum and leaned her cheek against the rim of the bath. Her face against it felt so cold she knew she must be very pale.

She stayed there motionless for several minutes, cold sweat trickling through the grooves under her eyes, between her breasts, down her back. Gradually, she became aware of the smell in the tiled room – of sick, but also of the stench which came from her own body, sweat and something else: the fishy smell of sex. As long as she lived, she thought, that smell would now mean betrayal and hurt.

She heard a sound and looked up. Gallaher's giant frame was filling the doorway, blotting out the dim nightlight from the corridor. 'Are you all right?'

Elizabeth did not have the energy to say anything but nodded. He came into the room and helped her up. 'Are you sure you're all right? Do you want me to get a doctor or anything?'

She almost laughed at that. *Yes, Doctor, I do feel faint and sick, it's because my lover has just announced he's a family man* . . . But she brushed off his hand. 'I'm fine. Leave me alone for a minute, will you, George? I'm just going to have a wash.'

'Well, if you're sure . . .' Like a shire-horse uncertain of what his master wanted him to do next, he backed out of the room.

Elizabeth shut the door, turned up the gas-lamp and, after cleaning the washbasin, stepped into the bath, not caring that the noise of the running water might wake anyone. And not having any soap or wash cloths with her, she had to use only her hands and water as cold as melted snow. But as she sluiced herself, wincing with the shock, she welcomed the torture on her body. It punished her for being such a fool.

She felt marginally better – at least physically – when she returned to the room.

Gallaher was again in bed, eyeing her from under the wings of his splendid eyebrows. Elizabeth marched over to her side. 'I'm cold,' she said, 'I have to get in, sorry.' She waited while he moved over to make room for her, but when he attempted to put his arms around her as she got in carefully and precisely removed them.

Gallaher was coaxing, trying everything in his consider-able armoury of charm and tricks to patch together what was left of their relationship but she found the strength to be adamant and to lie like marble as close as possible to the edge of the bed. Eventually, at about a quarter to three, he turned away from her and went to sleep.

For Elizabeth, the rest of the night passed in a fog of pain. Unable or unwilling even to cry, she lay unmoving in the dark, until the crack between the brown curtains grew grey, then pale, until the curtains themselves flamed briefly gold to fade again shortly afterwards with the arrival of

56

rain. She moved position only when the toes on one of her feet seized up with cramp and she had to brace them against the footboard of the bed to relieve them.

It was about half past seven when she slipped out of the bed. Although some part of her wanted desperately to stay, to kiss him again, to make love, to force those last few hours into oblivion, the greater impulse was for privacy. She had to escape and to put as much physical distance as possible between herself and George Gallaher.

'Elizabeth, please.' He woke up as she pulled her dress over her head.

'Don't, George, please don't.' Her back was to him and she did not turn round.

'But if you'd only let me explain—'

'There's no explanation necessary.' Once again, dignity was the thing. 'Really, I mean it.'

She finished with the dress. 'You were wrong not to tell me the truth,' she was pulling on her stockings, 'but quite right when you said you never led me on. It was me who was wrong there. I'll pay for my own mistakes.'

'At least let us say goodbye to each other. Can we be friends? Please?'

'To tell you the truth, George, I don't know.' At last Elizabeth faced him; the physical ache in her chest intensified but she had to be honest. 'There's not much point in being friends with someone you'll never see again, is there?' He made as though to answer but she held up her hand to forestall him and pretended to be hunting under the bed for her shoes.

When she straightened up, she saw his expression was again rather odd but she had no desire to prolong her own agony and did not pause to try an evaluation. 'Don't worry about it, George, I'm a big girl now.'

'Shouldn't we at least exchange addresses, Elizabeth?'

'What for? Anyway, do you know to what address you and your – your family—' Her voice wobbled. To hide her upset she bent low to strap the T-bars of her shoes. '—which address you and your family will be staying at in Hollywood?'

57

'They're not coming, I told you.' He was watching her very carefully. 'At least you can give me yours and I can send you a postcard when I'm settled.'

Elizabeth stuffed her nightdress into her bag. 'No, I don't think so, George.' She looked around the room. 'Well, that's it, I think. I'd better go, mustn't miss the bus.' Mallow was only twenty miles from Cork city and the bus service was good. There was one at eight.

'Come here, please.' His voice was soft, begging, as he held out his arms to her and, for a dangerous second, her resolve wavered. Then the wind flung a heavy handful of rain against the window, showing her an escape route. 'It's a terrible morning,' she said, 'you know how the rain affects the speed of those old buses and I don't want to be late for work.' The normality of the words seemed terrible.

'All right, if you insist.' He lay down again and closed his eyes.

Still she hesitated. Then did what she knew was completely wrong: dropping the bag on the floor, she flew to the side of the bed, took his head and kissed him swiftly on the lips. 'George, I love you.' Before he had time to react she had picked up the bag again, had left the room and was running headlong down the corridor, her bag bumping against the flaked cream paintwork of the walls.

Now as she walked along through the streets of Cork city towards her father's office, the memory of that final, horrifying lapse made her cheeks burn. They had never, either of them, uttered the word 'love' in all the weeks of their affair.

The wind was curling under her umbrella, tearing at the spokes but, like a yacht driving through hostile seas, she ploughed through it with head down until at last, with drenched feet and her bright hair lank and streaming, she arrived at the imposing building which housed her father's practice. To her intense relief, her father, unusually, was late too.

Elizabeth acted as a sort of under-secretary to two of the legal secretaries of the practice, both of whom were already cosily ensconced over a cup of tea and piles of paperwork. 'Morning,' said each of them without censure or even interest, as, apologizing for her lateness, she hung up her coat, shook out her umbrella and placed it open in a corner near a radiator to dry.

The square, high-ceilinged room had been furnished by Elizabeth's mother from auctions, in a style which, by 1937 standards, looked old-fashioned. Big enough to hold six enormous partners' desks, each with attendant mahogany coat-stand and personal locker, it reflected some of Corinne Sullivan's ideas of legal *gravitas*. She had curtained the two enormous windows which faced on to the street in brown, tasselled velvet and except for the door opening, one wall was lined with filing cabinets of highly polished wood; two walls were furnished floor to ceiling with well-filled book-shelves. Elizabeth's desk was in a corner, beside one of the windows, but today the light was dismal and although the cast-iron radiators clanked busily, the atmosphere in the room was chilly and damp, the latter condition not helped in that one of the radiators was leaking steadily, drip by drip, into a metal tray.

Elizabeth shivered as she pulled the cover off her typewriter but set her mouth in a grim, prim line. Work. That was the only solace. She would use work as a tool to exorcize George Gallaher, all his works and pomps. She pulled her in-tray towards her and began to clatter at the Underwood as though being pursued by a train.

She was well into the pile of typing by the time her father arrived. 'Morning, all!'

St John Sullivan was a man with a belly which he tried vainly to conceal under well-cut suits, fob chains and shirts a size too big for him. He was a hard worker, his meticu-lousness respected by clients, his partners and by those who led public opinion in the city.

'Morning!' chorused the two secretaries and the law clerk simultaneously.

'Good morning, Daddy,' Elizabeth said without look-ing up from her work.

'Filthy morning, isn't it?' Elizabeth's father peeled off his mackintosh.

59

Elizabeth sensed him looking at her, but St John Sullivan prided himself on treating all his employees equally and fairly, and rarely brought his domestic affairs into the office. This morning, however, was one of the exceptions to the rule. 'Oh, by the way, Elizabeth,' he said as he passed into his own office, the door to which fitted neatly into the surrounding bookshelves, 'your mother wants you to give a hand tonight with her card party.'

'Yes, Daddy.' Elizabeth kept typing. The command had been issued in pleasant tones but the underlying signal was clear. *You haven't been around all weekend so you'd better do what you're told tonight.*

As her father closed his door the document she was reading blurred before her eyes. She rooted in her handbag for a handkerchief and blew her nose. 'Sorry, it's this wretched weather,' she explained to no one in particular, 'must be getting a cold, sorry.'

Her father and mother need worry no longer, she thought. The way she felt now, she planned to stay home every night for the next ten years.

It did not quite work out that way. Because by Christmas, Elizabeth had found out she was pregnant.

She had suspected as much from the beginning of December but confided in no one, passing night after sleepless night alternately worrying and panicking, until on Friday 13 December she plucked up the courage to announce that the following day she was going to Dublin to do some shopping. Her real mission was to see a doctor who did not know her or her family.

'What's wrong with the shops in Cork?' Elizabeth's mother, daughter of one of the city's 'merchant princes', harboured a barely concealed antipathy towards the capital and never went there if she could avoid it. They were sitting in the big comfortable kitchen of the house in Blackrock, a prosperous suburb. There had been only the two of them for dinner that evening, Elizabeth's father was eating with a client at the Oyster Tavern.

Corinne Sullivan picked up their plates and got up

from the table. Willowy and languid, with the same colouring as her daughter, she dressed well and tastefully and patronized the top hairdresser in Cork. Elizabeth was wary of incurring her mother's displeasure; although Corinne rarely raised her voice, all her life, Elizabeth felt that in any conversation her mother was playing some subtext. The weekends with Gallaher had been the first open defiance of Corinne's wishes and she had been able to carry on with it only because, at the time, nothing else in the world had mattered.

After a brief attempt to dissuade her, Corinne had not spoken of it again. Yet, elated as she had been during that period, every time Elizabeth had met her mother's eyes she had not had the nerve to hold them.

'You barely touched your dinner,' said her mother now, bringing the plates over to the sink and scraping the remains into two Delph bowls for the family's pair of spaniels. 'What's the matter with you these days, Beth? You don't want to lose too much weight, you know. It's not attractive.' Attractiveness was high on Corinne's agenda of femininity. 'Maeve left tons of bread and butter pudding for us,' she went on, 'you'll have some?' Maeve was the Sullivans' cook-housekeeper whose half-day it was.

'Sure.' Elizabeth was anxious to please. 'There was nothing wrong with the lamb, Mother, it was delicious – it's just that these days I seem to have gone off meat.'

'Everything in moderation.' Her mother brought the pudding to the table.

Elizabeth tried her best to eat her portion with evidence of hearty enjoyment. Her stomach seemed to have shrivelled like a prune, however, and the amount she could get into it was minimal. 'This is wonderful,' she said, chewing energetically on the pudding which did not need chewing at all.

'Don't overdo it, Elizabeth,' said her mother, scooping a dainty spoonful from her own dish but before Elizabeth could expostulate she changed the subject. 'What kind of shopping are you planning in Dublin?'

Elizabeth looked sharply at her; was it her own guilty conscience or was that a loaded question? But she could

61

detect nothing untoward in Corinne's bland expression. She took another spoonful from her plate and did not reply until she had swallowed it. 'Oh, just – you know – Christmas presents, that sort of thing,' she said. 'What would you like, by the way?'

'Oh, anything, dear. You know me. It is the thought that counts after all, isn't it?' Corinne pushed her own, unfinished pudding away and Elizabeth smiled grimly. She knew very well that what the present was – and where it was bought – mattered a great deal more to her mother than the thought behind it.

'Well, I'll just surprise you, then, shall I?'

'Yes, dear, that would be nice. Tea?'

They drank their tea in silence. The kitchen was at the back of the house, in a half basement which ran the full width of the building and looked out on the garden which, although it was only seven in the evening, already glinted with frost. Inside, calm warmth radiated from the solid fuel stove against one of the walls; an old cat, almost fourteen years old now, dreamed the rest of her life away in front of it. 'When you're in Dublin, dear,' Elizabeth's mother replaced her china cup in its saucer, 'would you mind going to Bewley's for me? Maeve does so like those bracks.'

This, Elizabeth knew, was her mother's subtle way of checking that she was indeed going to Dublin and not chasing around the country after George Gallaher. After the weekend trips ceased, neither Corinne nor St John had ever enquired as to her intentions with regard to Gallaher but she had been aware of their delicate surveillance.

'Bracks?' she repeated. 'Fine.' Then some demon made her add, 'That's, of course, if I have time.' Her mother had no right to doubt her like that.

Belatedly, she realized that Corinne had every reason to doubt her. 'Of course I will, Mother,' she said, getting up from her chair. 'I'll buy three bracks, two for Maeve, one for us. How would that do?'

'Thank you, Beth, you're a good girl.'

Elizabeth was glad to escape to her room.

Next day, although the train she took was an express,

the hours it took to make the 160-mile journey to Dublin seemed to Elizabeth to take for ever. But by lunch-time, she was in Dublin.

And, in possession of three fruit bracks, by late afternoon she was emerging from the doorway of Bewley's in Westmoreland Street to walk back towards the quays and Kingsbridge station in plenty of time to catch the train home. Now that the stress of the visit to the doctor was over, she was weary.

It had been surprisingly easy. The doctor had been brisk and businesslike, had referred to her throughout the examination as 'Mrs Sullivan', and if he had harboured any suspicions about her Woolworth's wedding ring made no comment about it. He had promised to have the results of the pregnancy test available at the latest by the following Thursday.

It was already dark in the foggy street outside the café where a little crowd had gathered in high Christmas humour to listen to a pair of street musicians, a man who was so weatherbeaten he could have been any age from thirty-five to sixty-five and a tiny boy whose bare feet were black and horny with filth. The man played a tin whistle while the boy sang the carol 'Adeste Fideles' in a high, piercing treble; he sang it fast as though to get it over with, jigging from foot to foot in time with the beat. When it was finished, while the crowd flung ha'pennies and farthings into their caps on the ground, the little boy clutched his chest with both arms to control his shivering; in the freezing Christmas weather, he wore only short trousers and a torn V-necked jumper over a thin shirt.

Elizabeth took a ten-shilling note out of her purse and instead of throwing it into his cap, hurriedly pushed it into the astonished child's hand but before he could react, the man's hand had flickered across and the note had vanished. She did not wait to see what happened next. Pushing through the circle of spectators, she hurried away.

She must not cry, she must not. 'Just five more days,' she said to herself doggedly, 'just five more days and then you'll know the worst.' In her heart she knew what the worst would be but allowed herself the smallest, tiniest match-flame of hope.

At O'Connell Bridge she turned into Aston Quay, having to walk wide to avoid a huddle of beggars. She would be glad to get out of Dublin, she thought. It was difficult to believe that it had been only a few short months since she and Ida had partied here. Now she felt deafened and choked by the confusion of life in the capital: the fumes of coal smoke and car exhausts which overcame even the stench of the Liffey, the scurrying pedestrians and cyclists, the motor cars, the grave, clopping jarvey cars and drays and, over all, the sparking and clanging of the trams as they swayed around corners and sailed like kingly barges through the mayhem.

A few yards further on, she stopped in front of McBirney's windows. Over her head the coloured electric bulbs which sent a beaming Santa and his sleigh romping over the upper storeys of the building had been attenuated and haloed by the fog; at this proximity, they buzzed and popped alarmingly. The shop's window dresser had out-done himself: a full-sized decorated fir with piles of multi-coloured packages underneath took up the whole of one window; the others were a riot of red and green dashed with white and touches of bright tartan. Serried ranks of jumpers in red and green held fans of similarly coloured socks, gloves and mittens in their carefully folded arms; tartan scarves and hair ribbons were draped over red and green dresses, and, as if the seasonality had not been emphasized enough, holly sprigs and white fluffs of cotton wool had been scattered with abandon over the whole.

Shoppers hurried in and out of the store, their arms filled with parcels and paper bags; mothers pulled reluctant toddlers past the bright display; a man who had drunk too well staggered against the glass. It all seemed so innocent and carefree. Whatever happened now, Elizabeth thought, even if by the most miraculous chance she was not pregnant, she would never again in her life be carefree. If only human beings could see the unrolling of time ahead of them, it might make them appreciate the good times while they had them.

As quickly as she thought it, Elizabeth dismissed the maudlin sentiment. If she was to have any chance in the future, self-pity was one luxury she could not afford.

The air, which was borne off the Liffey on the tentacles of the fog, was stinging her cheeks and making her eyes water and she was glad to step into the warmth of the shop. For the next half-hour or so she bought fast and indiscriminately: a bottle of perfume for her mother, a pipe for her father, a pair of slippers for Maeve. Elizabeth's extended family was not large and her circle of friends had shrunk considerably in the two and a half years since she had left school. She added a lace collar for Ida, several bright scarves which would do for various relatives and, before she left the store, saw a small tartan rug which on impulse she bought for Bella, the aged cat.

What did it matter what she gave anyone, she thought as, outside again, she set out to walk back to the station. She had a fairly good idea how they would all react to the news that she was going to have a baby.

The Halfpenny Bridge seemed to be the limit of most of the Christmas activity; beyond it, the Quays were quiet and almost bereft of traffic. Down on the water, a Guinness barge chugged by, the noise of its engine dulled and its light eerie in the deepening fog.

Elizabeth came as far as Adam and Eve's, the Franciscans' church on Merchants Quay and, almost before she knew what she was doing, she had walked up the four shallow steps which led to the wooden doors of the church. Before going inside, however, she hesitated in front of them.

An old woman, dressed in black from head to toe and with a heavy shawl over her head, hobbled past her and, automatically, Elizabeth stood back to let her go ahead but having opened one of the doors, the old lady held it in one arthritic hand and looked back. 'Are you comin' in, love, or are you stoppin'?'

Elizabeth decided it was an omen. 'Thank you,' she said and taking the door from the woman she followed her into the lobby of the church, across a sort of ante-room and, pushing open another door, found herself in one of the transepts. It was dim and peaceful, the air smoky from the fog which had leaked in from outside and which seemed to muffle the sounds, the shuffling of feet, soft click of rosary beads, winter coughing.

Since it was Saturday and so close to Christmas, all the confessionals were in use and several people were making progress around the Stations, cast, unusually, in blue and white ceramic. The four confessionals on Elizabeth's side were busy; she scanned the names above them, Father Leonard, Father Victor, Father Bernardine, Father Livius. She settled for Livius as he had the longest queue and therefore had probably gained the reputation for going easiest on his penitents.

It seemed she had made the right choice; Livius' queue was moving faster than any other in the church and, within ten minutes or so, Elizabeth was only five people away from the box and starting to panic. She had not thought out what she was going to say. Yet she could not get up and leave now, everyone in the church would know she had lost her nerve and would think that whatever she had to confess was utterly heinous.

Fourth now. Could she pretend to be sick? The person on the other side of the box came out and the queue shuffled up on the seat. It was too late to do anything, she was third.

Then second . . .

She heard the slide in the confessional close, meaning that the next one in would be herself. 'Oh, God,' she prayed, 'help me,' then remembered she was in mortal sin and had therefore turned her back on God.

Her stomach churning, she closed the door of the confessional behind her and knelt on the hard wood of the prie-dieu. She felt oppressed, claustrophobic, as if in that tiny space the oxygen, breathed and warmed by so many bodies before her own, had already been used up; her blood

66

thumped in her ears as through the wooden slide she could hear the murmur of the Act of Contrition being made by the penitent on the other side and the answering deeper notes of the priest, his whispered, sibilant 'S's.

The whole box shook as the other penitent stood up and her own slide was pulled back.

'Bless me, Father, for I have sinned . . .' Elizabeth froze. She could not complete the formula, to say how long it had been since her last confession. She had not prepared. She did not know. She did not know what words to put on her sin.

The outline of the Franciscan's profile was all she could make out through the grille. It blurred and she knew he had turned towards her. 'Sorry, Father,' she whispered.

'How long has it been, my child?' his voice was perfectly pitched, not a whisper but a clear murmur in which a penitent could have confidence, knowing no other ears could make out the words.

Frantically, Elizabeth tried to remember. 'I don't know, Father,' she whispered. 'Some time this summer.'

'Don't worry, child, you're here now. What do you have to confess?'

'I – I find it difficult to say, Father.' Elizabeth was wrong-footed. She had been ready for a verbal attack.

'Let me help you. Is it to do with carnal love?'

'Yes, Father.' In the darkness, her cheeks grew hot.

'I see. Mary Magdalen was forgiven by Our Lord. So are you—'

'I think I'm pregnant, Father!' She blurted it.

'And you're not married?'

'No.'

'Engaged?' Then, when she did not reply, 'Is it possible for you to get married?'

Again he waited for a reply but Elizabeth's voice was choked in her throat.

'I see,' said the Franciscan. 'Do you love the man, daughter?'

'I – I don't know. I thought I did, but I don't know.' The admission seemed horrific. It was the first time she had brought it to the front of her mind. 'I did, Father,' she said in desperation, 'at – at the time, I mean—'

'Will your family help you? Will the man?'

'Maybe. Nobody knows yet, I haven't told anybody.'

'The first thing you must do is tell your family. You might be surprised at how they'll react. But even if they're harsh, remember that, as a Christian, you must have love for them, too. But your prime concern now is for the little baby you're carrying. To you, that little baby is the most important person in your life, in the whole world. Ask God and Our Blessed Lady for help. They won't fail you, child. I'll pray for you to St Francis every day. You will have courage. Your baby will give you courage. And remember there will be rejoicing in Heaven when your baby is born so you must rejoice, too. If you trust in God, that baby will be your strength, your consolation and your joy for the rest of your life. Is there anything else?'

'No, Father.'

'Go in peace, my child. And even when it seems you are, don't forget that you are never alone. Say the Magnificat for your penance. Think of the words as you say them. Now say your Act of Contrition. You are welcome back into God's family, my child.'

As Elizabeth mouthed the well-worn words of sorrow for her sin, an extraordinary thing happened; she felt her body grow lighter and lighter until her limbs were like vapour. She wanted to sing, to break down the mesh between herself and the old man and to hug him.

She realized he had finished his absolution. 'Thank you, Father,' she whispered, and just stopped herself from repeating it like a happy refrain: thankyouthankyouthankyou – *thank you*!

'Thank you, daughter. Goodbye now, God bless you, you and your little baby. He will.' The slide behind the grille closed and she heard the murmur as Father Livius bent his ear to the next penitent.

Although the body of the church was not fully lit, Elizabeth, carrying her packages, had to blink as she left the confession box. The glow from the sanctuary lamp flamed like fireworks, the brass chains suspending it glittered like gold, even the clothes on the backs of the poor of Dublin seemed to have lost their drabness and to spread now across the church like a colourful nosegay. She tried hard to come down to earth – to tell herself it was batty to be behaving as though all her problems were over instead of just beginning – but the exultation would not be tamped down; it coursed through her blood like a river about to burst its banks.

She knelt to say her penance but after the first few words: 'My soul doth magnify the Lord' ... could not remember the rest. She knew the prayer was easily found at home, however, in a missal or in her *Children of Mary's Manual*, put aside after her schooldays. She said a quick 'Hail Mary', genuflected to the altar, and left the church.

Outside, it was completely dark now and the fog had thickened. She wrapped her scarf around her mouth and keeping close to the buildings on her left-hand side, walked slowly along the Quays towards the railway station. It was impossible to see more than a few feet ahead; the city was invisible now, a presence which existed only at the margins of her consciousness. From time to time another human being, an indistinct sexless density, would loom out of the thickness and be as quickly gone, or the clopping of a horse cab, the putt-putting of a motor engine, would materialize briefly as a passing oval of light, but Elizabeth's isolation seemed to underline her feeling of airiness and she felt infused with resolve that no matter what faced her she could rise above it. Why hadn't she gone to confession before now? If this was coming back into the state of grace, she thought happily, it was almost worth going into mortal sin.

Her sense of well-being did not collapse until she was nearly back in Cork.

With an explosion of steam the train was pulling out of the station at Limerick Junction. As, puff by puff, it gathered speed, Elizabeth, who was alone in her carriage, lowered the window, letting the leather strap out to its furthest hole. She leaned out, inhaling the frosty air, tasting its sharpness at the back of her throat. Out here, far from any cities, there was no trace of the fog which had snuffed out the air over Dublin, the sky was so brilliant with stars, the high moon so white that she could pick out detail in the hedges and the roughness of empty fields and could follow the outline of the train's shadow as it travelled over the nearside ditches.

Ignoring the cold which made her eyes water, Elizabeth stayed where she was until the train went round a long curve and she was caught in the warm slipstream of smuts from the locomotive. Then she withdrew her head and closed the window but when she turned to resume her seat, found she was no longer alone. A woman was shepherding two small children on to the seats opposite. She had not heard them come in.

She smiled hello but, having no desire to enter conversation, pulled a copy of *Woman's Weekly* out of her shopping bag and opened it to an article on 'How to make the most of your appearance'. Covertly, however, she watched the actions of the woman opposite. One of the children, a little girl of about eighteen months, was grizzling and would not settle until the mother fished a minute patch of worn blanketing out of her handbag and closed the child's fingers over it, whereupon the little girl immediately ceased whimpering, shoved a corner of the patch into her mouth and promptly closed her eyes. The woman looked over at Elizabeth and, woman-to-woman, raised her eyes to heaven: *What can you do with them?*

Elizabeth smiled but her spirits plummeted. This was the reality of child-rearing: nappies and crying and sleepless nights. Her euphoria after her encounter with the priest now seemed stupid, a grasping at ephemeral straws of sentimentality and more childish than the habit of blanket-sucking.

Now she turned against herself and against the Franciscan who had so cruelly given her false joy. It was all very well, she thought, for a mendicant and celibate friar, snug in the cocoon of his little mahogany box, to talk about courage and little babies. What would he know? By the

70

time the train pulled into Cork railway station, Elizabeth was more depressed than she had ever been in her life.

Whoever heard of getting the Magnificat for a penance, anyway?

Yet she was too superstitious not to perform the penance and late that night, having discovered that the Magnificat was not in her missal, she started to hunt for her *Children of Mary's Manual*, not an easy task because her belongings were in their usual state of flux. By her own choice, her bedroom was in the attic and as Maeve had refused point blank to climb 'all them stairs' when she was cleaning the house, the room mouldered away to itself under a permanent layer of disarray. Only the costumes and starched blouses Elizabeth wore for work were placed in any order on the hanging rail which stretched the width of the room along one wall; the rest of her clothes could be anywhere under or over her old lacrosse sticks and tennis rackets, her first typewriter, the photograph albums, childhood teddy bears and dolls, even draped over the back of her ancient rocking horse. She hated to part with anything.

Up here, the noises from the rest of the house were heard only as distant echoes but she chose to sleep in the attic not only because of the privacy it afforded her but because the room was huge and lit by skylights. In this private place, Elizabeth's frame of reference was not the world but the universe beyond it; in the heat of summer, she opened her windows on the sky and imagined she was sleeping under the stars.

Apart from the bed, the dominant feature of the room was the undulating prairie of books, drifts and heaps of them, every book Elizabeth had ever possessed since babyhood, piled in no order all around the walls, spilling over the rest of the furniture, even shoved under the bed. Her irritation grew by the minute as she rummaged through them. Never having been exactly convinced of the strength of her purpose of amendment, she was becoming less and less so. Now she wished she had not gone to confession at all. She had been an idiot to have listened to that stupid

71

Franciscan. She'd need courage all right, but no stupid prayer would help her find it.

'Where *is* it?' she muttered aloud. Then, discarded in one corner, she spotted a pile of her old school books. She delved through the heap and found it, a dusty little volume, the top of the spine unravelled. 'Right,' she said, and finding the page, began to read aloud: '"My soul doth magnify the Lord . . ."'

Then, remembering the priest's injunction that she should think of the words as she prayed them, she shimmied across the room on her knees and assumed a prayerful position by the side of her bed. '". . . And my spirit hath rejoiced in God my Saviour. For he hath regarded the humility of his handmaid: for behold from henceforth all generations shall call me blessed . . ."'

Elizabeth's stomach again performed a nervous dance: Father Livius had either known what he was doing or he was having some sort of joke on her. She had forgotten that the Magnificat was the response of Jesus's mother to the news that she was pregnant.

Slowly, almost disbelieving, she read the rest of the words, mouthing them soundlessly:

'Because he that is mighty hath done great things to me: and holy is his name. And his mercy is from generation unto generation, to them that fear him. He hath showed might in his arm: he hath scattered the proud in the conceit of their heart. He hath put down the mighty from their seat: and hath exalted the humble. He hath filled the hungry with good things: and the rich he hath sent empty away. He hath received Israel his servant: being mindful of his mercy. As he spoke to our fathers, to Abraham and his seed for ever.'

'Amen,' she whispered.

She read the prayer again, concentrating. It was a song of such acceptance and joy that she felt it filtering through to her bones. When she had finished, she felt calm and empty. She stood up and began to remove her clothes.

She turned out the light and got into bed, lying on her back and gazing upwards at the skylight directly above her head. Hazed with frost, the glass had taken on the opacity of spun sugar and glimmered under the brightness of the moon. Maybe there was no need for all this apprehension and gloom? Maybe, when she rang the doctor, he would have good news for her? The mini-flame of hope that this was all a scare fluttered briefly.

Instantly and firmly, Elizabeth quenched it. She was pregnant, she knew it, and there was no getting away from it.

There and then she resolved with great clarity that she would not shirk what was to come nor prevaricate about it. There was no point now in whining or in being lily-livered. She had to look on the bright side, she told herself. No matter how difficult things were going to be, nothing could be as bad as what happened to the mother of Jesus twenty centuries ago. For instance, how did Mary's mother react to the news that her sixteen-year-old unmarried daughter was not only pregnant but pregnant by a sort of osmosis?

Try explaining something like that! Elizabeth smiled with grim humour as she turned over on her side. Anyway, she thought just before she fell asleep, no one was going to shoot her.

Chapter Five

Nobody did shoot her, of course, but there were occasions during the next two weeks when, despite all her resolutions, Elizabeth wished someone would. She longed to confide in someone, but Ida, who would have been the most likely candidate, had thrown up her dull job in Cork and was away seeking more exciting prospects in the United States; they had corresponded, but Elizabeth, in her letters, always pulled back from committing the news of her pregnancy to paper. Somehow, to see it written in black and white would have made it seem too real and permanent.

Although she had known that the telephone call to the doctor on the following Thursday would be a formality, she still dared to hope just a little. The hope survived until the Thursday morning when, to her dismay, she woke to the sound of a single magpie pecking at the putty in the window of the skylight above her head. Although she performed all the standard antidotes, spitting, giving the wretched bird a military salute, wishing it a loud 'good morning', in her heart she knew she was wasting her time.

Somehow she got through the day and then, pretending to have work to catch up on, waited until all the others in her room had left the office before dialling the Dublin number.

'So that's it,' the doctor said, having given her the approximate date on which, in his opinion, she would deliver her child. 'You'll be contacting your own doctor in Cork, I presume?'

'Yes.' It did not matter that Elizabeth had been prepared for this. It was still devastating.

'Congratulations, Mrs Sullivan!' If the Dublin doctor was being ironic, it did not show in his precise dry voice.

'Thank you.' With shaking hands, Elizabeth replaced the telephone receiver. Reflexively, she glanced at the closed door behind which St. John Sullivan still worked: how on earth was she going to break the news to him and to her mother?

He was in there right now. What was wrong with now? She remembered Father Livius and his exhortations: *No matter how difficult it is . . .*

'All right, St Francis or whoever you are,' she whispered, 'now's your chance. Let's see how good you are . . .'

But standing in front of her father's thick mahogany door she was seized with panic so strong she could hardly breathe. She would not be able to tell her father. Or anyone.

She grabbed her coat and hat from her coat-stand and fled the office.

The next few days passed in a haze of pain and indecision. She found it almost impossible to work normally and her powers of concentration were so much diminished that having read even the simplest instructions she would immediately forget what she had read and would have to go back to the beginning. And in light of the tremendous events which now concerned her, the verbose wording of legal documents seemed of no consequence, a ridiculous obfuscation of meaning. Her brain grappled with what she had to take in dictation and transcribe and frequently lost the battle for understanding.

She had decided on one thing at least: she would not spoil Christmas for her parents. But all through the feast, while she went through the well-worn motions of celebration, her emotions swung wildly between hope and despair.

She would have a miscarriage, it happened all the time.

No, not to her. Nothing but bad things now happened to her. She would be shut up in a Magdalen Home, incarcerated with the other wretches and outcasts of the county.

And all the time the *thing* was growing inside her. She had no sense of it except as an alien, malignant blob. At night, while she lay awake staring through her skylight,

75

she imagined it, fastened like a leech to the inside of her womb.

How could she have been so stupid as to imagine she loved that man? Yet, despite her terror, despite everything that had happened and was going to happen, the memory and thrill of the sexual acts between George and herself would not go away, and in the dead of night, insisted on being celebrated in her feverish mind and body. She did love him, she did. Then, in the next moment, her heart would fill with revulsion. She hated him. How could she have let him touch her?

Once, during one of those dreadful sleepless nights, she had resolved to contact George Gallaher – after all, it was his mess too. But next morning, she faced the fact that she had no idea how to find George even if he had not yet left for America. And to be fair, she thought, she had no right to add anything more to the difficulties of George's long-suffering wife.

Gradually, Elizabeth was overtaken by a sort of desperate stoicism.

As it happened, the confrontation with her parents, which she left until New Year's Day, had proved not to be the dramatic opera of her fears but a much more low-key affair during which her mother had sighed a lot and let spill a few tears and her father had seemed to be struck speechless.

Two days later, Cork being too small a place to consult a local gynaecologist without causing gossip, Elizabeth's mother had accompanied her back to Dublin to see a consultant there, a man who merely confirmed the diagnosis of the first doctor. Throughout the train journey there and back, during the consultation, for the whole of that day, Corinne Sullivan had not once met her daughter's eyes.

And for the following week or so, the little household had worn a wispy mantle of unreality under which everyone, even the housekeeper, Maeve – who, of course, had immediately found out what had happened – had acted as though life was quite normal. Yet Elizabeth felt that under this surface, a tentacled monstrosity was heaving around, waiting for the right time to rear through the surface and drag her into itself. Meal-times were the worst: the warm kitchen where she had spent such a pleasant childhood became a torture chamber in which silent recrimination served as a rack.

Round about the second week of the new year, she was summoned to the drawing room. When she opened the door, she experienced that little curl of air at the back of her neck which always signified that something of huge significance was about to happen. Her parents, like fire irons and just as immobile, stood at either side of the marble fireplace. On the couch, at right angles to them, sat a man whom at first Elizabeth did not recognize and whom she was too flustered to scrutinize.

'Come in, Elizabeth.' Her father was using his grave solicitor's voice. 'You've met Father Young before?' He indicated the other man.

'Oh, yes, I remember now . . .' The priest, originally from Bantry, a fishing port in West Cork, was a hunting acquaintance of St John Sullivan's. Elizabeth had not met him for many years and had not recognized him because of the woollen scarf he had wound tightly round his throat and which concealed his clerical collar. 'Sorry, Father, how do you do?' She realized her voice had started to wobble and consciously straightened her shoulders. 'It's been years since we've met, hasn't it?' she said, striding across the room with her hand held in front of her like a lance.

He stood up and shook the hand, seriously, as though to make sure that the gesture could not be misinterpreted as any ordinary old shake. 'Yes, it has, Elizabeth,' he said. 'Been years, I mean. How you've grown.'

The silence yawned before them all again.

'Let's all sit down.' Elizabeth's father crossed to another couch.

Elizabeth, feeling she was an actor in one of the Vivian Mellors Touring Company plays, sat beside the priest, folding herself into the angle of the arm-rest to get as far away from him as possible. Although the blustery January wind rattled the window-panes, she felt hotter than on the warmest day of summer. A priest! Except when they were relatives or guests at formal dinner parties, a priest's authority was brought to play in families in cases only of the direst emergency.

The dreadful day was here.

Her father cleared his throat. 'Elizabeth,' he began as Elizabeth looked at her feet, 'we've confided our predicament in Father Young here because we trust him and we know he is the soul of discretion. Nothing said or decided here will leave these four walls. Understood?'

Elizabeth nodded.

'Beth, your mother and I have looked at all the options facing us.'

It was here, she could see it already. The monster she had feared, it was coming up from the depths.

'And you know we want only the best for you.' In spite of the pompous tone, Elizabeth saw her father's face was lined with misery. She felt so sorry for him and for herself, too, that she wanted to tell him it was all a mistake, that they mustn't worry about her, she would just offer to go away and drown herself in the Lee. She glanced at her mother – but Corinne was gazing into the fireplace, away from the scene being played out in front of her as though it was no concern of hers. It was at times like this that Elizabeth thought she understood why she was an only child: she had wondered often how her fastidious, remote mother had managed to bring herself to go to bed even once with her father . . .

The bitter thought enabled her to hold on to her tears.

She sat very still while her father again cleared his throat. Hooking his thumbs into the armholes of his waistcoat, a gesture of confidence negated by the colour which flooded into his cheeks, he said in a rush, 'I won't waste time going through everything, you're an intelligent girl, you must have gone through all the possibilities already in your own mind. In conclusion, I believe – we *all* believe, Beth – that the best solution is for you to get married as quickly as possible.'

'But – but I can't, Daddy!' Elizabeth was stunned. In her deepest nightmares she had not envisaged this.

The priest made a little steeple out of his fingers. 'Why not, Elizabeth?'

'Because – because I just can't. The man – George, I mean, he's – he's –'

'Married already,' the priest finished gently. 'We all know that, Elizabeth. No, the option is to marry a good man at home. Well, near home,' he amended.

'What do you mean "near home"?' Good manners dictated that she had to stifle her growing outrage.

'West Cork. It's the same county, you'll be able to come home. As often as you like. For visits.'

'And you have a man picked out, have you? All of you?' Elizabeth could barely control her anger now as she gazed around at the three of them.

'At least consider it, dear.' Corinne was still looking into the fireplace.

Elizabeth took a deep breath. 'How about if I tell you I've already considered it and the answer is no?' Again she looked around the three of them. None would meet her eyes. She stood up. 'Suppose I say I'll just have this baby here? Right in this house?'

She knew the answer before it was voiced, she could see it in the way they continued to avoid looking at her. They had discussed the possibility that she might react like this.

The priest took up the running, confirming her view that this had been rehearsed. 'That won't be possible,' he said, coming to stand in front of her. 'I've something to show you.' He took a photograph out of the pocket of his coat and pressed it into her unyielding hand. 'Look at it,' he coaxed, 'just look at it, Elizabeth.'

Desperately, Elizabeth searched for escape. Her father's stricken face, bent to his chest, was drained of colour and looked like porridge; her mother's fingers plucked at her skirt. She could see there was no appeal.

Dignity. The old drum-beat at the base of her brain. Dignity. Dignity.

She turned away from the priest and walked to the window.

The road outside the house was lined on both sides with trees, bare now, branches extended before the wind like beseeching fingers. A young couple battled along the footpath, laughing, clutching on to their hats and to each other. As Elizabeth watched, they turned and walked backwards, the gale unwinding their scarves so the ends flowed off their necks like party streamers. An ordinary Sunday walk. The tears Elizabeth had been restraining stung hard now. Dignity, she must have dignity.

Slowly, she raised the photograph and looked at it.

The priest saw her do it. 'He's a widower, Elizabeth. And a decent man.'

The photograph had been taken in a studio. Two little girls sat together in a small armchair. A man, presumably their father, stood behind the chair; he held a baby of about ten or eleven months in his arms and beside him stood another little girl, aged, Elizabeth thought, seven or eight years old. She judged the children in the chair to be younger, perhaps six and five.

She felt the priest watching her. 'He has a farm in West Cork on the Béara peninsula,' he said, 'in a townland called Lahersheen, between the villages of Eyeries and Ardgroom.' The names sounded outlandish, even pagan. Béara was another country, and now that trains were so reliable and fast, was as far from Cork city in travelling time as the city of Dublin. She had been to Bantry a few times with her parents and once to visit friends in the yachting village of Crookhaven on the Mizen peninsula, but had never ventured as far as Béara.

She did not know what to do or to say and, to gain time, continued to examine the photograph. The little girls wore pinafores and starched bows in their straight hair, the baby wore a frilled bonnet.

The man was wearing a suit, his hair had been slicked with grease and his high collar seemed uncomfortably tight.

In nact all five in the photograph looked uncomfortable as they gazed solemnly up at her: they had obviously dressed up in new or best clothes for the occasion. Unexpectedly, Elizabeth felt a tug at her heart: all these little girls were orphans. Judging by the age of the baby, they must have lost a mother very recently.

And the man? He was thin, of average or below average size as far as Elizabeth could judge. She studied the long narrow face with its high cheekbones, the big hands which held the baby, and could not discern any character, good or bad, in the formality of his pose and expression.

This stranger was being proposed as her husband?

'You can't be serious!' With an air of finality she returned the photograph to the priest.

'We don't expect you to answer right away, Elizabeth.' The priest did not look in the least taken aback. 'All we ask is that you consider it.'

'We? *We?*' At last Elizabeth found her anger. 'Who's "we", might I ask?' She glared across at her parents for rescue but Corinne was still gazing into the fire and her father had shielded his distress by placing one hand to his temple.

'Your parents are *ad idem* on this,' the priest replied. 'They asked for my help because I have a little experience in these matters. You do accept that you cannot do as you suggested earlier, Elizabeth? You can't seriously be proposing that you stay in this house and have this baby, flying in the face of God's law and shaming your parents before the whole city?'

Elizabeth pushed past him, crossed the room and stood in front of her father. 'Are you, Daddy? Are you ashamed of me?'

He looked up at her, his eyes tragic. 'I'm not ashamed of you, Elizabeth, but I don't know what else to do.'

'Then why can't you stand by me?'

'Your mother – the practice . . .' He trailed off miserably.

'And you, Mother?' Elizabeth rounded on Corinne. 'What about you? Are you ashamed?'

Corinne smiled vaguely. 'Of course I'm not ashamed of you personally, Elizabeth, but we did warn you about

81

actors and the like. Oh, it's all such a bother.' She flicked dust off the arm-rest of the couch.

'What have actors got to do with it?' Absurdly, Elizabeth felt now she had to defend George Gallaher. 'It takes two to make a baby, Mother. I had something to do with it, you know. Quite a lot, actually, as it happens.' She wanted to punish her mother, punish them all.

'Spare us the details, Beth. At least have a little taste.'

Her mother's pained expression almost made Elizabeth laugh. 'Well, Mother,' she said, 'your cosy solution to *our* little problem won't work. I'm not marrying that man for your convenience and that's that.' Without a backward glance she stormed out of the room.

By the following Sunday, however, they had worn her down.

The priest came twice during the week. The first time, Elizabeth refused to speak to him at all, locking herself into her attic refuge. The second time she could not avoid him because he caught her unawares in the drawing room and stood in front of the door, blocking her exit, and for five minutes she was forced to listen as he attempted to persuade her once again that marriage to the Béara widower would be best for her, for her parents – and for her own baby. 'And think about those four little girls, Elizabeth,' he said at the end, 'four little girls who need a mother. Out of your disgrace, God has made an opportunity. He will bless you, if you listen.'

Elizabeth finally managed to escape and pounded up the attic stairs to the safety of her room. God was hounding her. They were hounding her with God. First it was the Franciscan in Dublin, now this earnest country priest.

Courage. She would have to keep tight hold on her diminishing courage.

However, on the Friday and Saturday of that week, she had her first bouts of morning sickness and on the Sunday, when the priest arrived for the third time, joining her and her parents for Sunday dinner, she was too tired, weak and wretched to maintain her defiance. Because in addition to her physical ills, unknown to them all, she had gone the day before to look at the outside of the Magdalen Home, the institution where the disgraced girls and women of the city went to have their sinfully conceived offspring. She had stood looking at it from the opposite side of the street trying to imagine what life inside might be, but although she waited for the best part of five minutes, no one went in or out through the massive gates, no face appeared at any window, no sound travelled from behind its walls. The building lay like a huge corpse across a corner of the city, repelling hope from all directions.

Elizabeth realized that passers-by were staring at her and walked away. The sight of this dreadful place now confirmed for her that there was no escape.

Nevertheless, at Sunday dinner when the priest again brought up the subject of the widower in Béara, she looked for one last time for help from her mother and father. 'Daddy? Mother?'

'For heaven's sake, we wouldn't be suggesting it if we didn't think it was the best solution! The *only* solution.' Corinne Sullivan's habitual vagueness was nowhere in evidence as she rejected her daughter's appeal.

Her father was gentler. 'Beth, what else can we do? If there was anything else, believe me . . .'

Elizabeth looked at him for a few moments, willing him to continue, to say he had changed his mind, to tell her she could stay, but he dropped his eyes to his plate. She looked out through the window into the garden, greying and forlorn under a shower of sleet. January had bleached the herb and vegetable plots of colour, the lawn looked rough and unkempt, the apple trees and deciduous shrubs sagged like old skeletons. Elizabeth felt as tired and scraggly as the plants, too tired even to search for a sign or an omen. 'What's his name?' she asked. 'How old is he?'

'Neeley Scollard,' answered the priest. 'He's forty-one.'

Father Young organized it so that the banns could be called in Bantry, and the wedding took place late one afternoon with only a handful of people present. There was no music.

Having tried in vain to talk Elizabeth into defying her parents and going to Dublin or even to London, Ida Healy, who had returned from America as a result of desperate homesickness, acted as reluctant bridesmaid. As late as their arrival at the door of the church, Ida had still not given up. 'It's not too late, Beth,' she whispered, 'we can still turn and run.'

Elizabeth shook her head. Since she had agreed to marry Neeley Scollard she had lived her life in a sort of determined detachment. This was punishment for past misdeeds. She had been stupid, hedonistic; now she must pay and she might as well get on with it.

She had taken no interest in what she would wear for the wedding, walking aimlessly along the rails of clothes in Cash's as her mother selected what she thought might be suitable.

Corinne had misinterpreted her expression as Elizabeth had inspected the garments she had taken out. 'Well, darling, you can hardly wear white, can you?'

Elizabeth did not bother to answer. 'This'll do,' she said, taking one of the outfits, a costume of dove-grey silk, out of her mother's arms.

'How about the yellow?' After bridge, shopping was Corinne's greatest pleasure.

'Whatever you think, Mother, I really don't care.'

'Oh, for goodness' sake, Beth, do pull yourself together and try to concentrate.' Corinne had insisted she try on both outfits and would have brought more, except that Elizabeth persuaded her that she loved the grey. And she had submitted without protest as her mother had selected a small, jaunty hat to go with the costume.

Elizabeth shivered now as she walked into the church porch with her father and Ida. Silk, she thought, was not at all a suitable fabric for a West Cork February. 'Think, Beth, think!' Ida was still whispering in her ear. 'I'd help you. You don't even know this man properly.'

'Please, Ida, let's do this and get it over with.' Elizabeth took her father's arm and pulled him into the body of the church ahead of her friend. As their footsteps echoed on the tiled floor, she saw Neeley Scollard look towards them from the top pew and then step into the aisle, followed closely by another man who stood beside him. Father Young was already facing them from the sanctuary. At the last minute Maeve, the housekeeper, had declined to attend the wedding – using a cold in the head as the excuse – so the only other person in the church was Corinne, standing resolutely in the pew across the aisle from Neeley's. Wearing a coat of turquoise wool with toning hat of aquamarine feathers, Elizabeth's mother glowed like an exotic jewel in the gloomy setting.

All the way up the aisle, Elizabeth could feel Ida willing her to turn back. And her resolve and detachment almost deserted her when her father squeezed her arm with his own. 'Are you all right, Beth?'

'I'm grand, Daddy.' But she had to blink hard.

Neeley Scollard had made an effort with his clothes, a pin-striped dark suit – in the shadows of the church it was hard to discern whether it was navy or dark brown – gleaming brown shoes and a shirt so white and stiff with starch Elizabeth heard a faint crackle as he took her arm.

After one brief, non-committal smile, she kept her eyes on the priest. She felt as she had on the day she came back to Cork from Gallaher, as though she was pushing hard through a headwind.

As there was no Mass, the ceremony was brief. Asked by the priest beforehand if she had any special requests, Elizabeth had on the spur of the moment asked that the Magnificat be said at the end. The request had been instinctive: somehow to say it seemed to allow her one private personal act which had nothing to do with the wedding itself. It had to do with the thing – she still could not think of it as a baby – inside her, the way it had been made and the feeling of euphoria in Adam and Eve's after her confession. Somehow, in a way she could not have explained, it had to do with a timeless celebration of what she had done with George.

Wearing Neeley Scollard's thin gold ring, she followed the words in her prayer book as the priest intoned them:

'My soul doth magnify the Lord. And my spirit hath rejoiced in God my Saviour. For he hath regarded the humility of his handmaid: for behold from henceforth all generations shall call me blessed. Because he that is mighty hath done great things to me . . .'

As the words rolled on, Elizabeth, recognizing that what she was feeling was not appropriate for a hurried wedding to a man she did not love or even know, nevertheless felt special and heroic, like the protagonist in a great drama.

As he spoke to our fathers, to Abraham and his seed for ever . . . Amen.

As she joined in the 'Glory be' which followed, she knew now why she had asked for the prayer: she was part of a chain of commemoration. Each time the seed was passed on was a triumph and added a link to the chain; physical love was a gift of life and as natural to human beings as to plants, birds and animals. Up to the time she had met George Gallaher, sex had been a whispered, giggled thing, surrounded by taboos and dangers but she knew now, George had taught her, that this was not what God had intended.

Elizabeth was not sorry she had made love with George Gallaher nor that he had taught her so well; she decided she would never be sorry again. In fact she felt quite the opposite: she felt victorious, as if she had won something which no one could ever take away from her.

Amen. The prayer finished the ceremony.

Elizabeth smiled at Neeley after they signed the register. 'Come on,' she said, taking his arm, 'it's very cold. I can't wait to get out of this church and get something hot to eat.' He blushed and as she felt his body tremble with tension, Elizabeth surged with unexpected sympathy.

She had met her new husband only once previously. As it had been too far for either of the parties to travel to one another's homes, they had met in the Eccles Hotel in Glengarriff, a small resort town at the junction of the Béara and Iveragh peninsulas. For Elizabeth that meeting had been almost surreal and she would have been hard put to remember many of the details, except that Neeley's hand had been wet when shaking hers. Her prospective husband had been polite, taller than his photograph suggested, with a bald spot at the crown of his head and, despite his seeming shyness, was almost comically eager to make a good impression. Yet, she kept reminding herself, he had been married before and had four children so he must have *something* to offer . . .

Her sense of unreality had been heightened because she had found it very difficult to understand him; like many people from West Cork, the words sprayed out of Neeley's mouth like bullets from the barrel of the Vickers machine gun she had once seen fired in an army display.

As she walked beside him now, Elizabeth realized that, up to this moment, she had not fully appreciated she was marrying a real person. In thinking about herself and her own plight, she had overlooked the fact that this could not be easy for Neeley Scollard either. Up to this she had treated him as though he were a paper man, of no substance, like the flimsy figures she used to cut out of magazines and arrange in lifelike poses round her bedroom to help fill the social gaps in her life as an only child.

Neeley was not George Gallaher, she decided, squeezing his arm, but he was a human being, of flesh and blood. All right, he was older; he was not rich; he was certainly not charming. He came encumbered with four dependants and lived in the back end of nowhere. But this marriage was real, Neeley was real. The prospect of spending the rest of her life with him frightened her but challenged her too. She had to make a go of this if her own life was to mean anything.

And she was going to.

'Look,' she whispered, as she and her husband walked out of the church, 'let's not spend too much time over the meal, let's get it over with as quickly as possible.'

'Sure.' Neeley glanced uncertainly at her.

The tiny group, caught by the wind from the grey sea, stood tongue-tied in the forecourt of the church and as no one else seemed about to make a move, Elizabeth tugged at Neeley's arm and began to walk towards the small inn where they were to eat.

The wedding breakfast, more properly lunch, was a short, awkward affair. Elizabeth's father was anxious to get back on the road before dark, and Elizabeth and Neeley were spending their wedding night in the hotel where they had met in Glengarriff which was a good hour and a half distant in the hackney that Neeley and his friend had hired to bring them into Bantry.

There were no toasts but when the rest of the company was listening to a long nervously related anecdote from St John Sullivan about the solicitor's lot in Cork city, Ida, who was sitting beside Elizabeth, surreptitiously raised her cup of tea in salute. 'I'm sorry for being so bitchy,' she whispered, 'you know I wish you all the luck in the world. He's not too bad, after all.'

'No,' Elizabeth whispered back. 'He could be worse, thanks, Ida.'

'You'll stay in touch?'

'Of course. And you must come to visit us.'

'As soon as I can. Depend on it.' Elizabeth realized that her father's story had come to an end and there was silence around the table. She turned away from Ida. 'We'd better start making a move?'

As though she had cracked a starting pistol St John Sullivan pushed back his chair. 'Now where is that waiter?' The words were too loud and to cover them he began to search ostentatiously for his wallet in the inside pocket of his jacket.

'Don't make a fuss, St John.' Corinne's voice was tired and remote.

'For heaven's sake, Corinne, I'm not making a fuss. They're never around when you want them are they?' Man to man, St John appealed to his new son-in-law.

Elizabeth saw that the hands which had at last found the wallet were unsteady and once again she had great difficulty in restraining her emotions. She squeezed her hands tightly together in her lap, wishing with all her heart that this phase of the event would pass as quickly as possible.

The little group emerged into the wide square, one of Bantry's most notable features. Today, however, under the low, blowing sky, the sea was uneasy, slapping at the hulls of the small half-deckers and open dinghies which bobbed around on its chop. 'Oh dear, it *is* dismal.' Corinne shivered delicately.

Elizabeth, seeing that both her parents were avoiding her eyes, pulled her coat tighter around her: 'Look, Mother, Daddy, don't let's hang around,' she said flatly. 'There's nothing much to say anyway, is there?'

Instead of replying, her father withdrew a small envelope from the pocket of his coat. 'This is for you – and – and Neeley,' he said gravely. 'Don't open it now,' he went on in a rush as Elizabeth made as though to slit it open. 'You'll have plenty of time later.'

Seeing his mournful expression, Elizabeth wanted to throw her arms around him, to beg him to forget all about this awful day, to bring her home with him. Instead, she put the envelope into her handbag. 'Thank you, Daddy,' she said quietly. 'I don't deserve this.'

'I'm *cold*, St John!' Corinne was looking away out over the sea as though, once again, the scene within her family had very little to do with her.

'Thank you, too, Mother, for everything.' Elizabeth pulled at her mother's arm, forcing her back into what was going on.

'For nothing, Beth.' For a second, Elizabeth saw in Corinne's eyes how great was her disappointment. But as quickly as her mother had shown her vulnerability, she covered it up. 'I wish you well in your new life, Beth,' she said formally. 'Do make an effort to stay in touch, won't you?' She kissed Elizabeth briefly on the cheek, leaving behind her the sensation of coolness and the scent of ashes of roses. She turned to Neeley and extended her hand. 'Congratulations, Neeley. I'm sorry the circumstances of your wedding were not a little more, well, auspicious . . .' She trailed off.

'Take care of her, Neeley.' Elizabeth's father turned away and walked rapidly towards the car.

Corinne watched him for a second or two then reached out her hand, first to the priest – 'Goodbye, Father, and thank you for everything' – then to the best man who was standing uncomfortably a little behind Neeley. 'Goodbye Mr – er –'

'Harrington,' the man supplied, taking Corinne's hand and shaking it vigorously.

For an excruciating moment, Corinne hesitated, unsure how to proceed further. Elizabeth helped her. 'Goodbye, Mother,' she said firmly, pecking her on the cheek.

'Be good, Beth . . .' As Corinne walked straight-backed across the square towards the car, Elizabeth had to resist a perverse impulse to run after her. For the first time in many years, she longed to throw herself into her mother's arms and to cry like a baby on her shoulder.

Ida was the last of the Cork city threesome to leave. She smiled and hugged Elizabeth and was almost at the car when, at the last minute, she ran back and threw her arms around her friend's neck a second time. 'You're a stupid oul' bitch, you know that?' She was crying. 'Why didn't you just take the boat? Something could have been organized.'

'Really?' Elizabeth hugged her. 'Come on, Ida. You know as well as I do I was in a trap.'

'I'm sorry I said all those things about you being thick. You know I didn't mean it. You're not thick, Beth, you've got a hell of a lot more guts than I do.'

'Oh, don't, Ida –' Elizabeth had difficulty with her voice. Although she knew she was secure in Ida's affection and support, the two of them had quarrelled frequently in the weeks preceding the wedding. 'Look,' she said, hugging Ida fiercely, 'I can't stand much more of this, let's just say goodbye, all right? And I'll see you soon. I'm not going to the end of the world, you know!' She let Ida go and, forcing herself not to look back either at her friend or at her parents, climbed in beside Neeley who was already seated in the back seat of the hackney car. 'Let's go, come on,' she whispered urgently to the driver.

With a great revving of its engine the big Dodge moved out of the square in Bantry and Elizabeth had to call on all her remaining reserves of strength to keep her face towards the west.

Chapter Six

On their wedding night, Elizabeth and Neeley sat over dinner like the strangers they were, their conversation polite to the point of being strained. Despite her brief moment of rapport with Neeley at the church, try as she might now Elizabeth could not grasp the total reality of her situation, of their situation together.

The food was good hearty fare, served in substantial portions but she was finding it difficult to eat. The only other diners were a party of three, seated at a table on the other side of the dining room; from their conversation, Elizabeth deduced that they were members of the Anglo-Irish gentry – or perhaps English visitors – here on a shooting holiday. By contrast to the loud and convivial sounds coming from their table, the one at which she and Neeley sat was an island of silence and tension.

The hotel possessed a generator and the dining room was brightly lit, which served only to highlight its emptiness. Doubling as a ballroom, the room ran along the front of the hotel and through the windows, as a mournful counterpoint to the bonhomie at the other table, Elizabeth could hear the subdued groan of the sea. Trying desperately to relax, she stared at the old-fashioned pattern on the carpet, memorizing the intricacies of its lines and swirls as though she were to be set a written examination on them.

She finally placed her knife and fork side by side on her plate. She continued to be a credit to Maeve, she thought, smiling sadly. As much as her parents, she already missed the old housekeeper who throughout her childhood had acted almost as a nanny, drilling her with correct manners and etiquette at table. She looked hard at her husband. It was now or never. She and Neeley had to break through to one another if they were to have any chance at all. And as it did not look like he was going to be the one to take the plunge, it was up to her. She took a breath and held it at the very top, counting to three. Then: 'We have to talk, Neeley,' she said, 'we didn't get much of a chance today – or even before.'

'Yes.' Bravely, he held her gaze. 'We're married now,' he said, 'in the eyes of God and man. We have to be able to talk like Christians.'

'Or like Muslims!'

He grinned in appreciation and Elizabeth rejoiced. Her new husband might be uneducated but he was not unintelligent, and although she already knew he was not in the least interested in books or anything cultural, she had sensed that, having lived his life in such a remote area, this was more a matter of his lack of exposure and opportunity to what had always been to her a normal part of city life. 'Listen, Neeley,' she said, leaning forward over her plate, 'I might as well be honest with you. I'm nervous about tonight.'

He looked at her for a long moment. 'Ditto,' he said.

The word struck Elizabeth as being so funny and incongruous in the circumstances that she laughed out loud.

'What's so funny?' His smile was uncertain now.

'Sorry,' she spluttered, 'it's just that word, not only that word but the way you said it.'

'Ditto?' He looked genuinely puzzled.

'The way you say it, Neeley, so fast like that, it sounds like "Diddo" – and it just strikes me as funny, that's all. Sorry.'

The laughter had eased the tension between them and they sat staring at one another, sizing one another up. 'Do you think it'll work?' Elizabeth said softly.

'Tonight, you mean?'

'Tonight, yes, but the whole thing, this marriage.'

He looked at her and she felt a subtle shift in his attitude, he was surer now. 'It has as good a chance as any of 'em.'

93

'Not a great start?'

'Why not?'

'I assume everyone knows? In Lahersheen, I mean.'

'Knows what? That you're having a baby?'

'That I had to get married.' Elizabeth still could not bring herself to think of the thing inside her as a baby.

'Sure it's no one's business except our own.'

'But won't they make it their business – a small place like that?'

'Listen, girl, you're not talking about city gossip now. We're a bit different on Béara.'

'No gossip?'

'Nothing that'll bother us.'

Elizabeth looked at him with new respect. This was not the tongue-tied peasant she had met a month ago in this hotel, nor the blushing groom who looked strangled by a new suit when he turned around to see her coming up the aisle.

He asked a sudden question, so quick that it passed her by and she had to ask him to repeat it. 'Does my age bother you?'

The question, reiterated more slowly, was nevertheless so unexpected that Elizabeth was startled into honesty. 'It is a big difference,' she admitted.

'Yerra, I'm young at heart! You'll see!'

He smiled but Elizabeth could see the bravado was assumed. He was as worried about their wedding night as she was. Elizabeth recognized for certain now how quickly she had grown up through the affair with George Gallaher. This man had fathered four children but before he had laid a finger on her, she was already absolutely sure she knew more about sexual love than he did. 'I'm sure you're as young as you look, Neeley,' she said softly.

'We don't have to – like – tonight, I mean—' He stopped, uncomfortable.

'Whatever you think.' She sat very still.

'Oh, no, I didn't mean—' He was clearly horrified at the thought she might believe he did not find her attractive.

94

'I know what you meant and thanks for the compliment.'

They were husband and wife now and there was no avoiding this. 'Let's just go to bed and see what happens, Neeley.' Making a calculated survey of the physically positive, Elizabeth looked deliberately at her groom, searching past the crooked nose, the weathered skin, the long narrow face and broken fingernails. Although Neeley would win no beauty contests, his wife decided now that he was not ugly; his mouth was full and mobile, his eyes clear. And now that he had taken off the jacket of his suit and loosened the strangulating tie, she could see his shoulders were broad and hard with work, his forearms strong.

'Come on,' she said, pushing back her chair.

Neeley followed her out of the dining room and stood aside to let her go first into their room. As she entered, Elizabeth's resolve was immediately shaken. In the period since they had placed their luggage in the room, its dimensions seemed to have changed; the walls were closer to each another now, the ceiling lower, so that by comparison, the bed, like the liner in a canal lock, dominated the space so completely as to appear monstrous.

To regain her composure, she walked over to the window and pulled aside the curtain to look out on the seafront of the town. It was only about eight thirty in the evening but, being February, there were few people about. The clouds had lifted and across the road from the hotel, the rowboats and pleasure craft rode as calmly as gondolas on the bay which gleamed under a frost-rimed moon. To the west, the charcoal mountains of Béara humped their secrets to themselves; Garnish Island rose like a dark mausoleum a little way out on the water.

Elizabeth longed to escape into the serenity of it all. 'It's a lovely night,' she said over her shoulder but when there was no response from Neeley, she let the curtain drop and taking a deep breath, faced back into the room and her husband.

Neeley was seated on the bed, watching her. 'Do you

want to leave it for tonight?' His voice was faint. 'I can sleep in the armchair there, if you like . . .'

The absurdity of Neeley's retiring to a chair for the night at eight thirty was too much for Elizabeth. It was on the tip of her tongue to say, 'We might as well get it over with,' but she stopped herself just in time. Instead she walked slowly towards him and put her hands on his shoulders.

Through the fabric of his shirt she felt he was trembling again, but was too apprehensive herself to discern whether it was from nerves or desire. She took his hands and raised them so they rested on her hips. He let them lie there unmoving for a few seconds; then, slowly, he buried his cheek in her stomach.

He smelt faintly of sweat. Time stopped while she stroked the crown of his head. Like a mother with a new baby, she arranged the hair over the balding parts, her fingers surprised by the softness of the strands. She felt now that she was in charge of this situation and the responsibility was bewildering. Had it been only six months since George Gallaher had taken her in his arms and had danced that slow exquisite waltz with her on the grass in Durrow? That Elizabeth was a lifetime away from the woman charged with leading this, very different, gavotte.

The silk on her hips was becoming hot and clammy under his hands, still as inanimate as hams. Gently she removed them and unfastened the skirt of her costume letting it rustle to the ground. He sat passively, his hands in mid-air and then looked up at her, his expression so peculiar she pulled back in alarm. 'What's the matter?'

'Nothing.'

'There is, Neeley, I can see it.'

''Tis nothing, nothing—' He was so agitated that she sat down beside him on the bed. 'It must be something, Neeley. Why are you so upset?'

'No why.'

She could see the conflict on his face. Could he be upset about the memory of his first wife, buried less than ten months ago? Had she completely misread the situation?

Perhaps he did not want sex at all? Perhaps it was too soon for him?

'Is it Agnes, Neeley?' she asked impulsively. 'Is that what's bothering you?'

Instead of answering, he jumped up and, to her horror, ran out of the room. Stupefied, she stared at the wood of the door, its slam resounding again and again in her brain. Her cheeks burned; she had been so stupid, her smugness about her maturity entirely premature. Yet her adventure with George Gallaher had led her to believe that all men, especially older men, were interested in sex. How could she not have seen that Neeley Scollard did not want her sexually at all, he had simply married her to have a free live-in housekeeper for his four children?

She lay down on the bed, not caring about creasing the jacket of her costume; and as she lay there, her humiliation was supplanted by a wave of loneliness and homesickness so intense she could not cry. She had not even said goodbye properly to Ida, to Maeve, to her parents. She pictured her mother and father, home by now, no doubt, seated in the kitchen on either side of the range, Bella curled up and twitching in her basket between them.

And here she was, married to a man she did not know and who did not want her, bound for the back end of beyond.

She lay unmoving for ten minutes then undressed and got into one of the new nightdresses Corinne had pressed on her as part of her bridal trousseau. Elizabeth had not wanted any 'bottom drawer' or any fuss made at the time. Now, however, she was grateful for the coolness of new lawn and for its distinctive clean smell as she turned off the lamp and slid under the bedclothes. She curled herself as small as possible on the very edge of the bed and tried not to think about her predicament.

She had not moved an inch when about a half-hour later she heard Neeley come back. Although he did not turn on the light she closed her eyes tightly, pretending to be asleep as she heard him stumble around and undress in the darkness. Then she felt the bedclothes being pulled back and the heave of the mattress as, breathing heavily, he got into bed beside her.

Every nerve and muscle in Elizabeth's body tightened and she stopped breathing. She felt as rigid and dark as a lump of coal. Then she felt Neeley's hand on her shoulder. 'I'm sorry I behaved like that.'

'That's OK.' This was not her voice. It was someone else's, high and tight.

'It's just that —'

'It's all right, Neeley, we'll sort it out in the morning.'

'No! I want to tell you!' He pulled roughly at her and she was forced to give a little.

'I couldn't do – you know – with the – with the —' His whisper tailed off into the darkness.

She turned round to face him. She could just about make out his features and, for the first time, noticed the smell of whiskey on his breath. 'With the what, Neeley?' She too was whispering.

'That other fella's baby!'

The outburst shocked her. He had obviously been expecting her to fight or argue with him because when she said nothing, he kissed her clumsily, his mouth landing somewhere on her cheekbone.

'It's all right now, it's all right now,' he whispered hoarsely, breath rasping in his chest, and before she knew what was happening, he had grabbed her and forced her round to face him completely, and pulling up the new nightdress had pressed her belly to his own. He was wearing a nightshirt, under which he was naked.

Instinctively, Elizabeth resisted but he was too strong for her, climbing on top of her and grinding her underneath him. The softly sprung bed sagged beneath their combined weight and Elizabeth felt she was being smothered. 'Neeley, Neeley, please!' she cried. 'I can't breathe!'

'Sorry,' he panted, raising himself a little off her but when she tried to struggle out from under him he took his penis in his hand and forced it between her legs.

Elizabeth closed her eyes and submitted to his probing. Her shock was subsiding and she felt that the less she resisted, the sooner this would be over. She opened her legs and guided him in.

It was finished in a matter of two minutes and he rolled off her to lie on his back, breathing hard. Elizabeth's heart was hammering like a piston. Carefully, anxious he would notice what she was doing and perhaps be offended, she lowered her nightdress and smoothed it over her stomach again and again as if the repetitive gesture could iron away not only the creases but the traces of what he had done to her.

'G'night, Elizabeth, see you in the morning.' Neeley turned his back to her and within thirty seconds, his deep, regular breathing signalled he was asleep.

Elizabeth turned her head away a little into the softness of the pillow. 'Oh, God,' she whispered into the tangled hair which covered her face.

When he awoke next morning. Neeley could not have been more conciliatory. He did not refer at all to the previous night, behaving as though it had never happened, and, without so much as laying a single finger on her, bounded out of bed, dressed quickly and left the room, promising to return with tea.

Elizabeth was groggy. She was also bursting to go to the bathroom, had been so for hours, but for fear of disturbing her husband and so drawing him on her again had not dared to get out of bed during the night. She had slept only intermittently. Once, coming to and thinking she was back in bed with George Gallaher, she had snuggled up to the broad back beside her only to realize her mistake immediately and to shrink back to her own side. Neeley's back, though hard and muscular, was half the width and not at all as commodious.

As soon as Neeley had left in search of the tea, she got out of bed and ran for the bathroom. She was back, pretending again to be asleep, when he returned bearing not only the tea but, she could see through slitted eyes, a toast stand as well. He stood over her. 'Here, Elizabeth,' he coaxed, 'wake up. Here's a bit of breakfast.'

She made great play of opening her eyes, stretching and yawning. 'What time is it?'

'It's after eight,' said Neeley, his face guileless and beaming. 'Did you sleep well?'

'Yes.' Yawning again to cover the lie, she accepted the tea-tray.

As she poured the hot tea, her husband crossed to look out at the day. 'It's raining,' he announced. 'Pity.'

'Mmm.' Glancing covertly at his back, Elizabeth felt this man to be more of a stranger to her than when first they met. The grotesque coupling last night, far from creating familiarity and intimacy between them, had physically alienated her so thoroughly she knew that from now on she was going to have great difficulty in touching Neeley Scollard, let alone allowing him access to her body.

On the other hand, from their brief, disjointed conversations, she felt instinctively she had reason to hope that Neeley was at heart a good man. And some time during the night she had determined that, hateful though it might be, she would simply have to knuckle under and perform what was euphemistically called her marital duty. After all, at present she was hardly in a position to do otherwise.

Perhaps after the baby is born ... At one stage during that long night, the thought, viscous as a deadly vapour, had inserted itself under the base of her brain and although she had tried to shake it off it would not dislodge. It surfaced now as she sipped her tea and as her husband came across from the window to sit beside her on the bed. She forced herself not to flinch as, shyly but proudly, he touched her shoulder. 'Will we do it again?' he whispered.

Her heart turned over. 'Do what?' Defensively, she wanted to play for time, to force him to say it. She was rewarded with a flush of scarlet to his face.

'You know—' As though she had poured the scalding tea over it, he withdrew his hand from her shoulder. He could not meet her eyes.

'No, Neeley,' she said, 'I'm afraid I don't know what you mean.' She watched him carefully, hating herself yet exultant at achieving a sort of revenge. Her triumph was short-lived as, abruptly, he got off the bed and walked to the other side of the room, picking up the socks he had discarded the night before and stuffing them into a holdall.

Instantly, she felt contrite, she had gone too far. 'Neeley,' she called, 'I'm sorry. Of course I know what you mean. It's just that—'

'I know what you mean too,' he cut her off, his humiliation palpable.

'No, you don't. Come here to me.' Half appalled, she reached for him: there was no going back now.

He hesitated and then walked slowly towards the bed. She put the tea-tray aside and patted a space beside her. 'Here.'

His face suspicious, he sat where she indicated.

'I'm sorry. I'm just out of sorts. I didn't sleep all that well. Forgive me?' Elizabeth took a deep breath and, closing her eyes, held up her face for a kiss.

Nothing happened for a moment or two but she remained as she was, face upwards, lips puckered. 'You're beautiful. I love your hair,' he muttered at last and kissed her hurriedly on the forehead.

She did not open her eyes nor return the kiss, but put her arms tightly around him, burying her head against his chest. Deliberately, she conjured up the feel and picture of George Gallaher. This was George's heart she heard hammering in her ears, George's hands which were kneading her back.

All the way through their lovemaking, never opening her eyes, she held tight to the picture and feel of George. And in that way she got through it.

Elizabeth's first glimpse of her new home came late that afternoon.

The last leg of the journey, from Castletownberehaven, had been a nightmare. Wrapped in a Foxford rug and oilskins, she was nevertheless soaked through, nauseous and shivering. The hackney had taken them only as far as the town and they had transferred, bag and baggage, into an open ass car owned by one of Neeley's neighbours. But throughout the entire ten miles as far as Lahersheen, the rain which had begun that morning, and which had never let up all day, swept over them in torrents; it obliterated mountain tops, swept in sheets into and through the valleys and blew this way and that in unpredictable eddies off the long swells and whitetops out at sea. With each mile, its force and density had seemed to increase; the peninsula was narrow, this part of it less than a mile across and the rocky landscape was exposed on three sides to the Atlantic. Almost the first thing which struck Elizabeth, accustomed to the lushness of North and East Cork, was the barrenness of the land and the absence of trees. She had never seen a place so ferociously hostile.

That impression was heightened on turning a bend in the steep uphill road, when, like four-eyed beasts, several Celtic crosses reared above and directly ahead of them as though barring their right of way; streaked pale grey against the dark sky, the tombstones had risen so suddenly in her sight that she had to restrain herself from crying aloud. 'Where are we going?' Frantically she pulled at the back of Neeley's coat. 'This is a graveyard we're going to—'

'That's Kilcatherine,' he shouted back. 'Not far now.'

Elizabeth huddled into her sopping rugs but as the ass battled on she saw that the road did not go through the crosses as she had thought but that, just as in other parts of Ireland where many otherwise straight roads describe half-circles around fairy raths, so the makers of this road had wound it around Kilcatherine cemetery. Nevertheless, she was seized with an irrational fear as they passed between the crosses and a piece of land which fell steeply away to the Atlantic, boiling over a black moonscape of rocks. The whole place seemed to her to be uttering portents of her life to come. Although they were symbols of Christianity, those crosses, louring in this alien place and presiding over such turbulence below, seemed set there as a reminder of a much older, more menacing and pagan way of life.

Then, just as they passed the last of the crosses, Elizabeth felt a small, transient fluttering just under her ribcage. When it happened a second time, she realized what it was: the baby in her belly had kicked. It was such an extraordinary sensation, so private and personal, that soaked and afraid as she was, Elizabeth felt a tinge of joy. Unexpectedly, the words of the Magnificat flitted through her mind. Two thousand years ago that woman, too, had felt this sudden announcing of life. Then a particularly violent squall hit her squarely in the face and she felt fanciful and foolish; for the rest of the journey she concentrated grimly on simple survival.

She could have cried with relief when they turned the last bend in the serpentine road and Neeley, excited and watching for her reaction, shouted over the drumming of the rain, 'There, Elizabeth, that's it. Over there.'

The ass was turned off the road and on to a narrow, muddy track which led to a five-barred gate. Squinting against the rain, Elizabeth looked at her home, or rather, at the back of it. The small, two-storey farmhouse faced south and they were coming at it from the north-west. Slate-roofed, with tiny windows, it was similar to many others they had passed along the road except that it was newly whitewashed. Neeley echoed her thoughts, 'I had it done up for you, Elizabeth.'

'I see,' said Elizabeth faintly. She was past caring. At least the place had a roof and four solid-looking walls.

'We'll get in and get you dry,' Neeley continued. 'I'm sure the childher is dying to see you. And I'm sure you're ready for a cup of tea.' Elizabeth nodded, although tea was the last thing on her mind. Her nervousness at the prospect of meeting Neeley's children for the first time was now superseded by the need to get in out of the merciless streams of water, laced with salt, which stung the skin of her face so harshly that she believed it would never again feel normal.

Half dead, she stumbled down off the ass car as soon as it pulled into the uneven, mucky yard behind the house, so newly decorated that around its base, the splashes of lime were running off with the rain in thin grey streams.

Neeley caught her arm and kicking off the attentions of a sopping black and white collie dog which ran to greet them, hurried her across to the door, ushering her into the warmth and welcome of the small kitchen.

At first Elizabeth was so preoccupied with removing her wet things and with mopping water out of her eyes, she did not see the little gallery of observers which regarded her with intense absorption from several parts of the room. When she did notice, she stood stock still, water puddling on the flagstones at her feet. 'Hello!' she said then, including them all.

Only one of the children answered. 'Hello!' said one of the smaller ones, who then stuck a thumb in her mouth and looked shyly at the floor. The others, even the baby, who was being held by a stout, frizzy-haired woman with chapped red cheeks, simply continued to gaze at her, their eyes huge in thin faces. The little girls were barefoot but neatly and cleanly dressed. All wore tartan ribbons in their thick straight hair, which, on the three older ones, had been cut short to just below their ears; the baby's still straggled to her shoulders in soft curls.

As Elizabeth and her instant family took stock of each other, she became conscious of the outlandish picture she cut, her nose and eyes streaming, hair plastered to her head in dark strings. Then the woman holding the baby bustled forward. 'Hello,' she said, 'I'm Tilly Harrington. You're very welcome.' At close quarters her eyes were bright and calm and she seemed younger than her hair and body indicated. Elizabeth, hazarding a guess that she might be in her early thirties, liked her immediately. 'Lord love you, you creature,' the woman went on, 'isn't it fierce outside? It's always worst when it's from the north-east. Come on over to the fire and get warm or you'll catch your death. Mary! Kathleen!' she commanded the two eldest children. 'Rattle up the cups there on the table!'

The two girls sprang into action as Elizabeth allowed herself to be herded over towards the open fire, fragrant with turf smoke. Like a dog, she shook her head so the drops of water hissed into the fire and sat gratefully into a small armless chair, clearly the best seat in the house. 'Thank you, Mrs Harrington,' she said, then, for politeness' sake, added, 'Are you any relation to Neeley's best man? He was Harrington too.'

The woman shifted the baby so she was sitting astride one ample hip, then moved the kettle on to the massive hook suspended above the fire from the chimney breast. 'Lord love you,' she chuckled, 'sure we're all Harringtons around here. Harringtons or McCarthys. No, we're not exactly related although I suppose somewhere we'd be far-off cousins, by marriage, that is. I'm one of the Sullivan Harringtons; Neeley's best man is one of the Danly Harringtons from Urhan and the fella with the ass and car that brought you here is one of the Cain Harringtons from Ardgroom Inward. Don't worry,' she chuckled again, 'you'll sort us out, it won't take long.' Vigorously, she poked the fire with a huge black poker.

The kettle started to sing and as the woman continued to work at the fire, from behind her, Elizabeth heard the soft clatter as the two girls set the table. Her head reeled. Her tidy city house and manicured city landscape were decades away from this. This, she thought, half dismayed but half fascinated, was like stepping into a woodcut illustration from a book written in the last century.

Neeley, who had been supervising the unloading and bringing in of the luggage, came in again. 'Where's your manners?' he roared at the unoccupied girl who still gazed open-mouthed at Elizabeth from a corner of the room. 'Don't stare like that. All of ye – come up and say hello to yeer new mammy!' This was a different Neeley from the shy bumpkin of Elizabeth's short acquaintance but the children seemed used to it. The baby merely grunted and put her head on Mrs Harrington's chest while the other three crowded in around Elizabeth. The tallest girl glanced sidelong at the other two as if giving a signal then all three whispered a concerted, 'Hello, Mammy, you're very welcome.'

It was so obviously rehearsed that Elizabeth's confused heart melted. 'Hello.' She smiled. 'I'm Elizabeth. Who's who here?'

The eldest took charge. 'I'm Mary,' she said, 'I'm the oldest, I'm eight. And these are my sisters.'

She pointed to each of them in turn. 'This is Kathleen, she's seven, this is Margaret, she's five and a half—'

'I'm five and three quarters,' corrected Margaret.

'And that's Goretti, the youngest.' Mary pointed at the baby, who, round-eyed, was craning around Mrs Harrington's back to watch the scene.

Mission accomplished, Mary took a step back. 'She's the baby of the family,' she added. 'She's one.'

Elizabeth felt a tug on her sleeve and looked down. Having achieved individual attention, this little girl stepped back a bit too. 'Are you from Cork?'

'Yes, Goretti,' Elizabeth felt her smile was becoming fixed. 'Have you ever been there?'

'I'm Margaret,' the child said in a matter-of-fact way. 'Have you seen Santy?' she went on.

'I'm really sorry, yes, of course you're Margaret. Sorry. It'll take me a while.'

'Santy doesn't live in Cork.' Mary gave her younger sister a little shove. 'I keep telling you he lives in the North Pole.'

'That's enough now, leave Mammy alone. Is the tea ready yet – what's keeping ye?' Neeley came up behind them and shooed them all away towards the table.

'I'll be saying goodbye, Neeley.' Mrs Harrington put the baby into a slatted pen constructed from pieces of mismatching wood and about the size of a large tea chest. 'The tea's drawing there on the hob,' she went on, 'and there's fresh soda bread and a little bit of bacon on the dresser. I'll come by tomorrow, see how everything's going.' She straightened her back as though it was giving her trouble: 'You're welcome to Béara, Elizabeth,' she said. 'You'll soon get used to us and we to you. See you tomorrow. 'Bye, Neeley, 'bye girls!' She shrugged herself into a raincoat, stuffed her feet into rubber boots and then battled through the back door into the elements.

The door closed behind her and Elizabeth was alone with her new family.

Chapter Seven

Over the years, Elizabeth and Tilly Harrington, the neighbour woman she had met on that first night, became fast friends.

But when, in late February 1944, Tilly first suggested that the two of them should treat themselves to a trip to Glengarriff to see the show being given by a touring company called the Liffey Players, Elizabeth demurred; although the resort town was less than thirty miles away, the prospect of the trip exhausted her.

It was not possible to hire a car for such a jaunt because of the petrol rationing; although the war which raged throughout the rest of Europe had exercised a marginal impact on neutral Ireland, many commodities were unobtainable or severely curtailed in supply, especially in remote regions like Béara. And if she could not be driven to Glengarriff, the alternatives – a voyage through winter seas on the steamer *The Princess Béara* from Castletownbere, or a jolting half-day bus ride across the mountain passes – appealed to Elizabeth not at all.

Six years of childbearing, childrearing and miscarriages in the Spartan conditions and tough climate had taken their toll; Francey, George Gallaher's son, although a good enough baby for the first year or so, was proving at nearly six to be quite a handful and when the current baby cried it was all Elizabeth could do to pick her up; as a result her days passed in a fog of fatigue. 'No, I couldn't,' she said to Tilly as strongly as she could, 'thanks very much, but I really couldn't. I'm sure you'll get someone else to go with you.'

But Tilly was having none of it. 'Oh, come on,' she insisted, 'it'll do you good. Look at you, Lizzie, only twenty-six and passing your days like this, never going out from your own fireside except to Mass. It isn't natural, girl.' She had appealed to Neeley. 'Isn't that right, Neeley? You have your football and your cards but she has nothing except all those old books of hers and the childher. You don't want your wife turning into an old woman before her time, now do you?'

'I don't mind, I'm sure, but who'll look after the care?' It seemed Neeley did not want to appear niggardly in front of his neighbour.

'The baby's weaned, isn't she?' Tilly retorted. 'And the big ones'll look after the little ones. And sure, won't you be here yourself, Neeley?'

'But we can't afford it.' In her turn, Elizabeth looked at Neeley, willing him to say she couldn't go. Frugality had become a way of life; the farm was very small and they lived just above subsistence level because, with the single exception of money enough to add a bathroom and scullery complete with running water to the house, Elizabeth had refused all help from her parents.

'Who said anything about affording it? You'll be my guest, you silly thing. Sure, I still have loads of the American money!' Six months previously Tilly had received a legacy from relatives in Butte, Montana, and every one of her neighbours in the townland had received some small benefit from it the previous Christmas. 'And, anyway,' Tilly added, 'I want to see the show, Lizzie, and I want you to come with me, so don't be selfish, now.'

And so Elizabeth gave in. Tilly was right. She had become a drudge. She had not even been home to Cork for at least a year. If it had not been for the books and periodicals sent every week to her by the ever-faithful Maeve, she might have lost touch with everything in the world bar the daily round of housework, children and making ends meet.

Tilly had insisted on making a 'proper holiday' out of the trip, so in addition to paying for the play and for the bus into Glengarriff, she was standing the two of them to a night in one of the town's guesthouses, 'One with a proper dining room, Lizzie, we'll behave like nobs.' The following day they were going into Bantry, taking the train into Cork, where they were to be met by Elizabeth's parents, and would spend the night in the city.

Now, sitting in the auditorium of the town hall in Glengarriff and infected by the excited buzz all around her, Elizabeth was glad she had been persuaded to come. Checking her programme, she saw that two plays, obviously deemed suitable for performance in Lent, were to be presented. One – the quasi-religious piece, *The Sign of the Cross* – was known to her; the first one, *The Mass Rock*, was new.

She gazed around: although the hall was already full, all seats taken and side-aisles packed three abreast, people continued to throng through the doorway at the back. Soft blobs of colour – a headscarf, the collar of a blouse – softened the darkness of the wartime clothing but, by and large, the women were dressed as austerely as the men in sludgy shades of grey, brown, black and beige. Looking down at her own poor attire, similarly drab and even more well-worn than many of the clothes of the people around her, Elizabeth longed for the butterfly colours and crisp smells of her girlhood dresses. Poverty and 'making do' had become so ingrained since her marriage that she had not fully realized until now how shabby she had become.

Five minutes later, however, she sat bolt upright as the curtain went up on a kitchen scene in which a priest stood in front of a small blonde girl who drooped consumptively in a rocking chair beside a fireplace.

Tilly Harrington dug her in the ribs. 'That girl's the spit of you, Lizzie!'

Elizabeth barely heard her; she was not looking at the blonde actress but at the man playing the priest. It was him. It was definitely him.

'Don't you think so?' Tilly whispered excitedly. 'Amn't I right?' Then she noticed Elizabeth's expression. 'Something wrong, Lizzie?'

'No,' Elizabeth whispered back, feeling the colour drain from her face. She had given the playbill outside the hall only the most cursory of glances but she would certainly have noticed had it mentioned George Gallaher. But even in the unlikely event of there having been two actors of George's size around, there was no mistaking that handsome, hawkish face, the leonine head.

'You look peculiar, are you sure everything's all right?' Tilly's concerned face was inches from her own.

'Ssh!' All around them, people were glaring in their direction.

'I'm fine, Tilly, just a bit tired, that's all.' Elizabeth was embarrassed to be the subject of public scrutiny. 'The journey was a bit of a marathon.' She attempted to smile at the other woman, then set her face to the stage, pretending to become engrossed in the play. For all she understood of what George or anyone else was saying, however, they might all have been talking Swahili.

How could he be here? He was supposed to be in Hollywood . . .

Elizabeth sat rigid as the piosities of the play wound on. If the truth be known, it was the religious theme of the evening which had originally deterred her from accepting Tilly's kind offer. The days had long gone when Elizabeth had been spiritually nourished by the ecstatic verses of the Magnificat.

Now, watching George Gallaher posturing in clerical garb as a Soggarth Aroon, was she glad she had come or not? All those hazardous feelings and emotions she had thought under control had been stirred up again and her attention was fixed on the massive figure of George Gallaher as surely as if she were a rabbit being lamped; for all she saw of the other actors on stage they might have been completely invisible. She felt galvanized, adrenaline pumping through her entire body so it tingled.

She had believed such electrifying physical sensations had been shut up for ever, entombed in the mausoleum of the lovemaking she underwent regularly with Neeley.

Neeley. She must remember Neeley.

Elizabeth conjured up Neeley's narrow, serious face,

110

the dependable strength of his back, his awkward hands which made her feel maternal towards him. Their sex life was adequate, she told herself; she had no right to expect more, a wife's duty was to her husband, and although he was volatile and sometimes had difficulty in controlling his temper, Neeley was never violent towards her or overtly brutish. Yes, she told herself, she was lucky. It could have been much worse between them.

Then, sneaking up on her as stealthily as a hyena, came the accusation that she was lacking in courage.

Like an automaton, she clapped along with the rest of the audience as George made a sweeping exit, his black soutane ballooning behind him.

She hoped she wouldn't meet him . . .

She prayed she would . . .

She would engineer it so she would . . .

She couldn't, she was a married woman . . .

The impulses flipped around in her feverish brain and always landed on the indisputable fact that no matter what her circumstances, no matter what she had told herself during the past five or six years, she wanted to touch George Gallaher again.

You're lusting . . . said her conscience. *He won't want anything to do with you, anyway* – hissed the insecure Elizabeth of long ago. *And even if he does, you'll be caught* . . . gloated the fraidy cat which lurked at Elizabeth's core.

'Are you sure you're all right, Lizzie?' Tilly was pulling at her sleeve. 'You're shivering.'

Elizabeth looked at her. 'Sorry, Tilly,' she whispered, 'please don't worry, I'm grand.'

'We could leave if you like,' Tilly said doubtfully.

'Ssh!' A man seated in the row in front of them turned round and frowned.

Tilly stuck out her tongue at him and, nonplussed, he stared for a second then swivelled his attention back again to the stage. 'Oul' bag!' Tilly hissed. Laying a hand on Elizabeth's arm, she stuck her worried face close. 'Are you sure?' she repeated, before being diverted by George

111

Gallaher's reappearance. 'Oh, my God, isn't he handsome?' Tilly, in high good humour, joined some of the rest of the audience in loud cries of 'Good Man the Priest!'

Had Hollywood not worked out? Although in films, California and Hollywood were always seen in black and white, in Elizabeth's fantasies, fed by magazine photographs and her own fertile imagination, George Gallaher was always stroking up and down a turquoise swimming-pool; or running to meet her on a beach golden with sand; or tumbling her naked body over and under his own in a white, deep-pile carpet.

She knew only too well that the images were clichéd; but while the south-west storms battered the house in Lahersheen and Neeley panted and huffed on top of her, these pictures of George, tanned, strong and laughing, made her feel warm and hopeful; her fantasy George was so gentle, tender and patient in his lovemaking that she could cope with Neeley's lumpish and unvarying routine of coitus.

Now, as George strode and twirled, Elizabeth knew full well that more than half the female hearts in the audience twirled with him. Nevertheless, sitting now on her wooden chair with Tilly beside her, with thick curtains on the windows of the hall because of the brown-out – as Ireland was neutral, the government had not imposed a full war blackout – and the sour smell of fusty wool and old gaberdine all around, she did not care who else loved him as the heat began between her legs, on her breasts, along her upper back.

She clenched her fists beside her on her seat. *This will pass*, she thought fiercely. *This will pass.*

It did not pass and by the end of the performance she was in such a state that she could not understand how Tilly had not recognized what was happening to her. Doing her best to cover over her confusion by trying to enter into Tilly's uncomplicated enjoyment of the evening, she responded as best she could to any comment her friend made. She even nodded and smiled as Tilly extolled George's handsomeness and presence.

112

And then, while the last tickets were being sold for the raffle, she saw George working his way inexorably towards their row. Seated as she was on the outside, there was no hiding place. As she saw him come nearer and nearer, she engaged Tilly in frantic conversation, so inconsequential and so different from her usual mode of speech that finally Tilly took notice. 'What's the matter, Lizzie? You're like a hen on a hot griddle —'

'Nothing, Tilly, nothing,' Elizabeth heard herself gabbling but could not stop. 'It's just that I enjoyed the plays so much,' she rushed on, 'it's probably gone to my head a bit. You know, I don't get out much. It's all your fault — you asked me, after all. You've a lot to answer for, you know —'

She stopped dead as, behind her, she sensed George's presence.

'Jesus!' Tilly breathed, finally understanding.

'Tickets, ladies?' The resonant voice was silky and casual.

Neither woman answered but Elizabeth was forced to turn round to look at him.

'Elizabeth!' His recognition was a little too theatrical but his smile was wide and friendly. 'My, my! After all these years.'

'Yes,' Elizabeth whispered. She was not a wife and drudge-mother. Again she was fresh and young. Before she could stop herself, she folded the fingers of her left hand into her palm to hide her wedding ring.

She was immediately ashamed of the action but if George noticed he gave not a sign. 'And how are you, Elizabeth?' he asked as though they were merely old friends. 'May we meet later, if you're not rushing off?'

Whether she imagined it or not, Elizabeth thought she saw his eyes flicker over her body; her clothes seemed to flake away like old paint, leaving her as vulnerable as she had been on the night they had first met. 'I – I – why not?' she stammered, attempting to smile.

'Wonderful!' His own smile widened. 'But for now,' he

113

said with a small bow, 'may I impose on both of you ladies to buy tickets? Elizabeth? You too, madam?' He smiled at Tilly.

'I'll buy them for both of us.' Her eyes like twin moons, Tilly extracted a shilling from her purse and handed it to him.

'All of it? How generous!' He counted out a wad of numbered tickets, some pink, some white. 'I hope you'll be lucky, ladies! Until later, then, Elizabeth?' He leaned across her to count out tickets for the couple seated beyond herself and Tilly, so close to her face that she scented his sweat and could see through the armhole of the toga he wore, clear down to where a belt held the costume to his waist. It was all she could do to keep herself from throwing her arms around him there and then.

The raffle proceeded and, to Tilly's delight, she won fourth prize, a tea-set, lavishly decorated with red roses. Beaming, she went up to the front of the hall to accept it from the manager of the company.

George, clapping along with the crowd at Tilly's success, immediately materialized beside Elizabeth. 'Shall I see you outside in ten minutes?'

'I'll have my friend with me,' Elizabeth managed to answer.

'I look forward to it.' He turned his back on her and shook hands with the woman on the other side of the aisle, accepting her congratulations on his performance. Others in the audience clamoured to shake his hand too and, like a victorious emperor, he moved off through the crowd towards the doorway at the back.

'Isn't this great? I've never won anything in my life.' Tilly was back.

'It's wonderful,' Elizabeth agreed, peering into the box containing the china and not seeing anything except a red and white blur.

'Sure, we're haunted!' Tilly took out one of the cups and held it up to the light. The prize had temporarily distracted her from anything she might have thought she had discovered and she applauded and cheered enthusiastically as all the other prizes, right down to the fifteenth – a half-crown – were won.

When it was all over and Elizabeth was about to join the rush for the exit, she felt Tilly's hand on her arm, detaining her. 'Right,' Tilly said, 'it's him, isn't it?'

'What do you mean?'

'That big actor. He's Francey's father.' The statement was so clearly that and not a question that Elizabeth knew the confirmation was written all over her face.

'I – I —' she stammered again but Tilly, leaning back to let others out of their row, cut through the protestations.

'Don't bother to deny it, Lizzie,' she said in a low, matter-of-fact way, 'it's written all over your face and, anyway, Francey's the spit of him.'

'I'd never have come—' As soon as she had said it, Elizabeth was not at all sure it was the truth.

But Tilly took it at face value. 'Sure I know you wouldn't, girl. I'm not saying for a minute you would.'

'I don't know what to do next.' Elizabeth longed for Tilly, for anyone, to take charge.

Their row was empty now but Tilly did not release the arm she held. 'I'll tell you one thing,' she said gravely.

Elizabeth quailed.

The other woman's face split mischievously. 'I wouldn't kick him out of bed meself! Sure, you've great taste altogether.'

Elizabeth glanced at her kind, homely face, the frizzy hair peeking out from under her beret like wisps of well-used steel wool. Somehow, just the fact that the whole thing was out in the open helped stiffen her backbone. 'I'm sorry about this, Tilly,' she said slowly but firmly, 'I didn't plan this, honest to God, but I'm going to have to talk to him. No, I *want* to talk to him. I'm meeting him outside.'

'All right by me, girsha,' Tilly patted her arm, 'just don't let certain parties get the wrong idea!' She jerked her head in the direction of the rear of the hall, where the rest of the Castletownbere party, chattering like a group of starlings, were making plans for the remainder of the evening.

'Tilly, you're wonderful. I won't be long.'

'Take your time, Lizzie.' Tilly hesitated. 'I'm going to have a lovely hot bath and a bit of supper. The landlady said she'd leave a cold plate out for us in the dining room.' Embarrassed, she stopped and looked down at her shoes.

Elizabeth, moved, heard the message: Tilly was giving her tacit permission. On impulse she kissed the other woman's lined cheek. 'Thanks, Tilly,' she whispered.

Tilly touched the place where the kiss had landed, then looked Elizabeth squarely in the eye. 'Be careful, please, Lizzie.'

'I promise,' said Elizabeth softly. 'See you soon.'

The stars overhead glittered like icicles, lending a Christmassy air to the little town, which was awash with happy, excited people who had travelled in to the show from the furthest reaches of the Cork and Kerry hinterland; milling around outside the parochial hall, backslapping and laughing, they stamped their feet and huffed into their hands against the cold as they renewed old acquaintance or greeted near neighbours as though they had not met for decades.

The playgoers had travelled to Glengarriff in the most extraordinary range of transport; while she was waiting for George to appear, Elizabeth counted three tractors, an ancient cement lorry, eight private cars and as many hackneys, some of these sporting huge gas cylinders on their roofs; most vehicles, however, were people- or animal-powered. Bicycles were piled a dozen deep against the walls of houses and shops, ass carts and pony traps were lined up on both sides of the roadway, their horse-power peacefully drowsing into nosebags. One enterprising soul had taken an old brougham out of retirement; resplendent with moth-eaten silk curtains, its equally moth-eaten steed drooping between the shafts, it reposed in a berth all its own at the fork of the road where Béara turns towards Killarney.

Elizabeth, even had she not had her own reasons for celebration, would have found it impossible not to become caught up in the frisson of uncomplicated enjoyment.

After a bit, the crowd began to dissipate, many vanishing through the doorways of the local public houses when, at last, Elizabeth spotted George's imposing figure coming towards her. 'Now, stay calm!' she muttered silently to herself as she braced herself to greet him.

'Elizabeth!' He had changed into a magnificent top coat, complete with shoulder cape, its cut and swing reminiscent of the previous century.

Elizabeth took a deep breath. 'Hello, George.'

She became aware that they were attracting attention from the knots of people who were still on the street. Let them look, she thought, she had done nothing wrong. *Yet* . . . whispered her conscience. 'I can't stay long, I promised Tilly—' she hesitated.

'At least a walk? Such a fine night! You'll be quite safe, Elizabeth. The good burghers of the town will see to that!' His smile was so wicked that Elizabeth giggled. She experienced the onset of that light, airy feeling she remembered so well but which in recent years had been absent from her life.

'All right, just a short one then I really do have to go in.' Still feeling the eyes of others boring into the two of them, she looked neither right nor left but allowed him to take her arm and propel her along the street.

He tailored his steps to her shorter ones and, side by side, they walked down the town. His physical proximity was working again on Elizabeth; she felt she was being pulled along beside him with no effort on her part. Except for the coldness on her cheeks and in her eyes, she was warm all over.

Expecting him to touch her covertly in the way he had when first they had met, she prepared herself with every step. 'So tell me,' she said brightly, 'what have you been doing with yourself? I thought you'd gone to Hollywood.'

'Hollywood?' He seemed taken aback then recovered. 'Ah no,' he said gravely, 'I'm afraid it didn't work out.'

'Did you actually go that time?'

'Well, no, commitments, you know?'

'You mean your wife?'

'Yes, my wife. Yes,' he repeated, 'family – all that.'

117

Elizabeth was puzzled at his tone but let it pass. 'So how come you're with this company now? What happened to Mr Mellors and the rest of the group? Are they still touring these days?'

'Haven't heard of them for years,' said George vaguely. 'And before you ask, Mr Mellors and I did not part on the best of company.'

'I see.' Elizabeth decided not to pry. 'So what have you been doing since?'

'Oh, a little bit of this, a little bit of that!' He looked quizzically at her. 'Ever heard of Ivan Eliovsky, the Russian Strongman?'

'What?'

'*Moi*, in a circus.'

'I can't see you being—'

'—and Condor the Tattooed Giant from the Amazon?'

'George!'

'That was me too. Acting jobs on the mainland are not what they used to be, you know. I even played part of a camel – the top part, mind you – in pantomime in Newcastle.'

Elizabeth digested this information. Even she knew how much of a comedown this sequence represented. It was hard to reconcile it with her fantasy images of George, so long held intact. 'So how did you come to be here, with this group?' she asked. 'I didn't see your name on the notice outside the hall.'

'Well, actually, you did. I'm George Stone now.'

'Why? What was wrong with Gallaher?'

'It's a long story, my dear, and much too boring to retell on such a sparkling night. Let's just say I was a little worried that Mr Mellors might have blackened my name in the business as a result of our slight – ah – contretemps.' He cleared his throat. 'This company has been good to me. And, as you no doubt know, being a citizen of another country I'm trapped here during what is elsewhere referred to as a world war but which you Irish so charmingly call the "emergency". And I must say that, if asked, I would be hard put to choose a better place to be marooned, especially now that companies like ours have no competition from abroad. A little more tea in the rations, an orange or two, and everything would be perfect. Yes, by and large, events have worked out quite well.'

They had reached the lower end of the town and by unspoken consent, had stopped at the little harbour opposite the Eccles Hotel which, due to the brown-out, rode the crest of its little hill like a phantom ship on a wave. Turning their backs on the hotel, they stood side by side facing out to sea. Beyond several small islands, far out near the horizon and bobbing on water made phosphorescent by the starlight, a pair of fishing boats seemed as fragile as toys. It was high tide and the shushing of the wavelets in front of them was so quiet that Elizabeth could hear the creaking of the boards in the rowboats tied to the small jetty.

She heard footsteps approaching where she and George stood and looked around nervously. Anyone going home to Castletownbere, Lahersheen, or any of the surrounding townlands would be travelling in the direction opposite to the one in which they had come; nevertheless, when she did not recognize the couple coming towards them, she was relieved – in the six years she had spent in West Cork she knew how fast word travelled. Loath to break the spell of the place, she turned her face back to the sea; she had the eerie sense that the world had split in two and that she and George Gallaher hung suspended in a canyon between both parts. In some way she knew that whatever happened in the next few minutes would be decisive.

'Enough about me.' George turned to her, cupping her chin in his hand. 'Tell me about you. I'm so glad you didn't cut your hair, by the way, you look as beautiful as ever, Elizabeth, a little thinner, however, if I may say so.'

'A lot thinner, George.' Elizabeth knew quite well she was a shadow of her former self.

'Oh, come now,' he said, 'such modesty. You're radiant.'

Despite her physical confusion at being so close to him, Elizabeth experienced the first tentacles of doubt about the

119

memory of her love for this man. In her recollection, George's gallantry had been as brilliant as diamonds yet now it seemed a little dull, like jelly too long in a mould. She squashed the unwelcome revelation. 'You don't look so bad yourself, George!'

'Thank you. Old Scotsmen wear well. All that porridge.'

Elizabeth picked up her cue. 'Oh, come now, George, you're not that old.'

'Forty-six!' he lamented.

Elizabeth did not quite know what to say. Surely he was wrong? He had been forty-six six years ago . . .

Then, catching her by surprise, he gathered her to him and kissed her so hard and deep she had to struggle for air.

'You haven't forgotten, I hope?' he asked, releasing her.

'No, I haven't,' she said but as he lowered his head to kiss her again, pushed him away. Scratching at the inside of her brain was the insistent thought that George Gallaher's kiss had not plumbed her in the way she had so many times re-created and imagined in her dreams and fantasies. In fact, if she was honest, her body responded not at all. Whatever she had felt for him a long time ago was dead; she had been fooling herself for six years.

The face above her own now seemed less handsome, the encouraging expression it wore less charming. It seemed now to be simpering. She needed to collect her thoughts. 'We haven't seen each other for so long, George,' she said, hedging.

'Milady!' He bowed and she found this to be an affectation. 'Perhaps,' he said then, 'you would prefer if we found somewhere a little more – ah – private?'

Still stunned at the discovery that what she had been telling herself was love had been no such thing, Elizabeth felt impelled to settle things one way or the other, yet she found herself reluctant totally to let go of the fantasy which had sustained her for so long. 'It's not that . . .' She hesitated. She was also becoming more conscious by the second of time running through her fingers – by now, Tilly would be wondering what was keeping her. 'George,' she

120

said recklessly, 'when we were together that time, did you love me?'

'Love?' He looked down at his feet. 'Of course I loved you—'

'I'm serious, George, it was not just a game to me.'

'Who said it was a game to me?'

'Was it? Please tell the truth, George. I was only nineteen.'

'Ssshh!' He placed a finger on her lips. 'Of course I loved you, my dear, but you know I mustn't.' He kissed the back of her hand.

With growing distaste, Elizabeth regarded the back of his lowered head. 'Please talk straight, George. Because you're married? Is that what you mean?'

'Of course.' He straightened. 'I was about to ask you the same question, by the way.'

Elizabeth's growing and seemingly irrational anger was forcing words to collect inside her like a flight of arrows in a bow. 'Yes,' she said bluntly. 'I'm married, all right. My husband's name is Neeley. Neeley Scollard. That makes my name Elizabeth Scollard.'

'I see,' he said. He patted her hand and placed it gently in one of her pockets. 'You must be cold.'

'I'm fine.' She watched him carefully, weighing up the rejection. It was still in the balance. There was just a chance. She had the feeling that if she could just stay still enough, quiet enough, she might yet be able to disarm them both, save something from this wreckage that was falling about her. But he turned away. 'My my! So here we are, Elizabeth, just two married people out for a conjugal stroll.'

His reaction was more than simple rejection; it was so trite it was an insult.

Like a mill chimney she had once seen being demolished, the last remnants of Elizabeth's elaborately constructed tower of fantasies and gorgeous illusion came crashing down around her, mortally wounding her pride. 'How is your wife?' She shot her arrows. 'Does she have a name, by the way?'

In the semi-darkness, she could see his mouth purse in

121

a half-smile: 'This is not the happy little Elizabeth I remember. Do I detect that this new married Elizabeth is not happy?'

Her anger grew like a mushroom but she held it. 'No,' she said truthfully, 'I'm not exactly unhappy but I'm not wonderfully happy either. I get by. We get by.'

'So did I.'

The use of the singular, plus something evasive in the way he said it clicked all the tumblers into place in Elizabeth's brain. 'You're not married, are you?' she said in a level voice.

'What makes you think that?' The recovery was too late; she knew she had guessed right and the knowledge that she had been such a fool was devastating. In the course of a few seconds, all the fractured dreams congealed in her memory, forming a lurid mass. Before she could stop herself she had reached upwards and had slapped George Gallaher's face as hard as she could manage.

Stupefied, he held his cheek. 'What the —'

'And I also think it's completely juvenile that you should lie about your age!' It gave Elizabeth some little satisfaction to watch him scramble for composure. Before he could achieve it she forged ahead to complete what she had started. 'Oh, by the way,' she said, 'there's something I've been meaning to tell you.'

'Yes?'

'It's just that you were not around, you see.'

'What is it, Elizabeth?' Still holding his cheek, he took a wary step back from her.

'His name is Francey.'

He frowned, puzzled. 'Whose name is Francey?'

'Francey Scollard. My son.'

'Quaint.'

She reeled him out a little. 'You approve?'

'Does it matter whether I do or not?'

Elizabeth gathered herself like a cat. 'No, I suppose it doesn't really matter all that much.'

'Well, then, that's a relief—'

'Except that he's your son too.'

She had the pleasure of seeing him rock on his feet. 'What?' he whispered.

'I think you heard me, George.'

'Why didn't you tell me before now?'

A small wave of warmth bathed the two of them as one of the gas-powered cars chuntered by. Knowing she had scored so heavily had taken all the sting out of Elizabeth's anger and humiliation. She waited until the car had gone out of sight, up the hill and around the bend. 'I'm sorry, George,' she said without looking at him again, 'I'm sorry.'

She began to walk away from him, back towards the guesthouse and Tilly. And sanity. All that time . . . Six years of her life . . .

Tears half blinded her as faster and faster she walked, past the lush, semi-tropical vegetation which flourished in this gulf stream climate, past a courting couple locked together in the shadows of a fuchsia hedge. He caught up with her. 'Elizabeth! What do you want me to do?'

She saw he was begging her for release but momentary pity for him gave way to revulsion. 'Don't worry,' she said, walking faster now. 'I'm not coming after you. My husband knows all about Francey's parentage.'

'But if he's my son, shouldn't I —'

'Shouldn't you what?' Elizabeth stopped dead. 'What would you do? What would you have done? Would you have behaved any differently?'

He was so put out that Elizabeth felt almost kindly. 'George,' she said, 'you were not meant for parenthood. You're not cut out for much, actually, are you? And since we're – no, since *I'm* being so honest,' she said, 'one thing I will say for you is that even though you are such an impostor and a failure as a human being, even as an actor – has anyone ever told you you can't even *act*, George? – you were born to make love. Stick with that and you'll be safe. I must admit that *sex* with you' – her use of the harsher word was deliberate – 'was very good. If the acting ever runs out on you, I'm sure you can make some sort of living in women's beds. So do take a bow on that, at least, Mr Gallaher!'

He grabbed her arms, imprisoning them. 'Elizabeth, you must give me time, it's been such a, well, such a *shock*!'

'Time for what? To concoct another wife, another gallant scene?' She shook herself free. 'Save it for the stage, George. No, better still, save it for the next poor hoor that comes your way.' The epithet gave Elizabeth, who rarely swore, a deal of delight.

As she walked rapidly away, she failed to see, behind George Gallaher and standing apart now, the open-mouthed figures of the courting couple, two citizens from Derryconnla, a townland abutting Lahersheen.

Chapter Eight

'This is ridiculous!' The man in the carriage with Elizabeth and Tilly sneezed as they were all covered with a film of pinkish ash, so fine it had drifted through the crack at the top of the ill-fitting window. 'I mean – I mean – it's ah-chOO!' He sneezed a second time and held a handkerchief over his nose and mouth.

Elizabeth waited until the remainder of the ash cloud which billowed past the window had settled and then opened it. The train had rolled to a halt in the midst of lush rolling countryside with not a house in sight; it was still too early in the year for cattle but a few sheep and lambs grazed in the patchwork fields and, as the locomotive puttered and huffed to a standstill, a chestnut mare inside the nearside hedge raised her tail and galloped off across the frosty grass towards the far corner of her pasture. She was followed by her startled foal who, as he ran, bucked and kicked with the joy of the chase. At the top of the paddock, the foal snuggled into the side of the mare as both animals turned to gaze at this noisy invader into the peace of their territory.

Elizabeth's breath plumed in the cold air as she saw that she was not the only one to look out through an open window. 'They're gone for turf again!' The groan began at the top of the train and ran swiftly through the row of enquiring heads along its length.

It was the second time since they had left Cork that the train had run out of fuel, forcing its crew to search along the line for supplies; the fireman, meanwhile, took advantage of the halt to shovel out heaps of spent ash, which, as light and invasive as talcum powder, puffed in large clouds down the line. Coughing, Elizabeth withdrew her head and

125

sat back into her seat. Since she had not been on a train for more than six years, she was unused to this wartime bunny-jumping progress. It would have been comical if she had not been in a hurry to get home.

'Don't say I didn't warn you.' In her own corner, Tilly was knitting. Childless at forty years of age, Tilly's abiding hobby was to produce hats, jumpers, socks, scarves and mittens for her numerous nieces and nephews. Even the younger Scollards passed their winters snug in the fruit of Tilly's fingers. 'Blame Chamberlain,' she said smugly, 'he's the one who got us into this mess.' Tilly, like many around the townlands of Cork where memories of famine and penal days remained fresh and nurtured, blamed the English for everything; and although her friend never went quite so far as to condone Hitler's invasion of Poland, Elizabeth had the suspicion that in order to teach the ancient enemy a lesson, she might sneakily like to see the Germans win the war.

She was too tired to engage Tilly in politics. 'Do you think we'll get a lift all right?' she asked. The train was so hopelessly late already she knew they had no chance of catching the bus.

'God is good,' said Tilly comfortably.

'At this rate it'll be midnight before we get home.'

'Nothing we can do about it, is there?' Tilly counted off her stitches. 'God, that Ida's a howl!'

'Yes.' Elizabeth smiled. Ida Healy – Ida Lavin now – whom Elizabeth had seen only twice since her own marriage, had called in to her parents' house the previous evening for a visit. Although the edges of her indefatigability had been blunted somewhat, marriage had changed her little; even in front of Tilly, she had continued to scold Elizabeth for everything from the thinness of her cheeks to her unfashionably long hair to the fact that Elizabeth, as her oldest friend, had not seen fit to come to her wedding the previous summer. 'You know the circumstances, Ida,' Elizabeth had protested, 'I was about to have another baby.'

'That's another thing,' Ida had retorted. 'When are you going to talk to that husband of yours? You can't keep on having babies and miscarriages like this, Beth. It's not healthy.' Ida had been so shocked when she heard that Elizabeth had been pregnant again with Johanna within three months of Francey being born that she had threatened to come to West Cork to sort Neeley out.

'Leave the poor girl alone!' Tilly had jumped to her defence. 'She just needs a tonic, that's all – isn't that all, Lizzie?'

'Well, it's just not *right*, Tilly.'

'Them that don't want 'em get 'em and them that wants 'em doesn't! That's the way of the world!' Tilly had laughed, disarming Ida and at the same time taking the sting out of her own childlessness. She and Ida, who was also as yet childless but not all that worried about it, had hit it off from the moment they had met and, as she heard them swap jokes and yarns together, Elizabeth had relaxed. She had been worried that Tilly might have let the cat out of the bag with regard to meeting George Gallaher the previous night but, to her relief, Tilly had remained discreet. In fact, except for a quizzical look when Elizabeth had let herself into the bedroom they shared in the Glengarriff guesthouse, Tilly had not indicated any interest whatsoever in the matter of Elizabeth and George and for that Elizabeth was deeply grateful.

The third occupant of the carriage, the man who was still sneezing intermittently, got up and left. Elizabeth watched him go.

The urge to talk to Tilly about what was on her mind was very strong. 'Listen, Tilly,' she began but stopped when another man put his head round the door of the carriage.

'I thought it was yourselves!'

'Hello, Mossie,' said Tilly.

'Hello,' said Elizabeth, without enthusiasm. Mossie Breac Sheehan was a neighbour from Lahersheen. A bachelor who lived with an old grand-aunt on a few acres of brackish land unsuitable for farming activity of any kind, he had been called Breac not because of this but because of a dense configuration of freckles on his forehead. Two of his fields, useless for anything except goats and one or two sheep, adjoined Neeley's and Elizabeth ran into him frequently while she was about her own chores. All the neighbours thought him decent enough and spoke highly of his obliging nature. Elizabeth was always civil to him but something about the way he looked at her made her feel uncomfortable.

It was not that he impinged on her day-to-day life, it was just that sometimes, when she met him on the roads or in the fields, she thought she detected a speculative look in his eyes as though he were thinking, *I know you*. At such times, she had the disturbing feeling that Mossie Breac should not be under-estimated – that there was more to him than the image he presented.

'You're coming from the city?' he asked now, walking into the carriage and sitting down beside her.

'Yes, Mossie,' said Tilly. 'We were up visiting Lizzie's parents' house.'

'And I heard you were in Glengarriff the night before.' He glanced at her as he said it, putting Elizabeth on alert.

Tilly seemed to take no notice. 'Oh, that's right,' she said, 'gallivanting. The last of the good-time girls – the Lahersheen Royalettes, that's us.' Tilly never tired of relating the story of her honeymoon in Dublin and its highlight, a visit to see the famous chorus line at the Theatre Royal.

'Neeley didn't come?' Mossie turned fully to Elizabeth now and as usual she had the feeling there was something more in what he said than just mere chat. She was unable, however, to decide whether Mossie knew something or whether it was just his normal layered way of speech.

'Are you coming from Cork yourself, Mossie?' she asked.

'Yes. Had to get a few bits and pieces, a blade for a scythe, that sort of thing . . .' Mossie examined his nails, work-roughened but clean. 'I could've got them in Harrington's in Castletown or even in Bantry, I suppose,' he went on, 'but seeing as how I was out, so to speak, the aunt wanted a few things from Cash's.' He smiled, a peculiar lop-sided smile which contrived to give him a sardonic air.

When Elizabeth did not respond but looked pointedly out through the window, he turned to Tilly.

As the two of them chatted inconsequentially, Elizabeth mulled things over; if Mossie was coming from Cork now he had to have gone up to the city at the latest last night. So he could not have heard anything about her – or could he? She did not dare probe.

The conversation petered out and Tilly began to concentrate on her knitting. Mossie got the message and stood up. 'Well, cheerio for now.'

'See you at the other end, Mossie,' said Elizabeth, trying not to sound too dismissive. After he had left, she threw her eyes to heaven. 'God help Ireland!' she said.

'Lizzie!' Tilly exclaimed. 'Mossie's a fine figure of a man. What've you got against him?'

'I suppose at least he has his own teeth!' Elizabeth regretted it as soon as she said it. Mossie Breac, unlike many another around the place, took fairly good care of himself. 'You're right,' she said. 'I shouldn't be catty.'

'There's many a young one around Béara would've had notions of Mossie in his day,' Tilly said owlishly, 'still would, I daresay – he's only about thirty-four.'

'I don't know what it is, Tilly, it's just the way he looks at me sometimes.'

Tilly glanced keenly at her. 'Well, you know how they all feel about land around here.'

'Well, that's nothing to do with *me*.' Elizabeth felt immediately defensive. Being from the city, she had not understood until quite a long time after coming to Béara just how passionate and obsessive people could be about acquiring and holding on to even the most miserable patches of scrub and furze. She had not been in Lahersheen long before she had heard about the bad blood between Neeley's family and Mossie Breac's. The families were distantly related and sometime in the middle of the previous century, Neeley's great-grandfather had inherited land which Mossie's great-grandfather had felt to be rightly his – land which, added to his own, would have made a substantial holding.

To make matters worse, Mossie's grandfather, the aunt's brother, had suffered from alcoholism and bit by bit the best of the original land had been sold, then the medium, then the borderline, until all that was left was what Mossie had now.

'You shouldn't dismiss Mossie, Lizzie.' It was Tilly's turn to sneeze as another fine cloud of ash wafted in through the ill-fitting window. 'He was disappointed a few years ago, you know.'

'Really?' Elizabeth replied without interest; when first she had moved to Béara, she had laughed at this colloquial term for being jilted but with other matters on her mind, was not now in the least inquisitive. She shed Mossie Breac Sheehan and his romantic misfortunes. 'Tilly?'

'Mm?' Tilly looked up from her knitting.

'There's something I feel I should tell you. You deserve an explanation for the other night.'

'Don't feel you have to tell me anything, girl.' Tilly's bright eyes became wary. 'Whatever it is is probably none of my business.'

'Maybe not, but I want to tell you. Anyway,' Elizabeth appealed, 'I have to talk to someone.'

'If you're sure you should.' Tilly tossed a skein of blue wool into Elizabeth's lap. 'Here, wind this with me while you're talking.'

Elizabeth looked out to where the mare and her offspring had ventured back to the hedge beside the railway track. Ready to take off again at a moment's notice, the mare stood with head held high, ears pricked and fluttering as her foal, snug against the safety of his mother's flank, gazed white-eyed but inquisitive at the stalled train. Elizabeth inserted her hands into the skein and stretched it taut and, as Tilly began to wind, she dipped first one hand and then the other to let the wool off, settling into a rhythm as steady as the ticking of a metronome. 'It's over between us, Tilly,' she said, after a few minutes, 'I found that out for sure the other night.'

'Lizzie, you don't have to —'

130

'Please, Tilly, I haven't been able to talk to anyone about this.'

'Not even Ida?'

'Ida greatly disapproved.'

Remembering George Gallaher's lies, her abject adherence to what had been as shoddy as some of the prizes on offer in the travelling show's raffle, filled Elizabeth with renewed humiliation. 'I've made a real mess of everything, haven't I?' She concentrated on the wool. 'I've loved him for so long – at least I've *fooled* myself it was love. And Tilly, the awful thing is, I found out the night before last that he wasn't worth it. It turns out he was as cheap as a tin watch. He lied to me about important things, really important things. In fact the whole thing was a lie from beginning to end. Oh, Tilly,' she said bitterly, 'I feel such a fool.'

'Don't. Whatever you are you're not a fool.'

'I can see now I was sort of mad.' Elizabeth reddened. 'When I *think* of it —'

'Look,' said Tilly, 'don't say any more. You're getting upset —'

'He didn't want *me*,' Elizabeth continued, ignoring the interruption, 'he never wanted me, he probably didn't give me another thought afterwards. Anyone would have done him, I was just handy at the time. But the worst thing of all is that I *enjoyed* it so much. Oh, Tilly, I feel so *dirty!*' More angry now than upset, with her forearm she brushed away the moisture from her eyes.

'Look, girl,' said Tilly urgently, 'whatever you feel, don't feel dirty. Because when that kind of passion happens, when you feel that way, neither God nor man can stop it.'

Elizabeth was stopped in her tracks. This was not the reaction she might have expected. 'That's not what most people would say,' she said.

'More people than you think. You might be surprised, Lizzie. It's just them that's never had it *right* who try to stop it when they see other people's happiness. Them that's had it rejoice.'

131

Something about Tilly's tone alerted Elizabeth. 'Are *you* telling *me* something, Tilly?'

'You might be surprised. I know I'm fat and I look like a bog-trotter but I wasn't always like this, you know.'

'Oh, Tilly—'

'Don't feel sorry for me. My man's a good man and I'm not sorry I married him. But I was . . .' Tilly hesitated, 'in, er – *love* just like you when I was a lot younger than you.'

Again Elizabeth hesitated; she had never thought of the other woman as having any life other than the one she presented to the world – that of settled housewife, good neighbour and universal friend. Although she was Elizabeth's closest friend in Lahersheen, in their relationship, Tilly had always played the role of adviser and there had always seemed to be a boundary between them which neither breached. Now she seemed willing to cross that line.

'What happened, Tilly?' Elizabeth asked softly.

'He went to Butte, Montana. He was killed in the mines eighteen months ago.' Tilly's eyes were fixed on her ball of wool, now almost completed.

The legacy. Thunderstruck, Elizabeth gazed at her friend. 'But, Tilly, I thought that money was from a relative—'

'And as far as Lahersheen's concerned it was.' Tilly looked up. 'Everyone in the townland has relatives, near or far, in Butte.'

'Why didn't you get married, follow him?'

'That was the plan. But he got a girl into trouble over there. He had to marry her.'

Elizabeth had no answer. She felt the last coil of wool fall off her hands. Tilly tucked in the end of the strand and put the finished ball into her knitting bag. 'I can see you're surprised, girsha, but it just goes to show you, you mustn't judge a book by the cover. Don't blame yourself for feeling the way you did, because since the beginning of time, men and women have died, have killed themselves and each other for what you've felt for that man.'

Elizabeth was open-mouthed. 'I'm amazed—'

'Of course you are, darlin'. "Good old Tilly, who'd have thought?" Isn't that what you're thinking?'

'N-no—'

'Of course it is,' said Tilly comfortably, folding her hands in her lap and settling herself against the back rest of her seat. 'All right,' she said, 'I know what the Church says and what the narrow-minded Nellies say and your man might be a bad one,' seeing Elizabeth's expression she corrected herself, 'so he *is* a bad one, but that doesn't take away from the goodness of what's happened. Listen, girl, why do you think the Church is so afraid of sex? Because if the women of Ireland dared to express themselves or what they felt about men, if they followed what they really *feel* in their hearts, the whole country'd crack open. Sure, we've let men run this country and our lives and men's only hope is to keep us split from each other and down under them. In every way and literally too.'

Pushing her wayward hair under the rim of her beret, she smiled mischievously at the astounded Elizabeth. 'So there y'are, darlin'! That's my story. I might have been sittin' over there in your position if things had worked out different, if it'd been me who'd got into trouble, I mean. And by the way it wasn't for want of – you know . . .'

As Elizabeth's jaw dropped further, Tilly's smile broadened. 'Anyway,' she continued, 'if you asked me if I'm ashamed or sorry about what I did with my lovely darling boy, I'm not. I'm only sorry he's dead.'

'Does Mick know?' Elizabeth found her voice.

'He knows all right but we never discuss it and it's in the past anyhow. We don't discuss much. We're happy enough the way we are and we leave well enough alone.' She hesitated and her tone changed subtly. 'And if you take my advice, you'll not say a word to Neeley about what happened in Glengarriff the other night. Just celebrate what you had and regard yourself as luckier than most.'

Elizabeth nodded slowly. She had not intended to say anything to her husband in any event. As she had lain awake in bed on the night after meeting George, she had gone over and over the scene, coming round always to the

133

resolve that something could be salvaged. It was not too late to make it up to Neeley.

Up to this, she had held Neeley up to George Gallaher's mirror and found him wanting; now, to her shame, she realized that, of the two, Neeley was by far the superior man. He was constant, faithful, within his means a good provider; and she had learned to live with his occasional drinking bouts and his uncertain temper which always blew itself out as quickly as it had erupted. She was an expert now in anticipating – and therefore avoiding – those eruptions, not only on her own behalf but on behalf of the children.

And in his own way, he had been patient, even kind, after her several miscarriages, the cause of which was unknown to the midwife who put them down to God's will.

Elizabeth told herself now that she had been falsely condemning her husband for his lack of sophistication, for his uneducated ways; for years she had been congratulating herself on staying the course with Neeley, an endurance course masochistically laid out by herself for herself as punishment for her own hedonism. But in light of her encounter with her former lover, she saw now how deeply unfair she had been to her husband: it was not his fault if he was not as sensual and experienced as George Gallaher; she had been blaming Neeley simply for being the type of person he was, which was, in the main, as good as, or better than, most Irish men.

And when seen objectively, her life was not so bad, after all, she had three healthy children of her own and Neeley's first family were fine girls. 'You're right, Tilly,' she said. 'Now I've got to go home and make up for all that lost time. Neeley deserves better than I've given him.'

'I'd say,' said Tilly slowly, 'that Neeley got the best of the bargain.'

In her new mode of missionary repentance, Elizabeth did not want to hear this. Embarrassed, she got up from her seat and went to the window. The empty, undulating landscape sparkled pale green and grey under a hard winter

134

sun, visible through a film of mist as a bright white disc; most of the frost had already been burned off but patches of it silvered the grasses, nettles and brambles under the hedgerows and in the more sheltered places in the fields. As if responding pugnaciously to wartime conditions elsewhere in Europe, Ireland was looking her gentle winter best.

'Since we're talking to each other,' from behind her, Elizabeth heard the tentative note in Tilly's voice, 'there's something I've been meaning to ask you, Lizzie.'

'Sure.' Elizabeth turned around.

'Please stop me if this is none of my business.'

'You've been a true friend to me, Tilly. I only wish I was as good to you. Go on.'

'It's just that, I was wondering if . . .' Again she hesitated. 'All right, I was wondering if everything is all right with Neeley these days?'

'In what way? Do you mean his health?' Elizabeth frowned. Had Tilly heard something?

'Well, yes, his health, I suppose you could call it that.'

'You're being mysterious, Tilly. What do you mean?'

'Look, I've been meaning to say this to you for months, years even, but I really did feel it was none of my business. It's just that once or twice in the past, people were a bit worried about him.'

'You mean his drinking?'

'Sure, they all drink.' Elizabeth saw that Tilly's expression was guarded. 'No, it's not just that, it's just that once or twice – like when Agnes died – Neeley got a bit, well . . . he suffered with his nerves a bit. And the drink didn't help, of course,' she added. She looked down at her feet. 'I'm sorry, Lizzie,' she said, 'but Mick says he met him drinking by himself over in Castleclough the other day and he thought he was a bit down in himself again and I just thought I'd ask you if everything was all right. We're very fond of the pair of you,' she added swiftly, 'Mick and me.'

Elizabeth thought back. There had been one or two occasions recently when she had thought Neeley to be unusually quiet but had put it down to the struggle he was

135

having with his unforgiving farm. 'Why are you telling me now?' she asked.

'Because I never got an opening before,' said Tilly simply, 'and, anyway, I thought I'd better say something in case you went running in to Neeley and telling him about meeting George. That's the real reason I think you shouldn't say anything to him. You'd never know what way any man reacts to that kind of thing.'

'Thanks, Tilly,' said Elizabeth, 'but to tell you the truth, I think Neeley's all right.'

It was nearly eight o'clock in the evening by the time she got home to the farmhouse. The bus from Bantry had long gone when the train finally pulled into the station there but out on the road a little, they had been lifted by an obliging builder from Adrigole. Driving his lorry on a homemade concoction of fuels which smelled lethal, the driver at least had enough of it and, in return for enough money to buy a bottle of whiskey, was able to bring them all the way to Castletownbere; from there they were taken as far as Ballycrovane by ass and car.

The night had become so densely foggy that the ass was allowed to amble at a snail's pace along the twisting road and they made very poor time. 'We'd have been quicker walking,' grumbled Tilly as, laden with packages, they set out to walk the rest of the way, both too tired now to talk and in any event having to concentrate in the fog on where they were going. Unconsciously, they fell into step, the sound of their combined footsteps like drumbeats against the deep organ note of the unseen sea.

When they came as far as Kilcatherine churchyard, Elizabeth transferred most of her parcels to one hand and slipped the other under Tilly's arm; no matter how many times she passed it or attended funerals there, she always felt uneasy in this place. Legend had it that there was an underground passage leading from one of the graves directly down to the shoreline but her discomfort was caused mainly by the presence of the Kilcatherine Head. This small object – less than a foot across at its widest point

136

– could hardly have been called a gargoyle; weathered by countless centuries of Béara weather, it projected about ten inches out from the top of one of the door openings and bore traces of a pair of eyes, a nose, or snout, an open mouth; many people said it was pre-Christian, some said it had to do with snake worship, no one knew for sure. But it exerted a profound influence on Elizabeth's superstitious soul.

Her first sight of it had occurred shortly after she had arrived at Lahersheen and, still pregnant with Francey, had attended the funeral of a local woman. The spring day was playing hide and seek with the sun, a strong wind sending clouds racing across the sky so that light and shade played like tumbling dice across the cemetery. As the priest was intoning the Rosary over the open grave, something had made Elizabeth look up towards the tiny ruined church. As she did so, the light had blazed suddenly, catching the Head at an oblique angle so the features stood out sharp and clear and had seemed to leer directly at her over the intervening headstones. For two seconds she and the malign thing had stared at one another. Then the light had died just as suddenly, returning the Head to passivity. The effect was so extraordinary that Elizabeth had clutched Neeley's arm.

The phenomenon had not occurred again but she had never overcome her fear of it, even though, from different perspectives, the Head could seem quite friendly. For instance, due to the way it had weathered over the centuries, when viewed at right angles it sometimes resembled nothing more sinister than the meekest of pet ewes.

'Are you all right, Lizzie?' Tilly's voice was unusually low as they trudged round the cemetery.

'Fine.' Elizabeth nodded vigorously as if energy alone could banish her growing feeling that danger was imminent.

'Soon be home now.'

They were exhausted by the time they came to the end of the boreen which led to Tilly's house and stopped to say goodbye. 'Tilly, how can I ever thank you?' Elizabeth hugged her friend. 'You won't tell anyone I met him?' She was suddenly anxious.

'Lizzie! I thought we understood each other.'

'Sorry. See you tomorrow?'

They parted and Elizabeth turned to walk the last quarter mile towards her own house.

She took a short cut through the upper haggard and was coming to a gap in the hedge when a small figure threw himself at her. 'Mammy!'

'Francey! What are you doing out here all on your own? You should be in bed!'

'I was waitin' for you. It's awful in there, Mammy – Daddy's in a terrible bad temper. He sent everyone to bed after tea. An' he slapped me with the stick. It's not fair.' Elizabeth's heart turned over: she hated it when Neeley hit any of the children, even those who were not her own. Although to be fair, he did not resort all that often to the use of the cane he kept hanging on a hook inside the back door, the threat of it usually being enough to deter any wrongdo-ing or cheek. Parental solidarity meant, however, that she had to support any disciplinary action he took. 'What did you do?' she asked. 'You must have been very bold, Francey.'

'I wasn't – I did nothin' – none of us did nothin'! Did you bring me a present?' He snatched at one of Elizabeth's parcels.

'Hey, easy there! Have a bit of patience. So you're all in bed?'

'The baby's up, she's crying. It's awful in there – I had to get out.'

Indulgently, Elizabeth smiled at his young outrage. Sometimes Francey sounded like a little old man yet he always pulled at strings in her heart that none of the others could reach. He was still pooching around at her parcels, trying to determine by feel what was inside. 'Francey,' she remonstrated, pulling them away from him, 'get your hands off and wait until we get inside.'

The fog muffled her voice as, side by side, they walked through the field next to the house. 'How'd you get out, anyway?'

'Through the winda!' Although his accent was as broad as Neeley's, he had George's smile. He was also going to have George's physique; he was already far taller than any of the other boys his age in the townland. As long as Francey was around, Elizabeth realized with a pang, she would never be totally shot of his father. 'Well, we'll just have to get you back in through the winda, then, won't we?' Playfully, she nudged him with one of the packages. 'You just go back in the way you came out and I'll see you in the morning.'

'But I want to see what you brought me!'

'Francey Scollard, you won't get anything unless you get back to bed this very minute.'

'It's not fair,' he protested again, but when he saw she was serious, scampered off out of her sight into the fog. She waited until she heard the sound of his running footsteps recede round the gable end of the house and then went to the back door.

Still smiling, she pushed in the door.

Her eyes took a second or two to become accustomed to the gloom of the kitchen as it was lit only by a feeble red glow from the range, the door of which was open to expose the embers. 'Why is it so dark in here? Is that you, Neeley?' She squinted at the figure slumped in her husband's chair by the side of the range.

Neeley did not answer but Elizabeth was distracted by the cries of the baby – and by the pungent smell coming from the same source. Abigail, confined in the ancient playpen on the other side of the range, was standing spread-legged, her nappy sagging so low it had obviously not been changed for a very long time.

'Oh, Neeley!' Elizabeth exclaimed, dropping her parcels on the floor and hurrying forward to pick up the child. 'The poor little thing!' Then, in lifting Abigail, Elizabeth noticed the bottle on the floor beside Neeley's chair. Although she had no idea how much he had taken, her heart sank: Neeley with any poteen at all inside him was an unpredictable animal. No wonder Francey had said he was in a bad temper.

139

Quickly, she lit the oil lamp on the kitchen table and attended to the baby's needs, soothing her with words and little pats so that the crying subsided to a series of shuddering hiccups. 'There now, Abbie,' Elizabeth hoisted her daugher on to her shoulder, 'isn't that better? Does she need a bottle, Neeley?' Keeping her voice bright she looked across the kitchen.

'Slut!' Although Neeley continued to look straight ahead, the word was so shocking and unexpected that Elizabeth almost dropped her daughter. 'What?' she whispered.

'You heard me,' he said in a low, venom-laden voice. 'Slut! Harlot! Whore!'

Carefully, Elizabeth put the baby into her cradle and covered her. She had to keep her wits about her; how much did he know? 'I don't know what you mean,' she said calmly, although she felt her face grow cold as the colour drained out of it.

'Yes, you do!' At last Neeley looked in her direction. 'You and that – that *actor*. That buckin' *actor*! Making an exhibition of yourselves all over Glengarriff. You couldn't keep away from him, could you? Holiday me backside, the whole thing was a set-up! And I suppose that Tilly Harrington was in on it! The whole of Lahersheen was probably in on it . . .' Throughout the speech, Neeley's voice gradually rose until by the end he was so enraged that blobs of spittle were shooting from his mouth and spraying round him.

Elizabeth held her ground. 'I still don't know what you —'

Neeley sprang out of the chair. 'It doesn't buckin' matter what you know or don't know. It's all over the village, you're the talk of every crossroads from here to Castletown.' For a few moments she thought he was going to hit her. Instead, he picked up the bottle of liquor, took a slug out of it and then flung it into the fire.

'Neeley, don't —' Elizabeth ran forward to take it out but she was too late. With a sound like a rifle shot, earshattering in the small kitchen, the bottle exploded in a sheet of bright blue flame.

Luckily he had thrown it with such force that it landed

right at the back of the vast fireplace and most of the glass shot upwards into the chimney to fall back harmlessly into the ash. Some shards did blow outwards, and although instinctively both Neeley and Elizabeth ducked, one piece caught Neeley just above the right cheekbone, narrowly missing his eye.

Abigail started to howl and, fearing the worst, Elizabeth ran to the cradle. To her relief, the baby was unmarked, her cries prompted by terror.

All the other children came running into the kitchen from the bedroom just off it. They crowded together in the middle of the room, the girls in their nightdresses, Francey still fully dressed. Mary, the eldest, was the one who spoke. 'What happened?' She looked from Elizabeth to Neeley. 'Daddy, you're bleeding!'

Stunned, Neeley touched his cheek and then looked at his hand, red with his own blood. 'Now look what you've made me do . . .' Sounding surprised, he took out a handkerchief and staggering a little, held it to his cheek. Instantly the white grew red.

Elizabeth, notwithstanding her profound shock at the speed and violence of events since she had come through the door, managed to pull herself together. 'Girls, get me the iodine —'

'Don't any of you move!' Neeley roared at the cowering children. Then he rounded on Elizabeth. 'You're not putting any shagging iodine on me. You're not coming near me, you bitch. Slut!' Addressing the children but pointing a shaking finger at Elizabeth, his voice rose to a scream. 'Ask you precious Mammy what she was up to in Glengarriff the night before last. Go on, ask her!' He seized the nearest girl by the scruff of the neck and pushed her towards his wife. '*Ask her!*' He gave the child, who happened to be Goretti, six years of age and by far the most timid of all the children, a violent shake.

She started to wail, 'You're hurting me, Daddy, you're hurting me!'

'Leave her alone!' Francey and Mary yelled it in unison.

'How dare you talk to your father like that?' Neeley let

141

Goretti go and rushed to the door. He grabbed at the cane which was hanging by a looped piece of twine but, whatever way he caught it, it refused to come off the hook.

All of the children, from the eldest to the youngest, now began to cry.

'Don't, Neeley, don't take it out on them!' Elizabeth ran to him and clawed at his jacket but she fell back as he turned and lashed blindly at her with his fists. Then he turned again to the door and continued his tussle with the stick.

'Quick, girls, Francey, into bed – quick!' Elizabeth screamed just as Neeley, pulling mightily, finally liberated the cane by causing the hook in the door to come off its screws, splintering the wood. Still wailing, the children scattered and ran for the bedroom as their father stumbled and turned round, swinging the stick with twine and hook still attached.

'Jesus Christ!' Roaring, he charged after them. 'Come back here, all of you!'

Elizabeth ran to intercept him, spreading her arms in front of the bedroom door to block his way. 'Stop this, Neeley!' she screamed. 'Stop it this minute.'

His face grotesque with rage, he raised the stick above his head as though to whip it across her face. Elizabeth closed her eyes in anticipation but did not lower her arms. For one see-sawing moment, smelling the stink of poteen on his panting breath, she waited for the blow to fall. Then she felt him turn away and opened her eyes to see him stumble across the kitchen towards the back door.

She waited until the door slammed behind him before finally lowering her arms. The sustained concert of screeching from seven terrified throats which rose throughout the house was unnerving but before doing anything about it, Elizabeth, herself weak from fright, paused for a few moments to gather her wits. She took several deep breaths, concentrating on letting the oxygen do its work; above all else now, she must keep her head.

She picked up Abigail and carried the hysterical baby into the children's bedroom. As soon as she opened the

142

door, the screeching intensified for a moment or two and then, when they saw it was she and not Neeley, Goretti ran towards her and buried her head in her skirt.

'Where's Francey and Johanna?' Elizabeth tried to make herself heard above the din.

'They're under the bed.' Margaret had collected herself the fastest; of the three beds in the room, she indicated the furthest from the door.

'Here, do your best with Abbie.' Elizabeth handed the baby to her and, with Goretti still hanging tightly on to her, made her way across the room and raising the bed-clothes on the bed Margaret had pointed out, peered underneath.

Arms around one another, facing inward, Francey and his sister were huddled together in the corner. At the sight of them, their backs shaking like cornered mice, Elizabeth nearly lost her composure. 'Johanna! Francey!' she called, having to shout. 'Come on, it's all right. You can come out now . . .' With great difficulty, because of Goretti's barna-cle-like grip, she reached in and took hold of the back of her son's jersey.

'Go 'way!' he shouted through his screams, holding tighter to Johanna. 'Leave us alone!'

Elizabeth realized he had not heard her and thought he was being pulled out by Neeley. 'It's me – Mammy!' she yelled. 'It's all over now, come on out, love.' He looked over his shoulder, and even though it was so dark, she could see how enormous his eyes were in his white face. 'Come on, darling,' Elizabeth said, 'come on out, every-thing's all right now.'

Bringing his sister with him, Francey crawled out on to the floor. The other children were also calming down; even Goretti loosened her grip on Elizabeth's skirt.

'Everyone out into the kitchen,' Elizabeth said. She was operating on instinct; although she was used to Neeley's bad tempers, his storming out like this was new and she had no idea when – or if – he would be back. The first priority was to settle everyone down, get them into bed and asleep before he returned.

143

The baby was the only one still crying when the children had all congregated in the kitchen, standing together uncertainly in a compact group. 'Would someone make Abbie a bottle? Mary?' Elizabeth turned towards the stove and threw in a few sticks of kindling and the remaining sods of turf from the creel. 'I think we all need some hot milk. How much is there?'

'Half a jug,' reported Margaret, as ever the practical one.

'Right,' said Elizabeth, 'that isn't enough for all of us, we'll just have to dilute it with water. Francey, I need more turf, Kathleen, you fill the kettle. Goretti, get the cups and you, Margaret, I want you to sweep the floor, make sure there's no glass lying around. Be careful, now . . .' With alacrity, they all did as they were bid.

A sense of normality began to return to the kitchen. By the time the baby's bottle was ready and she was sucking on it in Mary's arms, the diluted milk was warm too. Elizabeth doled it into the cups set around the table. She would have given a great deal of money for a cup of good strong tea but the tea ration was spread out on newspapers to dry from the last time it had been used and she felt she did not have the energy to deal with it. So she filled a cup of the milk mixture for herself too, then, with reckless disregard for economy, lit the other two oil lamps in the room, the one on the dresser and the one on the mantelpiece. She felt the need for as much light as possible.

After the storm which had racked it only a few minutes before, the peace in the kitchen was striking. Everyone, from oldest to youngest, responded gratefully to it and the only noises were the soft roar from the fire in the cast-iron stove and the sounds of children sipping their milk. Elizabeth could see, however, that they were all apprehensive and fully alert. She knew what was on their minds: they were all straining their ears for the sound of Neeley's footsteps in the yard outside.

'Mammy, what's a slut?' Margaret was the first to finish her milk.

Elizabeth was ready for it. 'It's not a nice word, lovey,

it's what men say when they're annoyed. They don't mean it.'

Margaret digested this in silence. Then: 'But why is he annoyed with you?'

'It's none of your business!' Mary put down her cup with a little bang.

'Daddy and our real Mammy never used to fight.' Kathleen was the only one of Neeley's four daughters by his first marriage who had ever shown any resentment that her mother had been replaced.

'That was most unusual, Kitty. Most people fight.' Elizabeth attempted to lighten the atmosphere: 'Even the Royal Family!' Kathleen, who of all the girls was the one most interested in clothes, fantasy and fairytales of all sorts, had cut a picture of the two little princesses out of a newspaper and had it carefully preserved between the leaves of her prayer book. While Neeley's strong nationalism permeated the ethos of the household, the British Royal Family seemed somehow personally exempt from odium, certainly among his daughters.

'When's he coming back?' It was Francey.

Elizabeth, looking around their faces, shadowed and golden in the lamplight, hesitated. 'He'll be home very soon now,' she said, then, feigning a briskness she did not feel, 'Are you all finished? Hurry up now and get back to bed or Daddy'll be cross again. I want you all tucked up and asleep as quickly as possible, all right?'

'What about the washing up?' asked Margaret. The chore of washing up always fell to the girls, who performed it in rotation.

'It's all right, Maggie, I'll do it myself tonight.' Elizabeth stood and took the baby from Mary's arms. 'Now shoo! Go on now!'

When they were all gone she extinguished two of the lamps, sat by the stove in the well of light cast by the one on the mantelpiece and put the bottle again to the baby's mouth. With her free hand, she stroked the dark hair which, never having been cut, straggled in soft ringlets to Abbie's shoulders. Both of Elizabeth's daughters were dark, like

145

Neeley, Francey was the one who had inherited her own strawberry blonde colouring. Although his eyes were violet and his physique far larger than average, the fairness mitigated, at least a little, his resemblance to his father.

Abigail, her eyes calmly fixed on her mother's face, sucked peacefully on. Since Francey's birth, this sensation of a small warm body in the crook of her arm, those guttural sounds of contentment as the baby balanced its breathing and feeding had always made Elizabeth feel warm and grounded. Tonight, however, the satisfaction it gave her was minimal; her worries about the developments with Neeley were uppermost.

He had said she was the talk at every crossroads. Mossie Breac? But she was virtually certain that Mossie had not been among the party which had attended the show. Somehow she had been spotted. What should she do?

She glanced around the familiar kitchen in which the corners and surfaces of various objects – a glass vase, a saucepan, the gilded frame on the picture of Neeley's first wife – gleamed in the limited light from the lamp above her head. The flagged floor was swept and clean, the chairs neatly ranged against the table. Except for the unwashed cups and the raw patch where the hook had been torn off the back door, no one could possibly have guessed that anything untoward had taken place here less than twenty-five minutes before.

Should she have it out with Neeley? As soon as the question posed itself, she discarded it. There was no point in having anything out with a man who was full of poteen.

The baby finished the bottle and yawned. Elizabeth yawned too; the false energy engendered by fear and the row itself had drained fully away to leave her limp and so tired that she could not think straight. The best thing, she decided, was to go to bed and pretend she was asleep; she would leave the dirty cups until the morning.

'Come on, lovey,' she said to Abigail, dragging herself out of the chair. She put the sleepy baby in the cradle, covered her and was just reaching up to quench the lamp when she heard a sound behind her.

146

'What — ?' She turned round.

'I can't sleep, Mammy.' Francey pulled at his forelock, a gesture he made when he was anxious.

Elizabeth looked down at his small plaintive face and had no heart to scold him. 'You haven't tried very hard, Francey, you've only been in bed for a few minutes. Come on, I'll tuck you in.'

'I hate him, Mammy!' The words burst from him before she could take his hand to lead him back to bed.

Elizabeth hunkered down to his level. 'No, you don't, you don't hate anyone, Francey. Hate is a sin, a very big sin. You'd have to tell that to the priest when you make your first Confession.'

'I don't care. I do — I *do* hate him.' His eyes filled with tears and his voice was as passionate as she had ever heard it.

'Come over here, love.' She led him to the chair she had just vacated and lifted him on to her knee. He cuddled in, but continued to pull at the front of his hair.

'Your daddy has a lot on his mind, Francey. Everything will be all right in the morning.'

He said nothing for a while but continued with his hair. Then he stopped and said, 'I'm going to get another daddy.'

The statement was so confident and positive that Elizabeth's heart jumped into her throat. She held him out so she could look in his face. 'Where would you look, darling?' she tried to sound jocose.

'I'll find one. *He's* not my daddy any more.'

'Francey, of course he's your daddy.'

'No, he's not!' Francey scrambled off her lap and, hands on hips, stood directly in front of her, challenging her to contradict him again.

At a complete loss as to how to deal with this, Elizabeth stared at him. From the time he could talk, Francey had exhibited an unshakeable belief in his own opinions. This one, so dangerously true, coming on top of the tumultuous events of the past forty-eight hours, was just too much to bear. She had no energy left for argument or persuasion.

147

'We'll talk about it in the morning,' she said, heaving herself out of the chair and taking his hand.

He allowed himself to be led back to bed but as she tucked him in beside Johanna, he looked up at her with George Gallaher's eyes. 'I won't change my mind!' he uttered in a piercing stage whisper.

His five-and-half-year-old certainty terrified Elizabeth. 'All right, darling,' she said, kissing him. 'We'll talk about it tomorrow.' Francey, squeezing his eyes shut, turned over on his side and within minutes, had fallen asleep.

Elizabeth eased herself out of the small gap between Francey's bed and the next one, but, burrowing her back into the heap of clothes hung from hooks on the back wall, stayed for a while longer in the room. Listening to the concerted breathing, she reflected that it would be no time before Abigail would be leaving her cradle by the fire to join her brother and sisters in here. She smiled a little at the image: what would her mother think of yet another body being squeezed into these three smallish beds?

Because none of the neighbours, certainly none of the children themselves, saw anything unusual with the way they lived, Elizabeth, whose family of seven was relatively small by Béara standards – where families numbering more than twenty were not unknown and where ten was unremarkable – had become accustomed to the lack of physical space in the cottage. Corinne, on the other hand, on discovering the sleeping arrangements in Lahersheen, had been aghast: the notion of six or even seven children crammed together in one room was so foreign to her idea of normality that she had been struck speechless.

'Goodnight, all . . .' Elizabeth whispered softly, leaving the room and closing the door with care. The children's slumbering faces – in sleep, even the older ones seemed younger than their years – had soothed her.

She thought she would not be able to sleep and indeed, as soon as she got into bed, her thought processes speeded up. But she had under-estimated the extent of her physical exhaustion and within a few minutes, had fallen into dreamless oblivion.

148

Chapter Nine

Elizabeth was pulled into groggy consciousness again when, some time later that night, she felt the blankets over her being disturbed.

'Neeley?' she whispered.

Grunting, her husband got into the bed and immediately rolled on top of her, snapping her into full alertness.

She closed her eyes and to shut him out, deliberately concentrated on making a list of what she had to do tomorrow, getting the children up and ready for school, cleaning the kitchen, making soda bread, feeding the hens, straining the milk . . .

Then she heard what Neeley was whispering in rhythm with what he was doing: '*Slut, bitch, whore, you're mine, you're buckin' mine, you slut, bitch, whore . . .*'

Appalled, Elizabeth's mental processes went into paralysis for a few seconds then, making a supreme physical effort, she threw him off her and slithered out from under him on to the floor. Quivering, she stood in the darkness, facing him. 'You may not use that language with me. I am your *wife*, Neeley Scollard. Your *wife*. Do you hear me? I do not give you permission to treat me like this!'

The bedsprings creaked as he sat up. 'You're a fine one to talk.'

'Did you *hear* me, Neeley?' Although she was aware of all the children sleeping in the bedroom on the other side of the wall, she was having difficulty in keeping her voice low. 'If you want to talk about it, we'll talk. But kindly give me the benefit of the doubt. I am not – those things you called me. I repeat, *I am your wife*. And I am not, repeat *not*, going to put up with this. I will be gone in the morning. And I'm taking my own children with me.' Past caring whether the children heard her or not, she rushed out of the bedroom, plucking her dressing-gown off the back of the door as she passed.

She expected him to come after her and, thinking she heard him, whirled round to face him.

It was not Neeley but Francey, standing uncertainly in the door, pulling at his blond thatch. 'I want a drink of water, Mammy.'

'Me too, Mammy.' Behind him, Goretti, too, was out of bed. How much had they heard?

She belted on the dressing-gown, went into the scullery and filled two cups with water. Coming back into the kitchen, she handed the drinks to the children and stood beside them while they drank. Goretti's eyes were concentrated on her cup but Francey kept his glued to his mother's face. Reading his expression, Elizabeth knew he had heard everything, or at least enough to make him fret.

'Back to bed now!' She took the empty cups and placed them with the other used ones on the table. Goretti, still without raising her eyes, took Francey's hand and led him back to the bedroom. And with that gesture, Elizabeth's fate was sealed. How could she break up this family which, against all the odds, had become a unit? Could she deprive Goretti and her full sisters of a mother, thus bereaving them twice in such a short space of time?

Throwing some sods into the stove she slumped into the chair beside it.

There were no further incursions into the kitchen and for the remainder of the night she did not go back to bed but dozed uncomfortably in the chair.

When dawn broke, knowing she would sleep no more, Elizabeth put the kettle on to boil, and, rubbing her burning, gritty eyes, went to the window. Except for a translucent film which crowned the hills on the Urhan side of Coulagh Bay, the fog had lifted; the sea was as grey and smooth as the skin of a seal and although the sun was not yet visible over the mountains to the east of Lahersheen, the withered winter growth had already taken on a pinkish cast. She must have slept more than she had thought because it was past time to wake the schoolgoing children. Neeley and his first wife had not believed in sending any of his children to school before they were six years old and although Mary was now fifteen, she was still attending and would not be leaving until July. Kathleen, ten months younger, was the exception to the rule; she had apparently been so energetic and inquisitive and therefore difficult to handle that at the age of only five she had been sent to school along with her elder sister, had been in the same class all along and was due to leave at the same time.

Elizabeth had had no objection to the custom and Francey, who would be six in May, was not starting school until September but as Johanna and he were almost inseparable, she would probably go with him.

It took the best part of an hour to sort everyone out, harrying the laggards out of bed, ladling porridge, tying pinafores, brushing hair, checking schoolbags; and when the older ones were gone and she was starting to see to the three younger ones, including Francey, the door to her bedroom opened and Neeley, fully dressed, came out.

Without a word, he crossed the kitchen, took his cap from its peg and went out into the morning.

Elizabeth gazed at the crossbeam of the door he had slammed behind him. Out of the blue, she remembered what George Gallaher had said to her so long ago: that love between a man and a woman was allowed; that joy was permissible. Hah, she thought bitterly, that was some joy last night between herself and the man who was her husband.

Tilly had not been joking when she made her remark about what would happen to the country if the women of Ireland admitted the truth about what they really felt. Tilly was right: the whole country would be rent apart. She looked around the kitchen. The rough walls seemed to come to malevolent life, pressing in on her, their very solidity a reproach to her self-imposed slavery to them.

She had to get out of this place, if even for a while.

Filled with renewed and blazing energy, she hurried the startled Francey and Johanna through the rest of their

151

breakfast. As soon as the baby was fed and changed, she bundled all three of them into their outdoor clothes. 'Where are we going?' Francey was watching her carefully.

'We're going over to Harringtons' for a visit.'

'At this hour?' Francey was using his little-old-man voice and Elizabeth felt a scream building inside her, one so big it would rip the sky asunder. She managed to control her voice: 'Yes, at this hour, Mr Smarty,' she said. 'Come on now!' Roughly, she forced Johanna's small feet into her rubber boots. She picked Abigail out of the playpen and wrapping her in a blanket, hunted the other two out through the door ahead of her. They had to trot to keep up with her furious pace as, clutching the baby to her chest, she half ran across the winter-roughened fields towards the Harringtons' farm.

'God, you're out early!' Tilly held the collar of an old dressing-gown tightly around her throat as she opened the door. 'Come in, come in . . . Nothing wrong, I hope?' She peered closely at Elizabeth's face as she closed the door behind them.

'No – yes – no – oh, Tilly!' Elizabeth hugged Abigail so tightly that the baby squeaked in surprise.

'Sit down, I'll make you a cup of tea. It's not all that old yet, only been used twice! Have ye all had breakfast?' Tilly addressed the two older children.

Francey and Johanna nodded solemnly. 'Well, then, in that case,' said Tilly, 'let's see what we can find up here . . .' Reaching upwards she took down a cake tin from the highest shelf on the dresser.

Elizabeth paced up and down in the confines of the small kitchen while Tilly took out three currant buns and gave one each to the children. Then she took a piece of brown wrapping paper from a drawer and tore it in half. 'Here we are now,' she said, placing the pieces in front of two chairs at the kitchen table and putting a pencil on top of each of them. 'Sit down there, now,' she addressed Francey and Johanna, 'and I don't want to hear a pop out of the pair of you until I see two real nice pictures.' As

Francey and Johanna, both chewing energetically, settled down to draw she busied herself with the tea while Elizabeth continued to move restlessly around the kitchen.

'God, you're in some form,' said Tilly, when the tea was ready. 'Come on into the room where you can tell me what's eating you. Be good now, you two,' she called back over her shoulder, as she led her guest into the parlour, rarely used except for company. She sniffed the stagnant air. 'I must open a few windows in here,' then, reaching for Abigail, 'Here, give me the baby – you drink while it's hot.'

Elizabeth surrendered Abigail. She wrapped her fingers around the hot cup and stared into the pale depths of the tea on the surface of which little globules of what seemed like grease floated. Tilly, dandling the baby, watched her closely. 'What is it, Lizzie?'

The depth and spread of her frustration and despair welled up in Elizabeth and she found she could not immediately put words on what had brought her here in such a state. She took a sip of the tea, which did not taste too bad; at least it was hot and had a flavour reminiscent of tea. 'I'm sorry, Tilly,' she whispered, 'I shouldn't have come.'

'Isn't it a pet day?' Tilly rose from her chair and went to the window, her back to Elizabeth. 'Would you believe it could be like this after yesterday—'

'I can't stand it any more!' Elizabeth hugged the cup to her chest as if its warmth could lend her comfort. 'I can't take another minute.'

Tilly turned slowly, regarding her over the head of the baby: 'This is my fault,' she said slowly. 'I shouldn't have insisted you come with me to Glengarriff.'

Faced with her friend's sympathetic eyes, Elizabeth felt truly wretched. 'Neeley's heard rumours,' she said. 'Already, before we even got back here last night, Tilly, there were rumours and gossip. All for nothing. And there was I – stupid, stupid, stupid! – planning a whole new start with Neeley. So *stupid*!'

Putting down her cup on the linoleum at her feet she

looked bleakly at the other woman. 'And there're all those children. I can't do anything which would hurt them. Tilly, I feel so *trapped*.'

'Neeley's heard? What did he hear?'

'What does it matter what he heard? Somehow he knows I met George. That's enough for him.'

'Did you talk to him about it?'

'I didn't get a chance.' Remembrance of the previous night rekindled Elizabeth's anger. 'He didn't *give* me a chance.'

Abigail, picking up her mother's distress, began to whimper.

Elizabeth took her. 'I'm sorry to burden you with this,' she said, rocking the baby from side to side.

'Is there anything I can do?'

'No, but thanks for the offer. It's not your problem. It's mine and it's me who has to do something about it. But I feel deep down that I have to take some action or I'll go mad. And that's not just a figure of speech, Tilly. I mean I really might go insane.'

'The first thing we have to do is get you away from here for a few days. Why don't you go up to Cork?'

Elizabeth thought briefly of the cosy, spacious house in Blackrock. Then she thought of her mother's pained and probing silences. 'But I'm just back from Cork,' she said. 'Anyway, running away's no solution, it'll all be here for me when I get home.'

'Lizzie, you're young, it'll pass . . .'

Elizabeth was tempted to shout at her friend but knew Tilly was as helpless as she. 'Maybe,' she said quietly, 'maybe I will go to Cork for a few days. But the difficulty is that I don't think I could stand being interrogated. Or even looked at!'

At the moment, even Tilly's kind, enquiring face seemed too much to bear; she brushed past her friend and pulled the lace window curtain aside. 'You're right, it is a beautiful day,' she said. The Harringtons' house was close to the shoreline and the view from this window was of the

154

sea and the mountains on the other side of Coulagh Bay. Compared with the turbulence in her soul at present, the calm permanence of rock, sea and headland seemed to offer Elizabeth both reproach and salve.

After her violent introduction to the weather on Béara, Elizabeth had gradually come to accept its quicksilver changes of mood. Vagrant days like this were not uncommon; in high summer there were always a few days which were so bitterly cold and stormy that they were reminiscent of midwinter, and in the worst depths of November or February some days dawned so warm, clear and still that visitors were heard to remark that the area reminded them of the South of France in spring.

'I hope you don't mind, Tilly,' she said slowly, 'but I think I need a bit of time on my own right now. If it's not too much to ask, would you mind the three of them for an hour or so while I go for a walk? I'll just be the hour, I promise. It might calm me down a bit.'

'Of course.'

Calling goodbye to Francey and Johanna, still bent industriously over their drawing, Elizabeth let herself out.

The air was warmer outside than in. A pair of hooded crows skrawked loudly and sailed away to a safe distance as, scattering rabbits, sparrows and starlings busy with their own affairs, she walked fast uphill, soon leaving behind both Tilly's farmhouse and her own. To her left, a quarter of a mile distant, she saw the figure of Mossie Sheehan. He was turning turf on his piece of turbary which adjoined their own above Derryvegill. He looked up and saw her and she waved but carried on without watching to see whether he waved back.

She was panting when she reached the topmost ridge of Knockameala where a small cairn of stones had been built to commemorate – what? No one had ever been able to tell her. She knew the Irish for Lahersheen was *Láthair Oisín* – 'the place of Oisín' who was a mythological Irish hero. Maybe this cairn marked the place where the warrior had slept . . . Some comfort here on a cold night, Elizabeth thought irreverently as she added a pebble to the mound. Already feeling better, she sat beside the cairn to think and to catch her breath.

The day was so clear that from this vantage point, she could see for many miles in all directions: to the north-east, the Miskish mountains and behind them the Cahas; to the north, the wide sea-inlet of the Kenmare river flowing between Béara and the misty blue Iveragh; to the south, the calm waters of Bantry Bay.

All around were the fields and tilled headlands of Lahersheen, Derryconnla and the other villages and town-lands of this part of the peninsula; Neeley's tiny fields, acquired piecemeal over the years and therefore largely unconnected to one another, were strewn around their own house like jigsaw pieces, most straggling upwards towards the low brown summit of Knocknasheeog or the higher one of Knockameala where she now sat. Way above her head a peregrine falcon, one of a pair she knew nested on the cliff near the wedge grave above Kilcatherine Point, glided in systematic circles. The cattle were not yet out, but the fields and commonage were alive with wings and tail feathers and the bracken at her feet buzzed with insects. This happy commotion contrasted so forcefully with her own brown and joyless existence that she was sorely tempted to succumb to tears of self-pity.

Elizabeth loved her children, all of them, Neeley's too, but all she could think of now was that she was serving out the time she was granted on this beautiful, light-filled planet as though it were something to be got through; not really living at all but grubbing like a beetle or a mole in her dark kitchen, muddy farmyard and musty bedroom. Her summers were filled with the round of farm work, her winters with survival.

Days such as this one came and went and she hardly noticed; if she went for a walk, even up to this glorious place, it was always with her eyes on the ground just in front of her or watching a baby; and when she came to the summit of the walk, she was always so tired and concerned about coming down again to start the next task that she never took time to look around. She did pay lip-service to each 'beautiful day', but the beauty habitually slid over and under her and never penetrated.

She threw herself backwards into the thick, scratchy undergrowth of furze, stunted grasses and brittle, withered ferns. 'I'm twenty-six,' she cried to the sky, 'I'm only twenty-six years old. What's happened to me?'

As she lay there, the sky seemed to poise itself, remaining still while she herself seemed nudged gently into motion, pushed slowly through its wideness in a slow arc. And here it came, that little curl of air around the back of her neck and under her hairline. Something was going to happen.

She heard movement a little to her right and pulling her legs under her, sprang into a crouched position; the sound could have been caused by a fox, a badger, or even a rat – Elizabeth was still citified to the extent that she was terrified of all rodents, particularly rats.

She waited for a few seconds and when she heard nothing more, relaxed a little. Then her eye caught a brief flash of light in the bracken about ten yards away. 'Hey!' she called, to scare whatever it was. 'Hey! Hey!'

'Mrs Scollard?' Carrying a broken shotgun over one arm, a young man unfolded himself from the undergrowth. Elizabeth recognized him as Daniel McCarthy from Lissacarrig, one of the local boys and one whom Mary, Neeley's eldest daughter, thought to be gorgeous. Known as Daniel Carrig to distinguish him from all the other Dan McCarthys in the area, he was eighteen or nineteen.

'Daniel?' Her astonishment at his appearance was followed immediately by exquisite embarrassment. This boy had heard her behaving like a madwoman calling aloud to the sky.

'I was hunting rabbits.' He bent and, picking up a brace of the animals to show her, walked across to within a few feet. Strangely, he showed no sign of being rattled. Perhaps he had not heard her?

'I see.' Elizabeth stood up and smoothed her skirt.

'Lovely day, Mrs Scollard?' Showing no inclination to

leave, he dropped the rabbits at his feet and stood looking at her.

'It is, isn't it?' Elizabeth felt vaguely discommoded as if he were the adult and she the child. 'Well,' she said briskly, 'I suppose I'd better be going.'

'But you just got here,' he pointed out.

'I did, didn't I?' She looked off over the mountain to where she could just see the gleam of Lough Fada. 'Mind you,' she was rapidly regaining her composure, 'I didn't know I was going to have company.'

'Oh, I come up here all the time,' he said. 'Great place for rabbits.'

She shot a quick look at him; was he poking fun at her? 'I didn't hear any gunfire,' she said.

'Got these about half an hour ago. I was just taking a rest. You know, enjoying the day.'

His composure was extraordinary and yet, not long after her first arrival on the peninsula, Elizabeth had noticed that the people of Béara, although quite often verbally shy, seemed to be filled with an innate self-confidence. And it was a quality seen not only in adults: children and adolescents, too, seemed blessed in this way. 'Well, I was, too,' she said. 'Enjoying the day, I mean.'

During the pause that followed, Elizabeth had to search for what to say next. But the boy got there first. 'You can just see the roof of your house from here.' He inclined his head in the direction of the farmhouse.

'Yes,' said Elizabeth drily.

'Snug house,' he remarked, seating himself.

'Do you think so?' Elizabeth hesitated and then herself sat down. Given the way the conversation was going, perfectly ordinary, person-to-person, there was really no reason to rush back. 'Do you know what time it is, Daniel?' she asked.

He squinted at the sun. 'About ten or half ten, I suppose. I've no watch.'

'Neither do I.' She smiled at him. Putting her hands behind her, she leaned backwards a little and raised her face to the warmth. When he said nothing more, she closed her

158

eyes and endeavoured to tune in to the symphony of twittering and chirping which, overlain by the solo outpourings of a skylark directly overhead, filled the air. And, like an echo in a distant cave, the air itself seemed full to bursting with the low sustained roar of the sea.

Elizabeth consciously let go, relinquishing her problems, sending them off on a short holiday.

After a few minutes she even let go of the fact that she was not alone.

'I heard you, you know. Saying that you're only twenty-six.'

Her eyes shot open. The boy's, she saw, were perfectly serious. They were dark brown and as Elizabeth looked into them she was aware of a momentary sensation, like burning, on the surface of her own. 'I'm sorry about that, Daniel,' she said quietly, looking away, oddly not embarrassed any more. 'As I said, I didn't expect I'd have witnesses.' In a way it was almost a relief that someone else, even this strange boy, had seen the extent of her unhappiness. 'What age are you?' she asked.

'Nineteen and a half,' he replied.

'Great age. I half wish I was that age again.' Elizabeth heard the words, spoken like an old woman. 'Well, maybe I don't,' she said then. 'I was married when I was that age.' Again that had come out wrongly. It sounded as though she regretted being married. 'Oh, don't mind me,' she said, lifting her face again to the sunshine.

'You have beautiful hair, Mrs Scollard,' he said after a minute or so. 'Like honey.'

She looked back at him in shock. Then: 'So do you, Daniel.' His thick curly hair was almost black.

'Thank you.' He accepted the compliment as though it belonged to someone else and his gaze did not waver. 'Do you know Irish?'

'A little.' Elizabeth's school Irish had never been up to much. Many of the older people on Béara used words and phrases in daily life, however, and by working out the context she usually understood them.

'Then you know that this mountain is "the hill of wild

honey". Its real name is Knockamealafin, Cnoc na meala fiáine, but everyone around here's too lazy to say it.'

'I see,' said Elizabeth, not knowing whether to be amused at the turn the talk was taking. 'There's a lot of peculiar place names around here,' she said, 'obviously, I know about Lahersheen, but what about Derryconnla for instance?'

'"The oak of the candles." Don't know what oak tree they're talking about there, actually. The first time I noticed your hair,' he went on, as though this was the most natural conversation in the world, 'was at Mass when your head-scarf slipped off. You were at the end of a row and I was two rows behind you at the other side.'

The air between them seemed to Elizabeth to take a sudden little jump. 'How long ago was that?' she asked faintly.

'About a year ago. Well, a bit less. March.'

'I see,' she said again, staring at him. 'Well, I'd really better be going.'

'All right.' He did not flinch under her gaze but, with the gun beside him as innocent as a hazel twig, lay seemingly relaxed in the furze. His body, she saw, was straight and strong.

She stood up and again smoothed her skirt. Then, looking around: 'It really is lovely up here, you know. I should come up here more often.'

'Yeah, 'tis lovely all right.'

'And you come up here all the time, you say?' She felt she was having to collect wits scattered by this very strange boy.

'There's rabbits all over these mountains,' he said. 'I get them all the way over to Derryvegill and down to Lough Fada. Sometimes, at night, I come up here to shoot foxes.'

'I see,' she said again, 'well, as I said, I'd better be off.' She turned her head away from him towards her house.

'Cheerio, so.' The silence between them grew denser.

Although she did not turn her head back and he did not move from his position seven feet away, she felt the touch of his lips on her own.

'Goodbye, Daniel.' She left him and plunged down the hillside.

What had happened back there? She really did seem to be going insane.

That boy was only that, a boy. Yet there had been something deeper in him, a sweetness . . .

Stop it! she told herself. *Stop it this instant.*

By the time she got as far as Tilly's house again she was somewhat calmer and had almost convinced herself that she had imagined the whole episode. But as she came within sight of Tilly's house, a pair of magpies, so close she could see the glossy, bluish tinge of their wings, flew directly across her path.

Two for joy.

Stop it! she said again but could not suppress the feeling that her body had become as light as a bubble.

Tilly noticed the difference. 'God,' she said, 'you should go for walks more often. You've even got a bit of colour in those cheeks of yours, God bless them.'

'Things don't seem so bad out in the fresh air, do they?' Elizabeth laughed. 'Come on, lovey!' Taking the baby from Tilly's arms, she raised her high above her head and swung her in a wide circle. Delighted, Abigail swam her fat little limbs and chuckled.

Bearing their drawings, the two older children came trotting away from the table, 'Look, Mammy, look, Mammy!' crowding in and pulling at Elizabeth's skirt.

'Let me see – oooh! Aren't these wonderful!' Placing Abigail on her hip, Elizabeth studied the drawings. Johanna's was a childhood standard: a tip-tilted house with curls of smoke coming out of the chimney, stick figures of cows, a dog and a cat in the fields around. Francey's was more complicated. His house, cramped into the lower right-hand corner of the paper, sported several long thin appendages, stretching like tentacles towards a human figure in the centre. The figure had its arms raised in fright; the mouth was open in a scream and the hair, long and savagely attenuated, stood straight up on its oval head. 'What's this, Francey?' Elizabeth was puzzled.

161

'It's the house monster.'

'It's very frightening all right. And who's the poor person?'

'Nobody.'

Elizabeth stared at him. 'Are you sure?'

'I'm sure. Can we go home now?'

Elizabeth felt too exhilarated to probe any further. She got the three children organized and, thanking Tilly for taking care of them, took her leave.

As they were coming through the upper haggard, she surprised the children by sitting Abigail down in a flat dry place. 'Come on,' she said to the other two, 'let's all play "Ring a Ring a Rosie".'

'Why?' Francey, unused to this strange mood in his mother, was cautious.

'Because it's a lovely day and I want to, that's why!' She seized Francey's and Johanna's hands, formed a circle with them and the three of them danced and sang the rhyme around the amazed baby.

'Asha, Asha, we all fall DOWN!' All three collapsed on the ground and Francey and Johanna dissolved in high-pitched giggles at the unusual sight of their mother with her legs in the air.

As she was getting to her feet, Elizabeth glanced upwards towards the summit of Knockameala. Rendered tiny by distance, a figure stood outlined against the sky. The weather was so clear, she could see one leg of the V made by the broken shotgun draped over his arm.

'Come on.' She picked up Abigail. 'We have to get home.'

'Ah, Mammy. I want to play again!' Francey stood with hands on hips. 'You *said*!'

'You *said*!' echoed Johanna.

'I know I did, lovey,' Elizabeth started to walk fast downhill towards the house, 'but I've changed my mind.'

She had the two older children seated to an early dinner at around noon and was just giving the baby a feed when Neeley came back. They all tensed and silence descended on the kitchen as he closed the door behind him.

162

He came across to Elizabeth's chair. 'Here,' he said, thrusting at her a small package wrapped in brown paper.

'What is it?' Surprised, she took it. It felt solid.

'Open it and see,' he said gruffly, turned on his heel and went into the scullery from where she heard him run the tap to wash his hands.

Elizabeth put the baby in her playpen and handed her the bottle so she could feed herself. She tore the wrappings off the package; inside, were two small bars of Cadbury's chocolate.

Elizabeth had always had a sweet tooth but chocolate was a commodity as rare as platinum in wartime Ireland. 'Where'd you get this, Neeley?' she called in astonishment.

'It's a present,' he called back.

She weighed it in her hand. *You're too late*, she thought.

That night, she had a dream of such pleasure and vividness that it remained with her in essence all next day. Try as she might, however, she could not remember any of the images or details. But throughout the day, she felt warm, as though she had been hugged by a dear friend.

It was only the following night, as she was suspended between semi-consciousness and full sleep, that the images recurred. She was facing towards the four-paned window of her bedroom when it seemed to brighten; reaching out, she was able to pull it towards her and to fit it around herself. Accepting this phenomenon without fear, she stepped through and into a jewelled landscape of such precision and hard-edged radiance that she gasped.

The mountains glowed with agate and amethyst and, down below, the sea threw pearls and emeralds against rocks of polished jet. The sky was a clear and brilliant sapphire, the whitewashed houses of their neighbours glittered hard under a diamond-white sun and instead of being pocked with rocks and thistles, the fields of Béara spread like jade-topped billiard tables around them; flowers of ruby, amber, aquamarine and citrine blew in the hedges, the roads and boreens shimmered between them with ribbons of opal.

As free and lighthearted as the birds which darted like spangles round her head, Elizabeth roamed through this enchanted countryside in which even the cows and calves seemed placed by a loving and exuberant hand.

Then, feeling herself beckoned, she came to Kilcatherine graveyard which was not the graveyard of her fears but an airy open place where the outlines of the crosses had been softened with flowers and ribbons so they resembled maypoles. Around them, a sort of ceremonial dance was in progress; it was being performed by people she did not recognize, men and women of taller than average height and great beauty. The women wore ground-length dresses in varying pastel shades which swayed against their legs as they moved; the men wore robes of silvery grey. Badgers, foxes and rabbits played together at their feet and all, even the animals, were bedizened with oak leaves; all smiled at her with such open welcome and friendliness that she felt their love to be palpable; it smelled and tasted like honey.

Elizabeth walked into the centre of this group and as she did so one of the women, dressed in some filmy stuff of turquoise, broke off from the dance and handed her an object. As Elizabeth gazed at it, she saw it was the Kilcatherine Head, not the awful thing of which she was so afraid but an orb of shifting texture and colour; now it was like smoke, now like fluid gold and the expression on the features she had thought so inscrutable and terrifying had liquefied into loving mildness. Elizabeth knew as she gazed at its shifting features that she was being asked to place her trust in it and that if she did irrevocable protection would be conferred on her.

This was all she could remember – she must have woken at that point – but as she played the details over in her memory, they again warmed her and gave her such a feeling of fulfilment that she turned and, with careful tenderness, kissed the sleeping Neeley on the cheek.

During that momentous day he had made further efforts at making amends. After she had thanked him for the chocolate – careful not to betray her real feelings – he told her he had been to see a solicitor in Castletownbere and had made out a will. 'It's all yours, Lizzie,' he said, 'lock stock and barrel.'

The issue of succession to Neeley's property had never entered Elizabeth's head, nevertheless, she was touched. 'Thank you, Neeley,' she had said, 'and if ever the worst happens, you needn't worry. I'll look after us all.'

Embarrassed, Neeley had left the room, leaving Elizabeth to wonder if she hadn't treated his gesture too lightly.

Turning round carefully now so as not to wake him, she snuggled down to sleep.

And as she lay basking, the last shreds of shame about her fixation with George Gallaher drifted off like gossamer into the night and she found she was thinking of him with considerable fondness, almost as though he was one of her children.

But her last waking image was that of Daniel Carrig's body stretched full length in the furze on Knockameala.

Neeley never referred again to George Gallaher or to what might or might not have happened in Glengarriff. And after a few days, during which Elizabeth watched his every move and gesture, on the surface their joint lives settled back little by little into a pattern of domesticity and work.

But there had been a fundamental change.

Although as a general rule she continued to submit to Neeley's lovemaking, Elizabeth never again allowed her husband to touch her when he had taken any drink, a situation Neeley accepted at first with bad grace and eventually with resignation.

Another more insidious change had occurred. Like persistent sea-mist, the sensations occasioned by the Kilcatherine dream clung to Elizabeth and, as she went about her daily chores, she found herself daydreaming back into them. And, despite her best and sternest efforts to banish him, Daniel Carrig McCarthy persisted in his invasion of her thoughts.

And then, a fortnight after her encounter with him on the summit of Knockameala, Elizabeth literally ran into him again. On her way out of the post office in Ardgroom, she was looking over her shoulder to say goodbye to the postmistress and cannoned into someone in the doorway. 'I'm sorry,' she said, then, 'Oh! It's you—' Caught off guard she felt the blood begin to rise in her face and was overwhelmingly conscious of the eyes of the postmistress on her back.

He seemed not at all put out. 'Hello, Mrs Scollard,' he said gravely, 'soft day.'

'Yes.' His clothes gave off a distinctive aroma, a combination of fresh air and strong tobacco.

'I think it might clear up later, though,' he said. His composure unnerved her as he stepped aside to let her pass.

'Thank you, Daniel,' she said, walking quickly and making her escape.

The exchange had taken perhaps ten seconds in all but as Elizabeth cycled home, she could not lose the smell of his clothes, the image of his eyes. She found herself wondering about his exact height; judging by his relativity to her own height of five feet eight, he seemed to be a little over six feet tall.

Hearing herself think, she was appalled. *This has gone far enough!* She dismounted from the bike at a particularly steep part of the road and leaning into the handlebars, pushed with all her might. *What are you doing? What are you at?*

She went at the machine so furiously she got to the top of the hill in record time. And as she freewheeled down again she made a determined effort to put Daniel Carrig McCarthy, his eyes, his height, everything about him, firmly out of her mind.

But on the following day, as she was pegging out a load of washing in the hill field to the east of the house, she felt the hair on the nape of her neck rise. Spinning around she looked up towards the summit of Knockameala. He was there, silhouetted against the sky.

The sheets already pinned to the clothes line cracked and flapped in the stiff breeze as they watched one another for a few seconds. Then, as though moving in slow motion, Elizabeth forced herself to turn away, to pick up a pillowcase from the basket at her feet. When she glanced back towards the mountain, he was no longer to be seen.

The weather turned foul that afternoon and she did not see him again for several weeks. During that period, Elizabeth strove very hard to keep at bay whatever spell she had imagined was being cast around her by Daniel Carrig McCarthy. She scrubbed the house from top to bottom, cleaned out cupboards, blacked the stove. Gathering the children round her like a protective screen, she read to the little ones at night, helped the older ones with their homework. She was considerate and loving with Neeley – even, to his astonishment, going so far on one night as to initiate lovemaking.

A few of the neighbours had been in for a game of cards. The evening had gone well but after she had seen the visitors out, noticing that the weather had at last lifted, Elizabeth had felt restless and more energetic than she usually did at such a late hour. She had delayed going to bed, saying that she needed a breath of fresh air. 'It's stopped raining,' she said to Neeley. 'I haven't been outside the door for days. You go on, I'll be in in a few minutes.'

A heifer lowed repeatedly at her from one of the outhouses as, joined by Rex, the family's dog who was surprised and happy that someone was going on a nocturnal jaunt, she crossed the farmyard, climbed through the little gap in the stone wall which bounded it and walked into the hill field which was still boggy after several days of heavy rain.

Since that pet day in February on the top of Knockameala, Elizabeth had made up her mind that somehow she was going to be more open to the sublimity which daily spread itself before her. Only half an hour ago, rain as hard as boat nails had been hammered by the wind into the rattling slates. But the storm had passed eastwards, and the landscape now revealed was serene and untroubled. Although the air held promise of more storms to come, as she walked uphill in this brief and magical lacuna, Elizabeth felt alert and tingling as though she was physically absorbing some of the luminosity of sky and sea.

167

All the time she tried to keep from looking upwards towards the top of Knockameala.

She called to Rex who was zigzagging far ahead of her; he lolloped back and, as she pulled his soft ears, gave her an ecstatic lick before bounding ahead again.

Elizabeth could not any longer resist looking upwards.

As far as she could see, the rounded, silvery grey summit was bare.

You're such a fool! Angry at herself for being so weak and stupid – what was she going to do about it if he was there, anyway? – she turned on her heel and walked fast downhill towards the house but just as she came to the boundary wall, the landscape around her echoed to a single shot.

She wheeled and looked back towards the mountain but it was bare as before. Sound was deceptive at night; he was somewhere else, she thought, searching. Or it was probably some other neighbour, supplementing the family pot.

Although she strained her eyes, she could see no movement of any kind, no glints or flashes of torchlight. The contours of the mountains, not only Knockameala but Knocknasheeog and Tooreennamna and all the others too remained as undisturbed as before.

Again she castigated herself. *For God's sake, woman!* You're a pathetic creature; first you degrade yourself with a liar and a cheat and waste half your life on him. And just when you're on the rebound from that, what do you do? You start fancying a boy – a child of nineteen years of age. Chilled, she caught her breath. Fantasies about Daniel Carrig McCarthy must remain just that – fantasies.

Elizabeth squared her shoulders and took a long look at the house. To air the kitchen after the smoke which had attended the card game, she had not latched the door when she had come out and a trapezoid of yellow light spilled into the farmyard, causing glints in the tiny puddles between the cobbles.

In there was where she belonged, not roaming the hills like a wanton ewe.

Purposeful and determined now, she walked across the farmyard. 'Hush, you!' she hissed at the heifer who, as she passed, again gave voice from its prison.

She latched the door behind her and went into the bedroom. Neeley was already in bed, his back, hunched under the bedclothes, was towards her. She had neglected this man shamefully, thought Elizabeth. No wonder he had called her a slut; in many respects he was right.

Undressing quickly, she slid into bed. 'Neeley?' She touched him on the back.

'Yes?' He did not turn round.

'Come here to me!'

'What?' His surprise was evident in the perceptible stiffening of his back.

'You heard. I said, come here to me!'

He turned in the bed and made as if to climb on top of her. 'Wait, Neeley, wait a bit.' She held him off. 'Hug me first.'

He put his arms around her and squeezed her to him so tightly she could barely breathe. 'That's nice,' she whispered into his chest. 'Can you feel me, really feel me?'

She felt him nod. 'Then kiss me, Neeley, gently now.' He held her, stroking her hair, kissing her deeply and with genuine tenderness. Elizabeth realized that in their entire marriage it was the most meaningful embrace they had exchanged. 'Isn't this nice?' she murmured as the long kiss ended and they snuggled into a comfortable position.

'Yes.' He kissed her again.

'This is the way I like it,' she whispered, 'slow and gentle. We've plenty of time, you know, we've no train to catch tonight.'

'Sure we haven't.' Delighted, he kissed her eagerly. A little more secure after a while, she responded with growing passion, taking his lower lip between her teeth and biting gently.

With this, she lost the battle. Like a stallion or a ram confronted suddenly with opportunity, he pulled up her nightdress and started to fondle her, kneading her breasts, thighs and stomach so roughly that her skin felt as though

169

it was being abraded. 'Neeley, Neeley—' with all her might, she willed him to slow down, to tune in to her again. 'Gently – gently . . .'

For a short while it seemed to be working. He stopped his kneading and again hugged her tight. 'Lizzie, oh, Lizzie!' But then, before she could stop him, he had entered her and as usual, within seconds it was all over.

After he rolled off her, he took her purpose of amendment, which had been shaky at best, with him; in its place grew anger so deep and complete that Elizabeth did not trust herself to speak. Her husband had rejected her as surely and clearly as if he had turfed her out on to the floor.

Her side of the bed was beside the window of their tiny room and she turned towards it now, away from Neeley; the curtains were not drawn and the four-paned window glowed with calm grey light, the cross of its wooden frame clear and black. Out there was life, the secret, pulsing life of animals and fish and planets and restless moving water, of furze and fern and insect.

Neeley turned towards her, cosying against her back, putting an arm around her: 'That was nice,' he whispered. 'I wasn't expecting that. You're full of surprises, Lizzie.'

Elizabeth knew then that his incomprehension was total and irreversible. With the knowledge came an easing of her anger. 'Yes,' she said quietly, 'goodnight, Neeley.'

His arm slackened and she knew he was asleep.

She stole out of bed and tiptoed to the bathroom to douche herself as she always did after sex with Neeley. As much as she ever prayed nowadays, she prayed to God with all her heart she was not pregnant again. For the past few years she had been lucky; her miscarriages, although messy and upsetting, had been a relief, and at least Francey and Johanna had been of manageable age by the time Abbie was born.

She looked out through the small bathroom window at the ethereal silver landscape and the prayers died in her heart. The attempted seduction of her husband had been a sham and hypocritical in the extreme.

For Elizabeth admitted to herself that she had known

full well there was no hope of fulfilling physical love with Neeley Scollard.

Daniel McCarthy.

She had wanted an excuse.

Chapter Ten

Next day, on going out into the yard carrying a basin of mash for the hens, Elizabeth saw Daniel outside the gate. She stopped so abruptly that Francey, who was following close on her heels, bumped into her and the basin fell, spilling a little of the mash.

'I brought ye a salmon,' Daniel called, putting a package, wrapped in brown paper, on one of the gate piers.

'Thank you.' Elizabeth's stomach contracted as she walked towards the gate. When she got close to him, she saw he was equally nervous. 'Come in, won't you?' she asked.

'Not at all, Mrs Scollard,' he said. 'I won't, but thanks all the same. I just came to leave this.'

'Thank you,' she said again, taking the parcel off the pier; it felt wet and surprisingly heavy. 'This is a big one.' She did not dare look at him but concentrated on the package in her hands. 'Wouldn't you eat it yourselves, Daniel? What made you think of us?'

'I caught it in the Cascades early this morning. We don't like salmon,' he said.

Elizabeth felt physically as though the sun had become warmer, reaching the bones within her skin. 'I do wish you'd come in,' she said, making an effort to sound casual, 'I've just taken bread out of the oven. And there's buttermilk. Neeley's gone into Castletown,' she added.

At last she looked up. 'He'll be sorry he missed you,' she whispered. They stared at one another.

Francey broke the tension. Running up to the gate, he inserted himself between them. 'Hello!' He beamed up at Daniel.

Daniel cleared his throat. 'Hello,' he replied. 'You're Francey?'

'What's your name?'

'Daniel McCarthy.'

Elizabeth unlatched the gate and held it wide: 'Come in for a few minutes at least.' Her voice sounded as hoarse as his. 'Francey,' she added, 'go on in and pour us some buttermilk.'

To make time to collect herself, she scattered the hens' mash around the yard and then rinsed the basin under the outside tap, taking longer than normal. But all the time she was unbearably conscious of Daniel's presence as, silent, he stood a little further away from her than would be customary for a neighbour dropping by for a simple chat.

When she had finished rinsing the basin, she went to pass him on her way to the door but he put out a hand as though to stop her. 'What is it?' she whispered.

He waited a little as though gathering his thoughts and, in the pause, Francey's clattering from the kitchen resounded like small explosions.

Eventually, Daniel spoke. 'It wasn't only to bring you the salmon I came,' he said. 'There's something I want to ask you. It may sound – peculiar.'

Elizabeth's already fast heartbeat speeded up until she could feel blood pumping high in her throat. 'I'd prefer if we talked inside,' she said.

Again it was Francey who saved her. As she cut two slices of bread off the cake, he sat beside Daniel at the table. 'Have you got brothers?' he asked.

'Four,' Daniel replied.

'I've none,' sighed Francey. 'It's all women here.'

Daniel, who seemed to Elizabeth to be calmer than she, did not laugh. 'It has its advantages,' he said. 'Where are they all now?'

'At school, some of them. Johanna's having a nap. And that's the baby.' Francey waved a dismissive hand towards the playpen over the top of which Abigail was gazing wide-eyed at the visitor. 'I'd definitely like a brother, though,' he returned to the subject.

173

'Why?'

'To play football.'

'What about your daddy? Doesn't he play football with you?'

'He's not my daddy.' Francey said it in a pleasant tone, as if this was a matter of no consequence to him.

Elizabeth placed the two slices of buttered bread on the table in front of them. 'Here, Francey,' she said and to her relief, her voice sounded passably composed, 'take your cut of bread out to the yard. And when you're finished, stay out there and play, it's a lovely day and you should be out in the fresh air.'

'There's nothing to do out there, Mammy,' Francey objected, but in response to a look from his mother, he took the bread and trotted out of the kitchen.

Elizabeth sat opposite Daniel. Behind her, Abigail began to play with a set of wooden alphabet blocks; through the hush which had descended on the kitchen, their clicking as she piled them on top of one another sounded as loud as the clamour from a shunting yard.

'How's the milk?' Elizabeth asked, finally dredging up something to say.

'It's fine, Mrs Scollard.' He took a sip.

'Thank you again for the salmon.' Frantically, Elizabeth realized her hand was itching to touch the back of his where it lay between them. His nails, she saw, were bitten.

Simultaneously, they turned towards Abigail as the baby let out a particularly loud coo of satisfaction and then Elizabeth jumped up and with a corner of her apron, wiped the drool off Abigail's chin. 'She's lovely,' said Daniel.

'I know.' Elizabeth concentrated on the baby.

'So's Francey.'

'Without knowing it, Francey's right.' Elizabeth returned to the table. She had the sense of jumping into the middle of a conversation, as though they were taking up where they left off. 'As you probably know,' she added, 'Neeley isn't the child's father.'

'Yes.'

174

'It's a notion he's got into his own head,' she continued. Now that they were actually conversing, she was finding it easier to look at him. 'As far as I know, no one told him. Unless he's heard gossip.'

'You shouldn't mind gossip. Corner-boys have little to talk about.'

'I don't. But maybe Francey has heard something.'

He drained the cup and put it down in front of him. 'Mrs Scollard, there's something I have to ask you—' He picked up the cup again and examined it minutely. 'I don't know do I have the right to say this to you. I probably shouldn't have come . . .'

The tension within Elizabeth stretched to breaking point. She started at the clatter from behind her as Abigail threw one of the alphabet blocks out of the playpen on to the floor. Then Daniel reached out deliberately and touched the back of her hand, just once. 'I wasn't able to sleep last night,' he said.

'Neither was I.'

The back of her hand stung at the spot he had touched. 'I walked up towards the mountain,' she said. 'You weren't there.'

He appeared to consider this, then, looking down at the table in front of him, 'What do you think is happening?'

Elizabeth exulted. 'I don't know,' she replied, then, impulsively, 'That's not strictly true. I want to be honest with you, Daniel. And the true answer is I don't want to say it. Not yet.'

'I do!' Boldly he challenged her. 'I think something happened between us, up there on Knockameala.'

'What do you think happened?' Elizabeth had to swallow hard.

'You liked me.'

Elizabeth noted that it was a statement and not a question. 'Yes.' She replied. 'All right,' she said then, gripping the side of the table, 'you're right. I am attracted to you. I'm attracted to you in a most fundamental way.' She gazed at him full in the face. His upper lip, she noticed, had become curiously rigid.

'Can it happen so quickly?'

'That's the way it seems to be. I'm sorry if that shocks you.' She refused to look away from him.

'You're a married woman, Mrs Scollard.' To her relief, he exhibited no shock.

'Yes. And my name is Elizabeth.'

'I find that a bit hard – it's a bit soon—'

' – you won't.'

'Are you wondering if I like you?' From several feet away, Elizabeth could feel the suspense vibrating through his shoulders, upper arms and hands. 'Do you?' she asked.

'I'm head over heels in love with you. I have been for ages.'

Elizabeth's blood leaped within its covering skin. But she smiled involuntarily at the curiously childlike expression. 'Head over heels?' she asked, hardly daring to breathe.

Obviously gauging her reaction correctly, he smiled back at her, a slow open smile. 'Is it all right?'

'Not only is it all right, Daniel, it's wonderful.'

He leaned forward a little and for a moment she thought he was going to kiss her. Instead, he jumped up from the table and threw back his head; raising his clenched fists victoriously he spun like a ballet dancer on the balls of his feet. Then he dashed across the kitchen and scattering building blocks, snatched the astonished baby from her playpen. Lifting her high above his head, he waltzed her madly round the kitchen.

At first Abigail was too taken aback to react then, afraid, she began to squeal.

Instantly, Daniel stopped the dance. 'I'm sorry, baby, sorry, sorry!' he handed her over to her mother. 'I'm sorry, Mrs Scollard,' he apologized again to Elizabeth. 'I didn't mean to frighten her.'

Abigail buried her head in her mother's shoulder, then, her terror forgotten, turned around to gaze at him:

'It's all right.' Elizabeth, caught up in Daniel's jubilation, laughed. 'She'll be fine. It's just that she's not used to being handled by a man.'

'She's lovely.' Daniel stroked the baby's hand, then bent ardent eyes on Elizabeth herself. 'So are you.'

'Enough for one day.' But Elizabeth's insides were churning with excitement. 'Listen, I have to think. This is all very fast – you'd better go –'

'Thank you for the bread and milk.'

'And thank you again for the fish.'

They smiled again at one another. 'Look,' Elizabeth said, 'let's not rush things.'

'I wouldn't dream of it.'

'I mean – let's just wait and see what happens.'

'Of course.' His brown eyes glowed. 'I won't do it now, but I can't wait to kiss you.'

Quickly she stepped back a few paces – for an instant she thought she heard Neeley's approach – and wondered why she was not feeling guilty. 'I'm serious, Daniel,' she said. 'Apart altogether from the fact that this is very, very dangerous, what I feel is that we shouldn't force anything. If we meet on the roads –'

'Or on the mountain,' he interjected.

'All right, on the mountain –'

'Be sure of it,' he said fervently. 'Be sure we'll meet.'

At the threshold of the door, he turned. 'I can't wait,' he said again.

'Ssh!' Elizabeth's stomach flipped over.

Accustomed as she was to moving events along, Elizabeth found it difficult to let them take their course. However, she felt very strongly that, for once in her life, she must not push but must listen to an inner set of instructions, which thundered at her not to be impatient. Although sorely tempted, she did not go again that spring to the summit of Knockameala.

Nor did she try to manoeuvre her daily comings and goings so that she might again meet Daniel Carrig by 'accident'.

But being human, she chafed. Not only at not seeing him, but at not knowing where he was, what he was doing, what he was thinking. If he was thinking of her.

Her physical obsession with him deprived her of sleep in a way that reminded her of the first days of her affair with George Gallaher; as she fed the hens, she fantasized about his shape, about his skin, about burying her fingers in his thick, dark hair; when cutting down a pair of Neeley's trousers for Francey or darning a basketful of holed socks, she saw not her own hands, but Daniel Carrig's and imagined how they would feel on the bare skin of her back.

The more time passed, the more – despite her firmest resolutions, despite the knowledge that being married she had no entitlement at all to such worries – she fretted that Daniel Carrig might meet a suitable girl and even leave the area. As the second eldest son in his family, he was unlikely to have any hopes of inheriting the family farm.

And then she overheard Mary, Neeley's eldest, talking to another girl out in the yard. Daniel Carrig, apparently, had taken a job from the Puxleys at the copper mines in Allihies. This renewed Elizabeth's confidence: Allihies was a fair journey from Lissacarrig and anyone who did that trip twice in one day on top of a full day's work could not have much time for travelling the roads or roaming over Knockameala with a shotgun.

By the time she did see him again, on 12 May, she was almost on the point of ignoring her instincts and seeking him out.

Mary was off school with a cold. Taking advantage of her presence in the house to mind the baby, Elizabeth went once again to the post office in Ardgroom where last she had encountered him. Today was a Friday and it had been a Friday the last time. She made sure it was the same time of day.

But she was disappointed, he was nowhere to be seen.

Having bought stamps she did not need, she made her way home and just before she crested the hill above the house, she heard Francey's happy shouts. And when she came to where she could see him, she saw her son was not alone: Daniel Carrig, with Francey in close pursuit, was kicking a football around the hill field.

The images and sensations of the jewelled-landscape

dream tumbled back into her thoughts. To prolong the feeling, she applied the brakes to the freewheeling bike and coasted only slowly downhill towards the gate of the farmyard.

'Mammy, Mammy!' The road skirted the field and Francey spotted her when she was still thirty yards away. 'Look at me, look at me!' Like a little dervish he threw himself full length on the football and rolled away down the hill with it, laughing and screaming at the top of his voice. Daniel watched him go then turned and looked towards where she stood by the hedge holding the handle-bars of the bike.

She had her emotions under control by the time she let herself into the yard and put the bicycle away in the shed. By this time Francey was away up at the top of the field again, lofting the ball as high as he could. 'Danny, Danny!' His excited voice was thin and shrill. 'I'm going to score a goal. Watch me!'

Elizabeth climbed through the gap in the wall and walked slowly towards Daniel; with every step she became more aware of the grass under her feet, of the feel of her clothes on her body.

Watching her approach, Daniel stood stock still.

'Danny!' From the far end of the field, Francey's voice was becoming petulant. 'Look! *Look*, Danny!'

'We're both looking, Francey!' Elizabeth called out.

'You're *not*!'

'Oh, yes, we are!' Daniel flashed a smile at Elizabeth then ran towards the boy. Expertly he hooked the ball away and, while Francey chased him, ran downhill with it, controlling it with feet and hands and keeping it in the air at all times.

Both of them reached her at once and while Daniel continued to pop the ball between feet and hands, Francey threw himself against her knees. 'I'm going to learn how to play real football, Mammy. Danny said. He said he'd bring me to Reen and he'd make the other boys play with me. And he said he'd bring me to a real match sometime in Eyeries or Urhan.' There were no official football pitches in

179

the parish but farmers were generous with their flatter fields when they were fallow.

'You don't mind?'

As Elizabeth bent to hug Francey, Daniel met her eyes. His were alight. 'I don't mind,' he said softly, 'I'd like to.' His expression told her in no uncertain terms what else he would like.

Elizabeth, controlling her urge to skip like a child, took Francey's hand. As she walked decorously between her son and Daniel towards the farmyard, she searched the fields for Neeley: he had set off this morning to turn the turf on their patch of bog near Derryvegill, but as yet there was no sign of his return. 'You got a job in the mines?' she asked, making conversation.

'Yes. It's just labouring. It'll do until something better comes along. I've a promise of a place on a seine boat out of Ballycrovane in the fall.'

'That's good.' Almost every village in the parish operated one or two seine crews, numbering eighteen men or more working in tandem boats, which fished seasonally for mackerel off the rocky coasts.

'One of the reasons I came,' he stopped walking and kicked at a spike of foxglove, 'I think Mossie Breac saw us together on the mountain that day.'

Elizabeth's heart jumped with guilt. Then she suppressed it. What had she been doing except sitting in the sun? 'There was nothing to see, was there?'

'You think it's all right, then?'

Elizabeth, far from being upset – she cared not at all for what Mossie or Neeley or anyone thought or saw – wanted to sing, to take Daniel's hand and play 'Ring A Ring A Rosie' with him as she had with her children. 'Yes,' she said, 'it is all right. We've nothing to be ashamed of.'

They walked on down the field as Francey frolicked to the right and left of them, hefting the ball and missing the kick more often than he managed to connect.

'How is it you're not working over, today?' Elizabeth asked as they stopped to watch Francey's antics.

'I went this morning but they didn't need me.'

'You never thought of going away?' Like everyone else in the parish, the McCarthys had sent many to Butte.

'I thought about it, but I'm not going now. Here's your husband,' he added quickly, picking up a stone and bending to scrape mud off his boots.

Elizabeth looked up. Neeley had just come into view around the side of the house. He stopped to wash his hands under the outside tap and looked up in their direction. 'Hello, Neeley!' she called.

Neeley did not respond but finished his ablutions and went into the house.

'I'll be going.' Daniel stood back to let Elizabeth and Francey through the gap. 'Keep the ball,' he said to Francey. 'You can practise with it.'

'All right, thanks!' Francey zoomed off across the yard, kicking the ball in front of him as he ran.

'Lovely smell,' said Daniel carefully, his tone entirely different from the one he had employed earlier. He indicated the display of wallflowers and sweet william Elizabeth had planted in an old feeding trough outside the door to the kitchen.

'They are nice, aren't they? Will you come in?' Her tone was uncertain; Neeley's proximity was dangerous.

'No,' he said, 'I have to be off.' He shot a glance at the open door of the house. Then, 'Are you coming to Jimmy Deeney's dance?' he asked quickly. 'Will you and your husband be there?'

The formality of the question brought home to Elizabeth how precarious her position was. She knew about the dance – it had been the talk of the district for months. Jimmy Deeney, a local man who had done well for himself in America, had bought a site at the crossroads of Castleclough, his home-place, and had donated funds for the building of a hall; this generosity was not unconnected with the fact that he was standing as a candidate in the forthcoming general election. The grand opening, originally scheduled for late June but hurriedly brought forward after the calling of the election, was scheduled for a week hence. It was to be a dance, to which everyone in the parish was invited free of charge; many of the Scollards' neighbours were going and it promised to be a great night.

Up to now, however, Elizabeth had not entertained any hopes of going; except for the card games which rotated around the neighbours' houses including their own, Neeley hated social functions of any kind.

Daniel saw her dilemma. 'Don't worry about it,' he said. 'Some other time.'

Elizabeth made up her mind. 'We'll be there,' she said firmly.

'May I ask you for a dance?'

'Of course.'

'I'm a very good dancer,' he said.

'I'm not too bad myself, you know.' She laughed. It was extraordinary how youthful she felt – almost as young as he – when she was around him. And how invulnerable. . .

'There's one more thing I want to tell you.' He was speaking very rapidly now.

'What is it?'

'I know I told you I'm nineteen and a half but I'm not far off twenty, you know.'

'Ancient!'

He smiled joyfully at her acceptance; he presented such a mixture of maturity and boyishness that to the ferment of Elizabeth's other emotions about him was now added a fine crust of maternal feeling. She saw him to the gate and, lest she betray herself, turned away as soon as he got on his bike.

As soon as she did, she saw Mossie Breac Sheehan coming down the hill from the direction of Ardgroom. That man seemed to be everywhere, she thought with annoyance. Then, remembering Daniel's warning and the undertones she had thought she detected in his talk in the railway carriage, she was briefly alarmed. What had he seen?

But tossing her head, she dismissed her fears as being the result of hypersensitivity, and reassured herself once again there had been nothing to see. 'Hello, Mossie!' she called out gaily.

This time, she did watch until he returned her wave.

But if he had seen anything of her encounter with Daniel Carrig, as far as she could discern it was not evident in his response. 'Lovely day,' she called then immediately walked away from the gate in case he thought she was encouraging him to stop for a chat.

Worried that Neeley might detect her unusual happiness, she was reluctant to go into the house and instead went into the byre where a sick suckling calf had been confined. The animal was shivering in a corner. She took a few wisps of straw and, channelling some of her own energy, was rubbing it briskly when she became aware of a shadow behind her. Neeley, hands hanging by his side, was watching her silently. 'I don't want that fella coming around here,' he said gruffly.

'Why not?' Elizabeth was taken aback. Surely she had given Neeley no cause to be suspicious?' 'He just came to play football with the child,' she said carefully.

'It's not the child I'm worried about.'

'Then what?' Elizabeth, standing stock still, became aware of the warmth of the straw in her hands.

'I just don't want pups like him sniffing around here.' He turned and left the byre.

Elizabeth flung the straw on the ground and ran after him. 'Neeley,' she called after him, panic rising, 'is it Mary you're worried about? Because if it is—'

'Maybe it is and maybe it isn't.' He walked away from her, round the side of the house.

A week passed, the morning of the following Friday dawned and still Elizabeth had not broached the subject of the dance in Castleclough.

Hoping to win him over, the night before she had again initiated lovemaking. But the result had been the same as always and when he rolled off her, she had been so disgusted with herself – she had acted like a prostitute – that she had not been able to continue with the pretence of closeness.

And Neeley was asleep before she could think up some uncompromising way of mentioning it.

'Mick and Tilly Harrington were asking me if we're going to the dance tonight,' she said as she gave Neeley his breakfast next morning. They were alone in the kitchen as the children were not up yet.

'I'm going to no dance. You know I don't dance, Lizzie.'

But Elizabeth thought she detected a chink in his armour. 'Please, Neeley. It won't cost anything and you know I don't ask for much.'

'What about Glengarriff?'

Elizabeth moved swiftly to head off any confrontation. She came up behind him and put her arms around his neck. 'That's all behind us, Neeley.' She kissed his ear, hating herself for her duplicity. 'Aren't we happy now?'

'I'll think about it,' said Neeley. Then, as she kissed him again, 'But if we do go we're coming home early.'

'Sure. Of course we will.' Elizabeth knew she'd won. She would worry about the logistics of the dance when they were actually there.

Apart from station Masses and their jolly aftermath in neighbours' houses, she and Neeley had been to only two or three public functions since their marriage and, as the day wore on, Elizabeth was afraid to show too much enthusiasm in case he changed his mind. But that afternoon she carefully ironed her best dress – of pale blue voile, a gift from Corinne – and washed and brushed her hair so that even in the small mirror in her bedroom she could see the way it shone. She was ready to leave about an hour before the dance was due to start.

Neeley, grumbling all the way, dragged his feet in getting ready so that she wanted to scream out loud. But, fearing to give him any excuse to back out of going, she curbed her impatience. At last he was organized and, with last-minute exhortations to Mary who was in charge of the children, the two of them set out on their bicycles. The evening was clement, warm and dry, and being only a month off midsummer, would be bright until very late. Elizabeth's spirits were so high as they called in for Tilly and Mick Harrington that she had to work very hard to avoid alerting Neeley that there was something more to this dance than met the eye.

On the way, the four of them were joined on the road by other neighbours, two more sets of Harringtons in a trap pulled by a jennet, a McCarthy couple in an ass and car, a bachelor by the name of Leahy on a saddle horse and two O'Sullivans, who were, like Elizabeth's immediate group, riding bicycles.

Mossie Breac Sheehan joined them when they were about half-way to the hall. 'That's a beautiful dress.' His patched and bulging tyres, the front one held on the wheel rim with binder twine, made a peculiar larruping racket as he fell into rhythm alongside her. 'Blue suits you,' he added.

'Thank you.' Elizabeth forced herself to smile. Mossie himself, in dark suit and snow-white shirt, looked unusually well and she was about to return the compliment but stopped herself. There was no point in encouraging conversation.

Mossie, however seemed determined to continue. 'Yes,' he said, 'it sets off your hair.'

'Nice of you to say so.' Then, before he could say any more, she slowed her pace, dropping back to cycle with Tilly.

'He's right,' Tilly said when they were moving along together. 'It is a lovely dress.'

'You can thank Mother for that.' But Elizabeth was watching Mossie scooting up to join the main bunch. What was it about that man that made her feel so uncomfortable? Despite Tilly's seeming to believe that his peculiar intensity was due to the long ago dispute about the land, she sensed something more, an underlying charge of suppressed energy she did not care to analyse. 'I wish he wouldn't watch me the way he does,' she said to Tilly now.

'Listen, girl,' replied Tilly, 'have you looked in the mirror lately? In this townland you're like a butterfly flying over a crowd of beetles. Mossie's not the only one who looks at you.'

'Yes, well . . .' Elizabeth, embarrassed, changed the subject and they spent the rest of the journey speculating about the coming dance.

By the time they came to within sight of the venue, their party numbered a dozen or more. In front of Tilly and Elizabeth, the chatter was loud and cheerful. Except for weddings and wakes, it was almost unheard of in the area that dances should be attended by so many married couples; marriage was customarily and swiftly followed by pregnancy and that always put paid to the dancing days of women on Béara. Elizabeth herself was talking so much that Tilly glanced sideways at her as they dismounted to push the bikes up a steep hill. 'What's up with you tonight, Lizzie?'

'Nothing. Why?'

'Don't give me that. This is Tilly you're talking to.'

'Nothing, really. How long is it since we've been to a dance, Tilly? It's been years. I haven't danced since the last station in Harringtons' – and that was in a kitchen, after all. This is the first real dance I've been to since I came to Béara. I'm just happy, that's all.'

'Hmm.' Tilly was not impressed.

Elizabeth thought it wiser not to prolong the conversation. 'Come on, we'll never get there at this rate!' Although they were not yet at the brow of the hill, she mounted her bicycle and pushed hard against the pedals. If she was that transparent already, she thought, she would have to be ultra-careful.

It was clear when they came within sight of the new hall that Jimmy Deeney's dance was going to be as popular as a Christmas fair. Castleclough, in reality just a crossroads strategically placed in the middle of the parish and boasting only a few houses and a shop-cum-pub, was so called because of the imposing, crenellated house of the same name, a decrepit ruin now. Built in the middle of the last century as a fishing lodge by an eccentric Englishman, it had been up for sale for over twenty years and mouldered quietly to itself on a hillside about quarter of a mile from the cross.

186

The dance was due to begin at nine and although it was half past by the time the group got there, there was no sign of a start being made to the proceedings. The door of the new hall was propped open and small groups of men and younger boys hung around outside under the huge banner which depicted a smiling Jimmy Deeney under the legend: 'VOTE DEENEY NUMBER ONE'.

On looking in, Elizabeth saw the hall itself was deserted except for a man who was screwing together a set of drums on the tiny dais at the far end and, to the left of it, two people setting up a baize-covered table. The Irish-American benefactor had also donated a mineral bar, a dance-hall luxury to date unheard of in Eyeries parish.

The pub across the road, however, was doing a roaring trade. Jimmy Deeney himself, six feet three and dressed in a white suit with green shirt, was holding court at the bar. Instead of a tie he wore a leather string held together at his throat with a glistening blue snake; beside him, inclining to stoutness, his blonde American wife looked into the middle distance as if she wished the evening was over. But Elizabeth paid the Yanks only the briefest attention because, one of a group of boys and girls, Daniel was standing at the far end of the counter.

As if in response to her presence, he turned and met her eyes. Elizabeth, afraid of betraying herself, dropped hers immediately. She accepted Mick Harrington's offer of a drink. 'I think I'll have a gin and tonic, if you don't mind, Mick.'

'Oh, begod!' said one of the other men, slapping Neeley on the back. 'That's a woman with expensive tastes you have there.'

'It's all right, Lizzie.' Tilly's husband was embarrassed for Elizabeth and turned away to order the drink.

Elizabeth did not care that any of them might damn her for her citified tastes as, resolutely, she turned her back on Daniel's end of the counter. But, exquisitely aware as she was that he was so near, every colour in the place, the women's dresses, the yellow of the whiskey in the glasses, even the dull reds and blues of the men's ties, was enhanced to such a degree that she might have been surrounded by a swarm of hummingbirds. In this state and unused to drink, her first gin and tonic went straight to her head and made her feel lightheaded and fizzy as she chatted and laughed with Tilly and the other women.

Although she had individual friends, Elizabeth generally found it difficult to integrate into a group of Béara women. No matter how hard she tried, it seemed as if she was and always would be different. It was not only the matter of her arrival on the peninsula in unusual circumstances; she had never been made to feel badly about that and Francey had been accepted as readily as any other child. Nor was it merely that she looked so different: she was taller than all of the other women and her striking blonde hair stood out from their dark heads like the mane of a palomino among a herd of bays. It was something more. The personal filters through which she viewed the world seemed to her to be different from theirs. But as she looked around them now, laughing and making jokes with one another, she remembered how Tilly had surprised her on the train. Her status as an outsider had definitely been her fault, she decided; from now on she would try harder to be a good neighbour.

They were all packed so tightly together that even raising an elbow to drink out of a glass was a feat. And it was so hot that after a few minutes, Elizabeth took off the white cardigan she had worn over her dress. Suddenly, she was aware of various men's eyes on her but did not care. 'Neeley, it's our round,' she called to her husband.

'Jays, you're in great form tonight, Lizzie.' Mick Harrington was a kind, bluff man whose red face now glowed with perspiration and bonhomie.

'And sure why not, Mick?' Elizabeth laughed. 'It's not often I get to go out in such dashing company.'

'Oho!' shouted one of the other men. 'You're made up now, Mick.'

'Careful, Neeley, you'd want to watch that fella!' another joined in.

Almost for the first time in her life, Elizabeth relished

being the centre of attention. *And why not!* she thought recklessly. *I'm young and on a night out.* Even the sight of Neeley's dark expression did not worry her.

At all times, although she kept her back to him, she was aware of Daniel Carrig McCarthy's movements. She knew when he was looking in her direction, when he had turned away; it was as if at some point between her shoulder blades, she had developed an additional sensor. And through it she also picked up the attentions of Mossie Breac Sheehan who was standing a little away from their group, a glass of whiskey in his hand. Turning once, she deliberately surprised him looking at her. 'Come on in, Mossie,' she called, challenging him. 'Join the party!' She felt she wanted Mossie where she could keep an eye on him.

'Thanks, but I'm going over now.' Mossie drained his glass and put it on the wooden counter which ran around the walls of the pub, then pushed his way towards the door.

Elizabeth fanned herself in the extra space afforded her as more and more people drifted out of the bar towards the hall. 'That's better!' she said, accepting a third drink from one of the other men in the group. Then, holding her glass aloft to keep it from spilling as a group of boys squeezed past, she saw under her raised arm that Daniel too was coming through. 'Good evening, Mrs Scollard,' he said when he reached her group, 'Mick, Tilly, John, Betty, Neeley,' acknowledging all those he knew.

To Elizabeth, his differentiation of her name had been glaring. She did not dare look at Neeley.

'How are you, Danny?' said Tilly. 'Going across now?'

'We'll see which way the land lies,' he replied.

'Ah, it's well for the young!' said Mick Harrington.

'For some of 'em, anyway,' said another man.

'Yes, isn't it?' Daniel smiled. 'Well, see you all inside!'

Throughout these exchanges, Elizabeth had kept her eyes studiedly on the floor but she could not resist looking after him.

As she did so, her eyes met Tilly's.

Chapter Eleven

By the time their group made their way into the dance, it should have been in full swing. The band, made up from local musicians, half traditional, half popular, was playing a slow set but there were very few on the floor. 'Come on, ladies and gentlemen, come on, boys and girls, let's see you out here . . .' The MC's urgings were falling largely on deaf ears as people stood around in groups, smoking precious cigarettes and chatting. Elizabeth's group divided immediately as was the custom; the women going to one side of the hall, the men to the other.

The structure was so new it still smelled of paint, but lit with Tilly lamps and decorated with paper chains strung from the struts of its corrugated roof, the atmosphere in the rectangular space, ringing cheerfully with the music and the hurricane of Cork voices, was festive and gay.

'Ladies and gentlemen! This is a *dance* not a fair day – for God's sake, people! I see the O'Sullivans from Lahersheen have arrived, now maybe we'll have a bit of action.' The MC and vocalist was small, fat and balding; from Derryconnla, he knew everyone in the parish. 'Come on, Raymond, Martha,' he pleaded, 'don't let Mr Deeney down, after all his generosity. Give a bit of example here! And because I know all you ladies are just dying to get up, I'm going to make this one a Ladies' Choice!'

As the MC began to sing, in a light tenor voice, his version of 'Red Sails in the Sunset' Elizabeth's senses sought Daniel. He was at the far end of the hall, his curly head the centre of a little group which lounged in front of the mineral bar placed to one side of the dais.

'Would you mind if I asked Mick to dance?' she asked Tilly.

'Mind? Off with ye! Mind your toes.' Tilly smiled indulgently. The exhortation was a joke because, having danced with him before in various kitchens in the parish, she knew Mick Harrington was nimble on his feet.

Before braving the expanse of empty floor between herself and the men's side of the hall, Elizabeth, instinctively needing a shield, or breastplate, threw her cardigan around her shoulders, buttoning one button under her throat so it should not slip off. Then, feeling all eyes on her, she walked across to the good-natured Mick Harrington who accepted her invitation. The rhythms of 'Red Sails in the Sunset' were not taxing and Elizabeth surrendered easily to his gentle piloting of her round the floor. She and Mick, comfortable with one another, did not talk through the set but, because they were joined by only four other couples Elizabeth, to keep at bay her feelings of vulnerability and of being on show, concentrated very hard on what she was doing. As they danced past Daniel's group, she averted her head but was conscious of the voile dress moving languidly against her legs; possessing only one pair of nylons, she felt very glad she had saved them for this.

When the set was over, Mick dropped her hand. 'It's a pity we don't get to dance more often, Lizzie, you're very light.'

'So's Tilly.'

'Yes.' Mick smiled fondly. 'We don't get out as much as we used – even the crossroads dancing is gone now. It's this bloodly endless war.'

'Blame Chamberlain!' Tilly's husband laughed and led her back towards the women's group before rejoining Neeley and the other men at the far side.

'All right, ladies and gentlemen, yiz are a disgrace!' The MC, working himself up to a lather, shouted it over the last part of Mick Harrington's sentence. 'We're going to have the Walls of Limerick and if that doesn't stir ye, nothing will.'

'Great!' Elizabeth seized Tilly's hand and the hand of the woman on her left.

The band struck up and played an introductory eight

191

bars over and over again until a sufficient number of dancers was lined up facing one another, women on one side, men on the other. 'That's better,' the MC roared, 'now, off we go!'

Elizabeth saw that even Neeley was in the men's line-up on the other side but as the dance began and the lines swept towards one another and out again, she felt almost sorry for him; dancing skills seemed to be inherent in most of the people of Béara and although Neeley was clearly doing his best, he was hopelessly outclassed; he had no sense of rhythm or timing and was completely out of step with the men on either side of him.

At one extremity of the line, Daniel Carrig, she saw out of the corner of her eye, was as erect and graceful as a swan.

When the time came to swing off in pairs, Elizabeth found herself being swung by Mossie Breac; he danced as well as anyone else but he gripped a little too tightly for her liking and she was glad to break away from him for the next set of communal steps.

When the Walls was over, she stayed beside Neeley in the middle of the floor and took his hand. 'The next one's the Stack of Barley, Neeley.'

But Neeley resisted. 'I'm going across for another drink,' he muttered, wresting his hand away.

'Ah, Neeley, come on . . . This is an easy one.' Elizabeth was dismayed. The last thing she wanted was Neeley under the weather.

'Look, I'm here, amn't I? What more do you want? Now, don't make a scene.'

Elizabeth saw they were isolated in the middle of the floor and that some of the others were watching. She gave in. 'All right, whatever you say.'

Turning away from Neeley she was on her way back to the women when the band struck up and she found Mossie Breac in front of her. 'Lizzie?' He held out an arm to her and she had no option but to take it.

As they paraded around the perimeter of the hall, she found herself two couples behind Daniel and a young redheaded girl from Ballycrovane. The two of them laughed uninhibitedly at one another and Elizabeth felt a stab of jealousy so intense it took her completely by surprise.

What else had she expected? she asked herself savagely as Mossie whirled her round in the next phase of the dance; she was an older married woman while this boy was young and carefree. Naturally he would have relationships with people his own age. Nevertheless, the sight of them being so openly happy together hurt so badly that her gaiety of only a few minutes before evaporated like steam. Perhaps she had misinterpreted the entire situation. She had made a fool of herself. How could there be anything between her and this boy, hardly more than a child? She was almost in despair by the time she and Mossie returned to the more sedate stage of the Stack of Barley but made a determined effort to stop looking at Daniel's back and to pay attention to her own partner. 'Enjoying it?' she asked brightly.

'Very much. You're marvellous,' Mossie danced easily at her side.

'Thank you.' Elizabeth, who wished profoundly that the man would stop the compliments, replied as curtly as she could without being rude. As the two of them spun to dance the backwards step, she saw that Neeley was back, talking to several other men clustered around the door. That at least was a good sign, she thought; in the short time which had elapsed, he could have had only one drink. Gritting her teeth, she threw herself fully into the simple routine, thereby hoping she was giving Mossie Breac – and her husband – the impression that she was just a normal housewife having a rare night out with the neighbours.

She got through the rest of the dance without further conversation. 'That was great,' she said when the band flourished to a halt.

'Maybe you'll dance with me again?'

She could not read Mossie's expression but there was something in it which made her feel so uncomfortable that she felt the telltale heat begin under the collar of her dress. 'Surely, Mossie,' she said, then found her own eyes betraying her in their automatic search.

'He's over there,' Mossie said softly, jerking his head imperceptibly.

'Who?'

Mossie smiled faintly and walked away from her towards the men's side of the hall.

Elizabeth, her face truly red now, watched his wide back recede through the crowd as the band struck up a foxtrot. She felt her arm being taken and, turning, found herself being asked up by Willie Bád Harrington, a pleasant, open-faced man in his early forties.

Over the next hour or so, to her relief, Mossie left her alone. She got no rest, however, as she was asked to dance set after set. Throughout, however, through the confusion of bobbing heads and pushing bodies, she remained acutely aware of Daniel Carrig's presence.

By half past eleven, the hall was so packed that the lines of sex demarcation were becoming confused. After one punishing quickstep, feeling hot and thirsty, Elizabeth escaped to the spot their group had made their own only to find Neeley was missing again. 'I'd love a mineral,' she announced to the company in general. 'Where's Neeley?'

'I'll get you a drink.' Before she had a chance to demur, Mossie Breac Sheehan was on his way to the mineral bar and she was left with no choice but to follow him as he shouldered his way through the crush around the bar and managed to get served ahead of his turn.

'Thank you.' She accepted the mineral as gracefully as she could. Then luck favoured her because the music started again and saved her the necessity of talking to him.

She was taking the first mouthful of her drink when she felt Daniel's light touch on her shoulder. 'Mrs Scollard? May I have this dance, please?'

'Will you mind this for me, Mossie? I'll be back for it.' Hurriedly she put the bottle into the other man's hand and walked on to the floor as the band got into its stride with a version of 'Moonlight Serenade', sounding slightly odd because the saxophone line was taken by the pair of button accordions.

Elizabeth would not have noticed or cared if the tune

194

had been played on African drums. All thoughts of Mossie, of Neeley, of everyone else in the hall, slipped away as she moved into Daniel's arms. His light hand on her waist felt as though it was part of her, his other hand held hers as though it were constructed with the delicacy of a spider web as he set a course for them around the perimeter of the crowd, a tactic which meant that even though the floor was so crowded, they could actually dance.

Perfectly balanced, they maintained the width of an oar between them and looked over one another's shoulders, careful not to let their eyes meet. But as they moved effortlessly round the floor, Elizabeth was aware of a current that crackled through their hands and completed a circuit through their bodies.

Sensitized as they were, however, to dance like this with Daniel felt in many ways as innocent to Elizabeth as holding someone else's newborn baby. The walls, the paper chains, the Tilly lamps, the smell of feet and of sweat vanished for her as they glided through the music as though a bubble of air had been constructed around them. So strong was the impression of floating that when another couple bumped into them the slight jolt was as shocking to Elizabeth as if someone had hit her with an axe. 'Sorry,' she said, not turning to see who it was. She closed her eyes to recapture the bubble, to preserve every instant of this experience, and immediately could feel Daniel's essence as if it were tangible. It blazed around her as hot and bright as a bonfire.

The ending of the music was like a small death but what survived in Elizabeth was the profound yet lucid knowledge that however much she might have been prevaricating with herself about love or finer feelings, what existed between herself and Daniel Carrig was obsessive and recip-rocal sexual passion; what was more, she now knew she could not resist it. Perversely, the recognition seemed to calm her.

'Will you dance with me again, Elizabeth?' His voice was low and urgent.

'Yes.'

She walked away towards her group from Lahersheen and Derryconnla. As the night had worn on, the dancers had become less inhibited and the floor was not emptying after each dance as men and women remained on it, chatting and laughing together.

As Elizabeth reached her group, Tilly pulled her aside. Turning her head so no one else could hear or lip-read what she said she hissed, 'Lizzie, please be careful —' then, 'Ahh! Here's the man . . .' With a wide smile and a complete change of demeanour, she looked over Elizabeth's shoulder. 'Where'd you run off to, Cornelius Scollard? We were all looking out for you! And here's Mossie with your lemonade, Lizzie.' She seized Elizabeth's arm and rotated her to face Mossie Breac.

'You forgot your mineral,' Mossie said levelly.

Elizabeth merely smiled. She was impervious to Mossie Breac Sheehan. Everything was so simple – and yet she had to protect herself and Daniel from harm. 'Thank you, Mossie,' she said with a smile as guileless as she could make it, 'sorry you had to keep it so long.'

'Excuse me, Neeley, Mossie, gentlemen . . .' Tilly again grabbed Elizabeth's arm, 'Lizzie and I were just going off to the ladies, weren't we, Lizzie?'

Elizabeth allowed herself to be propelled out of the hall and across the road towards the public house. Tilly locked them into the tiny enclosure and caught hold of her shoulder. 'What are you thinking of?' Her face only inches away, she gave her friend a little shake. 'Are you mad or what?'

'We only danced, Tilly.' Elizabeth kept her expression bland.

'Listen, girl, there's dancing and dancing. The whole place was watching ye.'

'We did nothing wrong.'

'Darling, ye were lit up like Catherine wheels. I've never seen anything like it in all my born days. And if you had to dance with him why didn't ye at least hide in the middle of the crowd?'

The toilet cubicle was so small that under the pressure of Tilly's hands on her shoulders, Elizabeth was bent slightly backwards with the bowl cutting uncomfortably into her legs. 'Please, Tilly,' she said, 'my back is breaking.'

Tilly eased the pressure a little. 'Please, please,' she begged, 'have a little consideration. It's not . . .' she hesitated, searching for the right word, 'it's not, well, *seemly*.'

Elizabeth frowned: 'Tilly, I don't want to be rude but, please, this is really nothing to do with you. I'm quite sure everything's under control.'

Tilly took a deep breath. 'Maybe this is unfair but I've got to make you see reason. At the time weren't you just as sure about George whatever-his-name-was? Where is he now? And now you have a husband and a family—'

'I know.'

'How do you think Neeley will react? I can see that even Mossie's noticed what's going on.'

Elizabeth felt as serene as a yacht on a quiet summer's day. 'Don't worry, Tilly,' she said, 'nothing bad is going to happen. All we did is *dance*, Tilly. One dance.'

'Don't dance with him again, Lizzie, please, I'm imploring you – not tonight. Dance with him all you like some other time but not tonight.'

'I promised him I would.'

Tilly shrugged helplessly. 'You're over twenty-one, there's nothing more I can say. But I'm begging you for one last time to reconsider. What's to be gained? One dance, three minutes, Lizzie . . .'

'Dancing with someone at a dance in full public view is not a sin. Even the Canon would say that. And he's in already, by the way.' This cleric, the terror of the district, was known not only for beating the ditches with a black-thorn stick to roust courting couples, but for policing dance halls and clearing them in ninety seconds if he detected fleshly pursuits. 'If we were close dancing or anything like that,' she went on, 'you can be sure he'd have stopped us.'

Tilly sighed. 'I've done my best.' Reaching behind her, she unlocked the door to let them both out. 'God be good

197

to all of you, that's all I'll say,' she added as the two of them walked back across the road and pushed their way back into the hall.

Elizabeth, who had passed the earlier part of the dance in a sort of haze, felt sharp and alert as they re-entered the hall, the walls of which were now streaming with condensation. She surveyed the present status of the dance: in the short time she and Tilly had been absent the communal mood had become, if anything, more spirited and the Canon, who had stationed himself half-way up the hall to keep an eye on the proceedings, need not have worried about moral turpitude: the band was now playing 'The Siege of Ennis' – far too fast and energetic for any possibility of sin. The younger people, who had carved an area for themselves around the bandstand, were whirling and carrying on with one another; women pushed strands of perspiration-soaked hair off their foreheads while shiny-faced farmers, contractors and fishermen loosened ties and deposited suit jackets in dark little heaps around the walls.

Within seconds, Elizabeth had spotted Neeley, a lost look on his face, standing alone to one side. Leaving Tilly, she threaded her way to him and having to shout to make herself heard above the commotion, tugged at his sleeve. 'Will you come out for this one?'

Her heart sank when he turned to look at her: he was flushed and his eyes were slightly glazed; although he was not yet drunk, he was well on the way. But he did go with her to break into the nearest group.

After a bit, Elizabeth, seeing how much he hated this, pulled him away again. 'Come on, we'll do our own dance!' and moved them into a corner of the hall. As she slowed them down to a rhythm Neeley could manage, the look of gratitude on his face made her feel more guilty than as if she had already been caught making love with Daniel Carrig. 'I love you!' she said into Neeley's ear, the treacherous words slipping out before she could stop them.

His uncomprehending look made her feel even worse and she covered over her confusion by giving him a hug to

198

which he reacted by pulling away in embarrassment. 'Everyone's looking!'

The music ended shortly afterwards and as the band stretched themselves and dismounted from the dais to take a break, the MC announced that Jimmy Deeney himself would say a few words. Like Caesar entering Rome, the Castleclough benefactor walked up the hall through an aisle of clapping, cheering people just as Mossie Breac Sheehan materialized in front of Elizabeth. 'Do you want your mineral now? If you don't want it, maybe someone else will . . .'

'Sorry, Mossie, I forgot all about it.' She accepted the bottle and then, by dint of watching Jimmy Deeney's triumphal progress, felt justified in turning her back. And when, sipping the unpleasantly warm fizz, she again looked round after the would-be politician began his speech, Mossie had gone.

She saw Daniel Carrig, however, pushing his way towards the door.

Was he leaving?

As of that moment, the drive to dance again with Daniel was stronger in Elizabeth than almost any other; it certainly meant more to her than her marriage or her desire to conserve her good name. And perhaps, if the eagle-eyed Tilly had not been watching her, she would there and then have abandoned her group and gone after him out through the doorway.

But Tilly detained her with a hand like a vice on her upper arm. And as something the Yank said occasioned a burst of applause, she hissed into Elizabeth's ear: 'Lizzie, *think*! Have a bit of sense and you'll live to see him again. Tomorrow is another day.' She was forced to let go then as Jimmy Deeney, announcing it was time for the raffle in aid of a new roof for the chapel, jumped down from the dais and the crowd around them shifted to accommodate the swarms of ticket-sellers who spread through it.

The extra sense Elizabeth had developed continued to serve her well. She turned around just in time to see Neeley, too, make his way out of the hall again, presumably to pay another visit to the pub. She deliberately relaxed; whatever was going to happen was going to happen regardless, or in spite of, how anxious she became.

The raffle proceeded and no one in their group won any of the modest prizes – a pound, ten-shilling note and a half-crown. As the band struck up after they had been awarded, Elizabeth was asked to dance for the second time by Mossie Breac.

As she took the floor with him, trying to conceal her reluctance, she saw Neeley, back from the pub, searching for her through the crowd. Then, mindful of Tilly's repeated warnings, she was seized with inspiration.

She could use Mossie Breac Sheehan to construct a smokescreen . . .

The vocalist was pouring his heart into the Judy Garland number 'You Made Me Love You' and many couples on the floor, with a watchful eye on the Canon, were dancing as close as they dared. And now, although no observer could have accused Elizabeth exactly of flirting with Mossie, she allowed her body to become pliant in his arms and smiled widely as though she were having the time of her life.

He did not react for a moment or two. Then almost imperceptibly, his grip around her waist tightened so that after a minute or so she could distinguish, through the voile of the dress, each individual finger on his right hand. She became worried she had gone too far. 'Oh, now, Mossie,' she said uneasily, prising the hand loose.

Immediately, too immediately, he slackened his hold and looked away over her shoulder and Elizabeth knew she had made a tactical mistake.

Concentrating on the steps as though giving an exhibition, they came apart on the instant the first dance of the set finished, at a spot quite close to the gathering point for their group.

The next part of the set was delayed as the MC made some announcements and while she and Mossie waited, she held her head high to cover her embarrassment. 'Thanks very much,' she said, 'that was grand.'

'You're very welcome, I'm sure.' Mossie's eyes, swivelling to the left of her, narrowed.

Glancing around, Elizabeth found herself facing Daniel Carrig. 'Daniel!' she said, forcing herself to sound surprised.

'Will you save the next dance for me, please, Mrs Scollard?'

'Sure, why not —' she began but in two strides, Neeley was beside her.

'You'll have no more dancing tonight. We're going home.'

He made as though to seize her arm but Elizabeth evaded his grasp. 'Ah, Neeley,' she said as lightheartedly as she could, 'just one more dance after this one. It's early. Sure, nobody's stirring yet – and anyway I still have to finish out this one with Mossie —'

'I said we're going home.'

'It's all right – I'm sorry, Neeley, Mossie —' Embarrassed, Daniel began to back away.

Elizabeth froze. The situation had changed. Now it was not only that she felt impelled to dance with Daniel Carrig because of her need to, the compulsion went even deeper than that and drove long-neglected reserves of independence to the surface. She would not be dictated to in this manner by anyone. 'Hold on a minute, Daniel.' Blindly she put out a hand to restrain him. 'One more dance after this one,' she said softly to Neeley, 'and then we'll go home.'

The MC droned on, as Neeley and Elizabeth, with a scarlet Daniel held by her side, stared at one another. The others in the group, becoming aware that something unusual was going on, fell silent among themselves.

It was Tilly who intervened. 'Sure what harm, Neeley?' she cried. 'We'll all have one last dance and we'll go after this. Won't we, Mick?' With her elbow, she gave her husband a dig in the ribs.

'Sure we will.' Mick Harrington was clearly as uncomfortable as the rest.

The MC finished at last and on stage, once, twice, the drummer in the band struck the metal rim of his snare, indicating the beginning of the next dance in the set. Elizabeth and Neeley continued to hold one another's eyes. 'I say we go *now*,' he said in a low voice, deadly enough to be heard over the first few notes of the tune proper.

'Don't mind the pair of them, I'll dance with you, come on, Danny!'

Tilly grabbed Daniel and pushed him in front of her on to the floor, leaving Elizabeth and Neeley still facing one another down like a pair of cockerels. As Elizabeth felt, rather than saw the other two go, she knew this scene between herself and her husband was seminal in some way as yet undefined and that she must not shirk it. 'You shouldn't have done that, Neeley,' she said.

'Are you coming or do I have to go on my own?' Just under the ears, Neeley's jaws were contracting and expanding.

'I'm not going.' Inside herself, Elizabeth heard a great hush, as if the blood in her veins had stopped moving.

He stared at her for another two or three seconds. 'Right, I'll see you later.' He turned and walked towards the door of the hall.

Irrelevantly, Elizabeth noticed a braces button on the floor near the spot where he had stood. As she stared at it, anger as black as oil welled insidiously through her whole body. She snapped upright and saw that Mossie, his eyes hooded, was still nearby. 'Shall we?' She held out her arms.

Mossie glanced after Neeley's retreating back but then took her out through the circle of watchers. 'Calm down,' he said as they moved off in the dance, 'he'll get over it.'

'Sometimes I could kill him.' Elizabeth's fury had overcome her standoffishness. 'Who does he think he is?'

'Oooh, be the hokey!' One of the men who had observed the entire sequence, and who with a partner had followed them out, thumped Mossie on the shoulder. 'Now's your chance, Mossie! In like Flynn!'

'Shut up!' Mossie, his face thunderous, whirled on the

man. Then he turned back to Elizabeth, dropping her hand. 'Maybe this is not such a good idea,' he said.

'Please, Mossie. It's important to me that I finish this dance.' Elizabeth picked up the hand again. As she led him with her, however, she was searching the floor for Daniel.

'I'm not sure I want to be part of this.'

Mossie spoke so quietly Elizabeth barely heard the words. Her public humiliation rankled so strongly that she snapped more forcefully than she intended at her partner. 'I don't know what you're talking about.'

They finished the dance in silence and then, as the band swung without a break into an old-time waltz, Elizabeth did not relinquish her hold on Mossie but, intent on reaching Daniel and Tilly, continued to lead him with steely determination through the steps. At about five feet eleven, he was only three inches taller than she was and although strong and muscular, offered little resistance to her piloting. Instead, his back stiff as a pole, he stared across her shoulder with a remote, fixed expression.

Within minutes, they had reached the other couple. 'Tilly?' Elizabeth immediately relinquished her hold on Mossie's hand. 'Would you mind changing partners?'

Tilly made one last effort. 'I would indeed,' she said, then, with a look at Mossie, 'Danny and I are having a fine old time, aren't we, Danny?'

But Elizabeth moved into Daniel's arms and seeing that the two of them were immediately oblivious of everything except the waltz music and one another, Tilly gave up. 'Come on, Mossie,' she said with a fair imitation of bravado, 'it's a long time since you and me stepped out together.'

After the first few steps in Daniel's arms, Elizabeth's anger dissolved to be replaced by a sense of urgent communion. She closed her eyes and when the music moved smoothly from the waltz to a slow foxtrot, felt no need to open them as she accommodated to Daniel's change of gait; she felt she was not dancing at all but moving upwards with him on a concerted and narrowing spiral of desire.

The illusion was violently shattered three minutes later

203

when she felt herself being wrenched backwards by the upper arm, an action which forced Daniel to drop her hand. The face on the husband who stood in front of her – and to whom other dancers were giving a wide berth – was contorted with anger. 'Neeley!' she said, genuinely shocked. 'I thought you were gone home.'

'I'm going and you're coming with me *now*!' he hissed, increasing his grip on her biceps.

Elizabeth removed her hand from Daniel's right shoulder. 'You're hurting me, Neeley,' she said softly.

'I said, come *on*!' With that he pulled her so hard she stumbled and would have fallen if Daniel had not moved forward to catch her under one elbow.

The gesture was too much for Neeley. With his free hand, he swung at Daniel and although the latter side-stepped the punch, Neeley recovered sufficiently fast to connect with a second, backhanded blow which caught the boy harmlessly in the middle of the chest.

The men in the immediate vicinity of the situation moved quickly to break up the fight but this proved unnecessary because Daniel, after one reactive moment when he clenched his fists and it appeared as though he would hit back, stepped out of Neeley's range, just far enough that Neeley, who was hampered by his continuing grasp of his wife, could not follow. But Daniel remained within a few feet, poised with hands a little raised from his sides as though ready to jump in at any moment.

The music continued without a hiccup as Elizabeth, her face scarlet, twisted this way and that in a fruitless effort to dislodge Neeley's fingers. The incident had blown up so fast that the circle of watchers seemed uncertain as to how to intervene in this silent struggle between husband and wife.

Out of the corner of her eye Elizabeth caught a flash of movement as Daniel stepped in again: her panic that the situation would escalate completely out of control lent her strength. '*Leave me go!*' she shouted, startling Neeley to such a degree that he released her. Panting, ignoring the shocked faces around her, she stood close to him. 'I'll be going home with you, Neeley,' she said, 'we'll talk when we get there.'

Then, to Daniel: 'I'm very sorry for what's happened.'

She did not wait for any more.

She was home and in bed half an hour before she heard Neeley come in. She had not quenched the Tilly lamp on the dressing-table and lay fully awake and alert in its flaring light.

She knew that whatever would occur in the next few minutes would be crucial and that the course of the rest of her life depended on it. It was not only the situation with Daniel Carrig McCarthy which was at stake but something much more complex. She was required now to make a choice between life for her own spirit and its slow death.

By the way Neeley was moving around in the kitchen, she realized he had had more drink. Contrary to her usual reaction, the knowledge calmed her, she swung her legs over the side of the bed and as he came through the door of the bedroom, was sitting facing him.

Just inside the door, he bent to fumble with his shoelaces, which gave her the opportunity to gauge the state he was in. She could see his anger had abated but although not so drunk as to be immediately belligerent, he had imbibed enough to be unpredictable. She would have to be careful. 'Before you get undressed or say anything, Neeley,' she said, 'I want to talk to you. Why don't you come and sit here beside me?' She patted the bed.

Straightening, he pursed his lips but came and did as she bid, sinking so heavily on to the springs that she bounced a little. 'Neeley,' she began, 'if that ever happens again, if you humiliate me like that again, I'll leave you.'

'If what ever happens again?' He said it truculently but she could see his heart was not in it. He was obviously ashamed.

'You know what I mean,' she said quietly. 'All I was doing was going out to dance with a neighbour at a public dance and under the eyes of the Canon. There was nothing on God's earth wrong with that, Neeley.'

205

'You were making a show of yourself – and me.'

Elizabeth was temporarily shaken by his echoing of Tilly's words and then seized her opportunity. Inferring he was referring to Mossie Breac, she kept her voice level. 'No, I wasn't,' she said. 'I was only dancing with a good neighbour. Like everyone else in the place.'

'I won't have my wife making a show of herself,' he insisted doggedly. 'It was bad enough that I had to put up with every dog and divil talking about your carry-on in Glengarriff—'

A simple kiss in Glengarriff with someone who no longer meant anything to her was so far removed from Elizabeth's concerns that now she felt justified in being outraged. 'Will you once and for all stop talking about Glengarriff?' she cried. 'I don't know what you heard but whatever you heard was undoubtedly exaggerated and it meant – means nothing.'

'Did you or did you not see that actor fella?'

'Yes, I did.'

'Alone?'

Elizabeth took a deep breath. 'For a few minutes. But out in the public street and in full view of the whole town. You must remember, Neeley, he's Francey's father. I couldn't just ignore him.'

'Did you – did you have sex with him?'

'What?' Elizabeth laughed in disbelief and for a few moments felt almost sorry for him. Then she remembered her public disgrace at his hands. 'I told you I was in full public view the whole time.'

'That's what worries me about you, you don't care what anyone might think, you have no sense of – of—' Neeley pulled at his already loose tie as words deserted him.

'Of what, Neeley?' Elizabeth was getting dangerously close to the limit of what she could tolerate.

He failed to hear the danger. 'Of – of—' he waved his hands helplessly, 'of decency. You're a married woman, Lizzie.'

For the second time, Elizabeth was shaken by his uncanny repetition of Tilly's language then realized it was

206

what everyone would say and it crystallized the entire situation for her.

Married meant owned.

'No one owns me,' she blurted.

'What?'

'You heard me. No one owns me.'

'I never said anyone owns you. All I said was you're a married woman.'

What she was talking about was clearly so alien to him that she felt she had to spell it out to him. 'I am a woman, Neeley,' she said passionately, 'a person. I am not a cow or a sheep or a jennet. I may be married to you but you don't own me in the way you own your livestock.'

'Who said —'

'I follow the rules of marriage. I perform all the drudgery marriage asks of me. I am – have been – faithful to you, Neeley. But I will *not* be told how to behave in public or who to dance with at a legitimate public dance.' She was now so worked up she could no longer stay sitting on the bed but jumped up and started to pace around the limited space of the bedroom. 'I will *not* be told when I can or cannot go home from a public occasion. I will *not* be treated in public like you treated me tonight. Show? *Show?* Who made a show of himself tonight? It certainly wasn't me.'

He stood up too. 'And what's going on between you and that young pup McCarthy? Don't think I don't know that fella's sniffing around here. You thought I didn't see the pair of ye. Dancing, my arse! You were throwing yourself at him like a slut.'

Quivering, Elizabeth came to face him. 'I told you once before you may not use that word to me.' She slapped him across the face as hard as she could.

He reacted slowly and with surprise, putting his hand to his cheek. Then, with a roar, he seized her by the shoulders and began to shake her as though he were a terrier with a rat in its mouth.

Elizabeth's teeth felt as though they were loose in her head and she screamed with pain and fright. Her long hair, which was loose, whipped out and around her head and into his eyes, impeding his vision. Roaring now like a goaded bull, he let go of her shoulders and seized it, swinging her around until she thought her scalp would come off her skull. It seemed he was trying to force her to her knees. She would not give way, however, and despite the pain and being bent double, kept her feet.

Then she saw him reach for her dressmaking scissors on the dressing-table and thought he was going to stab her: 'No, Neeley,' she screamed, 'please, no, don't, please— No! No!'

'I'll fucking teach you to throw yourself around—' Still holding a thick handful of her hair in one hand, he hacked at it with the scissors. Her screams reached a crescendo as she felt it give way. Hanks of it fell on the floor around her feet.

With a crash, the door of the bedroom opened and Francey, followed closely by Margaret and Goretti, tumbled into the room.

Francey took in the situation in a second and flung himself at Neeley's back, fastening himself on like a limpet to the back of Neeley's shirt collar.

Maddened, Neeley flung Elizabeth away. She fell backwards against the iron rail at the end of the bed so violently that the air left her lungs as if expelled by an explosion. She could not scream any more and collapsed on to the bed as though she were a rag doll.

Still twisting and bucking like a bull in a pen, Neeley was trying to swat Francey off his back but he could get no purchase. The buttons on his shirt collar popped under the strain of the boy's weight but Francey's grip encompassed the tie as well and although he slid down Neeley's back a little, he clung on, kicking as hard as he could with both feet.

The noise was huge. As well as Francey's yelling and Elizabeth's fractured gasping for breath, all the time Neeley roared and roared, great, inarticulate roars which filled the whole house. The girls, all of whom were now awake and out of bed and who had retreated into the darkest corners of the kitchen, were weeping hysterically; the baby, too, had joined in, screaming from her cradle. The only person in the house who was not making noise was Mary, the eldest, who stood in the doorway to the bedroom, holding on to the frame as though to let go of it would pull the walls and roof in on top of them all.

Then Neeley, still flailing in an effort to dislodge Francey but not succeeding, turned and deliberately cannoned backwards into the wall.

The impact was so severe that even through the general mayhem, the crack of Francey's head against the stone sounded like a pistol shot.

He went limp and fell to the ground in an unconscious heap.

Neeley, free at last, turned round to look. Then, horrified at what he had done, he took a faltering step towards Francey as though to lift him up. But Mary was too quick for him. Scooping her step-brother into her arms, 'We'll have to get the doctor,' she tried to say as she carried him to the bed and laid him beside Elizabeth, but she was so frightened that all that came out was a gasp.

Elizabeth, still coughing in an effort to regain regular breathing, forgot her own pain and the lengths of hair which had drifted throughout the room like twists of golden wire. As a child, she had been in the Girl Guides and had learned the rudiments of first aid; she checked for a pulse in Francey's neck, it was slow but steady. The pupil of one of his eyes, however, was large and unmoving, blood oozed from under the hair just above his temple and more trickled like a tiny rivulet from a corner of his slack mouth. 'Run over to Harringtons', Mary,' she shouted, 'tell them we need their horse yoked up. I'll come after you with Francey.'

'Let me —' Neeley, whitefaced, stepped forward as Mary ran from the room but before he could touch him, Elizabeth snatched Francey away.

Springing off the bed with the boy clutched to her chest she confronted Neeley. 'Don't you lay a finger on him,' she breathed. 'Haven't you done enough?'

Although all the other girls, overcome with fright and by the speed of events, had stopped crying by now, the baby was still screaming in the kitchen. 'Kathleen, see to Abbie!' Elizabeth commanded as she wrapped Francey in a blanket and, pausing only to insert her feet into a pair of shoes and to throw a shawl over her nightdress, picked up his inanimate body and rushed through the kitchen with him and out into the night.

As she ran through the upper haggard, she could see Mary's white form flying ahead of her. And as she came within sight of the Harringtons' house, to her relief she saw their windows were lighted; it had not until now occurred to her that Tilly and Mick might not yet be home from the dance.

Chapter Twelve

'Oh, my God, Lizzie!' Tilly fell back in the doorway, her hand to her mouth. Fleetingly, Elizabeth realized how she must look, in nightdress and shawl, with some portions of her hair hacked off, some still streeling round her face. 'No time, Tilly,' she gasped. 'Is the horse yoked?'

Tilly nodded. 'Here, you're exhausted, let me carry him.' She went to take the inert Francey out of Elizabeth's arms but Elizabeth would not relinquish him. 'Tilly, I'll never ask you anything again,' she said as with Tilly beside her she set out for the stable, 'but would you and Mick go over to the house? God knows what Neeley'll do, I'm afraid for the rest of the children.'

'Mick's going to drive you in to the doctor—' Tilly had to run to keep up with Elizabeth as they went through the farmyard gate and into the yard where Elizabeth could see Mick tightening the horse's harness. Mary was holding one of the shafts of the light cart.

'I'll be all right.' Elizabeth stumbled on a loose flagstone and Francey's head lolled free from her shoulder. She caught it and righted herself. 'Please, Tilly, I'm afraid of what's going to happen over there. Mary can come with me.'

Hearing the instruction, Mary climbed into the cart and Elizabeth heaved Francey up to her.

'Thanks, Mick.' Elizabeth accepted Mick Harrington's help in getting into the cart herself but fear had lent her such energy and determination that she did not really need any aid.

'At least let me get you a couple of coats. Mary'll catch her death and so will Francey.' Tilly ran back towards the house as Elizabeth gathered up the reins and clicked furiously at the horse.

211

Tilly caught up with the horse and cart just as Elizabeth was turning it out of the farmyard gate and into the roadway. She flung a pile of coats and rugs over the tailboard. 'Don't worry, we'll look after things here. God look after you. We'll say a prayer.'

Elizabeth did not hear the last words as she flicked the whip at the horse's rump.

She was operating now on instinct and not on fear; her only thought was to get help for Francey. She had not had many opportunities to drive horses but had driven this one a few times when out with Tilly. Luckily, the balmy evening had turned into a gentle, bright night and although the road was too rutted and winding to go any faster than a trot, she concentrated on keeping the horse on as fast a course as she dared. The doctor was ten miles away in Castletownberehaven but, if she was lucky, the Canon may not have left Castleclough. The Canon had a car.

'Is he all right? Check to see if he's breathing.' She glanced behind her to where Mary was sitting on the floor of the cart, her back braced against one of the wooden seats, Francey held tightly in her arms. Mary had wrapped the two of them in one of Tilly's rugs. She bent her head to Francey's mouth. 'Yes, he's breathing all right.'

'Come on, horse!' Elizabeth clucked at the animal and responding to the determination in her voice, he pricked his ears and lengthened his stride.

Twice they passed small groups of people coming from the Castleclough dance but Elizabeth did not even notice who they were or how they reacted to her headlong passage. As for what they thought of her bizarre appearance, she did not care.

To her intense relief, the Canon's Riley was still parked outside the new hall; she could see the shadowy figure of the Canon himself, distinguishable because of his soutane and burly stature, standing outside the new structure and deep in conversation with Jimmy Deeney and his wife.

All three looked in her direction as the horse careered towards them. She registered their looks of shock as she pulled the animal to a halt but again did not care. Shouting

212

at Mary to stay where she was for the moment, she jumped down into the roadway and in a few strides was beside the Canon. 'I'm sorry to bother you, Canon,' she said, the words tumbling out so fast she willed herself to slow down, 'but there's been a bit of an accident at home and we need to get my son to the doctor in Castletown.' Not waiting for his reply, she ran back to the cart and climbed up to take Francey from Mary's arms.

Both the cleric and Jimmy Deeney were at the side of the cart by the time she handed the boy down. Deeney took him while the Canon ran to the car and cranked the starting handle. Elizabeth did not wait to ask whether Mary could come or not but pushed the girl into the back seat of the car ahead of her. By the time they were in, the engine had roared into life; saying that he would look after the horse, Jimmy Deeney handed Francey in and Elizabeth cradled him on her lap.

Although ever after, she cringed at the memory of how she must have looked to passers-by and at how she had ordered the fearsome Canon around, try as she might during the rest of her life, Elizabeth could not recall a single detail of the final phase of that mad dash to Castletown-berehaven. To give the Canon his due, Mary told her afterwards, he drove the Riley like a man possessed, hauling the heavy machine around the tortuous corners, honking the horn at shadows which flitted in and out of the weak beams from the headlamps.

But in the back seat, Elizabeth's world had shrunk to a fierce, concentrated point as she held Francey tight to her chest and willed the force of her own life into him.

His eyes flickered open at one point, but although she spoke to him, calling his name, he did not respond and lapsed again into unconsciousness.

The doctor, who answered the door in his pyjamas and dressing-gown, took charge as soon as they arrived at his house. He carried Francey into his surgery and examined him. 'That's a bad cut,' he said, 'I'll put a stitch in it but he'll have to be got to a hospital for X-ray. There might well be a fracture. What happened?'

Elizabeth, conscious of the Canon's presence, told him that Francey had slipped on a greasy patch of the kitchen floor and had fallen, hitting his head on the flagstones.

'I see,' said the doctor thoughtfully, and she knew well he did not believe a word of it. She pulled her shawl tightly round her as again the doctor felt gently around Francey's head. 'Could you tell me what part of the head he hit?' he asked.

'The back of it, I think.'

'Right,' he said, 'just give me a moment.'

He vanished behind a small screen and when he came back, was carrying a small tray of instruments. Elizabeth averted her eyes as Francey's head was shaved around the cut, still oozing blood, and as the doctor stitched it. 'That'll hold it,' he said then. 'He's stable enough, Mrs Scollard, try not to worry. I'll just get dressed and get my car out. You'll need clothes. I'll get my wife.'

He called to the Canon who was sitting on a chair just outside the surgery door. 'We're going to Cork, Canon, could you bring Mrs Scollard's daughter back to Lahersheen?'

'Certainly,' the Canon nodded, 'if we're not needed here, we'll go straight away. Try not to worry, Mrs Scollard,' he added. 'Little children are tough and God will look after your son.'

'I don't know how to thank you —' Elizabeth began.

'Nonsense,' the Canon interrupted. 'Come on, Mary. And perhaps,' he added pointedly, 'Doctor's wife might be able to give you a hat too?'

It was the first time since it had happened that Elizabeth had taken serious cognizance of what had been done to her hair. But with more urgent matters on her mind she did not dwell on it. 'Thank you again, Canon,' she said, then turned to Mary. 'Whatever happens,' she said, 'you're a great girl. I'm so proud of you.'

Mary's white face crumpled but she did not cry. Elizabeth saw that although she still held Tilly's rug around herself, she was shivering. 'Go on, darling,' she said, 'and don't be afraid. Tilly and Mick will be there when you get back. Nothing more is going to happen.'

'I'm sorry, Lizzie,' Mary whispered, 'your lovely hair – Francey . . .'

Elizabeth realized that this was the first time the girl had used her name instead of calling her Mammy. She grasped her by the shoulders. 'You're a great girl,' she repeated, 'and I love you. I love you all. Now go on with the Canon. I'll see you soon.'

Mary flung her arms around Elizabeth's neck and hugged her briefly, then turned and, followed by the Canon, left the doctor's surgery.

A few minutes later, dressed in clothing much too small for her and with a headscarf covering her ruined hair, Elizabeth accompanied the doctor as he carried Francey to his car. He had constructed a makeshift head restraint from bandages and boards and carefully, as though the boy were made from eggshells, laid him full length on the back seat. Although there was not much space, Elizabeth got in beside her son, squeezing herself into a corner of the seat. She wanted to hold Francey's hand but found she could not reach it and had to content herself with holding on to his skinny ankle.

During the long, nightmare trip which followed, the doctor stopped the car several times to examine Francey. And once, when Elizabeth thought she detected his eyes opening, she called out but he had lapsed again into unconsciousness before the doctor had reached him.

Cork was a hundred miles distant and as the hours passed, Elizabeth resolutely fought the panic and fear which every so often threatened to overwhelm her. In a low, urgent voice, she talked non-stop to Francey, reaching out to him with every fibre of her will to force him to stay with her and not to die. Secure that the doctor could not hear her over the throbbing of the car engine, she talked to him about football, about her own childhood in Cork city, about her parents' hopes for her, about Ida Healy and other childhood friends, about her schooldays.

Leaning her forehead on his bare feet, she told her son that if he stayed and did not go, she would make it safe for him for the future, that Neeley Scollard would never lay a finger on any of them again. Recalling her dream of Béara transformed, she told Francey about it, describing the colours and the feelings, describing to him the glory of a planet he must stay to see and feel; she told him about his real father, about how beautiful George Gallaher was and how Francey himself had been conceived in such physical joy.

She remembered the words of the Franciscan priest, whose name now escaped her but who had talked to her when Francey was an object of terror and not happiness. 'You will have courage,' the priest had said. 'Your baby will give you courage . . .'

Elizabeth prayed, the only prayer which now meant anything at all to her. In a very strange way, as she felt her son's waxy skin under her forehead, it seemed appropriate: 'My soul doth magnify the Lord . . .'

She raised her head to look at him. In the darkness of the car his pale face with its alien white headdress seemed already to have left this world.

She made a tremendous act of faith in the sturdiness of Francey's spirit and of her own. Gazing at him, building a bridge over which she tried to lift him, she whispered the next few words of the prayer. 'Francey, Francey, don't go, you're going nowhere, please stay with me. "My spirit hath rejoiced in God my Saviour. For he hath regarded the humility of his handmaid: for behold from henceforth all generations shall call me blessed . . ."'

For the first time since the dreadful events in the house, she felt the tears begin to flow but forced her eyes to stay wide and fixed on Francey's face: 'Are you listening, lovey can you hear me? "Because he that is mighty hath done great things to me: and holy is his name. And his mercy is from generation unto generation . . ."'

At that she broke down and, no matter how hard she tried, could no longer continue.

The doctor, who apart from the occasions when he had

examined Francey had concentrated entirely on his driving and had not spoken directly to her since they had left Castletownbere, now heard her sobbing. 'Are you all right?' he called over his shoulder.

'Y-yes,' Elizabeth managed.

'Not long now, only another twenty minutes or so. How is he? Any change?'

'No, Doctor, I don't think so.'

The last part of the journey was the worst for Elizabeth. When at last they pulled into the entrance of the Mercy Hospital, she was trembling with tension and fatigue. But it was a relief to give Francey to the medical staff who, with gentle efficiency, bore him off through a set of double doors.

As Elizabeth went to follow, one of the nurses detained her. 'They'll need him for a few minutes, Mrs Scollard, then of course you can go to him.' She led Elizabeth into a small waiting room. 'You look all in, you poor thing, let me get you something hot to drink. The tea's a waste of time but we've a drop of Irel. Is that all right?'

Left on her own, Elizabeth sank on to one of the wooden benches in the room. Now that she was here and she had surrendered control of the situation, she was hit by the full import of what had happened back at the house.

When the nurse returned bearing a tray, she found her with her head in her hands, shoulders shaking. Putting down the tray, she went to sit beside her. 'Try not to be too upset, Mrs Scollard, I've seen them come in here and there wouldn't be an inch of them recognizable for the blood and the next thing you know they're sitting up in bed looking for their breakfast. Children are amazing, honestly.' She put an arm around Elizabeth's shoulders and as she did so, her wrist caught on the back of the headscarf so it slipped down. 'Jesus, Mary and Joseph!' she exclaimed. 'What did you do to your hair?'

'Nothing.' Quickly, Elizabeth pulled up the headscarf again.

The nurse, who was young, made no comment. She crossed to where she had left the Irel, filled two cups, and without asking what Elizabeth's preference was, added sugar and milk to both. 'It's my break,' she said. 'Any excuse!'

'What are they doing to him?' Elizabeth sipped the hot sweet liquid which, for all she tasted of it, might have been any beverage from dandelion wine to hot whiskey.

'X-rays, I should imagine,' answered the nurse. 'Try not to worry, I just bet you he'll be fine. He looks a grand, healthy little chap. How old is he – about eight?'

'No, he's not even six, he'll be six in a few days' time –' Elizabeth's voice wobbled again.

'God, he's big for his age, isn't he? Mrs Scollard,' the nurse looked away, 'I know it's none of my business or anything but sometimes it helps to talk about these things.'

Elizabeth hesitated; the temptation to unburden herself was very strong. But pride again held her back and in any event she was not ready to trust anyone. 'Thank you, Nurse,' she said, 'but I'm all right. All I'm worried about is Francey.'

The nurse looked back at her, then, speaking very carefully, said, 'Would you like me to tidy up your hair? I cut all the lads' hair at home.'

Elizabeth had not seen her hair but it was obviously very bad – and very noticeable. 'Thank you,' she said simply.

The nurse got up and was back within a minute or so, carrying a towel, scissors, and her own handbag. She locked the door of the waiting room from the inside. 'This is nobody's business,' she said, 'turn sideways on the bench.' She took a comb out of her handbag.

Elizabeth did as she was told and swiftly the nurse put the towel across her shoulders and went to work, snipping and combing. Within minutes she was finished. 'There, now, I don't have a mirror,' she said, 'but you can take it that you're quite respectable. You've beautiful hair,' she added quietly.

Remembering the day Daniel had paid the same tribute on Knockameala, Elizabeth grieved so strongly she feared she might disgrace herself again with tears. She had not until this moment realized how much of her own image of herself was bound up in that hair, long since childhood. The nurse noticed her distress. 'It'll grow again,' she said gently. 'Take lots of cod liver oil.'

Elizabeth tried to help her clear up the fallen strands but the nurse would have none of it. 'Take it easy, Mrs Scollard, you just finish your drink there.' She swept the hair into a neat pile with a piece of paper, and put it into a waste-paper basket.

'I'd better unlock this door,' she said then. 'Are you feeling a bit better?'

'Yes, thank you, Nurse,' Elizabeth whispered.

'Arrah, don't thank me, that's what we're here for. And if there's anything else —' She stopped, then looked at the floor. 'Would you like to see the chaplain?'

'No.' Elizabeth had not meant to be so emphatic. 'Not just at the moment,' she amended.

'All right, so. I'll go and see what's happening with your son, Francis, is it?'

'Francey.'

'Won't be long.' After a last, sympathetic smile, the girl was gone.

More for distraction than because she wanted it, Elizabeth sipped at the Irel, now cold. Beyond the door, she could hear subdued night-time sounds, the distant flushing of a sluice, the rustle of a passing uniform or habit. The hospital was run by nuns and their stamp was everywhere, in the holy antisepsis of the waiting room – crucifix, Sacred Heart and Our Lady of Lourdes on the walls, floor gleaming, benches in symmetrical rows – in the sense of quiet, the smell of polish. Finishing the drink, Elizabeth closed her eyes and willed herself to be calm. There was no point in being overwrought. When he came round, *when* he came round, she repeated fiercely to herself, Francey would need her.

She stood up as the door opened and the young nurse, accompanied by the Castletownbere doctor, came in again. Frantically, she searched the doctor's face for an indication of news and, as though she had been pushed, collapsed

219

backwards on to the bench when he told her Francey had come round in the X-ray room.

He came to sit beside her. 'It's good news, Mrs Scollard,' he said, 'but he's very disoriented. Of itself it doesn't mean much at this stage but it's a start. He'll be through in a little while and then you can go to him.'

But it was more than an hour before Elizabeth, her heart full, was sitting by Francey's bedside. The X-rays had shown a hairline fracture and his head, partly shaved, had been immobilized in a type of metal cage. He no longer seemed large and sturdy, but defenceless and very, very small. He was also drowsy, drifting in and out of consciousness, and the nurses on the ward were checking on him every ten minutes or so.

The sun was streaming through the ward windows and the breakfast bustle was under way when once again, he came to and looked up at her. 'Mammy?' It was the first time he had spoken since the incident in the house.

'I'm here, lovey.' She took his hand. 'You're going to be all right. You're in a hospital in Cork city but you're going to get better soon.'

He tried to sit up but, confined by the head cage, could not move. She saw the panic in his eyes and moved to comfort him, sitting up on the bed beside him and, as far as his encumbrance would allow, taking him in her arms. 'You've had a bang on the head, lovey, and you're not allowed to move it until it gets better.'

'I want to go home!' Francey rarely cried but the tears started in his eyes now.

His fright prompted tears in Elizabeth's own eyes. 'You can't go home just now, Francey, you have to stay here and get better.'

'I want to go home, Mammy!' His panic increased and he wound his arms around her neck so tightly he was hurting her.

'You have to be brave now, Francey,' she had difficulty in disengaging him, 'you have to be like Robin Hood. He was afraid too, I'm sure, but he didn't want his Merrie Men to see that he was afraid and that made him brave —'

The words were of no avail, he started to sob as though his heart was breaking. One of the nurses hurried to the bedside. 'Hush now, Francey,' she said, 'you'll disturb all the other sick people. They have to get better too. Would you like a drink of milk?'

But nothing, not bribes, cajoling or any of Elizabeth's attempts to calm him could distract Francey. His crying grew towards hysteria and although his head was so closely confined, he thrashed around with the rest of his body until the nurse became seriously concerned that he would further exacerbate his injury.

A nun in a white habit came to the bed. 'It would be better if you'd leave, Mrs Scollard,' she said firmly, her authoritative tone cutting through Francey's weeping. 'He'll calm down after you go, we can manage him.'

'I can't leave him!' Elizabeth, on the verge of hysteria herself, was appalled.

'Believe me, Mrs Scollard, it's for the best.' The nun attempted to take her arm.

'I won't go!' Elizabeth resisted.

When he realized what was going on, Francey reached his arms towards her as far as his cage would allow. 'Don't go, Mammy, please, please, don't go, don't leave me! I'm afraid – I'm afraid, Mammy –' His screams pierced whatever defences Elizabeth had left and she broke down completely.

'Come on, Mrs Scollard, he'll be all right in a few minutes.' The nun, her grip like pincers, took her arm. Elizabeth tried weakly to shake her off, but could not and found herself being led out of the ward. She managed to look back from the door; Francey, whose screams had reached such a pitch as to appear unearthly, was being held down on the bed by the younger nurse.

'Mammy – Mammy –' The screams followed her down the corridor as, weeping, she was piloted by the nun towards a small office and shepherded inside. Yet even after the nun had closed the door she could still hear him.

She sank into a chair and wept uncontrollably.

'Mrs Scollard, Mrs Scollard!' The nun squatted on the

floor beside her. 'It'll be all right in a few minutes. He'll be all right, I promise you. Here,' she took a handkerchief out of the pocket of her white habit, 'blow your nose like a good girl and pull yourself together.'

'I – I can't help it, Sister.' Elizabeth reacted to the note of authority as though she was fifteen years old and back in school. Obediently, she blew her nose.

The nun, patting her hand, stayed crouched beside her until she had regained some semblance of control. Then she squeezed Elizabeth's forearm. 'Listen' she said. 'What did I tell you? He's quieter already. I know it's hard on you but he'll be right as rain in no time.'

Elizabeth held her breath, but the nun seemed to be correct. Francey's screams had died away and all she could hear were the routine sounds of the hospital.

'There, you see?' The nun stood up. 'Now,' she went on, 'you've had quite a night of it, you must be exhausted. What are your plans? Have you somewhere to go?'

Elizabeth was still straining her ears for Francey's voice.

'Mrs Scollard?' the nun prompted.

'I haven't thought about it – about anything,' Elizabeth replied eventually.

'Dr Troy had to go back to Castletownbere,' said the nun, 'but he said to telephone him if you needed him to arrange anything for you. I'd say you need a good sleep first. Have you relatives in the city?'

'My parents,' said Elizabeth. Already, feeling that some-one else was taking charge, she felt a little calmer.

'Do they have a telephone?'

'Yes, they do.'

'Well, then, that's settled. We'll telephone them. What's the number?'

Elizabeth recited the number and within a minute or so was talking to her surprised and sleepy father.

After she had explained the situation – leaving out why exactly Francey was in hospital – St John told her to stay where she was and he would collect her within fifteen minutes.

After a few more words of kindness, the nun left her to

wait and bustled off about her own business. Elizabeth paced around the small office; the urge to go back to Francey was almost impossible to resist. Quietly, she opened the door and looked up and down the corridor. It was empty. Moving quickly in case the nun or anyone else should spot her, she went back towards the ward. At the door, she stopped. Perhaps the nun had been right and to see her might upset him all over again. Hesitating, she peered through a small glass panel in the door of the ward.

Francey's bed was in the middle of a row on the far side of the long room. Because of the cage structure around his head, she could not see his face. She could, however, see his hands, plucking at the bedclothes which were mounded around him like a smooth white sarcophagus.

Broken-hearted, Elizabeth walked slowly away.

When her father arrived, she was waiting for him just inside the main entrance door of the hospital. 'Elizabeth,' he hurried across to her, 'what a terrible thing. How did it happen?' He hugged her then held her off. 'And what happened to *you*, darling? You look terrible. And you cut your hair too.'

'I'm dreadfully tired, Daddy, I'll explain everything later.' Elizabeth just did not feel up to going into details. In any event she was undecided as to what, or how much, she should tell her parents. For once, she was grateful for her father's phlegmatic nature. St John asked no more questions and drove them home in silence.

Six hours later Elizabeth woke up in her attic bedroom. The sun was shafting directly on to the bed from the skylight above her head and for a few seconds she luxuriated in the warmth and contentment of having had a good sleep.

Then, she remembered where she was and why she was here, and shot out of bed.

She had been too tired to undress and, looking down at the wrinkled and too-small dress lent her by the doctor's wife, she felt guilty. She would have no opportunity now to have it cleaned. She had to visit Francey and then get back to Lahersheen as soon as possible.

223

While she had slept someone had laid out towels, toiletries and a fresh set of clothing for her, skirt, blouse, cardigan and underwear. Examining them Elizabeth saw they still bore the Cash's tags; her mother had obviously gone shopping on her behalf. The kindness caused a prickling behind her eyes but before it could take hold she ran down the attic stairs and into the bathroom where she scrubbed herself hard as though she could erase the awfulness of what had happened and of what still faced her.

Back in her room she dressed quickly. The skirt was a little loose but other than that, everything fitted perfectly. Corinne, she reflected wryly, had not lost her touch.

Her mother was in the drawing room. In a chair by the window, she was gazing out into the street and, unusually, she was sitting in a complete silence. Normally the BBC provided all-day background accompaniment to the comings and goings in the house and Elizabeth could see by the glow from its fascia that the radio was switched on. Her mother must have turned the volume down. 'Hello, Mother,' she came across the room to kiss her mother's scented cheek, 'thank you very much for the clothes. They fit perfectly – you're very good.'

'Elizabeth.' Corinne fixed her with an unusually challenging stare. 'What's going on out there?'

'Nothing I can't handle, Mother.' As soon as she had said it, Elizabeth longed to retract it. Normally so self-reliant, like her son she now badly needed a mother to make things better. But the chance to ask for help seemed to fly over her head before she could grasp it.

Corinne's blue eyes did not waver. 'At least tell me what happened to Francey. He's my grandson, after all.'

'He fell and hit his head.'

'So you apparently told your father on the telephone. How did he fall?'

'He slipped – you know . . .'

'In the middle of the night? And by the way where did you get those perfectly dreadful clothes, Beth?'

'Yes, in the middle of the night. And those dreadful

224

clothes, as you call them, were lent to me very kindly by Dr Troy's wife.'

'I see.' Corinne got up from her chair. 'I don't believe you about Francey.' She crossed to the radio, set on an occasional table in a corner of the room. Tinny and overlaid with hiss, the strains of a Strauss waltz swelled into the room as she turned a knob. 'Maybe I'm wrong,' she kept her back to Elizabeth, 'but it sounds very suspicious to me. And it's not only Francey, you look dreadful, Beth. I don't mean just that appalling haircut,' slowly she turned round to face Elizabeth, 'it's your face. You look as though you've just come single-handed through the war. Why can't you tell me the truth?'

'Because you sent me out there in the first place!' Elizabeth's hands flew to her mouth. But it was out now and so vehemently that she knew there was no taking it back.

'I see.' They stared at one another and the feeling of mutual dislike in the air between them was so strong that Elizabeth felt cold. 'Mother, I'm sorry—' she began, trying to patch it before it was irreparable but Corinne held up her hands.

'Don't bother, Beth,' she said crisply. 'I've never understood you. I probably never will.'

Prompted by fatigue or stress, Elizabeth abruptly felt the need for confrontation, long postponed. 'This has nothing to do with understanding me or not understanding me, Mother, has it?' she blurted out. 'But since we're talking about it and since we never have before, I would like you to know how I feel about the marriage you and Daddy and that priest arranged for me.'

'We did it for—'

'No, you didn't, Mother.' Elizabeth cut her off. 'You did *not* do it for the best for me. You did it for the best for you. For your bridge cronies, for Daddy's colleagues.'

Corinne toyed with the pearls around her neck. 'It wasn't like that—'

'Please, Mother, don't treat me as though I'm stupid. At least grant me that.'

'Have we – have I ever denied you anything, Beth?'

'No, I suppose not, at least not in the material sense.' She took a step forward, fists clenched by her side as the words tumbled out of her mouth like hot stones. 'But you did deny the one thing I needed more than anything else and that was your undivided attention. Mother,' she cried. 'Is it any wonder I fell into the arms of the first older man who was nice to me?'

'That's not fair!' Corinne fell back a little, her face paling.

'Maybe it's not, but is it fair that I am twenty-six years old and the mother of seven children?'

It was Corinne's turn to cry out. 'I – I –'

She was so distressed that Elizabeth's anger abated somewhat and she felt almost contrite. But something inside her had been dammed for so long and she was not about to allow her mother to escape now. 'For all his faults,' she said, making an effort to be more controlled, 'Neeley Scollard knows more in his little finger about being a parent than you do in your whole being.'

Her mother sat heavily into the chair behind her. Making an effort to recover some ground, she folded her hands in her lap and straightened her back. 'You've gone too far –'

'Have I?' cried Elizabeth passionately. '*Have I*? A little bit of courage, Mother, that's all it would have taken. One flurry of courage. I'm your only daughter, your only child. But because you couldn't make that one little act to stand out against your friends, you condemned your only child.'

'Beth – Beth –' Her mother covered her face with her hands and for the first time, Elizabeth noticed that the skin on the backs of them, meticulously tended for all of Corinne's life, had begun to show her age. With that discovery came a degree of pity. Elizabeth knew that, of all people, Corinne would not be able to bear the knowledge that she was losing her youth. 'I must go, Mother,' she said. 'I have to see Francey at the hospital and then I'm going back to Lahersheen. I don't know what's in store for me when I get there but I'm going back because I have children there and I love his children too. They all need me, now more than ever.'

Torn between pity and the need to finish what she'd started, she hesitated, then: 'You're right not to believe me when I try to lie or to cover up what happened last night.' Corinne looked up from her hands and her expression was so piteous that Elizabeth found it difficult to push her any further.

She could not stop now, however. 'I hate being nasty like this, Mother,' she said, 'but I've needed to say these things for a long time. I'll just say one more thing and then I'll leave you alone.' She took a deep breath. 'Don't think for a moment that you're not responsible for what Neeley did to your grandson – and, incidentally, to me.'

Corinne inhaled, a long shuddering breath as though she was going to say something. Elizabeth sprang towards her and took her by the shoulders. 'Don't bother, Mother,' she said, 'I've said it all now and maybe it's me who was lacking in courage. Maybe I should have had the courage to say all this sooner.' She felt no triumph at having scored so heavily. On the contrary, seeing the silent tears streaking the powder on her mother's face, she felt empty and sad. A strand of her mother's blonde hair had become loose from the French pleat in which she habitually wore it and as Elizabeth tucked it back in place – 'I'm sorry, Mother, I'm really sorry' – both knew the phrase covered more than Elizabeth's outburst.

'Oh, Beth.' Corinne made an abortive little gesture with her hands as though to put them around her daughter's neck in a hug but could not surmount a lifetime's habit of reserve and the hands fell helplessly again by her sides. 'It's all right, Mother, I understand.' Elizabeth kissed her cheek, then, all passion spent, crossed to the door. 'I want to thank you for the clothes, not only these ones, but all the clothes you send for me and the children,' she said. 'And for the money you and Daddy sent me to do up the house – I don't want you to think I'm not grateful for all of that. I suppose in your own way you do your best.'

In the centre of the sunlit room, her mother's

immaculately attired but sagging stance was like that of an old mannequin discarded by a window-dresser. 'I'm sorry,' Elizabeth repeated sadly before going out through the door, 'but money was never what I needed.'

As Elizabeth's father drove her back to Béara that evening, she was so distressed she was physically in pain. Compounding the profound remorse about her attack on her mother and her anguish at having to leave Francey at the hospital was the fear of what faced her when she got back to the house.

Her father seemed to pick up her mood and throughout the journey did not ask any leading questions or instigate conversation of any length or importance. Elizabeth was grateful. She did wonder once or twice how much he knew, although she was fairly sure that her mother would not have confided in him, but with so much immediately to worry her she was thankful for his tactful silence.

It was well dark by the time the car pulled up outside the farmyard gate. The house was in darkness, too, which served to exacerbate Elizabeth's anxiety.

When she pushed open the door she found that one of the paraffin lamps, its wick turned down almost as far as it could go, was glowing feebly on the mantelpiece. Neeley was asleep beside the cold stove. Of the baby there was no sign.

Elizabeth was across the kitchen in two strides. 'Neeley Neeley,' she shook him by the shoulder, 'where's Abigail?'

'Wha —' Blearily he looked up at her. In the dim light she saw he had not shaved.

'I said, where's Abigail?' Elizabeth repeated roughly.

'She's over in Harringtons'.' Neeley started, then spotting St John Sullivan hovering in the background, hauled himself to his feet. 'Mr Sullivan!'

'Come in, Daddy,' said Elizabeth. 'Will you pull out the settle?' She addressed a spot somewhere above Neeley's head. 'Daddy's staying the night.' Now that she saw her husband, her anger at what he had done was growing like a bush fire. 'Where are the other children?' She walked across to the door of their bedroom which was always kept ajar and, looking in, saw they were all safely asleep.

Carefully and deliberately, afraid that in her anger she might slam it, she closed the thick door fully; she did not want any of the girls to wake and hear what she was going to say. By the time she had turned to face Neeley again she was trembling with fury. 'Aren't you going to ask about Francey?' She did not care now what her father did or did not know. Reaching up, she turned up the lamp to its fullest extent.

'You're welcome, Mr Sullivan,' said Neeley to Elizabeth's father, then, muttering, 'How is he? Is he with ye in the car?'

'He might die,' said Elizabeth baldly. From behind her she heard her father's gasp but she moved quickly so her face was only inches away from Neeley's. 'That's how Francey is, Neeley, he has a fractured skull. He's strapped into a metal contraption and he can't move.'

The lamplight, wavering in a draught, played feebly across Neeley's horror-stricken eyes.

'Surely, Beth—' Her father took a step towards her.

'Daddy,' Elizabeth interrupted him, 'this is between me and Neeley.' All need to hide her domestic shame was gone and, in a way, her father's presence gave her courage to face whatever her husband might dish out.

While continuing to address St John, she kept her face set on Neeley's. 'I'm sure that by reading between the lines, Daddy, you've gathered by now that what happened to Francey last night was not an accident. It was Neeley who broke Francey's skull. And one more thing,' she said, 'Neeley also did the barber job on my hair . . .'

Like a tigress stalking a deer, she lowered her head and stared at Neeley from under her eyebrows. 'I haven't decided yet,' she said, 'whether or not to inform the Guards of what you've done. I'm going to wait and see what happens to Francey.' From neighbourhood gossip, she knew full well that the Guards rarely became involved in domestic rows but her desire to scare Neeley – and to protect the rest of the children – was too strong for factual niceties.

Yet she did not expect Neeley to react as drastically as he did. With a cry somewhere between a roar and a sob he reached blindly over his head towards the mantelpiece and seized the first thing that came to his hand which was the paraffin lamp. Raising it, he flung it across the kitchen, dashing it against the far wall. For an instant, the splintering globe sprayed hundreds of tiny rainbows through the air then the paraffin, spilling through the wick-holes of the lamp itself, ignited, running along the stone floor like a blue and yellow river.

Elizabeth's father was the first to move. Tearing off his suit jacket, he flung it on the fire and stamped on it, at the same time righting the lamp, in which the wick still burned steadily. The kitchen was filled with the smell of singeing but the manoeuvre had proved successful and the fire was out. St John picked up the lamp and placed it on a chair, underlighting all of their faces so that the three of them looked as though they were wearing wren boys' masks.

After a second or two, Neeley rushed across the kitchen, pulled open the door and ran through it, slamming it behind him.

Both Elizabeth and her father looked after him as the slam reverberated through the kitchen.

'How much of this has been going on?' St John's voice was level.

Elizabeth took a sweeping brush and began to sweep up the shards of glass. Now that the scene was over, she felt once again drained and empty – and more tired than she could have imagined. 'To be perfectly honest, Daddy, not all that much. I don't want to exaggerate. But lately he's getting quite moody.'

'Did he really injure Francey deliberately?'

Elizabeth detected the subtle adoption of her father's formal, solicitor's voice. 'Yes,' she said simply. 'But it was in the middle of a fight.'

'A fight with you?'

'Yes. Francey threw himself on his back. I suppose he was trying to defend me, and Neeley couldn't shake him off. And as far as I know – you've got to understand there was a lot going on – Neeley deliberately backed into the wall.'

'And he cut your hair?'

'Yes.'

'You have him for assault, Beth. No question about it. And if you want a witness, I was here and saw—'

'Please, Daddy,' Elizabeth leaned on the handle of the sweeping brush. 'Tomorrow, please. I can't think any more tonight.'

'If I'd known – if we'd known—' St John Sullivan punched one fist into the palm of his other hand.

'It's a bit late for that,' said Elizabeth, trying to keep the bitterness from showing. In any case it did not seem important any more. Nothing now mattered, not her worry about Francey, not the prospect of Neeley arriving home drunk once again. What was urgent was the need for immediate sleep. The sweeping brush proved a necessary prop as she felt her knees become weak.

Her father noticed her swaying. 'Let me help you into bed, Beth.' He put an arm round her and led her towards the bedroom.

'Would you do me a favour, Daddy?' she asked as, fully clothed, she climbed under the bedcovers.

'Anything, Beth, anything.'

'Will you stay in the room, please?'

Elizabeth was asleep before she heard any reply. And she did not see her father put his head in his hands to sob like a baby.

231

Chapter Thirteen

Neeley's flight from the house took him downhill towards
the crossroads about quarter of a mile from his house. He
was walking so fast that he was panting. Hearing the
murmur of voices as he came close to the cross, he stopped
dead; leaning on a gate, two of the neighbours were
chatting together. Neeley turned abruptly and retraced his
steps, past the house and uphill. Where the road curved
seawards, he left it and walked on to the commonage
skirting the lower slope of Knockameala.

Above and behind his head, stars spread thickly over a
deep sky; the moon, two nights off full, hung close to the
brow of the mountain and slightly to one side of it as
though apologizing for its less than perfect shape. Neeley
did not look up to appreciate its beauty but was enabled by
its light to move steadily up the slope. Without breaking
his stride, he picked up a pebble and added it to the cairn
as he passed.

A few minutes later he sat for a breather on a flattish
south-facing rock. The sea drummed faintly through a
small breeze which eddied around his ears, but Neeley did
not notice this or any of the other night-time noises, the
barking of a distant dog, the screech of a rabbit caught in
jaw, claw or snare. From time to time, when money was
particularly scarce and his own stock not yet ready for
killing, Neeley himself set rabbit snares but, at this moment,
he did not care anything about rabbits or in whose snares
they might be struggling. Hands on knees, his face a mask
of despair, he sat as immobile as the cairn he had just
passed. From this spot, he could not see even the roof of
his own house and the only artificial light showing in the
dark mass of the mountains was a single pinprick burning

in the schoolteacher's house at Derryconnla more than two miles away.

Gradually, despite his preoccupation, Neeley noticed minute movements and sounds which did not belong to the legitimate night-life here on the mountain. He sat taller on his rock and strained to distinguish them: there they were again, a small rustling, a metallic clink, so slight as to be inaudible to ears which belonged to anyone other than Neeley, a countryman to his fingertips.

'Who's there?' he called sharply.

There was no reply.

'Who's there?' he repeated, standing up.

After a short period of unnatural stillness, he heard a more definite, stronger sound, the sound of a human being.

Above him to the north a tall figure appeared, blackly cut into the bright sky. The moonlight reflected off the barrel of the shotgun in his hands.

A few minutes later, back in the house, St. John Sullivan started upright in the chair he had placed beside his daughter's bed and in which he had been sleeping fitfully. Was that a gunshot? He listened hard but the sound was not repeated.

St John looked across at Elizabeth's pale, sleeping face. The bedcovers had slipped off her shoulders. Moving carefully so he would not disturb her, he leaned across and, inch by inch, pulled them back over her, tucking them tenderly around the back of her shorn head.

Up on Knockameala, Mossie Breac Sheehan, who had been setting his snares, stood looking down at Neeley Scollard's bloody corpse. Half the head was blown away. The shotgun lay beside it.

Mossie had been bent double working on one of the traps when, a hundred yards away or more and just on the other side of the hill, he had heard the sound of arguing. Thinking he recognized Neeley's voice and wondering if his neighbour needed help, he had left what he was doing and had hurried towards the sound of the row.

233

He came to the ridge just in time to see and hear what had happened.

Looking away from Neeley now, Mossie watched the dark figure which was bounding like a hare down the mountain. He watched it until it reached the road and, still running headlong, vanished from his view around a bend.

Then he looked down again at the corpse.

The sight of the exposed teeth gleaming through the sticky dark ooze which until a few moments ago had been his neighbour's skull caused his gorge to rise and he vomited over a nearby pillow of furze.

Elizabeth woke only slowly. The sunlight flooding into the bedroom was so warm that she threw off the bedcovers. Then she realized she was still fully dressed and, turning her head, saw what had woken her: Mary and Kathleen were standing uncertainly in the doorway.

'Grandad Sullivan's out in the kitchen,' said Kathleen. 'Where's Daddy?'

'It's Sunday,' Mary chipped in. 'Will I tell the others to get ready for Mass? Where's Francey, how is he?'

Elizabeth pulled herself partially upright. Although she had slept well, she felt lightheaded and remembered she had not eaten anything substantial for more than twenty-four hours. 'Get me a cup of milk and a cut of bread, one of you, will you?' she asked, sinking back on to the pillow. 'Francey had to stay in hospital, he has a fractured skull but he's going to get better. Grandad Sullivan drove me home but it was too late for him to go back last night.'

'Where's Daddy?' Kathleen persisted.

'I don't know, Kitty. I've just woken up.'

'And what about Mass?' Mary asked.

For the people of Lahersheen, going to Sunday Mass in Eyeries involved a trek through the hills to Ballycrovane, a boat ride across Coulagh Bay and then a further walk. Elizabeth could not have faced it. Neither could she have faced the looks in the chapel and the sympathetic questioning afterwards, the murmurs behind her back. She had no doubt at all that news of Francey's hospitalization, embroidered with details even more lurid than the facts, had already spread throughout the parish and beyond. And although the family's absence from the chapel would be noted, at present she could not have cared less how much this would fuel even further speculation and gossip.

'God'll forgive us this once,' she said, stretching her arms and legs, 'so how about that bread and milk?'

As the two girls went back into the kitchen she turned her head towards the sunlit window. Where was Neeley? Had he come back during the night and left again? If so where had he slept? She turned back to check: Neeley's pillow was smooth.

'Good morning!' Her father's stout figure loomed in the doorway. 'Do you feel a bit rested?'

'Thanks, Daddy,' said Elizabeth. 'Was the settle all right for you?'

'I stayed in here.' St John indicated the chair, which was a wooden one he had taken from its place at the kitchen table. 'You asked me to, remember?'

Elizabeth was horrified. 'Daddy!' Again she struggled upright. She had no recollection of asking her father to sleep in a chair. 'You couldn't have got any sleep at all.'

'I'm all right.' St John came to the side of the bed and gently eased her back on to the pillow. 'Stay there for a while, the girls will look after things. They're marvellous, you know, Beth. They're a credit to you.'

'And to their mother, I suppose,' said Elizabeth. She nearly added Neeley's name to the list of tributes but refrained. 'Is Neeley outside in the kitchen?' she asked carefully.

St John dropped his eyes so his daughter could not read his expression. 'I don't think he came back, Beth,' he said, 'I would have heard him if he had.'

At that, Johanna, still in her nightclothes, trotted into the bedroom and climbed in beside her mother. Nuzzling in under Elizabeth's shoulder, she stuck her thumb in her mouth and peered shyly at her grandfather. Elizabeth stroked her warm tousled head. 'Do you want to go to Mass, Daddy?' she asked. 'We're not going today, I couldn't face it.'

He sat on the chair. 'I think I'll leave it too for today.' St John Sullivan was a Knight of Columbanus and a pillar of his local confraternity and for him to miss Sunday Mass was unheard of. Elizabeth appreciated full well the significance of the gesture. He wanted to stay around in case there was any more trouble and she was grateful in a way she would not have thought possible a mere two days ago. Blood ties really did count after all, she thought. The girls came in then with the meal and after they had given it to her sat quietly on the bed, watching while she devoured it; and although Elizabeth despised the dark wartime flour she was forced to use for baking, she was so hungry that even the bread tasted appetizing.

'It's *Sunday* and it's the middle of the *day*!' From the door, Margaret surveyed the unusual scene in the bedroom. 'Mammy! You're in bed with your *clothes* on! Oh, hello, Grandad Sullivan,' she added, seeing him only then as he was partially hidden behind the open door. She took a few steps into the room. 'What's going on?' she asked the company in general. 'Did Francey come back last night? Where's Daddy?'

'You might as well join us, Maggie.' Elizabeth patted the bed. 'Francey's going to be fine although I had to leave him in the hospital. As soon as I'm sure everything's under control here, I'll probably go back to him.'

She yawned. 'I'm too tired to think about Mass today. We're all just going to have a quiet day.' As she drained the last of her milk, she wished fervently that by saying it she could make it come true.

'Oh, good!' Margaret settled herself on the bed between her sisters and hugged her knees.

'What's happening?' Goretti, rubbing sleepy eyes, padded into the room.

'We're all going to have a quiet day. We're not going to Mass,' pronounced Margaret.

'Is it not a mortal sin?' Goretti looked worried.

236

'Not today,' said Elizabeth, 'come on over,' she held out her free arm. Competitively, Johanna nestled deeper into her mother's side as Goretti climbed aboard, pushing and shoving for position. Eventually, the bed sagging, they had all settled into and around each other like a litter of puppies.

Everyone was still as the sound of the Mass bell from the chapel in Eyeries drifted into the room; the village was more than two miles away across the bay as the crow flies and it was not often they could hear it but now it chimed sweet and clear like the chinking of a sugar spoon on the side of a china cup. 'The wind must be from the south this morning,' Elizabeth remarked.

'Who cares?' retorted Kathleen, elbowing for more space between her sisters.

'Shut up, Kitty,' snapped two of the others, accustomed to squashing Kathleen's contrariness. But as peace descended on the room again, Elizabeth felt its transience and knew that, very soon, she would have to pry herself away from this nest to face the harshness of the day. The more she thought about it, the more fearful she became of the consequences of last night's confrontation with Neeley. She had better find him as soon as possible in order to patch things up; she needed him to be calm and co-operative so she could get back to Francey in the hospital.

She was reluctant, however, to break into the quietness in the bedroom. Her father had his back to them and was standing stock still at the window, gazing out at the sunlit land. Even Margaret, normally so garrulous, seemed affected by the atmosphere as, cradled between two of the others, she listened to the sweet, remote peal of the bell. Nevertheless, Elizabeth might have guessed Margaret would be the one who would bring up the subject of her hair. As the pealing died away, Margaret, glancing round the others with a fierce look as though to head off any disagreement, spoke with forced casualness. 'Your hair suits you short, Mammy.'

Her father was right, reflected Elizabeth, these were fine girls. It could not be easy for them to have their loyalties so divided. 'Thank you, Maggie,' she said quietly. 'I don't agree with you at the moment, but we'll see. And, anyway, it'll grow again in no time — What's that?' – this in response to the sound of someone from outside knocking on the kitchen door.

'It's probably Mrs Harrington with Abbie,' said Mary, getting off the bed and going to answer the door. 'She said she'd bring her back first thing this morning before Mass.'

She returned in seconds, her face like chalk. 'Mammy, you're wanted,' she said.

'Who is it?' Elizabeth swung her legs out of the bed, wishing her clothes did not look so crumpled.

But Mary was so upset she could not answer and Elizabeth's heart turned over. *Francey. Something had happened to Francey during the night.* Pulling the cardigan round her, she raced into the kitchen.

Standing in the open doorway was a Garda sergeant and the curate from Eyeries.

Elizabeth's heart sickened: the curate from Eyeries should be saying Mass at this time. 'It's Francey, isn't it?' she cried. 'Oh, my God!' Her legs gave way and she clutched the edge of the table for support. The sergeant removed his cap and stepped in as though to be able to catch her should she fall.

'Can we come in, Lizzie?' The curate followed the sergeant across the threshold. 'It's not Francey we're here about,' he said gently, taking Elizabeth's hands and leading her over to the chair by the fire. 'But I'm afraid you're going to have to be very brave. We do have bad news for you.' He put pressure on her hands as though to force her down into the chair.

Elizabeth resisted. She looked from him to the sergeant whom she had never seen before and whose expression mirrored the curate's gravity.

'It's your husband,' the curate said. 'It's Neeley.'

Elizabeth did not comprehend. Neeley? What about Neeley?

It wasn't Francey – they were not here about Francey.

She let out a great sob of relief. 'Thanks, Father,' then,

'Aren't you supposed to be saying Mass – we heard the bell –'

'Did you understand, Lizzie?' The curate was taken aback at her reaction. 'We're here about poor Neeley . . .'

Elizabeth heard one of the girls cry out and saw her father come across the floor to stand beside her. *Poor Neeley*, the man had said – they were here about *poor Neeley*. To make it real, she shoved the knuckles of her right hand in her mouth. 'What's happened?' she whispered through her fist.

'Your husband was found up in the hills, ma'am.' The sergeant spoke for the first time. 'I'm afraid he's dead.'

'Oh, no –' The girls, crowded into the doorway of the bedroom, began to weep. Johanna ran across the floor and buried her face in her mother's skirt.

'I'm sorry, ma'am, sorry for your trouble,' murmured the sergeant.

'Sit down, Lizzie, I'll stay with you a while.'

Again the curate attempted to push her into the chair and again Elizabeth resisted. 'No thank you, Father.' This whole situation was so new and unexpected she needed to think. She could not get her brain to function in sequence. She felt like Alice in the story she had read aloud so often to her children that she knew it virtually by rote. She was growing and shrinking, growing and shrinking. And all the furniture in the kitchen had seemed, within the past few seconds, to have changed also, to have swelled monstrously until it crowded the room in an untidy jumble; the sounds, too, were outlandish and inappropriate, the wailing of the girls, the crackling of the new fire they had so recently laid.

She realized she had missed something the curate had said. 'Sorry, Father?' Even her voice sounded like a child's, like Alice's.

'Is there anything you need, Lizzie?' the curate repeated. 'Anything at all?'

Elizabeth still could not focus. 'No,' she whispered. 'Thank you, no – I don't need anything.'

'How did it happen?' St John Sullivan addressed the policeman. 'I'm Elizabeth's father, by the way,' he added.

239

'How do you do, sir,' said the sergeant. 'My name is Clancy. I'm normally stationed in Cork but I'm in Eyeries on relief, the regular sergeant's in hospital with a broken leg.' The two men shook hands.

'We're not too sure exactly what happened yet,' he continued. 'He was found about eight this morning. There was a gun beside him,' he added carefully.

'I see,' said Elizabeth's father. 'Where is he now?'

'They'll be taking him to Cork,' said the sergeant. 'There'll have to be a post-mortem of course, and an inquest.' Then, looking at Elizabeth, 'But the most immediate problem is identification. I'm sorry about this, ma'am, but someone will have to come with us into Castletownbere to identify the body . . .' Delicately, he let the sentence hang.

'I'll do that, Sergeant.' St John spoke briskly. 'My daughter will have to stay here with the children.'

Throughout this exchange, Elizabeth realized that the curate had been watching her closely. She felt claustrophobic; the conversation, the girls' sobbing, even her father's serious and unusual presence in the kitchen of the Lahersheen house seemed so unreal as to be preposterous.

Then she realized the sergeant was again addressing her. 'Sorry?' she said.

'I'll come back some other time,' the policeman repeated, 'I appreciate what a dreadful shock this must be for you, ma'am, but you do understand I'll have to ask you a few questions.'

'Of course, Sergeant,' St John answered on Elizabeth's behalf.

The curate looked from Elizabeth to her father. 'Do you think I should send out for the doctor?'

'No.' This time Elizabeth answered for herself. 'I'm all right, we're all all right.'

'Maybe a drink? You've had an awful shock —' The cleric glanced at the kitchen dresser. 'Is there any brandy in the house?'

Dumbly, Elizabeth shook her head. Neeley kept – *had*

240

kept – poteen but the last thing she wanted or needed was a drink.

'At least let me help,' the curate asked. 'Who do you need to contact? I can do it for you on the presbytery telephone.'

'Thank you, Father.' St John again took over, 'I think Beth's mother should be told. She'll want to come down, of course. Tell her to hire a hackney if necessary. I'll drive my own car into the town and will come back here.'

'Certainly, Mr . . . ?'

'Sullivan. St John Sullivan.' Elizabeth's father never went anywhere without a small notepad. He took it and a fountain pen out of his inside pocket and wrote down the telephone number of the house in Cork.

'How about Neeley's relatives in England and America?' The curate looked again at Elizabeth.

Still feeling her physical self to be mutating and reconstituting itself at unnerving speed, Elizabeth detached the clinging Johanna, crossed to the dresser and took down the yellowed list of addresses. As she did so, the stub of a raffle ticket from the night of Jimmy Deeney's dance fluttered to the floor.

Every hair on her body stood upright and unable to move or to pick up the stub, she stared at it as, like a dying moth, it flickered on the floor.

Daniel.

She became aware of the curate's solicitous presence by her side. 'Are these they?' he asked as, gently, he took the address list from her hands.

'Yes,' she whispered.

'I'll take care of this.' He patted her shoulder. 'And I'll stop in to the Harringtons on our way past to let them know you may be needing a bit of help.'

'Thank you, Father.' Elizabeth made a tremendous effort to shake off this sense of unreality, to grasp at what was really happening in the room, but she failed and the curate's concerned face remained as blank to her as the face of a full moon.

'How about Ida Healy, Beth?' Her father grasped her shoulder. 'I'm sure you'd like her to know?'

Elizabeth nodded assent and, from another pocket, St John took a small address book and added the telephone number of Ida Healy's parents to his own.

With further expressions of sympathy and concern, the priest and the sergeant turned to leave the kitchen but stood aside as Tilly Harrington, Abigail in her arms, rushed in. 'I came as soon as I heard – oh, Lizzie –' Seeing the three men, she stopped. 'Hello, Father, Sergeant – hello, Mr Sullivan. I didn't know we'd be meeting again so soon and in such circumstances.'

Somehow, Elizabeth found the strength to put one foot in front of the other and to take the baby from her friend's arms. Abigail felt solid and substantial in her arms, something to grasp. She supposed she should be experiencing a feeling of grief, but all she felt was this numbing sense of distance from everyone in the crowded room.

And an overwhelming sensation of danger. It pricked her scalp as though there were barbed wire entangled in her hair.

By late that Sunday afternoon, everyone in the district knew that Daniel Carrig McCarthy's shotgun had been the weapon found beside Neeley Scollard's corpse. They also knew that Daniel had vanished.

It fell to Tilly to break the news to Elizabeth.

By five o'clock, Elizabeth felt she was drowning in the deluge of callers and sympathizers who were passing through the kitchen. The curate had secured extra petrol for her father and he was away in the car on some errand or other; her mother was expected shortly. Remembering how they had parted, she was not looking forward to that particular visit. The world seemed now to be filled with faces and eyes, and lips murmuring incomprehensible words. All that seemed to be required of her was to sit and nod and to stay suitably quiet and passive.

Tilly and two other neighbours had taken charge of the stove, the scullery and the kitchen table so that no one who called was neglected. The girls, white-faced and solemn, helped out too. After the first semi-hysterical outburst of crying, which fed one off the other, they seemed uncertain what demeanour to adopt – all except for Kathleen, who was inconsolable and who had shut herself into her bedroom. From time to time, Mary, Tilly, and even Elizabeth had attempted to comfort her but no one could penetrate the thicket of grief which the girl, lying face down and immobile on one of the beds in the room, had constructed around herself.

As none of the women in the kitchen would allow her to lift a finger even to pour a cup of tea for a new arrival, at about a quarter past five, Elizabeth, feeling completely redundant, went again into the children's bedroom. Knowing Kathleen would not permit even a touch, she sat dumbly on the side of the bed, hoping that the girl would sense her presence at least.

Then she heard a sound behind her. Looking around, she saw Tilly standing in the doorway and knew immediately by her friend's expression that there had been some further development. 'What now?' she whispered.

'Come on out, Lizzie, I have to talk to you alone.' Tilly's voice was cracked and hoarse.

The neighbours in the kitchen hushed into silence as, obediently, Elizabeth allowed her friend to lead her through the kitchen and out into the yard. The older woman waited until they were at the gate and completely out of earshot then turned to face her. 'I've got to tell you this before you hear it from anyone else.'

Elizabeth waited quietly.

'It's Daniel Carrig,' Tilly went on without further preamble. 'The Guards are looking for him. It was his gun Neeley was shot with and now he's missing. It looks bad, Lizzie.'

Elizabeth took a few steps away from her friend and looked off towards the sea across a fuchsia hedge; the profusion of red and purple bells, the flooding larksong above her head, the sea's glitter, all seemed so incongruous in her present situation that again she felt herself detaching.

243

Tilly touched her arm uncertainly. 'Did you hear what I said, Lizzie?'

'I heard you. Do you know where he is, Tilly?'

It was Tilly's turn to move away. 'Honest to God, Lizzie, I don't.' She stared hard at Elizabeth for a few moments then took a breath. 'To tell you the truth,' she said quietly, 'even if I did know where he was, I don't know I'd tell you.'

'Look,' she came back to within inches of where Elizabeth stood, 'I know what you're feeling, darling, but for God's sake, don't make things even worse than they are.'

'I know you mean well, Tilly,' said Elizabeth, hearing as she said them that the words sounded final, like a farewell.

'Don't say that,' cried Tilly, 'please, just for once, listen to me – if you'd listened at the dance the other night –'

Elizabeth held up her hand. 'I'm truly sorry, Tilly, I truly am. But I don't want to hear any more.'

'Lizzie.' Tilly tried again, pulling at her sleeve.

From somewhere in the direction of the Knocknasheeog, Elizabeth heard the repeated call of a cuckoo and looked towards the sound. 'I'm really grateful to you for being the one to tell me.'

As she looked back to see her friend's face crumple, her detachment deserted her. 'Tilly,' she hugged the other woman, swallowing repeatedly between words to control her voice, 'you're a great friend, you've been the only true friend I've had here.'

'What are you going to do?' Tilly's body was as rigid as a coffin board.

'I don't know. Nothing for the moment.' Elizabeth's mind had at last clicked fully into place.

'I'll just say one more thing,' Elizabeth felt Tilly's shoulders rise with tension, 'the Guards know about the row at the dance.'

So much had happened within the previous twenty-four hours and Elizabeth's mind was so focused on the present that she had difficulty in discerning what Tilly was talking about. Tilly saw her incomprehension. 'The row, you remember? Between you and Neeley when Daniel asked you to dance?'

For Elizabeth, the contretemps, the cause of her present predicament, had been eclipsed in her mind by subsequent events. She stared blankly at Tilly, then nodded. 'Thanks for telling me,' she said, 'but I've one last favour to ask you. Will you look after things when I go back to Francey in Cork?'

It was late that night when she recognized the significance of the dance-hall row in connection with Neeley's death and Daniel's disappearance.

Because of the distance involved and the difficulty of wartime transport, Neeley's funeral did not take place until the following Wednesday by which time Elizabeth's detachment had deserted her. Harassed by Kathleen's continuing impermeability, frantically worried about Francey's well-being in the Cork hospital, by the morning of the funeral she felt she might disintegrate entirely.

And to add to this confusion of emotions, in the matter of Neeley's death, Elizabeth felt like a hypocrite. Although from time to time, particularly during the long sleepless nights, she had tried hard to feel some proper mourning for her departed husband, she could not summon up any emotion more profound than regret that his life had ended so messily. To stimulate grief she had even tried to force herself to picture the horror of his last moments, his terror, the knowledge that he was about to die; but each time she attempted that, her mind slid guiltily away.

For that moment had clearly involved Daniel and, despite all circumstantial evidence, Elizabeth could not bring herself to believe that Daniel Carrig McCarthy had murdered her husband in cold blood. Detecting an undercurrent of excitement in the words and expressions of the sympathizers who called unceasingly with condolences and offers of help, she knew, however, that her faith in Daniel was a minority one and that she was the talk of the county.

At least her mother was no longer around to add to her

tension. Throughout Corinne's short visit to Lahersheen, the image of her pale, reproachful face had lodged under Elizabeth's skin like a nettle.

But when, on the Tuesday morning for what seemed the thousandth time she had heard her mother's refrain, 'But is there nothing I can *do*, Beth?' her restraint had snapped.

'Yes, Mother,' she had answered, 'as a matter of fact there is. You could go back to Cork and take care of Francey. I'm very worried about him. He'll feel abandoned by now.'

The look of relief on her mother's face had been so naked – 'Are you sure that's what you want me to do?' – that Elizabeth had had to stop herself from smiling. 'Yes, Mother,' she had said soberly, 'I'd really appreciate it. But don't tell him yet about Neeley. I'll tell him that myself.' An hour later, in a flurry of scarves, bags and boxes, Corinne was getting into her husband's car. St John was to drive her as far as Castletownbere where he would organize the hackney to take her back to Cork. He had insisted on staying.

Now on the Wednesday afternoon, at the quayside at Castletownbere where the *Princess Béara* had just tied up, St John stood beside his daughter like a small solid rock. The cries of a dozen seagulls and the creaking of the wooden vessel were the only sounds as the coffin was unloaded; the day was blue and brilliant, the beating sun making a mockery of the sea of dark clothes worn by the mourners, the headscarves and long-sleeved coats and jackets of the women, the wool suits and constricting ties of the men.

Elizabeth held Abigail in her arms and to one side of her the rest of Neeley's pale daughters huddled together, their eyes fixed on their father's coffin which was being borne ashore. Ida Healy and her husband stood to Elizabeth's other side, just in front of a large group of Neeley's relatives; although, because of wartime restrictions, none of the emigrants had been able to return, the group numbered as many as sixty or seventy. They were integrated at the edges with an equally large group who were related to Neeley's first wife.

And the enormous crowd which spread behind the family and into the main street of the town was drawn from all over the peninsula; almost everyone who was able-bodied in Eyeries, Ballycrovane, Ardgroom, Kilcatherine, Lahersheen and Derryconnla had travelled but Neeley's nearer neighbours were augmented by people from Bere Island, from Rossmackowen, Adrigole, Urhan, Garnish, Allihies and from as far away as Dursey. It was not that Neeley Scollard was the most popular person on Béara, it was just that the community was so tightly cemented together that the death of one – especially death in such tragic circumstances – was a blow to all.

The Canon, purple stole around his shoulders, flicked liberal sprinklings of holy water from the aspersorium he carried as he moved forwards across the quay to receive Neeley. Elizabeth felt her father take her elbow as though to lead her forwards, too, but the squat finality of the coffin, its brass handles flashing in the sunshine, seemed to her to be obscene, a grotesque, slithering thing she did not want to be near. Involuntarily she tightened her arms on Abigail who started to whimper in protest.

'Come on, Beth, I'll be beside you.' It was Ida, whispering into her ear.

Elizabeth closed her eyes and with Ida holding one elbow, her father the other, allowed herself to be taken to her husband.

Later, as the obsequies were ending in the cemetery, to distract herself, she looked up from Neeley's open grave and towards the small ruined chapel. From this angle, she could not see the Kilcatherine Head but, clear as a photograph, she received the smoke-and-gold image of it which had been granted to her in her jewelled dream. And just as she had been in that dream, Elizabeth was once again comforted by the Head's pagan, protective presence.

The day dragged interminably on through late evening when at last the little house, which had been crammed with

247

people since Neeley's death, emptied slowly until only Elizabeth, her father, the older Scollard girls, the Harringtons and Ida were left in the stifling kitchen. 'I'm going to bed.' Elizabeth felt so exhausted she could barely drag herself out of the chair beside the stove. 'I'm all in. I hope you don't mind?' she appealed in a general way to the people in the room.

'Go ahead,' replied Ida as Tilly nodded agreement, 'we'll clear up here.'

'Mick and Mossie have checked the stock,' added Tilly. 'Everything's in order so you go and have a good sleep for yourself, Lizzie.' Since Neeley's death, Mick Harrington and other neighbouring men had been looking after the Scollards' animals and poultry. Neeley had kept only one milch cow to supply the family's domestic needs and it had always been the task of the three eldest girls to do the milking, a task which they continued to rotate.

'You go on, Tilly.' Tired though she was, Elizabeth continued to be conscious of Tilly's watchfulness. Her friend was waiting for her to do something rash with regard to Daniel and Elizabeth now found the vigilance irksome. She smiled, however, both at Tilly and at Ida. 'I don't know what I would have done without you both.' She turned towards her father to give him a hug. 'You, too, Daddy.'

'I'll be up first thing in the morning,' said Ida. Because the Scollard house was so small and crowded, she, along with Elizabeth's father, was staying with the Harringtons.

'Thanks, I'll go in, so.' Elizabeth turned to Neeley's daughters. 'You should go to bed too, girls.' Solemnly, Mary and Margaret nodded but Kathleen, who, stony-faced, was sitting in the furthest corner of the kitchen, ignored her completely. All day, Neeley's second eldest daughter, rejecting any touch of comfort offered to her, had wept without respite but she appeared at last to have cried herself to tearlessness. For that at least, Elizabeth was grateful and too tired to coax a response, left the kitchen and went into her room.

She expected to fall asleep immediately but as soon as she lay down, her brain shot into wakefulness as images of the past five days succeeded one another in dizzying rotation: the transcendental physical contact with Daniel at Jimmy Deeney's dance, the feel of the toilet bowl at the back of her legs as Tilly tried to shake her, the wild dash in the Canon's car, the metal cage around Francey's head, Neeley's sunlit coffin below the wheeling seagulls, the slow trip to the graveyard, the days and days in the crowded kitchen.

But mostly faces: Francey's unconscious, Neeley's suffused with hatred, her mother's shocked, bitter – and later, in Lahersheen, bewildered – Tilly's watchful, Ida's and her father's concerned, the sergeant's careful, the neighbours' ambiguous, all turned towards her as though she were the centrepiece of a bizarre public exhibition. Elizabeth shifted on to her side and tried to shut them all out. After a while her physical exhaustion overcame the turmoil in her brain and she drifted into sleep.

Some time later she found herself struggling into consciousness again. For a few moments, as she groped for reality, she did not know where she was. She felt she was drowning; her limbs felt weightless, as though she was floating just below the surface of the sea, but above her head, something was breaking the waves, an oar or the prow of a boat; it was making soft, regular sounds.

Making a great effort, she shook her head and came finally awake. She was in her room. And the sound was real. Someone was tapping softly at the window.

Heart pounding, Elizabeth sat up. Framed against the window-pane was a human torso.

It was Daniel.

For some reason she could never afterwards identify, she checked the luminous dial of her wristwatch and saw it was twenty past four in the morning. She jumped out of bed. As she did so, the figure vanished.

Afraid he might have run away, Elizabeth, trying not to make too much noise, ran to the window and struggled with the sash; it had always been stiff and would not yield without her having to give it such a tug that the racket might have alerted the entire household.

But through the window she saw he had shrunk into the hedge beside the cow byre and made frantic signals that he should stay where he was, that she was coming out to him. Snatching a coat from a hook on the wall, she opened the bedroom door as fast as she dared and peered into the kitchen. Except for the small red glow of the Sacred Heart lamp, the kitchen was dark. Throwing the coat over her shoulders, Elizabeth flitted towards the door, bare feet making no sound on the flags. Pausing only to check that Abigail was safely asleep in her cradle, she let herself out.

Outside, the air was sharp and still; even the drone of the sea seemed hushed as the tatters of night yielded to the new day and she could hear the breath pounding in her throat as she ran towards the hedge.

He took a step towards her as she approached and her heart constricted at how bedraggled he was. His longish hair was unkempt and although it was still dark, above the stubble on his face, she could see how deep were the shadows under his eyes. 'Daniel,' she whispered hoarsely. 'Oh, Daniel, what's happened to you? Where have you been?'

He spread his hands helplessly. 'I had to talk to you – I have to explain –'

'Not here.' Urgently, she caught his hand and pulled him towards the gap which led into the upper field. 'Come on up out of this yard.'

She stubbed her toe as she climbed through the gap but, terrified that one of the girls would waken and find her missing, did not stop. 'Come, come quickly,' she urged, still pulling at his hand.

She stopped running only when they were well away from the house and inside the roofless stone walls of a ruined cabin which in famine times had housed Neeley's great-grandfather and his family; she was panting from the run, her injured toe throbbed and her feet, already sore from her passage across the uneven land strewn with stones and pebbles, were finding it difficult to stand comfortably on the thistled ground. Disregarding all discomfort, she seized both his hands. 'Tell me,' she cried, 'tell me what happened, where you've been. I've been worried sick about you. And it's not safe here, you know that, you shouldn't have shown yourself like this.'

Daniel hesitated. 'I – I had to see you – I was afraid you'd believe them.' He sounded younger than he normally did.

'Believe them about what? That you would kill someone? That you're a murderer?'

'It was terrible—'

'Daniel, *please*.' Almost before she knew it, Elizabeth had pulled his head down to her and was kissing him, pouring into his mouth and body every ounce of passion and longing in her own. He responded instantly, locking her full length into himself.

'I'm sorry, I'm sorry, I shouldn't have done that!' Elizabeth broke away. She was finding it hard to breathe.

'I'm not—' He went to take her again into his arms but she held him off. 'This isn't the place – you know that. And we haven't much time. Please. Daniel, tell me what happened up there that night.'

He retreated from her until his back was to the wall of the ruin. 'I was up there with the gun—' His voice shook at the memory and he stopped. Elizabeth, the kiss still coursing through her veins, did not help him but waited tensely; it was as though she was poised at the edge of her own life and that what he would say next would pitch her either into it or out of it. A local saying rose in her mind: *Better the trouble that follows death than the trouble that follows shame* . . . She suppressed it, willing Daniel to continue.

As if he had heard her, he straightened his shoulders. 'I have nothing to be ashamed of, Elizabeth,' his voice was strengthening, 'what happened up there was not my fault.'

'Just tell me the truth.'

'I was up there with the gun,' he repeated, 'and I didn't know there was anyone else there. I thought I heard someone setting snares but I thought it was Mossie Breac – he goes up there quite a lot. It wasn't until I came over the hill that I saw it was Neel— your husband.'

'What was he doing?'

251

'He was just standing there. He called out, "Who's there?" twice, I think, or maybe three times, I can't remember . . . When he saw it was me, he – he sort of flew into a rage.'

'What did he do?' Elizabeth felt cold.

'He – he called me all sorts of names . . .' Again Daniel hesitated.

'Please, Daniel,' Elizabeth said again, 'I know how Neeley can be, please just tell the whole story.'

'The awful thing,' he cried passionately, 'is that he had every right—'

'He had no right!' The vigour of the denial surprised Elizabeth herself and startled Daniel so much that for a second or so he appeared nonplussed.

'Anyway,' he continued eventually, 'he was calling me all these names and he was coming towards me and he pushed me so that I fell down.' Reliving the experience, he began to pace the length of the tumbledown stone wall. 'I didn't hurt myself or anything, but he wouldn't let me get up, he was swinging at me, at my head and I was putting up my hands to defend myself. Of course I still had the gun in my hands.' He stopped pacing and turning his back on Elizabeth, leaned his forehead against the wall.

'Next thing I knew, Neeley was pulling at the gun and I was pulling it back from him and it became a sort of tug of war between us. I was still on the ground and he started kicking me, chucking the gun, trying to get it away from me and all the time kicking me with these boots he had on. And he never stopped shouting—'

As soon as Elizabeth heard his voice break, she was behind him and had wrapped her arms around his waist. 'Don't get upset, Daniel, please don't get upset, I can't bear it.'

'I can't help it.' He was sobbing now. 'I didn't mean to kill him, honest to God, it just happened.'

'How did it happen? Tell me, Daniel, you must tell me – finish the story . . .' Elizabeth pulled him round to face her. It was lightening to the east and she could see the trails of the tears on his face. 'Tell me!' Pulling him with her, she

252

sank to the rough, scratchy ground so she was able to cradle his head against her breast and shoulder. Shuddering, he clamped on to her, encircling her waist with his arms while she stroked his hair and covered his temple with gentle kisses.

After a minute or so he was able to go on. 'Somehow I managed to get to my knees and pull it away from him but – I don't know how it happened, honest to God I don't – some way or other my hand must have slipped or something and I pulled the trigger and the barrel of the gun was right up against your husband's face. Oh, God –' he wept fully now, great racking sobs. 'I'm sorry, I'm sorry, I'm acting like a baby – I've no right –'

'Hush, darling, hush. It's over now, it's over.'

She continued to rock him until, gradually, he began to calm. And as she held him, she became conscious that, second by second, the light was growing stronger. Although the cabin was roofless it had been almost completely covered with brambles, thick creepers and other greenery, so much so that from where she sat, all Elizabeth could see of the sky was a small triangle, now translucent, like mother-of-pearl. And as Daniel became quieter, she heard again the call of a cuckoo, probably, she thought, the same one she had heard the morning before. Other birds around, sparrows, a blackbird, starlings, magpies, were beginning to flex their morning voices. She knew she would have to go back to the house very soon.

She forced herself furiously to think. There had to be some way she could sort out this situation.

Quiet now, Daniel pulled away from her. 'I'm very sorry,' he said, 'I shouldn't have come to you.'

'Nonsense,' she said fiercely.

'I'll just go away, I'm sure my brother would help me.'

'I'll help you.' Pretending a confidence she did not feel, Elizabeth put her hands over his, forcing him to look at her.

'I'm not going to involve you in this,' he said softly, 'this is my mess.' His eyes, although still bleary from recent tears, were steady.

'It's mine too.'

'I made the mistakes, I shouldn't have run, for one thing.' He sprang to his feet. 'You did nothing wrong.'

'No, you shouldn't have run.' Elizabeth looked up at him. In the growing greyish light his haggard face was old beyond its years. The sleeve of his jacket was ripped and one side of his shirt collar stood higher than the other. She longed to tidy him up, to wash his hair and comb it, to shave the growth off his cheeks. *Watch it!* she told herself, you're not his mother. 'We're going to go to the police,' she said firmly.

'They won't believe me.' Although his expression was doubtful, she heard the hope.

'They will.' She stood up to face him. 'I'll make them. It was an accident, Daniel, we have to make them see that. I'll make them see it.'

'But it looks so bad – because of the dance hall and all –'

'Daniel, listen to me.' Elizabeth took a deep breath. 'Get this into your head. You and I did nothing wrong in the dance hall. We *danced*.'

He stood very still and so did she; even in this incongruous place, the memory of that dance crackled like distant lightning between them. Now she could see the confidence flowing back into him. 'I heard about your hair,' he said, 'and about Francey. How's Francey?'

'He's going to be all right.' Not only did Elizabeth no longer feel like Daniel's mother as, only inches apart, they continued to stare at one another, she felt younger than he. 'I have to get to Francey as soon as I can,' she whispered. 'He's so small. He must be very frightened.'

'Give him my love.'

'I will.'

'And your hair suits you short.'

In the pause that followed, she saw that there was a small gash on his temple. 'Thank you,' she said. 'It'll grow again.'

'It's still beautiful.'

254

The conversation going on above and underneath this one had little to do with hair.

'Have you been home?' Elizabeth asked after another pause. Anything to defuse a tension stretched nearly beyond endurance.

'No.'

'Who knows where you are?'

'Just one brother, the eldest. He works over at the mines and I knew when he would be coming home down the road. I hid in the hedge.'

'Where have you been sleeping?'

'There's a half-sunk boat near a cave at Cleanderry – I was comfortable enough.' Throughout, they had been standing as rigidly as cats taking the measure of one another and now the stilted words finally curled up and died. 'Are you hungry?' Elizabeth whispered.

'I'm always hungry!' For the first time Daniel smiled, a wry, self-deprecating smile which made havoc of Elizabeth's intentions.

Before she could stop herself, she had reached up and touched her mouth to his but pulled away again before he responded. 'Look,' she said rapidly, 'we don't have time to play games.'

'I didn't think we were.'

'We both know what's been going on between us. At least, I do.'

'I do, too.' Again he was very still.

'We've already acknowledged it. What's happened – what is happening – between us is awkward and inconvenient and unconventional but as far as I'm concerned it's real and it's here.'

'Elizabeth—' He went to take her in his arms but she caught them.

'No! There's no time. We have to sort things out first, you understand? And I haven't had an opportunity to think further than the next minute.'

'It's real?' This time his smile was so wide and happy that it lit his face like a blaze of candlelight. In the course of

255

just a few seconds, the transformation from youth to confident young man was astonishing. The electricity between them was recharged so strongly that Elizabeth, feeling as though his forearms under her hands were actually pulsating, felt impelled to step back and break the contact.

But Daniel followed her. Weakly, she tried to fend him off but this time he brooked no refusal and took her in his arms. '*A chroí*,' he whispered in Irish, '*mo chroí ghlégheal* . . .'

The endearments, followed by a slow deliberate kiss, took Elizabeth's strength away to the extent that her legs felt rubbery. A faint glimmer of George showed itself somewhere deep in her memory. 'This is wrong, we have to be careful!' Breathless, she broke from him at last.

'I know —'

'My husband was buried today – I mean yesterday.' She backed away, stumbling over a clump of blackberry bush.

'I know.' He pursued her, putting out a hand to help her regain her footing but she pushed it away and continued to back off.

'We're in trouble, we have to wait, Daniel —'

'I know —' He reached her, put his arms around her and kissed her until she felt her blood run like milk.

Chapter Fourteen

'Where were you?' Kathleen's accusing face burned like a lantern in the recesses of the kitchen as Elizabeth came through the door.

'Kitty! You're up already? It's very early.' Elizabeth tried to collect her scattered wits. She knew she must look a fright, her bare feet scratched and muddy, nightdress crumpled, bramble-snagged and stained, hair probably standing on end. Guiltily, she hoped her lips showed no sign of the sustained kissing they had just received.

'Where were you?' Kathleen repeated.

'I couldn't sleep.' The lie sounded unconvincing even to Elizabeth herself. 'I went for a walk.'

'Abbie got sick! She was crying for you!' Kathleen, her contempt obvious, turned on her heel and went back into the communal bedroom.

Although as far as Elizabeth could see, the baby was perfectly happy sitting in her little cot and playing with her wooden blocks, she scooped her up into her arms. 'Come here, Abbie.'

'Mama!' Abigail smiled and patted her mother's face.

Elizabeth hugged her tightly then took the bottle Kathleen had set to heat on the stove and after testing a few drops of the milk on the inside of her wrist, sat into the chair and put the teat to the baby's mouth. Although Abbie was now quite heavy, the warm sturdy feel of her body calmed Elizabeth as it always did. 'There, Abbie, there you are, my big little baby,' she murmured as, slurping rhythmically against her breast, Abigail fixed wide eyes on her own. As she settled into the feed, Elizabeth's thoughts formed themselves into some sort of order. She and Daniel had agreed to meet again at the ruined cottage after dark

257

that evening and in the meantime, she had promised to go to the police to see how the land lay. As she sat and watched Abbie's absorbed little face, she tried to underpin her confidence in the idea that when she explained what had actually happened, the Guards would see she was telling the truth.

What then? The thought sneaked in.

Was she absolutely certain that she loved Daniel Carrig McCarthy? Enough to alienate her parents yet again, disturb the children, scandalize the neighbourhood? Were the two of them together strong enough to stand alone against the world?

From the first time her eyes had been burned by Daniel's on the summit of Knockameala, Elizabeth had recognized her own physical fallibility. Could she be tough enough now to tell herself to have sense – that enough was enough? The moment she asked herself that question, Elizabeth knew what the answer would be: the fact that her relationship with Daniel was beset with obstacles and social taboos made no difference; she could turn the tide at Ballycrovane sooner than she could withstand the pull of her own body towards his.

'We'll just have to wait and see, won't we, baby?' She spoke aloud to Abigail, who, having finished her bottle, was struggling to get down on to the floor. She had been walking for a while now and, for her own safety, Neeley had constructed a walking frame, a square wooden cage without wheels which restricted her movements and was too wide to go through any of the doors leading out of the kitchen or to allow the baby to bump into or reach for the hot stove. He had made similar contraptions for the other children, all of which had served their purpose well until they came apart through over-use and had been broken up for firewood. As Elizabeth strapped the baby into her mobile prison, she felt the first genuine stab of mourning for her dead husband. Whatever his shortcomings and faults, in his own way Neeley had cared a great deal about his children's welfare.

She watched as, noisily stumping the frame along with

her, Abigail toddled around the kitchen. What kind of father – stepfather – would Daniel make? *Easy!* she cautioned herself. Don't get ahead of yourself . . .

Happy that the baby was safe enough, Elizabeth left her to her own devices in the kitchen and went into the bathroom to wash. Then, in the knowledge that she had to make a good impression on the sergeant, she dressed with care, but conservatively: she did not want to appear to be adopting the role of merry widow. Corinne, ever-dependable when it came to clothes, had brought with her from Cork an entire suite of black mourning outfits, skirts, cardigans and dresses in good, lightweight fabrics but of suitably sombre cut.

Elizabeth chose one of the dresses; of linen and softly gored, with a discreet V neckline, it fitted her perfectly. She put on her only pair of stockings and her court shoes, brushed her hair so that it lay sleekly against her head and fastened around her neck the gold cross and chain her parents had given her for her twenty-first birthday.

Then she stood back to regard herself critically in the mirror in her bedroom. She was too pale for the dress and there were purple patches under her eyes but by and large she felt she looked quite elegant: that on the outside, at least, she could do no better. She looked at her watch. Her father and Ida would be along shortly. She hoped St John would not be too inquisitive about her reasons for wanting him to drive her to the police station. In the event, he asked no questions at all.

The sergeant received them courteously as they entered the public office in the Eyeries barracks and showed no surprise when Elizabeth asked to speak privately to him.

St John, wearing his solicitor's expression, backed away. 'Take your time, Beth,' he said. 'I'll wait for you in the public house across the road.'

Having seen her father out, the policeman hovered by the door and Elizabeth already had the uncomfortable feeling that his eyes were sizing her up and were missing nothing. 'Would you like a cup of tea, Mrs Scollard?' he asked.

'No, thank you,' she said briskly, trying to convey a confidence she did not feel. Now that she was here the situation did not appear as straightforward as she had thought when she had been mentally rehearsing it. She glanced around the room: simply furnished with a small wooden table, four chairs and a filing cabinet, its only concession to décor, apart from the usual Garda warnings about control of dock, thistle and ragwort, was a calendar on one wall. In itself the place was not intimidating but its very spareness caused her heart to quicken.

'Right-oh,' said the sergeant. He closed the door and, pulling out one of the chairs at the table for her, waited politely until she was seated. Then, folding his hands in front of him, he sat in the chair opposite. 'Are you managing all right, Mrs Scollard? It was a fine send-off your husband got yesterday.' His tone was grave and mannerly but Elizabeth's conviction that he was watching her more carefully than might be warranted, had he seen her merely as the victim's grieving widow, was growing.

'Yes, it was,' she agreed. 'We're very grateful for all the help. We have good neighbours.'

'Anything I can do, please don't hesitate to ask.'

'I won't.'

'The inquest will be in about six weeks' to two months' time. If there is anything troubling you about it, I'll be happy to answer any questions. About procedures, I mean.'

Although Elizabeth searched his face, she could not find anything other than politeness. Nevertheless, she was now flustered. 'Thank you,' she said uncertainly, 'but that's not what I'm here about. Well, in a way it is, I suppose.'

'Yes?'

'Actually, I – I do want to talk to you about what happened that night.'

'Oh?' The sergeant smiled encouragingly but to Elizabeth's ears, the word had a slightly forced intonation. 'Do you mind if I take notes, Mrs Scollard?' he went on, taking a small notebook out of the breast pocket of his uniform.

This was something for which she had not bargained. The formality of it alarmed her further. 'Do you have to?'

'It's just to prompt my memory, you understand. And of course we would like to clear up what happened that night. So anything you could help us with . . .' During this he had retrieved a pencil from his pocket and now held it poised above the notebook.

'Well, if you need to . . .'

Convinced now that the man knew more about the situation than he acknowledged, Elizabeth also knew there was no going back.

'Yes, Mrs Scollard?' As she searched for a way to begin, he prompted her, letting the words fall like lead.

'I don't know where to start.' In an effort to collect herself, she looked away from him towards the calendar. The current week was displayed under a lurid print of a basket of flowers. Thursday. Today was Thursday. She hung on to that fact.

'Let me help you,' said the sergeant. 'You were at home in bed when your husband was shot.'

'Yes, I was. My father was in the house too – I was all in, you see, I'd travelled from Cork that day. And I'd been up all night the night before.' She heard herself starting to gabble. 'I was tired,' she repeated, forcing herself to slow down.

'Did you hear the shot?'

'No, I knew nothing about it until you and the curate came in. But I think my father heard it, all right.' She wanted to appear as helpful as possible.

'Yes, we know that . . .' While the policeman scribbled something in his notebook, Elizabeth gathered her courage. 'Look, Sergeant,' she said as strongly as she could, 'I'm here to tell you I don't believe Daniel McCarthy deliberately killed my husband.'

'Oh?' The sergeant suspended his writing and looked at her with eyes sharp as needles. 'I don't believe I mentioned Daniel McCarthy.'

'I know what's being said around the countryside.' Elizabeth straightened her back. 'It's what the dogs in the street say.'

'I see.'

261

'It was an accident, Sergeant.'

'You know this?'

'I know Daniel Carrig. He would not deliberately kill another human being. And, as Neeley's widow, I'm convinced Daniel did not kill my husband.'

The sergeant's stillness and lack of reaction unnerved her to the point where again she heard the words gathering momentum as they spilled out of her mouth. 'I believe there was a row between them, all right. And that Daniel was up on the mountain that night with his gun – he goes up there all the time shooting rabbits. But it really was an accident – you can take my word for it.'

'You know how it happened?'

She attempted to stare him down. 'Yes, I think I do.'

'Forgive me, Mrs Scollard, but you weren't there at the time.'

'No, but neither were you nor anyone else.'

'Would you mind if I asked you on what you base your belief?'

'On my observation of human nature,' Elizabeth whispered, then, more strongly, 'Do you not think it could be possible there was a struggle between them and the gun simply went off?'

'Plausible enough,' said the sergeant, pausing to allow his implication to sink in.

'What do you mean?' Elizabeth jumped to her feet.

'Forgive me, Mrs Scollard, but unless the young man comes forward, this is mere speculation. Perhaps,' he, too, stood up, 'he already has?'

'I beg your pardon?'

'Again, forgive me, but could I ask what your personal interest is in this?'

'I should think that would be obvious.' Elizabeth's heart was hammering now in her chest.

'Oh?' He raised one eyebrow.

'I – I want to see justice done.'

'Do you know where he is now?'

The suddenness of the question took her breath away. She stared at him, at his shrewd, knowing eyes. There was no point in appealing to this man's humanity. 'No,' she said quietly.

'Are you sure? Mrs Scollard, I know you've had a shock and I don't quite know how to put this, but are you aware that if you know where this young man is you are obliged to let us know? That not telling us might make things, well, *awkward* for you?'

'I don't know where he is,' Elizabeth repeated, her voice hoarse.

The sergeant dropped his own voice until it hummed like a cello. 'Again, I don't mean to be indelicate, ma'am, but there are stories about an earlier incident involving the young man and your husband. Something to do with yourself and a dance in Castleclough, I believe? Your husband was a lot older than you, was he not?' This time the innuendo was unmistakable. 'Could I ask you once again, Mrs Scollard, if you could help us by telling us where Daniel McCarthy is at present?'

Elizabeth stared at him, at his hateful, smooth face. Her naïveté had been monumental. She could see it now through his eyes, the conspiracy cooked up by the wife and her young lover to dispose of the awkward and inconvenient husband.

Dignity, dignity . . . The old drumbeat came to her rescue. Slowly and deliberately, she unclenched fists involuntarily squeezed to her sides during the tension of the interview and let her hands fall open and loose by her side. At the same time she stretched her spine until she was as straight as a sapling. She was no longer frightened. This was a contest for very high stakes. Daniel was the trophy and she was not going to hand him over without a struggle. 'I'm sorry I've wasted your time, Sergeant,' she said quietly, 'it's obvious now that I, too, have wasted mine – and that coming here was a mistake. I probably should have guessed that since you do not know him – and since you are so new to the area – it's quite conceivable to you that Daniel Carrig could have murdered my husband. All I can say to you, *repeat* to you, is that I know he did not.'

263

He said nothing, just continued to stare. His eyes, she saw, were a very pale blue.

'I'll be going now.' She inclined her head as though she were a queen and he an ambassador from a particularly lowly colony.

'Thank you for coming in, Mrs Scollard.' He moved to open the door for her.

She paused before moving. 'I'm sorry now I did,' she said.

'Just one thing.' He held the door ajar but not wide enough for her to get through without pushing past him. 'I'm sure you can understand how much we would appreciate it if Daniel McCarthy were to come to us on his own behalf.'

'That is outside my influence, Sergeant. And, if I may say so, if it were up to me and if I did know where Daniel was, coming in here would be the last thing I would now advise him to do.'

The sergeant ignored the irony. 'Nevertheless, Mrs Scollard, I can assure you it would be in the young man's long-term interest to come forward of his own accord. We will find him, you know.'

'Will you?'

'And you are not planning to leave the peninsula in the next while yourself, are you, Mrs Scollard?'

'As a matter of fact, Sergeant,' Elizabeth's nervousness had yielded to cold anger at the man's impertinence, 'at the earliest opportunity – certainly by tomorrow at the latest, I will be going to Cork to visit my son who is in hospital there. Is this permissible, do you think?'

'Of course, how insensitive of me.' The policeman smiled apologetically. 'Naturally you will be going to Cork. How long do you think you will be staying?'

'That depends, Sergeant, on how ill my son is when I get there. Now, if you'll excuse me, my father is waiting for me.'

'If you change your mind and decide to let us know where we can have a few words with the young man – again I assure you it will only be a matter of time . . .' The sergeant paused to let the import of the threat sink in, then opened the door wide and stepped back to leave a clear passage. 'My condolences again, ma'am, and we will be in touch in the near future, I'm sure.'

Shaking, Elizabeth left the barracks and walked fast towards the public house where her father waited. She realized that dressed in long-sleeved black on this glorious May morning, she could not have looked more conspicuous had she tried, and she kept her head down until she reached the pub. Inside, her father was slumped at the counter in front of a glass of whiskey.

The moment he saw her he stood off his stool and, leaving the rest of the drink behind him, accompanied her out into the sunshine. Taking her arm, he led her across the street to where he had parked the car and, clearing his throat as he opened the door for her, asked gruffly: 'Did you get your business done?'

The direct question wrong-footed Elizabeth who had not planned to reveal anything about her audience with the sergeant. 'Yes, Daddy – actually no—' she blurted, 'oh, Daddy, I'm in a terrible mess!'

'Wait till I start this and then you can tell me everything.' Shooing away a small gang of fascinated children, St John cranked the motor and when it was turning over let himself into the driver's seat.

'Daddy, I don't want to get you involved in anything,' Elizabeth said as they motored slowly out of the village, 'it's my problem, not yours. I'm a grown woman.' Despite the words, she was longing to confide in someone.

'Whatever you think, Beth. Don't tell me if you don't want to.' Carefully, he negotiated the car around several tethered horses and carts and a pen full of young calves.

'You might be shocked.'

'I've been a solicitor for a long time. Very little could shock me.'

In her mind, she tried to organize the story so that it would come out correctly and in the right order. 'The interview with the sergeant didn't go well, Daddy,' she said.

265

'Oh? Even on short acquaintance, I would have thought he was quite an able fellow.'

'He is,' said Elizabeth, 'probably too able. That's just the problem. It was me that made the mess of it.'

He glanced swiftly at her and then, letting her take her own time, turned back to concentrate on the narrow, twisting road.

They drove along in silence for a few minutes. Then: 'Damn!' Coming around the second leg of a sharp S bend, he braked hard to avoid running into a ewe and two fully grown lambs which, having been browsing on the ditches, skittered panic-stricken across their pathway. 'Damned animals!' St John swore again. 'The owner of those creatures should be brought before the courts. Are you all right, Beth?'

'Yes, I'm fine.' Elizabeth had been concentrating so hard on her problems that she had barely noticed what had happened.

'This is a dreadful country!' Cautiously, Elizabeth's father put the car into gear again. Neither spoke again until they were rounding the bend into Ballycrovane when St John once again asked if she was all right.

Based on her previous relationship with him, the extent of her father's kindness and solidity in recent days had been a revelation to Elizabeth. But she was less frantic than she had been in the immediate aftermath of the conversation with the Garda sergeant and to confide any more in her father than she already had done would have felt forced and false. Their developing intimacy was still too new and delicate to withstand such testing. 'I'm fine now, Daddy, honestly!' She touched his arm reassuringly.

She spent the remainder of the journey sunk in thought. The passage of a motor car was still a great rarity on Béara and to absolve herself of the obligation to return the stares and greetings of all those they met on the road, she closed her eyes, opening them again only when they purred to a halt at the gate to the farmyard. Before letting the engine die, her father spoke again. 'I don't mean to pry, but are you sure there's nothing I can help you with, Beth?'

'I may need you, Daddy, but not just at the moment.' Then, with a hand on his arm she detained him as he was about to open the door. 'I may not have a chance to say this again, but I just want to tell you how truly grateful I am for all your support.'

To her horror, she saw his face turn red. 'Beth, I'm your father!' His discomfort threatened to make smithereens of her fragile composure and hurriedly, she got out of the car on her own side.

'I'll just stay out here for a few moments – breath of fresh air, if you don't mind.' St John walked quickly away down the road.

'Surely, Daddy.' Her throat constricted, Elizabeth watched him go; his suit was too well tailored, his shoes too polished, his tweed cap set too firmly on his head for life in Lahersheen. And at this moment, she loved him with all her heart. The love contained within it the seeds of loss. In a way, she missed him more now that he was with her than she had in all the years they had been apart.

Inside, the household was quiet and under control. Abigail was asleep in her cot and none of the other girls was in evidence. 'Where's everyone?' From the doorway, Elizabeth addressed Ida and Tilly who were sitting at the table.

'I sent them all over to our house.' Tilly heaved herself on to her feet and crossed to the dresser. 'Mick is bringing them all for a long drive in the horse and car. It's a beautiful day and they're all so sad and there's nothing much for them to do around here. So I thought they needed a bit of distraction. I hope you don't mind?'

'Mind?' Elizabeth kicked off the court shoes, 'I'm very grateful.' She seemed to be spending all her time thanking people, she thought wryly.

'For what it's worth, Lizzie, I think you should send them back to school tomorrow.'

'I will,' said Elizabeth. 'But they'll have to do it on their own.' She flopped into one of the chairs by the table and accepted the mug of buttermilk Tilly placed before her. 'I hate asking you again but will you watch the little ones,

Tilly? I'm going to Cork in the car with Daddy and Ida first thing tomorrow morning. Francey will be really upset by now.'

'I'll stay,' said Ida impulsively. 'Of course you have to go but Tilly will need a hand and there's nothing to take me back immediately.' Ida, whose husband had left directly after the funeral, lived a life of comparative ease and luxury. 'I'll stay with you until you find your feet, Beth.'

'It's too much—'

'No, it's not,' replied Ida. 'Beth, for once in your life, accept a bit of help. For the children's sake if not for your own.'

Dumbstruck, Elizabeth looked at these two women, both of whose advice she had stubbornly refused to take – to her cost. Neither had ever said, 'I told you so', and both remained loyal and giving. Then there was her family; she had betrayed her family with her selfishness and hedonism but they, too, were faithful to the last; even Corinne, to whom she had been so recently and horribly abusive, continued in her own fashion to show her concern.

And what about Daniel? Her consuming and dangerous obsession with Daniel Carrig had resulted directly in his present predicament, yet he, too, seemed undeterred and did not blame her.

She brought nothing but trouble to those around her, she thought in a swirl of self-recrimination; she did not deserve such love. To hide how she felt, she took a long swallow of the buttermilk. 'I think you know how I feel about the two of you,' she said when she could at last trust herself to speak.

'Ah, shut up, y'oul' *amadán*!' Tilly covered her embarrassment with a wide grin. 'Sure, the Lord sent you to the two of us to try us!'

'Yeah,' Ida agreed. 'What else were Tilly and me put on this earth for except to mollycoddle Princess Elizabeth Sullivan?'

'I mean it.'

'Sure, we know you do,' said Ida, 'and we love you too, don't we, Tilly?'

She gave the other woman such a strong nudge that Tilly remonstrated. 'Hey! That hurt!'

'Sorry,' said Ida blithely, then, hands on hips, continued to Elizabeth: 'Now finish up that milk and then I think you should take a nap before they're all back in on top of us again.'

All the lost sleep and the helter-skelter of emotions she had gone through within the past week finally caught up on Elizabeth as soon as she got into bed and she slept for the rest of the day, waking with difficulty only when Ida gently shook her shoulder: 'Beth! Beth! Here's a bowl of soup for you.'

'What time is it?' Elizabeth raised herself on one elbow.

'It's after eight in the evening.' Ida plumped up the pillows behind her head. 'I didn't want to let you sleep on too long because then you'd be waking up in the middle of the night all alone again. Now, sit up and get this down you.' Elizabeth did as she was bid as her friend settled a small wooden tray on her lap.

'The girls!' The full import of what had been happening hit Elizabeth only then and she made as though to get out of bed.

'Relax.' Ida pushed her back. 'Everything's running like clockwork out there. Everyone's had their tea and Tilly's brought Abigail home with her again. Your father's happy as a sandboy. I found a drop of poteen in the dresser and gave it to him after his meal. I hope that's all right?'

'I'll get up as soon as I've finished this.' Elizabeth smiled gratefully at her friend. 'Oh, Ida, I don't know what I would have done without you.'

'You're welcome, Your Royal Highness!' Ida dropped a mock curtsey and went back into the kitchen.

Left alone, fully conscious now, Elizabeth felt appallingly guilty. How would Ida feel if she knew that in just a few hours' time the friend to whom she was being so supportive was planning to meet the fugitive who was implicated in her husband's death? For a few moments, Elizabeth toyed with the idea of confiding in Tilly and Ida, both of whom had had the tact not to ask why she had gone to the police station that morning. But then she told herself it would not be fair. But as she sipped the thick vegetable broth, she knew this was not the truth. She did not want to tell them because she was afraid they would try to dissuade her.

Through her window, she could see the sky had lost little of its light. She had many hours yet to wait. She finished the soup, pulled on a dressing-gown, and went into the kitchen.

The evening was so warm that the door to the outside had been propped open; the light shafted through it on to St John Sullivan's greying head. Watching listlessly as two hens pecked at the channels between the flagstones just inside it, Mary and Margaret, both holding balled handkerchiefs in their hands, sat sad-faced on a bench seat by the window. By contrast to the expression on her sisters' faces, Kathleen's was hard and set; she was sitting bolt upright on a kitchen chair a little way away from them but got up immediately as Elizabeth entered and made as though to go into the bedroom.

Elizabeth glanced into the scullery where Ida, drying dishes, was being as unobtrusive as possible. 'Don't go, Kitty,' she said, restraining Kathleen as the girl went to push past her, 'I want to have a word with all of you.'

'About what?' Sullenly, the girl refused to meet Elizabeth's eyes.

'About plans for the next few days,' said Elizabeth calmly.

'I told Mick Harrington I'd go with him for a pint.' St John stood up and stretched himself. 'I won't be long, Beth.'

'Take all the time in the world, Daddy, and thanks for letting me sleep.'

'If you're in bed when I get back, we'll leave as soon as we get up in the morning, if that's all right with you?'

'Fine.'

Kathleen, who, face averted, had stood sulking as St John picked his cap off the hook by the back door and went out, was the last to sit down beside her sisters at the table. Elizabeth waited until they were all settled and then, pretending a matter-of-factness she did not feel, said, 'Look, girls, as you know I've got to go to Cork tomorrow morning to see Francey.'

'Tomorrow's his birthday,' Margaret volunteered.

In the turmoil, the approach of Francey's sixth birthday had completely slipped Elizabeth's mind. 'I hadn't forgotten,' she lied quickly, 'and, of course, that's one of the reasons I have to go – I couldn't let him spend his birthday by himself in hospital. Now you know that this is a difficult time for all of us —'

'Can I be excused?' Kathleen pushed back her chair.

'I want to talk to all three of you,' Elizabeth felt that if she lost Kathleen now, she would never regain her. Her relationship with Neeley's second child had never been as good as with the rest of the girls but she was damned if she would give up trying. 'Sit down, Kitty, please.'

'I do *not* want to be called Kitty any more,' cried Kathleen passionately. 'My name is *Kathleen*. I am nearly fifteen years old and my name is Kathleen. Do you all hear that?' She glared round the table before stalking off into the bedroom and closing the door.

Mary half rose to follow her but Elizabeth stopped her. 'Let her go. She'll come around.'

'Daddy always called her Kitty, I suppose that's it,' said Margaret.

'I'm sure you're right,' agreed Elizabeth. In a way it was a relief to talk to the others without Kathleen's spiky, aggressive interventions. The other two sat quietly as she gave instructions about practicalities like the routines for getting all of the schoolgoers out in the morning.

Then Margaret put the question that had probably been uppermost in the minds of all of them. 'What's going to happen to us? Are we going to have to sell the farm?'

'I don't know,' said Elizabeth honestly. 'Your father left a will all right and as far as I know I'm getting the farm but whether we'll be able to work it on our own is another matter. So the honest answer is I don't know what's going

271

to happen. But there's a solicitor in Castletown,' she added comfortingly, 'who's going to sort things out for us and Grandad Sullivan's also a solicitor and when he gets back to his office, he's going to help too.'

'Are you going to get married again?'

'*Shut up!*' Too late, Mary pucked her sister in the arm but the question, put as baldly as only Margaret could, had hit Elizabeth so unexpectedly she felt almost winded.

'What do you mean, Maggie?' she managed.

'We've heard talk,' said Margaret bluntly.

'Don't mind her, Mammy!' Mary rushed the words. 'We haven't heard any such thing. You know her – nothing to do except gossip over the gates.'

'Well, are you?' Margaret persisted, her eyes boring into Elizabeth's.

Elizabeth's protective instincts snapped into place and she felt as alert as a hare. 'Of course not,' she said, feigning indignation. 'Of *course* not.'

'Well, then, why are they saying things?'

'What exactly are they saying?' she countered.

'They're saying nothing, Mammy.' Desperately, Mary tried to maintain the status quo. 'One more word out of you, Maggie Scollard,' she rounded on her sister, 'and I'll – I'll *hit* you!'

'It's all right, Mary,' said Elizabeth, 'let her be. It's just as well I know what they're saying about me.'

'I can't listen to this.' It was Mary's turn to push back her chair and rush from the kitchen into the bedroom.

Elizabeth listened out for evidence that Ida was still engaged with the dishes then cupped her chin in both hands and stared at Margaret. 'Now, Maggie,' she said, 'tell me what they're saying.'

Faced with her own weapon of the direct approach, Margaret quailed. 'It's nothing much,' she mumbled, 'and, anyway, I don't believe them.'

'Don't believe what?'

'Mammy, it's only one thing I heard. It's just a saying —'

'*What?*' Elizabeth's patience was almost worn out.

272

'Marry a scalder and she'll want to rove the world.'

Margaret mumbled the words so indistinctly that it took a moment or two for Elizabeth to figure out what she had said. She was familiar with the saying: 'scalder' was a colloquial word for an unfledged bird. 'I see,' she said. She had no desire to allow a conversation to develop along this line. 'I'm glad you know it's just idle gossip, Maggie.'

'It's Kitty that told me.' Margaret blushed a deep red. 'She told all of us that that's what they're saying everywhere. She said you were a scarlet woman.'

Elizabeth almost smiled at the terminology but the situation was too serious for levity. 'Do you think I am, Maggie?' she asked softly. 'Do you know what it means?'

'Sort of. She said it's when you have a baby and you're not married. Or when you're married and you have a boyfriend as well.' There was no stopping Margaret now. 'She said something else. She said that even a tin knocker will shine on a dirty door. She said that's why Daddy cut off your – your—' Suddenly, she was unable to continue.

Her distress was so abrupt and shocking that Elizabeth ran around to her and crouching beside her, took her in her arms. 'Oh, Maggie, darling Maggie. Don't cry, don't.'

'I can't help it.' Margaret sobbed against Elizabeth's shoulder. 'I don't know what to do, tell me what I'm supposed to do . . .'

'Nothing, darling, nothing. We'll all have to get through this together. Cry your heart out, you poor thing.' Her own tears threatening to flow in sympathy, she rocked her stepdaughter like a baby.

After a minute or so, as Margaret was at last calming down, Elizabeth realized they were no longer alone in the kitchen; Ida was standing awkwardly a few feet away in front of the stove. 'Is she all right?' Her friend's face was creased with concern.

'She'll be fine, she needs this. We'll all need time.'

'Yes,' said Ida slowly and Elizabeth's guilty heart lurched. Was this a warning? Had Ida too heard the gossip?

She concentrated on Margaret, whose sobs had quietened to the extent that she was making no further noise.

'Why don't you go and lie down on my bed, Maggie?' She hugged the girl tightly. 'It's lovely and quiet in there in my bedroom.'

'All right.' Margaret got up and trailed sadly into the room and closed the door.

'I've finished in there,' Ida indicated the scullery, 'but would you like me to stay on a bit longer?'

'No, that's all right.' Well-meaning though they all were, Elizabeth longed now to be alone. There was still an enormous expanse of time before darkness fell but she felt surrounded by a closely woven mesh of watching eyes and needed badly to escape. 'I can't tell you how much we all appreciate all you've done,' she said, turning away to sweep non-existent crumbs off the oilcloth on the table into her open palm, 'and thanks to you, everything here's grand now. To tell you the truth, I'm still tired and I'll probably go back to bed. As you know I've an early start in the morning.' She continued her redundant cleaning while keeping her head low to avoid looking Ida in the eye. 'You go on over to Harringtons', Ida, and I'll send Daddy over there when he gets back from the pub.' Promising to return in the morning to help the children get out to school, Ida gave Elizabeth a bear-hug and left.

Somehow, Elizabeth got through the next hour and a half or so until her father's return. When she had had the bathroom extension built, a door had been cut through to it from the children's room and for a time she heard them coming and going, but soon all noises ceased and she assumed they were in bed. She busied herself arranging and rearranging the Delph on the dresser and when there was no more she could do there, scrubbed the kitchen table until her hands were raw. Then, thinking how they would feel to Daniel, she smoothed cream over them. Every so often, through the open door, she checked for the onset of darkness. The world remained maddeningly visible and full of light.

She was ironing clothes already crisp when her father came back at about a quarter to eleven and when he, too, was safely dispatched to Harringtons' she stood in the middle of the immaculate kitchen and, to calm her nerves, breathed deeply and consciously, drawing the air down into her lungs.

Feeling marginally calmer, she looked in on the children. 'Hello, Mammy,' Goretti whispered, raising herself from one of the beds.

Elizabeth put a finger to her lips. 'Hello, darling,' she whispered back, 'are you all right?'

'Yes. But I'm not sleepy.'

'Hush now, close your eyes really tight and it'll be morning soon. Did you say your prayers?'

'Yes.' The child nodded solemnly. 'When's Daddy coming home from heaven?'

'We'll talk about it in the morning. Now close your eyes like a good girl.' Elizabeth knew she should probably take Goretti out of the bed and talk to her, but the twilight outside was deepening at last.

She glanced across to where Kathleen snored lightly beside Mary.

She would have to be very careful and very quick . . . 'Goodnight, Goretti,' she whispered. 'Sleep tight.'

'Don't let the fleas bite!' replied the child, smiling and subsiding back on her pillow.

Elizabeth went to the door of the kitchen and looked out into the yard. She never would have thought to be cursing the magical brightness of summer evenings on Béara. The gloom inside the house had been deceptive; although it was after eleven o'clock, it was still bright enough to see.

But telling herself she could not wait any longer, she ran across the yard and into the upper field. She strained her eyes as she came within sight of the old cottage, until she thought she detected movement there and checked herself; just in case it was not Daniel it would not do to be seen running towards the ruin. She again broke into a run as Daniel's unmistakable figure stepped out from the shadows.

As she came close, she saw that, since morning, he had made some effort with his appearance: at least his hair was tidier and he had managed somehow to shave.

'Daniel!' After one breathless kiss, she dragged him into the heart of the cottage. 'We've got to be careful,' she gasped, 'the sergeant is looking everywhere for you.'

'What happened?'

As quickly and succinctly as she could, Elizabeth related what had transpired between herself and the policeman at the barracks that morning. Daniel listened in silence, the whites of his eyes gleaming in the half-light, made greenish by all the foliage. At the end he drooped visibly as though someone had drawn all the energy out of him with a syringe. 'There's nothing left to do except turn myself in.'

'I'm so sorry, Daniel, it's all my fault.' Elizabeth turned away from him. Assailed by a wave of anger, she ripped a great handful of ivy off the wall and shredded it between her fingers.

'You did your best.'

'Not only this morning, the whole thing. I shouldn't have—' She was so frustrated with the situation and with her own disastrous part in it that she could barely string words together in a coherent sentence.

'Shouldn't have what?' He was behaving once again like the older of the two.

'I could have had more self-control.' She flung away the remains of the ivy. 'I could have had more sense.'

'Are you sorry we met that day on Knockameala?' Knee-deep in the furze and coarse grass, he stood like a dark statue.

'Of course not!' Elizabeth's instincts were to fling herself into his arms but restraining herself, careless of the possibility of being stung by nettles, she sank to the ground on her haunches and covered her face with her hands.

'Elizabeth, don't!' He was beside her, trying to prise her hands away, covering the backs of them with kisses.

'Please, Daniel, you must save yourself. I'll get money from my father. You must go away.' Uncovering her face, she seized his hands in her own. 'Daddy said he'd help—'

'You told him about me?'

'Not yet, but he'll help, I know he will. He has very influential friends. Daniel, you could go to America.' Working it out as she spoke, Elizabeth sprang to her feet again. 'Yes, that's it, America.' She began to pace the confined space. 'And not Montana, because everyone here knows someone in Montana. Somewhere like New York or Boston – or even Chicago—'

'I'm not going to run away from this.' His emphatic tone stopped her in her tracks and she looked back at him. He was standing again, hands by his sides. She ran to him and put her arms around his unyielding body. 'You have to, Daniel – they'll put you in gaol. They might even *hang* you!'

'They won't hang me. I'm innocent, Elizabeth. I couldn't run away,' he said quietly. 'I ran once and look what happened. And, anyway, I wouldn't take your money.'

'Money's only money. It's only bits of paper and cheap metal. You could earn loads of it in America and pay us back.'

'No.'

No matter how she put the proposition over the next few minutes, he rejected it flatly and after a while she came to see that she would get nowhere. Surrendering, she laid her head on his breast. He tightened his arms around her and lowered his cheek to rest on the crown of her head. They stood there for a minute or so. 'How did you manage to shave?' she asked irrelevantly.

'My brother,' he said.

'Would he help?'

'He would if he could but there's nothing much he can do, is there?'

Elizabeth became aware of the regular thud of his heart against her ear and the vision of that heart stilled by judicial decree, of this boy's hooded body dangling at the end of the rope, rose before her eyes so starkly that she had to stifle a cry.

As if he had read her thoughts, she felt his body slacken in her arms. 'I'm very tired,' he said.

Clutching him to her fiercely, she was filled with remorse for nagging him so hard. 'You poor thing,' she said, 'Look, everyone's asleep at home. Come on down to the house with me and I'll give you something to eat.'

'I couldn't!' He recoiled. 'I'm not getting your family involved in this.'

'Don't you think we're involved already?' she asked. 'Now come on, that's an order.' Having re-established some sort of moral authority, she felt better. 'I'll go in first and make sure everything is quiet,' she insisted.

She stepped cautiously outside the cottage to check that no one was about. As she did so there was a low-pitched hissing somewhere to the left of her and out of the corner of her eye she saw something move. 'Oh!' This time she did cry out as, like a wraith rising from the rafters over the rubble of what had been a chimney breast, a barn owl glided on silent wings into the open field. Drifting across the twilight, after a few seconds it vanished as completely as though it had been party to a magician's trick. 'Did you see that?' Elizabeth's heart was thumping.

'It's just an owl. There's not many of them around here.'

'Do you think it's an omen?'

'I don't believe in omens. I told you it's just an owl.'

But Elizabeth could not shake off the feeling of foreboding aroused by the sudden appearance of the creature. Very jittery now, she scanned the field for other signs of movement and took Daniel's hand only when she was sure that except for ruminating cattle, nothing large was stirring. 'Come on,' she whispered. 'Hurry.'

They walked fast across the field but as they came to the hedge dividing it from the upper field close by the house, Daniel stopped and again pulled Elizabeth into his arms. 'We may not get a chance to do this again for a long time.'

Elizabeth found the strength not to contemplate that prospect – or the worse one that they would probably never see one another again. 'I'm going to Cork tomorrow to be with Francey,' she whispered.

'And I'll go to the police station in the morning,' he said in a clear, determined voice as he bent his head to kiss her.

'I'm glad to heard it!' From the other side of the hedge stepped the sergeant and a younger policeman.

Chapter Fifteen

On several occasions during the next ten days, Elizabeth thought she would not survive. To be allowed to visit the fretful Francey only twice a day was bad enough – the child's screams as she left the hospital every evening would have been enough to cause heartbreak – but on top of that was the knowledge of what was happening to Daniel.

Before she left for Cork with her father a few hours after Daniel's apprehension by the Gardai, she had gone to Harringtons'. Ida had not been up but Tilly was in the kitchen with Abigail.

'Elizabeth!' she had exclaimed in surprise. 'I didn't expect to see you for a few days!'

'Something's happened, Tilly.' Swiftly, Elizabeth bent to pick up the baby. 'Something so dreadful that I have no time to beat around the bush. I have to ask you now to be my friend and to do something for me that I know you'll disapprove of. Just say yes or no, Tilly, but if you say no I don't know what I'll do. You're my only hope.'

Tilly had listened without change of expression or interruption as Elizabeth outlined for her as clearly and unemotionally as she could what had happened over the previous twenty-four hours. 'Do you believe me that I'm telling the truth? Do you believe that Daniel's telling the truth?'

'Yes.'

Tilly's unambiguous reply was such a relief to Elizabeth that she put the baby down and threw her arms around her. 'I'll never be able to thank you.'

'What do you want me to do?'

'All I'm asking is that you go to the post office in

Ardgroom or Eyeries every so often to telephone me and let me know what is happening.'

'The whole parish'll know then.'

'I'm gone beyond caring about the parish.'

Tilly had hesitated and Elizabeth had known instantly that what she was asking was impossible; that no matter how much Tilly might want to help, she could not, she had to think of her own position and that of her husband and relatives. As surely as if she had written it in the sky, Tilly had spelled out just how isolated was the position in which Elizabeth had placed herself. She was a blow-in; Neeley Scollard, seed breed and generation, had been a Lahersheen man.

'It's all right,' she had said, again hugging her friend, 'I'm sorry, I'm sorry, Tilly. I'll find some other way, it was very mean of me to ask you and please don't hold it against me. I just wasn't thinking very straight.' She had held Tilly at arm's length. 'But at least I'm going away knowing you believe us.'

'I do. And, Lizzie, I'll find some other way of ringing you if I hear anything, I promise. I'm sorry.'

'I know you will.' Elizabeth had rushed to reassure her. 'Anyway,' she had gone on, 'sure, I don't know what I'm thinking of, I'll be closer myself. I'm sure he'll be in Limerick – or even in Dublin.' She had not been able to bring herself to say the word 'gaol'.

She had picked up Abigail. 'Give us a kiss, lovey,' and after Abbie obliged, had said goodbye to Tilly. 'And please, forgive me for asking?'

'Of course.'

Elizabeth had stopped at the door. 'Everything comes around, Tilly. Some day I'll be in a position to repay you for all this.'

'Go 'way outa that!' Tilly's plump face had gone pink.

Throughout the following week, Elizabeth had been able to gather together only fragments of what was happening. On the second day she was in Cork, Tilly – dear, valiant Tilly – had managed to get the use of the doctor's private telephone in Castletownbere. After reassuring Elizabeth that everything was under control within the family and that Ida was managing grand, she had gone on to say that on the night he had been arrested, Daniel had been brought before a Peace Commissioner at a special sitting in Eyeries and charged with murder. He was taken by the Gardai to Limerick prison and would be appearing a week later in Bantry district court for further remand. No one seemed to know when or where the trial would be.

Daniel's family, Tilly had added, was in an awful state and the whole of the peninsula was talking of nothing else.

'What are they saying?' Elizabeth had been almost afraid to ask.

'Don't worry about them, girsha,' Tilly's voice was coming and going over tremendous static, 'you have plenty of friends here. Mick and me's speaking strongly on behalf of Daniel.'

'That means everyone else thinks he's guilty?' Elizabeth's heart had plummeted further than she would have thought possible.

'Hold on to the truth, Lizzie. Right will out in the end.'

Through his legal contacts, Elizabeth's father was able to fill in more of the details. The Gardai, having questioned, it seemed, half the parish, were proceeding rapidly with the book of evidence and would be in a position to forward it to the State Solicitor within a month; in the meantime, Daniel McCarthy would be appearing in court for weekly remand.

'They'll want a statement from you too, Beth.' Her father had avoided looking her in the eye. 'As soon as you feel up to it I'll bring you down to Union Quay.'

It took all of Elizabeth's inner resources not to betray herself. 'I couldn't,' she said quietly, 'not yet.'

'Well, whenever . . .' They were sitting in the kitchen. St John Sullivan had taken to coming home in the middle of the day for lunch and, from the scullery, they could hear the comforting sounds of Maeve beginning the washing up. From deep in the recesses of the house sounded a faint tinkling; Corinne had recently resumed her piano lessons. The atmosphere was domesticated and comfortable and as far removed from the events in Lahersheen as anyone could have imagined. 'Are you sure there's nothing you want to tell me, Beth? Like that day in the car after your visit to the barracks?' St John concentrated on the precise placing of his fork beside his dessert spoon on his clean plate.

Elizabeth had come to rely on him so much in recent days that she did long to tell him. Yet she knew that her disciplined father and enigmatic mother could never understand nor accept her obsession with Daniel Carrig and that this further revelation about their daughter's flawed character would have been almost too much for them to bear. 'No, Daddy,' she said, 'not really.'

'You're the boss.' St John looked at his watch and got up from the table. 'You know where I am if you need me.'

'Thanks.'

Day followed night followed day in barely discernible order, the only fixed points being the difficult visits to the hospital. Strenuously objecting to her mother's mild suggestions that she should look up some of her old friends, but needing to get away from the stifling atmosphere of the house – even the concerned eyes of the ever dependable Maeve were getting on her nerves – Elizabeth spent hours walking the streets and hills of Cork until her feet were sore. She did agree, however, to Corinne's suggestion that she should visit a hairdresser to have her hair properly styled but took no interest in the shingled result.

And as if to mock her trouble, the early June weather continued to be glorious. Elizabeth's over-active imagination tortured her with the vision of how all this light and brilliance must appear to the nature-loving Daniel through what she envisioned as the closely barred and meagre square of his cell window.

On the eighth day, her father telephoned from his office to tell her that Daniel's first remand in Bantry had been disposed of by the court in the space of two minutes. After he had hung up, Elizabeth sat staring at the heavy Bakelite receiver. She had just returned from the day's first visit to

Francey and the next one was not due until seven o'clock. She replaced the receiver and snatching up her handbag but without bothering about coat or hat, rushed out of the front door. She got on the first bus which passed and alighted in Patrick Street. Now what? She looked across to the Savoy: the cinema was re-running *For Me and My Gal* with Judy Garland and Gene Kelly. Elizabeth had not been in a cinema for years but her mother had seen the film and had loved it and at least it would pass an hour or two. She crossed the road and bought a ticket.

Less than forty minutes later, severely shaken, she emerged from the cinema into the warm sunshine. She had not waited for the feature; the newsreel had been her first serious exposure to the reality of what was going on in Europe and the Crimea where, according to the chapter of horrors she had just seen, forty-seven prisoners had been shot trying to escape from a German prisoner-of-war camp, the Soviet army had re-captured Sebastopol, the Allies had won a great victory at an Italian town named Monte Cassino and were pushing on to Rome. The grainy scenes, despite the clipped, unemotional tones of the English commentator, destroyed for ever the romantic resonances of the placenames.

Although newspapers were read and re-read avidly on Béara, Elizabeth had always been so busy and so full of her own concerns that she rarely bothered with them and had somehow managed to relegate the war to the status of an inconvenience. Busy about her chores in Lahersheen, her own needs were simple, she had never smoked so could smile at the national obsession with finding enough good quality cigarettes and 'The Emergency' simply meant no oranges or chocolate, the occasional gritty taste of sawdust in over-used tea.

Many of the young men in the vicinity had joined the Local Defence Force or its equivalent marine body, Maritime Inscription, not least because of the high quality of the uniforms and boots and the pulling power of military uniforms at dances. Until the total ban on travel imposed between Britain and Ireland the previous year, some local lad would occasionally return to the parish on leave from France or England. To Neeley, a diehard Republican, the khaki uniform of the British had been an affront, and, although Elizabeth had not cared one way or the other, the Scollards had never associated with those to whom he had insisted on referring as British Tommies.

As a result, the stark images of mud, wounds, coffins, devastated landscapes, grave faces of politicians or exhausted ones of soldiers were a shocking discovery and by contrast her own problems appeared puny and unimportant. The faces of some of those boys under the grimy helmets had reminded her so poignantly of Daniel that the longing to see him grew until it became unbearable. She knew, however, that this would cause him problems of such magnitude that she would be well advised, for once, to control her treacherous impulses. Yet she had to contact him in some way, to let him know he was not alone.

She decided to write to him. And the more she thought about it the better the idea became because, assuming it would be pre-read by the prison authorities, a letter might well be a good opportunity to plant the truth. In a fever of impatience, she waited for the bus home and when she got there, sped immediately upstairs to her room to begin.

She spent the rest of the afternoon in careful composition; while trying to maintain a conversational style, she set out the whole story as clearly as she could. From the time of their first meeting on Knockameala up to Daniel's arrest, she included her version of what happened at Jimmy Deeney's dance at Castleclough, Daniel's gift of a salmon to her and Neeley, his game of football with Francey. In fact she omitted nothing except their physical caresses.

You may wonder, Daniel

she wrote in conclusion and for the benefit of the authorities,

why I am going over all this again in such detail. But it's to show you that if and when you come to trial you have nothing to worry about. All you will have to do is to tell the truth and I'm sure you can see that you will be believed.

My husband was, as you know, basically a good man. He had his faults like we all do – and he should not have spoken to you the way he did that night at Castleclough. And as the whole parish knows, his temper sometimes let him down. But he was certainly a fair man and he would have been the first to speak up for you had he known that the incident would have resulted in your being falsely accused of his murder.

I hope you're staying healthy, Daniel, and that you are not too depressed. Tilly Harrington has told me that, understandably, there is great talk in the parish about what has happened but that many, many people believe the truth. Soon you will be able to put all this behind you.

She stopped writing, chewing at the end of her pen. She had to put in something which would mean something to only the two of them, a code. After considerable thought, she continued:

Have courage and confidence. Soon you will be back with your family and with us all on Knockameala.

Then she remembered that Neeley had died on the mountain and tore up the page, redrafting the last words as,

Soon you will be back with your family and with us all on Béara. Everyone there is thinking about you all the time.

It was clumsy, she knew, but she hoped it would convey something privately to him of what she felt. She thought again about how to sign off and settled for:

God bless you,
Your very sincere friend,
Elizabeth Scollard

On her way to post it, she held the letter tightly against her breast, concentrating on it as though to imbue it so thoroughly with her own determination that Daniel and anyone else who read it would be positively affected. And after dropping it in the slot, she stood in front of the pillar box for a few moments, willing it to be a beneficial emissary, leaving only when another woman, after giving her a peculiar look, said loudly, 'Excuse me, please.'

At least she received some good news that day: the staff nurse on Francey's ward had a message for her when she arrived at the hospital half an hour later. She could take him home the day after tomorrow.

First there was the matter of the statement at the Garda station. On the day before she was to go home to Lahersheen – the day she was to collect Francey – St John Sullivan accompanied his daughter to the barracks at Union Quay. 'Let me do the talking,' he said urgently as they walked into the public office.

Because of her father's stolid presence and reputation, the ordeal was less intimidating for Elizabeth than it might otherwise have been; the young Garda who took her statement was deferential and seemed a little embarrassed. Having mentally rehearsed what she was going to say, Elizabeth made her statement as short as possible; she outlined what she knew of the situation, how she had found out about the death of her husband, including a brief version of what she believed to have happened. Steeling herself to speak in her father's presence, she stated that this belief was based on two conversations with the accused man, the first at his instigation, the second by arrangement. To her relief, if this was a shock to her father he showed no sign of it.

The Garda made no comment when she had finished but merely read the statement back to her. He then asked her to read it again before signing it; she did so and that appeared to be that.

However, on the way to the hospital – they were walking to conserve the black-market petrol her father had managed to procure for the trip to Béara – St John opened the topic. 'Elizabeth, I understand you wrote to him, to Daniel McCarthy.'

'Yes.' Elizabeth was so astonished she was taken off guard. 'How do you know?'

'That doesn't matter,' her father said. He stopped walking and looked over the quay wall into the Lee. 'I think it's time you told me the truth,' he said quietly. 'I can't help you if I don't know the full facts.'

Elizabeth was silent. The bicycles, the horses, the buses and taxis, the sunlight sparkling on the shifting brown diamonds of the water below, came into sharp relief. Nervously, she brushed a strand of hair off her face until her hand discovered there was none there.

'I'm waiting, Beth.' Her father grasped the curved grey stone of the wall in front of him.

'All right.' Elizabeth lifted her chin. 'We love each other, Daddy, Daniel and I.' She realized as she said it that 'love' was a word neither she nor Daniel had ever used, and that, given the nature of her own obsession, 'love' was hardly correct.

'Where did I hear that before?' St John's bitterness was like a spear.

'I'm sorry, Daddy, but that's the way it is. And if you want to have nothing more to do with me, I'll understand.'

'How far has this gone?'

Elizabeth did not bother to expostulate. 'Not where you think, Daddy,' she said simply. 'If you mean have we made love, we haven't. We wouldn't. It wouldn't have been appropriate.'

'Well, that's something, anyway.' The folds of flesh above St John's collar reddened. This was so difficult for him that Elizabeth wished with all her heart she could save him from it. He still would not look at her as they resumed their walk. 'Well, at least we know the worst. You should have told me earlier, Beth.'

She wanted to tell him why she did not: that she had wished passionately to retain the new equilibrium between them and to build on it, that after a lifetime of feeling emotionally and physically out of touch with him how much she had rejoiced in the delicate, exploratory tendrils which had bound them together in recent weeks. But in the sunlit day, walking a tense twelve inches apart from him across the bridge towards the South Mall, she could not bring herself to say any of this. The only thing she could say was the weak and terrible, 'I'm sorry, Daddy, I just couldn't.'

'Leave it with me,' he said, taking her arm to cross the

road. Elizabeth looked sidelong at him, desperately seeking clarification of what he meant, but his face was stern and inscrutable and she did not dare ask any questions.

Francey, his shaved head swathed in a pristine white bandage, was dressed and waiting for them when they got to the hospital. 'Did you bring me a present?' he demanded as soon as he saw them.

'No, now you be a good boy.' Elizabeth kissed him. Spoiled by the nurses and the other patients in the ward during his stay, he was going to be a handful.

The three of them took a taxi back to the house in Blackrock where Maeve made a tremendous fuss of Francey, piling cream on wodges of apple tart and in the wartime absence of lemons for her home-made lemonade, plying him with glass after glass of blackcurrant cordial made from her carefully tended bushes in the back garden.

'He'll get sick!' Corinne, having joined Francey and Elizabeth at the kitchen table, watched in fascination as her grandson, bandage gleaming like a beacon against the warm umber of the brick hearth behind him, scoffed plateful after plateful of the tart.

'No, I won't, Grandmother,' he said through a mouthful. 'I'se a big boy now and I loves it.'

'For goodness' sake, Francey, talk properly,' Elizabeth remonstrated.

'I am talking properly,' he protested, shoving another spoonful in on top of the last. 'That's the way everyone talks.'

'Beth, can I have a word?' Her father stood in the doorway.

'Will you stay with him, Mother?' Elizabeth got up from the table.

'Yes, dear, don't be long, will you?'

Although because of the present crisis, Elizabeth and Corinne appeared to have brushed their differences under the carpet, her mother's personality continued to grate against Elizabeth's to such a degree that she had to grit her teeth to avoid retorting that she and her son, who were clearly such trouble, would be gone shortly. 'I'm sure I won't, Mother,' she replied sweetly, following her father out into the dim lobby which led from the kitchen.

'Come into my study.' From the top of four steps which led into the hall proper, St John beckoned to her.

He closed the door and then went behind his enormous desk as though she were a client and he was about to have a consultation with her. 'What's the matter, Daddy?' Elizabeth was alarmed. What more could possibly go wrong?

Her father waited until she was seated across from him, then, steepling his fingers, he gazed severely at her across their joined tips. 'Don't ask me how I did this, but if you want to pay a short visit to young McCarthy before you go back to Lahersheen it will be all right. I don't know where I'm going to get petrol to go to Limerick, though. I've exhausted all my contacts. We'll have to take the bus or hire a hackney.'

Elizabeth was so stunned she could barely take it in; he had spoken so harshly he might have been telling her she was forthwith to join her lover on the gallows. Then she jumped up joyously. 'Daddy!' making as though to run around the desk to kiss him.

'Control yourself, Elizabeth!' The dourness of his tone strengthened.

'Yes, Daddy.' Demurely, Elizabeth sat down again. 'When?' she asked.

'At half past six this evening.' St John Sullivan looked at his watch. 'It's nearly one now. We'll take a taxi.'

'Thank you, Daddy.'

'I warn you, it will be a very short visit and heavily supervised. And,' he sighed, 'it's going to cost a fortune.'

'I'm sorry, Daddy.'

'Perhaps it might not be a good idea to mention this to your mother.'

'Of course not.' Elizabeth's heart began to thump with anticipation laced with fear at what she might see, her mental image of prisons being heavily conditioned by her reading of Victorian novels. As decorously as she could, she walked back to the kitchen and explained to her mother that in connection with Neeley's affairs, she and her father had to go together to his office.

'There's a lot to be done, Corinne.' St John spoke from behind her. 'We'll probably eat at the Oyster. Don't wait up for us, it might be midnight before we get back.'

'Can I come?' Francey shot to his feet.

'What a lovely idea!' Corinne smiled benevolently at him.

'No, lovey,' said Elizabeth hurriedly. 'Grandfather and I have very private grown-up things to talk about,' she appealed to her mother.

'I'm sure he'd love to come. Are you sure you can't take him, Beth? He'd love to play with all those lovely type-writers, wouldn't you, Francey?'

Her mother's plaintive tone again caused Elizabeth to grind her teeth. 'I'll tell you what,' she said, forcing herself to sound casual, 'I'll ask Maeve to keep an eye on him if you're too busy.'

'That won't be necessary, darling,' her mother said, getting to her feet with a sigh. 'Come on, Francey, I'll show you how to play a scale on the piano.'

The interior of the gaol was even more intimidating than Elizabeth had imagined. As she and her father waited in a small visiting room for Daniel to be brought in, she tried not to look at the thickness of the walls, at the uneven floor. She and St John were seated on hard wooden chairs at one end of a scarred table; they faced a single empty chair at the other. Behind that, a small stool had been placed to one side of the heavy iron door, presumably, Elizabeth guessed, for the guard or the warder or whoever in authority would be watching. The tiny barred window was placed too high up in the wall behind them to allow much light, so even on this magnificent evening a bare electric bulb, of such low wattage that its usefulness was in doubt, burned over their heads.

One of the legs on Elizabeth's chair was considerably shorter than the others – or the floor was particularly uneven under it – and every time she moved she thought she was going to over-balance. 'This is ridiculous,' she said eventually, 'they said half past six,' she looked at her wristwatch, 'and it's ten to seven.'

'Patience,' said her father. 'They're doing you a favour, kindly remember that.' It was the first thing he had said since they had been shown into the room.

The aroma of the place, a grim amalgam of disinfectant and damp stone overlaid with cooked cabbage, was overpowering. 'Ugh,' Elizabeth shuddered with distaste, 'how can the staff stand that awful smell?'

'I warned you!'

Elizabeth subsided, but the longer she waited the more edgy she became. By the time the door in front of them creaked open, she was so nervous she was almost unable to breathe.

Daniel stopped just inside the door, a succession of expressions flitting across his face. Dullness was followed by incredulity, followed again by joy. 'Elizabeth!' He seemed to be about to run forward and Elizabeth half rose, but he glanced at the uniformed man who had come in with him and checked himself.

'Oh, my God!' Elizabeth remained frozen in her stance, half standing, half sitting; Daniel was wearing handcuffs.

Beside her, her father got to his feet: 'I'm Mrs Scollard's father, Mr McCarthy,' he said in a formal tone. 'I'm also a solicitor.'

The use of her married name hit Elizabeth like a cudgel. Evidently, despite his initial generosity, her father was not going to make this easy. The knowledge of what she was up against steadied her nerve and she leaned forward on her hands, cutting her father out of her picture. 'How are you, Daniel?' Beside her, she felt her father resume his seat.

'I'm fine, Mrs Scollard,' Daniel replied and Elizabeth wanted to weep. Instead, she allowed all her nervousness to evaporate in a hot geyser of anger. She was furious with her father for his insensitivity, with Neeley for dying, with the police, with everyone who was conspiring to put herself and Daniel Carrig in this situation. 'Can he sit down?' She had to restrain herself from barking the request at the uniformed official.

'Go ahead.' The man nodded Daniel towards the vacant chair.

Elizabeth tried hard to control her temper while both Daniel and the warder took their seats. Daniel kept his cuffed wrists underneath the table. 'I got your letter,' he said hesitantly, his eyes flickering towards her father.

'I'm glad. I'll write to you again the minute I get back home.'

'When are you going?'

'Tomorrow.'

Silence descended on the little room and as fast as it had spurted, Elizabeth's anger drained away, leaving her limp and so sad she could almost taste the feeling on her tongue. *Oh, Daniel*, she cried silently, *come with me! Say this is not happening and come with me . . .*

'How's Francey doing?' It was he who broke the silence.

'Bold as brass,' she croaked. 'The nurses have spoiled him. He's all bandaged but he's going to be fine.'

'Tell him I was asking for him . . .' His voice trailed off.

'I will.'

'I never brought him to that match.'

'You will.'

This was dreadful, this was far, far worse than not seeing him at all. The handcuffs, the two of them caught between the twinned sets of spotlights burning in the eye-sockets of her father and of the warder.

Out of the corner of her eye, Elizabeth saw the warder check a pocket watch. Surely their time was not up? She gathered all her reserves and cut directly through to Daniel. 'Please trust me,' she said, her voice vibrating with conviction. 'I know things look dark, but I promise you, *I promise you* that they will turn out all right in the end. I *promise* you, Daniel.'

She took a deep breath before continuing – and then made up her mind. Now was not the time for the subtleties of sexual obsession versus love. She could continue with her internal dialogue on that at some future time. 'I love you with all my heart,' she whispered.

'We never had time to say that to one another,' she continued, ignoring her father stiffening beside her in his chair. She strained against the table and its edge cut painfully into her diaphragm. 'To say it to you for the first time in this stinking place is terrible, but I've no choice at the moment.'

At his end of the table, Daniel too was leaning forward, his dark eyes alight. 'Elizabeth—' he began but she cut across him.

'Hush,' she said softly, 'I'm not finished.'

She lowered her voice still further and in an effort to tunnel it secretly through the distance between herself and Daniel, narrowed its range, picturing it going through like a spear: 'We don't have much time,' she said, 'so I want you to remember this moment always.' Ceremonially emphasizing each word, she repeated the avowal: 'I love you, Daniel McCarthy.'

Before anyone could say anything else, the warder had come off his stool and was taking Daniel's arm. 'Time's up, son.'

Violently, Daniel tried to pull his arm away from the man's grasp but Elizabeth stood up swiftly. 'It's all right,' she said, 'go with him, it'll be all right.'

Daniel, who was a head taller than the warder and a lot stronger, allowed himself to be led to the doorway but despite the man's insistent pull on his arm, he had no difficulty in stopping just inside the open door and turning back to face Elizabeth. 'I love you, too.' He smiled with such radiance that, in Elizabeth's overactive brain, his whole body seemed to burn like a torch.

'Daniel—' She took a step towards him, but the warder pulled more strongly.

'Whatever happens, I love you too, *a ghlégheal*!' Daniel said again, his face and eyes blazing. He smiled for another instant, then turned and, with a little gesture of surrender to the warder, allowed himself to be taken away.

As the door closed behind him, Elizabeth listened for a

few seconds, trying to hear his footsteps. But all she could hear was the muffled clang as the warder and his prisoner passed through an iron gate or a door. She waited another second or two then turned blindly to her father and crumpled into his arms.

St John hesitated for a second or two and then stroked her head. 'It'll be all right,' he said awkwardly.

St John was tight-lipped on the way back to Cork and did not bring up the subject of Daniel until they were more than half-way back to Lahersheen the next day. Yet as they bowled along, the possibility of her father's disapproval of the scene in the gaol hung over Elizabeth's head like the blade of a guillotine and she was grateful for the presence of the revitalized Francey who, bouncing and chattering in the back seat, proved suitably distracting.

As they were crossing the mountains above Glengarriff, Francey at last fell asleep and St John cleared his throat. 'I've been thinking, Beth.'

'Yes, Daddy?' Elizabeth's heart rocked.

'I'm worried about you.'

'Don't be. Please, Daddy, I know what you're thinking—'

'I wonder, do you?' St John slowed the car to a crawl to negotiate an S bend. 'You truly believe in this fellow's version of what happened?'

'I do,' Elizabeth said passionately. 'Oh, Daddy, I do. Is there anything you can do to help?'

'Well, in court it seems it will come down to his word against the Guards' and from what I can gather, Beth, the circumstantial evidence is pretty damning.'

'Yes, but it doesn't add up to cold-blooded murder. Daddy, Daniel did not murder Neeley and that's the end of it. It was an *accident*.'

St John glanced sidelong at her. 'How old is he, this chap?'

'Twenty,' said Elizabeth.

'Perhaps this is none of my business, but isn't he a bit young?'

'You're right, it is none of your business.'

'Mind your manners. If I'm to help, keep a civil tongue in your head.'

'Oh, Daddy, I'm sorry.' Elizabeth knew she had gone much further than she should have. 'Are you really going to help?'

'I can't promise anything. But I'll have a word with a few of my colleagues. He has a solicitor already, there's a matter of professional ethics here.'

'Yes but with someone like you on his side – oh, Daddy, would you?'

'I'll see what I can do,' her father promised. 'At the very least, I'm sure we can get the charge reduced to manslaughter, but he may have to plead guilty. And then we can appeal for reduction of sentence.'

'But, Daddy, he's not guilty.'

'Elizabeth,' said St John patiently, 'the law deals in facts and evidence. The only evidence so far is not good: his gun. The row in the dance hall – to which there were, I understand, many witnesses; the damning fact that he ran away. Your – ah – interest in him . . .'

When it was put as baldly as that, Elizabeth's heart sank. 'Oh, Daddy!' she said despairingly.

'Don't be too downhearted,' her father said. 'I've seen many surprises in court. I'm not all that busy at the moment, I'll go to see him again in the next few days, all right?'

He would not be drawn any further then, but on leaving the following day to go back to Cork, he rolled down the window of the car: 'Please, Elizabeth, don't do anything rash – anything else rash – for your own sake, if for nothing else. I doubt if your mother and I could cope with much more!'

A week later, remembering her father's admonitions, Elizabeth wondered whether the expedition on which she was now embarked could have been called rash.

Having flailed around for days, alternately moping and panicking, she had overheard a conversation between Tilly

Harrington and Tilly's cousin in Eyeries about one of the area's tarot readers, an Englishwoman resident in Caherkeem across the bay. Before she knew it, she had grasped at the notion of having a reading done for herself. Anything, she had thought, which might give her some hope.

'Are you sure?' Tilly had looked doubtfully at her. 'You have to be careful with the tarot.'

'I think it's a great idea – and Mrs Charlton Leahy's brilliant!' Tilly's cousin, a motherly woman in her late fifties, was a devotee of the cards.

Elizabeth already knew Alison Charlton Leahy by reputation. Having come on holiday to Béara before the war, she had fallen in love with the area and with a Béara man but as she was a Protestant and, even after taking instruction, had refused to convert, she and the Béara man had to be married by special dispensation.

She was not the only one in the district who read the cards. Béara seemed to attract the more mystical type of foreigner and many of the 'blow-ins' had more than a passing interest in the paranormal and the occult. Although these practices were greatly frowned on by the Church – even the gypsies and fortune-tellers who set up shop during the bazaars and fairs were strenuously opposed – as Mrs Charlton Leahy and many others of her bent were not Catholics, there was little the clergy could do to restrain them, short of making their views known to their own flocks. Mrs Charlton Leahy was regarded locally as one of the best readers on the peninsula and despite the efforts of those who would put a stop to her gallop, had never been short of clients.

And so, on a blustery day, Elizabeth found herself being shown into the Englishwoman's warm, comfortable kitchen. 'Isn't it wonderful?' The woman beamed. 'Looks like the whole bally thing'll be over soon!' Elizabeth smiled assent. Béara, remote as it was from the action, was nevertheless buzzing from coast to coast with the excitement of the progress of the Allied invasion since D-Day just over a week previously.

A few minutes later, as she watched the woman

297

concentrate on the spread of cards on the table-top between them it struck Elizabeth that Mrs Charlton Leahy was as far removed from her image of a fortune-teller as it was possible to be. Thin and large-boned with wispy dark-blonde hair, mild blue eyes and extra-large hands and feet, this woman would have looked at home not in a Romany caravan but in one of those blurred society photographs at the back of the *Tatler*. Even the setting was far removed from what Elizabeth had imagined it would be: the cards were spread on an ordinary deal table in this ordinary farmhouse kitchen furnished with the usual dresser, crockery and fireplace. The only concession to Mrs Charlton Leahy's art was the small pot of incense burning at the end of the table. Mrs Charlton Leahy herself was wearing wellington boots.

As the time ticked by, Elizabeth became more and more nervous. She was concerned not only about what she might find out but also because half the parish probably knew within minutes of her arrival that she had come for a reading. Like a beacon, the Harringtons' horse and car stood outside the house. The weather had made it impossible to cross the bay by boat.

The long-suffering Tilly was waiting in the parlour.

'When's your birthday, dear?' Mrs Charlton Leahy did not look up from the cards; her voice was soft and breathy.

'The eighteenth of August.'

'Ah, Leo,' she said, 'it fits. Now, dear,' she continued, 'you must concentrate again just as you did when you were cutting and selecting the cards. This is not a one-way operation, your questions and comments are important to the accuracy of the reading. The more open you are to me the better my interpretation. All right?'

Elizabeth's stomach gave an unexpected leap. The palaver of cutting the cards three times with her left hand and all the rest of it had made her feel distinctly foolish, but she saw now that the woman was in deadly earnest and, for the first time, examined in detail the brightly coloured and ornate cards in front of her, many of which contained human figures. One, in the centre of the spread, seemed to jump off the table at her; as far as she could see it depicted

298

a man hanging by one ankle; she immediately connected it with Daniel.

'Don't take the cards out of context, dear.' Mrs Charlton Leahy had uncannily read her thoughts. 'The Hanged Man is not necessarily what he appears, it depends on where he appears and what's on either side of him. In many cases he signifies that you have accepted or will accept a difficult situation and make a sacrifice – an unselfish act. But this card is what we call "ill-dignified" dear, so I would say that this sacrifice you have made or will make is, unfortunately, not voluntary.

'But we're getting ahead of ourselves and as I said, I don't want to take this card out of context. When I go through it all, it will be clearer. But I will say that, by and large, while there are certainly difficulties – which of us hasn't difficulties? – this is an encouraging, positive spread, so don't be alarmed, all right?'

Elizabeth nodded and the woman looked shrewdly at her: 'Now I've got to say, dear, that of course I know who you are. You're that unfortunate girl whose husband was killed by a shotgun. Is that why you're here?'

'Well . . .' Elizabeth was loath to admit it but she need not have worried.

Mrs Charlton Leahy answered for her. 'Yes, it's here all right,' she said comfortably, 'the Tower signifies you've had an appalling loss and a sudden dramatic change in your life. But,' she went on, 'this card also signifies that in some way this has purged a situation which could not go on. Only you will be able to know how – and how you can turn it to your advantage. You see,' she glanced keenly at her client, 'all I will be able to give you is choices, my dear. The cards will tell you what is happening and what will probably happen; they will give you trends and directions and likelihoods – but you are in charge and it is up to you whether you wish to change your own destiny or not. And remember *you* chose the cards; outside your conscious mind you were *guided* to choose these particular cards and in this order. That's why I asked you to concentrate so hard and to pick only those cards that seemed to "speak" to you. But no matter what the cards say or how I interpret them for you, you do have free will, you must never forget that.'

'I understand.' Mrs Charlton Leahy's tone was so matter-of-fact that Elizabeth was regaining confidence. As the reading progressed, she forgot her nerves and became fascinated. She and Tilly had arrived at this woman's house without an appointment so unless she made it her business deliberately to find out everything about everyone on the peninsula, she could not possibly have known all that she was saying without there being some sort of extra dimension in operation. Elizabeth knew it was all too probable for Mrs Charlton Leahy to have heard about her first love and her first child not being her husband's – everyone on Béara knew that – but, in the same unjudgemental way, she seemed to understand a great deal about Elizabeth's loveless marriage.

She also sensed the situation with Daniel Carrig, referring unemotionally to that situation as 'a recent, unusual and very deeply physical relationship, strewn with obstacles'.

'How is it going to turn out?' Abruptly, the seat of Elizabeth's chair felt as though it had grown tacks.

Mrs Charlton Leahy hesitated. 'It's not that I'm avoiding your question, my dear, but it's a bit premature.'

'I see.'

Again the reader studied the cards: 'Yes,' she murmured to herself. 'The Four of Coins, ill-dignified . . . the Knight of Cups . . . the Moon . . . yes . . . the High Priestess . . . How do you feel about remarriage?' she asked suddenly.

Joy flamed through Elizabeth. This was more than she could have hoped for, everything was going to turn out all right. 'It's what I want, more than anything—' she began fervently but Mrs Charlton Leahy put a moderating hand on hers.

'It looks like there will be delays and difficulties,' she said, 'yes – delays.'

Of course! Elizabeth thought. She was officially in mourning and could not think of remarrying for at least a year.

Again, as if divining her client's thoughts, Alison Charlton Leahy made a curious damping-down gesture with one hand as though to cut across them. 'The obstacles are many, and perhaps not what you now think or see. But they are not insuperable. Again, this is up to you. The cards show that at present you have tremendous strength and courage. Wisdom, too,' she added, 'but you must stay alert. There is an indication here that you may not see danger before it is too late. Because, as well as the obstacles that are obvious and open, there are hidden ones too. This is very, very important for you to remember, you must stay fully vigilant. Perhaps you have a tendency in general to leap before you look?'

'That's true.' Elizabeth smiled.

The woman nodded. 'You see this card here? This is you – the Queen of Wands; and this person here – the Empress – her advice is to be listened to. She is protective of you, probably an older woman. Your mother?'

Elizabeth smiled involuntarily. 'Hardly,' she said, then immediately thought of Tilly. Mrs Charlton Leahy watched the succession of expressions. 'Well,' she said, 'you must watch out for what this woman will say.'

'How long before this marriage?' Elizabeth was more interested in Daniel than in Tilly.

The woman looked steadily at her. 'I asked how you felt about remarriage, my dear, because it looks like you will marry twice. And that one of these matches will be for commerce.'

'Twice?' Elizabeth was stunned, 'you mean my first marriage and now another one?'

'No, two in the future. One for commerce,' repeated Mrs Charlton Leahy. 'Now, remember, I told you you have free choice in all matters. But that's what is on the cards.'

'Which – which one will be for commerce?' Elizabeth was now totally drawn in.

'The first one. But in some way this first marriage will confer benefit on the second one.'

'Do you mean I'll marry for money?'

'You'll have the *opportunity* to marry,' corrected Mrs

Charlton Leahy. She studied the cards again. 'It's definitely commerce. I can't say whether it will be for money or not, but definitely some sort of business transaction.' Her pale eyes sharpened on Elizabeth's as though trying to see through. 'It appears it's imminent, my dear. Perhaps it's already happening? Are you sure this is not why you came to me? You're trying to make up your mind?'

Elizabeth was too overwhelmed to answer coherently. She sat back in her chair, trying to work this out. 'No,' she whispered eventually, 'it was not in my mind at all.'

But was that a true statement? Had she not, deep in her heart, been hoping that she and Daniel Carrig could become man and wife?

And then something else struck her. If the marriage was imminent that meant that Daniel was going to be released soon. But the happiness occasioned by this thought was short-lived: how could a marriage to Daniel be for commerce? And much more sinister, having married him, why would she want to marry a third time?

Unless he too was going to die —

Mrs Charlton Leahy's expression softened as she looked with compassion at her querent's all-too-evident consternation. 'Let me stress once again,' she said, 'that the eventual outcome of all of this is positive. You will go through difficulties and hardships – even tragedy, I'm afraid – but you will win through in the end. Love is very very strong in these cards, a love that won't be broken even if you try. I would go so far as to say it is in place now.'

'Why would I try to break it?' Elizabeth was incredulous.

'Only you can know that, dear . . .' Bending her head again over the cards and injecting reassurance into her voice, she repeated what she had said previously. 'Yes, very strong. And, incidentally,' she added jovially, 'there's travel here, too, across deep dark water.'

Elizabeth stared at her. Something about this was deeply upsetting, and it was all far far more than she had bargained for. Up to now, reading cards had been to her in the same league as divining tea-leaves, a practice that even

302

Tilly indulged in occasionally as a sort of parlour game and which dealt only in the vaguest of generalities. She had not been expecting to believe this woman or to hear such definite forecasts. It was all much too close to the bone and she giggled nervously. 'Deep dark water? That's probably the boat back to Lahersheen!'

Mrs Charlton Leahy did not even blink at the flat joke. 'Are you happy enough with the reading, my dear?' she asked, as though Elizabeth had not spoken. 'Would you like me to do another spread? No extra charge,' she added.

'No, thank you!' Elizabeth almost shouted it. The first reading had been alarming enough.

'Very well. Now, my dear, I've two dozen hungry pullets to feed.' The other woman got up and blew on the little incense pot. The substance glowed red and then expired in a plume of fragrant blue smoke. 'It's a pleasure to do a reading for someone so open and responsive,' she said. 'This, I gather, is your first time?'

'Yes.'

'Well, as you no doubt know, nothing in this life is accidental. People like me are never surprised when people come to us for the first time. Although querents, those asking for readings, generally do not admit to it they never come unless they are ready. There is tremendous change going on in your sphere at the moment, my dear, and it's not a coincidence that you came to me for guidance.'

Elizabeth paid her and calling Tilly from the parlour, Mrs Charlton Leahy ushered both of them towards the kitchen door. When she opened it, the blast of cold wet air from outside was a shocking intrusion into the warm scented cocoon they had just left. 'Now, remember, dear,' Mrs Charlton Leahy patted Elizabeth on the arm, 'I've only given you the information. Use it – it's like a road map. It's up to you which way you go.'

Chapter Sixteen

That evening something happened which brought the afternoon's tarot reading into sharp focus.

Helped by Mary and Margaret, she was clearing up after tea when Francey came running in from outside. 'Mammy, you're wantin'.'

'Wanted,' corrected Elizabeth automatically. 'And put your cap back on.' Francey himself had removed the bandage from his head but Elizabeth still fussed over him, insisting he keep the shaved part covered in case he caught cold. Wiping her hands on her apron, she went out into the yard.

Although it was still windy and unseasonably cold for June, the rain had cleared away. Mossie Breac, his cap in his hand, stood in the centre of the yard.

'Mossie.' Elizabeth smiled in welcome. His constant air of watchfulness bothered her still but since Neeley's death he had helped out greatly with the farm tasks and she could not be churlish.

'Evening, Lizzie,' he saluted her. 'Sorry to bother you . . .' He seemed unusually ill at ease.

'Not at all, Mossie,' Elizabeth said warmly. 'Will you come in? I'm afraid the kitchen is rather crowded at the moment.' Unlike many of the houses around, the Scollards' did not have a 'room'; the kitchen extended the width of the entire house.

'No, I won't,' although he was wearing his everyday work clothes his collar and tie seemed to be bothering him and he ran a finger under them as though to loosen them, 'thanks all the same. I just came by to tell you that your turf over at Derryvegill is grand.'

Elizabeth was puzzled. She already knew that the work

on the bog, which Neeley had dealt with before he died, was up to date. Perhaps Mossie was looking for payment for the work he had done since? It would have been unusual in an area where neighbours helped one another so readily but Elizabeth was still new to the role of head of the household and perhaps there were some customs with which she was not fully conversant. 'Thanks, Mossie,' she said carefully, 'I don't know how to thank you enough. I'm sure Neeley would have wanted me to show our appreciation in some real way. You wouldn't be upset if I offered you something to repay you for all your trouble?'

He was so scandalized – 'I wouldn't dream of it!' – that she moved swiftly to ameliorate the insult. 'Don't take it badly, Mossie,' she said, 'I'm still new to all this. You'll have to make allowances for me.' A gust of wind caught her thin dress and blew it up around her hips; she caught it just in time to preserve her modesty. 'Look,' she said, 'it's very cold out here. I insist you come in, at least have a cup of something. We've just got the new ration.'

He hesitated and she thought he was going to refuse. Then he seemed to think better of it. 'Thank you.'

Displacing Kathleen who had ensconced herself in the 'good' chair by the fire to read – since her father's death she had taken to burying herself in books, magazines, newspapers, any printed matter on which she could lay her hands – Elizabeth invited Mossie to sit down and busied herself scalding the pot. The other three schoolgoers were bent over their homework at the table and shooshing them to one end of it, she cleared a space and cut a piece of bread off a fresh loaf. Glancing automatically towards the fireplace to check on Abigail, she remembered that since Neeley's death she had moved the baby's cot into her own bedroom.

Racking her brains to think of conversation while buttering the bread, she remembered Mossie's grand-aunt whom she knew only vaguely. 'How's Bel these days?' she asked in an artificially cheery voice as, one on top of the other, she put two thick slices of bacon on the bread.

'She's grand,' Mossie again pulled at his tie, 'as well as can be expected.'

305

'They're saying the war's going to be over soon, by the looks of it.'

'I heard that.'

As she poured the water into the teapot, Elizabeth heard herself mouthing further inanities and wondered how long she could keep them up. She waited for the tea to draw – it seemed to take twice as long as usual – then poured it and handed him the snack on a small tin tray. She sat opposite him, hoping her demeanour was suitably hostess-like.

'You're not having a cup yourself?'

'No, thanks, we've just finished tea.'

Conversation died again.

Mossie took a mouthful from the cup. 'It's lovely to taste real tea.'

One of the children at the table moved in her chair, its wooden leg skreaking on the flagstones. Other than that, the scratching of pen nibs was the loudest sound to be heard. As the door was closed, even the wind outside was muted and the silence between herself and Mossie felt to Elizabeth like a heavy coat. 'Excuse me, Mossie,' she said, 'I'll put another few sods on the fire.' She took an unnecessarily long time over the task and when she turned back towards him, he was draining his cup. He stood up. 'I'll be going, so.'

'All right, Mossie, thanks again . . .' She hoped the relief did not show too much.

But just as she was about to close the door behind him he turned back to her: 'You're not going out anywhere later tonight?' His eyes wore that inscrutable, hooded look she remembered from Jimmy Deeney's dance.

'No, Mossie, why?' He was unsettling her.

'Someone I know wants to have a word with you later on.'

'Really? Who?'

'It's no one you'd know. Would it be all right if we came around ten or would that be too late?' he asked.

She was about to demur until abruptly she remembered the admonitions of the tarot reader about staying on the alert. 'All right, Mossie,' she said slowly. 'You're not going to tell me who it is?'

He hesitated and then smiling his crooked smile, replaced his cap. 'All will be revealed!'

As soon as she had cleared up again, Elizabeth put Francey and the two younger girls to bed, then went into her own bedroom to write that night's letter to Daniel. Now that her father, and presumably her mother, knew how they felt about one another, she was past caring who in the prison service read the letters.

All seven children were in bed and the kitchen shone with cleanliness when, a few minutes before ten, Elizabeth lit the lamps and sat down to await her visitors.

At five past, she heard the crunch of boots outside the door and went to open it.

Mossie's beaming companion was a sparrow of a man, perhaps not more than five feet tall, as narrow as Mossie was broad and lean as a whippet. Hair oiled, dapper in a navy blue suit and polished brown shoes, in the gloom of the dark evening he twinkled like a fairy light. Mossie performed the introductions. 'This is Johnny Thade, Johnny Thade Sheehan, a cousin of mine from Lacknaheeny beyond Adrigole – Mrs Elizabeth Scollard.'

'How do you do? Come in.' Elizabeth shook hands and stood back to let them go in ahead of her. 'You'll have something?' She went to move the kettle on to the stove.

'Actually, we brought something for you.' Mossie, she saw, was also wearing his good clothes; under the shadowy lamplight, the collar of his white shirt gleamed against his weather-tanned skin like fresh snow. Pulling a bottle of whiskey out of one pocket of his tweed greatcoat and a bottle of port from another, he placed them gently on the kitchen table. 'You'll have a glass of port wine?'

The formality of all of this was not lost on Elizabeth. The two were here to strike a deal of some sort. Mossie had been looking after the livestock since Neeley's death – perhaps he was going to make an offer to buy? Having discovered long ago that the grapevine in Béara was the fastest and most efficient in Ireland, she supposed she should not be too surprised that the whole parish probably knew that Neeley had willed the farm and the stock to her.

Her brain clicked like an abacus as she went to the dresser to take down three glasses. If Mossie wanted the cattle, he would also need grazing. It had already occurred to her that conacre might not be a bad idea and would give her at least some steady income. She could not expect her neighbours indefinitely to carry on with the farm work and, although she was becoming accustomed to it, Elizabeth had little appetite for looking after a household of seven plus a dozen or more demanding animals.

One thing she must not do, she decided, was to appear too eager.

Then something else struck her: if Daniel Carrig was to be a part of her future, what would he think? Would he want to work the land himself? 'Here we are.' She put the glasses on the table beside the two bottles.

Mossie made a small ceremony of pouring the drinks, the port first, then the whiskey, holding each glassful up to the lamplight as though to scrutinize the contents for impurities. Then, 'Your good health, Lizzie,' he raised his own glass, watching her over its rim.

'Amen,' Johnny Thade chirped up for the first time, *'go mbeirimid beo ar an am seo arís!'*

His piping voice exactly matched his physique, thought Elizabeth as she raised her own glass. 'Gentlemen!'

All three drank, then sat at the table.

'My condolences on your sad loss, ma'am.' Mossie's little cousin broke into the awkwardness which had enveloped them.

'Thank you.' Elizabeth took another sip from the glass. The port was warming and, even to her untutored palate, surprisingly agreeable.

'Good men are scarce.' Johnny Thade, merry eyes dancing, leaned forward for emphasis.

'They are.' Elizabeth wished the two of them would get to the point. She looked to Mossie. 'Well, Mossie,' she said briskly, 'thank you for the drink. What's on your mind?'

Mossie gazed steadily at her. 'My cousin has a proposition for you,' he said.

'Yes?' Elizabeth glanced back at the other man.

In response, Johnny Thade pushed back his chair a few inches and cleared his throat as though embarking on a recitation in a talent contest. 'When I say,' he began, his little chest swelling, 'that good men are scarce, Mrs Scollard, there is an exception to this rule. My cousin here, Maurice Breac Sheehan, is one such man.'

'So he is.' Intrigued, Elizabeth regarded Mossie, whose eyes were firmly fixed on his whiskey.

'No man the length and breadth of Béara is more honest, more dignified, more generous. And you may not know, Mrs Scollard, because Mossie's not one for blowing his own trumpet, that my cousin's a triumph of cleverality. In school, the master always said Maurice Sheehan was the best scholar on Béara. Oxford University, the Sorbonne maybe, the master said, if things in them days had only been different . . . Mossie Breac' – warming to his theme, Johnny leaned forward earnestly – 'is known within his own family and without as a good provider; careful, of course, but not mean. Ask any neighbour! A mean man, Mrs Scollard, is a sword in the side of nature.' He drained the whiskey in his glass. Mystified – what did all of this have to do with cattle and conacre? – Elizabeth refilled it.

Taking a sip of his fresh drink, Johnny Thade resumed his pitch. 'On our side we can furnish a certificate from the doctor that Maurice Sheehan suffers from no communicable disease. Seed breed and generation, the Sheehans were and are a healthy and prolific breed.'

At last the penny dropped for Elizabeth as Johnny Thade, surpassing even his own rhetoric, reached ever higher flights of eloquence in extolling the virtues of his cousin.

This was a marriage proposal and Johnny was the broker.

The situation was so preposterous she almost laughed out loud. 'I'm sorry to interrupt you, Johnny,' she said

gently, breaking in on the hyperbole, 'but am I to understand that you are acting as a matchmaker for Mossie?'

'This is not a professional matter,' the little man
answered, pulling his dignity round him like a shield, 'no
money has or will change hands between my cousin and
me. Mrs Scollard,' he was quivering with sincerity now,
'the Lord has sent you to each other. I hear you're a woman
with a problem. Well, my cousin here,' he indicated his
companion, 'is likewise a man with a problem. You see – '
Johnny put down his glass on the table and held both hands
in front of him, palms upward as though he were about to
juggle apples. First the right hand moved higher than the
left: 'You're a good woman with a darling farm and no
good man to work it for you . . .' The left hand caught up:
'Mossie's a good man with no darling farm to be worked
and no good woman to ease the ache of his lonely bed.'
Now he spread both hands wide in front of him as though
all the apples had fallen neatly into place: 'And as you
know, there was bad blood between yeer two families in
the olden times about this self-same land. This is a heaven-
sent opportunity to right this ancient wrong. You see?
What could be clearer?' Case proven, Johnny thumped the
table in front of him with both hands then picked up his
glass and took a large swig before continuing with his
enumeration of the advantages of the match, the tidy sum
Mossie had saved in the post office and would bring with
him, his skill with tillage and animals, the strength of his
physique.

Although she was aware that the object of all these
accolades was staring into the depths of his own whiskey,
Elizabeth, flummoxed, did not dare look directly at Mossie
but, like a rabbit transfixed by a snake, continued to stare at
Johnny Thade, who was apparently only getting into his
stride. 'Mossie Breac is, of course, of impeccable character,'
he uttered solemnly, 'moderate in drink and tobacco and in
the matter of morals, unbesmirched. No parish priest,'
Johnny cried, 'has ever had occasion to call, no girl's father
either; no girl has ever had to take the boat or be run pale-
faced to a convent. But let it be said,' he lowered his voice,

'at the risk of being indelicate, I can assure you, Mrs Scollard, that all apparatus is in perfect working order, if you follow me.' He paused to let the meaning of this last electrifying statement sink in.

'Now, what do you say?' Mossie's cousin sat back in his chair and, like a barrister who has moved his case to a point beyond all reasonable doubt, again thumped the table. 'Have we a match?'

Elizabeth had had enough. Pushing back her chair, she stood up and replaced the cork in the bottle of port. 'I'm sorry to disappoint you,' she said as civilly as she could, 'but I'm not considering remarriage at present.'

'Of course not, of course not.' Johnny Thade, undeterred, stood up too. 'All we're asking is indication of intent, if you get my meaning. 'Tis a betrothal we're after at present. With not a daisy showing yet above your poor husband, of course you could not contemplate a trip down the aisle. But there's no law of God or man which would rule out a promise sincerely given. And my cousin here is willing to bide his time.'

'I'm sorry, but the answer is no.' Elizabeth forced herself to remain polite. 'Thank you for coming and I'm honoured with the offer you've made me but I don't want to waste any more of your time.' Corking the whiskey, she extended the bottle to Mossie.

'You keep it, Lizzie.' It was only the second time he had spoken since sitting down. He was still avoiding her eyes. There was an odd tension about him which was not in keeping with the demeanour of a disappointed suitor. If Elizabeth did not know better, she would have thought Mossie had been expecting this. In defeat, he seemed not resigned but quiescent.

His cousin seemed equally sanguine. 'Yes,' he urged, 'keep the drink, Mrs Scollard, and now we understand each other, sure, maybe we'll talk again?'

Elizabeth had to bury any possible expectations. 'I don't think so,' she said firmly. 'Thank you for your interest but, as I said, I'm not even thinking about marriage.'

'Not at the moment, no.' The little man would not give

up. 'But can we have an understanding that we can come back? Surely the ice is broken?'

'There's no ice, broken or otherwise. Thank you for coming.' Elizabeth's tone brooked no further argument and this time Mossie's cousin took his cue. 'No harm done anyway, eh?'

'No harm indeed.' Elizabeth walked to the door and held it open.

Both men shook hands with her before they left. 'I'll be back, anyway, Lizzie, in the morning.' Mossie looked her full in the face then hesitated. 'The cattle,' he said slowly and then turned away. Left with the uncomfortable impression that he had been about to say something else, as she closed the door behind them Elizabeth was more than half convinced that she had not heard the end of Mossie Breac Sheehan's wedding aspirations.

And he might not be the last, she thought. There were many around here who would love to get their hands on thirty-five acres of usable land. If it had not been for the security of the children, she was beginning to wish that Neeley had not left her the farm.

Sleep evaded her as for hours that night the gnomic face and merry eyes of Mossie's cousin flitted in and out of her consciousness, the images interwoven with the mild, serious eyes of Alison Charlton Leahy. She strained to remember every word uttered by the tarot reader: *Obstacles, delays, a marriage for commerce . . . hidden danger . . .*

Clearly, the 'marriage for commerce' foretold by the cards had been the one she had just refused. And had not Mrs Charlton Leahy reiterated time and time again that she had free will and was entitled to make choices? Well, she thought grimly, her choice was definitely not to marry Mossie Breac Sheehan.

But, she thought, seizing on the hope, didn't the woman also say that this marriage would benefit her marriage to Daniel?

Next morning, tired and irritable, she was inclined to give short shrift to Mossie when, at about half past eleven, he again appeared at the door. Yet she could not be rude.

'Come in, Mossie.' She extended the invitation as curtly as good manners allowed.

The weather had improved in customary dramatic fashion, Francey and Johanna were out playing in the fields and the baby was having a nap. As Mossie came into the quiet kitchen, she noticed again the added tension that, from time to time recently, she had seen in him whenever she happened to meet his eye.

Refusing her automatic offer of refreshment and her invitation to sit down, he remained just inside the door, spreading his feet a little apart as though steadying himself. As she stood expectantly waiting for him to say something, Elizabeth noticed that his tanned face was unusually pale.

'I've something to say,' he said then without preamble. 'I've asked you to marry me – and I think we both know that I did it honourably.' His eyes, fixed on some point beyond Elizabeth's shoulder, assumed the remote look she was beginning to know. 'I'm asking you again now. Lizzie, will you marry me – please? I've been fond of you for a long time.'

The blood in Elizabeth's arms turned as cold as lake-water. 'I'm sorry, Mossie,' she said as calmly as she could, 'but I'm afraid the answer is still no. I'm grateful for all your kindness since Neeley died, there's no taking away from that – and I'm flattered by your offer—'

'Will you think about it?'

Although she did not want to be brutal, she decided there was no point in giving him any false hope. 'I don't think so,' she said gently. 'I'm sorry.'

He looked her full in the face and Elizabeth was shocked at the strength of the momentary blaze of hurt in his eyes, but it was so fleeting that a second later she thought she might have imagined it. Because now she saw a transformation. Mossie's expression froze and he seemed to grow in stature: the man who stood before her now was no supplicant.

'If you'll excuse me—' she began nervously but he cut her off.

'I think if you would allow me, I could persuade you,' he said levelly.

Elizabeth felt that, subtly, he now had the advantage. 'I told you —' she began.

'Perhaps if I put it to you another way,' he interrupted. 'I think it would be to your advantage to listen to me.'

'I'm sorry, Mossie.' Elizabeth tried to win back the high ground. 'I'm going to have to ask you to leave.' She gained strength. 'What do I have to say to make you understand that no means no?'

He stared at her. 'If I were you I'd listen.'

As she was again about to protest, he walked past her and, as she gaped at him, sat in the chair beside the fire. 'Once more, Lizzie,' he said, gazing into the hearth, 'I'm giving you an opportunity to agree. We still have time on our side.'

With this, Elizabeth knew real fear. This calm, authoritative person was not the Mossie she had thought she knew. She had tended to dismiss him, seeing him to be like many another bachelor or spinster forced to eke out a lonely existence in the hidden country places of Ireland. This, she now saw, had been a mistake. Mossie's complex personality, hitherto revealed only in snatches, was not to be patronized.

'You'll never persuade me to do something I would find so distasteful as to marry someone I didn't – I mean, the likes of you —' As it left her lips, she knew the insult had been a mistake.

'Is that so?' The legs of the chair groaned on the stone under them as he made a sudden movement as though to jump up. But he stayed where he was. Even by the relatively limited light of the kitchen, she could see the colour drain even further from his face. 'The likes of me, is it?' he said softly. 'You weren't always so particular, Miss Solicitor's Daughter from Cork City.'

'Get out!' Elizabeth breathed.

He turned so that he was fully facing her. 'I've tried to do everything reasonably, by the book. But you won't have that, will you?' He added, 'With your airs and graces, your soft frocks and your silk stockings, you won't have no truck with the *likes* of me. The peasants were always beneath you, weren't they, Lizzie?' He smiled. 'Saving for one only, of course . . . Maybe two? Or maybe more which the *likes* of me is too stupid to know about?'

Elizabeth, responding to the ring of truth, sat down speechless in the nearest chair, which was the one just at the window. Mossie leaned forward so far that he was almost bent double in his own seat as he regarded her from under his eyebrows. 'My family broke their backs on this land you now call yours,' he said, his voice throbbing, 'and a blow-in like you can't have any idea what it's like for me to live on a few hopeless scraws of rocks and rushes, and to see you, who wouldn't know a whin from a holly bush, sitting on this warm farm which is rightly mine and which is now going to go to rack and ruin because you won't dirty your hands to work it.'

Elizabeth saw that his hands were shaking with passion. Somehow, she found her voice. 'That was all a long time ago —'

'This farm is *in my blood*! . . . It's in my blood,' he repeated more quietly. Then, 'I wouldn't expect you to understand.'

In the hiatus, Elizabeth gathered courage. 'It's the land you want to marry, not me,' she said.

'Is it?' he asked softly, the expression in his eyes again remote.

'It seems perfectly clear to me,' she was gathering strength, 'and I think that it is a despicable reason for marriage. What do you think this is, the Middle Ages?'

'I knew someone like you couldn't possibly understand what land means to us,' he said. 'But when it comes to it, there's no one without their soft spot, their Achilles' heel, is there?' She tried to outstare him without success as he locked eyes with her: 'For instance take yours. Yours is the opposite sex, isn't it, Lizzie?'

She sprang from her chair as though to claw at his face but he was too quick for her, intercepting her rush and catching her by the wrists. Although he had remained seated, his grip was immensely powerful. And as Elizabeth stared down at the eyes below her own, grey as flint, she knew it was useless to remonstrate or to deny what he had said. Although she was finding it difficult to draw her breath, she hung on to what dignity she could salvage. 'You're entitled to your opinion, Mossie, but if I may point out, this is not the route to take if you're trying to persuade me to marry you. I'm sure you will understand that after this I would not marry you now if my life depended on it. And I'd thank you to let me go. You're hurting me.'

'You might marry me, after all, when I've finished my say.' He held his lock on her. 'I'm not finished.'

Slowly, he released her wrists then looked down at his hands as though they did not belong to him. 'This is not the way I'd have wanted it. But so be it . . .' He sighed and then became businesslike. 'Sit down there now and listen, because you might hear something to your advantage.'

Rubbing her wrists, Elizabeth was about to shout that she would do nothing of the sort when Mossie added, 'And to Danny McCarthy's advantage too.' Heavily, she subsided in the chair opposite his. She tried to say, 'I'm listening,' in as icy a manner as she could summon, but nothing came out.

Mossie waited a second or two. Then, when it was clear to him that she was not about to object, or even to respond, he spoke in clipped tones. 'I was on the mountain that night. I saw what happened.'

Tersely, as Elizabeth's heart crashed harder and harder into her ribcage, he outlined what he had seen.

'But that's exactly what Daniel has told the police,' she cried. Then she stopped dead. 'Why are you telling me only now? Why didn't you come forward?' Again her anger surmounted her confusion. 'You could have saved him from all this torture.'

'Maybe.' Mossie remained calm, but she could sense that underneath he was as taut as a violin string.

'We'll have to go to Castletown right away – we'll get the Harringtons' cob—' Then she saw the expression on Mossie's face. 'There's more, isn't there?'

'Yes,' he said. 'No point beating around the bush. I'll

go to the police and tell them what I saw *if* you agree to marry me. If you don't, I won't.' Mossie exhaled as though the words had released a rush of dammed breath.

'That's outrageous!' Elizabeth could not believe what she had heard. 'I'll go to the police myself, they'll force you to tell the truth.'

'Will they? You remember Jimmy Deeney's dance, Lizzie? The dance where you used me as though I was some kind of puppet in your play?' He shook his head as though the memory was buzzing around it like a vengeful wasp. 'But no matter about that now . . . In my hearing,' he went on, 'you yourself threatened to kill your husband. And not only in my hearing. What you may not remember is that another man heard you quite distinctly. That man happens to be a second cousin of mine. And, of course, everyone at that dance knows why you said what you did. Because your husband was objecting to your mad dash to throw yourself at Danny McCarthy.' Elizabeth felt like an animal caught in one of his snares as he continued without mercy. 'How does it look? You threaten to kill Neeley because he is preventing you from dancing with your fancy man and next thing . . .'

He paused to let the import of what he was saying sink in, then, 'Who do you think the Guards'll believe? You and Danny McCarthy? Or me and my second cousin and three-quarters of the parish?'

He got up from his chair. 'I'll leave you to think it over and I'll not come near this house again until you send me your answer.' He looked away from her now and said almost casually, 'But don't worry about the farm. I couldn't bear to see you let it go down, I'll still work the cattle for you.' He picked up his cap from where he had placed it by his chair and went to the door. Before stepping outside, he turned round, his broad shape blocking out the sunlight in the door frame and leaving his face in shadow. 'Remember, Mrs Scollard, I did try to do this the honourable way.'

Elizabeth's cheeks felt so cold they were numb. 'What about the law?' she whispered. 'If I called you into court as a witness you'd be under oath —'

'I'm surprised at you, Elizabeth. Fancy lawyers, fancy law the English left us! This isn't the city now – or haven't you learned anything since you came here? Necessity knows no law. There's *land* involved here.'

Elizabeth knew then that he really would perjure himself – and was prepared to let worse happen. Her breath was coming in painful gasps. 'But if I'd said yes last night,' she said, 'you would never have told me. You were going to let Daniel rot in gaol – or even hang.'

Taking great care, he put on his cap. 'Probably not,' he said, 'but you'll never know, will you?' The lines of his face relaxed into sadness. 'You see,' he said, 'I wanted you to marry me for me and not for him. You never know, we might have had as good a chance as most . . .'

He looked away from her and out into the golden day. 'But that's another story and it can't be helped now.' He shook himself like a dog rising from a sleep. 'My family always had that land,' he added then, so quietly she barely caught it, and, 'Don't forget – send me your answer.'

After he had left, Elizabeth's first instinct was to run across the fields to confide in Tilly Harrington. But she held herself in check. She needed to think this out.

Mossie's personal interest in her was a revelation – how could she have been so blind? Yet she had always suspected that something of that nature underlay the way he had looked at her over the years.

On the other hand its unveiling was so sudden that she was finding it difficult to work out the exact equation of her own attraction versus the farm; Mossie had told the truth when he said it was virtually impossible for her, not experiencing it in her blood as he claimed he did, to empathize with the peasant passion for land.

Could he have meant it when he vowed he would perjure himself?

For the sake of thirty-five acres?

Elizabeth knew the answers before her brain had had time properly to formulate the questions. And to strengthen his so-called case, Mossie clearly felt the land was rightfully his by birth.

318

She paced the kitchen, forcing herself to think intuitively, to try to put herself inside Mossie's mind and motivation. The only point of reference she could use to understand such an obsession was her own. The image of Daniel, his curly hair, his straight back, the remembered sensations of his mouth, the feel of his skin, rose powerfully before her. When it came to sexual attraction, as she had demonstrated only too well, she had a habit of bulldozing through all morality and reason. If Mossie's need for the land, so ingrained and of such long standing, was as pressing as her own desire for Daniel, he would probably go to almost any length to fulfil it.

Could she manipulate her attraction for Mossie in some way? Manage events so that he would agree to exonerate Daniel while dropping his demand that she should marry him?

Then, remembering how cheap she had felt after she had seduced Neeley to get him to go to the dance, Elizabeth rejected this option: she could not bear to feel like that again.

And yet . . . it was Daniel who was at stake here. Again she tried to put herself in Mossie's shoes. If he was prepared to go to any lengths why shouldn't she?

She stood stock still in the middle of the kitchen: could she not just *give* him the land? Then, solicitor's daughter as she was, Elizabeth knew that, even after the matter of Neeley's estate was settled and although no one could have stopped her, she could not give away the farm over the heads of Neeley's children.

She could sell it?

But Mossie would never be able to come up with the money.

For a nominal amount?

Then how would she and the children live?

Could she offer Mossie an agreement? Put it in writing that if he came forward to save Daniel, she would ensure that, by some means short of marriage, he would have rights to the farm?

Could she conacre the whole lot and give him lifetime

access? But even as she thought this she knew it was hopeless. Ownership, possession, was what attracted Mossie.

Could she go to the Guards herself and try to persuade them of the story? But if Mossie denied it categorically as he had said he would, she had no chance at all of being believed.

For the rest of that day her brain tore into the situation and when the children came home from school she was in such a nervous state that she could not help but harry and harass them so that by tea-time Kathleen had retreated in high dudgeon to the bedroom, Francey, Goretti and Johanna were huddled mournfully in one corner of the kitchen and Margaret was hiding behind her homework. Even the normally placid Mary had been reduced to sniffles.

Elizabeth caught herself just as she was about to launch another offensive on how lazy and useless they all were. She gazed around the kitchen at the havoc she had wrought and was overcome with remorse and guilt: not one of these children had done anything to merit such treatment. What's more, having suffered grievously, they deserved not an assault, but loving support and understanding. 'I'm sorry,' she cried, 'I'm sorry.'

'That's all right, Mammy,' said Margaret, looking nervously around at the others, 'we understand.'

'Here —' Recklessly, Elizabeth took the remainder of the sugar ration off the dresser and dumped it into a skillet. 'We've all had enough hardship to do us for a lifetime. The hell with it, we're going to have custard.'

As she broke the eggs into a bowl, they all crowded around her. They had not had custard, which they all loved, since the previous Christmas.

To go with the treat, she made a large bread pudding, the familiar ritual helping to keep her wild thoughts at bay. She was determined to make up to them for her previous behaviour and made a supreme effort to be calm and loving.

When the unusual meal was ready, even Kathleen was prevailed upon to join them at the table.

'What'll we do for sugar now?' asked Margaret, looking at the steaming dish in front of her. 'It's all gone.'

Elizabeth spooned up a mouthful of the soft sweet pudding. 'This war can't last much longer,' she said, 'it'll have to be over by Christmas. Everyone says so.'

'Yes,' Margaret persisted, 'but what are we going to do for the rest of this week?'

'What would you think about us getting a few bee-hives?' Elizabeth asked, spooning some of the custard into Abigail's eager mouth. 'Do you remember last summer I got some from a man over in Derryconnla? He'd help us, I'm sure. And if we had our own honey we wouldn't need sugar.' This diverted them all to such an extent that Elizabeth could retire from the discussion.

As she watched and heard the talk about bees and honey raging up and down the table, it was brought home to her that she was now solely responsible for all these young lives. Her manic twisting and turning in an effort to find her way out of Mossie's snare had been selfish: this farm and this landscape were all that these children had known; they were their security, the constants in their cruelly changing lives, and she could not be the means of whipping it away from them. She would not be able to live with herself should she cause them any more suffering than they had undergone already.

So, just as she had known several times in the past – as when she had threatened to leave Neeley – she knew that she was trapped.

With the knowledge, however, came the return of reason.

At about eight o'clock that evening, leaving Mary in charge, Elizabeth set off to see Mossie Breac Sheehan.

The boreen which led to the house of Mossie's aunt was too uneven to take her bicycle with any degree of safety and she was forced to dismount. Leaving it in the ditch, she paused for a second or two to collect her thoughts. In the pocket of her cardigan she carried two pieces of foolscap with which she planned to bargain for her future and for Daniel Carrig's.

Within the past few days, the fuchsia had come into full flower on Béara; the high, untrimmed hedges on both sides of the boreen in front of her were thick with tiny lanterns, its rutted green floor starred with red and purple. But Elizabeth, thinking hard and unheeding of the show, pulled absently at the flowers beside her, squeezing buds until they popped, shredding blooms already open. She pricked her finger on a thorn and as a trickle of blood ran crimson into the pinker shades of the ruined petals, she mentally rehearsed how she was going to handle the coming scene. She had to be assertive but, more than that, she had to be precise.

Dropping the flowers, she sucked her finger until it was no longer bleeding and then set off down the lane.

Mossie's house was like their own, two storeys and solidly built. The small farmyard was clean and tidy; marigolds, wallflowers and bachelor's buttons bloomed in neat beds under the boundary walls. Elizabeth had time to absorb little else about the surroundings as the top of the half-door to the kitchen was open.

Mossie's aunt Bel answered her knock almost immediately. 'Good evening,' Elizabeth said, 'I was wondering if Mossie's here – I don't know whether you remember me, ma'am? I'm Lizzie Scollard.'

'Indeed I remember you, come in, come in . . .' Bel's back was humped and twisted from arthritis. With gnarled fingers, she undid the latch on the door and opened it. 'That's a beautiful evening, thank God,' she said, 'and I'm sorry for your trouble, Lizzie. I wasn't able to go to the church, but, sure, wasn't Mossie there? I believe Neeley had a great send-off.'

'Indeed he did. Are you the gardener, ma'am?' Elizabeth, having no desire to get involved in the long gavotte of ritual sympathizing, indicated the flowerbeds in the yard.

'Not any more, girl, not since the rheumatics. Mossie has to see to it. But he's a good lad.'

In a pig's eye, thought Elizabeth but let it pass. This was not poor Bel's business.

'Yes,' Bel went on, 'Mossie always had green fingers, you know, everything grows for Mossie.'

'Indeed,' Elizabeth said, trying not to sound tart, 'is he in?' She was surprised that she did not feel in the least nervous.

'He's about the place,' said the old lady, shuffling painfully across the kitchen, 'and Johnny Thade with him.' Scrabbling at the catch on a window she succeeded in opening it. 'Mossie!' she quavered in her high, cracked voice.

For the first time since leaving her own house, Elizabeth's stomach fluttered with anxiety as she heard a faint answering call.

'He'll be in presently,' said Bel. 'You'll have something?'

'Thanks, but I'm not stopping. I just want a quick word with Mossie and then I have to get back to the children.'

'Musha, the poor fatherless crathurs!' Tortuously, Bel lowered herself into a large chair padded with worn cushions.

'I'll go out and catch him on the way in,' said Elizabeth.

'Grand. You'll forgive me if I don't get up to see you out.'

'God bless now . . .' Glad to escape, Elizabeth wondered what Mossie had had in mind for his aunt. Did he propose to bring her along with him? The woman was clearly in no state to look after herself.

Seeing Bel's incapacity had stiffened her resolve still further. As she waited outside in the yard, she saw Mossie approaching from across the rushy field beside the house and thanked God that Johnny Thade was not with him.

'I wasn't expecting you so soon,' he said, indicating his earth-stained work clothes as he came within earshot. 'I was trying to drain a ditch.'

'No matter,' Elizabeth said curtly. 'Is there somewhere private we can go?'

'The house is small.'

323

'Outside will do.' She looked around. 'Over there.' She pointed towards an old garden bench placed in a sunny position beside a shed.

'Have you thought about my proposition?' he asked when they were seated. Although the words indicated he might have been talking about an offer for a calf, Elizabeth sensed his stress.

To let him suffer, she took her time before replying. Then, clutching the pages within her pocket to give her courage: 'I have a proposition for you.'

'I'm always open to propositions,' he said wryly.

Elizabeth ignored him. Now that the moment was upon her she was finding little difficulty in proceeding. She pulled both pieces of paper out of her cardigan pocket and checking them, selected one and smoothed it out on her lap; as she did so, it struck her briefly how incongruous this bower was as a setting for what she was about to say. The side of the shed behind them, facing south and sheltered from the prevailing wind by other outhouses, was covered with creepers, including two varieties of small old roses in riotous full bloom. 'I want tó read something to you,' she began, glancing at him to see how he was reacting.

But if Mossie was surprised at seeing her document, he did not show it.

'I've thought this out carefully,' she continued, 'and it is not negotiable. Do you understand?'

He nodded imperceptibly.

Elizabeth raised the paper off her lap. '"For the present,"' she read, '"you, Maurice Sheehan, may work the Scollard farm as you choose, but since my children and I have to have an income, it will be on a conacre arrangement at a fair price. And after a period of fifteen years, when my youngest child has left school and is independent, I will make out a will which bequeaths the land to you. You will therefore own it outright during the remainder of your lifetime but on your death, the land reverts to Neeley's family. You will so bequeath it in your own will. Both wills, yours and mine, to be drawn up at the same time by a solicitor of my choosing, namely my father."'

324

She looked up. 'Is that clear?' she asked.

'Perfectly.' Mossie's expression was inscrutable.

'Do you agree?'

'No.'

'Why not?' Elizabeth, who had more or less been expecting this rejection, hence her second piece of foolscap, endeavoured to sound outraged.

'Your document says nothing about marriage.'

'I thought it was the land you were interested in—'

'That, too.'

Eye to eye, they studied one another and feeling she had once again under-estimated Mossie, Elizabeth was first to give in.

'That land belongs in my family,' Mossie said softly as she dropped her gaze to her lap.

Elizabeth admonished herself that, at all costs, she must not become angry. 'I am not a fixture on my thirty-five acres,' she said.

'That land belongs *in* my family,' he repeated.

Elizabeth, conceding defeat, did not even glance at him as she opened up the second piece of foolscap.

'"I will marry you on several conditions,"' she read, in as formal a tone as she could muster. '"Naturally, it will not be until the proper period of mourning is over which will be at least one year from now. The second condition,"' she took another deep breath and the paper on her lap trembled slightly, '"is . . . you agree that I will be your wife in law only and not in any other way, you will remain here in your house and I will remain in mine."'

Beside her, he made a small movement and she heard his intake of breath but plunged on. '"The third condition is that you will never, ever speak to anyone about the reason I married you. Not anyone. Given the unusual circumstances in which we will live, people will speculate, of course, but you must live with this and never break silence about it.

'"But under this agreement, I have the right to tell a small number of people I think have the right to know, but I guarantee not to disclose anything at all unless the party concerned undertakes in advance to give his or her solemn word also to maintain secrecy.

'"What's more, no one is to know we are even betrothed to marry until the banns are called. And that will be not earlier than one year and one week after Daniel McCarthy is released from prison.

'"The fourth condition is that I may lead my life as I choose without let or hindrance from you. In return for all of this,"' she was reading faster now, '"I will bequeath the land to you on condition that Neeley's children will always have a roof over their heads and in the meantime, between now and the time the banns are called, you may have the use of the land on conacre as I mentioned in the first document.

'"If you break any of those four conditions,"' she stopped reading and at last looked up, 'any one of them, Mossie – if I find you skulking after me around the countryside, for instance – you will never, I swear it, own one inch of that place. Not one inch. And, of course, it is all entirely dependent on you going to the Guards first thing tomorrow morning and clearing Daniel's name.'

A large bee lumbered noisily past Mossie's face but he did not blink nor make an attempt to swat it. 'One year and one week?' he said softly. 'You're a solicitor's daughter all right. And what guarantee do I have that you won't change your mind after he's out?'

'You've none,' Elizabeth replied, 'only my word – and these bits of paper. But I suppose they'll have some validity in law. I'll sign them and get them witnessed.'

'Witnesses? I thought no one outside this select few was to know?'

'Our signatures only will be witnessed.'

Again he studied her. 'You can tell people but I can't?'

'The people I have in mind are people like my father – and . . .' she hesitated for the first time.

'And Danny McCarthy,' he said quietly.

'I told you,' she went on doggedly, 'that I will tell *no one* who does not, in my opinion, have a *right* to know about our agreement. If that is not strongly enough worded in the document, I'll change it to your satisfaction. Is there anyone on your side who would have a right or a need to know?'

'What do you think, Elizabeth? Do you think I want it advertised that I had to coerce someone to marry me?'

She was savagely glad to recognize that at least he had the grace to feel some shame. 'This document,' she said curtly, 'will be signed *after* you've been to the Guards.'

'After I've been to the Guards?' He smiled his crooked smile. 'Elizabeth, do you think I came down with the last shower? I'll sign it *before* I go anywhere near the barracks – along with another one, which will guarantee that you will keep your word to marry me in a year. A formal betrothal document, Elizabeth.'

Elizabeth knew the implications of this full well: if she reneged on her promise to marry him he could win an action against her for breach of promise.

'I told you none of my terms are negotiable.' She folded the two pieces of paper and put them away again in the pocket of her cardigan.

But Mossie's determination matched hers and, with the image of Daniel dangling at the end of a hangman's rope never far from her mind, he succeeded in wearing her down to the point where she eventually agreed to compromise. 'All right,' she exploded. 'I agree to sign your bloody document. But don't even talk to me again. Ever.'

'I'll have to, if, as you demand, I'm to work the land on conacre for more than a year.'

'And I want everything on that land, every last rake and harrow, enumerated and written down so you can't cheat me or my children.'

Mossie looked sideways at her. 'You don't have a high opinion of me,' he said after a pause.

'What?' Elizabeth laughed in disbelief. 'What would you think, Mossie, if the situation were reversed? Blackmail is not an honourable occupation.'

'Is adultery?'

His swift response unnerved her but still she refused to back off. 'You could have no idea—'

'Couldn't I, now?'

'I didn't mean—'

'Oh, yes, you did, Elizabeth. But it's of no consequence. What matters to me is something a lot more permanent than a few turns in a hayloft – or even on the top of Knockameala. Neeley would have understood.'

'He would have understood blackmail?'

'I think in this instance, yes.' Looking off into the distance, he spread his hands on his knees. Elizabeth, seeing the roughened nails and skin, knew he was quite right. She did not understand and never could. But she was not giving up the fight. 'You've said that before,' she said, 'you're arrogant into the bargain.'

'I think, Lizzie,' he said quietly, 'if that's the case, you're my match in that department. And if you lie down with dogs, you'll rise with fleas.'

She stood up and looked at him with contempt. 'Anything to get your hands on a few miserable sods of earth.'

'I'll earn it with my sweat. I'm not the first and I won't be the last to go *cliamhain isteach* into a farm on Béara.' This was one phrase in widespread use that Elizabeth understood: it referred to a man marrying into a place where the woman was owner. 'Let's get this over with,' she said bluntly. 'You write out your paper and I'll sign it now. But there has to be a clause in it which invalidates it if you do not go to the barracks.'

'All good relationships are based on such mutual trust.'

Looking at his ironic smile, Elizabeth almost admired him. In the past she had certainly been smugly blind to Mossie Breac Sheehan's shrewdness and intelligence. 'Where's your cousin?' she snapped.

'Back at the ditch.'

'Get him, we'll need him and your aunt as witnesses for my document. The Harringtons can witness yours. Bring it over to my house later on. The Harringtons don't go to bed until about twelve.'

'Anything you say, Your Majesty.' He pulled an imaginary forelock. 'But won't they ask questions?'

'They will see the signatures only and as far as prying is concerned, is it customary for farmers in this parish to let other farmers in on their financial business? That much I *have* learned.'

'You've everything covered, haven't you, Elizabeth?' Mossie seemed to have something in his eye. 'Before we conclude our business,' he said while rubbing at the irritant, 'I want to assure you that Neeley's land will be well taken care of. You won't need any bits of paper to have my guarantee of that.'

'Just tell me one thing,' Elizabeth injected as much distaste as possible into her tone, 'I'm just curious. Why did you wait for so long before coming forward to reveal what you saw that night?'

He left his eye alone. 'You wouldn't believe me if I told you.'

'Try me.'

'Not yet.'

Leaving Elizabeth in turmoil – she did not know whether she should be furious at his self-confidence, fearful of her own situation, or rejoicing that Daniel would soon go free – he departed in search of Johnny Thade.

As soon as Mossie rounded a corner of the outhouse and was out of sight of Elizabeth Scollard and everyone else, he collapsed backwards against the creeper-covered stone, sank to his haunches in the shadow of a rainbarrel, covered his face with his hands and wept.

Chapter Seventeen

The next eighteen hours seemed interminable. For the second night in a row, Elizabeth hardly slept at all and, in the morning, practically sleepwalked her way through the breakfast routine.

Tilly, arriving for a chat just after half past eleven, found her nervy and hollow-eyed. 'I suppose there's no use my asking what's the matter?'

'Oh, just the usual!' Savagely, Elizabeth banged a broom off the flagstones of the kitchen.

'Who's that?'

'What?'

'Whoever you're killing with that brush.'

'Sorry, Tilly. I'm just in bad humour, I'm not sleeping very well. I suppose it's all catching up with me.' Elizabeth stood the broom in its corner. 'Have you heard anything?' She could not help asking; there was a fair chance that Tilly, her house being that much closer to the crossroads than the Scollards', might have heard rumours about developments in Daniel's case before they reached her.

'About what?'

'About Daniel Carrig's case for one thing,' Elizabeth replied, too defiantly.

'There's definitely something going on here that I don't know about.' Tilly sat down at the table.

'That's typical!' Elizabeth rounded on her. 'Why must you always think there's something going on? I wish everyone would just leave me alone.'

'That can be arranged,' said Tilly slowly.

'Oh, I don't mean you.' Elizabeth was instantly contrite. 'I really don't. Forgive me?'

'Do I have any choice? Do you want to talk about it?

330

Did that Charlton Leahy woman upset you in some way? You haven't been the same since – oh, good morning, Sergeant!'

'Morning, Mrs Harrington, Mrs Scollard.' The sergeant removed his cap as he stood on the threshold. 'Could I have a word, Mrs Scollard, do you mind?'

'Come in, Sergeant.' Now that it was here, Elizabeth did not know whether to laugh or cry.

The sergeant, who was tall and rangy, seemed to take all the oxygen out of the room as he stepped through the doorway. 'We won't be long, Mrs Harrington . . .' he said and Tilly, taking the hint, got up from her chair.

'I'll come back in a little while, Lizzie.'

After she had left, the policeman took out his notebook. 'May I sit down, Mrs Scollard?'

'Go ahead.'

Elizabeth sat opposite him as, with maddening slowness, he leafed through the pages in front of him. At last he looked up. 'I'm sure you know why I'm here.' He said it so suddenly that he might have been trying to trap her but she could not read his face. After her last encounter with this man, however, Elizabeth's defences were already as high as she could erect them. She did not flinch. 'I presume it has something to do with my husband's death?'

'You might say that.'

'Has something happened?'

'Apparently,' the tiny emphasis on the word was enough further to jangle Elizabeth's nerves, '*apparently*,' he repeated, 'there was a witness to the incident.' His pale eyes were so devoid of expression they might have belonged to a cod on a fishmonger's slab.

'Really? That's great news. Who was this witness?' Elizabeth felt that if she moved a fraction of an inch, her back would splinter in a thousand pieces.

'One of your neighbours. A man named Maurice Sheehan.'

'Mossie? Oh, yes. He's been very good. Helping out with the cattle and all that.'

'Apparently, he saw the whole thing. Or so he says.'

'Well, that's wonderful, Sergeant,' said Elizabeth firmly.

'It's a little curious, is it not, that he is only coming forward now, several weeks after the event . . .' he turned the pages of his notebook again, 'twenty-six days to be precise. Why do you think it took this man twenty-six days to come forward?'

'I have no idea, Sergeant. Why should I know?'

'Strange, is it not?'

'I'm not a native of this place, Sergeant, as you know. I'm still learning the way things happen here. Perhaps he was afraid to come forward?' Necessity had honed Elizabeth's brain so it felt as sharp and thin as a rapier.

'Why would that be?'

'Perhaps he thought *he* might come under suspicion?' Elizabeth folded her hands in her lap and waited.

'Perhaps.' The sergeant put his notebook back in the breast pocket of his tunic and rose from the table. 'Well, I'll be on my way.'

'Thank you for coming and letting me know, Sergeant.' She rose and was on her way to the door to show him out when he stopped her, his eyes like crystals. 'Are you interested at all in what this Maurice Sheehan says he saw that night, Mrs Scollard?'

Too late, Elizabeth saw the trap. 'Of course I am, Sergeant,' she said, 'what did he tell you? Why was he up there anyhow?'

'It seems half the countryside wanders that mountain after dark,' said the policeman drily.

'Surely not, Sergeant. I know Mossie — Maurice has traps up there and one or two of the men lamp rabbits or shoot foxes —'

The sergeant seemed to tire of the skirmish. 'Well, Mrs Scollard,' he said, 'it appears Maurice Sheehan's version of events is the same as yours — and the young man's, of course. As a matter of fact, there is remarkable unity in all three accounts.'

'That's wonderful news.' Elizabeth refused to allow him to rattle her any further. 'As I told you before, I never did believe my husband was murdered.'

332

'Yes,' said the sergeant slowly, 'so you said. At any rate, Mr Sheehan is now prepared to come forward as a witness in court to state this on oath.'

'Thank God!' Elizabeth, hoping she had struck the balance between surprise and relief, turned her back to him under the pretext of checking the fire in the stove. 'Excuse me a moment, Sergeant, I'm planning to bake bread. When is the court case likely to be held?' she asked over her shoulder. 'Of course, I'd like to be there if possible.'

'Of course. The book of evidence is already in the hands of the State Solicitor. I gather that the plea is now guilty to manslaughter. In light of this new development, and since a jury won't be necessary, I would imagine the case will be brought either at the next sitting in Bantry or, if everyone's ready, next Tuesday at Ballyfee. That'd be the twentieth.'

Elizabeth closed the fire door of the stove. 'What is this likely to mean? Is Daniel – Danny McCarthy – going to be freed?'

'That depends on the way things go in court,' said the sergeant. 'After all, a man was found dead by means of McCarthy's gun.'

'But surely if it was an accident –'

'The Gardai's responsibilities lie in gathering evidence. After that it is up to the courts.'

Elizabeth knew better than to betray herself any further. 'Thank you for letting me know,' she said distantly, standing very erect and looking off through the door.

'It's only natural you should take a keen interest, Mrs Scollard. You'll probably be getting a witness summons yourself.'

'When is Sergeant Coyle coming back to Eyeries?' Even in the knowledge that she was being reckless, she could not let him away with being so hateful.

'I understand he is making a good recovery, but the leg is broken in three places and he won't be back for another couple of months.'

'We miss him.'

'I'm sure you do.'

Elizabeth maintained her show of composure until she

had latched the door behind him. Then the tension snapped and she leaned against the wall. Without knowing it, she had been holding her breath and it released itself from her body in a long thin stream. She remained at the door until a few minutes later when she was roused by a determined banging against it. 'Let us in, Mammy, let us in!'

Wiping her eyes, she opened the door again to find, standing on the threshold, Johanna and an indignant Francey. 'You locked us out.'

'You locked us out,' echoed Johanna.

'No, I didn't.' Elizabeth laughed and swept the two of them into her arms in a fierce hug. 'Come in, come in, my little pets.'

'What's going on? We saw a policeman.' Francey struggled against the embrace. Sometimes, Elizabeth thought fondly, letting both children go, her son sounded older than her father.

'The sergeant was just paying us a visit, lovey,' she said. 'There's nothing wrong, everything's under control.'

'Are we going to be 'rested?' Johanna sounded not at all worried, merely interested.

'No, of course we're not going to be arrested. Now,' Elizabeth said brightly, blowing her nose, 'who's for a currant bun?'

'Me! Me!' they both shouted and at the same time Abigail began calling from her cot in Elizabeth's bedroom.

By dinner-time the news of Mossie's coming forward was all over the parish. 'Is it true?' Tilly burst into the kitchen where Elizabeth was presiding over the children's meal.

'Is what true?' Calmly, Elizabeth wiped Abigail's mouth.

'Don't be irritating, Lizzie, you know what I mean. The sergeant was here, wasn't he?'

'You saw him yourself. If you mean has Mossie Sheehan come forward,' Elizabeth relented, 'yes, that's true.'

'So it looks like Daniel's going to be all right?'

'If it was up to that Clancy, I wouldn't be too sure. Oh, Tilly, he was horrible.'

334

'Bad cess to him, anyway. But surely, now, with Mossie going into the witness box . . .'

'I hope so,' said Elizabeth. 'But, Tilly, if you never prayed before, you've got to pray now. The court case could be as early as next Tuesday.'

'I'll wear out me knees!' Tilly promised. 'Isn't he an awful so-and-so all the same?'

'The sergeant?'

'Mossie Breac. Why'd he wait for all this time?'

'Afraid, I suppose, you know how people hate going to the civic Guards.'

'Maybe. But all the same . . .'

Privately, as Tilly continued to speculate about why Mossie had waited so long, Elizabeth wondered how her friend was going to take the news that she was going to marry him. She could not summon the courage just yet to say anything about it. One thing at a time, she thought. And who knew what might happen in the year before the banns were called?

The following Tuesday, Elizabeth, in the staunch company of the Harringtons, travelled on the *Princess Béara* to the market town of Ballyfee.

They went immediately to the courthouse to ascertain the time the trial would begin; to allow enough time for him to make the journey from Limerick, Daniel's case was called for the afternoon session. It was just before dinner-time and as the three of them stepped inside the door of the courtroom, the judge, cutting across the mumbled speech of the young barrister before him, checked his watch and adjourned until two o'clock. After he had swept out, Mick checked with one of the Gardai who in turn checked with the clerk; the cases were running a little behind schedule. Daniel's was unlikely to be called before three.

They went then to meet Elizabeth's father in the restaurant of the local hotel. St John was not on Daniel's legal team but, true to his word, had lent it the benefit of his considerable experience and expertise. And since Mossie Sheehan's revelations, he had tried also to use his influence on the prosecuting side so that Elizabeth, who had been summoned as a witness for the state, would not be called unless something went seriously wrong. 'I think it's going to go all right,' he said, taking a spoonful of Brown Windsor soup, 'and I'm glad we've got Eager.' Eager was the name of the judge hearing the case. 'There's no guarantee, of course,' he added.

Elizabeth, who was too nervous to eat, refused the soup and only toyed with a piece of overdone mutton when the main course was served. Valiantly, Mick and Tilly kept the conversation going. The *Independent* that morning had been full of Hitler's latest weapon, the V-1 rocket. '"Doodlebugs", they call them,' said Mick, 'and they fly all by themselves. Shocking!'

As her father, who zealously followed the progress of the war on wireless news broadcasts from the BBC, took up the subject, Elizabeth paid little attention. She had spotted Daniel's parents eating at a table in the far corner of the dining room. Should she go over to them? But what would she say? She had met them only once or twice, and although she had heard that they were present among the huge crowd at Neeley's funeral, had not seen them at all since Daniel's imprisonment.

Covertly, she watched as, with eyes downcast and without speaking to one another, they ate quietly and tidily as if they felt they might litter up the dining room. They looked so lonely and bewildered that, not for the first time since becoming emotionally involved with their son, Elizabeth felt a dart of guilt. And no matter which way the case went, God alone knew how they were going to pay Daniel's legal bills.

She could not bear to watch them any longer. 'I'm not hungry,' she said, laying her knife and fork across the untouched meal. 'It's stifling in here, I'm going out for a breath of fresh air.'

'Do you want me to come with you?' Tilly pushed back her chair.

'No, you stay here and finish your dinner. I'd like to be on my own for a bit, if you don't mind, Tilly – collect my thoughts, so to speak.' As she escaped from the dining room, out of the corner of her eye she saw both McCarthys stop eating and watch her go. She had little doubt as to what they must think of her.

Apart from having the distinction of playing host to a cattle market once a month, Ballyfee's main claim to fame was its small ruined castle, once a minor seat of the O'Sullivan clan. The edifice, its ramparts and blind windows redundantly vigilant in the direction of the sea, rode a knoll at the top of the town. Most of the shops were closed for dinner hour and, after a few minutes' aimless wandering up and down the main square, Elizabeth set off to climb the overgrown pathway which led upwards to the castle. Half-way up she found she had to push her way through rampant elder which threatened to obscure the path altogether. Although she had tasted and enjoyed elderberry wine, she knew that to pick the flowers was considered unlucky. She hesitated. Suppose she snapped some of them off inadvertently? Telling herself she was being ridiculous, she took great care none the less as she made her way through the flat creamy clusters.

When she got to the escarpment in front of the castle, she discovered half a dozen cows. The tufted, rocky ground was treacherous with cow dung which, being in the shadow of the castle with mud so churned up by the cattle, probably never dried. Elizabeth, who did not want to ruin her good shoes, was just about to trek down again when, far below, she saw a car and a motorcycle turn a corner together and, sweep into the square. Although she was too far away to see any markings, she knew instantly that these were the Gardai arriving from Limerick with Daniel. As she watched, the two vehicles slowed down and nosed their way through the crowded square, then turned in through an archway beside the courthouse and vanished from her view.

It was only then that the full import of what might or might not happen in the next few hours was borne in on her. Daniel – only a few hundred yards away now – might this very evening be freed. Or, as her father insisted on pointing out, depending on the judge, he might be facing a long sentence of imprisonment in that horrible place in Limerick, the memory of which haunted her. He might even be remanded again, there was no telling. Ignoring the danger of ruining her good mourning clothes, she sat down abruptly on a tussock beside her. Her instinct, which she knew was misplaced, was to fly down to him immediately, to force her way in to see him. Instead, like the tourist she was, she looked around her. As a distraction, however, this proved futile because she knew that Daniel, of all people, would love it up here, would relish the feeling of space and airy solitude.

From where she was sitting, which was the highest point in the rolling countryside, she could see for miles in all directions except for what was obscured by the stone walls of the castle to her right. Compared with Lahersheen, this landscape was mellow. As it was dinner-time, few humans were about but cows grazed peacefully or chewed the cud in fields, some green, some faintly gold, parcelled out between trim hedges and running right down to the water. In a paddock to her left, two sleek horses stood nose to tail swishing flies off one another under the shade of a wych elm, and in the pasture just below the spot where Elizabeth sat, a donkey, eyes blissfully closed, scratched his chin against a gatepost.

Between where she sat and the town, which was to her left, ran a crescent of sand against which the sea broke in long white chains. The beach was occupied but not crowded: children ran in and out of the waves or bent industriously over enterprises that Elizabeth could not identify; a few adults threw a rubber ball around among themselves in a game of 'Donkey'. It was all so far from the dark and turbulent goings on in her own life that for a minute or two, she longed for such normality.

She stood up. 'Feeling sorry for ourselves again, are we?' she said aloud. Then, remembering the last time she had spoken like that on top of a hill, looked shamefacedly around her. She need not have worried: the only reply this time was the rhythmic tearing of grass as the cows in her vicinity fattened themselves.

Slowly, she retraced her steps, dragging out the time, becoming jumpier with every footfall.

It was twenty minutes to two by the time she got back to the hotel. She could see no sign of Daniel's parents but her father and the Harringtons were waiting for her in the lobby. 'We might as well go over.' St John buttoned the jacket of his suit and picked up his briefcase. Winter and summer his clothing never changed: a good three-piece suit, an old-fashioned shirt with a high collar and a carefully knotted tie. Her father's predictability, which had irritated her when she was younger, cut now like the beam from a lighthouse through the fog of Elizabeth's worry and confusion and, impulsively, she kissed his cheek. 'Whatever happens this afternoon, Daddy, I just want to say thanks.'

Surprised and embarrassed, he rubbed the spot she had kissed. 'Yes, well, if we're to secure our places in the public gallery, we'd better get a move on.'

The courtroom, which could hold a maximum of forty or forty-five people, including Gardai, legal representatives and the court officials, was already filling up when they got inside. 'Not too long now.' Tilly gave Elizabeth's hand an encouraging squeeze as their party of four squashed in together on one of the scarred wooden pews which served the public.

Elizabeth had been in a court before – her father had taken her now and then as a child to see the cutting edge of his business – but she had never seen such a run-down decrepit room as this, in which the dun-coloured walls were patchy with mould and damp, and all the mismatched furnishings were the leavings of somewhere else. Even the bench, raised high on a rickety platform and which more resembled a sideboard than a table of jurisprudence, might have been salvaged at some time in the last century from the dining room of an Ascendancy house – and a run-down one at that. The place smelt of cats.

At the other side of the tiny aisle which ran between the rows of public seats, she saw that the McCarthys, parents, brothers, sisters and others she assumed were relatives, had squeezed themselves into a compact mass at the front. Elizabeth was glad to be behind them and hoped fervently that Daniel's parents, at least, would not turn round and catch her eye.

'All rise!' Just after two o'clock, the judge swept in, the babble of voices died away and the proceedings began with the resumption of the speech by the unfortunate young barrister who had been prematurely cut off before dinner.

As the lawyer mumbled and fumbled his way through his presentation, Elizabeth, who was sitting on the outside of her row, could not concentrate on what he was saying. Thinking every sound behind her was Daniel being brought in, she craned around continually from her seat to check.

On one such occasion, her eyes met not Daniel's but Sergeant Clancy's. She let her gaze sweep past him and along the row of Gardai, defendants and witnesses who were lined up along the wall. Another time, the arrival was Mossie Sheehan from whose presence she instantly turned away.

There were many adjournments and remands and case followed case at a speed which would have dismayed her had she not been familiar with the anticlimactic way in which routine Irish law was conducted. She studied the judge, trying to weigh up how he would feel about Daniel's case. He seemed to be in his late fifties or early sixties, with a dyspeptic complexion and a habit of fiddling with his half-glasses when irritated – which was frequently. Any barrister who dared talk back to him got short shrift. On the other hand, he dealt kindly and respectfully with an elderly widow who was alleged to have assaulted a neighbour over the matter of an ancient right of way.

The next time Elizabeth turned around in her seat, she looked straight into Daniel's eyes. His face lit up when he saw it was she but she had to bite her lip before managing an answering smile. Although shaved and neatly dressed, his body seemed to have caved in on itself in the short period since last she saw him; his complexion was pasty, he had lost weight and, emphasized by the severe prison haircut, the bones at his cheeks and temples jutted prominently. He was handcuffed to a man in uniform, whom

Elizabeth judged to be a prison officer, and was put sitting between this man and a Garda on a wooden form at the back of the room.

During the next ten minutes, she frequently turned round to smile encouragingly at him. Quelling her own nervousness, she willed strength from her body into his. But her stomach heaved when, at long last, she heard his name called. It was just after ten minutes past three.

The atmosphere in the courtroom changed noticeably as Daniel walked to the front of the room and stood at the ancient dock which was little more than a modified lectern surrounded by a set of rails like stair banisters. Although the circuit court at Ballyfee handled all sorts, a case such as this, which was widely bruited to have resulted from a crime of passion, was sufficiently rare as to be a source of public entertainment.

Elizabeth greatly resented the sudden charging of the air, the attentive stillness all around her as Daniel took the oath. Although he stood tall and straight while repeating the words after the clerk, to her ears his voice sounded weak and strained. She clenched her fists in her lap. Beside her, Tilly noticed and made a small gesture of 'thumbs up'.

The barrister representing the state rose first and asked to approach the bench. After a few moments of murmured consultation, the judge asked Daniel's barristers to come up as well. Elizabeth, trying to distinguish individual words, sat forward tensely in her seat; she could hear nothing, however, except a general baritone hum leavened now and then by sibilances.

As the consultation between the huddle of men continued for what seemed like an interminable amount of time, her sense of frustration grew to the point when she felt she wanted to scream. Then the prosecuting barrister left the group, and while the others – augmented by every eye in the courtroom – watched, he bustled to the last of the public benches and whispered something in Mossie Sheehan's ear. After a minute or so, Mossie nodded uncertainly and half stood up from his seat but the lawyer pushed him gently back. Elizabeth's internal scream continued to swell as if a series of organ stops were being pulled fully out. But she managed to contain her voice to a strident whisper as she leaned across Tilly and Mick to ask her father if he could throw any light on what was going on.

'Sshh.' St John put a finger to his lips. 'Eager's a fair man, it's looking promising.'

As the barrister, gown flying behind him like the wings of a crow, walked the short distance back to his colleagues in front of the judge's bench, Elizabeth glanced back at Daniel. He was staring straight ahead. Following his gaze, she saw that his eyes were fixed on a point somewhere above the window on the wall opposite the dock. As clearly as though it was herself and not he who was up there, she felt his humiliation at being publicly exposed like this, particularly in front of his own family and neighbours who, sitting only seven or eight feet away, were close enough to observe every nuance of shame in his expression.

She could not bear to look any longer and closed her eyes.

She heard Mossie's name being called, his quiet footsteps on the boards of the floor, then his voice repeating the oath.

As Mossie recounted the beginning of the story she knew so well, Elizabeth did not open her eyes even to see which side was taking him through it. The thin skin of her eyelids was jumping and in her ears, the thudding of her heart sounded like the waterwheel she had once been brought to see as a child. She groped for Tilly's hand and, when she found it, gripped it so tightly she could feel Tilly's bones give.

Then, almost unconsciously, Elizabeth, who paid only lip service to prayer and religion in general, began to pray and inappropriate or not, the prayer which rose to her mind was the Magnificat. Over and over again, she thought of the first few lines, building them into the rhythm of the waterwheel, to the jumping in her eyes.

My soul doth magnify the Lord. And my spirit hath rejoiced in God my Saviour. For he hath regarded the humility of his handmaid: for behold from henceforth all generations shall call me blessed . . . My soul doth magnify the Lord, My soul doth magnify the Lord . . .

Fiercely, she concentrated, blocking out everything except this pouring out of supplication.

Because he that is mighty hath done great things to me: and holy is his name. And his mercy is from generation unto generation, to them that fear him. He hath showed might in his arm: he hath scattered the proud in the conceit of their heart. He hath put down the mighty from their seat: and hath exalted the humble.

She felt Tilly's hand squirm in her own and released it. But this battle between herself and her concentration had become vital. She felt that if she could concentrate hard enough she could influence the outcome of what was going on.

And his mercy is from generation unto generation.

The hesitant undertone of Mossie's voice broke through, competing for her attention and, redoubling her mental efforts, she batted it away. *Mercy, mercy, mercy . . .* she repeated it like a mantra.

Mossie finished his evidence and, stony-faced, left the witness box and went back to his seat. Elizabeth stared straight ahead as he passed where she was sitting.

Now the barristers were again consulting with the judge in whispers, a torture that went on for minute after agonizing minute.

Then they returned to their seats and the judge, seeming to be in no hurry, spread out a number of papers out in front of him on the desk, scrutinizing one after the other. In the hushed, stuffy room, the rustling of the pages was as loud in Elizabeth's ears as the rattling of loose roof slates on her house under the winter wind.

The judge made notes. He reached for a carafe and poured water into a glass; he took a thoughtful sip as he opened yet another file.

As the tension honed itself to knife-point, Elizabeth felt that if she made the slightest move or gesture, some cosmic equilibrium would be shattered and the entire place would blow up.

Then, just when she thought she would have to leave, Judge Eager looked up from his desk and peering across his half-spectacles towards the dock spoke to the defendant in a conversational tone as though he were chatting at a dinner party. He told Daniel he was convicting him of manslaughter and sentencing him to seven years, but that in light of the unusual circumstances he was suspending the sentence. He warned him to be of good behaviour and added that he was lucky to have such good neighbours.

Next case.

Elizabeth heard only as far as the phrase 'seven years'. And just as on the occasion of the visit from the curate and the sergeant when she had been told of Neeley's death, the people and objects in the room around her began to grow and shrink with alarming rapidity. She closed her eyes to stabilize herself and to take in the enormity of what was happening. Then Tilly was shaking her. 'Lizzie, Lizzie! Oh, my God, oh, my God!'

'What?' She opened her eyes at last. 'What?'

'Haven't you been paying attention? Oh, Lizzie!' Tilly put her hand up to her mouth so that Elizabeth did not hear the rest of what she said.

She looked round. People were talking excitedly to one another and the judge was banging his gavel repeatedly on the surface of the bench in front of him.

'SILENCE!' The roar from the court clerk, a very small man, would have done justice to the ringmaster of a circus.

Elizabeth risked a glance at Daniel. Looking into the body of the courtroom towards his parents, he seemed disoriented and physically uncomfortable as though he did not know what to do with his hands; he rocked slightly as though to take a step and then seemed to think better of it.

'What's happening?' Elizabeth leaned out and addressed her father.

'Aren't you pleased, Beth?'

'What? Pleased with *what*?' Her voice rose and again the judge banged his gavel.

'SILENCE IN COURT!' roared the clerk.

Then Daniel's senior barrister walked forward and shook hands with his client.

'Is he being let go?' Stupidly, whispering now, Elizabeth looked from Daniel back to her father.

'Ssh!' St John stood up to leave and, as Mick and Tilly followed suit, 'We'll talk outside.'

Elizabeth was reluctant to leave and as Tilly hustled her the short distance towards the door she looked back at Daniel who, still in the dock, was gazing uncertainly in the direction of the Gardai and prison officers who had brought him into the courtroom. She tried to catch his attention but both Tilly and her father were intent on bundling her outside and she had to heed her footing.

Just outside the door, Elizabeth's father was diverted and engaged in conversation by a friend from the legal confraternity while Mick Harrington could not wait a moment longer to light a cigarette and turned away from the prevailing breeze, cupping his hands over a match flame.

'Oh, Lizzie.' Again taking Elizabeth by the shoulders, Tilly half shook, half hugged her. 'Your daddy's so pleased. He says even he didn't really expect this. I don't know whether I should laugh or cry.'

'He's being let out? I thought the judge gave him seven years.'

'It was suspended, you goose!' Again Tilly hugged her.

'Suspended?' Elizabeth repeated. Half strangled by Tilly's arms, she hardly dared believe it, a light, bubbling feeling expanding in her until she thought she might float away. 'He's free? He's really free?'

'Yes!' Tilly shot a look at her husband who, always uneasy when exposed to the excessive emotional outpourings between women, had strolled over to examine a display of second-hand farm implements outside a blacksmith's forge a few yards away. 'Lizzie,' Tilly begged in a more circumspect tone, 'take things easy now, won't you? Won't you promise me?'

Elizabeth did not get a chance to reply because at that point, surrounded by his family, Daniel emerged into the sunshine.

Tilly put a warning hand on her arm but the restraint proved unnecessary, because when Elizabeth saw him, rather than running towards him as five minutes beforehand she might have expected she would, she shrank backwards a few steps. It was not only because she felt that she was being watched, by Daniel's party as well as her own, but also because it seemed as if the situation was too momentous to handle in its entirety but must be taken on in smaller, more manageable pieces. His release, so desired, so much hoped for, had come too suddenly and thoroughly.

The centre of his ecstatic, back-slapping group, Daniel, his pallor even more striking in the outdoor brightness, still looked dazed. He responded to all the congratulations with a hesitant smile and allowed his hand to be shaken as though it really did not belong to him. He turned to his mother, a small thin woman wearing an old-fashioned brown costume and cloche hat, and the look that passed between them as he put both arms around her made Elizabeth shrink back even further.

As Mrs McCarthy raised her arms to reciprocate the embrace, she stood on tiptoe and Elizabeth saw that the soles of her brown shoes were so new that the leather was still fawn; it was this detail which closed the damper on her own joy. What right did she have to bring shame on this good woman, on this family? At the same time, selfishly, she yearned for such a moment for herself. Such a tender moment between herself and Corinne would have been impossible to contemplate.

Then, over his mother's head, Elizabeth saw Daniel's searching eyes and knew he was looking for her.

At the same time she saw Mossie Sheehan come through the thick oak doors of the courthouse and take a few steps towards the voluble group of McCarthys; before reaching them, however, he stopped as though changing his mind.

Well he might be unsure of his welcome, thought Elizabeth bitterly as she turned and grabbed Tilly's arm. 'Come on, Tilly, please.' Trying to do it as inconspicuously as possible, she began to pull the other woman towards Mick and away from the scene.

Although she allowed herself to be moved, Tilly protested, 'What about your father?'

'He'll find us. I just have to get away.'

'I can't understand you, Lizzie Scollard,' Tilly hissed just before they came within earshot of her husband, 'you're a mystery to me. You'd try the patience of a saint.'

'I know,' Elizabeth hissed back, 'I'll tell you later. And anyway, I'm only doing what you wanted. You said I should take it easy, well, I am taking it easy.' Then, to the long-suffering Mick Harrington who had progressed from the forge to the greengrocer's display next door, 'I'm sure you're parched, Mick, let me buy you and Tilly a drink.'

The causes of Elizabeth's hasty departure were too complex for her to sort out without some serious thought: she had not wanted to give Mossie Sheehan the satisfaction of being publicly proven right about her and Daniel, but they went deeper than that. On one level, all her instincts told her that her first meeting with Daniel should be private, but on another she had been greatly shaken by the scene she had just witnessed between him and his mother. Because of her own uneasy family relationships she had not seriously seen until now what effect her love for Daniel had and would continue to have on other people, innocent people whose lives were full of self-sacrifice and loyalty. She needed time to sort all this out before she and Daniel fell unthinkingly again into one another's arms.

But this was not to be.

St John Sullivan found them in the lounge bar of the hotel and the four of them were settling in to their drinks at a table in a corner when the McCarthys arrived *en masse*. Elizabeth, who was sitting on the inside of her own group with her back to the wall, shrank down in her seat. The ever observant Tilly, who was sitting opposite her, noticed the movement and turned round to see what had caused it. When she turned back, she frowned at Elizabeth as though to say, 'Pull yourself together.'

Elizabeth's father was engaged in explaining to Mick Harrington how the legal processes had worked in the case and Elizabeth leaned forward, desperately trying to concentrate. Luckily, the bar, walls decorated with mahogany panels and flock wallpaper of deep crimson, was dark and crowded, their own corner was largely hidden by other people, and, as yet, none of the other group, still laughing and chatting vigorously, had noticed their presence.

All during her father's lengthy, detailed explanation, Elizabeth kept sidelong watch over the activities of the McCarthys. Daniel's father went up to the bar to order as the rest of them settled themselves in a compact horseshoe shape over an L-shaped banquette and some small stools, just inside the door, Daniel, who found a place on one of the stools, had his back to the room.

There was no way out of the place, she saw with growing nervousness, without running the gauntlet.

A few minutes later, it was one of Daniel's brothers, the one a year or so older than him, who spotted her. Out of the corner of her eye, she saw his head jerk in recognition and then, as he told the others, she saw the whole group fall silent and look across towards her corner.

She saw Daniel rise and thread his way across the floor of the lounge bar towards where she was sitting. He seemed to be moving unnaturally slowly, as though swimming underwater, and the sounds around her, her father's voice, the chatter and laughter and clinking of glasses, the busy movements of the two attendants behind the bar, merged and softened into one another until they, too, seemed to be filtered through gurgling liquid. And all her doubts and panicky analysis were tempered until she was left with the single certitude of his coming towards her. Seeing her expression, her father twisted round in his seat and so did Tilly. Mick Harrington lowered his head.

'Hello, Daniel.' Her instinct was to stand up and receive him; instead, she stayed where she was.

'I'm so glad you were here, Elizabeth,' Daniel said simply. He turned to Elizabeth's father. 'Mr Sullivan, I'll never be able to thank you enough. My own solicitor told me how kind you've been.'

'Justice was done.' St John cleared his throat.

'Can I have a word with you?' Daniel turned back to Elizabeth.

'Of course.' But it was still too soon for her: she could not yet face what she was sure would be the hostility of Daniel's relatives, and she was still none too confident that the hostility was not justified. 'Are you going home on the steamer?' she asked.

'My parents hired a hackney. I'll be going with them.'

'Then come round to the house this evening?' His eyes, so dark in his pale face, were gazing at her with such force that she was having difficulty hanging on to whatever shreds of sense she had left. 'I've invited Tilly and Mick up, too.' Tilly, to whom this was news, made an abrupt movement in her seat but Elizabeth ignored it. 'We're all delighted at the way things turned out,' she continued desperately. That was completely the wrong thing to say: how could she be delighted that her husband was dead?

'Thank you, I'll see you then, so,' Daniel said, then turned to her father. 'And thank you again, Mr Sullivan. My family and I are truly grateful to you.' The little speech was so old-fashioned, Elizabeth half expected him to bow.

Daniel's family, who had been watching throughout the conversation, continued to watch as he made his way back to them.

'The three of us should leave,' said Elizabeth urgently to Tilly and Mick, 'if we don't want the boat to go without us. And, Daddy, you probably want to get on the road.' The boat was not due to sail for more than an hour, but perhaps, she thought, if all four of her party trooped out in phalanx, it might make it a little easier to pass the McCarthys.

The other three finished their drinks in silence; since Daniel's intervention, conversation among them seemed impossible to resuscitate. Elizabeth left her own drink untouched. Contrary to the way she had felt less than half an hour ago, she was close to despair. Had Daniel thought she had rebuffed him? She was making a mess of this whole situation. She willed the others to hurry up.

At long last, her father, who was the last to finish, drained his whiskey and all three stood up. She let them go before her and keeping her head high, walked as straight and as erect as she could manage; but just before reaching the door, her nerve failed her and she looked suddenly to the right and behind her, as though spotting something tremendously interesting at the bar.

Then, having crossed the lobby of the hotel and finding herself safely outside again in the sunshine, she felt like the greatest coward who had ever walked the earth. She castigated herself: she should go right back in there and confront Daniel's parents; she should say something at least to break the ice between them.

Not waiting until she could again second-guess herself, she made the excuse that she had left something behind her and walked back into the hotel.

Her impulse never saw fruition because in the lobby, she crossed the path of Daniel's older brother just as he was heading for the men's lavatory. He changed direction when he saw her and stepped back to block her progress towards the door of the bar. 'Mrs Scollard?' His eyes, so like Daniel's, were polite and cold. 'Maybe it's not my place to say this but my parents and I would appreciate it if you left Daniel alone now.'

With a final glance from under his eyebrows which left her in no doubt as to how low he thought her on the scale of humanity, he continued on his way, leaving her standing speechless and mortified. After that, she knew she could never voluntarily face any of his family.

Just as Elizabeth, Tilly and Mick were about to board the *Princess Béara*, Elizabeth felt as though she was being watched. She turned round to find herself staring into the eyes of Sergeant Clancy. 'Congratulations, Mrs Scollard,' said the policeman softly, and Elizabeth knew by his expression that to his dying day the policeman would believe that she and Daniel were guilty of murder.

And that night, although she waited up for him until after midnight, Daniel did not come.

Chapter Eighteen

Overnight, the weather blew up from the north-east and by morning torrential rain was crashing in horizontal waves against the tiny windows of the house. It was so inclement that although it would normally have taken the unlikely event of an earthquake to keep Béara children home from school, for the first ten minutes or so after she forced herself out of bed, Elizabeth, exhausted and red-eyed, debated with herself whether or not to send hers out to walk two miles in such conditions.

But the prospect of having them under her feet all day in the kitchen changed her mind and she reminded herself of Neeley's conviction that of all the houses in Lahersheen, because of an indentation in the mountain behind, this one always got the worst belt from a north-easter. It was probably not quite so bad further down the road.

And north-easters were rare on Béara – this one would probably blow itself out in a matter of hours, perhaps less.

She roused, fed and readied the older girls as usual and, having swaddled them all in oilskins and rubber boots, was seeing them out through the door when, glancing over their heads, she saw a figure, fisherman's cape flying like wings, battling up the hill on a bicycle. The head was bare and unmistakably Daniel's.

Francey, who was hovering around her heels, recognized him at the same time. 'There's Danny McCarthy,' he shouted and, notwithstanding the weather conditions, ran inside, shouting that he was going to get his football.

Now that the moment of meeting Daniel was imminent, Elizabeth who, only a few hours ago had thought of little else, had to fight panic. The previous day's confrontation with the evidence of the havoc wrought on his family had awakened her laggard sense of responsibility and yet, at the instant of seeing him, her treacherous body pulled her towards him as surely as if she were a hooked salmon and he was reeling her in.

To give herself a little time, she acted as though she had not seen him and went back into the kitchen, having to force the door closed against the gale. Then she saw Francey was shrugging himself into an oilskin a few sizes too big for him. 'What are you doing?' She spoke more harshly than the situation warranted.

'I'm going out to play football.' He did not look up from his exertions.

'Don't be an *amadán*. You're not going anywhere on a day like this.'

This time he reacted. 'Why not?'

Elizabeth detested the whine Francey had adopted since returning from the hospital. 'Because I say so, that's why!' In three strides, she was across the kitchen and pulling roughly at the oilskin. He resisted and she gave him a slap, not hard, but severe enough to make him cry. Elizabeth could have counted on the fingers of one hand the number of times she had smacked her son; she hated physical violence of any sort and she was immediately overtaken by remorse. To make things worse, Johanna, who had been playing quietly in a corner, started to snivel in sympathy. Elizabeth, aware that any second now Daniel would knock at the door, felt paralysed with indecision. Her instinct was to comfort Francey but all parental theory revolved around the notion of consistency and strength. At the same time she was wondering if Daniel had seen her deliberately ignoring his arrival.

She was in such a state of emotional disarray that when she heard the knock at the door, she was afraid that as soon as he saw her Daniel would recognize her for the lunatic she had become. And as she flew back across the kitchen, she still had not decided whether to invite him in. But her opening of the door coincided with a particularly violent squall and she had to fight to keep it from blowing off its hinges. To help her, Daniel caught the door too and was inside before she had time to think or to utter a word. 'Hello,' she said hoarsely, finding her voice, as looking like a seal just beached, he dripped on the flagstones of the floor.

He made no attempt to wipe away the streams of water that ran into his eyes from his hair which, even blacker than usual from the rain, emphasized the pallor of his skin; Elizabeth could not help staring at the even paler tidemark which ran around his hairline under the prison haircut. The ribbon of white skin looked unused, like that of a baby.

She had not felt shy for many years but now she became absurdly conscious of her own appearance. Her bare feet were encased in slippers, her shingled hair was carelessly brushed and as she did not bother to wear mourning clothes in the house, she was dressed in an old brown cardigan which drooped over an even older summer frock. Yet the way Daniel looked at her was making the hair stand on her arms. 'Sit down,' she said, 'take off your wet things, you're drowned.' Turning away to hide her confusion she crossed to the still snivelling Francey and gave the child such a close and loving hug that, in his astonishment, he immediately stopped crying.

When she turned back to Daniel he was still standing just inside the door, his cape in his hands. 'Here, let me spread this out for you.' She hurried to take it from him and spent longer than was strictly necessary draping it over the back of a chair. 'Would you like a towel to dry your hair?' she asked.

'Thank you.' They were the first words he had spoken.

'Run and get me a towel from the bathroom, Francey,' she ordered and, as he scampered to obey, stood facing the door through which he would come back as though waiting for him to emerge with the Holy Grail. Johanna, affected by her mother's odd mood, had also stopped crying and blinked round-eyed at Daniel from her corner.

Handing him the towel, Elizabeth turned away towards the stove but remained acutely aware of his movements behind her as he scrubbed at his hair. As she fussed with the kettle and teapot, she used an old trick to compose

354

herself, concentrating on counting silently backwards from fifty; she had succeeded by the time she had got as far as ten. 'That's better,' she said brightly, turning back towards him and seeing him use his fingers to tamp the spikes of his hair into some sort of order. 'Sit down at the table, why don't you? The kettle'll be boiled soon.'

As Daniel sat, Francey immediately came forward and, leaning one elbow on the table, engaged him in conversation about football, parroting snatches of men's conversations remembered from eavesdropping at crossroads or at card sessions in the house.

'Let Daniel be, Francey, shoo!' Elizabeth came forward with a pot of tea brewed from precious new rations. 'Go over and play with your sister.'

'Aw, she's only a girl,' Francey grumbled, 'I want to stay here for a talk with Danny McCarthy.' But he departed peaceably enough when Daniel promised to come back to give him a proper game of football before the weekend if the weather cleared up.

For only the second time, Elizabeth found herself seated opposite Daniel at her own table. And, although she tried hard to hold on to the few remaining wisps of decency and responsibility which clung around her, she knew she was fighting a losing battle. 'You didn't come last night?' she asked.

'We got home late and then a lot of the neighbours came in. They've been very good to Mam and Da.'

'Of course I understand. My own neighbours have been very good too.' Then, recognizing the naked look in his eyes, Elizabeth could not unearth another sensible word. 'Tea?' she asked desperately, pouring the liquid into two mugs.

Daniel added milk to his and sipped, gazing ardently at her over the rim of his mug.

'Don't!' she cried softly, then glanced over her shoulder to see whether Francey or Johanna had heard, but they were absorbed in a complicated game involving building blocks to represent train carriages.

'Don't what?' Daniel's stare did not waver.

'Don't look at me like that.'

'Like what?'

'With your eyes like that.'

'Where do you want me to look?' he asked. 'When are we going to see each other?'

Her emotional life had been so chaotic that she had almost forgotten his extraordinary self-confidence in these matters. 'We're seeing each other now,' she said faintly.

'You know what I mean!'

Elizabeth's entire body seemed to turn over. 'Soon,' she whispered.

'Tonight.'

Responding to his gentle yet definite command, Elizabeth's agitation mushroomed. She was not ready yet, she should think of her position, of his family ... Then she heard her voice betray her as if of its own accord. 'Where?'

'The ruined cottage in the field above?'

'No.' Elizabeth remembered Mossie's admission of spying. With the die cast, she performed a fast mind-survey of the district to find some location where they would be unobserved and, like a siren, the smoke-and-gold Kilcatherine Head of the jewelled dream shimmered into her brain. 'I'll meet you in Kilcatherine graveyard,' she said. Now that she was committed, she no longer felt confused or upset. 'No one goes near there after dark.'

He did not seem to think it an odd place for an assignation. 'Today's the longest day, you know,' he said, 'it won't be dark until very late.'

'Listen to that weather,' Elizabeth countered. 'It'll be dark by half ten.'

But in typical Béara fashion, by early afternoon the storm of the morning might have happened on a different planet. And when, trailing oilskins and walking barefoot on the verges to avoid the baking stones of the road, the girls came home from school, they found Elizabeth pegging out a line of washing which steamed under sunshine so hot it would not have disgraced the islands of the Aegean.

The long bright hours of the afternoon stretched into even longer brighter hours of early evening until by eight o'clock, Tilly Harrington, dropping in for a visit, found her friend as jumpy as a kitten. 'Oh, it's you.' Elizabeth tried to conceal her tension.

'Who did you expect?' retorted Tilly equably. 'Gracie Fields?' Even in this part of Europe, so remote from the war, Our Gracie had her followers and Tilly was one of the more fervent. Her seemingly bottomless legacy had stretched not only to a wireless – one of the first on the peninsula – but to a gramophone and a small collection of records which made her house one of the most popular in the parish.

'Sorry,' sighed Elizabeth, 'of course I didn't mean that the way it sounded.' She continued to sweep an already spotless yard.

'Mm.' Tilly settled herself on a bench seat beside the rain barrel. 'How're things going, anyway?'

'Fine, grand.'

'I see Daniel was up.'

Elizabeth's immediate instinct was to round on her friend. Nothing or no one could move through this land-scape, it seemed, without passing through the sieve of Tilly's scrutiny. But she curbed her tongue and bashed away at the yard.

'Had he any news?'

Tilly was either being deliberately maddening, Eliza-beth decided, or she herself was so guilty and apprehensive that she was overreacting. She decided on the latter. 'No,' she said, 'nothing much.' Carefully, she stood the broom just inside the kitchen door. 'They were late home last night from Ballyfee and they had a lot of visitors. That's why he didn't come over.' Tilly and Mick had stayed faithfully put in Elizabeth's kitchen until almost eleven.

'I see.' Tilly looked off towards the hill field. 'Oh, there's Mossie. Evening, Mossie!' she shouted at the top of her voice, waving her arm over her head.

Mossie, who had been hammering at a crooked gate

357

pier at the far end of the field, straightened his back and rubbed it as though it ached. 'Evening, Tilly,' he shouted back, 'lovely evening.'

'Don't draw him on us, for God's sake, Tilly,' Elizabeth muttered venomously under her breath.

'What's poor Mossie done now? And what's eating you, anyway? As if I didn't know!' Tilly refused to be intimidated by Elizabeth's mood. They both watched as Mossie bent again to his task. 'He's a good worker, anyway, you fell on your feet there. He'll improve things no end. Not that Neeley, God be good to him, was a bad worker,' Tilly crossed herself, 'far from it. But Mossie's eager enough, all right. You made a good bargain there.' Elizabeth remembered that Tilly still thought the agreement between herself and Mossie concerned conacre.

The other woman moved the seat so it was facing the sun, still hot but bearing now towards the west. She closed her eyes and held her face up to the warmth. 'So when are you seeing him?'

'Seeing who? Mossie?'

'Don't play the innocent with me, Elizabeth Sullivan. Seeing Danny McCarthy, of course.'

For one moment, Elizabeth was tempted to confide in her – after all, Tilly had been such a good friend, she probably owed her the confidence – but her assignation with Daniel was so imminent she did not want to put the hex on it by dissipating it with gossip. 'We've no definite arrangements,' she said quietly, 'we said we'd just wait and see how things go.'

'Mm.' Tilly did not move a muscle. 'But if I were you I'd be very cautious, Lizzie. The ditches have eyes and ears around here.'

'Don't you think I know that? Now could we change the subject?' Elizabeth sat beside Tilly on the seat and imitating her friend, turned her face up to the sun and closed her eyes. She consciously tried to force herself to relax, to tune her ears to the summer evening sounds, the bumblings and buzzings of bees, flies and wasps, the steady *pukka! pukka!* of Mossie's lump hammer, the thin faraway calls and whistles of a man working his cattle dog, the noise of the football game in progress in the low field. Homework finished, the older girls had yielded to Francey's pleadings that they all kick his ball around. The house stood between the yard and the field, the flattest on the farm, but although it was a quarter of a mile away, the children's cries and shouts rang across the still air like a carillon.

'Nice to hear the young voices, isn't it?' But Tilly's voice was underlaid with a hint of sadness. Hearing her friend's wistfulness upset Elizabeth. What kind of a world was it, she thought, when Tilly, who was by nature so maternal and who would have given her little finger to have even one child, could not have any while she herself had seven – not one of whom was planned or longed for?

Horrified at the idea that had popped up in her brain like a malign jack-in-the-box, she hastened to reassure herself that she would not now be without a single one of them, Neeley's included.

But the wagon of her self-recrimination gathered speed: here she was, she thought, with one husband not cold in the grave and fending off a second man because she wanted someone different. Someone who was six years younger than she. What kind of a woman was she, at all? Thousands, millions, billions of women since the beginning of time had managed to control this perfidious sexual longing.

But not Elizabeth Sullivan. Not she.

And look at the trouble she had brought on Daniel's blameless family . . .

The peace of the evening receded beyond recall as she pounded herself with her flaws and sins: Mossie Sheehan had hit the nail squarely, and maybe so had Neeley. She was a slut and no mistake.

A calculating one at that: despite the balmy evening, Elizabeth shivered as she remembered the vivid fantasies about the tryst at Kilcatherine in which she had indulged during the day. Just how ruthless could one person be? Her self-abasement turned to full-scale flagellation at the extent of her perfidy: she was actually planning and envisioning to have sex in the place where the body of her newly dead husband lay.

'What's the matter, Lizzie?' Beside her Tilly was sitting up, an alarmed expression on her face.

'What do you mean? Nothing's the matter.' Elizabeth tried to control her shivering.

'You're shaking.' Tilly put a hand on Elizabeth's forehead. 'Have you a temperature, do you think?'

'I'm just fed up with myself, Tilly.'

Fed up or not, at half past eleven that night, Elizabeth found herself crossing the fields between her house and Kilcatherine graveyard. The salmon-pink and gold remnants of the day lit the sky to the west, and although the night was without a moon details of the landscape were still perfectly clear; even the rabbits had not yet gone to their burrows.

Feeling like a thief, she kept well in by the stone walls and hedges while, by keeping an even pace and swinging her arms, she tried to convey the impression to anyone who might see her that she was just out for a breath of fresh air. This is what, keeping her head averted, she had told Mary too. 'I'm smothering with the heat,' she had said, hoping her voice sounded casual enough, 'and I know I'll have trouble sleeping. I think after you're all safely in bed I'll go out for a little stroll . . .' And Mary, obliging and responsible as ever, had concurred with the request that if anything happened during the 'hour or so' her stepmother was out, she would consider herself in charge.

But, as if sensing her plans, tonight of all nights the children had been more skittish than usual and had employed a variety of tactics to delay bedtime until Elizabeth was fit to kill them all. But when at last they had all settled down for the night, rather on the principle that she might as well be hung for a sheep as for a lamb, she had prepared like a bride for her outing. Although she did wear one of the mourning dresses and a filmy black cardigan and covered her telltale bright hair with a black headscarf, underneath, the hair was washed and had been brushed until it shone. She had carefully swabbed the cleft between her breasts with cologne-soaked cotton wool. Her under-wear, saved from the trousseau Corinne had assembled in what now seemed like another lifetime, was silk.

Giving houses and outbuildings a wide berth, she stopped when she came to a place from where she could see clear across the little cemetery. To the left of where she stood, a single star flared like a solitaire over the summit of Knocknasheeog, to her right a few miles beyond the land's end, the black bulk of the Bull Rock floated in a rose-coloured sea but she was blind to anything except the wedge of ground directly in front of her. Standing in the lee of a thorn tree as though taking a breather, she strained her eyes in search of movement, not only in the graveyard but, mindful of Tilly's warning about ears in ditches, anywhere around it.

She looked particularly for evidence of Mossie Sheehan but all seemed still and empty; the flat slaty waters of Coulagh Bay glinted like mackerel scales in the last of the light, even the eyes of the Celtic crosses in the graveyard seemed blinder and more peacefully inward looking than usual. Before moving forward for the last few steps of her journey, as though she was about to go on stage, Elizabeth self-consciously smoothed her dress over her hips, the fabric slithering sensuously on the silk she wore underneath.

Then she started to worry: suppose Daniel had been spotted? She should have arranged some sort of signal with him. But he was well known for moving around the district at night, she reassured himself, and what could be more natural than that after his incarceration he should want to roam free?

Enough! she thought, moving forward into the open to cross the wide field in front of the stone-walled grave-yard, her eyes boring into every shadow. Then she was inside the graveyard and still saw no sign of him.

In case anyone was watching, she crossed the uneven ground to where Neeley lay. The earth was still mounded under a cap of fishing net, fixed over the wreaths of artificial flowers sent by Neeley's American relatives to secure them against gales. Due to the exigencies of the postal service they had only recently been received.

Brought up by Corinne to detest artificial flowers, Elizabeth hated these wreaths, their gaudy colouring, their oversized realism. But crouching low now, she pretended to adjust the piece of anchoring net while she listened out for sounds of movement. All she heard was the sea, so calm it sounded like a distant, elongated sigh.

Abruptly she heard Neeley's bitter voice: 'Ye'll have no luck!' It was so clear she shot to her feet and, looking fearfully over her shoulder, half expected to see his thin figure standing just behind her. In a throwback to her schooldays, she bent and snatched up the small bottle of holy water embedded just under the family headstone. Shaking a few drops into her hand she made a hurried Sign of the Cross, replaced the bottle and was sprinting out of the graveyard when she saw Daniel coming down the approach road.

He saw her just as she saw him and also broke into a run.

He came into the graveyard over the stone stile and they collided with one another just inside the eastern wall of the graveyard, their lips meeting frantically. 'I thought it would never be dark,' he gasped, between kisses which covered not only her face, but her forehead, her neck and her ears.

'Me too —' Elizabeth's heat matched his; her body felt starved, as though it had been through famine. 'Oh, Daniel, I was so scared you wouldn't come.'

Although her passion for him was fully alight and they were safely out of sight of any dwelling-house, the residue of the fright she had had when she thought she heard Neeley's voice prompted Elizabeth to break off. 'Not here, not here,' she gasped, pushing strongly until they were moving away from the wall. But his desire for her was so strong that, although he allowed himself to be moved, she was lifted clear off her feet as with one hand, he pushed back the headscarf and her hair, kissing behind her ear, the tender flesh under her jaw.

Still kissing, they moved across the graveyard. The wrought-iron gate at the western end was locked and, as he assisted her from behind to climb over it, the skirt of her dress rode up her bare leg and his hand encountered her thigh. Swiftly, he lowered his head to where the dress was ruched, catching the thigh and burying his lips in the soft skin behind her knee. The sensation was so exquisitely pleasurable that Elizabeth threw back her head and had to stifle a groan. 'Not here, not here,' she repeated, 'please—'

When he too was outside the gate, she took his hand and led him insistently over a ditch, into the field behind the cemetery and towards a small depression from which they could not be seen by passers-by unless someone walked in on top of them. When they reached it, she turned to him, allowing him to take her again in his arms, and they tumbled together into the hollow, soft with summer ferns and grasses which were still damp and redolent of the morning's storm. 'Elizabeth, Elizabeth,' he whispered, 'you don't know how much I've thought about this . . .' With one hand he searched roughly under her skirt and pulled at her hips, at her buttocks.

Elizabeth assisted him, wriggling, herself pulling at her garments to give him access to her skin, her belly, between her legs. Then she raked at his shirt, pulling it out of his waistband, her hands finding the smooth young skin of his back, the muscles hard and working underneath.

All the time, while his hands were travelling, kneading at her, he was grinding her underneath him with more kisses, hot, urgent kisses everywhere, into her neck, on her shoulders, her belly, between her breasts, coming back always to her mouth. His inexpert lips felt sweet and hard, his tongue too demanding, but she wanted him so badly now that she acceded completely to his claim on every part of her body.

Suddenly he stopped, gasping, 'I've never — I've never—'

363

'I know.' Her own breathing was barely under control. 'It's all right. It'll be all right . . .' Swiftly, Elizabeth removed her own underwear and pulling his head down again, kissed him while she felt for his buttons.

He was as still as he could be while she undid his trousers but in her arms, she felt his trembling grow. And when at last she liberated him and guided him towards her, he groaned, 'Oh, God, oh God —'

'Just one thing,' she held him in her hand, 'you'll have to be ready to come out when I say so.'

'Anything, oh, Elizabeth —' He gasped again when he slid into her, filling her so completely that, for a second, she convulsed and almost lost control, but she managed to retrieve herself and held him tightly and lovingly as he delved into her once, twice, and then she felt the mounting, ecstatic shudder which rived through his entire body. By rotating her hips, she managed to eject him just before his body, rigid as a board, arched over her own. As he came, his mouth opened and he uttered a long, low cry, like an animal in pain.

Holding him, Elizabeth felt exalted, delighted by his rapture. She kissed his neck as he subsided on top of her, and panting, buried his head in the side of her neck. 'I'm sorry, I'm sorry, oh, Elizabeth, I'm sorry . . .'

'What are you sorry for? Don't be sorry, my love, my little love, don't be sorry . . .' She stroked the back of his head, the tender island of skin between the hairline and the collar of his shirt. 'There's nothing in the world to be sorry for, you're wonderful, you're a lovely, wonderful man . . .'

Over his shoulder she saw that the stars had begun to emerge through the darkening sky, stars behind stars behind stars, in clusters and handfuls and dense, milky masses. It was the first time Elizabeth had noticed their colours, not only the hard icy white she expected, but subtle shades of pink and red and yellow, even green. Some shone steadily, some came and went, some pulsed, some seemed to tremble and even dance. In her elevated state it seemed to her as though some cosmic jeweller had spilled a trove of living diamonds at random across a display cloth of infinite, velvety blue.

Daniel was calming now and reality tugged feebly but insistently at her senses. Suppose someone came along? Suppose one of the children was sick?

He sensed the tiny change in her mood and raised himself on one elbow. 'Did I do it all right?' he whispered.

'Perfectly, my little darling, you were perfect.' During her marriage she had frequently cursed George Gallaher for teaching her too well about sex on the grounds that what she had not known about she would not have missed. But remembering her own first time with George, Elizabeth thanked him now for his experience; and she had never forgotten what he had said to her in the grounds of that castle: *What we did tonight is beautiful. Enjoyment is permissible. Love between a man and a woman is allowed* . . . Echoing George, she kissed Daniel. 'And it will get better and better for you, you'll see.' But as he went to kiss her back as though to start all over again she held him off. 'I've got to go, sweetheart, the children are on their own.'

'When will I see you again?'

'Not like this. This is too dangerous, Daniel. But I'll think of something, you'll see.'

'Today's my birthday,' he said shyly. 'You've given me the best birthday present anyone ever had.'

'Oh, Daniel. I never knew – your birthday's on the longest day?'

'The twenty-second. It must be the twenty-second by now.'

'Happy birthday, my dearest darling love.' But she kissed him in a way which indicated that she was serious about leaving him for now.

They stood up, adjusting their clothes. And although Elizabeth had so readily taken on the role of leader, she felt embarrassed nevertheless as she retrieved her silk knickers from where she had so wantonly thrown them, and she turned her back as she slipped her legs into them.

But her embarrassment dissipated as the image of her

mother popped like a genie into her head: what would Corinne think if she could see to what use part of her wedding trousseau – so carefully selected – had been put? Not only the wedding stuff but the mourning stuff too: she took off her cardigan and tied it by the sleeves around her waist to hide the stained front of her dress.

As she turned around again to face Daniel, he was tucking his shirt into his waistband. In the starlight she could see his eyes were glistening with emotion. He stopped what he was doing and raised his arms so he stood cruciform. 'I love you, I love you, I love you! This was the most wonderful night of my life,' he said in a voice vibrating with such energy that Elizabeth looked swiftly around to check that they were still unobserved. 'Daniel, this is a difficult situation,' she said, seizing his hands and pulling them down in front of him, 'but it feels right to me. Not slinking about the ditches, that doesn't feel right, but the situation itself. And if it's to be it'll be. We mustn't force the pace of it though, all right?'

'I want to marry you. Will you marry me, Elizabeth?' Then, seeing her expression, he faltered, 'Oh —'

Elizabeth moved quickly to put a finger to her lips. 'We'll have plenty of time to talk about things like that, Daniel,' she whispered. 'And – and I'm in mourning, you know.'

He took the hand which covered his mouth and held it away from him. 'I don't mean we should get married right away.'

She thought rapidly. 'Come to the house tomorrow evening after tea to play football with Francey.' Even if Mossie was around and read the truth, there was not all that much he could do about a football game with a child. She squeezed his hand. 'We'll talk then.'

'Are you sure you want me to?' His voice was anguished, reminding Elizabeth that despite his self-assurance he was still so much younger than she. 'Of course, Daniel.' She reached up and kissed him again, tenderly, reassuring him as strongly as she could. He responded quietly and gratefully and as they stood together in the stillness, Elizabeth experienced again the completion of that circuit she had first felt on the night they had danced together at Jimmy Deeney's dance in Castleclough. 'Now I really must get home.' Gently she detached herself.

'Until tomorrow.' Blowing him a kiss, she backed away a few steps and then set her face across the field and home. But after twenty-five yards or so, she turned to look back. He was still standing where she had left him and, although it was bright enough to see all around her without use of the torch she had carried with her, from this distance she could not distinguish his features.

He raised one arm as though to wave, then seemed to think better of it. Elizabeth blew him another kiss and then carried on across two planks which had been placed as a makeshift footbridge across a drain. And when, just before moving into the shadows cast by a tangle of blackberry bushes, she turned round a second time, he was gone.

As she hurried home, Daniel's essence clung to Elizabeth like mist; she could smell him from her body, of course, but less tangibly, something of him seemed to have lodged within her. But she had no time now for sentimental soul-searching because, as she made her way across the dark, quiet fields as fast as decorum would allow, her conviction grew that something was wrong at home.

She was walking so fast she was just short of running; the distance, less than half a mile, seemed twice that. She jumped at shadows and almost screamed aloud when a small bat flitted low across her pathway. All the time she tried to tell herself that, once again, she was just overreacting from guilt.

She stopped dead in relief, however, when on breasting a rise in the land, she saw the house was safe and snug. It was only then she acknowledged that, as retribution for what she had just done, she had been expecting to see the roof on fire or, at the very least, the children milling around outside in panic at her absence. 'Thank God,' she breathed and then, appreciating the irony of the situation, 'You're a fine one, aren't you? Preaching to other people not to be ashamed of sex while all the time deep down, you're thinking like a missioner!'

The previous year she had accompanied Neeley to the mission in Castletownbere. The church, as usual, had been packed to the rafters for 'sex night', the entertainment value of which was legendary in the district, and Elizabeth had gone largely as a secure and disinterested observer.

But when the Redemptorist got into full stride, painting in apocalyptic detail his visions of the macabre and specialized torments reserved in hell for those who committed sins of the flesh, Elizabeth had found herself powerless to resist. Although she had tried with all her might to shut out his howling torrent of horrors, she had been swept up with the rest of the priest's stunned yet voyeuristic captives and, like them, had emerged from the church as though she was punch-drunk.

Such was the missioner's talent that later that night, chaste on her own side of her marriage bed, Elizabeth had experienced relief that in the matter of physical sins of the flesh she had little now to worry about. On her side, her marriage to Neeley was snowily virtuous and devoid of lust; the only blemishes on her recently stainless soul had been her private thoughts and fantasies and, under the influence of what she had just heard, she had resolved to banish even those.

This, of course, had been before she went to Glengarriff with Tilly to see the Liffey Players. And before meeting Daniel Carrig McCarthy.

She moved off again, so close now to the house that she no longer worried about being caught out. Then she heard Rex, normally the most taciturn of animals, erupt in a frenzy of barking. What now?

Running, she got the gate of the farmyard just in time to see the dog jump the boundary wall and go haring off across the hill field as though pursued by the devil. 'Rex!' she called, trying to make her voice carry without shouting. '*Rex!*' The dog ignored her and carried on along a course straight as an arrow; the last Elizabeth saw of him was the white tip of his tail vanishing behind a hedge at the far end of the field. At least he had stopped barking.

Then, coming into the farmyard, Elizabeth heard uneasy clucking from the poultry house and knew what had agitated the dog: there was obviously a fox in the area. She pulled open the door of the coop but, although they were moving about on their roosts, the hens did not seem too panicked. She bolted the door securely and shone her torch around the base of the building, making sure there were no fresh holes in evidence. All was in order.

She let herself into the house and was tiptoeing across the kitchen when she almost kicked something on the threshold of her door. Propped against a milk jug where she could not fail to find it, was a note: 'I was talking to the teacher today,' the paper read without preamble in Kathleen's clear, upright hand, 'and she says she'll put in a word for me with the nuns. I want to go to boarding school in Cork to do my Leaving Cert.' She signed it simply K.

This was the first Elizabeth had heard of Kathleen's ambitions to go on to further education. She had been so caught up in her own affairs she had failed to keep track of what was going on in the family.

Then something else struck her: the note had obviously been placed at her door after she went out. Had Kathleen seen her leave? Worse, had she seen or heard the preparations and had she waited for her to go? Was this note Kathleen's way of showing such contempt for her stepmother that she no longer wished to stay under the same roof? Elizabeth listened hard but there was no unusual sound from the other bedroom, no sense of anyone listening or watching.

Still carrying the note, she was just inside her own bedroom when she heard a discreet but distinct knock on the outside door of the kitchen and wheeled around. Had Daniel followed her here? As she hesitated, the knock sounded a second time.

She tiptoed back across the floor and opened the door a crack.

Mossie Sheehan, standing about two feet away from it,

369

tipped a finger to his cap. 'Evening, Elizabeth,' he said as though it was seven o'clock and not half past midnight, 'I was coming down from Knockameala and I heard Rex. I just thought I'd check to see if everything is all right.'

'Everything's all right, Mossie, thank you.'

He didn't budge. 'Well, so long as everything's in order,' he said. 'By the way,' he paused for a fraction of a second, 'you'd want to be careful.'

'Of what, might I ask?' Elizabeth was almost speechless.

In the starlight, his broad frame seemed massive and more powerful than it did by day as he gazed at her without blinking. 'I hear there's a fox about,' he said evenly.

Chapter Nineteen

Elizabeth tackled Kathleen at breakfast the following morning. 'Are you serious about going to Cork?' she asked while ladling out the girl's porridge.

Kathleen, her expression sullen, kept her eyes on the bowl in front of her. 'I wouldn't have written it in a note if I wasn't, would I?'

'Mind your tongue,' Elizabeth rebuked her automatically then turned to Kathleen's older sister. 'How about you, Mary? Do you want to do your Leaving Cert too?'

'No.' Mary was already eating. 'I think she's mad. I can't wait to leave school.'

'Well, what do you want to do, then?'

'I dunno.' Mary shrugged her shoulders and looked at her stepmother as though surprised at the question.

Elizabeth realized then that she had to sit down with these two to talk seriously about their future. Somehow, the years had slipped down a drain-hole of routine and she had not paid more than cursory attention to what Neeley might have had in mind for his daughters. It was taken for granted around the parish that girls put in time somehow between leaving school and getting married, sometimes in jobs, sometimes not. Many, as young as fourteen, emigrated to relatives in Montana or England but, at present, when all travel between Ireland and Great Britain was banned, the latter was unavailable as a jobs outlet. And as Elizabeth had never met them, she would be reluctant to write to Neeley's American relatives out of the blue. Something would have to be organized for Mary and Kathleen – and as soon as possible.

As all four of the schoolgoers worked their way through their breakfast, Elizabeth chided herself that she should have been more alert; now that she was solely in charge of the children's welfare, it was time she took the responsibility seriously. 'We'll have a talk about it when you come home today, all right?' she said to Kathleen, breaking into the busy silence while starting work on Goretti's plaits.

'There's nothing to talk about!' Kathleen's voice was definite. 'I'm going and that's that!'

'I'm sorry to have to point out,' Elizabeth was nettled, 'that secondary school costs money.'

'I've written to Grandad Sullivan,' said Kathleen.

'*What*?' Now Elizabeth was really annoyed. 'You had no right to do that without telling me, Kitty.'

'Did I not?' Kathleen's face was insolent. 'Grandad Sullivan told me that I could write to him any time I needed anything.'

Elizabeth suspended work on Goretti's second plait. 'When did he tell you this?'

'During my father's funeral.' In the emphasis she laid on 'father', Kathleen left Elizabeth in no doubt as to where her allegiance still lay and how she felt about her stepmother. She slid off her chair. 'I'm going to get my school bag. Are you coming, Mary?' She marched out of the kitchen.

Elizabeth was torn between a desire to shake her and pity for the trauma which Kathleen, more than anyone else, had undergone since her father's death.

'Don't mind her.' Mary, standing up too, was apologetic. 'She'll get over it.'

'Get over what? She seems determined to go.'

'No – I mean – never mind. I'd better get my books too. I'll be late. Hurry up there, Margaret!' Mary shoved Margaret who was still eating, then seized the hairbrush left on the table by Elizabeth and began to use it so energetically on her own hair that Elizabeth was afraid to probe: Mary seemed to be aware of some agenda in Kathleen's mind, which was not so simple as grief at the loss of her father.

She thought then that her world was becoming far too complicated, that too many people's emotions were caught up in the vortex around her. She thought of her own enmeshment with Daniel, of the distress of his parents, of Mossie, of the delicate balance of her relationship with her own father, and within the house itself, of the sadnesses, hopes and desires of all these disparate individuals with their unique personality quirks.

Visited with an image of her house as an outsider would see it – snug and clean, its back securely to the sheltering mountain, a place of comfortable family and farmyard habit, which varied only with the seasons and the school term – Elizabeth was stuck by how deceptive this image was. Inside this stolid structure whirled forces as elemental and potentially destructive as the storms that so frequently swept over its outside.

It was the imperturbable Margaret who brought her back to the reality of the morning. 'I'll be wanting to do my Leaving too,' she announced while continuing to work her methodical way through her porridge and a second slice of soda bread. 'If *she* gets to do it' – she jerked her thumb in the direction of the bedroom – 'I want to too. I'm just warning you in good time, Mammy. So you can make arrangements.'

'All right, now hurry up, Maggie, or you'll be making arrangements with the teacher's strap.' Removing Margaret's bowl she tweaked her cheek affectionately. 'Ow!' Margaret protested. 'Don't *do* that, Mammy, I *hate* that . . .'

Elizabeth got rid of them all and turned her attention to the three younger ones. She would be glad, she thought, when Francey and Johanna went off to school together in September. To have only Abigail and herself in the house for most of the day would feel like a permanent holiday.

And with that thought came a sneaking companion; her outside life would be much easier to organize.

She helped them get dressed, washed up and then brought the breakfast scraps into the yard for the hens. It was another gorgeous day and, alone for the first time since she had got out of bed that morning, Elizabeth, scattering crumbs and scraps of oatmeal in handfuls around the yard, allowed thoughts of last night's encounter with Daniel to seep into her along with the warmth of the sun. Then, out of the corner of her eye, she caught a flash of something metallic and looked into the hill field. The solid figure of Mossie Sheehan was bent double over the gate on which he had been working the previous night; the flash she had seen was from a handsaw.

All the warmth was drawn out of the day as Elizabeth realized once and for all that this was her appointed lot from now on. As much as the low drystone walls built boulder by boulder by Neeley's ancestors to mark out their fields, Mossie Sheehan was now a fixture around the farm. And in the clear light of day she saw that, agreement or no agreement, Mossie's permanent presence would make life difficult for her and Daniel.

Not only that, there were the children to consider. She pictured them all as they had been that morning, Kathleen sullen, Mary peacemaking, Margaret matter-of-fact, the accepting disposition of the younger ones for whom she was still the centre of their lives. She had been mad to think she could arrange the world to suit herself.

And by stringing him along, she was not being fair to Daniel. If she truly had his welfare at heart, she had to tell him the truth. Elizabeth went back into the kitchen and began dispiritedly to scour out the porridge pot with ash; as she did so she tried to put words to what exactly this truth was.

Her physical passion for Daniel was so strong that she could not bear to think of separation from him – and, yet, could she really contemplate the installation of this boy, at the age of nineteen or twenty, or even twenty-one, as stepfather to seven children?

And how was she to explain to him that, barring an act of God, an intervention for which she now desperately hoped, she may first have to marry Mossie Breac Sheehan?

Did she want another husband at all?

She banged away at the pot and then went about her other chores as though the end of the world was coming and her kitchen had to be in order before Christ called her to account.

'Hello, Elizabeth,' she heard from behind her an hour

374

later. Engaged in relining the drawers of the dresser, the floor around her feet was littered with carving knives, serving spoons, twists of string, spent candles, matches, wicks, pencils and pens, half-bottles of ink, writing paper, old letters, doorknobs and other redundant items which no one could bear to throw out. Whirling to find Daniel leaning against the door jamb, her body leapt in treacherous recognition: his expression was the one she herself had borne seven years ago, as for months nothing on earth mattered except to get back to George Gallaher's side – and into his bed.

Daniel Carrig McCarthy looked so desirable she felt her doubts shrivel like a violet under a hot sun. 'Hello,' she whispered as the will to reveal the true state of affairs slipped away. 'I wasn't expecting you until after tea.'

'I couldn't wait,' he said softly, the retrospective intimacy shining in his eyes dealing the death blow to her determination. The white ring around his hair line did not seem so pronounced this morning; he looked fresh, invigorated – and confident. He had also taken care to dress neatly; although he was not wearing a jacket, a sharp crease ran the length of his trousers and shirt sleeves, and his collar was stiff with starch. Elizabeth's fingers, hot from manic use of carbolic soap and polish, itched to tear it off. She turned round to give herself a chance to retrieve her composure. 'Francey!' she called. 'Daniel's here to play football with you.'

But when she turned back again, vividly recalling the same sensations he was, she had to fight hard not to run to him and offer herself to him again there and then. Although unable to look away, she did make one last effort. 'Come on, Francey!' she called again over her shoulder. 'What's keeping you?'

'I'm in the bathroom,' came the muffled reply.

'He'll be out in a minute,' she said, pushing her hands through her hair until they encountered empty air. She still occasionally forgot it was short. 'No hurry,' Daniel whispered, unmoving. 'Sure, amn't I part of the gentry until the fall when I get on the seine boat at Ballycrovane?'

'Sit down.' Elizabeth tore herself away and, willy-nilly, threw their former contents back into the half-lined drawers.

'I saw Mossie Breac above,' Daniel said from behind her. 'I hear you're giving him conacre?'

'You hear right.' She was glad he could not see the lie in her face.

'Well, I hope you only gave him a year.'

'Why is that?' She knew she should grasp this opening.

'Oh, no why,' he said mysteriously, then, waiting until her clattering had subsided, added, 'That's for you to know and me to find out.'

His gaiety nearly broke her heart. With a crash, she closed both drawers. 'Listen, Daniel.' She turned towards him but the opportunity for truth vanished as Francey came running into the room.

'I'm ready now — are you ready, Danny? Where'll we go? The low field?'

'Anywhere suits me, come on, *giolla* . . .' Snatching the ball from the boy and bouncing it from foot to hand, Daniel ran through the doorway.

Francey followed him and, after a few seconds, so did Johanna, 'Me too, me too, wait for me, Danny!' running as fast as her fat little legs could carry her.

Elizabeth sat down at the table and put her head in her hands.

After a bit, she picked up Abigail and put her into the wooden pram Neeley had made and which had served well for many of the children.

Wheeling it, she was half-way down the roadway to Tilly's farm when she stopped to watch the football game in progress; one of the pastures which belonged to the Harringtons stretched between the roadway and their own low field but it was not large and Elizabeth could see clearly what was going on. Daniel was leading both children up and down the field in great sweeping arcs, heading the ball, kicking it and then, just in time to prevent Francey from getting frustrated, tipping it in the child's direction.

Johanna, arms held straight out from her sides so she resembled a little aeroplane, buzzed around after the two of them, doing nothing much, content just to be part of things.

As Elizabeth watched, Francey lofted the football directly at Daniel, who pretended it had hit his stomach with the force of a cannonball and to the enormous delight of both children, groaned theatrically and fell backwards on to the grass. Closely followed by Johanna, Francey piled in to wrestle the ball away and the three of them rolled over and over on the ground, the children's high-pitched shrieks competing with Daniel's loud cries of simulated agony. The horseplay was so artless and youthful that, as never before, Elizabeth knew as she carried on down the hill that she had to be the strong one in her relationship with Daniel.

For once, Tilly was not at home. According to Mick, who emerged from the horse's loose box on hearing Elizabeth enter the yard, Tilly had gone to Eyeries to see her sister. 'Nothing wrong, I hope?'

'Ah no,' Mick wiped his hands on his shirt, 'nothing like that. She just took a notion to go in.'

'Right-oh.' Elizabeth turned the pram and, refusing Mick's offer of refreshment, went out the way she had come in. As she turned the corner for the last uphill push home, she saw the football game was still in progress. This time, however, they saw her and all three came dashing across both fields to the hedge.

Francey was breathless. 'Did you see us, Mammy? It was *great*. We had great fun.'

'I saw you all right.' Elizabeth smiled across the hedge at Daniel. 'They must have you worn out. Oh, no,' she added in dismay, 'look at your good shirt.' Creased and streaked with grass stains, the garment bore little resemblance to its pristine self of less than half an hour previously.

'It's all right, it'll wash,' Daniel said easily. He, too, was breathing hard but his eyes were sparkling with health and robust good humour as, quickly unbuttoning the shirt, he pulled it off and whirled it around his head a few times like

377

a flag. If she discounted his brutally cut hair, in Elizabeth's eyes he resembled nothing less than an exuberant, arrogant young Celtic warrior who was celebrating a conquest.

Which, she thought wryly, was exactly what he was entitled to do. 'Come on down to the house,' she invited, moving off again with the pram, 'and I'll soak those stains in washing soda.'

Followed closely by the two children, Daniel trotted ahead of her along the inside of the hedge towards the gate of Harringtons' field. Walking decorously behind, Elizabeth could not keep her eyes off the way the sunlight highlighted the sweat which polished his smooth, muscled back. The hell with it, she decided then: on such a glorious day why should she resist? What woman, with such a boy so passionately in love with her, with a full-throated lark above her head and the sun warm on her face, could maintain pinchgut rectitude? 'Hurry up, the three of you!' Laughing like a young girl, she leaned into the handle of the pram, bowling it noisily past the gate. 'Slowcoaches!'

Daniel, who had been waiting at the gate for the children to catch up with him, vaulted over the top bar and running after her, caught the pram handle too. His added weight propelled the ancient vehicle at practically double its former speed so that Abigail, joggled unmercifully along the rutted road, clapped her hands and screamed with delight. 'Wait for us, wait for us!' Francey and Johanna wriggled out under the bottom bar of the gate and set off shrieking after the pram and its pilots.

When they came within sight of Elizabeth's back door, she saw Mossie Sheehan, the white of his shirtsleeves shining like beacons, standing as solidly as a traffic policeman in the middle of the yard.

The joyful procession halted abruptly and Elizabeth's first instinct was to turn immediately and run back the way she had come. Then she became savagely, irrationally angry. How dare Mossie Sheehan invade her life again like this, spoil such an innocent moment? The thought that 'innocent' was not the appropriate epithet for what was going on occurred to her but she quashed it before it could dilute her rage.

Leaving Daniel at the front of the pram, she walked round it and opened the farmyard gate. 'Wheel it in, will you, please, Daniel?' she commanded and swallowing hard to keep her voice under control, she walked right up to Mossie. 'Yes?' she asked in the coldest most chatelaine-like voice she could muster, before Daniel could get within earshot, she lowered her voice to a hiss: 'I thought we had an *agreement*.'

'Of course we do,' he responded in a tone at normal conversational pitch. 'That's why I'm here. I came to ask what you want done with those bullocks – there's a fair in Castletown next week. Unless you want to sell them to me?'

Elizabeth glared at his bland face. Behind her, she heard Daniel latch the gate and the rumble of the pram wheels as he brought it across the yard. Then something happened which knocked any further speech out of her. As Mossie looked over her shoulder towards Daniel, the lines of his face seemed to slacken – she checked to make sure she was not imagining it. Mossie Breac Sheehan was deliberately projecting himself as being far more simple than he was. She gaped as he smiled at Daniel. 'How're you, Danny, we didn't get a chance to talk at all the other day . . .'

Daniel brought the pram to a halt and cocked his head to one side, obviously not sure quite how to react. Slowly he put his arms into the sleeves of the shirt he carried and did up the buttons one by one. 'I'm fine, thank you, Mossie,' he said. 'But there is something I'd like to ask you.'

'Fire away, fire away!'

'How come you waited so long to tell the Guards you saw what happened that night?'

Elizabeth went cold.

'To tell you the truth, Danny,' Mossie replied, 'that's a question I can't rightly answer myself. I sort of blocked it out.'

'You mean you didn't remember?' Daniel's eyes were sceptical.

'That's right. I came to Lizzie here as soon as it all came back to me.' His deviousness – underscored by his reversion to her nickname – lit a new fire under Elizabeth's fury as he turned to her for confirmation.

But as Daniel, too, glanced uncertainly at her, Elizabeth decided that for the present, unless she was prepared to reveal everything right at this moment, it would be wise to stay out of the conversation. Schooling her face, she smiled at Daniel and shrugged.

Mossie, however, foursquare as a keep, seemed to be waiting patiently for someone else to speak next and she felt forced into giving Daniel the half-truth that what Mossie had said was indeed the case; that as soon as he had come to see her, she had urged him immediately to go to the barracks.

'Thank you, Mossie, better late than never, I suppose,' Daniel said slowly and seeing his guarded look, Elizabeth knew he was not accepting the story at face value.

'For nothing!' Mossie's façade was so convincing that he even had the gall to look self-deprecating. 'I'm only glad it all worked out.' He cleared his throat. 'Now you'll let me know about those bullocks, Lizzie?'

'I'll tell you tomorrow.' Not trusting herself to speak, Elizabeth seized the pram, wheeled it into the outhouse where it was normally kept, and unstrapped Abigail. When she emerged again into the sunshine, carrying the child, Mossie had gone.

'Are you going to sell him the stock?' Daniel fell into step beside her as she crossed the yard to go into the house.

'Probably,' she said curtly. 'Anything to get shut of him.'

'Did he really have that . . .' Daniel hesitated, 'block-age?' He looked off down the road after Mossie.

'Let's not trouble ourselves with the likes of him.' Elizabeth again shrank from the opening Daniel had given her. She went into the house and settled Abigail into a corner, giving her a set of old saucepans and mismatched lids to play with. The clashing and clanging which ensued from the corner made significant conversation difficult and for that she was glad. 'Give me your shirt.' She held out her hand.

'I'll give you more than my shirt!' Looking swiftly over his shoulder to make sure the two older children were nowhere within viewing distance, Daniel attempted to put his arms around her.

'Daniel, not now. I told you last night, we have to be careful and discreet.' He smelled of sunshine and fresh sweat but Elizabeth detached herself firmly.

'Well, when, then? I told you I *love* you, Elizabeth!' He stepped back and, although his expression was plaintive, she could see in his newly knowing eyes that his confidence had not been dented one whit by her temporary rejection. Her own morale, she thought gloomily, had been shattered beyond repair – for the remainder of today at least – by the latest encounter with Mossie Sheehan; she seemed to be swinging on some sort of giant emotional pendulum of which Mossie was controlling the trajectory. She would have to put a stop to that as quickly as possible. 'Soon, sweetheart,' she said to Daniel, 'soon.' She kissed him softly on his breast, just above the nipple; the warm skin tasted slightly salty. 'As soon as possible,' she whispered, 'I promise.'

But when, having scrubbed off the stains, she was spreading his shirt on a bush to dry, he pressed her to come again to Kilcatherine that night, she demurred. 'I can't, I'm sorry, I really can't.'

'But I love you, Elizabeth.'

'Well, my sweetheart, if you love me, you'll have to show me that love by having a bit of patience. I have seven children, Daniel. Seven!'

'Sorry.' He was instantly contrite. 'You need a man around the place,' he said, then, seeing the look of warning she threw at him, 'All right, all right – shut up, Daniel.' He picked up the football discarded in the middle of the yard and using it like a handball, bounced it once against the wall of the house. 'I'll come again tomorrow, though – at the crack of dawn. Oh, Elizabeth,' leaning forward, he traced with one forefinger a delicate line from her throat to the top of her breastbone, 'I can't wait.' And as she started in response, 'To play football, of course.' Wide-eyed as Abigail, he backed away from her and, bouncing the football off his head, called: 'Francey, Johanna!' Then, singing, 'Come out, come out, wherever you are . . .'

Later that afternoon, just before the girls were due home from school, Francey came running into the kitchen from the yard to tell her that a lorry was on its way up the hill. As usual, a motor-driven vehicle travelling through this part of the parish was a rare phenomenon, ever rarer since the war had put a stop to most mechanical transport of any sort and Elizabeth went as far as the open back door to watch it. All she could see of the lorry was a rusted roof which had once been green and which, trailing flukes of buff-coloured dust, seemed to hump like a wide caterpillar along the brilliance of the fuschia hedges. She could already smell the gas which powered it.

The spectacle had brought children running from houses for miles around and even over the groan of the protesting engine she could hear their excited cries as they followed its labours up the hill. Elizabeth had decided it was a new purchase by some fisherman who was on his way around the coast road to Cleanderry or Ardgroom Harbour when, to her astonishment, a minute after it came into full view, the lorry turned into the few feet of well-worn grass in front of her own gate and, with a squealing of brakes, came to a halt just short of crashing into the gate itself. Automatically running her hands through her hair to tidy it, she hurried forwards as, with a great shuddering, the engine cut out.

As the dust settled, she saw there were two people in the cab. The door on the driver's side opened and Elizabeth's anticipatory smile froze on her face.

The person who emerged was a dust-covered George Gallaher. 'Hello, Elizabeth,' he said, brushing his clothes with his hands. 'Lovely day.'

Elizabeth could not have replied if she had been given a million pounds. She was temporarily saved the necessity, however, as the door on the passenger side opened and a very small blonde girl who looked vaguely familiar got out and came around the bonnet to stand beside George, her head reaching only a little above his right elbow.

George turned to her and, taking her arm, led her forward as though she were a débutante. 'You haven't met Hazel, have you, Elizabeth? This is Hazel Slye. She's an actress,' he explained unnecessarily since as soon as he said the name, Elizabeth had remembered she had seen the girl on stage in Glengarriff.

Small and wiry, Hazel sported a thatch of spiky blonde hair which she wore as short as a boy's. By far the most distinguishing features of her oval, elfin face were her eyes: one was light brown flecked with green, the other a bright, vivid blue. Elizabeth found the effect of her direct, multi-coloured gaze disconcerting. 'How – how do you do,' she stammered, holding out her hand to shake the girl's.

'Hello, Mrs Scollard,' the girl said seriously, 'I'm glad to meet you. George has told me a lot about you.'

'Has he?' Elizabeth stifled the impulse to giggle. After all she had been through, the arrival of this comical, mismatched duo in their absurd chariot was the last straw. She became aware that all along the hedges and walls, for what seemed like miles around, a gallery of fascinated observers, now old as well as young, was watching the proceedings. 'Would you like to come in?' she suggested. 'Are you just passing through?' Again she had to stifle a giggle. The notion that anyone, particularly this pair, would be 'just passing' such an out of the way place as Lahersheen was farcical. Only then did the implications sink in.

Francey . . .

'Thank you, we'd love to.' George pulled a package out of the pocket of his jacket; flamboyant as ever, it was tailored in Nile green seersucker. 'We brought you a small present. A little tea, a little sugar, some raisins . . .'

'How kind,' said Elizabeth, taking the packet and forcing herself to remain pleasant, 'this way, please.' She turned and walked in front of them towards the house.

Francey, who had been standing to one side of the gate

during the initial transactions, dashed ahead of the little group. Elizabeth did not turn to see how George was reacting to the first sight of his son.

The amount of tea was quite substantial, most likely a month's ration. Elizabeth did not bother with the niceties of exclamation over George's generosity. Instead, having shown them into the kitchen and seated them, she busied herself making an *ad hoc* meal, slices of bacon and mutton with soda bread.

It was the girl who kept up some semblance of conversation, dandling Abigail on her knee, then getting down on the floor to play alongside the child with Abigail's array of extemporaneous toys.

Francey, meanwhile, seemed to be struck unnaturally dumb. He hung about with Johanna in the doorway of the children's bedroom, never taking his eyes off the bigger of their two visitors. Even if he had no inkling who George was, she did not blame Francey for staring; the child, she knew, could never have seen such an exotic creature in all of his short life. George's great bulk seemed to fill the kitchen; his green jacket and khaki-coloured trousers glowed in the relative gloom as he sat at the table; apparently perfectly relaxed, he smiled any time he caught anyone's eye, including Elizabeth's. She was daunted by his continuing silence but could not summon up anything apposite to say. When the food was ready, she brought it across to the table: 'Here you are,' she said. 'I'm sorry it's not more, but you can appreciate we weren't expecting you.'

'It's lovely, Mrs Scollard.' Lithely, the girl uncoiled from the floor and sat beside George. Her clothes equalled George's in exoticism, her tight black skirt and gold-coloured even tighter blouse were patterned in an animal print of black and brown; with a yellow bandanna around her light-coloured, tufted hair, she reminded Elizabeth of a small bobcat she had once seen in Dublin Zoo. She was heavily made up but underneath, Elizabeth thought, the girl looked not much older than Mary, or even Kathleen.

George Gallaher was clearly up to even more dangerous

tricks than when she herself had known him. 'Thank you, Hazel, please call me Elizabeth,' she said on impulse.

'Certainly!' the girl's triangular little face was transformed by her wide, slightly gap-toothed grin.

Elizabeth was pouring their tea when she noticed that Francey had crept up to the table and was staring right into George's face. 'Don't be rude,' she called automatically then, as she continued to cater to them, willed as strongly as she could that under the pretext of arriving for a casual chat, none of her neighbours would venture into the house to examine Lizzie Scollard's outlandish visitors.

Because except for the hair colouring, no one looking at George and Francey together could fail to see the resemblance.

'This is your son, Elizabeth?' George asked rhetorically.

Elizabeth spilled some of the tea on the oilcloth and wiped it with her apron. 'Yes,' she said.

'Forgive me, I can't remember what you said his first name was—'

'Francey Scollard,' Francey said immediately. 'What's your name?'

'George,' the actor replied, 'I've a present for you.'

'A present?' Francey frowned. 'Why?'

'Francey!' exclaimed Elizabeth. 'Where are your manners?'

'Have you a present for Johanna?' Francey asked, ignoring her.

Grimly, Elizabeth realized she had little part to play in this scene beyond an attempt to limit its scope. Remembering the occasion when Francey had renounced Neeley as his father, she saw that once again she was up against her son's indomitable will, which was rarely exercised but unshakeable once he brought it into play. Francey had the bit between his teeth and when he was like this, short of physical violence there was nothing she could do to avert him from what he wanted to do or say.

Hazel saved the situation. 'I have a present for your sister.' She pulled a gilt bangle off one wrist and pushed it across the oilcloth towards Francey, who picked it up, examined it gravely and then turned round to where Johanna was, as usual, acting as his shadow. 'It's a snake, Johanna,' he said, rather as though Johanna was a favourite niece and not just a year younger than him, 'there's the two eyes,' indicating two little green gemstones.

'She says "thank you".' He turned back to George.

'And this is your present.' To Elizabeth, George seemed taken aback by Francey's self-assurance. 'Be careful opening it.'

'Thank you.' Francey accepted a wooden container about the same size and shape as a cigar box which George had brought with him into the house. Obviously heavy, it was fastened by means of a brass clasp.

'Oh!' The little-old-man guise slid like yesterday's snow off Francey as he gazed in awe at the contents of the box. Reposing in moulded velvet was a scale model of a steam locomotive, perfect in every detail. 'I have the rest of the set out in the lorry,' said George, 'carriages, tracks, even a miniature station. It used to be mine when I was a little boy like you.'

Francey looked up at him. 'Why?' he repeated.

'I'm – I'm your uncle,' George said, 'and uncles always bring presents when they visit, don't they?'

A frown creased the space between Francey's eyebrows. 'Whose brother are you?' he asked.

'Well,' George hesitated and it was the very first time Elizabeth had ever seen him so completely nonplussed, 'I'm – well, I'm more of a cousin, really, one of your mother's cousins from England – er – Scotland.'

'What's your second name?'

'Gallaher.'

Francey studied him some more then closed the lid on the locomotive. 'Can I see the rest of the train?' Knowing Francey as she did, Elizabeth could see that the subject of George's exact relationship to the family was not yet closed.

George, though, looked relieved. 'Certainly,' he said, hefting himself upright, 'come on out with me and we'll bring it in together.'

'They're lovely, Elizabeth.' Hazel watched Johanna follow George and Francey out into the sunshine.

Elizabeth sat in the chair George had just vacated. 'Why now? And how did you find us?'

'There was an account of the court case in some paper,' Hazel explained. 'He saw it and recognized the name. He'd been going on about having a son . . . Sorry about your husband,' she added, 'it must have been awful for you.'

'Still is.' Elizabeth was coming to like this strange girl, despite her having the flat Dublin accent she had always associated with being common.

'I told him,' in full flight now, Hazel waved an arm in the direction of the door, 'that you wouldn't want anything to do with him at a time like this but nothing would stop him.'

'Are you – are you his girlfriend?'

'Sort of. You know George – well, yeah, you *do* know George, don't you?' She grinned, 'Men!' and threw her multicoloured eyes up to heaven.

She was so direct that Elizabeth found herself liking her more and more. 'What are you doing around here?' she asked.

'We're opening on Monday for a season in Killarney, our own company. George came into a few quid; apparently, his oul' fella cashed his chips some time last year. That's how we got the transport. Why don't you come? I'll get passes . . .'

To travel to Killarney was an even more daunting prospect than to go to Glengarriff. 'No, thank you,' said Elizabeth. 'Don't think I'm not grateful for the invitation, but I'm in mourning.'

'Ohmigod!' The girl's hand flew to her mouth. 'How could I be so stupid!'

'Please, it's all right,' then, 'What do you think George wants to do about Francey?'

'I dunno, really, I don't think he's thought beyond giving him that bleedin' train. To be honest with you, Elizabeth, I don't think he wants anything more than to reassure himself that he actually accomplished the great feat of reproducing himself. Maybe he's just getting old.'

Elizabeth smiled. 'George's age has always been a bit of a mystery.'

'Not a bit of it,' retorted Hazel, 'I made him show me his birth cert.'

'So how old is he?' Elizabeth was almost afraid to ask.

'He'll be forty-five next birthday.'

Elizabeth digested this. 'Why on earth was he telling everyone six years ago he was forty-six?'

'I think George likes to have his cake and eat it too. Forty-six sounded like a nice safe age to him, still young enough to get it up, if you know what I mean, but not young enough that any unfortunate girl would want to get serious about him.'

'Are you?' Elizabeth felt somehow she had the right to ask.

'I dunno.' Hazel shrugged. 'I'm seventeen, but I've been in this business so long that I feel older than George. I'm a hoofer,' seeing Elizabeth's look of incomprehension, she explained the term, 'dancer. Been on the stage since I was four. But I'm trying to get into straight acting.'

Elizabeth was still not reassured about George's intentions. 'So you don't think he's going to make any trouble?'

'If you ask me,' said Hazel earnestly, 'it's you's the one who should be making trouble. Now that he has a few bob, I'm telling you, Elizabeth,' she proceeded to strike the table, one stroke to each word, 'that – man – should – pay – for – that – child!'

The light in the kitchen darkened as George and Francey came back in through the doorway. Hazel looked around unabashed. 'Did you hear that, George?'

'Hear what?' The expression on his beautiful face was bland.

'Never mind, not now,' said Hazel firmly. 'We'll talk about it later,' and she wiggled her pencilled eyebrows meaningfully in the direction of Francey who, in high excitement, was busy stacking boxes on the table.

'Where can I lay all this out, Mammy?' Francey asked.

'We'll get your daddy to —' Elizabeth began without thinking, then flushed crimson. 'Sorry,' she said. 'Tomorrow when I see Mossie I'll ask him to fix up a bit of space for you in one of the outhouses. All right?'

'Aw,' Francey's lower lip threatened, 'I want to play with it *now* . . .'

'I said tomorrow,' Elizabeth insisted.

'Let me — may I?' George offered. 'If you'll show me where you want it?'

'Well, if you're sure,' said Elizabeth, thinking to herself that wonders would never cease. This was certainly not the George she had known.

As soon as she went out into the yard, she saw that many of the neighbourhood children still hung around the lorry and the gateway. Ignoring them, she led George and Francey across the yard to the stable, empty since the sale of the donkey. There were two boxes in the shed, and even if they got another donkey, one of the compartments could be used permanently for the train layout. 'They'll probably rust, Francey, so you'll have to bring them in in the winter, won't he, cousin George?' she added maliciously, unable to resist it. Gallaher, to give him his due, smiled ruefully.

But as he removed the Nile green jacket to allow him greater freedom to work, Elizabeth gazed at his gorgeous, well-shaped torso and wondered if something would stir in her.

Nothing did.

It was amazing, she thought, how quickly her physical desire for him had disintegrated, once the rot had set in; now George Gallaher appealed to her merely in an aesthetic sense, as if he were a prize exhibit in a show. She could even be fond of him, she thought, as though he really were her cousin.

Johanna came into the stable and Elizabeth picked her up. Quietly, the two of them watched George and Francey open all the boxes. Here was another strange thing, Elizabeth thought as she continued to puzzle out the changes in George: the mild, helpful behaviour of this lapdog of a man was so far removed from that of the Lothario she had met as lately as last February that it was difficult to believe they were the same person. Could it be possible that Mr Gallaher had at last met his match? She peeped through the doorway of the stable: Hazel Slye was sitting on the little bench seat in the yard, her tight skirt hitched up to expose little knees as pale as peeled mushrooms, eyes blissfully closed in the sunshine. She was no beauty, thought Elizabeth, and although her size might initially make her look vulnerable, anyone who thought that was making a mistake. Hazel was tough and funny and clearly took no nonsense. George had probably needed someone like her all along.

She was still watching the model railway take shape on the floor of the stable when she heard from Hazel's greeting outside that the girls had returned from school.

Putting Johanna down, she went out into the sunshine. Neeley's four daughters were standing in a loose row, their expressions varying from Goretti's shyness to Mary's out-right wonder as they took in Hazel's novel outfit.

'Are these all yours? You don't look old enough.' The actress's expression was unequivocal: she was gawping at them in amazement.

'I married into them.' Elizabeth smiled. 'My husband was married before. Say hello to our guest, girls,' she continued, 'this lady is Miss Hazel Slye. She's an actress.'

They all murmured their greetings except Kathleen, whose reaction was so unexpected and untypical that Elizabeth was taken aback: her face, normally so closed, blazed with animation. 'An *actress*?' she breathed, then, as if feeling she had said too much, clammed up again.

But Elizabeth had no time to ponder this, because as the others crowded curiously around Hazel, it struck her that she had not prepared for the eventuality of introducing them to George. Being older, it was unlikely that they – the three eldest ones at least – would be deceived by the story that the man so like Francey was her long-lost cousin from Scotland of whom they had never heard until now. She knew she had better get them all to herself for a few moments to explain George Gallaher away before he came out of the stable. 'Come on, girls,' she said briskly, 'leave

390

Miss Slye alone now. Into the house and wash your hands. Excuse us a moment, Hazel,' she added. 'I'll be back out to you in a few minutes.'

'Who's in the cabin?' Margaret reacted to the sound of George's deep voice as he explained something to Francey.

'I'll tell you inside. Now go on – shoo – all of you.'

Visitors from outside were a rare treat in Lahersheen and the girls chattered excitedly among themselves as they made the daily transition from school to home life. Watching them, Elizabeth was struck by the natural resilience of children; it had been not much more than a month since their father's funeral and yet although she occasionally found one or other of them glumly staring into space, they seemed to have recovered remarkably well. The exception, of course, was Kathleen, who was so introverted that Elizabeth could rarely figure out what was going on behind those closed features.

Even now, she did not participate in the general chat in the kitchen but seemed to have sunk into a private world of her own. Elizabeth noticed for the first time that her growth had spurted and that she was now a little taller than her elder sister.

The girls' chatter drained away as George Gallaher came into the kitchen. This time even Kathleen reacted in tandem with her siblings, her expression mirroring those of Mary and Margaret as everyone stared at the shirtsleeved vision in their doorway. The effect George was having would have been comical if Elizabeth had not been so worried about Francey – and if she had not recognized adolescent hero-worship when she saw it.

'Hello, girls,' said George, a trace of his former braggadocio instinctively resurrecting itself.

Elizabeth stepped in. 'Girls, this is George Gallaher, he's Miss Slye's friend. He's a sort of relative of mine from Scotland.' All the girls stood mesmerized but out of the corner of her eye Elizabeth saw Kathleen's hand go to her throat. Had she recognized the face? 'These are my other daughters,' Elizabeth went on.

George's eyes raked over them and Elizabeth, wondering how deeply buried were his naturally lascivious instincts, became protective. 'You've already met Johanna and Abigail and Francey, so that's them all,' she finished stiffly.

'I can't believe it,' George said, smiling his incomparable smile. 'Six girls and all so beautiful.'

Mary and Margaret giggled self-consciously and Elizabeth, knowing she was being over-sensitive, nevertheless thought she detected the word 'harem' written all over George's face. Again she took charge – she had to get the girls on their own. 'Were you looking for something, George?'

'Yes. The floor of the stable is uneven – would you have a flat piece of wood or tin or something?'

'I'll show you,' Kathleen said before Elizabeth could reply.

'No, you stay here and finish up what you're doing,' said Elizabeth authoritatively. 'Come with me, George.' She took his elbow and led him, still shaking his head in wonderment, back outside. As she crossed the yard she turned her ears to the kitchen. After a second or so of profound silence, there was an explosion of talk.

The girls were still talking at the tops of their voices when she got back, having found a set of boards for George. 'Right,' she said, 'we're being very rude, leaving Miss Slye out there to her own devices. Goretti, will you go outside and talk to her for a few minutes, please? I have a job for these other three,' she indicated the three eldest.

When Goretti had left, she called the other three to the table. 'There's something I have to tell you,' she said quickly, 'but it's very confidential. That means it's a secret – understand? Only between the four of us. I'm trusting you now.'

Mary and Margaret nodded solemnly, Kathleen pursed her lips.

'Is that understood, Kathleen?' Elizabeth's eyes bored into her.

'Yes.' Kathleen raised her eyebrows.

'George Gallaher is not a distant relative of mine,'

Elizabeth said flatly, 'he's Francey's father. But Francey's too young to know that just yet. All right?'

'Why are you telling us?' After a pause in which none of them moved, it was Margaret who spoke.

'Because you're old enough to know, that's why.' Elizabeth tried to make herself sound as though she was paying them a compliment. 'And when you look at George again, you'll see how very much like him Francey is. I didn't want you saying anything.'

'Why isn't Francey supposed to know who his father is?' Kathleen was twisting one of her plaits in between finger and thumb.

'I told you, he's too young.' She did not have any time to analyse Kathleen's reaction to this because again the doorway darkened, this time with the figure of Hazel Slye. 'Whew!' she said. 'It's too hot out there. Would you believe this is Ireland? Would you mind if I asked for a drink of water?'

'Well, it is summer – and this is Béara!' Elizabeth laughed, got up from the table and fetched the drink.

An hour or so later they all crowded into the stable to watch Francey's clockwork train set in operation. Elizabeth could see what a beautiful artefact it was: lovingly constructed by a master craftsman and correct in every detail, the windows of the carriages, in their smart livery of green and red, were of real glass, the enamelled locomotive gleamed with brass banding and the winding key, also of brass – which Francey clutched so proudly in his hand – was so ornately scrolled that it, too, was a small work of art.

George had laid the track in a figure-of-eight pattern and Elizabeth found it almost mesmeric to watch the repetitive circling of the train as round and round it bustled, brushing against the dangling hose, as thin as twine, of the water tower, trundling past the station platform on which tiny tin people, a nurse, a porter, a well-dressed Edwardian lady and her trilby-hatted husband waited eternally beside a diminutive weighing machine. As it clicked through its tunnel and, first one way then the other, clacked over the points where the loops of the eight crossed over, she felt soothed, almost hypnotized, and as though she could stand there all day.

Through her dreaminess, however, she became aware of an insistent tugging at her sleeve and turned around. 'Mammy!' It was Kathleen, whispering, her eyes unusually large.

'What is it?'

'I want to talk to you – in private. It's urgent.'

'Now?'

'Yes.'

Elizabeth followed Kathleen back into the house. 'What is it?' she asked.

Kathleen took a deep breath, then the words came out all in a rush as though sluice gates on a dam had been opened too suddenly. 'I've been talking to Hazel,' she said, 'and, Mammy, please, please – she says it's all right if you say so, *please* can I go with them to Killarney. I've always wanted to be an actress —' She faltered then as though she had said too much.

Elizabeth looked at her wild, pleading eyes. She had never seen Kathleen like this, nor had Neeley's second daughter ever spoken so directly to her, soul to soul. This was clearly of such vital importance that she knew she had to handle it very carefully indeed. 'I see,' she said. 'But what about your Leaving Cert – boarding school?'

'I discussed all that with Miss Slye – Hazel,' Kathleen rushed passionately on. 'She says what we could do is I could try it out this summer and if I'm no good or anything – I'd just be starting off doing odd jobs and little parts and things like that – then in the fall I could go to the boarding school. But, Mammy, please, I'll never know unless I try. Please, Mammy, *please* . . .' She wrung her hands in front of Elizabeth, so avidly in earnest that tears stood out in her eyes.

Elizabeth thought she could be fairly sure of Hazel, but what about George? Could she trust Kathleen to a company which included a man like George Gallaher? 'Darling, you're only fourteen,' she said softly, 'it's very young to be going off like that—'

'I'll be fifteen in September – but, Mammy, Hazel started when she was only *four*,' Kathleen cried. 'I know I can do it if only I get the chance. And I'll never, *ever* get such an opportunity again. I just *know* I won't!'

Elizabeth thought fast. Killarney, while not exactly just up the road, was at least within striking distance, and girls younger than Kathleen had been shipped off alone to England or America to work in domestic service for people neither they nor their families had known. She looked at the girl's face, so kindled with enthusiasm and desire, and knew that if she did not accede to this, she could forget any chance she had ever had of forging a relationship of some sort with her. And, yet, could she take this responsibility?

As she dithered, the expression on Kathleen's face changed. From one of open communication, it closed up again until it had hardened into lines of deadly suspicion and even hatred. 'You're not going to let me go, are you?' she said.

'I'm not saying that, Kitty – Kathleen – I'm just thinking about it, that's all.'

'Well, think about this, then. I know why you want this George Gallaher kept a secret around here. And it's not for Francey's sake!'

'What?'

'I know what you're up to with Danny McCarthy.' She lowered her chin until she was regarding Elizabeth steadily from under her brows. 'How would he feel if he knew what his precious lady love is *really* like?'

'Kathleen!' Elizabeth was so appalled she could barely articulate the word.

'So put that in your pipe and smoke it. And I'm going whether you like it or not. You can't stop me.'

Elizabeth swallowed hard. 'I'm sorry you feel you have to resort to this, Kathleen, because whether you believe this or not, I was going to let you go to Killarney. I was just considering it, that's all.'

Something of the truth of this cut through Kathleen's anger. 'Oh, really?' she said aggressively, but there was an element of doubt in her eyes.

'Yes.' Elizabeth wondered if anything could be retrieved from this mess. She remembered then Alison Charlton Leahy's warning about staying alert to hidden dangers: Mossie Sheehan had not been the only spy in the camp. But she knew now she could not let it pass. 'My relationship with Daniel is not your business, Kathleen,' she said.

'It was certainly my *dead father*'s business!' Kathleen retorted. 'Ye didn't think much about him, did ye?'

Elizabeth found the confidence to stare her down and when Kathleen's fierce eyes slid away, her voice was again steady. 'We were discussing you and Killarney,' she said.

'Well, can I go?' Kathleen did not look back at her.

'Yes. For a trial period.'

Again, Elizabeth thought the girl was going to cry. She closed her eyes and threw back her head, while at her side her hands made fists. 'Thank you,' she whispered and while she did not go so far as to embrace her stepmother, when her eyes opened she raised her arms a little and took a half-step forward as though she was going to; her eyes had miraculously cleansed themselves of hatred and were joyful, in Elizabeth's experience, an expression hitherto foreign to them.

It was not only Francey, who was a cuckoo in this crowded nest, Elizabeth thought, as she watched this succession of transformations, and blamed herself anew for not giving enough recognition to the diverse personalities of the children. From whatever genes it had sprung, Kathleen's character certainly contained a penchant for drama. 'I said a trial,' she warned now, 'and you can't go until the school holidays. But that's only a couple of weeks away,' she added hastily, not wanting to bring on herself yet another operatic onslaught. 'Anyway, if you're going to be away all summer, you'll need a chance to get ready.'

'Can I tell Hazel?'

'Yes,' said Elizabeth, *and I'll deal with George*, she thought privately.

Kathleen flew towards the door. 'Mammy?' She turned round before stepping outside.

'What?'

'I'm sorry about what I said.'

Elizabeth did not trust herself to speak and contented herself with a nod. Nevertheless, she knew that Kathleen's contrition, while undoubtedly genuine, was only for the moment. As the girl vanished into the brightness outside, Elizabeth made a resolution to redouble her vigilance and her efforts to be discreet.

That night as she collapsed into bed, she wondered weakly how many other women around the country were going through such turbulence. And although, predictably, her body longed again for Daniel, she was glad she had forbidden him to come round that evening. She was tired deep in her soul and doubted whether her emotions could have coped with any further demands, no matter how pleasurable.

At least she was fairly sure that, at least for the present, George would not pose problems in the matter of his son. She had spoken to him alone for a few minutes in the yard just before he and Hazel had left. 'I only wanted to see him,' he had said. 'Hazel thought it might be a good idea.'

Elizabeth could not resist it. '*Hazel* thought? That I ever thought I'd see the day, George Gallaher!'

He had had the grace to look sheepish. 'I know, I know,' he said, then, appealing, 'You know it never could have worked out for us, Elizabeth.'

Elizabeth had refrained from uttering the obvious retort which came so readily into her mind: there was nothing to be gained by beating George Gallaher to death with his own past inadequacies. 'People change,' she had said enigmatically and left it at that.

He had seemed grateful, his beautiful face lighting up. 'Do you think I could see him from time to time? And I'll send some money for him whenever I can.'

Remembering Hazel's revelation about George's 'few quid', Elizabeth had thought wryly that he had not changed

397

all that much. 'Whatever,' she said. 'You can see him whenever you like, but I reserve the right to tell him who you really are only when I believe the time is right. Agreed?'

'Agreed – and, Elizabeth?'

'What?'

'You turned out all right.'

'Thank you. One more thing, I'm trusting you with Kathleen, George. If I get a hint – *one hint*, George – that you're up to any of your old tricks with her, I'm warning you, big and all as you are, I'll break your jaw. Understand?'

'Elizabeth!' Placing both hands across his heart, he had made a little *moue*. 'Come on, have a little faith . . .'

'This is Elizabeth Sullivan you're talking to.' Elizabeth had thrust her face as high as possible towards his. 'She has her heart set on it and it appears I have no choice but to trust you. But she's not even fifteen and I'm serious, George. I'll follow you to the ends of the earth – even Hollywood or the BBC.' She had the satisfaction of seeing his eyes flicker but before he could reply they had been joined by Hazel.

Promising to send the lorry back for Kathleen in a fortnight's time, the two visitors had taken their leave.

There was a time, Elizabeth had thought as she waved goodbye to the two of them as they bumped off up the hill towards Castleclough, that even so niggardly a compliment as 'you turned out all right' would have thrilled her to the roots of her hair. People changed and no mistake.

For the rest of the evening, the excitement among the girls had been barely containable. Kathleen had basked like a celebrity in the unaccustomed attention and even now, when it was nearly midnight, Elizabeth could hear the excited whisperings emanating from the bedroom next door. 'Go to sleep in there,' she knocked on the communi-cating wall, 'I'll never get you up in the morning.' But her heart was not in the command and they knew it because all it elicited was a heightened discharge of muffled giggling.

She was too tired to be more insistent and, as she drifted towards sleep, one of her last waking thoughts was that at least Mossie Sheehan had been benevolent enough to stay away. Fuzzily, she envisioned a scene in her kitchen in which Mossie and Gorgeous George, each in his own style, misunderstood one another perfectly.

And, then, supposing Daniel put in one of his unscheduled appearances as well? All three of them could be locked together into her kitchen.

An infernal triangle, she thought, trying to imagine an uncontroversial topic of conversation between these three males, as different from each other as animal, vegetable and mineral. That was good. As she slid towards unconsciousness, Elizabeth entertained herself with notions of which of the three was animal, which vegetable and which mineral . . .

It seemed like a long time since she had been able to laugh; now she began to giggle as loudly as the girls in the next bedroom and was still chuckling as, finally, she fell asleep.

Chapter Twenty

Over the summer months Elizabeth's life settled into some semblance of routine.

For the fortnight after the visit of George and Hazel, her entire household became involved in Kathleen's departure for Killarney and the excitement continued long after that as everyone watched every day for the arrival of the postman.

Kathleen's new station in life seemed to suit her: although, to judge by her letters, most of her duties seemed to consist of running errands, mending costumes, doing laundry and operating a backstage device called a 'thunder-sheet', she was given small parts in the productions and filled page after page with vivid descriptions of audience reaction and the praise larded on her by her new friends, George, Hazel and another girl called Vanessa.

The language and liveliness of the letters were a revelation to Elizabeth. Accustomed to overseeing Kathleen's dull, formulaic school essays on topics such as 'The Life of a Ha'penny', she had had no idea that Neeley's second daughter was so imaginative. What's more, unlike the watchful, brooding personality Elizabeth had come to know since she had arrived in Lahersheen, the Kathleen in these letters was happy, even ecstatically so.

The Killarney season was due to end in early September and, increasingly, Kathleen's letters contained a subtext about wanting to make her career on the stage. Elizabeth's quandary about this was considerable; with her vow to take her responsibility for her stepdaughters seriously in the forefront of her mind, she was not convinced that the life led by strolling players was suitable for young girls not yet fifteen years of age. Yet Kathleen was so headstrong Elizabeth doubted if she would easily succumb to dictation.

She put off a confrontation – always unsatisfactory by letter – and also postponed making a firm decision. In the meantime, however, she made enquiries about boarding schools in Cork, and discovered that Kathleen had indeed approached St John for advice and help in the matter of secondary education and that he was more than willing to sponsor her.

Meanwhile, Kathleen's absence had lifted a small degree of pressure from her own day-to-day existence. Her relationship with Daniel Carrig continued to swing between extremes of joyful, obsessive passion on the one hand and deep anxiety on the other. Given Mossie Sheehan's peripatetic presence in Lahersheen and the endless light of the summer nights, she could not bring herself again to make love in the open fields or even, despite Daniel's urging, in the little ruined cottage on her own land.

As lovers therefore, they had no opportunity at all for privacy – even the haysheds in the area were too close to their owners' farmyards – and the school holidays meant that the children were permanently present in Elizabeth's house. Having to content themselves with covert, fraught kisses, their physical frustration grew in direct proportion to their ardour.

By late August, Elizabeth had still been unable to bring herself to tell Daniel the truth about her contract with Mossie Breac and, in answer to his pleas that they become open about their love, continued to insist that due to her mourning and, more pertinently, the circumstances in which her husband had died, an open flaunting of her relationship could with some justification be considered a scandal.

She found she was reluctant to confide even in Tilly, feeling that by doing so, she would be placing her friend in a difficult position, and as a result, the question of Daniel now hung like thin but impenetrable gauze between the two friends. Elizabeth fully understood Tilly's dilemma; she felt she had already called too often on her reserves of loyalty and generosity and, after all, Neeley's family and Mick Harrington's family had lived side by side and worked their adjacent lands for generations.

In all material respects, however, Elizabeth's affairs were in a better state than at any time since her marriage. Taking Tilly's advice, she had added a few ducks and geese to her poultry stock; they were less difficult to care for than she had imagined and would fetch a good price at Christmas. The only large animal she had kept was the milch cow to supply their domestic needs – responsibility for her milking was now divided between Margaret and Goretti – and of Neeley's other twelve cattle, Mossie had bought six and had sold the other six at the Castletown fair. The money from both transactions was safely banked and, in addition, her father, brooking no refusal, had insisted on placing a substantial sum of money into a separate 'insurance' bank account for her in Castletownbere.

What was more, although she hated to admit it, her land thrived under Mossie Breac's stewardship.

Tilly had been right about Mossie's ability as a farmer: seven days a week, in good weather and bad, he worked diligently from first light and even to Elizabeth's relatively inexperienced eye, the land and the stock on it were blooming. Although she continued to loathe him for the position in which he had placed her – and to mark with dread the dwindling of the months until she would have to declare publicly her betrothal to him – she had to admit to a grudging respect for his agrarian skills. He had even converted one field to the growing of root crops and, as well as turf, Elizabeth's fuel store was neatly stacked with kindling and firewood from his clearing operations along the boundary walls and ditches.

Of course, continuing to imagine his presence behind every hedge and furze bush in Lahersheen, she would never have dreamed of allowing Mossie to guess at her sneaking respect and, any time they encountered one another in field, farmyard or roadway, simply nodded curtly to him without speaking. In light of their pending nuptials, however, Mossie's work on the farm naturally proved far more complicated than the simple conacre agreement they had presented to the world and it was impossible to avoid all personal intercourse.

Whenever she did have to speak to Mossie Elizabeth made it perfectly clear that in her estimation his behaviour had been no better than that of a worm. Her contempt, however, seemed to be having little effect and no matter how icily or monosyllabically she behaved towards him, he continued to treat her with infuriating equanimity.

And whereas her relationship with Daniel had merely put a small dent in her friendship with Tilly, in her dealings with Mossie it kept her off balance and terribly unsettled. Because although she perceived it to be lying warily between herself and Mossie like a quiescent but poisonous jellyfish, Mossie himself seemed interested only in the farm business with which they had to deal together, and never hinted at or referred to the relationship in any way.

Elizabeth frequently longed for one major, blazing row but Mossie never afforded her the opening.

On the evening of 20 August, which was the day after her twenty-seventh birthday, she and Tilly were sitting not in the farmyard as they usually did on fine evenings but on kitchen chairs they had carried round to the front of Elizabeth's house. 'I don't know why we don't come out this side more often,' Tilly remarked, surveying the small stone walls and gentle undulation of the landscape as it fell towards Coulagh Bay.

'I suppose it's because we like to keep an eye on the comings and goings in the parish.' For once, Elizabeth's day-to-day stresses had subsided and she was basking in the glow of physical well-being. In a belated bout of spring cleaning, with the children's help she had scrubbed out the entire house; on the clothes line to her left, sheets, tablecloths, dusters and dishcloths hung motionless and golden in the light of the dropping sun; the fuchsia hedges were draped with rugs, blankets and bedspreads, and her hands smelt pleasantly of soap. 'I'll sleep well tonight,' she said.

'I know most people hate housework,' said Tilly comfortably, 'but from time to time, I dunno . . . it's kind of nice the way the house talks back to you, sort of thanks you. You know what I mean?'

'Mm.' Elizabeth did not entirely go along with her friend; in her view, housework was repetitive and exceptionally boring, but she had to admit that tonight she did feel satisfied, not to say virtuous. They lapsed into companionable silence, broken only by the faraway call of some forlorn cow and, nearer, the assonant note of a corncrake in a field of hay stubble.

'I suppose you heard the latest about Jimmy Deeney?' asked Tilly after a bit.

'No, but I'm sure you'll tell me.' Elizabeth did not like what she considered to be the man's vulgarity and had not voted for him. Deeney had, in fact, failed by quite a large margin in his election – despite his generosity, even the Lahersheen, Derryconnla and Eyeries boxes had not gone for him – but he fancied his chances next time round and was still to be seen buying drink all over the constituency in an effort to woo support for his next outing.

Tilly, who had voted for him, took no offence at Elizabeth's tone of dismissal. 'Well, he's bought Castleclough, apparently,' she said, 'lock, stock and barrel.'

'That old pile? What's he going to do with it?'

'Live in it, I hear, at least part-time in the summer. Now that he wants to be a TD, he feels he has to have some place in Cork South West. I gather the Yank wife wouldn't dream of living here permanently, of course, but she likes the idea of being lady of the manor. There's eighty acres with it, you know, and a good stretch of river. Not to speak of that little private harbour on the sea.'

'Yes, but it's beyond repair, surely?'

'No, that's the good part, there's no roof, but the basic structure is sound enough. So the good news is that the restoration means jobs for a few months at least.'

Elizabeth wondered if her friend had been hinting on

behalf of Daniel's employment prospects but, not wanting to enter any note of dissonance, let this pass. 'Did I tell you I had a birthday card yesterday from Kathleen?' she asked. 'Wonders'll never cease. She's certainly changed. Until now she wouldn't have given me the time of day. She's due home soon,' she added lazily, luxuriating in the warmth on her face. 'I don't know what we're going to do with her. I've the convent all set up in Cork but she doesn't want to go now. She's really enamoured of this stage idea. What do you think?'

'Is she any good of an actress?' Tilly flicked at a ladybird which had landed on her lap.

'I don't know,' Elizabeth shrugged, 'that's just the thing. I've never seen her. This whole thing was a great surprise to me. And I suppose Neeley'd turn in his grave.'

'Why don't you go and see her? Make up your mind then?'

'Sure, how could I?'

'Why not? The farm is ticking over grand under Mossie. And I'd help Mary out on the domestic side – they're all getting older and more manageable now, you know, Lizzie. And, sure, it'd only be for the one night.'

The more Elizabeth thought about it, the more attractive the proposition became. 'Would you, Tilly?' she asked tentatively. 'I hate always to be the one on the receiving end.'

'What goes round comes round. My day will come to ask you for a favour, you'll see. Anyway, it's no favour. I like looking after childher. You know that.'

Elizabeth's sense of settled domesticity deserted her as she examined the prospect of going to Killarney. Because, of course, if they planned it properly and were discreet, Daniel could come with her. Like she and George so long ago, they could stay in a hotel.

Glancing at Tilly to make sure she was not betraying herself, her mind sharpened up and began feverishly to lay plots: she could leave off her mourning clothes, make herself look a bit younger. They could book in as a honeymoon couple . . . 'Would you really look after things for me?' she asked.

'I just said so, didn't I? Off you go – and enjoy yourself while you're at it.'

And so it was that Elizabeth found herself sitting nervously in Killarney railway station waiting for Daniel to arrive. She had written to book them into the Great Southern Hotel, which was in the station grounds – the confirmation was in her handbag – and, according to the plans she had so meticulously laid, they would walk into the lobby as though they had travelled there together.

Twisting her wedding ring, which she had cleaned and polished until it looked as new as possible, she thought that George Gallaher would have been amazed at how easily the little girl he had known had fallen into the role of chief strategist in the matter of bamboozling the eye and ears of Lahersheen. For instance, knowing they could not be seen to eat together in the hotel or even a restaurant, she had brought sandwiches for Daniel; and, feeling delightfully sinful, she had even timed the trip for the days when she would be least fertile.

But her present anxiety came from the one facet of the project she had had to leave to chance: the plan had called for Daniel to travel courtesy of the goodwill he could find on the roads between Ardgroom, Kenmare and Killarney but as travellers, particularly motorized ones, were scarcer than ever, she was getting more and more worried that he had not been able to find enough lifts and was stranded on top of a mountain somewhere.

The other prospective problem, that someone from home would see them together in the short time it would take to cross the public concourse of the hotel, was so fearsome that Elizabeth's brain had shut it out altogether. But the longer the wait went on, the more nervous she became. Fearing that her continuing loitering in the station was becoming too conspicuous, she left her seat for the fifth or sixth time to check whether Daniel was approaching.

This time, to her relief, she saw him on the public road beyond the hotel just as he was jumping off the back of a trailer being pulled by a motorbike. Checking the urge to

406

run to him, she walked slowly and casually towards the wide entrance of the hotel.

As he came towards her she saw he was turned out like a new broom; he was wearing his Sunday suit and good shoes, and his curly hair, back to its normal length, was slick with hair oil. But if by shining himself up in this fashion he thought to make himself look older and more sophisticated, the effect he had achieved, she thought fondly, was to the contrary: he looked like an oversized candidate for Confirmation.

Elizabeth herself had dressed carefully: her own lengthening hair was caught back from her face with a white Alice band and under a light black raincoat, which she had taken off the moment she arrived in Killarney, she wore a belted, full-skirted dress of yellow and white cotton, more suitable to the farm belt of Oklahoma than the sombrely sartorial hills of Béara, but she knew it took years off her age.

She greeted Daniel soberly, squeezing his elbow to warn him against a public display of affection. 'But we're supposed to be on our honeymoon!' he protested.

'Plenty of time for that,' she hissed. 'If we've just got married, we'll be shy with each other, won't we?'

'Oh . . . Sorry . . .'

'Don't be sorry, just be ready.' She was beginning to feel giddy, like a schoolgirl mooching from school for the day.

'Oh, Elizabeth —' His expression kindled.

'Ssh!' She caught him by the arm and led him chastely up the steps in front of the hotel.

She handled the check-in procedures, surprising herself with her own ease, but as soon as the door closed behind the porter, who had shown them into their room, she leaned against it and exhaled a long, long breath she had not realized she had been holding.

Daniel was beside her in two strides. 'Wait, wait!' She held him off while she locked the door. But even as she was struggling with the stiff key, his hands were on her breasts and he was already kissing the side of her neck.

Their first lovemaking that day was, if anything, more

furious than in the grassy hollow behind Kilcatherine cemetery on midsummer's night. But just as had happened on that occasion – and despite her careful calculations – fear of pregnancy forced Elizabeth to watch with one side of her brain so that she placed reins on her own desire.

But when, after he came, she was holding him in her arms and stroking his damp, satiny back, her body seemed to continue working independently of her mind. Reacting, he was ready again within seconds and made as though to re-enter her but she twisted away. 'No, no, not now, just hold me tight, very tight . . .' Her breath was shuddering out of her lungs in small intense explosions and the sensations chasing through the rest of her body were like the tongues of forked lightning she had seen playing repeatedly over the summit of Tooreennamna on a hot afternoon during the previous week. Instinctively, she clutched one of Daniel's thighs between her own as, without warning, the second orgasm of her life rippled through her.

When at last she opened her eyes, Elizabeth laughed out loud at the thunderstruck expression on Daniel's face. He responded with an uncertain smile. 'Are you all right?' he whispered. 'You gave me a terrible fright.'

Riding on a wave of relaxation, she stretched her legs and spread her arms, pushing the hands against invisible walls to each side of her. 'I've never been more all right in my life. I'm lovely, I'm wonderful, you're wonderful. You're a wonderful, marvellous man.'

'Come here to me.' He grabbed her.

Their second time was slower and, since she felt that by now she could trust him to be aware of the need to be careful, was for Elizabeth far more erotic than the first. Nevertheless, she continued to maintain her watchfulness and, as before, twisted away to eject him seconds before he came. This time, after his breathing had returned to normal, he had enough confidence to complain. 'I wish we didn't have to do that,' he said into her hair.

'Me, too, but we have to and you know why.'

'It will be different when we're married,' he blurted out.

All the eroticism drained away and Elizabeth felt cold.

He felt the change and raising himself on one elbow, gazed down at her. 'Sorry, I know I shouldn't have said that without asking you first. But it's the truth, isn't it?'

Something of what she was feeling communicated itself to him because his look of youthful bravado peeled gradually away, leaving in its wake an expression of such anguished doubt that she could not bear to see it. On the other hand, he had now presented her with an opening and she knew she should avail herself of it; she was not being fair to him by not telling him the truth.

But again Elizabeth balked at it. Why spoil a lovely day, perhaps the only day like this they would ever have together? 'Look, my little darling,' she kissed his eyes one after the other, 'I can't talk, or even *think* about marriage in my present circumstances. Let's just try to live each day as it comes and be grateful for what we can get.'

'All right,' he said, recovering somewhat, 'but I'm warning you, Elizabeth, you're going to be my wife and that's the holy all of it. So I hope you're prepared.' He kissed her, but for Elizabeth the complications were now too close to the surface. 'Not just now,' she said, holding his head in her hands but keeping him away. 'I've got to go and find the place where Kitty's play is and buy a ticket.' Fearing to make her stepdaughter nervous, and also for reasons of discretion with regard to Daniel, she had not told Kathleen about her visit to Killarney.

'You've plenty of time for that.'

'No!' She tried to sound lighthearted.

'All right,' he said. 'But you'd better come back soon. You don't want to leave me here like this for too long, do you?'

Seeing he was ready yet again, Elizabeth laughed and slid off the bed. 'It's a machine you need – you bold thing, you!' She went off to douche herself and get dressed.

When she returned from the bathroom he was lying

exactly as she had left him, on his back, awash in the ruined sea of bedclothes like an otter she had once surprised taking a breather among the small waves of Glenbeg lake. 'You're lovely, Daniel,' she said softly, 'and I love you.'

'I love you, too,' he said.

Promising to be quick, Elizabeth left the room and descended the broad, carpeted stairway into the lobby of the hotel and out into the day, which was overcast and threatening rain.

Having left the hotel grounds and turned the corner into the street, the first person she saw was George Gallaher. There was no mistaking his massive frame as he strolled along the footpath, a girl at his side.

Elizabeth arranged her face and hurried her step.

She was within five yards of the couple when the girl with him turned her face sideways and upwards to say something. The girl was Kathleen.

Elizabeth was so shocked she stopped dead and then, to give herself time to catch her breath, turned to look in the window of a nearby shop. The window display – a satin eiderdown, bolts of oilcloth and furnishing fabric, dungarees, pinafores, wellington boots, threads, towels, tablecloths, dishcloths, sheets, pillowslips – whirled before her eyes in a multicoloured blur as she gathered her thoughts.

After a minute or so she ventured another glance at the couple. It was not surprising that she had not immediately known the girl: Kathleen looked entirely different from the schoolgirl who had left Lahersheen two months previously. Her dark hair was combed sleekly into a chic French pleat; she was wearing high heels and quite a lot of make-up and her red, polka-dotted sheath dress was cinched with a wide white belt.

Elizabeth's instinct was to run after the couple and snatch her stepdaughter away right there and then. Then she realized it was possible that she was making Everests out of one small molehill: why shouldn't Kathleen be in the public company of her boss? After all, they were working together.

There was also something else, she thought wryly;

given the small matter of her own lover stashed away in the Great Southern, the stench of hypocrisy hung about any moral calls she might now make on Neeley's daughter – or on George himself, for that matter. Yet Kathleen was under-age and fatherless. Elizabeth gazed intently after the pair who were about sixty yards away now.

They were not touching and she decided for the present to give them the benefit of the doubt but to stay fully alert. She also decided she would stick to her original plan by not announcing her presence in Killarney until after the show that evening.

She waited until George and Kathleen had gone from view around a corner before continuing on her own way. Killarney was a small town and she had little difficulty in finding the hall where the show was running. Having bought a ticket for the performance that night, she hurried back to Daniel.

Later that evening, Elizabeth was finding it quite difficult to make up her mind about Kathleen's talent for the stage. She played three tiny roles in the play, a transla-tion of a Russian drama that Elizabeth had never heard of and which she found so convoluted and slow moving that she wished several times for the simplistic but entertaining melodrama of *Conn The Shaughraun*. Kathleen appeared as a maid, as the niece of one of the minor characters and, in heavy make-up and crude grey wig, as a hunched old lady begging for alms. The niece did not speak at all and the combined lines of the maid and the old lady would not have amounted to more than half a page of script.

The maid, however, was the most substantial of the three roles; she did not have much to say or do with the action but she moved through quite a few of the scenes. At least, Elizabeth thought, Kathleen was able to move with grace and ease and she was certainly not lacking in confi-dence. Yet her talent, if such it was, was not of the variety which blazed across the rudimentary footlights so clearly that it would have immediately convinced her stepmother to let her have her way in pursuing a career as an actress.

George, as gorgeous but as wooden as ever, played the

unlikely part of a student; his lines indicated that he was perennially studying and that this was not unusual in Russia, so much so that Elizabeth wondered if this piece of script had been added to cover his age. Had she not at one time been a victim herself, she would have laughed at the palpable quickening in female audience attention every time he came on.

Hazel's performance was a different matter. Barely recognizable in dark ringlets which cascaded down her back, bearing no trace of the heavy Dublin accent which normally overlay her speech, she played the fey daughter of the house with whom George's character was hopelessly in love. She was really good, Elizabeth thought, wondering how long she would stay with such an undistinguished company.

But most of the play passed without engaging Elizabeth at all as she worried and harried at the problem of what to do with Kathleen.

She was still debating which way to approach it when the final curtain came down. She checked with the commissionaire by which door in the hall the players would emerge, then, decling his offer to show her backstage, waited outside for Kathleen to come out.

Because of the overcast sky, it was darker than normal in the street, a condition not helped by the brown-out. But Elizabeth was glad of the gloom: Killarney was only sixty miles from Lahersheen and, as a result of Neeley's death, she was notorious not only in Béara but in the whole region. She knew she had every right to be here to see her stepdaughter's performance, but because of Daniel's presence in the town the fewer who knew about it the better; for safety's sake she had even sat near the back of the hall but as far as she could tell, no one from home had been in the audience.

The actors, chatting and laughing, all came out together; Kathleen was last of the group. 'Hello.' Elizabeth stepped out of the shadows.

'Mammy!' Kathleen's hand flew to her mouth in surprise. 'What are you doing here?'

'I came to see the play. It's a public performance after all . . .' Elizabeth hugged her stepdaughter and, for once, Kathleen did not stiffen but, after some hesitation, hugged her back.

'Elizabeth, how nice.' George, fully back into his theatrical persona it seemed, kissed her hand. 'Hazel you already know,' he continued and then introduced the rest of the company, including Vanessa, the other 'girl' to whom Kathleen referred constantly in her letters who proved to be a tall willowy woman whom Elizabeth judged to be at least thirty. 'Congratulations, you were very good,' she said, including them all.

'We're all going to have a little party in Vanessa's room,' George volunteered. 'Of course you'll come along?'

Unsure how she should react, Elizabeth glanced at Kathleen but her stepdaughter's face bore no visible warning. 'All right,' she said, 'but just for half an hour.' She was conscious that it was now more than three hours since she had left Daniel mournfully eating sandwiches in the debris of their hotel bed.

To get to the Cork road where Vanessa lived, the group had to pass the entrance to the Great Southern. Elizabeth, aware from her own young years of the embarrassment of having to walk with your parents when your friends were around, had let Kathleen go on ahead with the main group and was lagging behind with Hazel, whose small stature in comparison to her own made her feel like a giraffe. She kept her face averted as they passed the hulking grey stone of the hotel building but, once safely past, took the opportunity to ask the other woman's advice about what to do with Kathleen. 'She's awful keen,' Hazel said in reply, 'but it's far too early to tell whether she'd make it or not. She's certainly not a dud and I think she could develop quite well, but to tell you the truth I think she should go to school. I'm sorry I didn't have a proper education. I'm moving on, did she tell you?'

'No, she didn't say anything. Where?'

'I've managed to save a bit of money and I'm going to London. I've an audition for drama school. I'm fed up with this lark.' She waved a small, contemptuous hand in the direction of the rest of the company.

'How'll you manage? I thought all travel was banned?'

'Oh, there's way and means,' said Hazel mysteriously.

'And what about George? I thought you and George—' It was said before Elizabeth thought about it.

'Fecker!' said Hazel passionately. 'That's all he is, a fecker. I can't stand the sight of him and I'm having nothing more to do with him. I have to stay here and finish the season because I'm a *professional*! Otherwise ... Sorry, Elizabeth,' she shot a look at Elizabeth's face, 'but he's — oh, nothing.' She clammed up.

Elizabeth's suspicions about George were re-aroused. 'Please, Hazel,' she asked, trying not to let her panic show, 'is there anything I should know?'

'Nothing, nothing,' said Hazel quickly, 'he's just a fecker, that's all. Like all men. But, of course, why I am I telling *you* that, you of all people?' She stopped in her tracks and clutched Elizabeth's arm. 'There is something and maybe I shouldn't tell you this – and please don't be upset about it, he's not worth it, but ...' Hazel took a deep breath. 'Do you know that he has kids everywhere?'

'What?'

'Well, I suppose that's a bit of an exaggeration. There's another besides your son,' she amended. 'It's another boy, by the way. That I know about,' Hazel added darkly.

Elizabeth did not quite know how to take this, not yet. To her surprise, during the first scan of her feelings it did not seem to matter to her all that much. 'How did you find out?' she asked.

'I'm a Dublin woman. I didn't come down with the last shower,' Hazel replied enigmatically. '*Fecker!*' She spat into the gutter. Then, dropping Elizabeth's arm, she searched her face, her own expression anxious. 'Are you upset? Maybe I shouldn't have told you – but I'm just so *annoyed*. Can't stand to be in the same *room* as him ...' She grimaced with distaste.

'Please, Hazel,' Elizabeth begged as they moved off

414

again, 'you'd tell me, wouldn't you? If there was anything else. Anything else I should know.'

'Of course I would,' Hazel replied but something in her expressive features did not match the words.

'I don't believe you,' Elizabeth clutched at her. 'It's Kathleen, isn't it? Kathleen and George?'

'Elizabeth' – as Hazel turned her face upwards Elizabeth was conscious, even in the weak, hooded streetlights, of the astonishing divergence of her eyes – 'don't ask me any questions about George Gallaher – *fecker*!' Again Hazel spat into the roadway. 'Sorry,' she said then, 'I can't help it. Every time I *think* —' Recovering, she picked her next words delicately. 'Please don't forget that Kathleen is a colleague now and she trusts me . . .'

Elizabeth knew that in letting the rest of the sentence hang she was as good as revealing the truth. 'Oh, my God!' Her hand flew to her mouth. 'I *knew* it!'

But as her rage at George started to flow like a red tide, Hazel put a restraining hand on her arm. Her fingers felt as strong as talons. 'You don't know anything,' she insisted, 'and I haven't seen anything – honest to God I haven't. I'm not just saying it. I think she probably has just a little crush – Elizabeth – please . . .'

'I'll – I'll —' Elizabeth was incoherent.

'Here's the house,' Hazel said urgently, stopping in front of a small iron gateway. 'Please, Elizabeth, not a word.' She thumped the side of her head with the palm of her hand. 'This is me all over. I shouldn't have said anything.'

'You didn't, Hazel,' Elizabeth choked back her anger, 'but thank you for telling me. I'll control myself. But don't let me be alone with him or' – she clenched her fists – 'I won't be responsible for my actions. Of course Kathleen can't stay here now —'

'I told you, Elizabeth, I saw nothing,' Hazel cried, 'and I'll keep an eye on her. It's only another two weeks.'

'Then I'm definitely going to talk to George —'

Now Hazel seized her by both forearms: 'If you do,

Kathleen might as well go home with you tonight. *Think*, Elizabeth. Do you think she'll ever forgive you?'

The words acted as brakes on Elizabeth's rage. She remembered her own 'little crush' on George Gallaher and her simmering resentment of her mother and father for all those years. 'Are you sure it hasn't gone any further than a crush?' she asked Hazel.

'I'm positive. She is very young,' said this seventeen-year-old. 'I'll watch her for you, I promise – and more to the point, I'll watch George. Neither of them will make a move without me seeing it.'

'How can I – I'm not sure I'd be doing the right thing by leaving her.'

'I promise you, Elizabeth, I'll mind her. I will. Now calm down, for God's sake, take deep breaths . . . Come on now, there's a good woman . . .'

Obediently Elizabeth, who found she was shaking, did as she was told. And after the third breath, she was indeed more collected. And having received further wholehearted reassurances from Hazel that for the next two weeks she would not let Kathleen out of her sight, after a few minutes she managed to go in through the gate and towards the party with some semblance of composure. 'You'll write to me if there's anything?' She stopped at the threshold of the front door.

'Of course. I promise.'

Everyone at the party – Vanessa's room proved to be a small bedsitter – was far too wrapped up in him- or herself to notice anything untoward in Elizabeth's manner. She was greeted warmly, handed a glass of beer and left to her own devices. Kathleen, who had been ensconced in a corner of the room before her stepmother arrived and who acknowledged her merely with a nervous smile, was subdued, even uncomfortable. *So well you might, my girl*, Elizabeth thought dourly, herself taking a seat on a divan.

Neeley's daughter seemed far less sullen than was her wont in Lahersheen; on the other hand she showed little sign of the vivacity she had displayed in her letters home; nor, to Elizabeth's small relief, no matter how keenly she

416

observed Kathleen as she listened to one of George's theatrical stories, did her stepdaughter's expression betray any special regard for him. George, Elizabeth saw, had reverted more than a little to type; tonight there was little of the lapdog so much in evidence during his visit to Lahersheen – how wrong she had been about *that*, she thought bitterly; nevertheless, he seemed happy simply to shine within the company in general and was not paying particular attention to anyone.

Or was that just a cover? But George, Elizabeth reminded herself, was not a good actor . . .

Catching Kathleen's eye, she raised her glass to her and then, as she tuned in to the latest of George's stories, tried to put herself in the girl's shoes: just fifteen years old, in her first, glamorous job, having an adolescent crush on the man who must rank as one of the most beautiful she would ever see in her life – and who had also been her stepmother's lover. And now being watched by this selfsame stepmother.

No wonder she was uncomfortable.

Elizabeth tried to relax her vigilance a little, and listening to the tone and unnatural colouration of the stories, seeing the casual way the actors hugged and touched each other, she experienced a sense of *déjà vu*. There was little to choose between these actors and those she had first encountered with Vivian Mellors. Theatrical people enjoyed themselves certainly, but Elizabeth wondered how self-confident they really were underneath all the bonhomie. For instance, when it came to it, just as Vivian Mellors had changed his name, how many of these Rogers, Hazels and Vanessas were really Dottys, Marys or Seáns? And what did that say about them? At least Kathleen had as yet shown no inclination to become Juliet or something even more fancy.

And once again it was proved to Elizabeth how much actors as a group differed from ordinary mortals. For instance, after her protestations of hatred for George, it might have been expected that Hazel would be a little tense when sitting only three feet away from him but this was not the case; the little actress was ignoring him but otherwise seemed quite at ease.

In spite of her worries about Kathleen, Elizabeth was conscious of the time flying and of Daniel waiting for her back at the hotel. But she could not leave too soon and it was nearly midnight when, taking advantage of a communal laugh, she stood up. 'I've really got to go now. Will you see me off the premises?' she added to Kathleen. Saying her goodbyes to the rest of the company and with Kathleen close behind, she left the room.

'Thanks for coming,' but Kathleen seemed to tense up again as the two of them stood in the recessed porch at the hall door of the house. Was she going to confide in her?

'You're welcome,' Elizabeth replied. 'I'm glad I came to see you, you were marvellous.'

'Did you really think so?'

'I did,' said Elizabeth, 'but we'll talk more when you get home at the end of next week, all right?' Then, sensing the girl's turmoil but not wanting to alienate her, she chose her next words. 'Is there anything you need, Kathleen? Anything you want to tell me – anything I can do for you while I'm here?'

'I don't want to go away to school!' Kathleen burst out, her veneer of being grown-up close to crumbling. 'I know I said I did but that was ages ago. Everything's changed and I don't want to now.'

'There's nothing written in stone,' said Elizabeth carefully. 'But it was your idea, you know. We've all gone to a lot of trouble and expense on your behalf. Grandad Sullivan—'

'I know it was my idea and I'm sorry. But is a person not allowed to change her mind around here? It's my life, you know.'

'Why don't you talk to Hazel about it?' Elizabeth asked evenly. 'She thinks, by the way, that you should go to school first, get an education. Then you could think about the stage.' She hesitated. 'And don't rush into anything,' she said softly. 'Don't grow up before you have to – you've plenty of time, Kathleen.' She hoped Kathleen would interpret the code.

But Kathleen chose not to. 'Easy for Hazel to say,' she retorted aggressively, 'she's going to London.'

'So she told me.' Elizabeth felt that once again she was right on the precipice of disaster with this intense girl. She had to tread delicately or lose whatever relationship she and Kathleen had cobbled together through their correspondence. The porch of the house supported a rose-covered trellis and to give her something else to do besides staring into Kathleen's eyes, she tucked in some of the plant that had trailed free. 'Kathleen,' she said calmly, 'I said we'd talk about all of this when you get home. But I might as well tell you right now that you're not even fifteen, and I think you are far too young to go to London. Anyway, there's a travel ban, you wouldn't be able to go until the war's over. But, as I said, you should talk to Hazel about it. She seems to know what she is doing.'

'I'm nearly fifteen and I'll never forgive you, *ever*, if you make me leave the theatre. I *love* the theatre. It's my *life*!'

'Please, Kathleen, don't overreact—'

'Please, Mammy, I'm begging you. You don't know how important this is to me. It's a matter of life and death.'

'It's only natural to feel that at your age. That's what you think now—'

'I'm warning you.' Kathleen's body assumed a stillness which did not bode well but nothing could have prepared Elizabeth for the deadly tone of the girl's voice when she continued. 'I'm going to make you regret this,' she said, 'and I can, you know.'

'You're jumping the gun, Kitty.'

'*And don't call me Kitty!*'

'All right!' Elizabeth had had enough. 'I'm sorry,' she said, just managing to hold on to her temper, 'but this is something you've just sprung on me. And this is hardly the time and place. I have to think over what your father would have wanted—'

'Don't bring my father into this. He's dead, thanks to you and your—' Kathleen, spitting with fury, stopped herself just in time.

419

Making a last supreme effort, Elizabeth held her tongue. 'Goodnight, Kathleen,' she said quietly. 'We'll talk next week. And I'll write to you tomorrow.'

'Well, don't expect a letter back!' Kathleen went back into the house and slammed the door.

As Elizabeth walked along the few feet of concrete which served as a driveway, she was stunned, not only at the viciousness of the row but at the speed at which it had erupted. It was as though Kathleen had not only provoked but had rehearsed it, including the part Elizabeth was to play. What was more, she thought, the row was almost too heated, as though the subject matter – of going to school – was only the crust over the cauldron.

Closing the gate after her, Elizabeth walked back along the dark streets, even the prospect of going back to Daniel doing little to lift her spirits. The altercation with Kathleen, on top of her worry about her, had taken all the joy out of the trip; and she was in no doubt that Kathleen would be quite capable of wreaking havoc if she was thwarted in the matter of staying in the theatre.

But what sort of revenge was she planning?

Her brain picked over the possibilities, each one worse than the other, as she trudged along. Although the end of August was still technically the summer high season in Killarney, there were very few people about. Between the house and the entrance to the hotel, she encountered only a woman walking a dog and two young men lounging against the high stone wall which ran around the periphery of the Great Southern grounds.

When she let herself into the room, Daniel was sitting on the bed which he had remade. Freshly washed and shaved, his curly hair gleaming in the glow cast by the bedside oil-lamps, he looked up from the book he was reading. 'I was getting worried,' he said, 'it's after midnight.'

Elizabeth's spirits lifted a little: he sounded so much more like her grandfather than her lover. 'Oh, Daniel, I've had such an evening,' she said, collapsing on to the bed beside him. 'Hold me, just hold me and don't say anything.'

Carefully, he put down the book and took her into his

arms, cradling her as though she were made of porcelain. 'What happened?' he asked after a few moments.

'I'm so afraid the whole thing is going to come crashing down around me.'

'What whole thing? Tell me . . .'

'You, me, us, the farm, the family, the whole thing.'

He stroked her hair quietly for a few moments. 'Must have been some play!' he said then.

'Oh, Daniel!' She laughed, turning her face to him for a kiss and marvelling once again that whereas sometimes he could seem so young, at times like this he could behave with such maturity and perception. Yet, when the kiss was over and he was again stroking her hair, she could not bring herself to tell him about her fears for Kathleen. She sighed. The whole issue was just too complicated.

Hearing the sigh, he hugged her to him as though she were a child who had cut her knee. 'Please don't be so upset,' he said, 'I hate to see you upset. I want to take care of you.'

As she snuggled in to him, he brought his lips in contact with the top of her head. 'It's only a matter of time before we won't have to be creeping around like two thieves,' he murmured into her hair, 'and then people like Kathleen can go to hell. The whole of the parish can go to hell. And I promise I'll never let you be upset when we're together for good.'

Elizabeth gazed up at his serious, loving face. 'Just kiss me,' she whispered.

Chapter Twenty-One

Elizabeth did not have long to wait before finding out exactly what Kathleen had in mind. Two weeks after her visit to Killarney – and on the day before Kathleen was to leave for the convent in Cork – she caught the girl in her bedroom.

Having left the house to visit Tilly but having progressed only fifty yards across the fields, Elizabeth found that the afternoon had turned chilly. Although still wearing mourning clothes, she had begun to ameliorate their harshness by adding splashes of colour: today, the skirt was worn with a blouse of pale lilac which, made only of fine cotton, gave no protection from the breeze which skirled up from the bay.

Returning to fetch a cardigan from her bedroom, she surprised Kathleen with hands deep in a square wooden box kept hidden under a pile of clothes at the bottom of the chest of drawers in which were stored birth and baptismal certificates, jewellery and anything else considered valuable.

Like the handwritten agreement with Mossie Sheehan.

'What are you doing?' She rushed towards Kathleen but the girl was too quick for her: 'I'm sure Danny McCarthy would be very interested in this!' She brandished the document and then put it behind her back.

'Give that to me at once!' By standing very still and concentrating all of her will into her voice, Elizabeth tried to intimidate her.

But Kathleen stood her ground. 'Fair's fair,' she said in an equally concentrated manner. 'You've ruined my life, now I'm going to ruin your little arrangement with your croppy boy.' She placed such a venomous emphasis on 'boy' that Elizabeth wanted to strike her pale, insolent face.

'That piece of paper is none of your business—' she began, only to be cut off by Kathleen.

'Oh, is it not, now, Mammy? Mossie Breac is to be – what is he to be exactly, Mammy? My step-stepfather? Or just another ride for my stepmother? Oh, I forgot—' turning her back and arching it protectively over the document to fend off any possible attack, she read as rapidly as she could: '"I will be your wife in law only and not in any other way – you will remain in your house and I will remain in mine."'

She whirled around again. 'No rides for Mossie, eh?' It was virtually unknown for women – especially young girls like Kathleen – to use the horrible slang but Elizabeth's only concern now was to get at the document. But as she moved forward once again in an effort to grab it, quick as an eel Kathleen ducked under her outstretched arm and backed up against the wall, the document still behind her: 'Thought of everything, eh, *Mammy*?' she taunted. 'How to have your cake and eat it too – eh? Or should I say your pound of flesh?'

Elizabeth managed to seize Kathleen's shoulders. She tried to pull her away from the wall but the girl resisted, kicking out.

Then Elizabeth, horrified at what she was doing – in the very spot where Neeley had cracked Francey's skull – stood back and as quickly as it had begun, the physical struggle stopped. Panting, they faced one another and Elizabeth was doubly appalled at the depth of hatred in Kathleen's young eyes. 'What have I done to you to deserve this?' she breathed.

'It's all your fault. If you'd let me stay in the theatre, none of this would have happened.'

'That is beneath contempt,' Elizabeth said quietly, retreating and sitting on the bed. 'Do your worst, Kathleen, I won't stop you. I hope you can live with the consequences.'

423

'I will. You can be sure of it!' But for the first time, Kathleen looked a little uncertain. Then she made an effort at recovery. 'Here's your precious paper!' She flung the two sheets of foolscap on the floor. 'I don't need it, anyway. And by the way I've known what's in it for *months*.' Turning, she ran out of Elizabeth's bedroom and into her own.

Slowly, Elizabeth bent and picked up the two sheets of paper. Folding them, she put them in the pocket of her skirt. The time had come to tell Daniel the truth. Before he found out from some other source.

She knew where he would be: the job on the seine boat had not worked out – six of Neeley's cousins were on the crew – but he had been given a start on the preliminary building work in progress on Castleclough. Putting on the cardigan she had come for, she left the bedroom.

'What was that all about?' Mary looked up from where she was colouring a picture with Abigail. 'I told her she shouldn't be going into your bedroom.'

'I can't tell you now, Mary.' Elizabeth heard the sharpness in her own voice and immediately apologized. She was guilty about Mary in general. Having left school, Neeley's eldest daughter showed no inclination to leave home or to look for work and, over the summer months, Elizabeth had come to rely on her more and more as an unpaid housekeeper. She knew that this was unfair and Mary's future was an issue she would have to address very soon. 'I'll tell you,' she promised, 'but I've to go out for a while. I'll be back to get the tea. In the meantime,' she hesitated, 'if Kathleen talks to you about it, will you please remember that there are two sides to every story?'

Mary nodded, obviously intrigued.

Strangely, as she cycled towards Castleclough with the most difficult task of her life ahead of her, Elizabeth's brain detached itself from the emotional import of what she had to do. It was as though it refused point blank to deal with the issue until it was faced inescapably with it.

She thought about what she had said so glibly to Mary

about two sides to every story. What exactly was her own side in this situation? Look at me now, she thought, survivor of three miscarriages, mother to seven children – including one who hates me on principle – my life a complete mess; infamously widowed, betrothed to a man I do not love, loving a man I can't have. And all because seven years ago I developed a young girl's crush on an unprincipled cad.

No, she thought, that was not fair. She could not blame George Gallaher for the directions her life had taken. The blame lay squarely with herself. It was not as if she had not been warned, by the church, by the nuns, obliquely by her parents. If only she had had more sense, more self-control . . .

And in all fairness, she thought, her life had not been all bad. For instance, insulated here from the war that still raged interminably in Europe, she was housed, fed, seriously wanting for nothing material. The children were healthy, unlike the unfortunate war orphans and refugees in the ghastly photographs she occasionally saw in the pages of the newspapers.

And she should not discount the joys she had been granted, of the glimpses she had had of true human love: of holding Francey when he was born, the other babies too; of the improvement, despite all her sins, in her relationship with her father and even, slightly, with her mother; of the warmth of her friendship with Tilly Harrington; of the physical celebration of sex with the right person.

With the right person.

She must not dwell on that or she would never be able to do what she had to do. 'Good afternoon!' She greeted a neighbour who was leading a donkey laden with turf creels.

In reply, he cracked a switch across the animal's rump and tipped his cap. 'Afternoon, ma'am! Lovely day, thank God!'

'Thank God!' This was another good aspect, Elizabeth thought as she leaned into the pedals of the bike to push it up a steep gradient: the gradual dawning that, in some way she could not quite define, people like the man she had just met had become familiars and the Béara peninsula had become home.

As she continued the clinical survey of the positive aspects of her life it came to her that if, ten years ago, someone had told the city-bred Elizabeth Sullivan she would put down roots in this wild, beautiful part of the earth, Elizabeth Sullivan would have thought him certifiable. But she now knew that Béara had lodged under her skin in a way the city of her birth never had or ever could. At the highest point in the road she dismounted and, under the pretext of planning what she was going to say, stood looking around her. Predictably, her brain again slid away from the trauma facing it and, instead, feasted on the glorious afternoon.

From here Elizabeth could see no dwelling houses at all, just the green and brown-gold landscape of rough bog stretching on one side of her towards the low summits of the Béara hills, on the other gently downwards towards the empty and glittering sweep of the Kenmare river. At this time of year, the violet peaks of County Kerry on the other side softened and blurred in the late summer haze so that they seemed to float independently of the land, as if they belonged to some faraway place created in the imagination of artists and dreamers.

And then as she looked across the blowing buff-coloured grasses and the year's last puffs of bog cotton Elizabeth was pierced with a sense of loss so acute the tears sprang to her eyes.

The same thing had happened two weeks before, when, just before dawn, she and Daniel had been lying quietly in one another's arms in their bed in the Great Southern. They had made love twice more that night and after Daniel had fallen asleep just before dawn Elizabeth, cradled in his arms, had pulled back a little to watch him in the growing grey light. His head was thrown back a little and she could see the gleam of his eyes under his eyelids; his lips, too, were parted slightly, fluttering as the breath came through them in deep regular waves. As she gazed at him, her sense of

426

physical repletion drained away to be replaced by the same sense of desolation she felt now. It was as if to be human was constantly to be reminded of transience and mortality. Happiness, once planted, always threw up the shoots of its own destruction.

The beauty around Elizabeth now became similarly unbearable to her and, remounting her bicycle, she free-wheeled round a bend until, sailing before her on its sea of surrounding trees like a square raft, the roofless turrets of Castleclough came into view. There could be no further escape into daydreams or emotional self-indulgence. Elizabeth's lips tightened with determination and, within minutes, she was cycling through the tall stone pillars at the entrance to the house.

The driveway had already been cleared: mounds of foliage, tree saplings and uprooted bushes lined it on both sides while its surface had been temporarily dressed with rough gravel through which the bald tyres of Elizabeth's bicycle scrunched loudly. Afraid she might get a puncture – even yet her detachment had not totally deserted her – she left the bike propped against a tree and set out to walk the rest of the way. Ahead of her she could already hear the ringing of tools and the faint sound of men's voices. After a hundred yards or so, she passed under an ivy-covered archway, emerging into the open space in front of the house against which the work party was busy erecting a wooden scaffold.

She saw Daniel immediately. Stripped to the waist, he was hefting a long plank across one shoulder, having taken it from a pile dumped on the overgrown lawn.

As she hesitated, Elizabeth was spotted by a man whose name she did not know but whom she recognized as being from Derryconnla. Obviously some kind of foreman, he was directing operations from the ground. 'Mrs Scollard,' he said in surprise, coming over to her. 'What can we do for you?'

'I have a message for Daniel Carrig,' Elizabeth said, holding fast to her conviction that if she wavered now, she would be lost. 'Is he around?' Not wanting to see whether or not the man reacted to this, she looked away from him towards the house.

'Danny!' he shouted. 'Come over here a minute.'

Elizabeth saw Daniel look over his shoulder and even from this distance, discerned the shock in his face when he saw why he was being summoned. She held her head high as the other men working on the building stopped what they were doing to observe what was going on. The only way she would be able to get through this, she thought, was to pretend that it was another Elizabeth Sullivan who was here and not herself.

Daniel lowered the plank he was carrying and then dropped it, the *thunk*, as it hit the ground, loud in the watchful silence of the workmen. His face was bright red with embarrassment as he walked across to where Elizabeth was standing with the man from Derryconnla. 'Hello, Elizabeth,' he muttered, 'is there something wrong?'

'I need to talk to you, Daniel,' she said. 'He won't be long,' she added to the foreman, who took the hint and left them, shouting to the rest of the men to get back to what they had been doing.

'I'm sorry to come like this,' she said immediately the foreman was out of earshot, 'but something has happened which meant I had to talk to you right away.' Not waiting to see how he reacted to this, or to check if they were still being watched, she turned and led him back under the arch towards the driveway. After a second or so, she heard his boots sounding on the gravel as he followed her.

When she was certain they could no longer be seen, she stopped and turned again to face him. 'Daniel, I don't know how you're going to take this – well, I suppose I do – but I have something terrible to say to you.'

'What?'

Forcing herself to ignore the fear in his eyes, she plunged on. 'I can't marry you,' she said harshly. 'And there's a very good reason for this. I have to marry someone else. I repeat, I *have* to. I don't want to. I think you know how I feel about you. That was no lie—'

She stopped as all the colour drained from his face so that his brown eyes looked almost black. 'You have to?'

Elizabeth realized that she had put it badly: 'having' to get married meant illicit pregnancy. She of all people should have known that. 'It's not like that,' she said hurriedly, 'it's something else.' Taking a deep breath, she fixed her gaze on the patchy gravel at her feet and told him the whole story. 'So you see,' she finished as though she were a reciting child and the grey stones at her feet the audience, 'I had to come and tell you in case Kathleen did. I had to be the one to do it,' she repeated doggedly, 'I'm sure you can see that. And I hope you understand why I didn't tell you before. It was very selfish of me. But I wanted to hold on to you for as long as possible – I couldn't help it, Daniel.' She glanced up at him and, although she had thought she was prepared, was aghast at the effect her words had had on him.

Daniel's bloodless face was sunk low into his chest and his hands hung uselessly by his side. His entire body was slumped in despair as though the substance had been drawn out of it.

The membrane of Elizabeth's assumed toughness split and she put her hands to her face. 'Oh, Daniel,' she cried, her voice muffled through tears, 'I'm really sorry, I'm so sorry.' But within seconds, she dashed away the tears with the heels of her palms. 'I'm sorry,' she repeated in a more normal voice, 'you can't imagine what it's been like trying to keep this to myself. Say something,' she begged as Daniel continued to stand as though turned to marble, 'please, please say something – anything . . .'

He looked up at her finally, the skin on his face like that of a cadaver. 'I'm going to sort out Mossie Breac Sheehan,' he said.

'No, oh, God – no!'

Elizabeth tried to grasp his arms but he evaded her. 'Leave me *alone*!'

'Just say you'll come to the house tonight,' she begged. 'We'll talk—'

'What have we to talk about now?' he asked, the

429

expression on his face so terrifying that Elizabeth cried out, 'Oh, Daniel, don't say that – I've never seen you like this—'

Again she tried to embrace him but he pulled away, holding his arms out from his sides to fend hers off. 'Please Elizabeth, don't. Don't humiliate us both.' He turned and walked away and Elizabeth knew that for the rest of her life she would remember the image of his rounded shoulders and clenched hands, his head thrust forwards on his neck. The work sounds floating to her ears from the unseen house, the jocular calling in the musical up-and-down accents of the peninsula seemed outlandish: why was there no physical reaction anywhere to what had just occurred? Surely it was inappropriate that only a few yards away, men were laughing and hammering as if nothing at all had happened?

She was able to hold herself in check until she reached her bicycle. Then, as she tried to mount it, the pedals slipped on the chain, which was loose, and although it did not come off, her shin cracked off the bike's fork. She was not really hurt but this small misfortune was the impulse which tipped her over the abyss. Her self-control and false detachment deserted her and although she made little outward noise, she wept as uninhibitedly as an abandoned infant, tears blending with mucus from her nose and saliva from her distended mouth. Straddling the fork of the bicycle, she pushed her head as low as she could force it until the handlebars cut painfully into her abdomen; she welcomed the pain and pressed harder, harder, as though to cleave herself in two. She clutched the perished rubber of the grips until she felt fragments of it coming off in her palms and bent her knees until her pubic bone was being crushed by the cold metal of the fork.

The paroxysm was too strong to last and after a minute or so it eased. She had no handkerchief and, looking blindly around for something to use, saw a stand of dock leaves; she pulled a handful, blew her nose and wiped the rest of her face with the sleeves of her cardigan. 'Right,' she said aloud, clearing her throat, 'come on now. You need to be in the whole of your health to deal with what's next.' Remembering Hazel's lessons in self-calming, she threw her head back and took a long deliberate breath, then a second and a third. The air shuddered at first through her lungs but she kept the posture, eyes closed, head thrown back, until she felt quieter.

When she was confident that her breathing had returned to relative normality, she opened her eyes; she happened to be standing in a portion of the driveway which boasted stands of mature trees on either side. The sky, framed by dense tree-top foliage, seemed to gaze impassively down at her like the blue eye of a Cyclops. 'Come on, now,' she said again, dismissing the notion, 'now's not the time for rubbish like that.'

She was grateful for the cooling effect of the breeze on her stinging eyes as she cycled away from the gates of Castleclough. Her face distorted and her calves burned as, expending as much physical energy as she could summon, she stood on the pedals of the old machine, torturing it, impelling it up the hill as though demons were in pursuit. 'Come on, come on, push, *push*!' she exhorted herself. 'Don't look back. Don't think. Think later . . .'

Activity was what was needed now. When she got home she would blacklead the stove, yes, that's what she would do. The cow byre could do with a good cleaning out. She had postponed that too long. She could whitewash the interior – there was still some lime left over from the last time Neeley had whitewashed the house. And there was a little window in the cabin which had previously been used for wintering the cattle. All that was in it now was the butter churn and the clothes mangle: maybe she should make up a set of curtains for the window, put a few chairs and a little table in it, fit it out as a sort of playhouse for the younger girls so that on a wet day they could get out from under her feet in the kitchen. And then Francey had been wanting her to help him make another tunnel for his train set . . .

And when all that was done she could look out all her old books, all the favourites she had brought with her and which, because she had been so busy since she came to Béara, she had not had an opportunity to revisit. She had read only one novel – *Rebecca* – sent as a Christmas present by Maeve, in the past two years. It would be nice to bury herself in her old friends . . .

The house came into view and behind it Elizabeth could see her geese, heads down, moving in unison across the lower field. That was another task, she thought, she was not at all sure of the security of the shed in which the fowl were penned at night. She would ask Mick Harrington to have a look at it.

By the time, exhausted and panting, she turned the bike in through the piers of the farmyard gate, Elizabeth had accounted for every minute of the next three weeks.

As she crossed the yard and entered the house, her legs were trembling from the punishment she had given them; they gave way just inside the door and she sank on to the chair beside the window to catch her breath. The aroma of baking bread filled the kitchen and on the table, cups, plates and cutlery glinted in the diagonal shaft of sunlight emanating from over her left shoulder: Mary had already started preparing the tea. The eggs were lined up and ready for boiling, the kettle was singing on the hob and, just as she had found it at Castleclough, all was normal as though nothing untoward had happened.

'Are you all right, Mammy?' Mary suspended the operation of scooping butter out of the crock on the dresser on to a plate and looked over at her with concern.

'I'm fine,' Elizabeth replied but it came out as a croak and she had to clear her throat. 'I'm grand,' she repeated, 'just a bit winded, that's all. Where's Kitty?'

'I dunno.' Mary shrugged. 'She went out.'

'And the others?'

'They're around somewhere. Maggie and Goretti are minding Abbie out in Francey's shed.' Mary went back to what she had been doing.

After a bit, Elizabeth struggled to her feet and crossed the floor to look into the children's bedroom. Kathleen's suitcase, still empty, lay open on one of the beds; her school uniforms, dressing-gown, slippers, nightdresses and sponge bag, all spanking new, were strewn carelessly over the floor and the other beds. Elizabeth, just barely holding on to her self-control, fought a fresh upsurge of tears, this time of frustration. The girl was supposed to have finished her packing by now: they had to be ready to leave the house very early the following morning.

She went back out to the kitchen. Using two butter spades, Mary was shaping the butter into a smooth cake on the dish. Her small deft movements had a calming effect. 'Want a hand?' Elizabeth asked. Action was what she needed now.

'Everything's done.'

If it could not be action it had to be distraction with another concern. 'Mary,' she asked, 'are you sure you're happy enough just working here in the house like this?'

'What else would I do?' Mary hesitated. 'I was a dunce at school, nobody's going to give *me* a job in a chemist's.'

'Don't run yourself down like that.' Mary's best friend, daughter of the shopkeeper from Castleclough, had gone straight from school to work as a counter assistant in one of the two chemist's shops in Castletownbere. 'You're not a dunce, you've got other talents.'

'Like what, Mammy?'

'Like running a house better than anyone I've ever seen, like dealing with children.'

'You mean like a housemaid?'

It was the nearest Elizabeth had ever heard to bitter words on Mary's lips; it had never occurred to her that Mary, dear dependable Mary, could be unhappy or frustrated. Once again she felt helpless: somehow, all these children were running through her fingers, they had grown and developed without her really noticing. 'Of course not,' she said stoutly, 'not a maid. Someone who is lovely to live with.'

Mary looked at her uncertainly, the butter dish still in her hands. 'I mean it, Mary,' Elizabeth insisted, 'you're a lovely person. And the man who gets you will be lucky.'

'Yeah, surely, that's me all right, the belle of the ball!' Mary turned away to put the butter on the table.

Elizabeth was soothed again by Mary's quiet, understated movements as she moved around the kitchen. As she sat at the table she felt scoured out, as though the crying jag in the driveway of Castleclough, followed by the physical exertion of the cycle ride, had abraded her emotional insides. She was not lulled enough, however, to think that she was going to escape the consequences of what she had set in motion. Should she warn Mossie?

She felt too tired to deal with that and allowed her overwrought senses to ride on the everyday sounds in the kitchen – the bubbling of eggs in a pot, the clunk of the oven door as Mary removed the bread, the inquiring cluck of a hen as it ventured across the threshold into the kitchen to peck at the cracks between the flagstones. She felt cut off from the outside world; the recent trauma at Castleclough, the possible dangers inherent in Daniel's reaction, even the reality of her relationship with him, seemed dim and contained by the normality of activity within this small, commonplace world, where the knife cuts and ineradicable traces of inkstains on the table in front of her were like milestones, and the small tear in the oilcloth which covered the mantelpiece was like a familiar friend.

As she watched Mary's quiet, efficient progress with the making of the meal, she made a mental note to help her shine up her appearance and to gain a little self-confidence. Unlike Kathleen or Margaret, Mary suffered little from vanity, contented it seemed to wear the same old clothes and shoes and never complaining about the state of her hair or asking to wear lipstick. Yet she had a sweet, heart-shaped face and a beautiful smile. Her stepmother saw now that this lovely girl was in danger of slipping by default into the role of drudge and that she herself had to take a great deal of the blame for that. It had been just too easy to rely on Mary. 'Will I call them?' she asked.

'I'll do it, if you like.'

'No, you've done enough.' Elizabeth's sore muscles complained as she stood up.

*

By eight o'clock, the whole family was seriously worried about Kathleen's whereabouts. At first, Elizabeth had dismissed her absence from the tea-table as just another sulk. It was only when on impulse she went through Kathleen's belongings, and found that her purse and make-up bag – a present from Hazel Slye – were missing, that she realized Kathleen had run away. As far as she could tell, her stepdaughter had not taken any clothes.

Her first reaction was one of profound irritation with the girl, followed swiftly by self-pity: she was now going to have to drag herself into the barracks in Castletown, get the Guards involved; the gossips of the neighbourhood would be fired up again. What more was she going to be asked to bear?

Then the implications of the girl's disappearance dawned on her. Suppose Kathleen really was in despair and did something foolish? Elizabeth sat down on the bed, the beautifully pressed uniform tunics mocking her as in her imagination she saw Kathleen's sodden body floating face down in the Kenmare river or in Coulagh Bay. Then she got a grip on herself: if her stepdaughter was planning to throw herself into the sea, she thought, she would hardly have bothered to bring a theatrical make-up kit with her.

Or would she? Kathleen was very melodramatic. Perhaps she was thinking ahead to when she was found and was going to make herself up before consigning herself to the waves so she would be found like Ophelia . . .

Elizabeth stood up. Kathleen was not the only one behaving melodramatically: she had been missing only a few hours and it was not yet dark. The likelihood, if she had indeed run away, was that she would try to go to George – or Hazel – or, failing that, to another theatrical company.

Or there was one further possibility. Kathleen was so angry with her stepmother that she might be simply trying to teach her a lesson and had taken the make-up to make Elizabeth *think* she was in earnest about running away.

The more Elizabeth thought about it, the more likely this latter scenario seemed.

She went back out to address the conclave of solemn faces which looked at her from all over the kitchen. Only Abigail was going about her normal baby business, building towers from a pile of old tin mugs in a corner of the room.

'Now,' Elizabeth began, 'we're not going to get all upset about this. Kitty's a sensible girl deep down and she'll come back, you'll see. What we need, though, is some idea of where she's gone. So, Margaret, I've a small job for you. I want you to go over to the Harringtons and ask Tilly if she happened to see Kitty leaving, and if she did, which direction she took at the crossroads. Got that?'

Margaret nodded gravely, aware of the importance of the task entrusted to her. She trotted out through the doorway and Elizabeth surveyed the remainder of her brood. 'The rest of you now,' she went to the dresser and lifted down a wad of brown wrapping paper from off the top of it, 'I think you should all be covering your books. You two as well . . .' She beckoned to Francey and Johanna who had started school at the beginning of the week and whose books, so far, numbered one apiece. 'Here's two pairs of scissors. Will you help the littler ones, Mary?' Elizabeth took the implements out of the dresser drawer. 'And Francey,' she continued, 'when you're finished with yours, don't forget the geese.' Elizabeth's son had been given responsibility for penning the fowl at night.

When they were all bent over their work, Elizabeth picked up Abigail and went out into the yard to think. As a treat, she stood the baby on one of the gate piers, allowing her to 'fly' by waving her chubby little arms around. She wrapped one of her own arms around Abbie's middle, drawing physical comfort from the warm compact feel of her small body.

Rex came over and plonking his front paws on the side of the pier, offered his head to be petted. Elizabeth pulled his ears and he licked her hand. Her whole body ached.

As it was now September, the evenings were beginning to draw in; the sun was almost gone and in another part of the sky a three-quarters moon was already visible as a diaphanous, misshapen disc tacked on to the end of a creamy-coloured streamer of cirrus. The quiet of a still evening, Elizabeth thought, was entirely different from that of an early morning. There was a palpable slowing down: the birds, on their final expeditions of the day, seemed less self-important, and even the waves from the open sea crashed with less urgency against the rocks at Cod's Head across the bay.

As she listened to the subdued chatter floating out from the kitchen, to Abigail's intermittent chuckling as, her fat knees folding and unfolding like little concertinas, she squirmed and jounced on top of the pier, Elizabeth re-affirmed her choice: her primary duty lay not with her own desires and needs but with this collection of people known as Neeley Scollard's children. In fact, she thought, remembering how, in the past, the children had kept her anchored when she felt like running away, the choice had been made long ago.

There was another aspect too: for the present at least, the choice between duty and inclination was no choice at all because, looking up at the placid sky, Elizabeth knew she needed a rest from emotional battering. She had no scruples or regrets about her affair with Daniel. And they could be together in the future, she thought, hope flaring at the memory of the tarot reader's assertion that she would marry twice. But at present, free will or not, she could intervene no more in the hand fate had dealt her; her emotional resources were depleted and she had to have peace.

She would see Daniel soon; if he did not come to her, she would seek him out as soon as she could recover some energy. And when they were face to face, if she could manage to stay strong, to explain that if they did not fight, everything would turn out as fate intended, she knew she could make him understand.

She was just about to lift Abigail down from the pier when her attention was caught by the sight of Margaret rushing back towards the house across the fields; she was running so fast Elizabeth figured she must have news about Kathleen.

The news preceded her, however, because a split second later Kathleen herself came into view on the road. She was accompanied by Mossie Sheehan.

On seeing the two of them, Elizabeth had to fight between relief and an upsurge of anger. Not only had Kathleen put them all through the mangle, she was now bringing Mossie in on them as well. What the hell was she doing with him?

It occurred to Elizabeth that Kathleen, unaware of her own visit to Daniel, was stirring things up still further. She clenched her fists at her side. But at least, she thought, the girl was safe.

Margaret reached her well ahead of the other two. 'She's back,' she panted. 'Tilly saw her going, all right, but it was me who saw her coming back down the road with Mossie.'

'Thanks, Maggie, I can see them. You're a very good girl. Will you take Abbie?' Elizabeth lifted the baby down and put her standing on the ground.

'Is there going to be a row?' Margaret, her chest heaving with the effort of her run, peered closely at Elizabeth's face.

'I don't know,' Elizabeth said through gritted teeth, 'but at this moment I'd like to strangle her.'

'She's probably upset about going away from us all, that's all.'

'I don't know why you're sticking up for her,' Elizabeth said sharply, 'and I'd like to point out that she didn't seem in the least upset when she was going away from us all to Killarney. Take Abbie in,' she added.

'I'm her *sister*! That's why I'm sticking up for her,' said Margaret with great dignity. 'Come on, pet,' she said to the baby in a completely different voice, one which was a fair imitation of Elizabeth's own. She took the baby's hand and walked solicitously beside her as Abigail toddled across the yard.

Elizabeth held her temper in check as she waited for the two on the road. She saw there was no conversation between them and if Kathleen had been up to mischief, it did not show in her dragging gait as she walked a couple of paces behind Mossie. Elizabeth waited until they were right at the gate. 'Where were you, Kathleen?'

Her stepdaughter, striking an insolent pose, looked off over her shoulder into the farmyard.

'I found her in Castletown,' Mossie intervened, 'she was trying to get a lift out the road.'

'Out the road here?'

Mossie looked at Kathleen and hesitated as though not wanting to betray her. But Kathleen spoke for herself. 'No,' she said flatly, 'the road to Cork.'

'Go inside,' Elizabeth ordered, 'I'll be in in a minute.'

Kathleen swept past her and, head high, marched into the house.

Elizabeth was doubly irritated now because by finding and bringing Kathleen home Mossie had put her under some sort of obligation. Notwithstanding that she had to swallow her pride. 'Thank you, Mossie,' she said stiffly, 'I appreciate your taking care of her.'

The lids hooded Mossie's eyes. 'You're welcome, Elizabeth,' he said, 'anything I can do to help.' Elizabeth knew she should ask him in but could not have borne the strain of it. 'She's going off in the morning,' she said, 'we're terribly busy getting her ready – I hope you don't mind if I go on in?'

'Not at all.'

'Thank you again,' she said as, saluting her, he turned to go. Elizabeth tried to tell herself that Mossie Sheehan deserved everything he had coming to him but could not in all conscience not warn him about Daniel's threat. 'Mossie.' She called him back before she had thought it through.

He turned and for a fraction of a second she thought she caught a glimpse of a vulnerability she had never noticed before. 'There's something I have to tell you about.'

'Oh?' The impression of vulnerability had been a mirage. Now Mossie stood poised a few feet away, inscrutable as ever. Elizabeth drew on her bottomless well of contempt for him and said stiffly, 'I've told Daniel Carrig about our arrangement.'

'I see.' He looked steadily at her. 'You have that right. Why are you telling me?'

'Because —' Elizabeth stopped. Then: 'He – he didn't take it well.' Something was happening to her resolve; Mossie's direct gaze was making it difficult for her to impart to him the gravity of the situation.

'I'm sure he didn't,' he said quietly, 'I'm sorry.'

'The thing is,' Elizabeth spoke resolutely now, 'he says he's coming to get you.'

Mossie laughed outright. 'He'd need to get up fairly early in the morning. I've a few spuds dug for you. I'll leave them in the yard.' Tipping his cap to her he walked off up the road, leaving Elizabeth speechless.

Kathleen gave no further trouble that night and, making a tremendous effort, Elizabeth did not pursue a quarrel with her. This proved to be a wise decision because Kathleen, although acting as though she was puzzled by the lack of recrimination, got on meekly with her preparations to leave for boarding school.

Elizabeth waited until her suitcase was closed and in the kitchen and Kathleen was in her nightdress and ready for bed. Then, aware that the others were probably listening from the bedroom, she asked her stepdaughter why she had run away.

'I just had to, that's all.' For an instant, Kathleen's eyes were as startled as a fawn's but then the habitual cloak of wariness covered them over.

'Why did you have to?'

'No why. It's my life.' Elizabeth heard the familiar belligerence and was too weary to pursue the matter. In any event, Kathleen would be safely corralled from tomorrow.

'All right,' she said, 'I won't badger you about it. Just tell me where you were planning to go.'

'Nowhere —' Kathleen began and then, seeing the look on her stepmother's face, changed her mind. 'I was going to Cork,' she muttered, 'to ask for help from Grandad Sullivan.'

'What kind of help?' The admission jolted Elizabeth;

her parents were the last people to whom she would have thought Kathleen would run.

'I wanted to go to London,' Kathleen said, lifting her chin.

Elizabeth gazed at her. She had to award some sort of prize to her stepdaughter in the matter of determination. 'Look,' she said, 'you put the heart across us all. Please, Kathleen, don't do anything like that again, sure you won't? I'll tell you what, I'll make a bargain with you. They say that this wretched war is really going to be over soon and if you're still as keen on the theatre this time next year, we'll discuss it, all right?'

If she expected gratitude or even surprise, she was mistaken. All Kathleen said in response was a low, 'All right.' She went then into her bedroom and for the second time that evening Elizabeth was left speechless. If she lived to be a hundred, she thought, as the door closed behind her stepdaughter, she and Kathleen would never understand one another.

Ten minutes later, the house was at last fully quiet and, too tired now to think of Kathleen or Daniel or anything other than the sheets and pillows on her bed, Elizabeth forced her bones out into the yard to check that the poultry were secure for the night.

Everything was in order and she was just going back into the house when she remembered she had left a sheet out to dry. She hesitated a moment, too weary to contemplate walking even the additional twenty-five yards the trip to the clothes line would entail, but it had been a good drying day and who knew what the weather might bring tomorrow?

She trudged across the yard and through the gap into the field. Having unpegged the sheet, which was so dry it was stiff, she was turning away with it when automatically, as she had done since meeting Daniel – even during the time he had been in prison when she knew he could not possibly be there – she glanced up at the moonlit summit of Knockameala.

He was there.

Even without the signature of the broken shotgun over his arm, it was definitely him.

Minutes passed as they watched one another. Elizabeth wanted to cry out, to wave the sheet, to perform any action which would break this terrible impasse.

But she felt paralysed with indecision and did nothing.

Then he was gone. Handicapped by the semi-darkness and the distance between them, she did not see him turn. He simply vanished.

Chapter Twenty-Two

Elizabeth had decided she would not stay overnight in Cork when bringing Kathleen to her new school but would spend some of her money on the luxury of a hackney all the way in both directions. But although the car arrived to collect the two of them exactly on time at eight the following morning, she spent longer than she had anticipated in the convent.

As she had never suspected that her stepdaughter was in any way dependent on her, her parting from Kathleen had been more upsetting that she could have imagined; she had been totally taken aback at the extent of Kathleen's emotional breakdown. When the time came to say goodbye, her stepdaughter had fastened her arms around Elizabeth's neck and, despite all she could do or say, would not let go.

They were in the sparsely furnished and shining parlour of the convent, stuffy on this warm day. 'What is it, Kitty – Kathleen? Come on, darling,' she coaxed desperately as her stepdaughter wept into her neck, 'it won't be all that long before you're coming home for Christmas. You're going to love it here – you'll settle down.'

But Kathleen was not consoled and would not let Elizabeth leave until one of the nuns, accompanied by a senior girl, came into the room and insisted she come with them for a tour of the school.

Her heart breaking for her, Elizabeth followed her out into the entrance hall as, tearfully, Kathleen allowed herself to be borne away. Although Kathleen was tall, she seemed very small as, flanked by her guides, she was walked away down an echoing corridor. Before she turned a corner, she glanced back at Elizabeth and gave a forlorn wave.

Elizabeth did not get back to Lahersheen until after

nine that night. Mary had everything under control: the smaller children were in bed and the kitchen was spotless. 'Thanks, Mary,' she said gratefully, kicking off her shoes and accepting the mug of hot milk put into her hand minutes after she sank into the chair beside the stove.

'Tell us everything, Mammy.' Margaret settled herself on a little stool in front of the chair and hugged her knees. 'Would I like it, d'you think?'

'It's too early to tell, Maggie, let's wait and see how Kitty gets on. It's a huge place, enormous . . .' Between mouthfuls of the snack meal, she answered as many of Margaret's avid questions about the convent as she could.

Mary listened too, but purely in the manner of interested observer and Elizabeth again resolved to turn her attention to Mary's future. After a while, she hunted them both off to bed, hugging each of them in turn. For a few minutes, she heard their quiet to-ing and fro-ing as they got ready for bed and then, before she knew it, lulled by the warmth of the stove and the hot milk in her stomach, she had dozed off in the chair.

Some time later she awoke with a start and checked her watch. It was after eleven, time she was going to bed. She was pulling herself out of the chair when the strong feeling swept over her that Daniel was nearby. Instantly alert, she was across the kitchen in three strides and already looking towards Knockameala as she ran across the farmyard. Rex, caught by surprise, popped a single bark and then, recognizing her, wagged his tail in apology and raced beside her through the gap and into the hill field.

He was there all right, immobile against the starry skyline, his distinctive figure rendered small by distance.

What was she to do? Elizabeth entered a panicky debate with herself: she could not call out for fear of waking up the entire household. Should she go running up the mountain? But as she dithered, just as had happened the previous night, Daniel vanished.

Again and again throughout the following day, Elizabeth was drawn to the hill field. As if to abet her, the weather held and she washed and hung out more clothes

444

that day than she had in the previous fortnight. But by mid-afternoon, the only human being she had seen was Mossie Sheehan, who had come into the farmyard bearing an armful of cabbages for her and to whose enquiries about how Kathleen was settling in, she replied in frosty monosyllables.

Tilly arrived for a chat at around four o'clock just as she was returning yet again from the clothes line. 'I think Indian summer's really my favourite time of the year.' Elizabeth's friend gazed appreciatively round the sunny farmyard.

'Yes,' Elizabeth agreed. 'Cuppa?'

She had brought a bottle of coffee substitute home with her from Cork and the two of them brought their steaming mugs out to the little bench seat in the farmyard. They could hear the clickety-clack of the clockwork train set issuing from the outhouse where Francey and Johanna were playing. 'That's some washing!' Tilly remarked, staring at the laden clothes line which stirred only a little in the light air. 'Any news from Cork?' she asked, settling herself on the bench.

There and then, Elizabeth decided she had to tell Tilly about her pact with Mossie. 'Listen, Tilly,' she began, 'I've something to say to you. I'm sorry I haven't told you before . . .' She went on to outline the facts as unemotionally as she could, omitting nothing. 'And now,' she concluded, staring into the depths of her mug, 'I'm afraid there's going to be another fight about me. Oh, Tilly, I'm jinxed.'

'I don't believe you're going to go through with it.' Tilly's eyes were round with shock.

'I gave my word,' Elizabeth said. 'It's written down – you and Mick witnessed it.'

'No court on earth would enforce that agreement. I can't remember what it's called now, something to do with being forced to agree to something against your will—'

'I gave my word,' Elizabeth repeated flatly. 'And I told you that with his document he could get me for breach of promise.'

'Yes, but—'

'Don't make it worse than it is, please, Tilly. Anyway, I'm surviving all right at the moment, amn't I? What'll be different? The children come first and you said yourself he's a great farmer – and at least we won't be under the same roof.'

Tilly clammed up. Then, 'God help ye all, that's all I'll say.' She cupped her hands around her mug of coffee substitute. 'But you've got to stop Daniel.'

'I know,' said Elizabeth. Then, defensively, 'What would you have done if you were me? Would you have let him rot in gaol?' Tilly did not reply. Instead she took a deep, meditative draught out of her mug.

Rex, basking, had stretched himself out at their feet; Elizabeth bent to pet his sun-warmed head and he thumped his tail in appreciation. Having related the story in the warmth and brightness of the day, with marigolds still in bloom in the trough beside her, for a few blessed minutes of relief her predicament seemed to retreat and shrivel until she could see it in its entirety like the final tableau in an absurd play.

It was not long, however, before her sense of reality returned and each night of the next four, Elizabeth went to stand in the hill field to watch Daniel Carrig watching her. He never stayed long, vanishing always within minutes of her arrival. So she had no idea how long he spent looking down at the house.

On the fifth night, as soon as the children were all in bed, she went out a little before half past ten and instead of going into the field, went out through the farmyard gate and up the road towards the mountain track. She had no way of knowing yet whether Daniel was *in situ*. At the angle at which she was approaching Knockameala, the summit was not visible.

Although it was now mid-September, the Indian summer continued and the night was balmy. An enormous yellow moon, a lovers' moon, so unusually large and pendulous that it seemed almost too heavy for the sky to bear its weight, lit her way as she left the road and climbed steadily along the track. The torch she carried became superfluous and she switched it off. Immediately, she became aware of a singular quietness; perhaps, she thought, it was because of her own overwhelming sense of the moon's presence that the night-time sounds, the scurryings and rustlings normally audible even in the lower places around the farm, seemed absent.

When she reached the cairn of stones she stopped to add a pebble to it and to search the terrain ahead of her. Although the summit was now visible, no outline of a human being broke its smooth round contour. She shivered; although it was not really cold and although at present she was as yet only a few hundred feet higher than the roof of her house, the night air in this exposed part of the landscape was much sharper. Half expecting Mossie Sheehan to rise up at her from behind a clump of furze – tonight, she would actually have welcomed a confrontation – she pulled her jacket around her and listened hard.

All she heard was the faraway breathing of the sea and, nearer, a small scuffling she knew could not be human. Not even a night bird called; it was as though every living creature on the mountain had bowed before the sovereign radiance of this harvest moon.

As she moved on, Elizabeth found herself so deeply affected by the atmosphere that she tempered her gait until she was almost tiptoeing through the thick growth of bracken and furze. Surrounded by that implacable, eternal light, she felt small and insubstantial, as if in the scheme of the universe she and her affairs stood equal in status only with the insects she crushed and with the stalks which snapped under her shoes as she passed over them.

Within minutes, she had reached the summit. A small night wind had come up, stirring her hair and the fullness of her black dress as, knee-deep in grasses and bracken, she stood as tall as she could for a few moments in order to signal her arrival to anyone who was around to see. She cared not a fig now whether Mossie Sheehan, or indeed any other neighbour, knew she was up here or why, but after a while when she had still heard nothing untoward, nor seen any movement other than the small drift of the foliage around her, she sat on a rock and settled down to wait.

In all the years Elizabeth had lived in Lahersheen, she had never been up here at night. When picturing Daniel here, the images largely based on his own stories of his hunting expeditions, she had imagined this mountain top to be darkly alive with rabbits, foxes, even owls and bats. Perhaps it was this particular night, she thought, but the reality was different and instead of teeming life, Knocka-meala presented perfect, silvery calm. The twin streams of the sea which flowed into Coulagh Bay and the Kenmare river on either side of the mountains glowed like phospho-rescent ribbons against the humped black shapes of the mountains of Cork and Kerry; nearer where she sat, the thick brushes of furze blossoms, bleached of colour, bent silently on their thick, woody stems under the light probing of the breeze.

'Hello.'

Her heart leaped with fright as she twisted around. She had not heard a single sound before she was addressed. In the moonlight, Daniel's face was shadowed and haggard, seeming to belong to a man much older than one of his twenty years. 'Hello,' Elizabeth said in reply. Feeling the inadequacy of it, she seized his hands and forced him down to her level so that he was squatting and they were face to face. 'I saw you every night,' she said.

'I know. I saw you, too.'

'Why didn't you come down?'

'I wasn't ready.'

'Are you ready now?'

'No.'

'Then why . . . ?'

'I just saw you here,' he said simply. 'I've been watching you for the last quarter of an hour.'

Keeping a tight grip on his hands, Elizabeth impelled herself forwards off the rock so she was on her knees and closer to him. 'I love you.' She felt it sounded a little forced and repeated it, investing in it as much urgency as she could. 'I *love* you.'

He did not immediately reply nor respond. Then, slowly, 'Do you, Elizabeth?'

'Do you doubt it?'

'You're marrying Mossie Breac.'

'Daniel,' she cried, 'that's not fair. You know why that came about. It means nothing at all. I told you—'

'You don't have to go through with it,' he interrupted, echoing Tilly.

Elizabeth bent her head so the top of it rested against his chest. 'He'll sue me for breach of promise,' she whispered, 'we've both signed papers that he can. I could lose everything, the children could lose everything—'

'Let him sue you. Let him!' Through his bones, she could feel the ferocity. In her hands, his stiffened like claws.

She looked up at him, pleading for his understanding. 'I can't – I couldn't face it. I couldn't put the children through anything else.'

'You could put me through it, though, couldn't you?' he said bitterly.

'Daniel, this isn't like you. You know I agreed to this because I had to get you out of gaol.'

Swift as a cat, Daniel shook away her hands and stood up. The moon was at his back and Elizabeth could not see his expression; from where she knelt, he seemed huge, looming over her like a dark monolith. 'I would have preferred to stay in gaol for the rest of my life than to be free and see you married to someone else,' he said.

'Daniel, please, let's talk—'

'We've nothing to talk about any more, have we, Elizabeth?'

'Please, at least give me a few minutes.' She stood up, too. 'I told you that this will be a marriage in name only,' she said desperately. 'We will even be living in separate houses. And Mossie has guaranteed – in writing – that he will not interfere in any way with my life.'

'What are you saying, Elizabeth? That it's all right by

449

Mossie Sheehan if you and I skulk around the hedgerows for the rest of our lives? That I may have you with his permission? No, thank you!'

It was on the tip of Elizabeth's tongue to tell him about Alison Charlton Leahy's prediction. But she bit it back: the timing was wrong and, since they had never discussed it, she had no idea how much, if any, credence he gave to the accuracy of the tarot. Instead, injecting as much confidence as she could into her argument, she tried to reassure him that the situation would resolve itself. 'It will, Daniel, believe me. If you'd only wait for me —'

'*What?*' He laughed disbelievingly. 'Until when, might I ask? I hadn't heard Mossie Sheehan is thinking of being so helpful as to die!'

'Trust me. I know something you don't know. I *promise* you it will turn out all right. Have a little faith, darling — trust me, will you?'

He looked at her sceptically. 'You know that's impossible.'

'At least will you give me your word you won't fight with Mossie over me?'

She attempted to put her arms around his neck but savagely he threw her off. 'So that's it, is it? You're protecting *him* now!' His body went rigid as he faced her. 'Well, I'll give you no word. I have my own score to settle with Mossie Sheehan.'

Then he stilled and they looked at one another in the mocking golden light. Elizabeth felt her own dreams, their passion for one another, which had seemed at the beginning to be so pure and right, sinking like lead between them. She felt paralysed, unable to say any more. Daniel covered his face with his hands. 'Oh, Jesus, Elizabeth . . .'

'Ssh!' She reached for him. 'Please, Daniel,' she begged, 'no more violence. For my sake.' As, this time, he allowed her to put her arms around him, Elizabeth felt the small stirrings of guilt as she recognized echoes of the opportunism she had displayed with Neeley when persuading him to take her to Jimmy Deeney's dance. Fiercely she suppressed it and hugged him to her.

450

'All right,' Daniel whispered, 'I promise – but he'd better not come anywhere near me.'

When they kissed, she could taste his tears.

Although she went out to the hill field over the next several nights, she did not really expect to see Daniel again on the summit of Knockameala. Finally she went out no more. And although she continued, against her inclination, dutifully to accompany the girls to Sunday Mass in Eyeries, she never saw Daniel in the chapel.

Over the following month or so, however, she caught sight of him on two occasions.

The first was when she had taken Johanna to the doctor's surgery in Castletownbere. Finished with the consultation, she came out into the main street and was walking towards MacCarthy's, where she planned to buy some groceries, when she saw him coming towards them across the square from the direction of the waterfront. He was with two other men and all three were dressed in workmen's overalls.

Holding Johanna's hand, she hesitated as though to wait for him but when he saw her, he wheeled and, leaving his companions, walked fast towards O'Donoghue's, one of the other public houses on the square. The snub was so obvious that Elizabeth's face burned and, pulling Johanna bodily along the street, she bundled the child ahead of her into the entranceway to the victualler's.

The second time was one Saturday afternoon when she and Tilly were in Eyeries, having gone together with an assortment of shoes to be mended by one of the cobblers in the village. Daniel, carrying a lath, was coming out of one of the carpenter's premises adjacent to the shoemaker's. This time, there was no avoiding him as they practically bumped into one another, circumventing physical contact only by dint of Daniel's stepping sideways out of the way. 'Sorry!' Elizabeth said involuntarily.

'Afternoon, Mrs Scollard,' Daniel said, his face blank. He had seen her before she him and obviously had had time to school himself. He had taken to wearing a cap like those worn by most of the other workmen employed on the restoration of Castleclough. He tipped it now, 'Ma'am . . .' and walked on. He was wearing bulky work clothes but during the brief close-up glimpse she had had of him, Elizabeth saw he had lost weight.

She waited for the impulse to run after him, to jump up beside him on the sidecar he was now untying, to tell him that no matter what the consequences, she would go to Mossie Sheehan and inform him that their unsavoury deal was off. Instead, she took Tilly's arm and, swallowing hard, oblivious of the stares of the other people in the short narrow street, led her quickly in the opposite direction towards Tilly's own horse and car.

'That poor lad,' was Tilly's contribution.

'I'm doing my best, Tilly, please!' Elizabeth gritted her teeth. 'What about poor me?'

'The remedy is in your own hands,' Tilly retorted. 'I'm not saying I altogether approve of the notion of you and Danny McCarthy together but I certainly don't approve of the way you're being stubborn about Mossie Sheehan. Have you asked your father about that oul' agreement? I don't think it's worth the paper it's written on.'

'No, I haven't,' Elizabeth said, hoisting herself up on the car. 'I'm sick of everyone telling me my business.'

'Sorry.' Tilly got up beside her.

'Look,' said Elizabeth, 'it's not you I'm upset about, it's myself.'

What was happening to her? Her body had not reacted to Daniel's as it would have less than a month ago. Was she so involved now in self-preservation that even her feelings were dead? 'It's the whole thing,' she cried, 'I don't know what I feel any more.'

Tilly pursed her lips and stowed her own packages under the driving seat. Eyeries was a compact, L-shaped village, nestling just above the sea in one of the loveliest parts of the peninsula. Clucking her tongue at the cob between the shafts of the car, Tilly drove him through the other parked cars and carts towards the elbow of the L and, turning him with expert hands, set him on course for home.

Elizabeth had to hold on to the sides of the car as it jolted heavily against the ruts of the road.

'Look,' Tilly said as the horse slowed to a walk while pulling his load up a steep hill, 'you've already told me to mind my own business and maybe I should. But you've involved me and I do care about you. I've been thinking about this a lot, Lizzie, so don't bite the nose off me if I tell you what I think.'

'I'm not going to be able to stop you.' Elizabeth knew she was not going to like what was coming. But Tilly was right – she did owe it to her. 'Go ahead,' she said, bracing herself.

'I think the shine's worn off your fancy for Daniel Carrig,' said Tilly baldly. 'I think if it hadn't you would have gone to your father long ago to send Mossie Sheehan packing. You're a passionate woman, Lizzie, but I think that in this instance so much has happened you're finding it hard to admit that what you dressed up as true love was physical desire. And now that it's past its prime you're feeling guilty. Whether you realize it or not, you're using Mossie as an excuse.' Tilly reined in the horse and pulled him into the side to let a haycart past. 'Afternoon, Eoin!' she called to the man leading the ass.

'Fine day,' the man replied, hitting his animal an almighty wallop with a stick.

Elizabeth, still holding on to the sides of the cart, hated Tilly at that moment as much as she hated Mossie Sheehan.

'Sorry to be so blunt,' Tilly said then, glancing sideways at her when they were again under way, 'but, Lizzie, why don't you ask yourself why you simply don't tell Mossie to shag off?'

This was the second time lately Elizabeth had heard a woman swear on Béara and certainly the first time since Elizabeth had met Tilly that she had heard such words – commonly attributed to the influence of the British army and thereby known as 'soldier's language' – fall from her lips. Her resentment of her friend drained away as she saw it for what it was: her antagonism was not towards Tilly but towards having the truth so brutally exposed.

It was staring her in the face that Tilly was right: having so blindly followed the dictates of her body she had been artifically draping her infatuation for Daniel Carrig with the flags of something more profound and this self-deception had helped her ignore the little twinges of doubt about the suitability of the relationship – her worry about his installation as stepfather to the children, for instance.

'Do you forgive me, Tilly?' she asked.

'For what? It's your life, girsha, you've done nothing on anyone except yourself.' Again Tilly had to pull the cob into the side of the twisting roadway, this time to let a pony and trap pass, and as she whipped him up again, Elizabeth was glad that the bone-jangling trot which ensued made further conversation impossible.

Although dry, it was a blowy day and to their left, hundreds of small white horses chased each other in front of the wind across the grey waters of the bay, slapping playfully against the hulls of the seine boats. From this part of the road could be seen the burned-out hulk of the coastguard station beyond Ballycrovane harbour; since reading *Rebecca*, its tall chimneys and blackened stone against the sea always reminded Elizabeth of the ruins of Manderley but today, as she held on grimly to the sides of the car to prevent herself being thrown on to the floor, she gave it not a second glance as, more trenchantly than was the norm even for her, she faced her own shortcomings.

Over the following month or so, she allowed herself a breathing space. During the daylight hours when she felt the onset of guilt or shame, she took it out, acknowledged it and then buried it in a welter of activity. Frequently, especially at night, she experienced a renewal of physical longing for Daniel but it did not dominate her thinking and feeling the way it used to and, little by little, she came to terms with the notion that her affair with Daniel Carrig was over. At least, she thought, it had not taken her six years to realize it, the way it had with George Gallaher. Perhaps she was maturing, after all. And although as her emotional turmoil subsided she was enabled to celebrate what they had had, she made a firm resolution that never again would she allow her physical self to lead her life.

After the turmoil of the recent months, she found she was savouring the newly reliable beat of her life. With Mary around to look after things as well as herself, the household ran as sweetly as Francey's clockwork train. The house had never smelled so much of polish; the girls had never gone to school with such tidy gleaming plaits, such well-ironed clothes, such beautifully ruled copybooks. Even the littlest scholars, Francey and Johanna, fell into the routine Mary set for them and, whatever the weather, left safely each morning with the others bang on time. When they had all gone, with the washing up and sweeping done, the day's bread in the oven, Elizabeth and Mary, like two old cronies, had fallen into the habit of sitting down together over a cup of whatever brew from the rations would taste the least revolting.

Elizabeth began to look forward to the quiet of the evenings, when, with Abigail tucked up in bed and Mary supervising, the rest of them did their homework around the table by the light of two oil lamps, one at each end. Preparing mash for the fowl, or holding a bowl in which she was mixing a cake of bread for the following day, Elizabeth frequently suspended what she was doing and, unobserved, surveyed all the heads, three black and one golden, as, individually idiosyncratic as always, they bent over the books.

Francey and Johanna insisted on sitting next to each other and consulted with one another all the time, Francey taking the lead, sometimes holding Johanna's small hand to guide her with her straight and slant lines; Goretti, who was a *ciotóg*, had to sit at the end of the table where her left elbow would not bump into her neighbour; the teacher was trying to force her to write with her right hand but Goretti's way of dealing with this was to write with her right hand in school but to do her homework with her left. Margaret had to have a neat square of bare table in front of her. She

455

could not work unless everything, pencils, compass, set square, pen and ink bottle were all lined up and just so before she started.

Although Elizabeth's emotions continued to be raw, during these domesticated evenings, particularly when the rain was battering against the doors and windows and the snugness of the kitchen was palpable, a feeling of contentment had sometimes stolen up on her, surprising her with its sweetness. There was a lot to be said for an unrippled life she had thought once or twice, and had then laughed silently, chiding herself that she must be getting old.

Even Mossie Sheehan was being merciful lately, she thought one Monday morning as she poured for herself and Mary two cups of tea so pale it was almost colourless. Here it was, nearly Hallowe'en and she had not·run into Mossie face to face for at least a fortnight. Long that it would last.

But even where Mossie was concerned, provided she had to have no truck with him, there was a certain satisfaction in walking the length of her own land and seeing tidy, well-cut hedges, taut fences and the neat drills of vegetables in the field Mossie had cultivated. Everyone in the parish had asserted that Neeley had been a good farmer but Mossie Sheehan, it appeared, was more than good. He had been born to it; more than once, Elizabeth had been reminded of his grand-aunt Bel's assertion, on that awful day she had gone to the Sheehans' house, that Mossie had green fingers.

All in all, with each day Elizabeth felt psychologically stronger. 'I've made up my mind,' she said to Mary as they sat down to drink their tea on this Monday morning at the end of October, 'next Saturday the two of us are going to Cork. We'll visit Kitty, and you're going to get your hair properly done and we'll buy a few decent clothes for you. You deserve a treat. How would you like that?'

Mary's face lit up with pleasure. 'That would be great, Mammy. But who'd look after things here?' She took Abigail up on to her lap and fed her a piece of brack.

'Tilly,' said Elizabeth decisively. 'She's always offering.'
They spent a pleasurable half-hour making plans.

Once again, Elizabeth had decided to hang the expense and hire a hackney. It arrived, as arranged, on the dot of six in the morning because Elizabeth wanted to get as much value as possible out of their day in the city. Tilly, reliable as always, arrived minutes after the hackney. 'Hello,' Elizabeth whispered, letting her friend in from the darkness outside, 'sorry for whispering but we don't want to wake the others.'

'Off with ye,' Tilly yawned, 'and don't buy up the whole of Patrick Street!'

The engine of the hackney sounded thunderous as they twisted through the dark, slumbering countryside. 'It feels like Christmas, doesn't it?' Mary, her forehead pressed to the glass of the window on her own side of the vehicle, had been too excited to sleep.

Elizabeth knew what she meant. Although since she had lived on Béara she had come largely to eschew formal religion, the early morning trek through the starry darkness to First Mass on Christmas Day appealed to her sense of mysticism and ritual. 'It's Christmas all right,' she said, 'I can't wait to get my own hair done – and as for shopping, none of your muck for us, my dear! We're going straight to Cash's!'

Mary giggled. 'Oh, Mammy! Poor Daddy – if only he could see us now, squandering all this money!' It was the first such reference Mary had made to her father since his death and the sentence fell between them quite naturally as they smiled understandingly at one another.

Afraid she would not hear the alarm clock, Elizabeth had not slept all that well. Now she laid her head on the soft pillowy leather of the seat back and, despite the frequent, jolting bumps and changes in engine noise as the driver negotiated the tortuous, hilly roads, was soon asleep.

She did not wake until they were beyond Bantry. In her own corner of the seat, Mary was asleep, both hands curled in on her chest like the paws of a squirrel. As it was

457

going to be a long day, Elizabeth let her be. The arrangement was that after the hair appointments, Elizabeth was to telephone the house in Blackrock and Corinne and St John Sullivan were to come to take them to lunch in the Oyster. After that, they would have their shopping time and then they were going up to the convent to see Kathleen.

They reached the centre of Cork city by mid-morning and the day flew. Even the lunch in the Oyster, which was the one aspect of the outing to which Elizabeth had not looked forward – she was still not fully at ease with her mother – passed off remarkably well. Corinne was as vague as ever but was putting herself out to be agreeable and nothing contentious arose in the conversation.

Mary, shy at first in such opulent surroundings, blossomed after a few minutes and chatted quite naturally to her step-grandparents. After sixteen years of hair straight as curtains, her new, shorter style, curled and rolled above her ears and round her temples, took a little getting used to, but it certainly softened her face and took the childish look off it. She had good bone structure and, now that it was revealed and enhanced, looked very pretty. In many ways, Elizabeth thought, watching her quiet, understated movements with knife and fork, Mary had become the younger sister she had never had.

She spent recklessly in Cash's. Corinne came with them, 'To guide you, Beth. Lord alone knows what you'll buy if you're left to your own devices! And Mary here doesn't mind. Sure, you don't, dear?' Mary, to whom this entire day was like a trip to fairyland, nodded happy acquiescence. But half-way through the spending spree, Elizabeth, to whom a shopping expedition was always more attractive in theory than in reality, was glad of her mother's foraging presence. She begged to be excused, telling Corinne she would go for a stroll in the street outside and would come back in half an hour to pay for whatever Mary had selected.

'An hour, please, Beth,' Corinne ordered.

Having escaped into Patrick Street, Elizabeth, reflecting that her present state of mind was far removed from the last time she had been here, when Francey was in hospital with a broken head and she was powerfully angry with her husband, quite enjoyed strolling the length of the boulevard. Now she could appreciate the cheerful uproar: the calls of the *Echo* boys, and of shoppers and browsers as they hailed one another, the shrill clamour of bicycle bells as their owners demanded passage through the buses, the jingling of horse traffic and the honking of the small number of private vehicles swerving their way around jaywalking pedestrians. After the ringing silences and deep skies of Béara, she found it all unusually stimulating and had no difficulty putting in the hour her mother had requested. She wandered in and out of the smaller shops, in one of which she bought a classy leather writing case for Kathleen; the remainder of her time was spent in Woolworth's, where she bought presents, including additional lengths of track for Francey's train set, for the children at home.

When she got back to the department store, Mary and Corinne were waiting patiently by the cash register in the women's clothing department, boxes and bags neatly piled on the floor all around them. 'There you are,' Corinne said, 'we were beginning to give up on you, weren't we, Mary?' She actually winked at the girl and, not for the first time, Elizabeth marvelled at how the process of shopping seemed to animate her mother. 'You said an hour, Mother,' she pointed out pleasantly, then pulled her cheque book out of her handbag. 'What's the damage here?'

'It's taken care of,' said Corinne.

'Mother!' Elizabeth was horrified. 'We have enough money, honestly. Daddy—'

'Put it away, Beth,' Corinne insisted. With one gloved hand she covered the one in which Elizabeth held the cheque book. 'Please. Let me help.'

She did not let go and Elizabeth knew immediately there was more to this than simply buying clothes for Mary. 'Thank you, Mother,' she said simply and was astonished to see tears springing into her mother's cornflower blue eyes.

As quickly as they had started, however, they were gone. 'For nothing,' Corinne said briskly, dropping Elizabeth's hand and turning away to pick up some of the packages. 'Now, let's get these to the taxi.' She led the way towards the exit and the penny finally dropped with Elizabeth. Her mother's presence was no impulse. In her own way, Corinne had been making a form of reparation.

'Happy with what you got, Mary?' Unexpectedly happy herself, she put one arm around Mary's shoulder as they followed her mother.

'There's too much,' Mary's eyes were round. 'I'll never get to wear them all. But she insisted, Mammy.'

'Of course she did and she can afford it so don't *you* worry about it.'

They said goodbye to Corinne as soon as the taxi, which was waiting for them in a side street, had been loaded, and then set off in it for St Brigid's, Kathleen's school.

'I hope Kitty won't be worrying about us being late.' They were running a little behind schedule and Mary sat up as straight as she could to see over the shoulder of the driver.

'The nuns know we're coming from a long distance away,' Elizabeth soothed. 'It'll be all right.'

When they arrived at the convent they were shown into the parlour Elizabeth remembered from when she had delivered Kathleen here almost seven weeks before; it was even cleaner and more antiseptic than she had remembered. The room was so unnaturally tidy that Elizabeth found herself lining up the edge of Kathleen's new writing case with the exact edge of the small table in front of the chair in which she sat. Even the hydrangea in a brass pot adorning a small table in the bay window of the room seemed to be standing to attention.

After a few minutes, there was a knock on the door.

Mary flew to answer it but as she opened the door the excited smile froze on her face. A split second later, she staggered backwards as Kathleen, bursting into tears, fell into her arms and held on as though she was drowning.

Mary reacted instinctively. She patted her sister on the back as she did when quieting Abigail and murmured, 'There, now, you're all right, what's the matter? You're all right now . . .' Her assurances succeeded only in provoking a fresh storm and she shot an agonized glance of enquiry at Elizabeth.

To give herself time to assess the situation, Elizabeth moved behind the two of them to close the door. Even allowing for the tears, and for Kathleen's melodramatic propensities, she was shocked at the girl's appearance: she had lost weight; her face was gaunt and pale and her hair, although obviously newly washed, had lost its lustre and hung around her small face in long lank strands. She was clearly not happy here. Her weekly, formulaic letters, which Elizabeth knew were read by the nuns before being posted, had given no indication of it.

Yet it had only been seven weeks – too early to tell whether or not she would settle down eventually.

Through the sobbing, Elizabeth thought she detected that Kathleen was trying to say something. Gently, she attempted to detach her arms from around Mary's neck but Kathleen resisted, clinging on the way a baby animal cleaves to its mother's fur. Eventually, the crying eased and she allowed Elizabeth and Mary, one on each side of her, to assist her towards a chesterfield couch. 'Here,' Elizabeth handed her a handkerchief, 'blow your nose, lovey, and tell us what's wrong.'

It took an age for Kathleen to quieten down but eventually, having blown her nose several times, her wild sobbing eased to a hiccup and twisting the sodden handkerchief between her fingers, she muttered that she was all right now.

Elizabeth prised the wet square away from her and used a second one to wipe her puffy face. And Mary, seated on the other side of her, took both her hands in her own.

Elizabeth stroked the lank hair away from her stepdaughter's face. 'What's wrong, darling?' she asked softly. 'Tell us, please tell us. We're here to help . . .'

'I – I –' Again Kathleen hiccupped like a baby.

'Ssh . . .' Elizabeth continued to stroke her hair, 'in your own time. No matter what it is.' She waited and waited but whatever it was that was bothering her, Kathleen could not force herself to say it. Each time she tried, she was overcome with a fresh bout of tears.

'Could you tell Mary? Is it that you don't want to tell me, Kathleen? Would you like me to leave for a few minutes?' Elizabeth, having to raise her voice to be heard over Kathleen's sobbing, was seriously worried now that there was something more to this than merely homesickness.

Her face screwed up piteously, Kathleen made a desperate effort. 'It's all – it's all right –' She hiccupped again and then she looked from one to the other of her visitors through swollen eyes. 'I think I'm pregnant.'

The succession of emotions which chased one another through Elizabeth's heart swung within two seconds from wanting to hit Kathleen, to the deepest, darkest pity and back again towards rage at George Gallaher.

Because of course it had been him. Who else?

But Hazel Slye had assured her in two separate letters after her own trip to Killarney that in watching both Kathleen and George like a hawk she was absolutely certain that nothing untoward had gone on between them. Unless it had happened beforehand . . . Elizabeth made a tremendous effort to speak in a level tone of voice. 'It was George Gallaher, wasn't it, Kathleen?' she asked, trying not to let her anger at George show too strongly.

Kathleen could not speak. She fixed her wretched, streaming eyes on her stepmother and if Elizabeth could have resisted the look in them, she would have been made of stone. She put her arms around the girl. 'It's all right, it's all right,' she murmured, 'even if you are pregnant, it's not the end of the world. People survive it – look at me!' She attempted to hold Kathleen off but failed dismally. 'You poor old thing,' she said, patting her on the back of the head, 'what you must have been going through . . .'

She thought furiously as she continued to rock Kathleen in her arms. Whatever her own situation had been with him, Kathleen was not yet sixteen. Elizabeth knew enough about the law to know that George Gallaher could be locked up for a long time. And her inclination was to pursue that option right to the end.

In fact if Kathleen had not been so upset, she would have got on the telephone to Union Quay Garda station right this very minute. 'There, there, hush,' she said as softly as she could manage while her brain dealt savagely with the thought that if, right at this moment, she had happened to discover a meat cleaver in her handbag, George Gallaher would be seducing no more virgins.

Ever.

Glancing at Mary from over Kathleen's shoulder, Elizabeth saw she was almost as upset as her sister. As always in a crisis, Elizabeth decided to trust her instincts for action. 'Kathleen, Kathleen,' she called into the girl's ear, 'listen to me, darling. Listen, I have a plan, all right?' She had no such thing but she hoped that the right words would come out of her mouth as soon as she could get Kathleen to stay calm long enough to hear them. 'Kitty, *Kitty*!' she called, louder, hoping the hated nickname would somehow cut through.

The ploy worked.

'Don't call me Ki—' Automatically, Kathleen sprang to the attack, lifting her head only to meet Elizabeth's eyes. 'Sorry,' she muttered, the edge of the frenzy blunted a little.

'I've a plan,' Elizabeth said quickly and as Kathleen's face crumpled again she caught her urgently by both wrists. 'Don't you want to hear it? You've got to pull yourself together, Kathleen. Do try.'

'I want to die!'

'Of course you do,' said Elizabeth. 'But do try to listen to me first. If you don't, Mary and I will just have to leave you here and go home. We do have others to consider.'

Kathleen responded to the tone of quiet authority. 'I'm sorry, Mammy, I'm so sorry.'

'I know you are. But we have to think ahead now.'

'What's the plan?'

'The first thing is to find out if you're really pregnant.'

'I am, I *know* I am . . .' Kathleen was off again.

'All right, all right,' Elizabeth held up her hand, 'but we'll still have to have it confirmed by a doctor. The second thing,' she rushed on in order to head off further protestations, 'is that you're coming home with Mary and me right away. Today. Now.'

'Can I? You'll take me *home*?' Kathleen's expression was almost incredulous.

'Why not?' Only then did Elizabeth fully comprehend the extent of the girl's distress. 'Oh, Kitty,' she cried, 'did you think for one moment I'd abandon you – me of all people?' She was devastated at the notion of what Kathleen thought of her as a mother.

For once, Kathleen did not respond to the nickname. 'I didn't know what to think,' she whispered.

'Are you sure it's the right thing to do, Mammy?' Elizabeth had almost forgotten Mary's presence.

'What do you mean?'

Mary lowered her tear-stained face. 'The family, all that . . .'

'You mean the so-called disgrace?' Elizabeth felt the leash she had placed on her rage beginning to unravel.

Mary nodded miserably.

'Listen here, Mary Scollard,' Elizabeth said intensely, 'and you too, Kathleen! This pregnancy – if indeed it *is* a pregnancy, by the way – is unfortunate. But that's all it is. It's an *accident* and it's *unfortunate* but there's no going away from it now. Have you got that? Both of you?'

They stared at her. And at least, she thought, she had managed to stop Kathleen's hysterics. 'Kathleen,' she continued, addressing her directly, 'you're still a lovely girl. That doesn't change just because you ran into a – a—' Elizabeth could not think of any word abominable enough to describe George Gallaher.

'And, Mary,' she whirled on the older girl, her passion rising, 'you're her *sister*. And don't you forget it. We're *family*! We're all going to pull together on this.' The leash was barely holding now. 'Under*stand*?' she hissed.

Elizabeth's fury with George was being vented on more than him alone; when she had been in this exact same predicament herself, she had not had the opportunity to show her contempt for those who would turn out their daughters. Kathleen's dilemma brought it back all too vividly. She was now so angry and in such a complex way – at herself, at her parents, at George, at Mossie Sheehan, at the whole shooting gallery – she could no longer stay seated. The leash snapped as she shot to her feet. '*Shag* the begrudgers!' She pounded a fist into the palm of her other hand.

'*Mammy!*' Neither Kathleen nor Mary had ever heard her swear before.

Trembling, Elizabeth surveyed their shocked faces. Tilly had been right to use the word – it mollified the tongue. 'Shag them all,' she repeated, a little more gently. 'Anyone who wants to take on the Scollards is going to have a fight on their hands. Right, girls?'

Chapter Twenty-Three

Elizabeth's mood of defiance carried her through the interview with the head nun and the drive home in the hackney. She had flirted briefly with the notion of telephoning her parents, but decided against it. One thing at a time, she thought grimly.

If the driver, the son of the regular hackney man from Urhan, had been surprised that he had an extra passenger and luggage to carry home, he did not say so. Tilly, however, showed no such reticence. 'Kitty!' she said, rising in astonishment from the chair by the stove as Kathleen followed the other two into the house.

Kathleen's response was to make a run for the bedroom. She had spoken hardly at all on the way home – none of the three of them had – and, worn out by emotion and worry, had fallen asleep on the other side of Adrigole, to waken only when they pulled up at the farmyard gate.

Elizabeth put a finger to her lips. 'I'll tell you later,' she whispered to Tilly, then turned to Mary: 'You're all in, darling, go on to bed. And take a lie-in in the morning. I'll take care of everything. Everything's going to work out fine, you'll see.' She smiled encouragingly.

'Where do you want these, ma'am?' The driver struggled through the open doorway carrying not only Kathleen's suitcase, but all the packages from Woolworth's and Cash's. Elizabeth indicated he should simply dump the whole lot in the middle of the kitchen floor. She had almost forgotten about the shopping: the idyllic few hours she and Mary had spent on their outing now seemed as though they belonged to another century. Poor Mary, she thought, some treat! And it was only then she remembered Kathleen's writing case, no doubt still on the table in the convent parlour.

She paid and tipped the driver and, when he was gone, again urged Mary to go to bed.

'All right, Mammy, goodnight. Goodnight, Mrs Harrington.'

Mary looked so woebegone that Elizabeth threw her arms around her neck. 'Cheer up, everything will look a lot better in daylight, I promise.' But as she trailed off to bed, Mary did not even glance at the stack of her new clothes in the middle of the floor.

'What's all this about?' Tilly stood in the position she had adopted when they all first came in. 'Why's Kathleen home?'

'It's a long story. But you might as well be the first to know.' She took a deep breath. Loyal and tolerant though Tilly was, Elizabeth knew that within the past year, some of the propositions Tilly had been asked to support would have tested the allegiance of a St Bernard dog. 'She thinks she's pregnant,' she said unambiguously.

'Oh, no, Lizzie!' Tilly sank into her chair again.

'I'm afraid so. I'm not a hundred per cent sure – she hasn't seen a doctor – but she's not stupid.'

'Who?'

'Guess!'

Tilly read the truth in Elizabeth's sardonic expression. 'Oh, Jesus, Mary and Joseph!' she said, then: 'What are you going to do with her?'

The question was loaded, as Elizabeth well knew. She watched Tilly carefully: a lot depended on her friend's reaction. 'What can I do?' she asked rhetorically. 'Another mouth to feed, I suppose.'

'I – I see. Oh, well, God is good.' Tilly's friendship reasserted itself after the tiny hesitation, and before she left to go home, she agreed to drive Elizabeth and Kathleen to the doctor in Castletown the following morning to have the pregnancy confirmed.

*

Elizabeth lay awake for a great deal of the night. Having heard the hesitation in Tilly's response to her declaration that she was going to keep both Kathleen and her baby at home, she had no illusions about just how difficult the road ahead was going to be for them all.

By the time she had seen the schoolgoers out next morning, she had decided that the only course open to her was to face the situation head on – and quickly. Within hours it would be all over the parish that Kathleen Scollard, the actress and scholar, was home unexpectedly from boarding school. It would not take a genius to put two and two together.

The visit to the doctor in Castletownbere later that morning passed off efficiently – Kathleen, although pale and frightened-looking, was docile – and other than to offer his services again should they be needed, the man forbore to make any untoward comments about this new misfortune which had befallen the Scollards. Elizabeth thanked him and ushered Kathleen out again in the street where Tilly was waiting with her horse and car. It was raining, that steadily pouring windless rain which seemed somehow to epitomize the month of November and Tilly, engulfed in oilskins, was sheltering in the doorway of MacCarthy's.

Elizabeth asked her if she would mind waiting another few minutes with Kathleen. 'I've a small bit of private business to do,' she added.

Tilly nodded assent. 'I've to go into Hanley's to get a few new tea-towels anyway,' she said. 'Come on in with me, Kitty.'

Elizabeth's business was with the Canon. One of the stratagems on which she had decided in the middle of the night was that, rather than have herself and Kathleen and the whole family living in dread of the man's inevitable visit when news of the pregnancy got around, she would take the initiative. To quell her nervousness as she hurried across the bridge over the sea inlet at the east end of the town, she drew again on her reserves of anger against the uncharitable system of sexual morality which had cast her here on Béara in the first place.

The presbytery was a substantial two-storey house in an enviable location overlooking the harbour; as Elizabeth knocked loudly on the front door, she tightened her lips: no child for whom she was responsible, she thought balefully, was going to suffer the fate she herself had been forced to bear.

Five minutes later she was still waiting for the cleric in the sterile front room of the presbytery; too strung up to sit down, as the minutes ticked on she began pacing the highly polished linoleum in front of the empty firegrate, with each pass having consciously to avoid meeting the sorrowful gaze of the Sacred Heart, whose image, over the chimney breast, was the only decoration on the pristine walls. The firegrate itself acted as a scourge to Elizabeth's already whipped-up anger; it was customary when calling on the clergy to bring fuel, at least a sod of turf. Elizabeth was delighted that she had brought nothing.

She had worked herself up to such a degree when finally she heard the doorknob turning behind her that, had the Canon smiled at her on coming in, she would probably have spat in his face.

He was not smiling, however, nor did he come fully into the room. Instead, he stood in the doorway, continuing to hold on to the doorknob with one hand as though he had been passing by and was merely looking in. 'I'm very busy, at present, Mrs Scollard,' he said severely. 'How can I help you?'

The cleric's brusqueness served her purpose well and strengthened her determination. 'I'm not sure you can help me, Canon,' she said. 'There is something, however, I'd like to *tell* you about.'

'Yes?' Still he did not let go of the doorknob.

'Do you have a minute?' she asked pointedly. 'This won't take long.'

He sighed and at last came into the room. He did not, however, sit in one of the chairs, or close the door behind him. 'What is it?' he asked, jingling keys or coins in the pocket of his soutane.

Elizabeth took hold of the scrolled back of the mahogany dining chair in front of her as she faced the Canon on the other side of the long table which took up most of the space in the room. She had decided when planning this visit that she would not use euphemisms like 'in trouble' which might give the Canon a psychological opening. 'In trouble' invited the offering of 'help' or 'solutions'. 'It's about my stepdaughter,' she said, 'or rather, one of them. She's pregnant.'

The clergyman regarded her for a long moment but, boldly, she held his stare. He broke first. 'Why are you telling me this? Are you looking for my help?'

'No, Canon,' said Elizabeth, 'but thank you for offering,' she added, knowing full well that both of them understood he had offered no such thing.

'Then why are you here?'

'I'm here because I knew that when you heard about it, Canon, as I'm sure you will quite soon, you would want to help,' she stressed the word slightly, 'and I just want to assure you that we can manage by ourselves. But thank you, anyway.' It was not elegant, she knew, but she saw she had made her point because one eyebrow twitched and his eyes slid away.

'I see,' he said again.

'So I just thought I would be the first to tell you,' she said.

'Well, thank you for that,' he said drily.

He may be autocratic, she thought, but he was no one's fool. 'I won't take up any more of your time,' she added and then, before she could lose the momentum, 'Thank you very much again.'

Not waiting to be dismissed, she walked round the table, left the room and let herself out through the front door of the presbytery.

Remembering the way in which she had been hounded by the priest her parents had brought in, she felt sneakily triumphant as she walked back to where Tilly and Kathleen were waiting. That's one chalked up for Elizabeth Sullivan, she thought. But the feeling was short-lived and drained away as she came within sight of Kathleen's mournful figure slouched under a rain cape in the horse car. The victory, if victory it had been, was putative. She might have won, or maybe only averted, a battle, but the war over the next few years was not going to be easy.

Later that day, Elizabeth decided that she could not forever call on the Harringtons for transport. In any event, the process of acquiring their own would be a positive distraction she could offer the family while the implications of Kathleen's predicament percolated through. At tea that evening, she announced that she was going to ask Mick Harrington to keep an eye out for a good horse and car.

There was an outburst of excitement around the table. Even Kathleen, who had spoken hardly a word since she had come home, looked up from her untouched meal with a flicker of interest.

'Why not ask Mossie Sheehan, too?' Margaret asked, after the initial buzz had died down.

Elizabeth looked sharply at her. 'Why should we?'

'It's only a suggestion, Mammy.' Margaret was miffed at what she took to be her stepmother's implied criticism.

'All right, maybe I will,' Elizabeth said, trying to make her voice sound casual. And then, while pouring milk into Abigail's mug: 'Have you been talking to Mossie?'

'Sure I meet him all the time,' Margaret replied, 'of course I talk to him. It'd be rude not to. Anyway, I like him,' she added, 'he's nice.'

'Had he any news?' Elizabeth, aware of Kathleen's sudden quickening of interest, paid great attention to wiping Abigail's mouth with her bib.

'What kind of news? It's not those kind of conversations, Mammy, it's just saying hello! Can I ask him the next time I see him?'

'Ask him what?' Elizabeth had temporarily forgotten the initial reason for bringing Mossie into the conversation.

'*Mammy!* About the *horse!*'

'All right,' she agreed reluctantly. And then, as speculation about their proposed acquisition ran round and round the table, she thought she had better make sure that Mick Harrington found a horse and car for them in double quick time.

She reckoned without Margaret. The following afternoon, she and Mary were taking turns to churn butter in the outhouse when Elizabeth heard Mossie's voice calling her name at the kitchen door. Knowing Kathleen would not answer – the girl continued to haunt her bedroom and Elizabeth thought it wise to leave her alone for the time being at least – she went out into the yard. 'Yes, Mossie?' she called.

'I believe you're interested in a pony and trap?' He leaned against the lintel of the door.

'A horse and car, actually . . .' There was no need to make the distinction but she was annoyed that Mossie had again taken the high ground. 'Are you selling one?' she asked coldly.

'I know where there's a good one reasonable.'

'Thank you, I'll keep it in mind. Now, if there's nothing else?' She half turned.

'Will I bring it over tomorrow morning? Maggie seems to think you're in a hurry for it.' He seemed undeterred by her deliberate discourtesy.

'Thank you,' she said, 'but I've asked Mick Harrington to look out for one for me. If that does not work out I'll certainly contact you.'

'It was Mick Harrington who recommended this one to me.'

He had said it before she could make her escape. Although his expression was bland, her irritation increased and in a perverse effort to regain some sort of control she lied. 'Tomorrow is not suitable,' she said. 'Please leave it until Saturday. This will be a family decision.'

Mossie eased himself off the lintel. 'Looks like rain.' He scanned the slatey sky. 'See you Saturday, so.'

When she got back into the outhouse, Elizabeth seized

the churn from Mary and churned so furiously that the butter turned rock hard.

The excitement in the house the following Saturday morning was barely containable. Francey, in particular, wore a track between the house, the gate and the top of the hill field in order to be the first to spy out the arrival of the new rig.

Other than the two ancient bicycles and the ass Neeley had used to haul turf, the Scollards had never enjoyed the luxury of their own transport and watching the enthusiasm of the children – even Mary and Kathleen were now fully involved – Elizabeth, whose well-to-do father had purchased one of the first motor cars ever to be domiciled in Cork city, reflected once again on the different upbringing she had enjoyed. She had simply taken it for granted that if she or her mother needed to go anywhere, her daddy would drive them provided he was not too busy at his office; and to her it had not mattered by what means: she had barely noticed even the periodic changing of the vehicles.

At last she heard Francey's shriek and went outside. Endangering his life, he was perched on top of the cow byre and waving his arms in the air. At the base of the building, Johanna, as ever his acolyte, was following suit.

'Come down off there at once, Francey Scollard!' Elizabeth shouted. 'You'll get killed—'

She did not need to repeat the order. Agile as a young chimpanzee, Francey scrambled to the edge of the roof, dangled by his hands from its edge for a heart-stopping second and then let go, landing lightly as if he had practised this every day of his short life. Not waiting for any further admonitions, he zoomed past his mother, out through the gateway and up the road to meet Mossie and the new horse.

Hearing the commotion, all the girls came running out of the house and crowded around the gate.

Elizabeth hung back. She knew it was quite irrational to be angry with Mossie Sheehan for what he was doing in this instance; he was, after all, only doing her a good turn. *Another* good turn, she thought grudgingly, hating him for

473

it. She also resented the fact that whether she liked it or not, he seemed to be worming his way into the credit ledger of the children.

From where she stood she saw Mossie's head coming into view over the top of the thick winter skeleton of the fuchsia hedge. He was not alone. Francey's beaming face bobbed along beside him and the sight added yet another emotion to Elizabeth's already full quota: one not a million miles from jealousy. How dare Mossie Sheehan act so familiarly with her son? She was so cross she felt like calling off the entire deal.

She had taken a few steps towards the house when she saw that not all the girls were at the gate. Kathleen, her face like thunder, was lurking just inside the kitchen door. In Elizabeth's mind, Kathleen's pregnancy had virtually obliterated her concern that the girl knew about the agreement with Mossie.

But it was too late now to warn her not to betray her knowledge. The horse was being turned in through the gate.

The girls fell back to let the animal and his passengers through but when Mossie pulled him up right in the centre of the yard, they crept forward again to stand around him, petting his nose and patting him on the flanks. The horse, chewing the bit in his mouth, tossed his head and snorted acknowledgement. Even Elizabeth, who knew little or nothing about horseflesh, had to admit that this was a lovely animal. A lean gelding, black as a raven except for a white star on his face and three white socks, his thick winter coat gleamed in the weak sunshine. 'His name's Snowball,' shouted Francey.

'It couldn't be!' Elizabeth, who was trying to show as little interest as possible, said it involuntarily.

Mossie Sheehan laughed. 'It's not,' he said, letting himself down off the car, 'I was just teasing the boy.'

'Well, what is it, then?' Francey was put out. He jumped off the car and came around to stand beside Mossie, looking up at him with hands on hips.

'It's Lightning,' Mossie replied, ruffling Francey's hair.

The familiarity of the gesture was like a goad to Elizabeth. 'I'll need to get an opinion on this, of course,' she said stiffly to Mossie.

'Of course,' Mossie agreed. 'But I can guarantee that, for the price, you wouldn't get anything as good as this fella on all of Béara.' He patted the horse's shining neck. 'He's a bit fresh but he'll settle down all right.'

'Who owns it?'

'I do,' said Mossie, 'I bought it off a tinker in Cahirciveen the day before yesterday.'

Elizabeth wanted to scream. Drawing on all her reserves, she turned to the little knot of girls who, enthralled, were fondling the horse's face and ears. 'Would one of you go and get Mick Harrington?' she said.

None of them volunteered.

'You, Margaret! Did you hear me?' Elizabeth snapped.

'It's not fair,' Margaret whined but after a look from her stepmother thought better of any further protests and scampered off.

'Can we go for a drive?' Francey asked.

'Yes, please, please!' Johanna chimed in and so, belatedly, did Goretti.

'Can we, Mossie?' Francey repeated, tugging at Mossie's sleeve.

'It's up to yeer mammy.' Mossie shrugged.

'No.' Then Elizabeth modified her tone. 'He's not ours, and we don't know yet whether we can afford him. Mr Sheehan's prices are usually quite high.' She did not look at Mossie as she made the gibe but walked away from him and around the car, which she saw was freshly painted, black like the horse but with bright red shafts and wheels and matching trim along the sides.

'I gave her a lick of paint last night,' Mossie said, anticipating her, 'be careful of your dress, Lizzie, some of it may not be quite dry on the underparts.' She ignored him and continued with what she hoped looked like a buyer's inspection. She had no idea what to look for, however, and

475

for something to do, kicked one of the wooden wheels, much in the manner she had seen her father kick an automobile tyre.

'It's a wheel, all right.' The irony in Mossie's voice made her want to up-end the whole thing over his head. But now that she had sent for Mick Harrington, she could not send Mossie away with a flea in his ear until after Mick had pronounced on the horse.

'Call me when Mr Harrington gets here,' she said to Mary. 'I've to see to something on the stove.' Without looking right or left, she walked past Mossie and into the house. She stopped just inside the door. Kathleen was sitting at the table, her head pillowed on her crossed arms. 'Do you not want to see it, Kathleen?' Elizabeth crossed to her and touched her on the shoulder.

'What?' Kathleen looked up and caught off guard for an instant, looked so vulnerable that Elizabeth's resolute anger against Mossie Sheehan softened and eased. But then, as Kathleen's face narrowed and assumed the contemptuous expression Elizabeth remembered from of old, her own feelings transmuted again, this time towards caution. 'The new horse, of course,' she said.

'I'm not looking at anything that fella brings here.'

'You and I have to have a talk, Kathleen.' Elizabeth sat at the table beside her.

'There's nothing to talk about.'

'Oh, yes, there is. Now, you're in trouble – and so, in a way, am I. We can help one another.' As she seemed to be doing so much lately, Elizabeth was flying blind, trusting her instincts.

'How could you do it?' Kathleen cried, banging the table with both palms.

'Do what? Fall in love – like you did, Kathleen?'

'That's –'

'Different?' Elizabeth cut in swiftly. 'What's different about it? Because I'm older, is that why?'

'No . . .'

'Well, why, then?'

476

'You're twisting everything – as usual!'

'Is it because I fell in love more than once? Is that it?'

'What about my father?' Kathleen covered her face with her hands.

The joyful sounds of the other girls outside, the clop of the horse's hooves as he shifted in the yard, sounded ironic in Elizabeth's ears. 'Oh, Kathleen!' She dared to reach out, touching the top of Kathleen's bent head.

'Well?' Kathleen made a token gesture of rebuff with her head but then submitted. 'What about him?' she sobbed into her hands. 'Did you love him at all? Even for a minute?'

'You poor thing,' said Elizabeth sadly. 'I loved him as much as I could. As much as I could, Kathleen,' she repeated when there was no response. 'And I always thought he was a good man and a great daddy to you all – you've got to remember that.'

'Even though he . . . your hair . . .'

'Yes,' Elizabeth said firmly. 'Come here to me, lovey.' She cradled Kathleen's head against her shoulder and let her sob her heart out.

Then she realized that her stepdaughter was uttering words into her shoulder.

'What is it, darling? I didn't hear you.' She listened hard. As far as she could make out, the words Kathleen was crying over and over again were, 'I loved him, I loved him.'

'Of course you did,' Elizabeth said soothingly. 'Your daddy was—'

'No!' Kathleen raised her head, 'George! I love him – I love George.' She subsided again on Elizabeth's shoulder.

There was a lot of crying ahead for poor Kathleen, Elizabeth thought as, cuddling her close, she kissed her gently on the top of her dark head. 'Hush, darling,' she crooned, 'you poor old thing . . . ssh . . .' If it had been possible at that moment to consign the actor to a physical hell, she would have plunged him unhesitatingly into the most fiery one she could envisage, one reserved for degenerates the depths of whose depravity left them with no possibility of escape or redemption.

Margaret appeared in the doorway. 'Mr Harrington's here,' she announced breathlessly then, seeing her sister's distress, 'Oh . . .'

'I'll be there in a minute.' Elizabeth nodded over Kathleen's head.

Kathleen responded instantly by jumping up and going into her room. 'What's wrong with her?' Margaret's worried little face looked a lot older than it should have at thirteen.

'She's just mixed up at the moment,' Elizabeth said, getting to her feet. Margaret knew about Kathleen's pregnancy for Mary had confided in her.

Outside, Mick Harrington, watched closely by the silent and fascinated circle of youngsters, was examining the horse and cart. The horse was getting restive, tossing his head and tugging at the bridle, pawing a little at the ground. He laid back his ears and rolled his eyes when Mick pulled his lips apart to look into his mouth but eventually submitted.

Mick ran his hands along the withers and then stood back critically to examine the animal's conformation. 'He's nice all right,' he said to Mossie after a bit, then, turning to Elizabeth, 'You could do worse, Lizzie.'

Elizabeth could feel the frisson which ran through the children at the verdict and knew that now she had no choice. It was she who had set this in train and she had no excuse to stop. 'How much?' she asked Mossie.

'We won't fall out over the price,' said Mossie easily.

'Will you do the deal for me, Mick?' Elizabeth asked Tilly's husband. Her implication that Mossie would cheat her if he got half a chance was clear and, for once, judging by the expression which flitted across Mossie's face, she had the satisfaction of knowing that she had scored. To add stress to the insult she smiled at Mick. 'I trust you, give him whatever you think is fair.'

Mick looked uncertainly from one to the other. 'All right, so,' he said uncomfortably.

'Thanks,' she said. 'I'll be in the house.' She swept past them.

*

478

Mossie had not been lying when he had opined that Lightning, who was only five years old, was 'a bit fresh'. Elizabeth found him quite a handful between the shafts as, taking their first outing, they moved cautiously along the road towards Eyeries. At the beginning she was afraid to let the horse go any faster than a walk, a restriction he resented greatly and tried to overcome by pulling hard and twisting his head in an effort to take the bit. Her shoulders and arms hurting with the strain of keeping the reins taut, Elizabeth was starting to regret her curt rebuff of Mossie's offer to drive them on this first occasion.

After the first few minutes, however, the horse calmed down a little and she began to relax and to enjoy the experience, returning the greetings of admiring neighbours, revelling in the exhilaration of the children all around her. The housework had been abandoned for the day and they had all come, even Abigail, clutched tightly on Mary's lap and round-eyed with delight. The only absentee was Kathleen.

The sun, which had been shining only intermittently all day, came out again from between the scudding clouds just as they were clopping southwards down the hill above Kilcatherine Point.

As Elizabeth watched, a patch of light blazed along the sea like an elongating sovereign and then climbed the land across the bay, illuminating first the clustered houses of Eyeries village, then picking out the dwellings, as small and scattered as children's toys, above the coastal strip through Urhan and Caherkeem and all the way to Gortahig and Cod's Head. It rendered invisible the curls of turf smoke emanating from the chimneys and caught, here and there, on patches of cultivated land so they glowed like irregular pieces of jade among the browns, golds and greys of the mountains.

Then the clouds rolled in again and all was as normal. 'Did you see that light?' She turned to Margaret, who was sitting beside her at the front of the car.

'What?' Margaret looked puzzled.

'The way the sun – oh, never mind.' Elizabeth supposed

that, having lived here all their lives, they were immune to the phenomenal beauty all around them.

They were rounding the hairpin bend above Ballycrovane harbour when Francey let out a shout. 'There's Danny McCarthy! Yoo-hoo, Danny!' he screamed at the top of his voice. 'Look – we got a new horse!'

Elizabeth glanced involuntarily over her shoulder. Daniel and one of his brothers, knee-deep in the seaweed uncovered by a low tide, were harvesting it with pitchforks. She saw him straighten and look over to the road before she had to look away again to keep Lightning on course.

'Why doesn't Danny McCarthy play football with me any more? He promised.' Francey was tugging at her sleeve.

'He's probably too busy.' Elizabeth kept her eyes on the road.

'Well, I'm going to go and see him and I'm going to axe him!'

'Ask,' Elizabeth corrected, then: 'You listen to me, now, don't you dare go to see him or ask him any such thing. If Daniel wants to come and play football with you, he will. Do you hear me?'

'Well, I'm just going to axe – ask him, I am,' Francey muttered, but low enough that Elizabeth knew she was not meant to hear. She let the subject lie: the sight of Daniel had unsettled her enough without arguing with Francey about him. She gave the horse his head a little on the straightish piece of road which ran along the harbour and as he trotted along, probed her own feelings now about Daniel. But she found the complicated wound was still too raw to bear much pressure and she made an effort to concentrate again on the task in hand.

They travelled to about a mile within the outskirts of Eyeries but Elizabeth did not feel confident enough yet to bring the horse and car right into the bustle of the village. She pulled Lightning up at a farm gate and dismounted to turn him. On the way home, she let Mary take the reins for a while. When they rounded the corner, and Ballycrovane harbour and the uncovered rocks at its end were in sight, she tensed up for a further sighting of Daniel, but saw to her relief that neither he nor his brother was in evidence.

Safely home, between them all they managed somehow to unharness Lightning. The horse seemed to like all the attention. While Elizabeth and Mary pulled the car into the cow byre to preserve it from the elements, he stood accommodatingly as the rest of them fussed with buckles and straps and unfamiliar lengths of leather.

In anticipation of the horse's arrival, they had already put straw bedding in the stall beside the one used by Francey for his train set; Tilly had given them a hay net and a small supply of hay and oats and it had been Francey's job to scour out an old iron bucket for use as a drinking pail. As if it had been his all his life, Lightning clopped into his new home behind Margaret and emptied the drinking pail within a minute and a half.

The normal Saturday routine of the household had no chance as, for the rest of the day, the Scollards and their new horse got to know each other better. Even Elizabeth found she was finding excuses to go out into the yard and each time she did, just happened to glance casually into the stable. She was trying to round up all the children for the ritual of the Saturday night baths when, on finding Kathleen to be the one that was missing, went across yet again to the stable.

Kathleen and Lightning were quite literally cheek to cheek in the horse's stall. She had her arms around his neck and had laid her face against his black one. Lightning was very still, except for his ears, which were flicking independently of one another as if deciphering Kathleen's thoughts.

The moment was so obviously private for Kathleen that Elizabeth, who had not, luckily, shone the torch into the stable, backed away quietly from the stable door, but Kathleen heard – or sensed – the movement and turned round. 'It's all right, Kathleen,' Elizabeth mouthed quietly, 'stay where you are. Come in for your bath when you're ready.' But Kathleen came to the half-door. 'Mammy,' she asked, her face pinched, 'when are you going to tell the rest of them about me?'

'Do you want me to? Are you sure the younger ones need to know?'

'I want to get it over with,' Kathleen said doggedly.

'I'll tell them tomorrow after Mass.'

'And the other thing is,' behind her, Lightning pulled a mouthful of hay from the net and crunched rhythmically on it as she shifted from foot to foot, 'what about that – that thing with Mossie Sheehan? When's that going to happen?'

'That'll be months away yet. *If* it happens,' Elizabeth added significantly. 'Don't you worry about that, Kathleen, but I've got to point out that this is something you should not know. You should never have—'

'Don't start!'

Elizabeth felt she had every right to start but held her tongue. 'All right,' she said, 'I won't.'

'And what about Danny McCarthy? Where does he fit in these days?' Elizabeth fancied she saw a malicious light in Kathleen's eyes and was almost glad: the tortured Kathleen over the past few days had been difficult to watch.

'That,' she said firmly, 'is definitely none of your business. And I don't want you to mention it again. Understand? Now, don't stay out here too long,' she added in a no-nonsense voice, 'it's getting very cold.' She hurried inside to supervise the rest of the baths.

Last thing that night, having done her security checks at the fowl house, Elizabeth looked in on the horse for one last time, shining her torch over the half-door of the stable. Lightning had company again. This time it was Francey, fast asleep in a heap of straw in the far corner of the stable; one hand, lying in the middle of his chest, was firmly closed over a clump of hay as though he was clutching a nosegay; the other, at his side, lay open under the locomotive from his train set.

Little monkey! Elizabeth thought. Her son could not have come out here without her seeing him unless he had been up to his old tricks of climbing out through the bedroom window. Then, deciding to let him be, she fetched a blanket from her own bedroom and covered him with it.

Over the following weeks, life at last seemed to settle down for the Scollards. The outdoor farm work was largely over for the year and, to Elizabeth's great relief, they saw little of Mossie Sheehan. And as the weeks passed quietly by, her projected wedding to Mossie took on an air of unreality; she began seriously to feel that if she did not think about it it would not happen. Once or twice, Tilly alluded to it but, when Elizabeth immediately changed the subject, did not pursue it.

With Christmas fast approaching, she immersed herself in preparations. She was determined that this Christmas, the family's first without Neeley, would be as festive as decorum allowed.

Unlike many families in Lahersheen, the Scollards did not keep a pig expressly to fatten for Christmas but this year they did have their geese. These fierce, hissing monsters, which were now the undisputed monarchs of the farmyard, had proved to be the worst investment Elizabeth had ever made because no one in the house, least of all herself, could face the prospect of harming – or causing to be harmed – a single feather on a single bird. This was one arena in which Elizabeth sorely missed her late husband: Neeley had always seen to the gorier side of farm life and since his death, the Scollard hens – and now the geese and ducks, too – could look towards a peaceful old age. So at the beginning of this December the Scollards ordered, not only the bacon and ham for the Christmas dinner, but someone else's goose as well. To be properly dead before any of them set eyes on it.

They tacked up Lightning and took him all the way into Castletown for the Christmas fair where they bought currants, raisins and as much flour as they could find. Elizabeth spent money as though it was sea sand. She bought new clothes for everyone – even Mary who had not exhausted the possibilities of the wardrobe she had brought from Cork; she sifted through the hardware stock in

Harrington's and bought new saucepans; she paid off the account at MacCarthy's, receiving in return the customary seasonal gift of a bottle of whiskey, and trawling through the stalls in the fair, she bought a complete new set of figures for the crib and the fattest Christmas candles on offer.

A major regret was that because of the continuing wartime shortages, she could find no oranges, always the traditional toe-filler for the Christmas stockings but towards the end of the day, she gave a shilling to each of the children and sent them all off with Mary to look around by themselves while she took advantage of their absence to buy Christmas presents for them, including stock for Santy's sleigh.

Tired, but as happy as she had been for a long time, she loaded everyone and all the pucks and parcels into the car for the trip home. But as Lightning leaned into the traces and bore them up the hill out of the town, she was conscious of an odd tugging at her emotions. It was only then she recognized that throughout the shopping trip she had been subconsciously watching out for Daniel; she could not decide now whether not seeing him was disappointing or a source of relief. On the one hand she had learned to enjoy the few weeks of relatively uncomplicated serenity, but on the other, she was going through one of her periodic bouts of physical longing for him.

Over and over again in her mind, as she went through the events of the previous seven months, she had come to date all her misfortunes not from the time she had first met Daniel on the summit of Knockameala but from Jimmy Deeney's dance. If only she had heeded Tilly . . . 'Would you drive for a bit?' She handed the reins over to Mary whose turn it was to sit beside her on the front seat of the car. She was wearing gloves but her hands were very cold and to warm them she crossed her arms and placed them into her armpits.

Although it was only just after four o'clock in the afternoon, it was dark. 'Is everyone all right?' Turning her head, she surveyed the throng, faintly lit by the lanterns which swung fore and aft from the car. Abigail was already asleep in a little nest which had been made for her out of the softer packages on the floor. Francey and Johanna were huddled together under a blanket, Goretti and Margaret under a second one. All these human beings, Elizabeth thought again, all trusting me . . .

She turned back and before the thought could overwhelm her, made up her mind to make the most of this period of domestic calm because within only four or five months, all hell could break loose again, with the birth of Kathleen's baby – and with the calling of the banns for herself and Mossie Sheehan.

Poor Kathleen, she thought. Although to Elizabeth's eyes, the pregnancy was not yet showing, Kathleen believed herself to be huge already and rarely went beyond the farmyard gate. She had given up going to Mass on Sundays. In vain did Elizabeth point out to her that this was tantamount to carrying a sign on her back calling attention to her trouble but Kathleen had been adamant and Elizabeth had not pressed the issue.

The children had taken the news with equanimity. The littler ones were largely unaware of the disgrace of it anyway and Margaret, fiercely loyal as always, had dealt with it by taking it upon herself to nag Kathleen about eating properly. With a pang, Elizabeth saw that this was probably what she remembered about her own mother's pregnancies.

Christmas Eve dawned bright and cold and she rousted them all out of bed early to help with the final preparations. 'Who's to stop us?' she retorted, when Mary, seeing her go through the doorway to cut holly, wondered unhappily about the propriety of putting up decorations.

Elizabeth enjoyed cutting the holly; the shrub grew in such profusion in Lahersheen that it might have been the holly capital of the world she thought, as, her cheeks tingling in the sharp air, she found a suitable specimen in a hedgerow less than two hundred yards from the house. 'Francey? Johanna?' On her return with a profusion of berried, glossy green branches, she gave the two some crêpe paper and scissors, and showed them how to cut out paper chains. She put Mary and Margaret in charge of peeling a miniature mountain of potatoes, some of which was to be used to stuff the goose, while Kathleen and herself got on with preparing the rest of the vegetables.

The house buzzed with activity all that day. Even Abigail got a job as, deciding not to wait until the more traditional Christmas morning, Elizabeth decreed that the baby Jesus would be born in His manger as soon as it got dark. So, just after four and with enough exhortations and physical encouragement from her older brother and sisters to launch the *Queen Mary*, the plaster figure was put into Abigail's fat little hand and baby Jesus arrived safely in his wooden cradle.

Because of the morning there were no Christmas cards this year so when the postman arrived with the last batch of post Elizabeth did not open it but put the envelopes in the pocket of her pinafore and promptly forgot about them.

By eight o'clock that evening the air was full of steam from the boiling pudding, holly sprouted from behind every picture and along the top of the dresser, the crêpe paper streamers stretched from side to side of the kitchen and the crib, complete with wobbly tinsel star stuck to its roof on a piece of wire, reposed on a small table in a corner of the room. The good shoes, buffed to a high shine, were lined up on the flagstones in front of the stove, all the stockings had been hung from the mantelpiece and most importantly of all, the goose, covered with a piece of muslin, lay in the centre of the table ready in its bastible for roasting.

The last task of the day again fell to Abigail. As Elizabeth guided her chubby little hand, she lit all the Christmas candles set in earth-filled bowls in the recesses of all the windows in the house. 'Good girl!' Elizabeth blew out the taper and picked her up and with the others crowding behind her, brought Abbie into the yard to listen for the sound of Santy's sleigh approaching Ireland from above the stars.

It was only when they were all bathed and safely in bed that Elizabeth remembered the letters in her pocket. She still had the stockings to fill but decided she deserved a break. Pouring herself a nip of sherry, she set the glass on the table and, sitting down, pulled the lamp closer and sat down to read. There were five envelopes altogether; one was obviously from the bank, another was a bill. These two she put aside for post-Christmas attention and opened Ida's letter first. Her friend's great news was that she was pregnant. Page after page, her large, flamboyant script described her feelings of joy and apprehension, her physical symptoms, the reaction of her husband and of her family. Elizabeth was delighted: Ida had never been one to bemoan her lot but she had really wanted a baby.

The second envelope contained two letters, one from her mother, with a postscript and a cheque from her father, the other from Maeve, the housekeeper, who, since Elizabeth had moved to Béara, had written faithfully on the first of every month. Her mother's letter was chatty and warm: she was making serious efforts to be friendly and maternal. Of course, Elizabeth thought gloomily, Corinne did not yet know about Kathleen. Sipping the sherry, she scanned the cheque: the amount was substantial. Her father, she thought affectionately, seemed to think that to live in such a place and in such numbers constituted certain destitution. She resolved that next time he came on a visit she would bring him on a tour of the other cottages in Lahersheen, pointing out the ones which housed families numbering fifteen, eighteen or twenty children. Several households of her acquaintance numbered even more.

Not immediately recognizing the script, she had left the third letter until last as a sort of Christmas surprise to herself. As she slit it open, she saw it, too, contained money – two five-pound notes.

The address was simply, 'London', and the letter, in reality only a note, was from George Gallaher:

My Dear Elizabeth,
I hope this finds you well. The compliments of the season to you and your family and enclosed, please find a small offering towards Francey's Christmas cornucopia.
Yours as always,
George

Before she could second-guess herself, Elizabeth had bounded across the kitchen and had flung the note, the envelope and the money into the stove. Her heart pounding, she watched the flames lick at the bank notes until they curled and were devoured. It was only then she knew to what extent she had buried her head in the sand in the matter of dealing with George. Just as he had eight years earlier, he had been allowed to continue in blithe unawareness of the havoc he had caused.

Discovering that it was far easier to be determined on Kathleen's behalf than it had been on her own, Elizabeth decided then and there that first thing in the New Year, after telling her parents about Kathleen, she would ask her father to track George down so that once and for all he could be properly confronted with his perfidy and made to pay for it. She finished her sherry in a single gulp. That was next week's work, she decided. In the meantime, George Gallaher must not be allowed to ruin the magic she had worked so hard all day to create. To calm herself down, she went out into the yard to check the fowl house. It was not cold and having seen that all was well, the beauty of the night was such that she was loath to go back inside. Instead, she walked a little distance into the hill field.

The scene all around her might have been an artist's template for an illustration of Christmas Eve on Béara. Standing on a little hillock of grass and breathing deeply, Elizabeth inhaled the pungent aroma of turf smoke as it rose visibly to the sky in pale straight columns of vapour from a hundred all-night cooking fires. Between Lahersheen and the other side of the bay, the glimmering slash of the sea was still, and to illuminate the journey of the Holy Family, the windows in every house for miles around were lit with candles, hundreds of points of gold mirroring the silver of the stars. After a few minutes, Elizabeth's temporal concerns and worries floated away; she felt free as though she were drifting weightlessly through the delicate web of lights.

Although he was perhaps seventy yards away, she could hear Lightning shifting quietly in his stable and, to bring herself back to earth, decided to check that Francey had not come out again to sleep with him, a habit in which he indulged with disturbing frequency. The horse whickered at her as she opened the top of the half-door and shone her torch inside; the beam caught the star on his face and the sheen of his eyes. 'Happy Christmas, horse,' she whispered and then, feeling foolish, shut up the stable.

Back in the kitchen, she added more boiling water to the pudding and proceeded to the last job of the day, the filling of the Christmas stockings from the sacks she had hidden in the loft above the kitchen. First she went along the line, substituting apples and hazelnuts for the unobtainable oranges and was going back to the first stocking again to start filling it with its designated toys when she thought she heard a soft knock on the door. She suspended what she was doing and listened: sure enough, there it was again. She debated whether or not to answer it – the hour was late, she was tired, and she had to get up very early in the morning. Then – it was probably Tilly – sighing, she put down the sack of presents.

When she opened the door, it was not Tilly who stood there but Daniel. 'I didn't know whether to come,' he said quickly, 'but I saw you outside in the field and I knew you were still up . . .'

'Come in,' she said faintly, holding the door open. Daniel was the last person on earth she had expected to see. She turned to face him after he entered. For some reason, he seemed taller than she remembered. They were standing only inches apart and Elizabeth experienced the rash visceral leap she both welcomed and dreaded.

'I've missed you.' In the lamplight, his brown eyes shone with intensity. 'I had to come to give you this.' He pulled a small package out of the pocket of his coat.

She took it without looking at it. 'Daniel, I wasn't expecting you – I've nothing for you.'

'Open it, please.'

She pulled the wrapping off what proved to be a jeweller's box and then prised this open. 'Oh, my God!' Standing proud of a white satin mount was a gold ring set with two amethysts and a single, tiny diamond. It was an engagement ring and, modest as it was, to buy it Daniel must have spent practically all of his wages from the job at Castleclough.

'I'm sorry it's not bigger,' he mumbled. 'Will you marry me?'

The succession of emotions – chagrin, remembered love, horror – which tumbled through Elizabeth's brain left her physically dizzy. This could not be happening, not now, not when she had her life so well under control. The little jewellery box open in her hand, she played desperately for time. 'Let's have a drink – for the night that's in it?'

He was not to be so easily put off. 'Will you marry me?' he persisted.

Elizabeth panicked. Not having had any expectation of this and therefore having had no time to sort out an appropriate reaction, she smiled tentatively at him while her brain ticked furiously. He did not smile back and she could sense the coiled tension in his body; he looked like a wild animal ready to pounce. 'What about my agreement with Mossie?' she whispered but he cut her off abruptly.

'I've promised you no violence and I'll keep my word, but if you agree to marry me, I'll take care of Mossie Breac. You can leave him to me.'

Elizabeth felt cornered. She looked up at Daniel's face; he was so close to her she could smell the turf smoke from the outside air off his clothes and hair. Her physical attraction to him stirred again – she could feel its pulsing deep in her stomach – but not so strongly that she wanted to rush gladly into his arms. How to turn him down without fatally wounding his pride? All the protestations of love she had made that night in Killarney . . . He would have every right to call her every name under the sun . . .

'It's a beautiful ring, Daniel.' Her voice shook as she moved the box this way and that so the little gems caught the light from the oil lamp on the mantelpiece. Then, looking back up and him and putting as much appeal into the words as she could manage, 'Could I have a little time to think about it?'

to now, darlin'. We've had this conversation several times before, remember? You know my views about this kind of thing.'

'Say it – say it, Tilly! For once say the word "sex"!'

Maddeningly, Tilly counted off the stitches on one of her needles. 'What are you so angry about?' she asked when she was finished.

'I'm not angry.'

'Do you know what I think, Lizzie Scollard?' Tilly smiled slightly. 'I think that deep down, you're a prude.'

'What?' Elizabeth was at first flummoxed, and then defensively outraged. 'How dare you!'

'Yes,' Tilly went on imperviously, 'I think you're afraid to be truthful with yourself. As I said before, I think that, like many another, when your body cries out for what's only natural, you feel you have to dress it up in something else and then you feel like Old Nick himself.'

Elizabeth snorted but felt embarrassed that Tilly knew her so well.

In the midst of the general chat at tea-time that evening, Margaret's latest news bulletin from school revealed that Danny McCarthy had left for Butte, Montana, the day before. Disciplining herself not to react immediately, Elizabeth waited until they were all busy with homework and clearing up after the tea. She went into her bedroom and stared at herself in her mirror, exploring herself for a truthful reaction.

The truth turned out to be multi-faceted. She was sad he had gone without saying goodbye, upset at the notion that she had hurt him so badly – and, being as scaldingly honest with herself as it was possible for her to be, she also admitted that she would miss him because now she had no lover.

Elizabeth called up Mrs Charlton Leahy's reassurances about everything coming right after obstacles and delays. If Daniel wasn't to be her third husband, who was?

Two days later, Mossie Sheehan came to call. 'Excuse me,' he said politely when she answered the door, 'I'm thinking

495

of putting in a few *scilleáins* and I was wondering if you wanted me to plant a few for the house?' He opened the sack he was carrying to show her the prepared seed potatoes, already sliced in two between the eyes.

Lately, in some respects because of her huge self-doubt, Elizabeth was finding it difficult to maintain the glacial air she had adopted for her dealings with Mossie Breac. As time passed, the urgency seemed to be draining out of her hatred, and while she still felt she could never forgive him for what he had done, she was beginning to see him as an ordinary imperfect human being and not as a beast. 'Sure, Mossie,' she said listlessly, 'thank you.'

He looked swiftly up from the sack and she was surprised to see a puzzled expression in his grey eyes. Then she recollected that this was probably the first time she had spoken to him normally, without patronizing him as she had before the agreement, without demonstrating anger and contempt as she had since. 'Will you come in?' she invited.

'Are you sure?' He hesitated.

She bridled at that. 'Oh, well, if you don't want to!'

'I think we'd better leave it,' he said quietly.

Elizabeth was so put out about what she now saw as her magnanimous gesture being thrown back in her face that she hardened. 'I'd like to talk to you, as it happens,' she said.

'Yes?' His habitual look of guardedness had returned.

'About this marriage,' she began, watching for his reaction, 'you don't seriously think that we should still go ahead with it? Aren't we managing all right as we are?'

'An agreement is an agreement.' Mossie's strong frame seemed to grow larger as, resolutely, he closed the mouth of the sack and rolled it over on itself.

'Yes, but you're not going to hold me to it, are you?' Elizabeth remembered Tilly's words on first hearing the news. 'For instance if I decided to take this to court, I'm absolutely sure I could prove I signed that agreement under duress.'

Mossie looked off across the farmyard. The day was

bright and windy but very cold. He took a pair of fingerless woollen gloves out of his pocket and slowly drew them on. 'An agreement is an agreement,' he repeated, studying the backs of the mittens as though the stitches were of immense interest, 'there are witnesses.'

Elizabeth had had no intention of pursuing this today, and had Mossie come into the house in response to her invitation she would probably not have brought it up. Now she folded her arms across her chest. 'Yes, Mossie,' she said doggedly, 'but do you not think you'll be making a laughing stock of yourself? Everyone in the parish will know it's a sham and that you're doing it only for the land.'

'I don't care about everyone in the parish,' the lids dropped over his eyes so the expression in them became as enigmatic as that carved into a marble statue, 'and my reasons are my own.' Elizabeth knew then she had taken the wrong tack. She would have to come up with something better than appealing to Mossie's non-existent fear of public opprobrium.

Her day-to-day existence continued to jog along. The only storm warning was the impending birth of her step-daughter's baby. Fed on blood-curdling tales in school, Kathleen was terrified of the physical pain involved in giving birth and, although Elizabeth did her best to soothe her fears, as her time came inexorably closer, Kathleen was unable to sleep and took to walking the floor of the kitchen into the small hours of the morning.

Elizabeth's parents had taken the news of the pregnancy not half as badly as she had expected. Reading her mother's first letter of reply after being told about it, she thought sardonically to herself that a few years previously she herself could have done with some of this Christian forgiveness and tolerance. Better late than never, she thought then, understanding that, by being loving now, her parents were trying to make up for how they had behaved towards her.

St John had written twice on her behalf to George Gallaher's last known address in England. He was currently pursuing him through Actor's Equity in London. Elizabeth's instructions to her father had been simple: if George

497

Gallaher ever tried by any means to contact any of the Scollards again, she would sue for paternity both on her own behalf and on Kathleen's. At first she had wanted to sue George in any case – but, having thought it through logically, had decided that on balance they would all be far better off if they never saw a hair of his head again.

She had still not told her parents about Mossie Shee-han, however. In one sense, she was hoping for a *deus ex machina* to sort out the entire situation, but knowing one was highly unlikely to present itself, she decided to take matters into her own hands and to try again herself.

One fine day, she went out to where he was working on the potato drills. 'Would you mind bringing Lightning in to the blacksmith's in Eyeries to be shod?' she asked, making herself sound as conciliatory as possible as she handed him tea she had brought out in a tin mug.

He drained the tea in a continuous draught. 'Thank you,' he said, handing the mug back to her, 'yes, I'll do that.' When she made no move to leave he raised a questioning eyebrow. 'Is there something else?'

'You know there is, Mossie.'

He was silent.

'Can we talk about it – can you not just try to see my point of view?'

'Can you see mine?'

'Of course I can,' she said swiftly. 'You've put a huge amount of work into this farm already, Mossie, and don't think I don't appreciate it. I'd see you were well compensated—'

His face darkened. 'That's not what I meant.' Deliberately he turned his back to her and bent again to the potato drills.

Elizabeth's automatic impulse was to become angry: Mossie had the capacity to make her feel permanently wrong-footed. What's more, he was giving her the distinct impression that he felt he was already in charge. She knew, however, there was nothing to be gained by antagonizing him further and held her temper in check. 'I'm sorry if that insulted you, Mossie,' she said to his back.

'That's all right,' he said over his shoulder but without missing a beat of the work and Elizabeth felt she was left with nothing further to say on this occasion at least.

She would have to plan a lot more carefully.

She made her next attempt a few days later when Mossie brought the newly shod Lightning back from Eyeries. 'Can we talk about this like adults?' she asked as, with the horse stamping and blowing between them in the yard, she helped Mossie with the harness.

'Fire away,' he said from behind the gelding's flank as he unbuckled the girth.

'You go first,' she said, feeling absurdly like a child.

'You know my position,' he said. 'It hasn't changed.' He slipped a halter over Lightning's head and led him into the stable.

'Listen, Mossie,' she said, following him, 'I have moral right on my side, you know I do. I could take you to court but I don't want to go through all that. Could we make some sort of deal?'

'I think the deal we have is fine.' He looped the reins and hung them from their hook on the wall.

Seeing his insufferable calm, she did not know whether to kick him or to beg.

He finished what he was doing and turned to face her. 'Elizabeth—' he began but she cut him off.

'That is a liberty you have been taking. I have not given you permission to call me by my first name.' Then, as he stared at her, she knew the outburst had been childish and had lost her some ground. 'Sorry,' she muttered.

'There's no point in fighting this,' he said quietly.

'All right!' she hissed, managing — barely — not to scream. 'When would you like to *coerce* me to become your wife? And don't think I won't let everyone know what happened and why.'

'That's your privilege but that would be breaking the agreement and, anyway, you already know I don't care what anyone else thinks. As for when, the agreement says a year and a week after—'

'I know what the agreement says!' she cried. 'Stop quoting the bloody agreement at me!'

'It was your idea,' he pointed out.

Elizabeth pulled on all her reserves of dignity. 'If you won't let me out of it,' she said, 'if you won't behave like a gentleman, well, then, as far as I'm concerned the sooner it's over with the better.'

He looked at her for what seemed to be a long time and to her annoyance she felt herself redden as she divined what he was thinking. 'Of course,' he said mercilessly, proving she had guessed correctly. 'Danny McCarthy's out of the picture now, isn't he?'

'Do you have to be so nasty?'

Then she thought she detected a hint of amusement in his eyes as he gave Lightning a farewell pat, which infuriated her beyond the bounds of all reasonable debate. 'You'll thank me some day,' he said. 'Now, if you'll excuse me . . .' Unruffled, he walked past her without another glance.

Elizabeth picked up a handful of hay and rubbed the horse down so furiously with it that he danced away from her.

That night, having calmed down, Elizabeth decided to stop kicking against the destiny the tarot cards had foretold. *If* she believed in it, she told herself, she would have this second, presumably happy marriage to look forward to in the future – increasingly she believed it would not be to Daniel – and in the meantime her daily life could continue on an even keel exactly as it did at present, peacefully and calmly with the farm well looked after.

The following Saturday, she took advantage of a station in a neighbour's house to buttonhole the curate, who was a nice enough man. All through the Mass, she planned what she was going to say; her opportunity came as the refreshments were being handed around and the curate, who had been served first, was temporarily alone in a corner of the kitchen. 'Excuse me, Father.' Handing him her envelope containing the oats money, her contribution to the feeding

500

of his horse, Elizabeth asked if she could have a quiet word with him.

'Surely!' The priest put down his cup and followed her into the parlour where lately he had celebrated the Mass.

She wasted no time on a preamble. 'I'm in a strange situation,' she said. 'As you know I'm a widow since last June but I'm getting married again and I'd like the banns called. I know I should wait a year but as this will be purely a marriage of convenience, I'd like to get the whole thing over and done with as soon as possible.'

'Well, as you probably know there's no canonical bar on getting married again any time you like but it's the custom around here to wait for a decent period—'

'Saving your presence, Father,' she interrupted, 'I don't care about the custom. It's going to be a quiet wedding – there will be no guests. In fact, Father, I would greatly appreciate it if you could do it for us very early in the morning.'

He paused before replying and she knew exactly what he was thinking. 'I'm not pregnant if that's what you think all this is about,' she added brutally.

'Mrs Scollard! I wasn't—'

'Sorry to be so blunt, Father,' she said. 'But I just thought I'd get that out of the way. I don't blame you, by the way – faced with a request like that it's what most people around here would think.'

'Well, all right,' he said faintly. 'Will you organize letters of freedom and so forth?'

'Yes. Thank you, Father. And thank you mostly for not asking any questions.'

She stayed away from the chapel on the three Sundays the banns were called from the altar. And after the first Sunday, knowing she was yet again an object of gossip in the parish, she kept as much as possible to within the precincts of the house and yard.

Feeling, however, that the children had a right to know before they heard it broadcast from the rooftops of the parish, she did tell them that she was thinking of getting

501

married again. The reactions varied from indifference from the littler ones, through perplexity from Margaret – 'Mossie's nice but aren't we grand as we are?' – to acceptance from Mary and, predictably, outrage from Kathleen. Elizabeth was prepared for this and faced down Kathleen's truculence, pointing out curtly that she herself was in no position to condemn.

The wedding was conducted at six o'clock on a Saturday morning in the second week of April. Johnny Thade and Tilly were witnesses and the only other people in the chapel besides the priest were Mick Harrington and Mossie's bewildered aunt Bel. Despite Tilly's last-minute urgings, Elizabeth refused to allow confetti or flowers or anything which might indicate that this was a joyful occasion. She had deliberately chosen a Saturday because no one had to be called for school. And she managed to get back into the house without being missed. The family's first sight of Mrs Mossie Sheehan was when she called them all for breakfast.

But she was under no illusion about how quickly news would get around the parish and so that the children would hear the news first from herself, she kept them busy with chores around the house until she could orchestrate a suitable opportunity.

The kitchen was humming with the routine of Saturday night: while Elizabeth and Mary were preparing food for the Sunday dinner, Francey was cleaning the brass paraffin lamp, Johanna was scrubbing the table, Goretti was polishing all the shoes, Margaret was ironing. The only one not busy was Kathleen who was stretched out in a chair, reading as usual. Although the others complained, Elizabeth had lately decided to leave her intractable stepdaughter to her own devices, finding this preferable to constant rowing and nagging. She looked around her at all the activity and decided that now was as good a time as any to make her announcement. Putting handfuls of marrowfat peas into a bowl to steep, she kept her voice casual. 'I've something to tell you all.'

When she was sure she had their attention, she sluiced

the water around with one finger as though this task was the most important in the world. 'Mossie Sheehan and I got married this morning.'

Pandemonium ensued as they all started talking at once. 'Hold on, hold on!' Elizabeth held up her hands for quiet.

'You might have told us!' Margaret would not be silenced. 'I could have been bridesmaid.'

'Me too, me too!' Goretti and Johanna chimed in, while Kathleen heaved herself clumsily out of the chair and trod heavily towards the bedroom, making no secret of her disdain. In case Elizabeth did not get the message, she muttered, 'Typical!' under her breath when passing the table where Elizabeth still stood.

'What do you think, Mary?' Elizabeth appealed to the loyalty of the one she felt she could most count on.

'I think it's Mammy's life!' Mary rounded on the others. 'I think you're all very selfish. What difference does it make to you?'

'Of course it makes a difference.' Then, spotting the obvious, Margaret stopped. 'If you're married to him, why isn't he living here, then?'

Elizabeth was prepared for that one. 'Mossie's aunt Bel is very old and can't manage on her own. He has to stay there and look after her. After all, we don't have any spare room – unless you all want to get out of the bedroom and sleep out here?'

As she watched them argue about that one, she heaved a sigh of relief. That was a hurdle she seemed to have cleared quite well.

In the days that followed, life jogged along much the same as it had before. Elizabeth's new husband was scrupulous in his observance of the agreement between them and, although his influence on the life of the farm continued to be benevolent, she saw him as infrequently as she had before they were married.

The only differences the wedding had made to Elizabeth's life, it seemed, were that she now wore two gold bands instead of one and that on her infrequent visits to the village or to town people in shops fell silent as she walked in. This difficulty she could cope with quite well as she knew it would pass, lasting only until the next nine days' wonder came along. Where it came to land meeting marriage, unorthodoxy – as it might have been known elsewhere in the world – was not uncommon. She had even heard of a case in Derryconnla where a man of fifty-nine who had married *cliamhain isteach* into a snug farm, was sent packing back to his ninety-year-old mother five years later when he proved unable to sire an heir.

But although the circumstances had nothing at all to do with her new status, one day towards the end of April, she did feel close to the end of her tether. The day – three days after Mary's seventeenth birthday – had been unusually busy. Margaret, Goretti and Johanna had woken up the previous day with a stomach upset and both Mary and Elizabeth had been run off their feet tending to the needs of the sickroom for more than twenty-four hours.

In addition, Kathleen had been unusually cranky and, while this was understandable, her brooding presence did little to help the mood in the house. As, covertly, Elizabeth watched her hugely heavy stepdaughter struggle to retrieve a comb she had dropped on the kitchen floor, she abruptly felt the need to scream. 'Will I help you?' she asked as the comb dropped through the girl's fingers for the second time.

In reply, Kathleen began to cry. 'Oh, for goodness' sake!' Elizabeth ran across the floor and picked up the comb. 'It's nothing to whinge about!'

'I've a pain in my stomach!' Kathleen sobbed.

According to the doctor's best guess, Kathleen was not due to deliver for another month and there was every possibility that she was suffering from the same stomach complaint which had hit the other three – but, Elizabeth thought, anything could happen with a girl this young. 'Is the pain coming and going?' she asked.

'No, it's just *there*.'

Elizabeth relaxed a little. 'Sit down there at the table,' she said, 'and I'll warm you up a cup of milk.'

'I don't *want* a cup of milk.'

'Well, go and lie down, then.' Elizabeth's already fragile patience thinned further. 'If the pain's not gone in half an hour we'll see what we'll do.'

Sniffling, Kathleen trailed off into the bedroom.

It was in the course of seeing to Goretti, who had vomited yet again, that Elizabeth decided that, for safety's sake, Kathleen should see someone. 'Is it no better?' she asked, looking across at the bed on which her stepdaughter lay. 'No.' Kathleen curled up.

Not for the first time, Elizabeth wished they were nearer to a telephone. No one in the district had one and the public telephone in Eyeries was the best part of half an hour away. She put her hand on Kathleen's forehead: it was perfectly cool so it was unlikely that she was suffering from the same ailment as the others. 'Would you feel up to going to see the midwife?' she asked. The midwife, who lived near Castleclough, was less than half the distance from the house than was the doctor in Castletownbere. 'I have to stay here, but Mary can drive Lightning. I'll tell her to take him very easy, just to walk him.'

'People'd see me!' Kathleen cried.

Although everyone in the parish knew about the pregnancy, Elizabeth, remembering her own public shame, empathized with her stepdaughter's reluctance to go out. 'I think it's important, Kathleen,' she coaxed, 'and it's chilly enough out there so if I lend you my cape no one'll stare at you.' She knew Kathleen coveted the cape in question, made of light wool. 'Come on,' she urged, 'you haven't been outside these four walls for weeks. Apart from anything else, the fresh air will do you good.' She continued to work on Kathleen and after a few minutes persuaded her to go.

Tilly arrived about half an hour later as she was helping Mary tackle up the horse. 'Going somewhere?' Her friend watched the operation.

'I'm sending Kathleen in to the midwife,' Elizabeth replied. 'Whoa there!' she admonished the horse. Lightning, who was newly out on grass and had not been in

505

harness for quite a while, was snorting and stamping with impatience; he had been quite difficult to catch and for once Mossie, who might have helped, was nowhere in evidence. Everything today seemed to be conspiring against her, Elizabeth thought irritably as the gelding raised his head so high that she practically had to jump to catch at his bridle.

'How's things?' Tilly surveyed the scene in the yard.

'Not great.' Elizabeth fastened the final buckle ensuring that, at last, Lightning was ready. Mary held his head while her stepmother called out to Kathleen to hurry up.

Kathleen emerged immediately, the voluminous cape doing little to disguise her size; it was a good thing, Elizabeth thought, that there was no full-length mirror in the house. She and Tilly helped Kathleen mount the horse car and then stood back while Mary, who had become quite a good driver, climbed into her seat.

'She's awfully big. Are you sure you should let her go?' Tilly said dubiously in an undertone as Mary clicked her tongue at the horse and waved them a cheerful goodbye.

But as Lightning stepped briskly through the gateway and then leaned into the traces to take them up the hill away from the house, Elizabeth thought she detected that Kathleen was already looking a little more animated. 'She'll be fine,' she replied. 'Don't forget now,' she called after Mary, 'take your time. There's no rush. If you're not back at tea-time I'll keep something for the two of you.'

'So what's wrong?' Tilly asked as they turned away to go into the house.

'What's *not* wrong today? Come on in and I'll tell you all about it.'

Although it was a little early in the year, April had been a dry month and Mossie was working turf on the Scollards' plot above Derryvegill. It was one of the tasks he enjoyed most each year, getting into the rhythm of cutting and turning, cutting and turning, relishing the good clean line of the sods which came off the edge of the *sleán* like oversized slabs of shop butter.

He was not the only one on the bog: Mick Harrington, too, was taking advantage of the good drying weather and was working about a hundred feet away in an adjacent plot.

Mossie had been working for about an hour when he stopped to take a slug of milk from the mineral bottle in his pocket. The sweat on his forehead dried quickly and coldly in the northerly breeze which swept across the Kenmare river from the mountains of Kerry. Wearing only a shirt, Mossie shivered.

He was just about to slide the *sleán* into the turf again when he thought he heard a noise that did not belong in the countryside. Leaning on the implement, he listened hard. The sound was coming and going on the wind but it was undoubtedly a woman screaming. It seemed to be coming from the direction of the lake. 'Did you hear that?' Mossie shouted across to Mick Harrington.

'What?' Mick was south-west of Mossie and the wind whipped away his voice.

'Listen!' Mossie called.

Both men strained their ears. There it was again, definitely a scream. 'Jays, I heard it that time!' Mick Harrington, shoving his own *sleán* into the earth so it stood upright, broke into a run.

Mossie did likewise, sprinting towards a small ridge which at present hid the lake from his view.

But when he got to it, standing scanning the landscape, he could not see anything.

The screaming, stronger now in his ears, seemed to be coming from below a steep, grassy cliff which rose to the road from a marsh on the western side of Derryvegill lake. Closely followed by Mick, Mossie came off the ridge and sliding on loose pieces of earth and stones, careered down the hill towards the road. He was so busy keeping his footing that it was only when he was about twenty feet away from it that he saw, lying on the verge above the edge of the cliff, a woman's open handbag, its contents spilled over the grass. 'Jesus,' he shouted as the other man caught up with him, 'someone's gone over.'

Mick crossed himself as both men peered over the edge of the cliff, which was about forty feet high.

'Oh, Christ!' They said it simultaneously.

Lying in a jumbled heap under the broken horse cart at the bottom of the cliff lay the two eldest Scollard girls. It was Kathleen who was screaming. Having been thrown clear during the fall, she was lying on her side, clutching her stomach with both hands; one leg was bent behind her at an unnatural angle. Only the back of Mary's head was visible under the glistening spars of black and red wood. She was very still.

A little way away, Lightning, still in the traces, thrashed his hind legs and rolled his neck from side to side as he tried to rise. Both of his front legs seemed to be broken.

Mossie took all this in in a second or two. 'Get help!' he yelled over his shoulder as he began frantically to search for a way down the cliff, which was a sheer embankment.

'I'll be as quick as I can.' Mick sprinted off in the direction of the nearest house which was about five hundred yards away down the road.

'And bring a gun!' Mossie screamed after him but began his precipitous descent without waiting to hear whether or not Mick responded.

Kathleen saw him coming and redoubled her screams. Dragging her bent leg, she began to crawl towards him on all fours. Mossie was descending as fast as he could; once he lost his foothold and saved himself only by catching on to one of the tough clumps of furze which sprouted here and there on the face of the embankment. But when he was still ten feet off the ground, one of these clumps gave way and he tumbled the rest of the way, landing heavily on his right shoulder.

He was up in an instant.

Kathleen had almost reached him, her open, screaming mouth like a dark red scar in her white face, the huge bulk of her pregnant stomach dragging through the marsh. As Mossie covered the last few feet between them he realized she was trying to say something. 'Calm down, calm down,' he shouted.

The babel of glottal sound coming out of Kathleen's mouth reached unearthly heights but through it, Mossie thought he detected the word 'feeling', or perhaps 'bleeding'. He seized her by the shoulders. 'Are you bleeding?' he yelled.

'Ye-eee-ees!' Like a drowning swimmer, she threw her arms around his neck.

It was only then that Mossie saw the dark stain spreading through the lower part of the cape she wore, which itself was a dull red. With some difficulty, he prised her arms from around his neck. 'Listen to me, Kathleen, listen to me!' He held her wrists and shook her.

'You're hurting me!' she wailed, then, 'Oh, Jesus!' She spasmed with pain, her undamaged knee jerking upwards, 'I think the baby's coming—'

Mossie loosened his grip. 'You've got to listen. The baby won't be here for a while yet. Hold on, Kathleen. There's help coming. Do you understand?'

But she carried on screaming. 'Oh, Jesus! Jesus! The baby!'

'I've got to go see how Mary is,' he cried, trying to make himself heard above the noise she was making. 'You sit here and stay as quiet as you can. There's help coming. Stay as quiet as you can!' he repeated, manhandling her into a position where she could support her back against the embankment. 'I'll come to you in a minute.'

Mary had not moved but the car under which she lay jerked up and down on top of her with the thrashing of the injured horse. 'Easy, Lightning, easy . . .' Mossie, crouching low, inserted his left, unhurt shoulder under the upset sideboard of the car and heaved with all his might. It shuddered and moved a little, exposing the upper part of Mary's torso.

Making an enormous effort, Mossie, neck corded, muscles behind his eyes stinging with the strain, pushed again – and then, supremely, one more time until he had managed to push it clear of her.

When he stood up, his eyes seemed to explode with a sunburst of red and gold; he felt he was going to faint and hung his head low for a few seconds until the dizziness cleared. When he could see properly again, he saw there was still no move from Mary.

Mortally afraid of what he would find if he examined her closely, Mossie looked involuntarily back towards Kathleen, who was still screaming, but at slightly diminished volume. Eyes closed, both hands clutching her stomach, she was rocking herself rhythmically from side to side against the grass of the embankment. The stain on the cape seemed larger now. 'Oh, Jesus,' Mossie prayed, 'please send help soon . . .'

With that, he bent to check on Mary.

Mary was dead.

'She can't be, she can't be!' Instinctively, Mossie picked up the lifeless head and pushed the fine dark hair back from Mary's face. The eyes were round and open as though she had just had a great shock. One of the top teeth had come through the bottom lip and a small trickle of blood ran from the wound down her chin. Otherwise the face was undamaged.

But by the way the head was lolling, loose and unconnected, Mossie already knew what had killed her. Her neck was broken.

Gently, he replaced the head. The skirt Mary wore had ridden up over her hips, exposing her knickers and bare thighs. Having to lift her slightly, Mossie pulled down the skirt as far as it would go.

Lightning was getting weaker. The foam from his mouth was flecked now with blood as he lay panting on his belly, his useless front legs splayed in front of him like those of a drinking giraffe. 'Easy, boy!' Mossie put out a hand to stroke his nose and the horse whinnied, jerking away and rolling his eyes. 'There's help coming . . .' Mossie covered his own eyes and sinking to his haunches, cried like a baby.

After a while, hearing sounds, he looked up. Mick Harrington, accompanied by two men and a young boy, was running across the marsh from the head of the lake. 'We've sent for the doctor,' Mick shouted when he was still fifty yards away.

'Over there!' Mossie pointed towards Kathleen. 'It's too late here—' He was overcome again.

'Oh no!' While the other two men – each was carrying a wooden door to act as a stretcher – ran over to Kathleen, Mick bent to examine Mary. 'She's gone all right,' he said, straightening up. 'Did you say the Act of Contrition for her?'

Mute, Mossie shook his head.

Mick squatted by Mary's head and whispered the prayer into her ear. Dimly, Mossie was aware of the men behind him persuading Kathleen to get on to the makeshift stretcher. The floor of the marsh was sheltered here from the wind by a rise in the land at the sea side; in light of the devastation all around, Kathleen's continued screaming, the struggling of the horse, the broken car, the relative calmness of the air seemed to Mossie to be an insult. 'Is that thing loaded?' he asked almost angrily, pointing to the old shotgun being carried by the boy, who was not more than twelve or thirteen years old. Grey-faced, the boy nodded.

'Give it here.'

Mossie waited until Mick had finished the Act of Contrition.

Lightning seemed to know what was coming. He stopped struggling and lowered his beautiful head so it rested on the ground between his ruined legs. Flanks heaving, he waited quietly for Mossie to lift the gun.

Mossie's eyes were so blinded with tears, he could barely see enough to aim properly. His hands shook.

'Do you want me to do it?' Mick asked in a low voice.

'No!' Mossie replied violently. 'He was my horse, and I brought this on the Scollards.' He took a deep shuddering breath and fired.

Elizabeth and Tilly were gossiping companionably at the table when Elizabeth heard the familiar cry from the bedroom. 'God!' she groaned. 'I know they can't help it but this'd try the patience of a saint!' She dragged herself out of the chair and, picking up fresh bedlinen from the pile set ready on a chair by the stove, went to investigate.

A few minutes later, Goretti lay back wanly as Elizabeth sponged her forehead. 'Thank you, Mammy.' Beside her Margaret, on the mend and reading, asked who was outside in the kitchen.

'Tilly,' Elizabeth replied.

'Yes, but who's the man?'

'What man?'

'The man who's out in the kitchen,' Margaret repeated patiently as though her stepmother was a moron.

On going back out, Elizabeth discovered that there was not one man but two in the kitchen. One was Mossie, the other was the curate.

Mossie looked around when he sensed Elizabeth's presence behind him in the doorway and at the sight of his ravaged face, her heart felt as though it had stopped.

'What? What is it?' she cried.

'I'm sorry, Elizabeth, I'm so sorry,' Mossie whispered, 'we were too late – Mick and me – we were too late . . .'

Elizabeth looked from him to the curate. 'What's going on?'

'I'm afraid you have to prepare yourself.'

The priest moved forward as though to touch her but Elizabeth shrank back. 'Tilly?' she whimpered.

Tilly's face was as white as the basin Elizabeth still held in her hand.

'Kathleen's on her way to hospital,' Tilly said and then could not continue.

For a few seconds she struggled for composure. 'There was an accident,' she said then. 'Mary – she's – she's . . .' Making a huge effort, Tilly gathered herself. 'I'm afraid she's dead, Lizzie.'

The china basin slipped from Elizabeth's hands and crashed to the floor, breaking into pieces and spewing water all over the flagstones.

Chapter Twenty-Five

Of all the vicissitudes in her life so far Elizabeth was hit hardest by Mary's death.

In many respects, everything else that happened to her, the unplanned pregnancy, Neeley's death, even her ill-starred passion for Daniel Carrig, had occurred as a consequence of some action and could be seen either as reaction or retribution.

But Mary's death seemed so unutterably pointless and undeserved. Neeley's eldest daughter had moved sweetly through her short life, seeking little attention for herself, offering a haven to the more turbulent spirits around her in the house. In retrospect, Elizabeth saw that in many ways Mary had been the steadily beating heart of the household.

All this she saw too late. It was of little use to Mary now that Elizabeth been planning to get around 'soon' to do something for Mary's future, to pay back some of the unflappable loyalty and support without which she herself would have had a much tougher time than she did. At the beginning, however, she managed to impose an iron control on herself and would not allow the tears to come.

When Mary was brought home to be laid out, she thanked the neighbours who offered to do it but insisted on performing this last service for Neeley's eldest daughter. She had never done it before and Tilly, who knew the routine, stayed in the room with her to advise her.

But as far as Elizabeth was concerned, although she was objectively grateful for Tilly's supportive presence, she and Mary were alone together for the last time. She spoke quietly to Mary as she washed the young body, said all the things she should have said when Mary was alive. She told Mary how lovely she was; how she herself could not have managed to get through the last terrible year without Mary's unselfishness; how grateful she was for all Mary's tacit love and support right from that first stormy day when she had arrived on Béara. How she had forgotten to thank her on the occasions when Mary was worried about the appropriateness of something Elizabeth was doing but, out of loyalty, subsumed her own preferences.

As she pared the nails she remembered Mary's deft movements around the kitchen with butter spades and sifters, the pride she took in the smallest of Abigail's achievements; the way she had become a second mother to her half-siblings and even to Francey with whom she had no blood ties at all.

She remembered the shy light in Mary's eyes – now weighted down with copper pennies – when, from the hairdresser's chair, she had looked around to see what Elizabeth thought of her new style. 'Oh, God.' Elizabeth gave in at last, bending low over the perfect waxen skin of Mary's face. 'I don't know what I'm going to do without you . . . Mary, darling Mary,' she wept, 'I'm going to miss you so much . . .'

From behind she felt Tilly's arms creep round her shoulders.

Once she had started to cry, it seemed Elizabeth could not stop and eventually Tilly sent her husband to telephone for the doctor to come. When he came, he gave her something which made her sleep for sixteen hours.

He came again in the morning before the funeral and whatever he gave her this time made her feel so groggy and disoriented that the funeral passed without any recognition from her of its reality. In the church, everyone around her seemed to glow and then fade, to advance and recede as though they were participants in an ethereal gavotte; she heard the priest's intonations as though from a great distance and, when accepting condolences, sometimes had difficulty in remembering people's names. Even the children seemed like strangers to her.

514

In the cemetery, she found her father's constant presence irksome. He was holding on to her arm all the time when all she wanted was to go off by herself; it was a lovely day, she thought at one point, it would have been nice to walk up Knockameala. Looking away from the open grave, which meant as little to her as did the vast numbers of people thronging around, she gazed towards the summit of the mountain, just visible to the north-east behind the folds of Knocknasheeog. She remembered Daniel Carrig standing there and saw him there again but although she attempted to pull away from her father, other hands restrained her.

She was aware that Ida and Ida's husband had come from Cork with her parents and, back in the house, heard herself smiling and congratulating Ida on her pregnancy, now well advanced. That was nice of Ida to come.

But where was Mary now that she was needed to help with catering for all these people? Three times in an hour she looked around the crowded kitchen and asked for Mary but nobody would tell her where Mary was.

Then she asked for Tilly, because she could not find Tilly either. She went right up to Mick and asked him where Tilly was but Mick said that Tilly had gone to Cork to be with Kathleen who was having her baby in hospital there.

Even to take this in was a struggle. Was it not Ida who was having the baby? Why was Kathleen having a baby in Cork too?

Mulling it over, Elizabeth decided she herself wanted to go to Cork to be with Kathleen and went out to the stable to harness Lightning only to find the stall empty. Something about Lightning was pulling at the edges of the fuzz around her brain. Something about a ram that had jumped out in front of him near Derryvegill. But there were no rams on the farm . . . Not any more, anyway . . .

She was trying to figure it out when she heard someone come in behind her.

It was Mossie Breac.

515

'Someone's stolen Lightning,' she said severely to Mossie but to her surprise, Mossie said nothing, just took her by the elbow and led her gently back towards the house.

She balked at the doorway. There were too many people in there and none of them was doing anything about Kathleen's baby or about finding Lightning. 'Get the Guards!' she said to Mossie.

'In a little while,' he said. 'I'll go to town in a little while.'

'Do you promise?' she asked.

'I promise.'

She decided she might as well trust Mossie as anybody else so she let herself be brought back inside.

The doctor was there again. Was the doctor at the funeral? Elizabeth could not remember. He seemed to be coming to the house a lot lately. She saw Mossie and her mother talking to him and now he was giving her something warm to drink and telling her to lie down for a few minutes. 'But what about the tea?' Elizabeth looked around at the hordes in the kitchen. How on earth was she going to feed them all? She was not even sure if they had enough rations.

'It's not tea-time yet,' her mother was patting her shoulder. 'You take a nice rest, dear, we'll look after things out here.'

Elizabeth was very confused. She knew it must be tea-time by now. But she went obediently into her bedroom and lay down. For a few minutes she tried to remember why everyone was here, why she was in bed in the middle of the day. She must be sick, she thought, like Johanna and Goretti and Margaret. But she did not feel like vomiting, she was just very sleepy. Maybe she had a sleeping sickness. As she drifted again into drugged inertia, the subdued babble of the crowd outside the door swelled and faded like the waves on the sea until the tide went out and there was nothing to be heard except echoes.

Some time during the blackest part of the night, Elizabeth woke to find her bedroom flooded with light as bright as from the electric chandeliers under which she and

Ida had danced in Dublin so long ago. The light was golden and warm; if she raised her arms it yielded only slowly on her skin. Like honey, she thought, remembering Daniel Carrig. The memory was soft and clean.

Lazily, she turned her head on the pillow. Mary was there, in a corner of the room; the light was coming from Mary, whose face was as radiant as the sun. 'Hello, Mary,' Elizabeth said, surprised.

Mary did not reply but smiled so sweetly that Elizabeth wanted to run to her as though she were the child and Mary the mother instead of the other way around. But she found she could not move.

Mary, her hair lit from within so it glowed like a halo, was dressed in a one-piece garment which fell in soft folds from her shoulders to the floor; like a patchwork quilt, it was sewn from thousands of multicoloured diamonds of fabric, so vivid and bright they seemed to pulsate. Then Elizabeth saw why: Mary raised her arms and the garment disintegrated; each diamond flew individually into the air and the room was filled with clouds of hummingbirds, flashing prisms in the torrents of glorious light.

Naked now, her long limbs gleaming like alabaster, Mary raised her ecstatic face as some of the tiny, glistening birds came back to her, burrowing into her hair, tipping to and fro on her shoulders and outstretched arms, covering her breasts with pillows of living colour. Two, the first cobalt, the second jade, came to perch on her eyes.

But they were Hazel's eyes – where was Hazel? Hazel was to mind Kathleen – where was Kathleen?

'Where's Kathleen?' Elizabeth asked Mary but Mary smiled and shook her head so that her bird-filled hair wheeled like spangled feathers around her face. And, although she laughed with joy, no sound came out of her mouth.

Instead, a breathy, sustained chord, like the soughing of wind through telephone wires, grew and grew throughout the room as the beating of the birds' wings combined in unison. The chord filled Elizabeth; it entered every orifice, every pore until it pierced her heart. She found she

517

was crying because it was so beautiful. She tried to tell Mary about it, to ask if she felt it too but when she turned again to Mary, Mary was gone.

The chord continued. She felt herself being lifted physically by it, as though she was floating. The birds whirled round her own head now, faster and faster: they were taking her up with them off the bed ... Then something harsh broke in, her own name splintered the harmony so that it became cacophonous. 'Elizabeth! Elizabeth!' Someone was calling her back, pulling her down ...

'Elizabeth!' The awful sound was louder now, more commanding. The comedown was shocking. Elizabeth wanted to rise again into the colours and the music but the voice would not let her.

'Elizabeth!' Now she was being shaken by the shoulder.

'Please,' she whispered, 'please ...' But the voice was insistent and eventually she opened her eyes.

Her mother was standing by the bed; there was no golden light in the room, just an ordinary spill of lamplight from her own lamp on the dressing-table. 'You were dreaming, dear,' her mother said gently. 'Here, the doctor said you're to have this.' She held out two tablets on the palm of her hand.

'No.' Elizabeth tried to say it vehemently but her mouth was as dry as ashes and all that came out was a weak croak. 'No more pills,' she whispered, then, too groggy to make another full sentence, 'Drink, please.'

Corinne helped Elizabeth drink the water, holding the glass to her lips and supporting her head. This close, she smelled exquisitely of freesia. 'Are you sure it's wise not to do what the doctor says, Beth?' she asked.

'Too much.' Elizabeth sank back into the pillow. 'Time, please?'

'It's just after midnight. Everything's under control. That nice Mr Sheehan has sorted everything out for us and we're going to stay in the Béara Bay Hotel in Castletownbere. He says he'll stay here for the rest of the night to make sure everything is all right.'

Elizabeth, to whom reality was returning all too

518

quickly, tried to struggle up on one elbow but the effort was too much and she subsided. 'Not stay the night,' she blurted.

Corinne misunderstood. 'You don't have to worry, darling, we're in a *hotel*, do you understand?'

'Mossie!'

Elizabeth was so obviously agitated that Corinne herself was getting flustered. 'Now now, don't upset yourself, darling,' she said nervously. 'He says it's no trouble. You just close your eyes and go back to sleep.'

Elizabeth was too befuddled and weary to press the argument. She closed her eyes. Then like the brush of a butterfly's wing, she felt the touch of Corinne's cool lips on her forehead. 'Mother?' Her eyes opened again in surprise.

'Ssh . . .' Corinne put a finger to her lips. 'Goodnight, darling, see you in the morning. And please God by then we'll have good news about Kathleen from the hospital.'

Although she was not as confused as she had been earlier in the day, Elizabeth's brain was still having great difficulty in focusing. Time had become elasticated so she could not yet fully separate the past from the present. It was only after she heard the outer door close behind her mother as her parents left for the hotel that the significance of what she had said penetrated the fog. She managed to get out of bed and although the floor was as unsteady under her feet as the deck of a boat in a rolling sea, made it as far as the door. But once there, she felt dizzy and had to hold on to the jamb for support.

Seeing her, Mossie, who, on his haunches in front of the open fire door, was banking down the fire for the night, rose and came towards her. 'You shouldn't be out of bed.'

'What about the hospital?' Elizabeth gasped. 'My mother says . . .' But her head was spinning so much she was afraid she was going to faint, something which had never happened to her in her entire life and she was forced to allow Mossie to support her while she made for a chair.

He dashed into the scullery and ran water into a glass. Returning, he handed it to her.

After a few mouthfuls, Elizabeth's head felt a little

clearer and she handed back the glass. 'Tell me about Kathleen,' she said, having to make an effort with each word.

'I thought they told you?'

'No.' In fact, she did now remember something vague about Kathleen and hospital but she had to keep her sentences short and uncomplicated.

In the lamplight, the circles under Mossie's eyes looked as deep as craters. 'She's had a baby boy,' he said.

'Is she all right?'

'She has a broken leg.'

'Baby?'

'I think he's going to be all right, too.'

Elizabeth's head was spinning again. 'Water, please,' she said faintly.

Again Mossie handed her the drink and stood over her while she drank it. 'You have to get back to bed,' he said, 'please, Elizabeth.'

Elizabeth allowed herself to be helped by him into the bedroom. 'Thank you,' she said, climbing gratefully between the sheets. She noticed she was wearing a night-dress and a cardigan but could not remember having got into them. 'Thank you,' she said again. She tried to tell Mossie he could go home now, that she and Mary could manage by themselves but as she drifted off again into unconsciousness, all she could get out was the single word: 'Home . . .'

When next she awoke it was bright. For a few moments, she felt relaxed and cosseted under her warm bedclothes. Automatically, she looked to the corner where Abigail's cot stood: it was empty.

Where was Abbie?

A cold wave of grief rolled over her as, clearly this time, she remembered the accident and its consequences. Unable passively to lie there while the terrifying memories flooded back, she threw off the bedclothes and tested her footing on the floor. Although slightly lightheaded, she was quite steady and pulling on her dressing-gown over her night-clothes, went out into the kitchen.

To her horror, Mossie Sheehan was asleep in the chair beside the fire.

She looked at the clock on the mantelpiece: it was just after six in the morning. What was Mossie Sheehan doing in her kitchen at this hour? She did not hesitate: 'Mossie!' She shook him roughly by the shoulder. 'Mossie, wake up.'

Mossie woke up slowly and for a moment or two looked at her without recognition. Then he sprang to his feet. 'What time is it?'

'Where's Abigail?' Elizabeth asked abruptly. 'She's not in her cot.'

'Your friend Ida took her to stay down at the Harring-tons'.' Mossie stood up. 'How are you feeling?' he asked.

'Never mind how I'm feeling, what are you doing here?' Elizabeth concentrated all her energy on this one thing: if she could channel some of her feelings in this single direction, she would not yet have to think about Mary. She was almost glad Mossie was here as a target.

Mossie cleared his throat. 'I thought you might need help,' he said quietly.

'Well, thank you very much but I don't need any more help. We'll all be fine now.'

He seemed about to say something then, but rubbing his hand across the stubble on his chin thought better of it. He picked his jacket off the back of the chair – he was wearing his good suit, Elizabeth noticed – and retrieved his cap from the pocket. Donning both garments, he paused again. 'Don't be too hard on yourself,' he said softly.

'That's my business, Mossie, but thank you again for your concern.' Elizabeth felt that if he did not leave quickly her fragile composure would splinter and tip her into madness.

Mossie crossed to the door. 'I'll check back later,' he said, and before she could again object, 'just to see if anything heavy needs doing or, for instance, if you'd like me to send a message to Kathleen in Cork.'

521

'What about Kathleen in Cork?' Then, at the back of her memory, Elizabeth was nudged by some obscure reference to a baby boy. 'Has she had the baby?'

'Yes, a baby boy. Everything's all right, as far as I know – except for Kathleen's broken leg, of course.'

'Why didn't someone tell me?'

'We did – I did, last night,' he said gently.

His forbearance forced Elizabeth abruptly to face the fact that she had been gratuitously boorish. She could not bring herself to apologize but called him back as he was opening the door. 'Mossie?'

'Yes?' He turned round.

'What happened to the car?' she asked quickly in an effort to make amends.

'I burned it,' Mossie replied.

'And – and – the horse?' Elizabeth could not bear to use Lightning's name.

'That's taken care of,' he said quietly.

'Thank you, Mossie.' She felt the tears springing behind her eyes. 'I really appreciate all you've done.'

He rubbed his hand over his stubbled chin again, whether out of embarrassment or not, she could not tell, and simply nodded. When he was gone, Elizabeth looked around the quiet kitchen. Everything was in its place, she thought, just as if Mary –

Bawling, she sank into the chair Mossie had just vacated.

'Mammy?'

Elizabeth looked up: Francey's frightened face was swimming in front of her. She took a handkerchief out of her dressing-gown pocket and blew her nose. 'Come here, lovey,' she said. He ran to her and climbed on her knee. He was far too large and heavy for comfortable cuddling but he threw his arms around her neck and buried his head against her. 'Don't cry, Mammy, don't cry.' He, too, wept.

'I'm better now, darling,' Elizabeth said, rocking him. 'We both have to be brave. We'll help each other.'

'Mammy,' his tear-stained face was inches from hers, 'is Lightning gone to heaven, too?'

'Of course he is. Mary took him to heaven with her.'

'What are they doing up there?'

Shreds of Elizabeth's hallucinatory dream returned to her. 'You wouldn't believe how beautiful it is up there, Francey,' she said, wiping his tears with the sleeve of her dressing-gown. 'Everything is gorgeously coloured – like a big garden full of flowers and birds and sunshine. Lightning has plenty of grazing and plenty of space to gallop around as fast as he likes . . .'

'Will someone give him oats?'

'As many oats as he can eat.'

Francey lay against her shoulder and contemplated this vision of heaven. 'How did he get there?' he asked.

'When someone dies –' Elizabeth's throat threatened to close over but she swallowed hard. 'When someone dies,' she repeated, 'it's like opening a mussel shell. You know the way the little mussel is all soft inside the shell?'

'Yes.' Francey nodded.

'Well, this body' – she touched his chest – 'is like that shell but the real person, the *real* Francey is inside, just like the little mussel. And at death, the person's shell is opened up and the real person inside is free then to go to heaven. He doesn't need the body any more and it's left behind, just like the old mussel shell.'

'Do they fly up?'

'Sort of. It's hard to explain but if you can try to imagine them spreading out on the wind and the wind then takes them up beyond the stars . . .'

'But if Lightning leaves his body behind how can he gallop when he's up there?'

'The real Lightning can do anything he wants now. You know the way that even if you run as fast as you can, it's still not as fast as you'd like to? Well, that's because your body is not free. Lightning's free now and because he doesn't need his body any more, he can gallop faster than he ever galloped before, all over the universe.' She stroked his tousled hair. 'The next time you look up at the stars, Francey, if you concentrate very hard, you could probably hear Lightning galloping through them.'

523

'Really?' Francey's eyes were large with wonder. 'Is is sort of like magic?'

'It's definitely like magic.' Elizabeth needed to change the subject or she might again break down. 'Would you do me a favour, darling?'

'What?'

'I haven't had anything to eat for a long time, would you mind getting me a bit of bread and butter, please?'

He climbed down off her lap and as she watched him butter the bread, tongue stuck out in concentration, she knew that she could no longer afford self-indulgence.

When Ida returned Abigail, she found Elizabeth dry-eyed, mentally recovered – at least on the surface – and resolute. 'Are you sure you're all right, Beth?' And when Elizabeth tried to assure her that she was – 'It's all that sleeping' – Ida offered to stay for another few days. 'It's very soon, Beth,' she said, 'I know you seem to be all right now but there's bound to be a reaction.'

'I'm not alone, I have the children. We have to face it sooner or later, it might as well be now,' said Elizabeth.

'And what about your husband? Since you didn't see fit to tell me about him.' Ida pursed her lips, 'I wasn't going to mention it.'

'I see Mick Harrington's been talking,' Elizabeth said, 'but, Ida, I wanted as few people to know about it as possible. My parents still don't know so I'd appreciate it if you'd be discreet.'

'I never heard of such an outlandish arrangement in all my life.'

'It's turned out all right, it really has. He doesn't bother me. And, as it happens, I now see I couldn't possibly have managed the farm by myself.'

'But —'

'Please, Ida.' Elizabeth could see Ida gearing up for an argument and she did not trust her own shaky equilibrium to hold.

'All right, all right!' Ida immediately backed off. 'But

keep me posted,' she said gently, 'I'm your best friend, Beth.'

'I promise. This was a special circumstance.'

'So I believe,' Ida replied drily. 'Beth, I know it's a bit soon to say this, but I hope things will settle down now. You've had enough troubles for ten lifetimes.'

'Well, I did have six years of nothing—'

'I wouldn't call several miscarriages nothing.'

'I suppose when you're going through it it's just one thing at a time and it doesn't seem so much.' Having said it, Elizabeth was surprised at how truthful this was. 'You just have to keep going. And if I didn't keep going, if I caved in, what would all the others do?'

'I just wish you could do something for yourself for a change.'

Elizabeth managed to smile. 'That's what has me in this mess with Mossie Sheehan.'

'I can't understand this whole thing. He's very nice, Beth. I don't know why you don't—'

'Don't start, Ida!' Again Elizabeth felt the cracks developing in the surface of her self-possession. Hurriedly she changed the subject. 'Be sure and let me know how things develop with the baby.'

Ida took the hint. 'I will,' she said, then, 'I was just thinking of you.'

'I know.' They hugged one another and Ida left, promising to visit Kathleen as soon as she got back to the city.

At breakfast, as was to be expected, only Abigail behaved as she did every day, talking quietly to herself, banging her spoon experimentally on the side of her porridge bowl to see what would happen. The other three sat hollow-eyed and silent, toying with their food. Elizabeth, whose head was now throbbing with a violent headache, was finding it difficult to eat. Yet as she looked along the sad, lost faces, she knew they were looking to her for some sort of lead. 'I want you all to listen to me,' she said, as strongly as she could.

Abbie, lost in her own world, dug her fingers deep into the goo in front of her but three pairs of eyes turned instantly in Elizabeth's direction. 'What has happened is absolutely terrible,' she said, 'but it has happened and we all have to go on. You know there's a saying around here that a death brings a new life? Well, in our case, that's certainly true. We all loved Mary very much,' her voice wobbled but she carried on regardless, '*very* much. We'll all miss her. But we all have a new job to do now. There's a new baby coming into the house soon, Kathleen's little son. Kathleen herself will probably have to stay in hospital for a while because she has a broken leg, so we'll all have to look after this new baby boy.'

There was silence for a few moments, then Margaret displayed a flicker of interest. 'What's his name?'

'I don't know yet. That's up to Kathleen. But maybe that's something we can all do today. We can write letters to Kathleen and tell her how we're looking forward to seeing the baby and maybe suggesting what we would like to call him?'

Her suggestion was greeted with continuing silence. 'She's probably very lonely there, too, in the hospital all by herself without us,' she prompted.

'Do we have to go to school today?' Again it was Margaret.

'No, darling. Today is a day we all need to be together.'

The suggestion about the letters turned out to be a good one because after the breakfast things had been cleared away and washed, they settled down at the table with paper, pencils and pens. And, as the inevitable arguments began, their sadness dissipated and Elizabeth was impressed with how resilient they seemed to be. Notwithstanding that, she would have to watch them carefully. While they had seemed to get over Neeley's death quite well, she felt that Mary's gentle day-to-day presence would be missed incalculably more.

As it happened, the names they came up with for the new baby were not very imaginative. Johanna was naturally *ad idem* with Francey: their suggestion was Charlie. Goretti offered Seán and Margaret had a hard time deciding between Rodney, Richard or Roy. In the end, persuaded by Elizabeth, who pointed out to her that none of the three names had much to do with Béara – or even Ireland – she eventually decided on Michael.

All day, the kitchen was again occupied by a stream of solicitous neighbours calling to see if Elizabeth needed any help or service, or simply coming to sit and talk. Her parents came, too, to say goodbye, but they were so obviously relieved to see that, in the circumstances, she was again behaving relatively normally that the farewell was not as much of an ordeal as Elizabeth might have expected. 'We'll come down again in a fortnight,' her father promised, 'just to see how things are.'

'Yes,' Corinne agreed, 'and we'll go in to the hospital to see poor Kathleen. And the baby, too, of course,' she added.

'Thank you, Mother.' Elizabeth did not care now whether her mother recoiled or not: she hugged her.

'Daddy.' She hugged him, too.

'Oh, I wish this bloody war was over,' he said, so irritably that she knew he was moved. 'Transport is so difficult,' he continued. 'Come on, Corinne . . .'

'It soon will be by the looks of things, dear –'

'What?' St John appeared to be having difficulty with his watch.

'The war, dear, it's only a matter of weeks now, everyone says so.' Corinne patted his arm with her gloved hand.

They were making such valiant efforts to behave like an agreeable, supportive unit in front of her that Elizabeth was deeply touched. 'Go on,' she choked. 'I'll see you in a fortnight.' She ran into the house.

It was only minutes, however, before another neighbour woman arrived and she was again diverted.

In one way and another, she was kept occupied all day. But that evening, when at last only the family was left in the kitchen, she was left with a sense of incompleteness. Not remembering anything at all about the funeral, she felt

527

a great need to go to Mary's grave, so, when the three youngest children were in bed, she asked Margaret if she felt up to being in charge for an hour or so. 'Where are you going?' The expression on Margaret's face betrayed her insecurity.

Elizabeth was reluctant to leave her but the need to visit Mary was very strong. 'I'll only be gone an hour or so,' she said, 'I'd like to go to the graveyard for a little while.'

Margaret's face crumpled but immediately she controlled herself. 'All right,' she said.

As Elizabeth started across the fields towards Kilcatherine graveyard, she saw Mossie baling potatoes in the vegetable plot. It was only then she realized that he had not again called into the house as he had said he would. Had her ingratitude insulted him? She had no desire to talk to him but he had been kind and she should not have been so churlish: she should probably make things up with him. As she hesitated, debating whether to go across to him or not, he saw her and, making the decision for her, put down his spade and came towards her. 'Did you want me?' he asked while still a few yards away.

'I just wanted to say I'm sorry I was so unappreciative this morning,' she said quickly before she could change her mind. 'You were very good to stay the night.'

He stared at her. Then, 'You're welcome,' he said.

'Yes, well – thanks again.'

'Are you going to the grave?' he asked.

'Why not?' Immediately she knew there had been no call for that. 'Yes, I am,' she corrected herself, 'I don't remember much about yesterday.'

'May I come with you?'

She looked at his serious face and could think of no polite way to refuse other than to tell the truth. 'I'd prefer to be on my own, if you don't mind,' she said quietly.

'I understand,' he said. 'Goodnight, Elizabeth.' He turned away and walked back towards the vegetable field.

When she got as far as the wall of the graveyard, her courage temporarily deserted her and, although she was conscious of Margaret waiting for her at home, she stopped just outside the entrance gate. A new and restless breeze curled up from Coulagh Bay, stirring her hair against her face; the good weather had held for more than a week now but as dusk pushed the light towards the west, bulging, peach-coloured clouds were piling up on the seaward horizon.

She forced herself to walk through the gate.

Her sense of fear and unease increased as she approached the grave, which was on the eastern side of the cemetery and in line with the small ruined chapel; in the dusky light, the mound of earth, raw as an open wound, seemed alien, darker than it should be as if it was turned inside out. But it was only when she was standing right beside it that she remembered she herself was the alien. Mary had been buried with her father and her mother. She was the one with no claim to Mary, the intruder on this completed family. The thought ripped apart the carefully constructed control she had exercised on herself all day. For a while she tried to hold on to it, to say meaningless Hail Marys and Our Fathers, to pray for Mary like she knew she should.

But it was no use. The words made a mockery of her despair and loneliness and something else she had not until now acknowledged.

Guilt.

Guilt that it was she who had sent kind, loving Mary to her death by asking her to drive Kathleen that day. 'Oh, God, I'm sorry, Mary, I'm sorry . . .' Elizabeth sank to her knees and buried her hands up to the wrists in the soft clay as though she could reach Mary, could channel her contrition directly into the coffin below. 'Oh, God,' she wept out loud, pulling up handfuls of clay and smearing it over her forehead, down her nose and cheeks and chin, down over her neck and breasts.

She looked up and saw the Kilcatherine Head, an affront to the living because when the living were gone it would still be there, eternal and knowing. Elizabeth wanted to pull it down, to bury it, to throw it in the sea. She remembered the way the thing had invaded her dreams, seducing her with illusory, chameleon colours. Folding double, she rested her forehead on the clay and wept to Mary, for Mary, for herself. As she wept, aloud she begged Mary for another chance.

A voice cut into her consciousness, a male voice. 'Elizabeth! Elizabeth!' She looked up and it was Mossie, standing at the other side of the grave. 'I'm not spying on you,' he said urgently, 'please believe me, I'm not spying. I was just worried that it was too soon for you to be coming here all by yourself.'

Elizabeth sprang at him, clawing at his face, beating at his chest with both fists. 'You bastard, bastard! It's all your fault.'

'I tried my best to save her, Lizzie, I really did. I ran down to her as quick as I could.' Mossie made no effort to duck her blows.

'Go away!' Elizabeth screamed, pounding at him. 'Go away! I don't want you near me, near her. If you hadn't brought us that horse—'

'Do you think I don't know that?' he cried, seizing her by the shoulders and shaking her. 'How do you think I feel?'

Something of his grief penetrated hers and, shaking herself free, she backed away from him across the grave, stumbling on the soft clay. 'Oh God,' she swung her head from side to side as though it were a pendulum. 'I'm sorry, Mossie, it's not your fault, it's mine – it's mine. I sent her that day, it was me – oh, God – what am I going to do? What am I going to do?'

He ran around the grave and caught her again by the shoulders. 'Stop being so hard on yourself. It's not your fault. Please, Elizabeth, I can't stand it . . .' When she did not respond but continued to swing her head like a robot, he again shook her a little. 'Listen to me, listen, if you won't think of yourself, think of the other children. You can't go back looking like this. At least wash your face.'

This did have an effect and she stopped the manic movement of her head. She gazed at Mossie for a minute then down at her filthy hands, at her ruined clothes. 'How can I?' she asked dully.

'Here.' Mossie extracted the bottle of holy water embedded in the clay under Agnes and Neeley Scollard's headstone and, having unscrewed the cap, held it out to her. 'I'm sure the Lord won't mind.'

Elizabeth held her face to the sky and poured some of the lemonade bottle's contents over her face, scrubbing at it then with the hem of her cardigan. 'You're only making it worse, let me help you.' Mossie produced a crumpled handkerchief. 'Don't worry, it's clean.' He took the bottle from her and poured water from it on to the linen. Like a child Elizabeth obediently screwed up her face as he cleaned it gently. 'Give me your hands,' he said then and when she held them out, poured more of the water over them, scrubbing at them with a clean part of the handkerchief. Then he passed the bottle back to her. 'There's some left,' he said gruffly. 'Maybe you can do something with your dress.'

The breeze was really freshening now and she began to shiver as, hiccupping in the aftermath of her crying, she regarded the wide russet-coloured stains on her black dress. 'They're too bad,' she said, 'but thanks.' As she handed him the nearly empty lemonade bottle, another hiccup caught her and she dropped the bottle. It fell on its side so the rest of the holy water poured out through the neck and seeped instantly into the clay. This small setback upset her all over again. 'See? I can't do anything right.' She covered her face with her hands.

'Don't *say* that!' Swiftly, he retrieved the bottle, recapped it, and put it back where it belonged. Mossie then did a curious thing: he grabbed hold of the tombstone with both hands and pushed as though he would overturn it. 'Are you feeling a bit better?' he asked over his shoulder. His voice sounded peculiar, as though he was having difficulty breathing.

Elizabeth hiccupped. 'I think so.'

Mossie, standing on the grave, was facing the road.

'There's a gang of the Derryconnla Harringtons coming,' he said. 'You don't want anyone to see you like this.' From where Elizabeth was standing she could not see anyone but then she heard a girl's high giggle. Mossie stepped down from the grave to stand beside her. 'Come on, Elizabeth,' he said gently.

'All right.' She was shivering quite hard now.

'Here, take this.' He took off his jacket and put it around her shoulders. Although he did not attempt to touch her again, she felt, as he was walking beside her out of the graveyard, that he was leading her.

'Goodbye, Mary,' she whispered under her breath as she went before Mossie through the gate. The tears which flowed this time were quiet and cleansing.

Mossie did not speak again as they walked back towards the house through the gathering darkness and when they came to the gateway of the house and she gave him back his jacket, he simply turned and walked away. Elizabeth did not wait to watch him go as the rain, which had been threatening for an hour now, finally lashed in with the suddenness of summer.

When the new baby boy came home with Tilly two days later, they found out that none of them had prevailed in the matter of what he would be named: Tilly announced that she had stood for him when he had been baptized and his name was for ever Desmond Mary Cornelius. But within minutes of coming home Desmond Mary Cornelius naturally became Dessie.

All that evening, the girls and Francey took turns holding him, exclaiming in delight when he did anything at all, like opening his milky, sightless eyes, or yawning, or uncoiling tiny starfish hands. They quarrelled over whose turn it was to feed him, change him, pick him up or put him down in the little wooden cradle, now reinstated beside the fire. He never cried because he never got a chance at it: at the smallest chirp, someone rushed to sort him out.

For Elizabeth, Dessie's arrival was a welcome distraction from her own sadness; she seemed to have cried herself out and now moved through the days in a spirit of empty resignation. Worried that Abigail might be put out by this usurpation of her position in the family, while keeping an eye on the new baby Elizabeth made it her business to pay her special attention; although she had been planning to, she did not yet move Abbie out of her bedroom and in with the other children.

Placid as ever, Abbie displayed no jealousy and seemed merely as interested in Dessie as all the rest. At one point Margaret, whose turn it was to be in charge of the infant, brought him over to where Elizabeth was sitting cuddling the former baby of the family on her lap. 'Look, Abbie!' Margaret said joyfully. 'Look at your new brother!' She thrust the baby so enthusiastically at Abbie that Elizabeth was afraid she might drop him. Anxious to maintain Margaret's confidence, however, she forbore to intervene. Neither did she point out that Dessie was not Abbie's brother but her nephew. And since that did not seem to have occurred to Margaret, the logician, it seemed unlikely to be important to anyone else. Dessie became a baby brother to the family that night and remained so, even after Kathleen came home.

In any event, about a month after the accident when she did eventually come back to Laherseen, Kathleen was so incapacitated by the cast on her leg – she had also sustained three broken ribs – that she was unable to do much for him, even had she been willing. This, Elizabeth thought, was a moot point; Kathleen seemed less interested in her son than were the rest of the children and, for the baby's sake even more than Kathleen's own, Elizabeth saw little point in forcing her to go against her natural instincts.

And so Dessie was almost by default installed in the pecking order simply as the latest addition to the family. And after a while, even Elizabeth had occasionally to remind herself that he was not hers.

She began to worry that Kathleen might secretly resent this communal takeover of her son. One night, when Kathleen was reading in bed and the rest of them were squabbling in the kitchen over whose turn it was to feed

533

Dessie, Elizabeth went into the bedroom. 'Is it sore?' she asked, standing by Kathleen's bed and indicating the unwieldy cast which encased the girl's leg from hip to toe.

'Itchy,' Kathleen replied without looking up from her book, which, Elizabeth saw, was her own copy of *Rebecca*.

'Anything you need?' she asked.

'Tell them to be a bit quieter out there, will you?' Kathleen said shortly.

Elizabeth felt she could not let her stepdaughter get away with this. 'They're looking after *your* son, Kathleen,' she protested.

'And I suppose you think I should be doing it?' At last Kathleen looked up from the book. 'That I'm neglecting him – is that it?' Her eyebrows beetled together.

'I didn't say that,' Elizabeth replied quietly. 'Look,' she added, 'maybe it's time you and I had a bit of a talk. We haven't had much of a chance since the accident.' For a moment she thought Kathleen was going to respond with her habitual negativity but then an astonishing thing happened. Kathleen's face cleared and levering herself off her pillows on to one elbow, with her free arm, she hugged Elizabeth fiercely, dragging her down by the neck. 'What's this for?' Elizabeth was so astonished her voice squeaked.

'I just want to say thank you, Mammy. I had a lot of time to think in that hospital,' Kathleen released her, 'and when I'm better,' she said gruffly, 'if – if you like I'll try to do all the things Mary used to do to help you around the house. I know I won't be as good, though . . . And I'll take over Dessie too, but I'm no good with him, Mammy, you'll have to teach me.'

'Oh, Kitty!' Elizabeth was deeply moved. But she did not dare push the situation and resisted the impulse to hug the girl. 'Of course I will.' She contented herself with smiling. 'There's something else we should discuss too,' she added, deciding to strike while Kathleen was apparently so malleable.

'George,' Kathleen said flatly.

'We have to, darling. Just let me speak, you don't have to say anything,' she rushed on, 'I'll just tell you what I've

534

decided, but obviously you have a say in the matter too.'
She watched her stepdaughter carefully as she continued.
'Granddad Sullivan is tracing him in England. At first I
thought we should take him to court —'

'Don't, *please*, Mammy! I – I —'

'All right, let me finish . . .' Feeling she might be
crowding Kathleen by standing over her, she backed away
to sit on the next bed. Then: 'I'm not going to give you any
lectures about George Gallaher – who am I to talk, after
all?'

Knowing she was on dangerous ground, again she
paused, watching the struggle on Kathleen's face. 'I think,'
she said carefully, 'I've decided now that it's' – she had
almost said 'he's' – 'not worth the trouble. So I've changed
my mind about the court. What do you think?' She held
her breath.

'I agree.' The appeal in Kathleen's eyes was heartbreak-
ing. It'll probably take you six years just like me, poor
darling, Elizabeth thought sadly. 'So anyway,' she resumed,
'will we just put it all behind us? Dessie will be perfectly
happy without him. Just like Francey . . .'

Kathleen, whose face appeared to have aged since the
accident, shot her a wry look and then smiled. 'We're an
unusual family, aren't we?'

Elizabeth relaxed. 'We certainly are. Even for such an
unusual place as Béara.'

Despite all that had happened, life in Lahersheen gradually
resumed its normal day-to-day beat. The regular weather
changes, the demands of feeding and caring for her pecu-
liarly assorted brood, Tilly's unstinting and staunch support, even the occasional visits from her parents, helped
Elizabeth come to terms with what had happened. She was
determined that within the house Mary's death would not
be pushed away into a sealed vault of silence and although
she herself found talking about it painful, she encouraged
the children to vent their feelings.

This was more successful in some cases than in others.
They all clearly missed their sister but after the promising

rapprochement in the bedroom that evening, Kathleen, although she made efforts to keep her word, reverted to type and refused point blank to discuss the accident at all. Any time anyone mentioned it, she hobbled off into her bedroom; Francey seemed more concerned about the loss of Lightning and the younger girls were sadly inarticulate.

Margaret struggled hard to express what she felt. And after a while, it dawned on Elizabeth that her stepdaughter was under the impression that despite Kathleen's hit-and-miss efforts to help around the house, everyone in the family now expected her automatically to slot into Mary's place as ministering angel. 'Darling, of course not!' Elizabeth reassured her, trying to make herself heard above the happy din from another part of the kitchen as Goretti and Johanna tried to play peep with Dessie. 'If that's what you think,' she said, 'please don't. No one can replace Mary and no one's going to have to try. You're yourself, Maggie, and yourself is great, just the way you are.'

To her chagrin, Margaret burst into tears of relief.

If there was one thing she had to learn, Elizabeth thought later as she was giving Dessie his night-time feed, it was that she must from now on be permanently vigilant about bolstering all the children's self-esteem. The lesson had been learned too late for Mary but perhaps the others could now benefit.

And so, little by little, the sharpness of her grief over Mary's death dulled. And as her interest in the wider world revived, like everyone else in Lahersheen, she became vitally interested in the winding down of the war, which was over now in Europe but still grinding on in the Far East. She invested in a wireless set and although the reception blurred and crackled so that at times it was virtually indecipherable, it proved to be a wonderful toy for everyone, not only in the family but for neighbours and neighbours' children as well.

After a little while, she summoned up the courage to make another visit to the graveyard. Mossie had brought her a magnolia cutting from his aunt Bel's garden and, although in Kilcatherine there was no tradition of placing flowers on graves – there was no florist west of Cork city and the wind from the sea near by was usually too strong – she planted it over Mary, earthing it up well and building a small wall around it with pebbles and stones to shelter it until it took root. She talked softly to Mary as she worked, telling her the news, of Dessie, of her sisters, but although she did weep, it was softly and not with the frenzy of a few weeks previously.

Having made that leap, she began regularly to go to the grave, usually during school hours, when Tilly would take Abigail and Dessie for an hour or so.

The farm continued to thrive. Strictly speaking, under the terms of the agreement, Mossie Breac did not have to give Elizabeth any of the produce off the land. But he seemed unconcerned about this nicety and continued to supply her with a steady stream of vegetables. He had also bought a pig, which was housed in his own sty, and had offered some of the bacon to the Scollards for the following Christmas, an offer Elizabeth had accepted. In return for all this, she gave him a little of their buttermilk and some surplus eggs, as his aunt could no longer move about well enough even to look after her own few hens.

At three months old, the baby was alert, constantly smiling and, Elizabeth had noticed, with the exception of his reddish-brown hair, beginning increasingly to resemble Francey. One evening in the middle of July, she was watching Abigail amuse Dessie by shaking a wooden rattle over his head when the doorway darkened and Mossie Breac called out from the threshold, 'Anyone home?'

'Hello,' Elizabeth got to her feet, 'are you coming in?' She found she was talking a lot more easily to Mossie these days: the passage of time had blunted her resentment so much that to keep it in peak condition she would almost have had to groom it daily. If it had not been for their bizarre arrangement – and the way it had been born – she might even have come to like him. She had certainly come to depend on him.

'I won't come in.' He indicated his workclothes and muddy boots. 'Look,' he went on, 'this is a bit embarrassing. I don't know how to put it,' he looked at the boots.

'Try using words of one syllable, Mossie. Sorry,' she spread her hands in apology when he glanced reproachfully at her, 'hard to break the habits of a lifetime.'

'It's just that Maggie has invited me to tea this evening.'

'I don't believe you!' Elizabeth was more amused than taken aback. 'When did this happen?'

'Last week. I've been putting off telling you.'

'Well, I suppose if she asked you . . .' she said doubtfully.

'I'm sorry, it was nothing to do with me.'

'Sure, what's the harm?' she said then. 'Come around six, all right?'

'Thanks.' As he walked off, Elizabeth could not decide whether he had been relieved or further embarrassed by her half-hearted endorsement of Margaret's largesse.

She accosted her stepdaughter when Margaret next came into the kitchen. 'Where were you?'

'In the train shed.' Since the family no longer had a horse and, in spite of Francey's pleadings, was unlikely to have one for quite a while, this was the new name for the stable.

'Did you take it on yourself to ask Mossie Breac here to tea?' Elizabeth put her hands on her hips.

Margaret's hand flew to her mouth with dismay – a little too quickly for Elizabeth's liking. 'Sorry, I forgot,' she said.

'Why did you ask him, Maggie?'

Margaret cocked her head to one side as though considering her answer.

'Come on, I'm waiting.'

'Because I wanted to, because I like him – he's very nice – and because today's his birthday.' She had obviously thought this out. 'And, anyway, he's sort of a relation, isn't he?' When Margaret was angry or indignant or nervous her voice always strengthened; it was shooting up and down the scale like a slide whistle.

This time Elizabeth was certainly taken aback. 'How do you know today's his birthday?'

'He told me ages ago.'

'I see. Well, I suppose we'd better make a cake.' She gave in as gracefully as she could in the circumstances. 'And since you're the one's doing all the inviting, you can stay in here with me and help me.'

So much of Elizabeth's good china tea service had been broken over the years that there was no longer enough of it left to serve a couple, much less a large family. But Margaret insisted on putting a tablecloth on the table and using an assortment of mismatched saucers under the mugs. They did not have time to ice the cake but instead, using even more of their precious sugar than had been squandered on the cake itself, Margaret whipped up an entire bowlful of cream and slathered it all over the cake until it resembled a large meringue. When that was done, she went out into the hill field and picked handfuls of ox-eyed daisies and from the hedgerow nearby, a large spray of dog roses, arranging them all together in a large white milk jug and placing them in the centre of the table. 'My!' Elizabeth stood back to admire the finished table, 'Mossie Breac won't know himself,' she said drily, 'he'll think it's his birthday . . .'

Margaret searched her face. 'It *is* his birthday, Mammy,' she said uncertainly.

'I know, I know.' Elizabeth was repentant. 'Don't mind me.' She looked up at the clock, it was almost six, the guest of honour would be here shortly.

Surprisingly, she found she was a little nervous. It had little to do with Mossie, she reassured herself, more to do with the fact that she had rarely entertained anyone in all the years she had lived in this house. Social life in Lahersheen was casual, neighbours dropping in on one another unannounced or, more formally, to play cards; it certainly did not revolve around tea parties.

Nevertheless, after she made sure everything was in order in the kitchen, she went into her bedroom and changed her clothes.

*

Mossie arrived exactly on time, dressed in his good suit and a shirt so white and stiff Elizabeth suspected it was new. He carried a small posy of pink and white roses. 'Thank you for the invitation.' He gave them to Margaret to her delighted confusion. To Elizabeth he gave his other gift, a packet of precious, unused tealeaves. 'We've been saving it,' he explained. 'Bel doesn't drink it any more, anyway, because of the rheumatics.'

'Thanks, Mossie,' she said, putting the tea high on the dresser. The odd formality of the occasion was intimidating her and so that he did not discern that she did not quite know what to do next, she picked Dessie out of his cradle although he had been peacefully asleep.

The baby woke up immediately, smiling beatifically around at the entire company, all of whom were standing awkwardly around the table as if awaiting orders. Joggling him in her arms, using him almost as a shield, Elizabeth managed to take charge, assigning places to everyone, seating Mossie between Margaret and Kathleen. When they were all settled, she herself, still holding Dessie, took the chair at the top of the table. 'Let's all start!' she said briskly.

'What about grace?' Margaret demanded.

Elizabeth shot her stepdaughter a quick look which, had it been a poisoned dart, would have killed her on the spot. 'You lead us, so, Maggie,' she said sweetly.

Margaret bowed her head and reverently folded her hands: 'Bless us, O Lord, and these Thy gifts, which of Thy bounty we are about to receive, Amen.' Triumphantly, she looked back up the table. 'Amen,' Elizabeth said, already planning what she was going to say to Miss Margaret Scollard after the meal. Grace was not routinely said in the Scollard household.

'Amen,' everyone else, including Mossie, echoed.

Since the meal consisted of hardboiled eggs, potato salad and strips of streaky bacon, the bustle of passing dishes and cups, or pouring tea and milk occupied the next few minutes. They were all on their best behaviour and conversation was stilted and desultory, totally unlike the subdued uproar which usually accompanied meal-times in the Scollards' house.

Elizabeth ate very little. Still using Dessie as a cover for her nervousness, she picked at some of the potato salad while she watched that their guest had everything he needed – and while she tried to sort out her feelings.

It seemed peculiar to have a man sitting at the table again; the deep voice was predominant over all the lighter ones as they said 'please' or 'thank you' or 'Pass the salt, please.' Strange, she thought, how she had not fully noticed until now that the house was one of women and children. She knew it, of course, on the surface, but it had not struck her as abnormal until this very moment.

She shook off such musings and cut up a piece of egg for Abigail. At least, she said to herself, the children were being mannerly. 'It's warm, would you mind if I take off my coat?' Mossie looked up at her across Margaret's head.

'Certainly, go ahead.' Both Kathleen and Margaret immediately turned to help him as he struggled out of the suit jacket.

Seated in his shirtsleeves among all the slender young bodies, he seemed suddenly massive, as out of place as a bull in a henhouse. The suit jacket had somehow acted like camouflage, or a uniform. Now that the width and strength of his shoulders and chest was exposed, his maleness was somehow shocking to Elizabeth. Her nervousness increased.

She was relieved when it was time for the cake: it meant the end was in sight. Glad to have an excuse to leave the table, she passed Dessie to Kathleen and went to fetch her silver cake slice out of its velvet box. It was one of the few good pieces of cutlery she had taken from the house in Blackrock when, before her wedding to Neeley, Corinne had invited her to take anything she liked. It had seldom been used but she kept it clean and polished.

Margaret and Goretti cleared away the used plates while she brought the cake and the slice across to the table. 'This is wonderful, thank you,' Mossie said, gazing down at the creamy confection in front of him.

Standing so near, she picked up the tension in him; he was clearly as uncomfortable as she was. 'Would you like to cut it?' she asked.

'Oh no! You go ahead.'

She felt that the two of them were participating in manoeuvres as formal as those of the old-fashioned quadrilles the nuns had taught the girls at school in Cork. Mossie was about to sink the slice into the cake when Margaret cried out, 'Not yet!' she turned almost accusingly to her stepmother: 'We have to sing "Happy Birthday", Mammy.'

Elizabeth looked at Mossie with a small *moue* of apology. Then, getting it over with, closed her eyes so she would not see his embarrassment, or he hers, and struck up the first bars of the song. They all joined in in ragged chorus, even Kathleen. Just before the end of the song when Elizabeth opened her eyes again, she caught Margaret looking at her with an expression of calculation on her face which would have done justice to Lucretia Borgia. It vanished within a split second to be replaced by a look of angelic innocence but not before Elizabeth finally understood what was going on. She remembered Margaret's pretended amnesia, her nervousness.

As clumsily in her own way as Mossie's cousin Johnny Thade, Elizabeth's stepdaughter was matchmaking.

The song ended and over the next few minutes, as her hands were busy helping Mossie distribute the cake, Elizabeth's brain whirled with the implications of what Margaret thought she was doing – and why.

She did not take any cake but took Dessie in her arms to leave Kathleen free to eat hers. Had Mossie noticed what was going on? 'May I leave the table?' Johanna spoke immediately she finished the last mouthful of cake on her plate. She was followed in close succession by Francey and Goretti and, taking Abigail between them, all four scampered out into the yard. Kathleen, stumping her plaster cast, vanished into the bedroom.

Margaret plucked Dessie out of Elizabeth's arms. 'I'll just take the baby out for a breath of fresh air.'

'What about the dishes?' But Elizabeth was talking to

the empty air. It had all been so closely orchestrated that now she was sure every one of them had been carefully coached by Margaret. She looked with dismay at Mossie across the littered table. 'I'm terribly sorry, I don't know what they're all at.'

'I should think it's obvious.' He looked up at the ceiling. The tension she had noticed earlier in him seemed to have grown. His face was set in long lines, like a carving.

'Yes, well, I'm sorry. I had no idea —'

'I'm sure you didn't.' He spoke quietly, still gazing at the ceiling. Then he looked directly at her. 'Let me help with the dishes.'

'No!' She was horrified. Then she modified her tone. 'Of course not, you're the guest. Anyway, there's enough of them here —'

'I'd like to.' He cut forcefully across her and picking up his own plate and mug, carried them through into the scullery. Within seconds she heard him running water into the sink.

Short of physically evicting him, Elizabeth felt she was faced with no option but to clear away the rest of the dishes and to let him at it. Just wait until he was gone, she thought murderously, that stepdaughter of hers was going to be one sorry girl.

Wanting to spend as little time as possible in the scullery with him, she took as long as she decently could in stacking the rest of the dishes on a side table in front of the door to the scullery, shaking the crumbs off the table, folding the tablecloth and then sweeping the floor in long, careful arcs.

When she could no longer avoid it, she brought the rest of the dishes out to him. He had finished washing up what was out there and was half-way through drying them.

'I don't know where to put these —'

'Here, let me —'

They spoke simultaneously.

'You first —'

'Sorry – no, you go first!'

The scullery was very small, although not so small that

it did not quite often accommodate four or more of the Scollards. But, again, the dazzling shirt created an illusion of immensity and Mossie seemed to fill all the available space. 'Excuse me.' Elizabeth, feeling she was squeezing around him, described a slight half-circle as she went to the sink. Mossie took a step backwards in an exaggerated and unnecessary effort to make room for her.

Elizabeth plunged the plates she was carrying into the soapy water in the sink and started to scrub at them. 'Oh,' she said, 'this water isn't hot enough – I'd better get some from the kettle.' The banality dropped between them like a heavy rock. She made as though to hurry past him again but he blocked her way.

'Elizabeth –'

'What?' she was whispering but would not meet his eyes.

'I can't stand it any more, I'm going mad.'

'What?' Still she did not look at him. 'What do you mean?'

'You know what I mean. I love you. I've loved you since the first day you came to Lahersheen. I haven't been able to think of anything else except you for the past eight years.'

'This is preposterous.' Elizabeth refused to let him go on but to her horror the palms of her hands were beginning to sweat and her treacherous heart was up to its old tricks again. It had been almost a year since Killarney and, as if her brain was irrelevant, her body was reacting to Mossie's overpowering masculinity. At last she looked at him. 'This is madness . . .'

'Is it?' he breathed. He was so near that she could smell the fresh sweat which was beading on his forehead. She backed away until she felt the cold stone of the scullery wall at her back. 'We're enemies, Mossie Sheehan, you did a terrible thing to me, to us – to the whole family –'

'It was the only way I could get to marry you.'

'Rubbish!' But Elizabeth's heart was now beating an urgent tattoo against her breastbone. 'You were prepared to let Daniel –'

'Of course I wasn't. But I had to gamble.'

'Why did you wait so long to come forward?' She was whispering.

'I needed to think, I needed to be sure you'd accept – I really didn't mean to let it go on for so long, I kept putting it off. You're a formidable person, you know, Elizabeth Sullivan.'

'Me?' The revelation was astonishing. To herself Elizabeth was as timid as a mouse. Why else did she get herself into such messy situations?

'Yes, you—'

Seeing his mouth bearing down on hers, Elizabeth made a huge effort. Placing both hands on his chest, she held him off. 'You wanted the land, Mossie Sheehan.'

'Yes, the land, too. I told you honestly about that. But, oh, God! Elizabeth, I wanted *you*.' He had inched forward again until her wrists were bent under his strength and the front of his shirt was so close to her breasts she could feel his heat. He stretched out his arms and placed his hands so they splayed on the wall on either side of her and at the same time, arched his body so that he was still not touching her.

Elizabeth dropped her hands but flattened herself against the wall. 'Let me go, Mossie, don't do this—'

'I can't help it. It's all I've been dreaming about since I saw you for the very first time. You were pregnant and sitting on that little seat out in the yard. You wouldn't remember but I do, your eyes were closed and you were holding your face up to the sun. I don't think you even saw me passing. Your hair was loose. You were wearing a navy dress with a big white collar and your feet were bare. I had never seen any living creature so beautiful in all my life. You came between me and my sleep that night and many nights since because I fell in love with you that day, Elizabeth. Completely and for ever.'

Without taking his hands off the wall, he moved so he was crushing her breasts with his hard, heavy chest and his thighs were pressing against hers. 'If only you knew the torment of how I felt when I saw you up on Knockameala with Danny McCarthy –'

'Don't,' she cried.

' – how I would have swung for him that night I saw him kissing and cuddling you in that ruin above—'

'Mossie, please—'

' – how I died every time I saw the way you looked at him—'

Elizabeth let out a sob. She tried to twist out from under him but faced with his strength, hers was as a bird's. Her hands were pinioned beneath him so she could not close her ears with them so she closed her eyes instead.

But his words went on as inexorably as the running sea. 'Or how badly I wanted to kiss you when I was cleaning your face in the graveyard that evening.'

'Why didn't you?' It was a stupid question, asked without thinking, and he did not answer it. Instead, he fastened his lips to hers with such a direct and hungry passion that, instinctively, her body strained into his. The kiss continued for several seconds and then, abruptly, it was over. 'Marry me, Elizabeth!' he said huskily.

The shock of his stopping, followed by the absurdity, caused her to laugh. *'What?'*

'Marry me! Properly this time, at a proper time of day with guests and flowers and music. I want the world to witness that I'm the husband of Elizabeth Sullivan.'

Elizabeth heard a sound and behind his head saw three smaller ones peering through the tiny window above the sink. All wore broad smiles, Margaret's broadest of all. She tried to push him away. 'We're being watched,' she hissed.

Mossie looked around. 'Scram!' he ordered. The heads vanished with an explosion of giggling.

'That's that, I suppose!' He shook himself like a dog and cleared his throat a number of times. Then he turned back to her and after another swift kiss, stood away from her. 'I'm going now, Elizabeth, but I'm coming back at ten tomorrow morning. And I'm going to come at ten the next morning and the next morning after that and I'll keep coming until you say you'll marry me. One more—' This time he put his arms fully around her and kissed her so hard that after he stopped her lips throbbed in protest. 'Until

546

morning, then.' Leaving her breathless and wrung out, he walked quickly out of the scullery and picking up his jacket off the back of his chair, left the house.

Elizabeth heard him calling goodbye to the children.

She leaned against the wall of the scullery, unable to think, only to feel. She was bewildered, upset, confused, thrilled, excited, sad . . . everything in her life, everything she thought she had worked out so satisfactorily, where was it now?

She was still leaning against the wall a few moments later when Margaret, incandescent with glee, stole into the doorway. 'Well?'

'Well, what? You're for it!' Having to make an effort, Elizabeth prised herself off the wall.

Margaret's answer was to hug herself in a paroxysm of giggling. Behind her, Johanna and Goretti had to hold one another up due to the hilarity of catching Elizabeth in a compromising position.

Elizabeth was in no state for retribution. In any event, such communal joy had been so long absent from this house that to see it was infectious. 'Come in here and help me with the rest of this washing up,' she said. 'Rascals!'

By five minutes to ten the next morning, her state of confusion had multiplied a thousandfold. One minute she was thrilling to the physical memory of Mossie's passion, the next, infuriated at him for his audacity. As objectively as she could, she examined how she now felt about what he had done to Daniel. And to her surprise, she found she could forgive him at last. If, as he had claimed, his passion was so all-consuming, she knew more than most to what lengths he had been pushed. And then, all over again, she became angry. Who did Mossie Breac think he was? She was the one who was in control here . . .

By the time he arrived, she was so agitated she could not sit down. 'How dare you?' she raged at him before he had had a chance to say even good morning. 'How dare you put me in this position?'

'What position? I've told you nothing more nor less

547

than the truth.' Mossie adopted what seemed to be his favourite position, leaning against the jamb of the door. 'I love you, I've loved you for years. And I guarantee you no one ever has, nor ever will love you like I do. Where are the children?' He looked beyond her shoulder into the house.

'Out.' Preparing for this scene, she had sent all the children out with Abigail and the baby, telling them she did not want to see hide nor hair of them for an hour. Fortunately, it was a lovely day.

Mossie eased himself off the door and came right into the kitchen. Seizing her, he kissed her hard.

'Don't *do* that!' She wiped her mouth with the back of her hand as though he had contaminated it.

Ignoring her outburst, he seated himself on the table. 'I know you, Elizabeth,' he said softly, 'don't forget that. The schoolteacher used to say it was a shame I couldn't get to a university to do a degree but I've done a degree after all. It was a long course – eight years.'

'You don't know the first thing about me —'

'I'm afraid I do. I tried to say it last year, but I put it very badly. I botched it last time because I was very emotional about your carry-on with Danny McCarthy. He's a lovely lad, Elizabeth, but he's not up to your level.'

'And you are, I suppose?' Somehow in the face of his deadly seriousness, the taunt fell flat.

'Remember I've had eight years to prepare,' he said.

'I'm not the marrying type,' she said then, almost appealing to him.

'Depends on what type of marriage we're talking about. I'm talking about a marriage of equals. I think that's what you would like, too, but you've never tried it. You're afraid marriage to me would be just more of the same. And may I point out,' he added drily, 'that we have been married for over a year now. Have you felt crowded by me?'

She looked at him, understanding at first hand for the first time in her life, the meaning of the expression about jaws dropping. 'Maybe this might help you make up your mind . . .' Swiftly, he got off the table and picked her up as easily as though she were a doll. 'How much time do we have?' he asked.

Elizabeth was too surprised to tell him anything but the truth. And her body was again rejecting the messages from her brain. 'An hour,' she said faintly.

'That should be plenty.' He carried her through to the bedroom. 'Don't forget,' he said, lowering her on to the bed, 'it won't be a sin, we're married!'

Elizabeth began to laugh. She laughed and laughed until the tears ran down her face. He joined in, giggling at first, then laughing as uproariously as she.

'Do you know what the funniest thing of all is?' she spluttered when finally she managed to utter a few coherent words.

'What? What?' He tried to kiss her tenderly on the lips but she was laughing so hard her lips bounced off his as though they were made of inflated rubber. 'That – that *woman* in Cahirkeem told me—'

'What woman in Cahirkeem?' He was puzzled.

'That – that Englishwoman—' Again she was off uncontrollably.

'What Englishwoman? Please, Elizabeth—'

'Mrs—' The giggles swelled and swelled until they filled her like balloons.

'Come on – try!'

'Mrs Charlton!' She was laughing so hard she felt lightheaded. 'Mrs Charlton . . . bloody . . .' The balloons burst and the tears rolled down her face. '*Leahy* . . .'

'Oh, her?' Mossie was again giggling empathetically. 'What about her?'

'She said – she said—'

'Elizabeth Sullivan, I'll strangle you.'

'She said it was in the c-c-cards I'd marry twice and I thought – I thought—' Her stomach felt as though it was being forced through a colander as the laughter took over again. He silenced her the only way he could, by kissing her hard. The mirth shook her under him for a few moments, then it began to subside as she began to respond to him.

Quickly, hands shaking, he undressed her but it was

not quick enough for her and she helped him. 'Oh, Jesus, you're beautiful,' he whispered when she was lying naked in the debris of her clothes.

Elizabeth then became so self-conscious, she reached for his face.

His lovemaking was strong and confident and, after an initial shyness, Elizabeth's sensually starved body drank him in. His muscular bulk was viscerally satisfying; his chest against hers, his weight, the way his torso completely filled the span of her arms conspired to make her feel more female than she had ever felt before.

When, a little while later, he was lying supine in her arms, he took a strand of her hair between his fingers. 'We have a saying here on Béara,' he said softly. '"After the settlement comes love." Did you ever hear that one?'

'No, I did not. I assume you're referring to our famous bloody agreement.'

'Indeed! Well, I know that saying well. And I knew if I gave you time, you'd get used to me.' He nuzzled the hollow between her breasts and smiled wickedly up at her. 'And do you know what's even funnier?'

'No!' she kissed the top of his head. 'But I fear you're going to tell me!'

'I've been taking dancing lessons.'

LOVE LIKE HATE ADORE

In memory of Nellie

✦ Acknowledgements ✦

As always, profound gratitude is due to many people. To my sister-in-law, Mary Purcell, who helped with research and who was assisted by my terrific brother, Declan. To Aldiscon Information Ltd, and Barry White, SC, who gave generously of their time and expertise. To my mother, Maureen, who found the correct words of 'Kitty from Coleraine'. To the dedicated person – you know who you are – who helped with detail about Mountjoy Park. To Joe from Cheekys Kissing Telegram Company, to the long-suffering Fiona from Reprocentre, to the three Pats – the brilliant Pat Brennan, loyal Patricia Byrne, ever-loving Patricia Scanlan.

Thanks to my agents Charles Pick, Martin Pick, Treasa Coady – and to Amanda Kiely of Townhouse. To my superb editor, Suzanne Baboneau of Macmillan, to Hazel Orme, and to Ian Chapman who bemused me with his enthusiasm.

Finally, much love to all my kind, supportive friends. And to my family, particularly Simon, Adrian and Kevin.

✦ One ✦

Every second of this summer hammered a spike into my memory. It is bizarre that so much could have happened. It is still August and the first intimations of disaster came on a Saturday in early May. Three months. As slow as a century.

I thought I'd tell it all to you before the finer details blow away like dandelion clocks.

By the way, you'll forgive me if sometimes I use what you might think are inappropriate words. Or at least words above my station! I'm not all that educated and my grammar or tenses may not always be the best, although I do watch out for the inflexible rules, like, *never* a comma after an 'and' – and so forth. But I adore the words themselves, always have, they're piled higgledy-piggledy in my brain. In ordinary life, or what passes for it nowadays, I have to squish a lot of them when they pop into my mouth in case people think I'm showing off. I learned this lesson early, where I grew up, in the flats.

That was some tough area of Dublin. There you didn't dare be different or you'd be in danger of getting your head chopped off. I got used to kids shouting after me, There goes Angela Devine, she swallowed a dictionary. I'd die. I'd pretend I didn't care, but I'd die.

Well, I still love dictionaries. They're so fat and full of possibilities. And I'll tell you another thing, I'm a natural speller. For some reason, I never had one bit of difficulty with spelling, right from the start-off at school in Low Babies. It's something to do with the sound and the shape of words on the page. I can even see some of them, some are like smooth Christmas balls that you can't resist touching and stroking and holding up to the light so they glitter.

I don't want to go on about it. Just take it that however it happened, from the very beginning, my brain sort of hoovered up every word it could find and stored it like you'd store good wine or cheeses. (Strange as it may seem, I know a bit about wines and cheeses. It's because of one of my jobs – of which more anon . . .)

Enough apologias. To get to the story.

Day one, that Saturday. Afternoon.

The bus was crammed as usual. I was coming home from one of my jobs, the Saturday morning one in the deli – a southside deli – and I was wrecked because we had been particularly busy.

You know the type who rush into these delicatessen shops as if they're on their way to a fire? They usually have the small-bore Merc or Volvo runaround – Beemers are now *out*, apparently – parked with one wheel on the footpath outside. Stuck at about age thirty-four, sound like they're asking for poppyseed rails instead of rolls. Designer track suits, the smoothed wide-eyed look that gives them all faces like Dolly Parton. They're the type who give out about the price of balsamic vinegar even though it's far from balsamic vinegar many of them were reared. I call them Samanthas. Marks, if they're men.

Because it's Saturday the Marks wear Nikes or Adidas runners and waxed jackets.

Now, in fairness I have to say I have met one or two real people named Samantha and Mark and they've been grand. But you know what I mean. It's my personal shorthand.

That morning we'd had a lot of Samanthas and Marks and by the time I'd had to run across to the jewellers' for the fifth time to change the fifth twenty-pound note, I was ready to scream. What's more, it was raining that day and on the way home I'd had to wait thirty-five minutes for the bus.

I could have walked, often do — because we live very close to town — but as I told you I was wall-falling with tiredness, soaked to the skin, and my feet were killing me from all the standing and from my new shoes. Which got even tighter in the bus. It's funny how your feet swell in buses, isn't it?

I defy you to tell the difference between chain-store shoes and shoes from a real shoe shop. I suppose I should feel guilty about them, though. They're real leather and at the price I bought them they had to have been manufactured by some tiny little boy or girl in Bangladesh or East Timor or somewhere. Who was probably whipped into producing them. Literally.

So as you can imagine, I could have done without any more hassle that day.

When the bus eventually came, the omens were not good. The minute you stepped inside you were assaulted with the smell of damp and wet feet. And buggies and crying babies, and dozens of crabby, snotty toddlers — not to speak of exhausted women with Roches Stores' bags clamped between their ankles to stop them spilling over every time the bus went around a corner. You couldn't see a sausage through the windows with all the steam from the coats and the umbrellas and the breath.

Actually, the way those bus drivers throw these double-deckers around corners, I find it amazing that they don't keel over. What's big and green and lies in a ditch? A dead bus. That's the only joke I ever remember Mammy telling. Of course that's when the buses were all green, that long ago I can only vaguely remember them. Now they're like mobile funderlands, painted all over with brilliant colours. I love the Birds Eye one with the peas tumbling over it from top to bottom.

By the time we got to my stop, I was glad to get off, I can tell you.

Mountjoy Square is going all yuppie these days and it seemed to happen overnight. Trees growing out of windows one day and then, shazam! next day there are acres of phoney frontages with apartments behind them. Some of these apartments cost more than a four-bedroomed house. Half the space for a hundred times the rent.

I have to admit the Square is not a bad environment to live in if you're forced to rent privately. At least it's very nice outside. We have a terrific park in the middle of this square.

But why anyone would want to live in a flat, even when it's called an apartment, is beyond me. Call me a snob but I certainly wouldn't live in an apartment if I had the choice of buying a house.

Even that day I wouldn't have been surprised if Reddy, our so-and-so of a landlord, came to tell us he wanted to get us all out of our place. I'd say given half the chance, he'd knock our whole place down. He could probably get some kind of a grant for knocking it and building an eggbox like all the other eggboxes around here because this is a tax-designated area. I've never quite understood what that is, but it seems people who have money to invest in Ireland can buy apartments in the inner city and can then rent them out, paying no tax at all. Like in Temple Bar. Temple Bar is the new centrefold of Dublin that we're all supposed to be very proud of, full of pubs and trendy restaurants and as for the yuppie apartments across there! People queued all night to buy them at *huge* prices.

Not that I'd know. I've never been to Temple Bar, even though it's less than a mile from where we live. Temple Bar is not for people like me. I hear from James, who's nineteen, that it's a young person's place, full of tourists and English fellows puking at their weekend stag parties and kids as young as fourteen drunk on three beers sprawled all over the footpaths. You see articles in the paper about it all the time – it's supposed to be our Left Bank.

Well, that day I would have wished Reddy luck with trying to get us out. At the time in question I was, speaking generally, full of vim. Even though he had given us only a month to month lease, if he'd tried anything, if there'd been a peep out of him, I would have been prepared to take him to the Supreme Court. To Europe if necessary. We were going when we were good and ready and not a day before. In this country, thank God, the courts always take a lenient view of people like us when it comes to the landlord–tenant relationship.

And anyway, even if he did try something, it takes donkey's years for anything even to get near a court. James and I would have had plenty of time to find somewhere decent of our own.

As I walked away from the bus stop I saw there was a sale on in Discount Electrical. Nothing unusual, there always seems to be a sale on there. Another one in D.I.D. Electrical a few houses away. (That electrical

business is cutthroat in Dublin. You'd think that everyone in Ireland has enough tellys and microwaves by now.
But no. Soon they'll be giving them away with pounds of
rashers.) At least it had stopped raining.

When I got to the steps leading to the front door of
our place James's bike was not locked into its usual place
on the railings. I'll tell you who James is in a minute,
you'll be hearing a lot about him. This is his story I'm
going to be telling you, not mine. I always hated that
bike. He came off it more than once – I was always
telling him that those Kawasakis are too powerful, and
half the time he wouldn't wear his crash helmet. He had
to when he was working, he's a courier by profession,
but he thought it was cissy to wear it when he wasn't on
duty even though it's the law that he has to. Once or
twice I had thought of reporting him to the cops to
frighten him into it, but then I'd think of his face in the
police station and I couldn't.

I knew I'd have to get over thinking of him as a baby.
I'd already started working on it.

It was a bit odd that the bike was gone that day,
because normally on a Saturday an earthquake wouldn't
wake him. I half thought it might have been nicked, but
when I got inside, I saw he was gone all right. Amazing.
Only three o'clock! I'm not being sarcastic here,
honestly, James always tended to stay in bed a lot if he
didn't have to do anything. (And sometimes even when
he did. For instance, I had to go on at him or he would
have slept away his appointments at the dental hospital.
He has great teeth and I aimed to keep them that way.)

I suppose if I'd had more money, I probably should
have been sending him to a counsellor, or at least
someone who would identify if there was anything wrong
with him. Like, was this behaviour normal for a nineteen-
year-old? I mean, I wasn't competent to decide whether

or not his long silences, black moods, staying in bed a lot, would qualify as depression or what. There's a lot about James I can't precisely pin down, he's a loner, certainly, but a loner who goes out to clubs and parties and stuff. Who seems to have friends. And yet whose loneliness you can feel almost a hundred per cent of the time when he's in the same room as you. Does that make sense?

Counsellors are all the rage these days but in our circumstances where we'd have to go public, it was a non-starter because you'd be waiting years for an appointment. So we had to muddle along the best we could.

About money. I'm prepared to admit that I have an ambivalent attitude towards money. With all my jobs, we should probably have been doing better than we were at that stage – but I was saving hard. Probably too much. (Although as you'll see I haven't succeeded all that well. Twenty years' working and only a few thousand to show for it! However, it's something . . .) I was putting it away towards that place of our own. And for something else that I find hard to talk about. For some reason, I find it very difficult to spend money on myself, even when I have a few bob over. I sort of have to put it away towards the future. I've analysed this and I think it has a great deal to do with security. Some day James was going to go off on his own and I've always known – from day one – that I couldn't rely on him to look after me if I got sick or anything. I wouldn't have asked him to anyway. Having seen the state of Mammy for so many years, who could? Enough said.

He has a very strong personality as you will see. It can be difficult living with someone like that when they're under your feet a lot. Don't get me wrong, though, I adore that kid.

That first Saturday, when I got in and found him gone, I have to admit it was nice to know I'd have a bit of peace for a while.

Now I'd like to be able to say that when I let myself into the flat I was aware that something was amiss. That's what you read always in books. The main character always finds something amiss when he lets himself into his home. Mind you, there's usually blood smeared all over the walls or a funny smell of gas or something. Not in this case. Everything looked normal. Like a tornado blew through the window and out through the front door. Typical. I always found it like that when James went out and I hadn't been there to nag at him.

I always got a bit of a kick in the teeth when I let myself into the flat. Somehow, when I was out, I managed to develop this sort of rosy feeling about going back home again. You know, looking forward to snuggling back into my own little nest. Well, each time I actually did get in – I leave it to your imagination.

If I was to use words like damp or brown or peeling, would they fill in the picture for you?

I did my best. I've a lot of books and the bookshelves were arranged in front of the worst of the wallpaper. And I'd hidden what upholstery there was under white candlewick bedspreads I bought (for half-nothing – fair play!) at the Daisy Market.

I picked up the wet towels in the facilities – Reddy's word, not mine, it's a cubbyhole partitioned off the room but the so-called walls are so flimsy you can hear *everything*. (I usually turned up the radio or the telly when James went in. You have to have a little bit of privacy in your life.)

Then I kicked off the famous shoes and did a bit of tidying before I put the kettle on and laid out the bits of grub I'd brought home from the deli. I look forward to that on a Saturday. Have myself a posh little picnic. I'm allowed take the heels of cheese and the bits of salami that fall off the slicer, stuff like that. On Saturdays I make an exception to my miserly instincts, I buy myself a couple of rolls. I vary them. Sesame. Tomato. Onion. Garlic. Et cetera. I have a special tray that I use, it's Chinese laquered, with a lovely picture of a spreading willow tree, green on black – more turquoise really or, that lovely word, aqua. The colour of the sea just before a storm.

Isn't it amazing how life works out? Every so often I stop and wonder how someone like me, Angela Devine from the flats, came to be able to talk knowledgeably about chorizo and prosciutto. And even more than that, came to be eating it *by choice*. God, if Mammy could see me now. Of course James wouldn't be caught dead eating any of it. He's into fast foods, like them all at his age. Personally I can't stick burgers any more, especially since I saw on the telly that when you're eating them in some places you're eating cow's abscesses. Yuck.

I should have sat down immediately that day and started to study. I was preparing for my Leaving Cert – I'm doing it bit by bit as a mature student – and with the exam so near I had no business behaving like the Queen of Sheba with my tray and my little bits of finger food. But I was so damp and cranky, I couldn't face into the books straight off.

Anyhow, I was pretty well on top of things. *Hamlet* was on our cycle this time in English, although during the course of that year our teacher, Mr Elliott, had made us study *Macbeth* as well. We weren't all that keen, of course, because it was not going to come up in the paper, but he insisted. It would be greatly to our benefit, he told us, to know more than one play if we were to have any idea of the context in which Shakespeare was writing.

According to him, studying just the Shakespeare on the curriculum is simply not getting a proper education and this school, he goes, puffing out his chest like a cockatoo, prides itself on not being merely a crammer. Whatever. I just wanted to get the exam. I was dreading it, of course, the weeks were flying by. I did OK in maths last year. Pass paper naturally, but I got a C3. High normal. Not bad for someone who never went to secondary school, if I do say so myself.

On that Saturday in May I was still continuing to study Irish as well, although looking back on it now, I was mad ever to think I could do Irish and English in the same year. I suppose it was because at the rate of only one subject a year it'd be the millennium before I got the bloody certificate. It's beyond me how kids can do six or seven subjects all together.

Here's another thing – I'm quite glad it's only at this age (I'm thirty-six) I got into Shakespeare. Because if I was doing those plays when I was sixteen or seventeen, like normal kids have to do them, I don't think I'd have understood half of what was going on. Ireland is a very peculiar country. There's people all over the place giving out about porno videos and *Playboy* magazine and all the rest of it but do they know what their kids are studying in English for the Leaving Cert? Do they have any idea what *Hamlet* and *Macbeth* are all about? Like incest?

Anyway, I said feck it to the books and turned on the telly. I took my tray and my cup of coffee over to sit in front of it. There's usually a good Bette Davis or Cary Grant on BBC2. I love Kirk Douglas. We got the cable last year, it's expensive but I think it's worth it, you have to have some nice things in life and it was mostly for James. I put my foot down, though, about us getting Sky Sports. Over my dead body. Twenty-four hours a day of Italian bobsledding or motocross? No way.

But we might as well have had Sky Sports that Saturday, it was nothing but sport, sport, sport. Even BBC2 had cricket. God help us, I thought, when the Olympics start in July.

At least Sky News had one of those fashion programmes, this one was from Milan. It was fantasy gear, stuff I wouldn't wear in a million years. Couldn't. You'd have to be seven feet tall like Naomi Campbell or Elle MacPherson. They all come to Dublin a lot, you know, or at least they used to when Naomi was engaged to Adam Clayton. Dublin is where it's all at these days, I keep reading it in the paper. For fun and music and clubs and stuff. And they're all making millions out of the music. That Cranberry girl is a millionaire already in her early twenties.

But what I think is really gas is that they all make the money out of giving out. Their childhoods and their upbringings and their abuse and their deprivation. The whole shebang.

In that case I should be a billionaire. I should give a seminar.

I must have dozed off looking at the telly because suddenly there's one of those American news programmes on and I didn't even remember the end of the fashion one. Still no sign of James. I'll kill him, I thought. He was supposed to be here this afternoon, I'd extracted a promise out of him to help me bring a bunch of stuff down to the launderette. Winter duvets and covers. They're not all that heavy but they're very bulky and it's a fairly long walk.

I was damned if I was going down to that snooker hall again to haul him out of it. He had too much loose change from his job, in my opinion. But I just couldn't help being so soft with him. I mean, he grew up not remembering one iota about Mammy. How could he? He wasn't even three months old when she died. I mean, with all her troubles, she was his mother and everyone needs a mother. All these years, even when he was in nappies, I never let him call me Mammy. He'd had a mammy and it wasn't me.

I made sure he knew all about her, all the good bits. I didn't hide the truth from him, I couldn't anyway, even if I wanted to, not with all the social workers around. But I made a point of telling him how nice she was underneath.

I should have insisted he gave me his paypacket and then I'd give him back pocket money. Mind you, even though he was old enough to vote and to get a mortgage he was still a child, really – and I suppose I was so thrilled he had found a job that he continued to get out of bed for, I didn't want to rock the boat too much.

Speaking of being just a child, in some ways I quite often feel like one too, if I'm being honest. I don't know how I got to be this age, I really don't. When you look at it, I'm only two years younger than Mammy was when she died. God, I wonder how she felt when she was thirty-six. Did she know she had only two years left? Too far gone, I suppose.

One day I'll always remember about Mammy. I was going in the bus along O'Connell Street – as far as I can recall I must have been about ten or eleven. I'd seen Francesca and Justine and Nicola on an access visit and I was in the bus with my own social worker going back to her office. The three had all just been moved from one foster home to two separate ones, Francesca in one, the other two in another. Nicola, in particular, was pretty upset and she had started to cry when she saw me. Then the other two had started as well. It had been a real waterworks party.

Anyway, I'm going along in this bus afterwards and

I'm not feeling the greatest, as you can imagine, and I look out through the window beside me and, my God, there she is. Mammy. Absolutely straight. Walking perfectly, no wobbling. And she has a kind of suit on, an outfit I never saw before. It's a lovely sunny day, I remember. Her hair is shining, it looks as shiny as a crow's wing. Tears come into my eyes for some reason, and I remember thinking, My mammy is beautiful. I look hard at all the other women in O'Connell Street – we're just outside Clery's – and I'm thinking, None of them, not one of those other women, is a patch on her. It gives me the most extraordinary feeling.

The social worker sees there's something going on with me. Is everything all right, Angela? she asks.

Fine, I say. I don't want to tell her I saw Mammy. I can't explain even now why not. It was something to do with keeping the perfection of it.

To this day I don't know whether she was really there or whether it was a vision. For instance, I never saw that suit again. Like, I get home a few hours later after spending a while with the social worker in her office. Mammy's in her usual slacks and jumper and the wobble is back in the walk. I saw you in O'Connell Street, I go, that was a lovely suit, Mammy, where'd you get it?

But she just looks at me. Blank. No one home.

Ah well, I thought, that Saturday sitting in front of Sky News, no point dwelling on the past. So I was thirty-six. Big deal. We were managing OK and we weren't having to humiliate ourselves by being on the Labour. And at least I wasn't looking at the world through the bottom of a bottle or the butt of a syringe. I certainly could be. Funny how I'd managed to keep James straight too, I thought. Not funny at all, pretty damned lucky.

It started to spill again and never stopped for the rest of that whole day. You couldn't even see out with the condensation on the window, and the bucket under the drip in the ceiling of the facilities was nearly full. There was something new too – a patch of damp over the sink, spreading by the minute so that by half past seven it was as big as a small continent.

Another thing for Reddy for next Friday night, I thought, adding it to the list, which included not only the drip but the blown ring on the breakfast cooker. It was only a two-ring one. You try cooking a full meal with one ring! It always gave me great satisfaction to withhold some of Reddy's money until he fixed things. There was nearly always a reason to withhold. These were going to do nicely for this week.

I love that phrase. I wonder what it would be like to have an American Express card. (Of course, James would probably take it and buy himself a Harley Davidson. That's all I'd need.)

My second job was being a kissogram person and I had a 'bunny girl' gig that night so I couldn't spend any more time lounging around.

Before you jump to conclusions, I have to assure you it's not as seedy as you might think. Some very respectable people (like me!) do the work only because they need the money.

By eight o'clock I was almost ready, I had my raincoat on over my outfit and I was just putting my ears and other bits and pieces into my bag when I heard his key in the lock. Where were you? I'm sounding aggrieved before I can stop myself. Even though I know as sure as eggs that it's the worst possible thing I can say and the minute I've said it I regret it.

I'm also thinking how hilarious this would look to an outsider – this deranged woman in a raincoat and a cheap rabbit's outfit, giving out to this big six-foot hunk in leathers.

Nowhere, he says and pushes past me into his room. He got the bedroom in the flat — it was only right, I suppose, raging male hormones et cetera — while I used the bed-settee in the lounge.

I was tempted to barrel in after him but I knew that I might as well save my breath to cool my porridge. I'd smelled the Heineken off him. I consoled myself that this was not too bad, at least it wasn't spirits. So I contented myself with just hmmphing and glaring and slamming about a bit.

Before I left, I took the precaution of lifting his keys from where he threw them on the table. If he went out again he wouldn't kill himself on that bike.

Please God, I thought as I left for the gig, he'll go asleep now and stay asleep until I get home. I had only three kissogram calls booked in — so I wasn't going to be home too late.

→ Two ←

The third job at the beginning of this summer – I still had it then – was by far the most fun. Myself and my friend, Patsy Jennings, had been doing gigs for a few years, singing at weddings, if we could get them (big party-weddings seem to be going out fashion in this country) but mostly pubs. Sunday mornings, that sort of thing.

She's brilliant, Patsy. A really strong voice and she plays three instruments, keyboards, guitar and clarinet. Although to tell you the truth, the clarinet isn't much use. It's too soft for the kind of clientele we play to. I felt privileged to be singing with her because my own voice is not a patch on hers, a bit above average, I suppose, although I did once get a second place in the Feis Maitiú when I was about nine.

I suppose I shouldn't boast but kids came from all over the city for that Feis, so it was a bit of a feather in my cap. It was held in the Father Matthew Hall in Church Street (I suppose that's why they called it the Feis Maitiú). Being on the north side, it wasn't as posh as the Feis Ceoil, and not as specialized, because the Feis Ceoil did only music whereas ours had compeititions for Irish dancing and elocution and God knows what else.

Patsy wasn't in for it that day, lucky for me or I would have only got third! I sang Kitty From Coleraine. Those days you had to act out the songs so the nuns found me a little three-legged stool and a milking bucket but they had to show me what to do with a cow. I couldn't *believe* that you actually have to put your hands on. Yuck.

> When beautiful Kitty one morning was tripping
> With a pitcher of milk to the fair of Coleraine,
> When she saw me she stumbled
> And the pitcher it tumbled,
> And all the sweet buttermilk watered the plain.
> 'Twas hay-making season, I can't tell the reason,
> Misfortune never comes single 'tis plain.
> For very soon after poor Kitty's disaster,
> The divil a pitcher was whole in Coleraine!

Picture it. Me sitting on this little stool milking this imaginary cow into my pitcher before standing up and tripping. Nobody seemed to mind that we'd got completely the wrong end of the stick. That song is supposed to be sung by a boy. A boy from the country. The adjudicator never mentioned it.

The nuns put ringlets in my hair for the occasion because, of course, the way poor Mammy was at the time she wouldn't have been able to twist a ringlet if you'd paid her a tenner. But those days you had to have ringlets if you were to have any chance of a medal. And little white socks.

. Even though I only got second, the way Sister Marita was carrying on you'd think I'd won the Nobel Prize for Singing. It was a brilliant day. She brought me and another girl who got a Highly Commended down into town and we had chips and a Wimpy and as much Coke as we liked. I still have the medal somewhere. The winner got a plaque. In a way I'd prefer medals, I think plaques are a bit vulgar.

Patsy and I called ourselves PA System. Get it? P for Patsy, A for Angela. On a good day with the light behind her, as the fella says, Patsy would pass for Goldie Hawn. She's tall and blonde. 'Statuesque'. We'd known each other since High Babies.

We did lose touch for a few years after national school but then she turned up at Mammy's funeral. She told me one of the nuns rang her. I know people give out about nuns and how narrow-minded they were during that era but in my experience they were brilliant. With one notable exception, which I'll come to soon.

That Sunday morning, the second day of this story, PA System had no gig lined up so I was free to potter about in the flat. It was so small, you could fix it up in a trice but sometimes I liked to play house. You know, when it's real peaceful, and maybe raining outside, or even when it's sunny like it was that morning, you polish and hoover and shine everything up and when you stand back and look at it, the place sort of talks back to you. I always imagined the lounge twinkling and saying, 'Thanks, Ange!' I was using a brand new yellow duster, the kind you get as free offers with Flash. I love them, they're so soft, like the kind of gloves you'd buy only in Brown Thomas's. And the colour is so pure. I'd always planned that when James and I got a place of our own I was going to paint the walls that colour because then there'd be sunshine all the time *inside* the house. No more wall-paper. I hate frigging wallpaper.

I hate going into Brown Thomas's. I feel everyone there is looking at me and asking themselves who let me in.

Now it may have been poxy in the damp and drips department but we had a lovely high ceiling in that flat.

Georgian. Dublin's famous all over the world for being Georgian. I went to the Abbey once to see *Shadow of a Gunman* by Seán Ó Casey – one of the things that's great about living in Mountjoy Square is that the two best theatres in Ireland are right on your doorstep. I nearly fell out of my standing when I went into the Abbey that night and saw the stage. The room that the gunman was staying in? You'd think they'd copied the décor from our gaff. Right down to the peeling wallpaper.

I believe that in all those new apartments the ceilings are so low they're oppressive.

Well, that Sunday morning, as I told you, I was really enjoying myself tipping around. *Hamlet* was sitting there reproachfully on the arm of the bed-settee. I was ignoring him. That man's heart was too dark by half for such a lovely atmosphere. As a finishing touch, I put fresh water and a Disprin into the vase of motorway daffodils James nicked for us and then I put them inside the net curtains, between them and the glass. Patsy made those curtains for me on her electric machine. They're ruched and that morning, maybe it was the ruching, maybe it was the sun outside, they instantly turned gold when I placed the daffs behind them. The effect looked brilliant. You wouldn't see it in a magazine.

People are always giving out yards about Dublin Corporation and the County Councils and so on, but I think credit where credit is due. They've done a fantastic job with those motorways. I remember the first spring I saw the way they were planted, we were on our way to a gig in Patsy's car and I couldn't believe the sight of my own eyes, four wide ribbons of flower stretching for miles and miles, like four Yellow Brick Roads.

Years ago, in primary school, we did that poem by Wordsworth about daffodils. I thought it was useless, to tell you the truth.

I have another memory about daffodils, which is not great. I was only about eight, and here we come to that bitch of a nun, Sister Concepta, the only termagant nun I've ever come across in my whole life. That nun hated me. Well, maybe she didn't, in fairness. But when I was eight, I was *sure* she hated me. She was always sucking up to the kids who had money. At least, that's what it seemed like to me. Most of us in High Babies came from the flats but there were a few who came in from private estates in places like Glasnevin and Fairview. I suppose, looking back, their parents were socialists or something. They were the pets and you'd want to see the shop flowers they brought in for the May altars. (I suppose sucking up goes two ways.) When it came to that altar, the rest of us had make do with robbing Michaelmas daisies or snapdragons or tulips out of people's gardens. That was in the days before the motorways.

I'll give you an example of this one's bitchery, it has to do with daffodils, that's probably why I'm remembering her at this point. I wrote the word jonquils in a composition for her. Now remember – I was eight years old.

You mean 'daffodils', she says to me. How often do I have to tell you that you don't use big words just because they're big? Stop looking for notice.

I blush to the roots of my hair and insist that I mean jonquils. That jonquils are a different species to daffodils. I say I saw it in a gardening book.

Big mistake.

What gardening book? she pounces.

One I got out of the library, Sister. Now I'm in real deep. And I'm terrified.

Oh, the *library*, is it? she goes, is that right? Well, Miss Notice Box, bring it in so we can all see.

Of course there was no gardening book and I'd used

jonquils because I loved the sound of it. I have no idea where I heard it. How was I to know it was the French for daffodil? In my mind a jonquil was as different from a daffodil as a daisy from a dandelion. A jonquil was soft and quiet with petals like ferns.

She wouldn't let it go. She pursued me on it day after day. And of course I ended up getting slapped because of looking for notice and lying.

But the worst of all was the day she announced that the school was having a jumble sale in aid of Biafra or some other unfortunate place, I can't really remember, and that our class was having its own stall. She asked us – looking down at the pets – to bring in our unwanted toys and unused household items.

That was a laugh where I was concerned. Unwanted toys? Crap tyres and chipped steelies and bits of frayed rope from the docks which we used as skipping ropes. And as for unused household items, the mind boggles.

Mind you, we weren't all that deprived. Those steelies were lethal against real glass marbles. (A friend of mine was friends with McHugh Himself, the bicycle man, who gave her the best part of a bucketful of ballbearings he didn't need. Fair dues to her, she divvied them out.) And our dock ropes lasted a hell of a lot longer than the cissy skipping ropes you'd buy in a shop. Particularly when they were used for swinging around lamp-posts. They killed your hands, though.

But to get back to Concepta, I did have one lovely thing, my pride and joy. One of our social workers had given me a doll. I didn't even play with her, I didn't dare in case I ruined her. Her frock was made of stiff organdy in pale blue and she had real hair on her eyelashes. I called her Susie and I kept her hidden from the others. I hate to say this, because it sounds disloyal, but I didn't let even Mammy know where I kept her. Because you know what would have happened. Susie would have gone down to me uncle's in ten seconds flat and that'd be the end of her. Poor Mammy. The pawn was always her best friend.

So when Sister Concepta asked us about our unwanted toys—

I know, I know . . . You're way ahead of me here.

It wasn't even a struggle. I didn't even have to imagine how awful it was for the poor children of Biafra or wherever it was.

I don't know what got into me. I suppose deep down I was insecure enough to want her to like me. Whatever.

I ran home at little lunch, even though we weren't supposed to leave the grounds of the convent under pain of *death*. The flats were nearly a mile from the school and when I say I ran, I mean I really legged it. Little lunch was only twenty minutes.

I must have got home in about six or seven minutes because I could barely breathe when I was going up the steps to our door. And wouldn't you know it, just my luck, Mammy had a friend there.

She looks up all bleary-eyed when I run in the door and I can see him there on the sofa behind her, even more bleary-eyed. I ignore the both of them and run straight to where I'd hidden the doll.

On the way out they don't even look up. But the baby, it had to be Justine at the time, she's sitting in the middle of the floor with that look on her face, which meant she was probably going to cry in a minute. She smells, too, but I don't have time to change her nappy. I just put her soother back in her mouth and run.

I get a stitch half-way back and I have to stop. A very nice lady asks me if I'm all right and I have so little puff I can barely answer her that I am. When the stitch eases up a bit I have to run as though my life depended on it.

Which in a way it did. We were always strapped for being late. Even half a minute.

I manage to get back in without being noticed. Things were freer then, nobody worrying about baby-snatching or drugs in school playgrounds or suchlike, and the double gates were always wide open. The bell is just ringing for the end of little lunch and they're all going back inside. And as soon as I get inside the classroom I run straight up to Sister Concepta and give Susie to her.

Thanks, she says, and turns around to chalk something on the blackboard.

Thanks!

All during the rest of the day, I couldn't take my eyes of that doll where she'd put her beside the duster and the bell on top of the cófra. Yes, that same cófra where she kept not only the chalk and the copies and things like that but her best stick, her strap, and our knitting bags (I *hated* knitting with a *passion*), also the toilet paper you had to ask her for when you were going outside, making a show of you. That cófra symbolized everything I hated about that nun. And there was my beloved Susie sitting on it. A prisoner. Not only that, she was looking at me all the time. *How could you?*

Thanks.

It would be hard to exaggerate the effect that incident had on me. It was trivial, I suppose, and it happened so long ago, I should be able to let it go, shouldn't I? But it genuinely haunts me. I can still feel all the feelings, fresh as the day they arrived. Rage, sorrow, misery, and an overwhelming sense of injustice. I was also furious with myself for being such an eejit.

To get back to the Sunday in question. I had the radio playing low. 2FM.

I'm a big radio fan, as you'll discover. One of the stations, Classic Hits – or was it FM104? – used to have

The Golden Hour on Sunday mornings, I used to listen any time I could because it was a complete programme of the songs from the seventies and eighties that Patsy and I always used in our act. But now they're all doing chart shows. I just can't take techno or dance. I hate it.

All the time I was keeping an eye on the bedroom door. He likes to get up and go to meet some of his pals in the Millrace for a few pints before Sunday dinner. When PA System has no gig, I like to have Sunday dinner, the real thing, with Bisto and marrowfat peas. It makes me feel we're like a proper family.

So, sure enough, the door opens on schedule, about a quarter to twelve. I keep my mouth shut. Because I want him to come home for the dinner. The moods he's been in lately, you'd never know how he'd react if you said anything at all. A joke can be taken as an insult. You can't look crooked at him. All he's looking for is an excuse to storm out. And with the motorbike, I'm always afraid.

How'ya, I say to him, I know I'm walking on eggshells here and I try to place my tone just right. Not too cheery, no hint of enquiry in case he thinks I'm being intrusive.

He just grunts back and despite my best intentions, I get goaded. Oh, very nice, I say. Yes, Angela, I'm fine, thank you for asking. And what a lovely day it is outside and how are you doing yourself?

There's no point, I'm talking to myself. He's already gone into the facilities.

When he comes back out I ask him if there's anything wrong.

Nothing, he says.

I know better than to go on at him. Whatever chance I have of him coming round, I've none if I nag. Those hormones, probably. I have to make allowances, I know that.

Although I used to think naïvely that at nineteeen he should have been over the worst of them. I kept on telling myself that some people are just late developers, yet sometimes during that period, I used to find myself fantasizing we were having a real chat like real people. You know, having a laugh about the kissograms or the gigging or the cleaning (my main job) or the Samanthas and Marks I've met that week. And then he would be telling me about funny things that happened to him on his deliveries.

There had to have been some crack to be got out of that job of his. I've seen bunches of those courier lads sitting in their leathers, chatting and smoking there along the canal near where Patrick Kavanagh is supposed to have sat. (According to Mr Elliott we should all be making pilgrimages to that spot. Apparently Kavanagh wrote some of his best poems about that district around there and he used to spend a lot of time in some bookshop on Baggot Street Bridge.)

Now he grabs a heel of a loaf and eats it raw.

Will he have an egg or a rasher? Or even cornflakes?

I'm to get off his back and leave him alone.

At least he does say he will be home for the dinner. Well, so long as he stays on the Heineken, I suppose it'll be all right.

I tell him to be back for half two on the dot. He says he might.

A peculiar thing is that during that period I prayed a lot (if you could call it prayer, because I'm not practising and I'm not a bit religious. I don't even much believe in God, to tell you the truth). But I found myself all the time saying stuff like, 'God, if you're up there, please keep him safe . . .'

I worried a lot about drugs. Not for myself, because since I was old enough to notice the kind of thing that was going on around me, the last thing in the world I ever wanted to see was a cap or a syringe. To this day I try to manage without tablets when I have a toothache. It's sort of a principle with me. But there's no getting away from it in this city and where we're concerned, of course, there's heredity. Genes. Apart from Mammy altogether, I'd be willing to bet that James's father was a druggie. It stands to reason. From the time he was about twelve, I searched James's bedroom on a regular basis when he was out and once or twice I did find cigarettes broken up but I didn't really worry about that. That meant only hash. They all do that.

I'm humming away to myself over the dinner when he comes in about ten to three. Not late enough for a row but not on time either – tardy enough to show me I can't be interfering in his life.

I remember thinking, that day, God help his wife – and then wondering how I'd get on with her. A fantasy . . . Even at that stage I'd figured he did have a girlfriend although I hadn't dared open my mouth about her. There were little signs.

What little signs? Big signs! Like condoms in his jeans pockets. And him asking me to bring him back Lynx deodorant when I went to the shops.

The dinner went OK that day – he even talked to me a bit about some of his pals. There was one, Ferdia, who had a car, he worked for his father's computer business, and on the odd time I've met him he seemed to be a decent bloke. James tells me that they're all planning to go down the country, to Wicklow, to stay in a mobile home that Ferdia's parents have near Brittas Bay.

That brought me back. I was there once on the August Bank Holiday. One of the social workers arranged a supervised access visit for Mammy with the three in care and she let me go with them. She had a new Toyota car – well, new to her – and we all fitted in quite comfortably. She'd even brought a proper tartan rug so we could all sit down on it together.

Brittas Bay that day was crawling with kids, frolicking in and out of the waves and digging for shells and making moats for the tide to fill. I was fascinated to see the way the water came into the little channels, creeping in like fingers wearing white lace gloves. Although I'd been to Dollymount a few times I'd never noticed this before because every time I was there the tide was so far out you'd need binoculars to see any water.

Yes, it was brilliant. Mammy was grand that day, she even paddled with us. And on the way back she sat in the front holding Francesca on her knee and the whole lot of us were on our best behaviour.

I'd love to live somewhere nice like that. One of my biggest fantasies is of winning money in the Lotto. I'm not looking for a fortune, half a fortune would be enough! Patsy got three and a bonus once. Great lot of use eight quid was to her when she estimated that over the years she must have spend hundreds.

I've always concentrated on the scratch cards myself, I feel the odds are better. And I've won loads of two poundses, two fours and once even an eight. But I have to tell you getting those three Frees is useless. You're wasting your time going back in to claim the free card. It's just a way of prolonging the agony. But James got a twenty-five just before Christmas.

No matter what happened or happens to me I never lose sight of my belief that one day I'll get the three stars. Then I'll go on *Winning Streak* and I'll win that quarter of a million. Funny how most of the people on the programme are from the country. I suppose they've more money to spend on the scratch cards. The EU and all the rest of it. Headage. You'd have to laugh. Here's me from the inner city and I could hold my own with the best of the culchies in the matter of slurry and first-cut silage and headage grants. Isn't the telly very educational all the same?

By the way when I do get to go on *Winning Streak* I'm going to be very strict as to what my supporters in the audience can put on my posters to wave for me. Some of those posters are really stupid. 'Go for it, Deccie', or Joe or Nessa. Stupid. What do those people think the contestants are going to do? Not go for it? Why do they think they're on the ruddy programme?

Maybe we'll have our own mobile home in Brittas Bay someday, I say to James, as I'm ladling out the gravy. You know, of course, that I'm going to win the Lotto—

Huh, he goes. You and what army?

You just wait and see, I say. Maybe you'll be married by then, and have a couple of kids and I can mind them in the mobile home while you and your wife go to the pub for a bit of a break.

He lets me know what he thinks of that little scenario with a look that'd kill an elephant. So I shut up. Typical, give me an inch and I'll take a mile.

Three

Don't laugh, but there was a time when I was in danger of getting married myself. I was just turned seventeen. Nowadays seventeen would be seen as far too young, and of course it is, but it would have been a great way to go, eh? And it was legal. We're allowed to get married when we're fourteen, they've to wait until they're sixteen although maybe they've changed it now. Last I heard about it they were talking about raising the age of both sexes although, being a bit lax as far as being a Catholic is concerned, I'm not up to date on it.

I met him at the zoo, of all places. It was another Sunday and James was in hospital. It was just before Mammy died and he'd been taken in the day before 'for observation'. I knew what that meant. He was going into care too, like the other three. He was only two months old. He had been left with us as a sort of trial to see how Mammy'd get on.

But what did they expect?

There'd been murder in the flat that Friday night, the night before the zoo. Mammy wouldn't give James to the social worker and the police had to be called to get him away from her. I was screaming at them to get out, she was screaming, the social worker was screaming, that rat of a boyfriend was screaming. He pulled a knife on the social worker, and the police jumped on him. Complete bedlam.

The neighbours in on the act, gawking in through the open door. It was most likely one of them that reported us. Busyfeckingbodies. Sorry for the language but that kind of nosiness really gets on my wick.

I can still feel sick when I think of that night. I ran out of the place to get away from it. From them all. Afterwards when I realized I'd left them all to it I nearly died with the guilt. Any of them could have been killed. At least when I was there they'd listen to me. Most of the time anyway.

I spent that Friday night walking the streets but I did manage to get a bit of a kip down at the Irish Life Mall, there are a lot of nooky places in there and you'd be amazed who you'd meet. The Simon people came on their food run but I hid. I didn't trust them not to report me. I've always looked younger than I am.

But when I went home the next morning to face the music no one was there. I really panicked then. I was afraid to go to the police station and there was no way in the world that I was going to go down to Killarney Street to the social workers. Not yet. So for some reason that to this day I can't fathom, I got on the 10 bus and went up to the zoo.

I suppose I felt I'd be safe. They'd never think of the zoo – they'd know I'd be starving and they'd probably be looking for me in fast-food joints. I knew the zoo had a café and I did have a bit of money in my pocket to cover food and the entrance fee – I was working in the stockroom at Dunne's at the time and we'd just got paid.

Even still, I think that something stronger than the ordinary made me go to the Phoenix Park that day. It was like fate.

I saw Tom Bennett the minute I walked in through the stiles. He was gorgeous, in a chunky kind of way. His hair was slicked back straight in a DA and, although the Brylcreem darkened it, you could see it was red. Wet-coppery. I went weak at the knees. I always go for the Viking-type – you know, freckles, reddish or blond thick hair. And shoulders. Kind of like Brendan Gleeson or Liam Neeson. And if they wear glasses, particularly granny glasses, I'm done for. Don't ask me why. He was wearing glasses, black horn-rims. Like James Dean, or was that Buddy Holly?

He was with another bloke and a girl and they were strolling along by the lake there on the left-hand side, not the one with the flamingoes, the one with the ordinary swans and ducks. There were loads of seagulls there that day too, I remember. I suppose they were hoping for a free meal.

I walked casually after them, watching them. I don't know what I thought I was doing. I mean, my whole life was upside down and I knew that sooner or later I'd have to go to the police or the Eastern Health Board or at least Temple Street – although I hate hospitals with a passion – to find out what was happening with James, but here I was, passing the time of day in the zoo like a real person. I even forgot I was hungry while I was trying to work out whether "my" fella or the other bloke was the one with the girl. She was a bit of a chrissie, to tell you the truth, a bottle blonde with very thick kohl around her eyes and the platforms she was wearing made her spindly little legs look like ants' feelers. I would have been very disappointed in him if he'd been with her.

I needn't have worried. The other bloke, whom I subsequently found out was called Jason, kissed her and put his arm around her shoulders and since there was no aggro about it, I knew then that the fella I was interested in was free.

They stopped at the monkey house and he said something to the other two and then he laughed. Not sneering laughing, like you'd hear from a smart alec, but real, chuckly laughing, like he was saying something appreciative of the monkeys.

I dawdled along beside them, holding on to the metal rail in front of the cage and pretending to read the notice that told you what kind of monkeys they were.

And then the miracle. He turned around to me and he asked me if I'd like to join them. Just like that.

I was flabbergasted. I mean, I didn't even know he'd noticed I was there.

Well, you *are* all on your own, aren't you? he goes.

I can't remember what I said. Since then I've gone over that scene in my mind trillions of times but, as God is my judge, I could have answered him with the ten times table as far as I can tell. And the funny thing is that later, when we tried to remember together, he had no idea what I said either. We agreed it must be lurve!

Anyway, I joined them and the four of us had coffee and chips in the café. It turns out I was right about the girl. Common. No manners at all. She and Jason were eating each other – and this is with kids all over the place watching. And when they weren't eating each other they were bopping monkey nuts off each other's faces – that was in the days when you could buy monkey nuts in little twists of paper.

I was very embarrassed and I think so was Tom. It turned out that he wasn't a close friend of either of them, they were all just part of a big gang of people who knew each other and who had been supposed to go to the zoo that day. Only these three had turned up. So the two of us ignored the two of them as best we could and got on him. Don't worry, I go, I'll just be in the bedroom. I glare over at the cops. Suddenly the room seems awfully small. Did you ever notice how even one policeman can fill up a room?

Seeing the way James is I'm not at all as confident as I'm trying to portray.

I pick up *Hamlet* ostentatiously. I won't be far away, I make the point again as loud as I can without sounding as if I'm trying to start an argument with the cops. I don't say anything more but I hope these two get the message that I know what's what and I won't tolerate any messing. I've long had the impression they pick on fellas James's age just out of spite.

Then I go into the bedroom and close the door.

Here I'd like to be able to write that I could only hear a murmur through the closed doors, or that I had to strain to hear what was being said. It would probably sound more like a real story. But not a bit of it. It's not only the facilities, all of Reddy's walls are like tissue-paper. They're only partitions. James threw a saucepan once – he was angry about something, I forget what – and it made a huge dinge. The wallpaper tore and there were splinters all over the cooker. I had to get a mirror down at the Daisy Market to cover the hole. I'm going to leave the mirror to Reddy when we move out of here, pretend I forgot it. He'll be so delighted to get something for nothing he won't bother to check under it. Otherwise he'd probably dun us for every penny of the security deposit.

And the doors are the cheapest you can buy.

I could hear perfectly what was going on.

I can't write here what was said. I just can't. It's too hard. The words were like brass knockers on my skull and still are. I can't put them in proper sentences on paper because I'd dissolve.

Sexual asssault. Police station. That's all I can manage. Even that's after taking me ten minutes.

I nearly collapse when I realize. I'm holding *Hamlet* so hard that the cover has got hot. I can't stand it any longer. I crash out through the door. What's going on?

The two policemen look across at me as though I'm someone they'd never seen before. But I'll never forget James's face. Never. He's staring at me with eyes like craters in the middle of this white moon of a face and he looks about three years old. Like he did the first time I brought him to that Eastern Health Board playgroup and had to leave him there. I want to batter those cops to within an inch of their lives and take him in my arms and hug him to pieces and never let him go for as long as both of us lived. How dare they. Who do they think they are.

Will someone tell me what's going on, please?

The taller of the two stands up and says that they have to bring James to the station to ask him a few questions. That there had been allegations.

What allegations? I say.

They tell me. Some girl has filed a complaint. Rape.

That was the word I couldn't write before. It's still difficult.

James, I go, tell them. Come on, tell them—

He can't say anything. He's still looking at me with those eyes, like an alien, he's getting younger-looking by the minute. And the odd thing is, I notice for the first time that his jeans are pressed. How come I never noticed that earlier, when he got up or when we were washing the dishes. Who ironed your jeans I? say.

Still he can't answer. And it's only then that the penny drops. This is a boy who up to a few weeks ago wouldn't even wash a sock of his own.

Ironed jeans.

He'd pulled a few all-nighters recently, telling me it's

twenty-firsts and parties and clubs and so on. I should have taken the condoms and the deodorant more seriously.

We have to go now, says the smaller cop. Sorry, Missus, he says to me.

Something happens to me inside, a sort of cool wash feeling, and I get very sharp. I'm getting him a solicitor, I say. He's entitled to a solicitor.

Thanks be to God for the telly.

Hang in there, I say to James and for the first time he blinks. I see the rims of his eyes have gone all red. It nearly does me in but I manage to hold on. I wouldn't lower myself in front of these other two gougers.

That's your prerogative, says policeman one. But at this stage we only want to ask your son a few questions.

He's not my son, I say. They look a bit surprised at that. Maybe I'm not as young-looking for my age as I think I am.

It's the small things, isn't it? My image of him being taken away is of the back of his neck with the collar up on one side.

Wouldn't you know it, the first phone I try is out of order although it wasn't vandalized, just ordinary out of order. It used to be awful, you could never get a phone that worked, but since they got card phones in Dublin and put in those steel cables and took out the glass in the boxes, the gurriers don't seem to bother. They still smash the glass in those nice new bus shelters, though. Why they do that I don't know, because you'd think they wouldn't want to get wet any more than the rest of us. Maybe they don't travel in buses. It's probably faster for them to get where they want to go if they rob a car.

The next phone box is OK. I'm still thinking sharp. Since it's a Sunday, I know there's only a duty social worker on and I know there's no point in ringing her.

They're always snowed under with work and they take the emergencies first so problems like mine are always sliding down the queue. The best thing is to go straight to whom I want. Luckily I have Pat McCartan's number still, from the time he sorted James out with that bit of trouble he got into when he was sixteen. I don't care that he was a politician as well as a solicitor at the time. I'm not one of those begrudgers that says people shouldn't be allowed to make millions. If they're good at what they do they deserve everything they make and, as far as I'm concerned, Pat was great that time. He got the Probation Act for James. And James hasn't been in one bit of trouble since.

Unfortunately he was out that Sunday but whoever was there, I don't know if it was his wife, she gave me the number of another solicitor to ring. This fella's name is Patrice Murphy. I find it hard to believe that this is a real name. He was probably a Patrick and had to change it to distinguish himself from all the other Pat Murphys.

I don't want to go on too much about the rest of that day. I was able to keep going because I'd things to do to help James. I got the solicitor and I have to say he was very efficient. I mean, he came down to the cop shop at Fitzgibbon Street right away and he had a nice car so he had to have had a bit of success. The thing was, though, he did look like he was only James's age. At least Pat McCartan has grey hair even if he does have a young face. Solicitors nearly always have young, well-padded faces, have you noticed that?

James was arrested.

And despite Patrice Murphy's best efforts to get him released into my custody, he was put into a cell for the night. We were going to have to wait until the morning until we knew whether a judge would give him bail. I can't remember much of what the room was like where they eventually let me see him. I think it was quite small.

The cops themselves were quite good as it turned out, they let me bring in his own pyjamas and toothbrush and his ruddy deodorant. And of course I had to bring in his good clothes for the court. Luckily we'd been able to buy him a new jacket for the previous Christmas.

Neither of us can think of anything to say at first when he's brought into the room where I was told I could see him. Eventually he asks me would I ring his work first thing in the morning to say he wouldn't be in for the day. Say I'm sick, he goes.

Of course I'll ring them, I go. Although it wasn't going to be easy doing that. We're watched like hawks on the cleaning job in case we lift anything. And making free phone calls is regarded as lifting. Anyway, I wouldn't want anyone to know our business. They're nice, the crowd at work, but I like to keep a bit of distance.

Silence again.

Don't sign anything, I say to him next. It's your word against hers. Who is she anyway—

He's looking at the floor. Muttering something.

What?

He says louder that he knows there's no point in denying anything, even if what he's being charged with isn't true. That women have it all sewn up. That I'm pathetic. That I don't know what it's like in the modern world. You only have to look crooked at some girl now and she and all her mates are crying rape.

I don't know what to believe, of course, but here and in this situation is not a place to get into an argument about greater society. Tell me what happened, I go, in your own words.

You won't believe me either, he says. Sort of hopeless.

I get that feeling again, a fierce wave, where I want to smash open the walls with my bare fists and let him out of there and the two of us fly away to Spain or Timbuktu or somewhere safe.

Tell me, I say again, at least try me.

He looks at the floor. I can't, he says.

I wish there wasn't a damned policeman standing at the door only three feet away from us. Then James looks back up at me and there are now big tears in his eyes. I haven't seen tears in that fella's eyes since he was seven. It turns me inside out but I certainly don't want to start blubbing in front of him or the policeman. I stand up and say as steadily as I can that I'll see him in the court tomorrow.

Can I give him a goodbye hug? I ask the policeman, who nods.

I go around the table and I put my arms around him but he doesn't stand up. He just sits there like a rag doll. Well, not a rag doll, his shoulders and chest feel like a hollow drum. Except I can feel his insides shaking.

Just tell me one thing, I whisper to him while I'm still holding on to his shoulders. Is this why you've been in such bad humour for the last few weeks? Did you know something like this might happen?

No, not really, he says back, but I was worrying about why she suddenly changed towards me.

Well, at least that's something, I go, I wasn't just imagining things. The policeman then tells us it's time for James to leave and that moment has to rank very near the lowest in my life.

→ Four ←

Patrice Murphy comes to the flat that night. He asks
me about my means and whether, if the judge grants
bail, I can come up with it. He tells me I'm going to have
to show that I can.

The hell I can. If I've to rob a bank I can.

Well, do I have a bank book or something to show I'm
good for the money in case James skips the jurisdiction?
And do I know two people who could give indpendent
sureties? The usual would be about ten thousand in all.

Ten thousand? I can't believe it. My brain is skipping
and hopping over the figure. To me that's Lotto money.
I promise you James won't skip the jurisdiction, I say but
my voice sounds as weak as a baby's. Anyway, he doesn't
even have a passport.

Patrice Murphy looks at me as though I've lost it.
There's England, he says, very quietly.

He won't go to England, I say. That's a definite.

Have you any means at all, bank books? Any valuables?

I tell him about my post-office bonds. As I told you,
I've been putting money away, into those bonds because
I believe they're the safest. There would be a couple of
thousand, I go, actually two thousand eight hundred and
fifty. But nothing near what we'd need—

Is there no one at all you'd know? Do you have a bank

account? Could you go to the manager? What about friends? Employers?

I shake my head. Employers? The only possibility is the deli owner but I'd be very hesitant there.

Then I think of Patsy, but I reject the thought as quickly as it's occurred to me. Patsy and I are best friends but I wouldn't even consider asking her for money. For a start she's always going on about how Martin's business is going from strength to strength, yet how as a family they never have two pennies to rub together what with the drain on them from all the children's activities.

But even if she wasn't always talking like that, I would never put myself under an obligation to her. This is a disaster. How much time do we have? I ask Patrice Murphy.

He purses his lips as though he's trying to look wise. The judge will have to be satisfied in the court tomorrow if we're to get James out after the hearing. Bring the bonds along with you tomorrow. How about valuables? Jewellery? He looks around the flat. Looks back at me. His face says it all.

I think. Review my measly possessions. Maybe another thousand, I say, one thousand two hundred?

Well, that makes four you can come up with, he says. We'll see. I'll try to talk to the other side. Bring everything with you tomorrow, will you? He's still putting on the wise act but the matter-of-fact language impresses me. He seems to know his stuff.

I see him out. Sit down to draw breath. I start feeling sorry for myself, why is it always us, what are we going to do, et cetera . . .

I catch myself at it. Hate it. Self-pity has to be by far the most destructive of emotions.

Right, I say to myself and stand up again. Shut up. Stop whingeing. James is not dead. He doesn't have terminal cancer. He's not on heroin, he's only in trouble. And he's just accused not convicted. Look on the bright side, it could all be a misunderstanding, it could all be cleared up in ten minutes. We have a great solicitor and who knows, we might get a great judge tomorrow who'll trust me when I say James will turn up.

And the time factor was working in our favour, so that was in the plus column too. Carthy's Pawnbrokers in Marlborough Street opens at half nine and James's court appearance wasn't due until half ten. Luckily I get off work every morning at nine. There was going to be enough time. Just.

I do a quick mental survey of our hockable items. James's bike is on the drip but we've paid off a mere six months of it – anyway, he needs it for work – and the telly's rented. So they're out.

But the haul turns out to be respectable enough. The payments are finished on the video, and on the microwave and on the coal-effect electric fire. They're ours and we can live without them. All biz now, I make out a list in order of preference. Jewellery and video first, I'd get most money on them. Electric fire next – luckily it is the summer.

Thank God I've resisted the temptation all these years to cash in Mammy's bits and pieces. Sentimentality, I suppose, because God knows there were times when James and I could have used the money. I think some of them are quite good, particularly the Victorian mourning brooch and the rose-gold neck chain and garnet ring. There's a silver christening spoon as well.

There's one thing that I'd part with only as a last resort, though – a tiny marcasite brooch in the shape of a peacock. I always wear that, I change it from lapel to lapel. She told me once that marcasite is diamond chips and of course I believed her until I looked it up one day in my dictionary and found otherwise. I never told her, though, because she thought her peacock brooch was the most valuable thing she owned and she always told me it was for me after she was gone and I was to mind it.

I don't care whether it's valuable or not. It was diamonds to her.

Anyway, I have to have something left belonging to her, don't I? Just in case I can't get the rest of the jewellery back out . . .

Isn't it funny how things go in circles in your life? First of all, Carthy's was the pawn Mammy used, I had a path worn to it from our place. And second, with the exception of the peacock brooch, I never wore any of that jewellery, it just never looked right on me somehow and now I know why. It's fate. I was meant to save it. In a strange way she was saving it for me for when it was needed to help James.

It goes to show that she's still looking after us in her own way.

I bet you're surprised that she had such quality jewellery.

You see, Mammy came originally from a well-to-do family down the country in Birr, Co. Offaly. Believe it or not she was a Protestant. She never practised, of course. Where could you, if you were living in the flats? Even if she wanted to – or if they'd have her which, of course, was unlikely. And I suppose she had us baptized Catholics because it was simply easier for her. There were more people to look after us that way, like there were more schools.

One thing I have to hand to her is that with all her vicissitudes the jewellery never got hocked. Not once. (And I'd know because I'd be the one sent with it.)

She even had it hidden away from all the so-called friends. I suppose somewhere deep down she felt that to own a little bit of good jewellery would maintain some shreds of her dignity. The temptation must have been huge, though, especially when she was having a hard time and moaning for relief. Wouldn't you have to admire her?

Now here was I hocking it.

Oh well, I thought that Sunday, the stuff won't be in for long. And I reckoned that with a small amount of luck it wouldn't be necessary to give in the other electrical appliances. Like her, I wanted to keep up a certain standard if at all possible.

I suppose it's because she was a Protestant that Mammy knew unusual hymns. She had a very nice voice – that's probably where I got it. There was one time when she was just out of Coolmine and she was straight for a few weeks – that was a brilliant time, they hadn't taken Nicola, the youngest, yet – she taught me one of those hymns. Abide With Me. I believe they sang it on the *Titanic* when it was going down.

Or was that Nearer My God To Thee? I saw *A Night To Remember* on the telly the other night. I should be able to remember which hymn they sang. Wasn't it a brilliant film?

Anyway, she taught it to me and I remember she was holding Nicola on her lap at the time and feeding her like a real mother. Oh, it was fantastic. I can still remember the words, every single one of them.

But my favourite was Starbright. On her good nights she used to say it to me when she was putting me to bed. Starlight Starbright First Star I See Tonight. I Wish I May I Wish I Might, Have The Wish I Wish Tonight. And then she'd kiss me on the forehead. I can't bear to think about it.

It's funny how you remember things you learned at that age. I even remember the first verse of Wordsworth's bloody daffodils. And An Old Woman of the Roads. Although she was a homeless poor old thing, I was quite easily able to put myself in her position. It's funny, but when I got sentimental about the kind of place we were going to get for ourselves I always saw us in a little house with the stool and all, just like her.

> *Oh to have a little house*
> *To own the hearth and stool and all*
> *The heaped up sods upon the fire*
> *The pile of turf again the wall . . .*

Et cetera. In my imagination, the wind was always howling outside my little house and the rain was bashing against my snug little windowpanes. We never had sods stacked up ourselves, of course, but our nun – *not* Concepta, I hasten to add – described what turf should look like and I could just see it. She said it smelled pungent and wrote the word on the blackboard. For days I was trying to find ways to slip pungent into sentences.

> *I could be busy all the day*
> *Cleaning and sweeping hearth and floor . . .*

Because of that poem, I even practised sweeping up in our place. (That was a riot, you'd want to see our place!) I'd found a brush handle outside in one of the entryways and I pretended it had bristles. Imagination is a great thing, isn't it?

But to get back to the jewellery. The neck chain and the mourning brooch were Mammy's own grandmother's. That would have to make them more than a hundred years old.

Unfortunately that Birr, Co. Offaly, branch of the family wants nothing to do with this branch in Dublin and I wouldn't know any of them if they stopped me in the street. I wouldn't blame them for disowning us, I suppose. Still, it must have been hard. I know she tried her best.

I suppose at this stage you're wondering why I wasn't taken into care when all the others were?

Well, I just wouldn't stay anywhere, that's the holy all of it. I kicked up murder and I ran back to her all the time. And in the beginning, anyway, things weren't too bad and they kept giving Mammy chances. I slipped through the net, sort of.

And by the way, no one could say she ever, *ever* abused me. I'd kill anyone who said that. She never abused any of us. All right, under the definition of neglect, I suppose in some ways we were neglected but she did her best. She certainly did her best when she was able to.

Some of the boyfriends weren't all that bad at the beginning either. There was one – I'm nearly sure he was Francesca's father because he was the one who lasted the longest. About three years. And Franscesa was born sometime around then. This fella, his name was Joey, he was from Kerry or somewhere and he was a bit of fun. He even bought clothes for us. The only problem was he kept disappearing for weeks at a time. And when he'd come back there's be some other fella there and there'd be an almighty row and the social workers'd come again and I'd be delivered up to my regular foster family and I'd run away after a day.

I must point out that no blame should attach to those people, the foster parents, I won't tell you their names because I'm not sure they'd want to be associated with us any more. They were kind, and they had a nice house, lovely and warm. I loved having a real bath.

I absolutely hated the real children, though. And I know they hated me. They'd hold their noses when I came in the door. Behind their Mammy and Daddy's backs, of course.

Another thing was, I could never get used to a Daddy around the place, giving orders.

I keep meaning to try to re-establish contact with Francesca for one last try, but I just haven't got around to it. I did make efforts for a while, wrote regularly, but she kept rebuffing me and eventually I lost heart. I know she's in England somewhere because she's in touch with her foster family and the mother told me a couple of years ago she was still there. The woman wouldn't give me the latest address, though, she said that'd have to come from Francesca herself.

I suppose I can understand it, she set off on her new life and she wanted a complete clean break with the old stuff. We'd all be painful reminders of what she has escaped from. She'd be about thirty now. She might even be married and I might even have nieces and nephews.

Justine and Nicola were always a twosome. They're in Australia, and although I have their addresses and I make sure to remember their birthdays, I get only a Christmas card from Nicola and maybe a postcard, once in a blue moon, from Justine. At least it's something. Neither of them is married, although in her last card Nicola dropped a hint that she had a boyfriend. Isn't it terrible the way people of the same flesh and blood — or half it, anyway — can so easily scatter?

Some day I'll go out to Australia. The girls haven't invited me yet, but I'm sure they'd be delighted. I have this lovely fantasy about my fiftieth birthday, that I'll have a bit of money put by and we'll have a real reunion, all five of us. Dream on, Ange!

It was very lonely that Sunday night without James. It was unusually quiet outside with hardly any traffic and whatever way the wind was blowing I could hear

Eason's clock chiming into the early hours, all the way from O'Connell Street. It wasn't like the times he'd pulled all-nighters, this was completely different. This time I knew where he was, you see, I could picture him. I kept seeing his white face and those big eyes, and wondering was he sleeping. I doubted it. The papers are always full of how awful these remand cells are and how kids are always committing suicide in them. I had a terrible time visualizing. Graffiti. Concrete. A really hard mattress. A toilet bowl in the corner. No seat or lid. Stink. All night I saw worse and worse things. I couldn't wait for five o'clock to come when it would be time to get up.

I'm not usually introspective but in between thinking about James I did bring up a lot about my own life all that night. And oddly enough one of the people I thought about a lot was Tom Bennett. There was never any real chance we'd get married, I see that now. But, as I think I said earlier, I did have high hopes at one stage. I thought Mrs Angela Bennett had a great ring to it.

When I got back to the flats after the zoo that first day I met him, there was nobody in our place and I had to go around asking. It killed me, you could see their little smiles and their little slitty eyes. They were all delighted that the Devines were out at last. Nobody said so, of course, with their phoney sympathy and their where-*were*-you-love, we-were-looking-for-you.

They were in their eye. Couldn't wait to get rid of us. As if we were the only dysfunctional family in the place.

I couldn't avoid it any longer, I had to go up to Temple Street to ask after James. To keep me determined I kept my mind fixed on a bright thing – I had a date with Tom Bennett to go to the pictures on the following Wednesday. He worked most nights, he was a shift worker in Cadbury's, but he had Wednesdays and Fridays off.

They were all right to me in Temple Street. They were used to it, I suppose.

But James was already gone. To a family, somewhere up on the Navan Road. The nurse wasn't supposed to tell me that but she was nice. She saw how upset I was, I guess. I was used to the drill by then, of course. The new family was an emergency homing; they'd keep him until he went to a proper foster home.

Something snapped in me. Over my dead body. I was old enough to look after him – all right, I wasn't his mother but I'd certainly had enough practice at it. And I was seventeen. All you had to be was sixteen for you not to have to go into care yourself. I was a responsible adult and I knew the provisions of the 1908 Children's Act. He was my little brother. I wanted to mind him and that was that.

Apart from anything else, it was something to do, a project to keep my mind off where Mammy might be or what might be happening to her. So I pushed and pushed until I managed to persuade the powers that be that he'd be better off with me than with strangers. I had a brilliant social worker that time. (She left to go to the North afterwards and I really missed her. This was the same one who brought us all on the picnic to Brittas Bay with the tartan rug.) She was always on at me that I had to develop a life of my own and stop worrying about all the others, but when she saw I was absolutely set about James, she came on my side and some way or other she managed to get her bosses to give me a chance.

She got James back out of the emergency foster home and I was allowed bring him home with me on a trial basis. It was the same evening I was to meet Tom Bennett and she even babysat for me when I went down to explain that I wouldn't be able to go to the pictures with him as we had planned. I bet that was against the rules of the Eastern Health Board. That's why she was brilliant. She used her noggin instead of always going by the book. I know they have to have rules because otherwise they might be left holding the baby. Joke. Ha ha. But I'm not like that and she knew. She trusted me.

I rush to Eason's to meet Tom Bennett. All the way down I'm peppering. I wouldn't blame him if he did a runner. I mean, who wants to take on a girl with a two-month-old baby? Especially in that era – this was nineteen years ago.

He's here, waiting already – and he looks fabulous. He has on this crocodile jacket and a black polo-neck and very, very tight jeans. He isn't wearing his glasses. He wears contacts because he plays football. I'm very flattered, I can tell you, that he put in the contacts just because he was meeting me. (Even though, of course, I love fellas in glasses as I told you already.)

And he's great about what's happened, he really is. (I never blamed him afterwards. It was nobody's fault that it didn't work out with Tom Bennett and me.)

I explain the whole thing to him. Well, not the *whole* thing. I don't tell yet about Mammy being missing again, and the boyfriend, and the other three in care. I just say that, owing to circumstances beyond my control, I have to mind James for a little while. It's a desperately windy evening, and my hair keeps blowing around my face so I have to talk to him holding it back with both hands.

There's one awful moment when I'm finished and he doesn't say anything. A bit of litter blows around his legs and sticks there and he has to bend down to peel it off.

Even the top of his head is gorgeous.

Don't worry about it, he says. We can meet some other time. Then he says he understands about James. That he himself is the youngest of twelve and although his mother is still alive there are so many of them that one or other of his sisters always had to mind him too when he was growing up. (I already know they live in Finglas. There are lots of huge families up there.) When, I go, when can we meet?

In for a penny in for a pound. I'm not in a position to be shy about this, I don't have time.

He doesn't back off like most of them would have, doesn't just say, See you, or I'll be in touch. No, he makes another definite arrangement with me for the following week. I know I'm home and dry when he asks me would I have time now just for one quick coffee.

Sure, I say, although I had promised the social worker I'd only be half an hour.

We go to the nearest place, I can't remember whether it was Cafolla's or Forte's or Wimpy's or what. And as for remembering what the coffee was like, it might even have been tea.

Another plus. His manners. He makes me sit down while he goes up to the counter.

He comes back with the two cups and sits down, gives me this smile of his. It pulls me in feet first like going down a warm water slide.

We start to chat. Usually I'm the one that talks the hind legs off a donkey but I find I hardly have to talk at all (even if I could!). He doesn't ask a thing about my family and in my opinion this is very tactful. Instead, he tells me about his family and his job in Cadbury's and how he's seen so much chocolate he'll never eat another square of it for the rest of his life. You wouldn't either, he goes, if you saw what we have to deal with. Big brown lakes of the stuff. I leave it to your imagination as to what it'd remind you of.

I'd like to be tested, I say. I've always had a sweet tooth.

I don't have a sweet tooth at all, but that'll give you an idea of how I was behaving that day.

Afterwards, he kisses me goodbye, right there in the open in O'Connell Street. Not a snog, a respectful, gentlemanly goodbye kiss.

That night, when I'm alone and James is sleeping, I do the cross-off game. (I'm not sure if it's just a Dublin thing, I don't think so.) You know it? Where you write his name, and then your own name directly underneath, and then you cross off the common letters and you count off what you're left with. *Love Like Hate Adore Kiss Court Marry* . . .

It came out that for him it was Court and for me it was Love. Not great, I think you'll agree. Court is up against the wall, slam, bam and thank you, Mam.

So I redid it as Thomas Bennett versus Angela Devine. Much, much better! Almost the best of all! (Which would have been for both of us to have come out as Marry.)

Would you believe this time I came out Love and he came out Marry?

It was cheating in a way – it's supposed to be the name you're known by, but Thomas was his real name, after all.

I whirr across the floor and into bed. Two feet off the ground, like I'm an angel.

Five

James was all smiley and cuddly when I got home and the social worker had bought us a block of ripple ice cream to celebrate our homecoming and she even gave me a bag of Babygros, hardly used. She explained all about my entitlements — actually they were James's entitlements — but she needn't have bothered. I knew them backwards, everyone in the flats did.

I listened, of course, I didn't want to be impolite. It paid off. Because there was one entitlement I didn't know about — we could apply for some money to buy a little pram or a go-car. Nowadays I see them all with those Lolita buggies. Ten a penny. Fifteen- and sixteen-year-olds (that's why we call then Lolitas) proud as punch walking in pairs down Henry Street with buggies that wouldn't disgrace a millionaire. But back then the buggy thing was still only in its infancy. Ha ha!

Poor Mammy could have done with this particular entitlement. Maybe if she'd had a buggy or a little pram she might have had something to do. You know, push us down to the river for a walk or something. But I suppose they couldn't have given her a buggy because it would have gone down to the pawn first thing.

I asked her once how she came to Dublin and why she didn't stay with her family in Birr, Co. Offaly. She said she'd tell me when I was older. She never did, of course, she was dead before I asked her again.

But there's no point in dwelling on what might have been. I believe in looking to the future. And I was born with certain advantages. Like I always knew that if I ever sincerely wanted to discover my father's identity I was in a far better position than any of the others. Their fathers flitted in and out – flies amongst flies whose names none of us really knew and who probably ended up in the morgue.

But mine wasn't one of them. She told me once I hadn't been conceived in Dublin, only born here.

And over the years she'd say other things to me when she was relatively well and feeling soft, little starry things, like teasing me about being a bit of a culchie. Or she'd warn me to watch out for romance with the boy next door. They seem to be the nicest, she'd say, but they're always the most deadly. And she'd get this wistful look on her face.

There was enough of that nature so that when I put them all together I'd have to conclude that to begin a search for my father I'd have to start in Birr, Co. Offaly.

Of course I couldn't be *absolutely* certain, only ninety-nine per cent.

But one thing for definite. I definitely knew I'd be looking for someone with fair hair, since I'm the only one of the five of us with it. Mammy's was black – did I tell you that already? Maybe it's because of my father that I always go for the Viking type! Mind you, I always figured that if I ever did find him, the first thing I'd do is I'd probably give him a dig.

Then I'd think it needn't necessarily have been his fault. He could have been very young. He mightn't even have known about me, Mammy was only nineteen when I was born, the same age James is now. My father might have been only seventeen, or even sixteen – or so I fantasized when I was in a forgiving mood. For some reason I saw him always in a meadow. With cows and daisies and buttercups and skylarks joyously trilling overhead, like in an Emma Thompson picture. Birr, Co. Offaly, had a hell of a lot to live up to in the picturesque stakes if I ever got there.

But as a matter of fact I can't stand that Ode to a Skylark by Percy Bysshe Shelley.

That Sunday night when I was lying awake in bed and picturing James in his hard, horrible little cell, I realized how much I was going to have on my plate with this court problem. So I decided I was going to pull out of doing the Irish exam. There would always be next year.

It was a great relief. Irish is too hard. In the Inter, I only wrote my name on the Irish paper. Just my name in Irish and not another comma.

At least with some of the other subjects I did try. But that time I couldn't wait to get out of school – legally you had to stay there until you were fifteen and I suppose I was just marking time. Mammy was bad during that period so I had a lot more to think about than history and geography. Certainly more than Irish.

There are too many haitches, like Devine in Irish is Ní Dhaibhín. I think they put in the haitches to keep Irish exclusive. I get the feeling that those Gaeilgeórí are a secret society, like the Masons, and their secret sign is that they all wear jumpers.

Maybe I'm prejudiced but did you ever notice that they seem to think they're comedians? Éibhear Ó Súilleabháin, our teacher, was always making a joke out of my name. Angela Devine. Divine. Angela. Angel. Get it? Angel Divine. Maybe it was Mammy's sense of humour.

But I was furious that it took someone in a jumper to point it out to me. I'm not *that* thick, am I?

Ping pong ping pong, pong ping ping pong . . . Eason's clock down in O'Connell Street again. I thought the dawn would never come that Monday morning and then, when the alarm did go off, I was afraid of the day.

James won't be in this morning because he's sick. I'm looking over my shoulder, with the telephone right up to my mouth. Thank God this particular courier company believes in starting early. It's seven o'clock and I'm standing there with the polisher going full blast, pushing it round and round in circles so this bit of lino will nearly have a hole in it by the time I'm finished. That bitch of a supervisor creeps around. I'm sure you won't believe this but she wears slippers. I swear to God, she comes in in her shoes all right but then she changes into her slippers. Real bedroom slippers with blue fur all around the uppers. You never hear her until she's right behind you.

I'm passed on to the base controller and I'm sure I can hear your woman coming so I hang up.

I polish as though my life depends on it but it turns out to be a false alarm. I move to the next desk and dial all over again. Hello, it's me again, I was holding on for the controller and got cut off.

He takes like a million years to get on. Hello, who's this?

This is James Devine's sister. He's sick and he won't be in this morning. I'm sorry for the short notice.

Heavy sighing on the other end. Look, I go, I'm just his sister. Don't shoot the messenger. And I put down the phone.

We're six floors up and the sky outside is gorgeous so I feel a bit better about the day coming up. Pink and gold. It's a late dawn because it was cloudy this morning but it's still lovely.

You may have gathered by now that yellow, and gold in particular, is my favourite colour. I love skies in the summer-time. No matter what the weather is going to be like for the rest of the day – and it could be howling when we're being picked up in the minibus – it very rarely seems to be raining when the sun comes up. We're usually working somewhere where there's a huge amount of glass. Most days, certainly from February to October, I manage to see the dawn or at least the early sun. I regard it as one of the perks of the job. (That's unless she puts me working on the western side of the building out of spite – she's caught me more than once mooning out, Dreamy Drawers, she calls me. She should talk. In her slippers.)

It makes you humble. No matter what happens, that sun will come up tomorrow morning and that sky will still be gold under whatever clouds are there. Our little problems don't amount to a hill of beans, eh?

Today is so lovely I hope it's an omen.

I'm dusting now and I can't stop wondering how James is feeling. He'll get bail anyway – that solicitor seemed very confident.

The little so-and-so, I'll kill him when I get him home. He'll tell me every last detail, I'll make sure of it. I've been in court before so I'm much better off than some poor bitch who's going in there for the first time. That was the children's court, though, which is supposed to be much better than real court.

Still, I'm quaking. I hope she won't be there. She probably won't, isn't she just a witness, or something, and don't they try to spare her until the very last minute.

I wonder what she looks like, the girl? What's her family like?

I never met Tom Bennett's family. Wait 'til you hear why!

Time and again he said he was going to bring me up there but he never did. About six months after we started going out together I asked him what was the mystery. Was he ashamed of me? Of us coming from the flats? He was really upset that I'd even think of such a thing.

Well, why not, then, I go, do you have something to hide up there, maybe? Are you all on the game or into something else hookey? I was only joking, naturally. Someone as straight and respectful as him couldn't come from that kind of a family.

It was the only occasion during the whole time we knew each other that I thought I was in danger of getting a clatter from him. He didn't, of course, but he looked like he might. If only I'd known then what I found out later I wouldn't have been making such an eejit of myself.

He dashed away from me and then came back – we were in Talbot Street, I remember – and he stood in front of me and denied vehemently that he was ashamed of me or anything like it. He was yelling. Everyone was looking and I was mortified.

Now that I think back on it, he was probably *too* upset. That usually means you've hit the nail on the head. It should have set off my alarm bells.

I let it go, though, because I didn't want to provoke him any further.

It wasn't the only row we had, of course. They never started that way, always about something else. Usually tiny little things. I remember one day we were in Bewley's. James was in a high chair and he had jam all over his face. (Tom Bennett was good about that. Half the times I saw him I had to bring James along.) We'd had a lovely day. It was a Sunday. We'd been for a bus ride all the way out to Dalkey and back. James had been as good as gold.

Anyway we started arguing about whether the sugar in the packets was Irish or English. Pathetic. A little thing like that to develop into an almighty hoo-hah! What started with packets of sugar ended up with us having a fierce row about the English still being in the North of Ireland and whether Patrick Pearse should have held the Rising or not in 1916. This is one of the reasons I hate politics in this country. You can never have a calm conversation with anyone about the subject.

Up to that moment I wouldn't have put Tom Bennett in the Republican camp. And to tell you the truth, I probably shouldn't have argued with him at all because he didn't say anything I hadn't heard a million times before in pubs or at a sing-song. Roddy McCorley's Going To Die On The Bridge Of Toome Today? How many times have you heard that one? Heard the passion? Especially from someone with the few jars on . . .

I suppose a lot of our skins are very thin in that North of Ireland department.

It later turned out that he didn't care a fig one way or the other about Patrick Pearse or the Rising. It was just argument for argument's sake. I think I must have had a bit of PMT because, looking back, my reaction was completely out of proportion. I whipped James out of the high chair and stormed out of Bewley's and I didn't give a sugar, no pun intended, what anyone thought of me. He didn't try to stop me.

Of course I was sorry by the time I got to O'Connell Bridge. I ran back straight away. He was gone. I can still see the empty chair where he'd been sitting.

I was frantic. I ran up and down Westmoreland Street and D'Olier Street and then ran the length of O'Connell

Street to where all the 40 buses left for Finglas. Poor James got a terrible bumping around in his buggy.

It was no use, Tom Bennett seemed to have vanished into thin air.

I rang Cadbury's the next day but they said he was on a day off.

He turned up at the flat the following night and even though I had my rollers in I threw myself at him the minute I saw him in the doorway, and cried and couldn't say enough how sorry I was.

That was the first night we ever had sex. And we got engaged the next morning.

Our flat that time wasn't bad, thanks to that brilliant social worker I told you about – and to the Vincent.

Poor Mammy always hated having the Vincent.

Come to think of it, maybe she didn't like them because she was a Protestant. Maybe she thought they'd put a hex on her something, or make her say the Rosary with them (of course, they never do) but I think it's more likely she hated accepting charity. Towards the end, she didn't care and ironically, the place was never better furnished than when she was too far gone to appreciate it.

She shouldn't have minded, she could have been killed in the rush. More than half the families in our flats got help from the Vincent de Paul.

That morning we got engaged, I fed and changed James and put him into his playpen and then Tom Bennett ordered me back to bed. That gave me the greatest feeling. Fluttery and excited. Even sexual. But strange, too. I wasn't so sure I was going to be able to let anyone, even Tom Bennett, boss me and James around even in a nice way.

He was taking another day off, even though he wasn't

supposed to. He didn't even ring. Feck it, he says, it's not every day a fella gets engaged.

Suppose they sack you, I go. We have to start saving up immediately and we can't have you unemployed.

Not at all, he goes back. Will you stop worrying. Leave the worrying about our future to me, I'm your man now and you'll have to trust me to take care of us all.

It was a single bed and before I got back into it, I insisted on changing the sheets. They were all stained. Sex was not like I expected. It was very smelly for a start. But it didn't hurt half as much as I'd been led to believe. I quite enjoyed it, although I believe you're not supposed to enjoy it your first time. I didn't ask him if it was his first time. I didn't care a damn — that was all in the past and the future was what was on our minds. It was pretty obvious that it was my first time so he didn't have to ask me!

The second time I was sore from the previous night but I got over it. And from then on I knew it was going to be OK. Tom was avid for it. I knew that morning I was going to have to work miracles and get a washing machine from the Vincent! Or, failing that, I thought I might try the *Gay Byrne Radio Show* fund. You do that through your social worker and they seem to specialize in washing machines, or they did at that time. I wouldn't tell them why I needed it, mind you. If they knew the reason I wanted it they mightn't think I was all that worthy a cause!

Now will you bring me up to meet your family? I say, when we're standing at the window having a cup of tea afterwards.

Of course, he says.

When?

On my next day off.

I'll never forget that moment. The window in our

place looked out over the yard and for once it was really respectable-looking, as pristine as a new twenty-pence piece. The Corporation had just removed all the graffiti, and for good measure, they'd cleaned away all the rubbish, the oil and dog dirt and broken glass, even the burned out Volkswagen that had been there for years. They'd put concrete tubs in, filled with wallflowers which, so-far-touch-wood, the gurriers had left alone. And the scent! You could have got drunk on that scent. The sun was shining after a spell of rain and those wallflowers wafted all the way up to our balcony. There were kids on the swings.

This was the Communion season and there were two little girls in their Communion outfits sitting together on one end of the see-saw, heads bent over the Communion bags as they counted their lolly. It didn't matter that morning how long the yard was going to stay like this because looking down at it all, the scene and the moment became fixed for me. I was going to meet Tom Bennett's family and at last have a real family to be part of.

The only fly in the ointment was, would they take to James. He said of course they would, there'd be no problem. Weren't they well used to kids? Anyway, who wouldn't take to him. He was at a lovely age.

He sure was. Then.

I know every mother since Eve has said, 'If only they'd stay like that . . .' And if I feel that, and I'm only a sister, I hate to think how a real mother must feel when she looks at the scowling hard chaw who's suddenly shot out of her little chuckling baby. It's like being related to The Incredible Hulk.

They were very decent at the pawn that Monday morning, they gave me exactly five hundred for the jewellery and the christening spoon and fifty for the video – although the pawnbroker himself said he should only be giving me twenty-five. They even remembered me from years before and asked after James.

Grand, I said, he's grand, never better. Stroppy, of course, you know how they all are at that age . . .

Even in the middle of my panic about the court and what was facing me in the next hour, I felt a pang parting with Mammy's jewellery. Naturally, I was going to do my damnedest to get it all back. I had six months to redeem it but I'd no illusions about how difficult it was going to be. The case probably wouldn't come up for months and months. There's a terrible backlog, according to Patrice Murphy, and not half enough judges.

I was going to have to find something else to do that'd earn money. A bit of private cleaning, maybe. The pay is lousy but it's into your hand.

Some of the women at work are always bitching about the deductions from our wages, but to tell you the truth, I don't really mind. Like, where is the Government going to get the money for the social welfare entitlements and all the rest of it if it's not from the PAYE worker? From farmers? Give us a break.

We're all socialists until we get a few bob. (Come back to me after I've won the Lotto!) But for the moment anyway, I fervently believe in helping those less fortunate than ourselves – after all, I've been there, done that, got the T-shirt. At the very least, my own deductions are an investment in our future. The old-age pension or invalidity if anything ever happened to me.

The dole is different. I'd die rather than queue up for the dole. As long as there's breath left in my body et cetera. I'd do anything, skivvy in McDonald's, *anything*. We've paid our way since I was able to and we're going to continue to do so.

Like everyone else, though, money into my hand is what I really want.

It was a quarter to ten when I got out of Carthy's and rushed over to the GPO to buy more certs and bonds with the cash. I never had that much cash before, I never *saw* that much cash before. I held on to my handbag for dear life, I can tell you. I still had sixty from my own bits and bobs of wages and from a few spare notes and coins I found in James's room so we were going to be OK. I kept ten back for us to live on until next Friday. So, all in all, I was bringing evidence that I could come up with three thousand four hundred and fifty pounds into the court. I hoped it would be enough.

I was in rag order when I got to the court because I had to run all the way down the Quays to the Four Courts.

The girl wasn't there, thank God, but her mother was. With her pussycat bow under her chin.

No, I have to be fair. The poor woman looked shattered. That's how I knew who she was immediately, that and the way she stared straight ahead the whole time and because she held her handbag upright in her lap, like a headstone. She wore a donkey-brown pull-on hat, the kind you buy for the winter and then don't wear.

She was older than me. A lot older. She was very small, like a little wren, and she had that skin that looks like creased tissue paper. In fact, she looked old enough to be the girl's grandmother. I couldn't look the woman in the eye, of course, but I was sitting at the end of the row in the public gallery and I knew I could see her if I turned my head. There was another woman sitting beside her and you could see that she was with her. I found out later she was from the Rape Crisis Centre. Apparently that's what they do, they always have someone sitting with the victim in the court cases.

It was awful to think of someone being a victim of James. Before I could go too far down that road I blanked out my mind deliberately. I had enough on my plate without feeling sorry for everyone else in the courtroom.

The public gallery is not really a gallery at all. I don't know why they call it that. It's just a row of chairs at the back of the room. And the room is nice, I was surprised. I don't know what I was expecting. Bars and a cage and whips, maybe? Like the zoo? It was actually a bit like the children's court, sort of open plan with light-coloured wood furniture. Quite like those office blocks we clean. Beigey.

At least there were no plants. I always think that poor plants absorb the atmosphere around them. A plant in a courtroom must have a terrible time.

James wasn't anywhere to be seen as the court was called to order. The Devines were never at the top of the queue for anything.

Patrice Murphy takes me outside and asks me have I arranged the bail money. He shakes his head when I show him how much I have, tells me I'll probably have to go into the box to convince the judge. He also tells me her name is Madden. The girl. Rosemary Madden.

It gives me an awful land. Mammy's name was Rose. It's also my middle name, after her.

And that's Mrs Madden inside, he goes, you may have noticed her.

Then he gives me the bad news. Apparently this Rosemary Madden has waived her right to anonymity. It's unusual, he says, highly unusual. He doesn't know what her motivation could be, doesn't want to hazard a guess. He warns me that one of the consequences of this is that sooner or later the papers are going to name James. So we're to brace ourselves.

Has he no idea at all why she's done this?

No, he hasn't. It could be because she's so angry, that very occasionally happens. It could be because she's under pressure from someone else. It could be because she's playing some complicated role within her family. But since we'll probably never know why she's doing this, he says we're not to waste time with wondering, it's not our concern, we've to take care of our own problems, keep our eyes on our own ball. This waiving will have no bearing on the trial. It's the facts and the truth that count inside the courtroom. And we're not to be distracted by the media, they won't be making any decisions, the judge and jury will.

Yeah, sure, I think, but only to myself.

Then he has to race back in for other cases so he can't tell me any more. I follow him in and if I tell you my heart is leaden it's an understatement.

The two of us had to sit there, the girl's mother and I, while the other cases came and went. They were all remand or for mention and they went up and down quickly. I hated to see those boys in their 'good' track suits or their cheap suits. They tried to look so cocky and failed miserably. There's a particular look about being poor, I don't know if you've ever noticed. They're always thin. (But it's not that, I find that the richer people are the thinner they are.) No, the poor have cheekbones like knife handles. They protrude under their eye sockets. It's an absolute mystery to me. The rich have cheekbones, of course, but they're not like knife handles. I wonder if it could be something to do with their teeth?

On the odd occasion when I've ventured into Grafton Street or the Powerscourt Centre, I've used that information to pick out who shouldn't be there. Knowledge like this comes in handy, you know when to watch your handbag.

Anyway, up they came, one after the other, those boys with the knife-handle cheeks and the pimples on the back of their necks. There wasn't one girl or woman up for anything that morning, although if you were to believe the *Evening Herald*, there are women being thrown in jail big-time every day, just for nicking something like a pair of tights.

Mrs Madden didn't move a muscle, as far as I could see.

When he came up at last he looked terrible. I could see he was trying to be calm but he was shaking. And the collar of the new jacket was standing away from the back of his neck like it was too big for him. He looked around for me and when he saw me it was pitiful, the expression on his face. I couldn't help myself, I gave him a little wave. Then I stopped my hand. I didn't want Mrs Madden thinking I was the type of person who didn't care about rape.

Six

Patrice Murphy was right on the button about the bail. Ten thousand. He gets the judge to agree to hear me.

I'm afraid I want to draw a veil over my appearance in the box, it was one of the most humiliating experiences I've ever had and I never, ever want to go through anything like it again. The judge was lovely, but in a way it didn't help. She was quite gentle and said I was obviously a hard-working woman and provided I could guarantee James would fulfil absolutely all the conditions, she would post bail at three thousand pounds and would accept me as sole surety.

I felt like a real charity case, sitting there in the silence while she was scrutinizing my pathetic little bonds and my new receipts. All those eyes. Having to admit in public how poor we were. It was like being naked in the middle of O'Connell Street.

I was still beetroot when I was signing the bail bond. I mean, I never in a million years thought I'd be in a situation where I'd be in a courtroom bailing out someone who was charged with rape. It was dreadful. The registrar was terribly matter-of-fact about it, which helped in one way and in another way made it worse. I mean, did they think we were just common criminals like the rest of the dross that were hanging around that place?

James smiles at me when we get out on to the street. The first real smile I've seen on him for weeks. I get another land because I really see the resemblance in him to Mammy. Really see it as opposed to just half noticing or taking it for granted. She had the loveliest smile and here she is, smiling at me out of James.

I have to harden my heart, though. Don't you smirk at me, I say, we're not going to lower ourselves to talk here in the street but you're coming straight home with me and you're telling me exactly what happened.

He gets stroppy immediately. Tells me to eff off.

I'm outraged. Don't you talk to me like that, I go, and for once, to my surprise, he takes me seriously. Maybe something in him recognized subconsciously that I meant it this time.

Sorry, he says.

Now that was a moment to treasure. The only other time he ever said sorry to me since he came to be a teenager was one night when he was fourteen. I'd been saving up so he could go to the Gaeltacht with the rest of the class and he stole the money out of my drawer and went out and bought a ghetto-blaster. Everyone else had a ghetto-blaster and I suppose he didn't want to be different. I was so shocked when I found out I couldn't even be angry.

I didn't need to be because he got his comeuppance in the end. When the time came, all his pals went off to the Gaeltacht without him and he was miserable for the three weeks. A lot of them got scholarships from Gael Linn. I was working, of course, and I didn't even try for a scholarship for him. That time I thought if you were working you were eligible for nothing.

We get home after the court case and after he tells me his side of the story, I don't know what to believe.

The girl, Rosemary, is a bit older than him, she's just turned twenty and she's doing a bookkeeping course on a FÁS scheme or a Youth Employment or something like that, he doesn't know which kind of scheme it is. They're all hookey, as far as I can see, just a way to keep the unemployment figures down and then you're back to square one. The family's pretty well off. The father's in the printing business and she's the only daughter.

He met her at a club, where else. According to him, she was a goer. They nearly had sex on the very first night. I have to listen to this without saying a word of criticism because who am I to cast the first stone in that regard.

I wait until he pauses for breath. What did he mean 'nearly'.

Nearly, he says, use your imagination.

Where did you do it? I go. I'm trying to strike a balance because being straight up — as if this is the kind of thing we talk about all the time — and showing him that in general casual sex is not on. He's about to tell me to eff off again, I can see it, but he stops himself. And he says, quite humbly, that where they nearly did it was in your man Ferdia's car. The whole gang of fellas were at the club that night, apparently, and two of them clicked and this fella Ferdia lent his car to both of them.

Together? I ask, and I can't help sounding scandalized. Because I am. This is the same Ferdia that wanted to take them all down to a mobile home in Brittas Bay. Over my dead body.

James looks at me as if I'm mental but then he realizes that he's not exactly in a great position to argue with me and he tells me that they took turns.

It's a relief, of sorts. Right, I say. Go on.

Well, according to him, he and Rosemary Madden 'nearly' do it again two more times. Once at a party in a free house, somebody's parents were in Majorca on holidays, then again, the day after another party. In another free house. (There was always someone in the gang whose parents were away, it seems.) The two of then went to the Furry Glen in the Phoenix Park. In broad daylight. He skived off work and she skived off her FÁS course and he took her up there on the bike. That's the time she alleges he raped her.

Now, I'm not stupid. I know about date rape and all the rest of it. The newspapers are full of it and Marian Finucane has it on all the time on the radio and not for a second would I not agree that the woman has every right to say no. Every right.

Why did she think he raped her this time? What was different? He just shrugs. I dunno, he goes. Beats me. I didn't even come.

I nearly die. Don't be so vulgar, I say. And it's not good enough just to say you don't know. What do you mean you don't know? She didn't just make it up out of thin air. Or did she?

As far as he's concerned she did.

But what about her statement? According to Patrice Murphy, her statement is totally detailed.

That's nothing to do with me, he goes. I know what happened. When they wanted me to sign a statement saying I did it—

Don't you sign *anything*, I yell at him. Look what happened to the Birmingham Six.

After I calm down I try again. There must be something to it, I say to him. You must have done *something* to her. Otherwise why would she complain—

He's definite he did nothing to her he didn't do before. Only a bit more so.

Well, for instance, did she say no? At any stage?

He can't remember. But as far as he was concerned she was definitely as willing as he was. I can feel his temper starting to go – Look, he says, we didn't do it properly – we've never done it properly.

I keep cool. Was there a tiff? He shrugs again. Nothing more than the usual.

What does the usual mean –

You know, he says, the usual. A bit of slagging. Sniping at each other, nothing serious.

Could he elaborate, please? It was nothing serious, nothing – he's getting angry now – nothing, all right?

And no matter how I cajole, I can't get any more out of him. As far as he's concerned everything was hunky-dory that day. Apparently he thought they were in love and he thought she thought so too. After the alleged rape, they came back from the Furry Glen on the bike and he left her off near her house in Drumcondra and he went back to work. End of story. And as far as he was concerned, she was probably still a virgin.

Well, I'm on dangerous territory here and I don't want to go much further into this. I mean, what am I supposed to ask him next? How did he know she was still a virgin if he says they never did it? Maybe he used a magnifying glass?

Then I think I see another avenue of enquiry opening up. If everything was so great then why was he going round with a face on him like the back of a bus for the last couple of weeks?

He has an answer for that. She wouldn't see him any more after that day and he couldn't understand it. When he went to meet her at their usual place the following weekend he waited for three-quarters of an hour before he realized he'd been stood up. He tried to ring her a few times but she wouldn't come to the phone.

His last try – even though he would have been livid if any of his mates had seen him – came when he brought a presentation-size box of Cadbury's Roses up to her house. But when he knocked on her door, the mother answered it and said none of them wanted to see him around their house ever again. And then she closed the door in his face.

Did she slam it?

No. He looks surprised. She just closed it.

I'm thinking now maybe I should go and see her. Maybe we could sort this out, woman to woman.

But Patrice Murphy, when I ring him to ask him about it, thinks that would be an awful idea. He tells me not to go near her.

Still, I don't know. Sometimes a personal approach isn't such a bad idea.

James goes out after our so-called chat and I pull out the bed-settee for a bit of a nap. I'm wrecked. No sleep the night before, as I told you, and all the drama of the morning. I bring *Macbeth* into bed with me because I have a class that night – it's the last time we're going to do *Macbeth*. After tonight we're going to concentrate on the texts for the exam itself. But Mr Elliott wants us to be so familiar with *Macbeth* that, no matter what comes up about *Hamlet*, we'll be able to show off a bit in the paper, compare and contrast.

I can't concentrate, though. We're supposed to be studying the really famous bit in the play, the bit where she's wringing her hands and thinks she can't get the blood off them. But when I crack open the book, absolutely by chance, I find myself looking at the part, right after the murder of Duncan, when Macbeth is on about never sleeping again.

I find that a lot. I'll be thinking about something and then it happens. Patsy says that everyone is psychic although they don't know it. It's only when you give in to it that you notice all the strange things that happen. I've long been enamoured of pathetic fallacy, it's my favourite device of the English language. But it's not just a device, that's what's so brilliant. If you're watching out for pathetic fallacy in real life you'll notice that it really does happen. For instance it usually rains when I have my period. At least one of the days. (And no smart remarks, please, about this being Ireland where every day would be a lovely day if it would stop raining.) *Macbeth* is *full* of pathetic fallacy. Maybe that's what I love about it.

It also has a terrific story, like *Pulp Fiction*. I got the video of it out once, although when I got home I discovered it wasn't the play at all but the opera. Opera! But I'd paid good money for it so I watched it anyway. There were subtitles in English and I could follow it and guess what – the story was the exact same as in the play and believe it or not, watching that opera helped me with an essay Mr Elliott had given us to write. It clued me in to the atmosphere of the time, and I got a B. It was the first B I ever got in English and I was dead chuffed. Actually, it was the first B I ever got in anything.

Shakespeare was a genius, there's no doubt about it. 'Sleep that knits up the ravelled sleave of care, The death of each day's life, sore labour's bath, Balm of hurt minds, great nature's second course, Chief nourisher in life's feast'. Who else could come up with all that? I can certainly identify with 'sore labour's bath'. What woman couldn't?

I'm just drifting off to sleep and it comes to me. Maybe

the Rape Crisis Centre can help us too. After all, it's a rape crisis for us as well. Patsy did a sponsored parachute jump for them and she must know someone.

Well, maybe not. They're pretty implacable about rapists from what I hear.

Anyway, I hadn't made up my mind at that stage whether to tell Patsy or not. We tell each other a lot but not everything. Like, I have the feeling that although she goes on about how lucky she is, everything isn't all rosy in her garden. And James says he saw her husband one night in one of his clubs.

I was dreading the *Herald* that evening. I didn't normally get it on a Monday but of course I had to that day. I was praying they wouldn't use our name.

You know the way when you sleep in the afternoon sometimes you have really bright, weird dreams. That day I dreamt about Tom Bennett. After all those years. You would have thought, with all the trouble we were in, I would have dreamt about courts or jails or something like that but no.

He was a golden lion in the dream and I was there in the dream with him but I was invisible. Nothing much happened. He was just there, sitting on the grass, and I was just there, watching him, I could see him but he couldn't see me. Nevertheless it was still very vivid. I suppose the lion bit was because we met at the zoo.

Tom turned out to be an orphan.

I couldn't believe it when he told me. He left it right until the last minute. What last minute, last millisecond! We were all set, or so I thought, to go up to meet this supposed huge family of his in Finglas. I'd washed my hair until it hurt and I was wearing one of Mammy's linen dresses. She had two linen dresses that she must have brought with her from Birr, Co. Offaly, when she came to Dublin. They were always hung up, even when we'd no wardrobes. I only saw her wearing one of them once, for my Confirmation.

I was the exact same size as her when I was nineteen so both of them fitted me. They were perfect too – linen lasts for ever. And they were shirtwaisters so they never went out of fashion. I wore the blue one. I'd ironed it very carefully but of course I knew it would be creased again in ten minutes – that's the trouble with linen. Still, it's very classy.

You'd think blue only goes with blue eyes. But oddly enough, it really suits me. I'm one of those peculiar people with dark brown eyes which you don't normally get with fair hair, which, by the way, was long at the time. For that day, I let it stay loose. I thought I looked good, although I do say so myself. Or at least the best I could look.

James too. I'd scrubbed and polished him to within an inch of his poor little life, God love him. I was damned if I was going to let Mrs Bennett, who'd reared so many of them, think I couldn't take care of a baby properly.

It took us all morning to get ready. And that was getting up at half seven. More fool me.

He whistled at me when he saw me. I could see he really meant it, too. That shirtwaister did suit me, I have to admit, because I was quite slim. I still am but I was really slim then. And I was taller than Mammy so the dress wasn't too long on me. In fact, it was just above my knees, just right. And I wore my good sandals.

Are we right, he says, very jovially. I must say you look terrific. He goes to put his arm around me but I scream at him not to touch me or he'll crease the linen.

I have butterflies in my tummy. You'd think I was going to see the Pope. (Not that I give a damn about the

Pope. I'd like to see him manage to live in Dublin on our
income. What I earn wouldn't keep him in tassels for his
throne.)

I pick up James and put him in his buggy. I've washed
the upholstery of that too. Last night, so it would be
dry.

I wheel James out on to our balcony and turned
around expectantly so that Tom Bennett can help me
carry the buggy down the steps to the yard. I freeze.
He's not coming after me. He's still standing at the door.
His face is crumpled up like an old orange.

I'd better come back inside. He has something to tell
me.

Somehow we managed to get through that first week
James was on bail. I leave it to you to imagine what his
mood was like. Reluctant to go to work, that kind of
thing.

At least I had the usual routines to distract me. The
cleaning, a couple of night classes for the Leaving – it was
such a relief not to have to show up for the Irish, it
clashed with *ER* anyway – the deli on Saturday morning.

The hardest was on the Sunday. PA System had a gig,
in a pub in Rathmines. I had to act my head off. Our next
remand was on the Monday morning and of course I was
going to run into Mrs Madden again. And that's all that I
could think of even while we were singing.

By the way, all the time was I growing up I thought the
southside was posh. Not any more. Not if you've played
some of the pub venues we've played. The rugby crowd
is by far the worst. I believe rugby is a working-class
game in other countries (and in Limerick) and it's only
here and across the water that it's upper class. I'm not
surprised. We do everything baw-ways here. And how-

ever they behave during the matches, they certainly
lower the tone here with their working-class manners
when they've had a few scoops. Give me soccer any day.
Or even GAA, God love them, although I've heard that
the prostitutes around Fitzwilliam Square say that their
best business comes with the All-Ireland Gaelic football
finals. Must be the excitement of all those country
bachelors coming up to the Big Smoke!

The pub is already raucous when we get to it and
we're completely ignored for our first set. Come on
now, everyone, Patsy starts to yell at them, this is
supposed to be a singalong, you're all supposed to be
singing with us. Otherwise we might as well just go
home—

Big roars from the floor. None of it printable.

You have to hand it to Patsy, she rolls with it. What's
that? Keep 'er going, Patsy? We have a comedian in our
midst, do we? There's always one – oh, very droll. How
long did it take you to dream up that one, Einstein?

She rolls her eyes at me, then, now, come on, fellas,
give us a break. Everybody ready? You ready, Angela?
Dha-dhah! All together now – one two three – Keep
Your Mind On Your Driving Keep Your Hand On The
Wheel – And Keep Your Snoopy Eyes On The Road
Ahead—

I'm singing away but my brain is clicking like an
abacus. It's desperate having to pretend that I'm having a
great time. I'm really glad it's a church wedding next
weekend and not another gig like this. Right now, I hate
showbiz with a passion. I know Patsy sees right through
me. She's keeps looking at me, she's probably wondering
what's wrong. I still haven't made up my mind whether
to tell her . . . Kissin' And A Huggin' With Fred. Up a
dupp a-dum. Dee do dee dum dum, dee do dee dum
dum, dee do dee dum dum *dum*.

At least they listened that time. They're even applauding – wonders will never cease . . .

We go through the routine and get mercifully near the end. They're getting drunker by the minute. Here goes Patsy again, she's really very good at this crowd-control lark. Some of you down the back there a bit fragile from last night, eh? Or are yiz practising for tonight? Poor babies, eh, Angela? Now, let's hear you on this one. Clean out the sinuses. Right up your street, boys – and girls! One two three – *and* . . .

Two Little Boys Had Two Little Toys . . . Both Had A Wooden Horse . . . Daily They Played Each Summer's Day . . .

Poor Patsy, she's been carrying me through the whole of this gig. I can't stave her off for ever. I'll have to tell her sometime.

I like the harmonies on this. Did You Think I Would Leave You Dying, When There's Room On My Horse For Two . . . Please, Sacred Heart, be kind tomorrow at the remand. Let the *Evening Herald* not be there . . .

That was great. They're great, aren't they, Ange?

They sure are, Patsy. They were great.

Nearly there. We can go home soon.

Now, ladies and gentlemen, this next one is our penultimate song – that's the second last for those of you who don't have the Irish! But seriously, folks, we were only joking when we were giving out to you – you've been a lovely crowd. And at this point we're going to slow things down a bit. We're going to give you something from our native Irish culture. The old ones are the best, eh? And for this we need a bit of hush.

O Danny Boy, The Pipes The Pipes Are Calling . . .

*

The remand hearing next morning. She's there again, Mrs Madden. Still not looking at me although she'd want to be incredibly thick not to know who I am. She knows all right. I know she knows by the way she keeps staring straight ahead. From the minute I come into the room to the minute I leave.

I can't stick it. I make up my mind. I have to go and see her.

→ Seven ←

He was moping around in his cacks, looking at the *Big Breakfast*, when I got home from the job on the second Tuesday. So far he'd got away with being late for work on the Mondays by saying he had appointment in an outpatients' clinic.

When I had a go at him he got defensive immediately, said he couldn't face it. I bawled him out of it, told him he'd be sacked. All right, so it was only an old courier job but it was me had to go guarantor for the loan on that bike. Anyway, I told him, going to work would keep his mind off his troubles.

After I calmed down we both had a bit of breakfast.

We'd also got away with it so far where publicity was concerned. For some reason the papers weren't showing any interest in the case. Maybe rape is just ordinary now, what with all the crime against the elderly and child abuse and murders and all the rest of it. Or maybe his rape, on the scale of things, wasn't too bad when you consider the horrific injuries some poor girls have to contend with.

When we were on our second cup of tea, I told him what I was going to do and asked for the Maddens' address.

Well, he went ballistic. No way was I going to go up

there, no way. He started to throw things. It's what he does, he has a terrible temper. (But at least he always throws inanimate things if that's the right word. No one ever gets hurt. He wouldn't hurt a fly, you know, that's why this thing is so absurd. That's why I think that if I go and see Mrs Madden we'll be able to sort this thing out between us.)

Of all the boys in the world, James a rapist?

I remember when he was little, from six on, he was besotted with wildlife. We had quite a decent telly, the good old Vincent again, and he absolutely loved all those Richard Attenborough programmes. I was delighted with him. I mean, other kids were into nothing but *Star Trek* and *Neighbours* or cop programmes and the more violent the better, but the worst punishment I could ever threaten on James was not to let him watch his nature programmes. He still watches them, even in preference sometimes to his MTV. He always said that when he grew up he wanted to be a vet. Some hope he had, with the points you'd need from the Leaving. Even if we'd any chance of him staying on at school to do the damned Leaving.

I never discouraged him though. I thought it showed high aspirations. And anyway, who knows, I thought at that stage, maybe by the time he was leaving school the points would have come down and you wouldn't need to have been a farmer's son and to have gone to Rockwell or Clongowes or somewhere.

I did try to get him into Belvedere, they had a scholarship scheme for poor kids, but he didn't do well enough in the entrance exam. It's just around the corner. When he didn't get it I told myself I was just as glad, Belvedere is a rugby school and you know what I think of the rugby heads, but I was only fooling myself. I would have given my eye teeth to have got him in there. The

Jesuits give a great education but more than that, they operate a brilliant old boys' network. I'd say if you did a survey, you'd find very few Belvedere boys in the ranks of the unemployed. It would have been really handy too, he could have walked.

I wouldn't allow him to have pets when he was a kid, and I'm sorry now. At the time I thought I'd enough to mind, without a load of animals around the place. Mind you, he took no notice of me, all the time bringing home mongrel dogs and bloody kittens and I was all the time ringing up the cruelty people to come and get them and then there'd be murder. He'd swear he hated me and he'd never speak to me again as long as he lived.

Once it was a hamster. He said he swapped it for a Hallowe'en mask. I gave in and let him keep it but it died. Died of love, I'd say. He stuffed it with food and never let it get a minute's respite. Played with it every blessed waking minute.

Now, does that sound like a rapist?

He wouldn't give me the address so I had to go to a pub to look it up in a telephone directory. It wasn't hard, they were in under Madden Colour Printers. I knew from what the solicitor had told me that they ran the business from behind their house.

I know Drumcondra a bit, it's not that far and Patsy and I have done gigs at the Regency Hotel and another pub up there near where the Lemon's factory used to be on the river. I'm not old enough to remember Lemon's factory but I do remember the sweets. Mammy loved the soft chewy fruit ones, especially the lime. Her teeth weren't great towards the end and I suppose she had a bad taste in her mouth from the drugs. The lime taste probably cut through it. I think now that she might have been HIV but this was back in the time when it wasn't heard of.

It's one of the things I keep meaning to do. I'd like to have a long chat with a doctor sometime, describe the way she was. Because I've seen a few documentaries about HIV and you'd think they were talking about Mammy. When did that HIV come in to Ireland?

She was only barely alive when I met Tom Bennett that day in the zoo. Maybe that's why I latched on to him so quickly.

Of course, I see now I'd been living in cloud cuckoo land where Tom Bennett was concerned. It did occur to me right at the beginning how peculiar it was that a fella coming from a magic family like his would have any time at all for people like us. But then I've told you I was naïve. And when Mammy died soon after I met him and when Tom found out about her and about James and didn't do a runner, I thought our luck had just turned. Simple as that.

I just stare at him when he tells me he's an orphan.

It takes me a minute. You mean there's no family? (I know I sound stupid. How can you have a family if you're an orphan?)

He shakes his head. Mumbles something. He looks ashamed, I give him that.

I look out over the yard. The concrete tubs are still there but as for the wallflowers . . . History. And someone's tastefully redecorated the tarmac with a few broken bottles. Devine's variation of pathetic fallacy. Never lets me down.

I go to wheel the buggy inside again and Tom steps out of my way. Poor James. All that scrubbing for nothing. He's looking at me – James, I mean, not Tom – like I'm off my rocker. I thought we were going out, his eyes go at me above his soother. He's too surprised to cry.

Right, I go, closing the door. What gives? I'm not yelling, not shouting. Calm as a nun.

It turns out he didn't think a girl, I quote, as good-looking unquote, as me, would go with an orphan. He was brought up in an orphanage and he thought there was a stigma attached to that. So he reinvented *The Waltons*.

Stigma? Jesus, had he taken a look around our place lately?

No relatives at all?

None that he's aware of, anyway, although he does admit that it stands to reason there must be someone he could trace if he put his mind to it. Like he knows he didn't arrive on this earth like a dalek. Even Superman had a family, according to the film. The Brothers were my family, Tom goes, as though saying it is like saying you're an alcoholic.

Now I've heard what went on in those orphanages run by the religious orders. They were brutal, in every sense of the word. So immediately I'm beginning to see the other side of it and I can't stay mad at him.

Was he traumatized? I'm already picturing him in little short pants with his poor little legs black and blue from all the beatings the children were supposed to get in those places for the slightest thing. And crying for his Mammy in his bed that night and being afraid to wet his bed in case he'll get another beating.

Before Tom can answer, James throws his soother on the ground, in protest I suppose, and starts yelling and I have to deal with him. Sit down and we'll talk about it, I go to Tom, while I'm unpeeling James's outer layer. Ah, what the hell, I'm thinking to myself, we have each other. Or so I think that day. Lord, when they made me they threw away the mould.

Drumcondra's not a bad little place although it's always stuffed with traffic going to the airport and beyond to

Belfast – my bus was crawling. I've never been to Belfast, not yet anyway. I was going to go during the ceasefire and Patsy was dead keen to go up to see President Clinton when he lit the Christmas tree up there but I couldn't go that day. So I went to see President Clinton in College Green in Dublin the following day. It was freezing.

She was lovely, I thought, no matter what the papers say about her being a bossy-boots. Why wouldn't she be bossy, what man ever got anywhere without a good, bossy woman, eh? She looked as if she was feeling the cold too, although, thanks be to God, the sun shone the whole time. It's a pity they didn't bring Chelsea. I always feel sorry for that poor kid. Did you ever, in all your twist, see such horrific train tracks? And she has such a little mouth. But I believe the tide is turning for her now.

Do you know what I heard from one of the women in work? That there are actually orthodontists in America making a *fortune* out of putting braces on kids' teeth *for show only*! Would you believe that? They're real braces all right, but they're not tightened because the kids don't need their teeth straightened one iota. They're put on just to be a status symbol.

Clinton was grand, quite handsome and much taller than I'd imagined – but I'd put a question mark over his hair. And he has this sort of smile where you wouldn't know whether he's going to cry or not. Patsy thinks it's an act, I'm not so sure. I was only a few yards away from him and I watched him very closely and I really believe he was sincere in what he said.

Not that he said all that much but I suppose he can't, with the delicacy of the situation in the North. We didn't care anyway, me and the thousands of others who turned out to make eejits of ourselves waving the little plastic American flags his secret-service people gave out. He could have recited Mary Had a Little Lamb and we would have cheered him every bit as lustily. Dubliners always give visitors a great welcome. We take things personally, I think, we feel responsible for people having a good time and bringing home a good report about us.

By the end of it even those secret-service guys were smiling at us. And I hear they thought the Dublin crowd was the best of any foreign crowd he ever addressed – or so the papers said. Our own papers anyhow, I didn't read any of the rest.

President Kennedy certainly thought the Irish were the best. It's hard to believe that I was alive when he was here. That's always heartrending in the old programmes to see him telling us at Shannon that he'll be back to see us in the springtime. And waving. When now we all know when we watch it that he's standing there and he's only a few months left to live. And he's looking as though he hasn't a care in the world. Hasn't a clue about what's in store for him.

Another great occasion, apparently, was when the Pope said Mass in the Phoenix Park. I say apparently, because I wasn't there. I wouldn't bother my barney going up there to see him. He's sincere enough, I suppose, but I don't approve of his views on contraception.

Abortion is a different matter. I'd never have an abortion for myself – it's very hard to imagine how you could, once you've known what a baby really is. It'd be different if you'd never had one, I'd imagine.

I have known a fair few who've taken the boat to England, God love them. Some of them not a million miles away from work. We have a tea-break every morning and that's when the truth comes out. I think it's to do with the oceans of shiny floor all around us and us huddled in the middle like castaways with our teabags and our kettle. It makes you feel intimate.

I don't know what Patsy's views are on abortion. It's one of those things you don't really talk about with your friends, only your acquaintances.

I couldn't believe it when Patsy showed up at Mammy's funeral after us not seeing one another for nearly nine years, not since First Class. It was a pretty sad day, of course, mourners pretty thin on the ground and the church was huge. It looked like Croke Park on the day of a GAA camogie final. Patsy and I went to a camogie final once because she had a friend who played for Kilkenny so that's how I can make the comparison.

Hurling is a good game but there's something really weird about camogie. I know they put their hearts and souls into it, just the same as the men, but when you hear the thin, high-pitched shouting from the bare sidelines, it doesn't seem to match up. Does that make sense?

At the funeral the four of us girls – James was being minded – were sort of huddled together in the front row of the church with the director from the Eastern Health Board. The nuns were spread out in the row just behind us, God bless them, and behind them again a few of the social workers and the foster families who had some of their friends and relations with them. To give them moral support, I suppose. None of her so-called boy-friends showed up. Not one.

Nor was there a single relative of Mammy's, although the notices were in the papers. I'd been half hoping but I wasn't surprised.

To be fair, a good few of the neighbours did come along. I was pretty bitter about a lot of them at the time, God forgive me, particularly the vigilante types, and I remarked to my own social worker that they'd probably

come to make sure she was really dead. Or to drive a
stake through her heart.

I'm not bitter any more, by the way. I can now see
their point. I'd nearly join the Concerned Parents myself
now if I thought James was in serious danger, and I
totally agree that pushers' lives should be made as
difficult as possible.

> **Devine, Rose Alice**, late of Dublin
> and Birr, Co. Offaly. After a short
> illness, bravely borne, in the loving
> care of the sisters and staff of
> Our Lady's Hospice. Sadly missed
> by her five sorrowing children,
> Angela, Francesca, Justine, Nicola
> and James, and a wide circle of
> friends. At Rest.

There's a lot of emotion in death notices, isn't there?
Bravery, love, sadness, sorrow, all in a couple of lines. It
was the head nun at the Hospice who suggested putting
'At Rest' at the end of Mammy's death notice, and I
thought it was lovely. I still have the cutting. I keep it
under 'D' in my *Concise Oxford Dictionary* because it's the
book I use most and I like to be reminded of her.

None of the others wanted to but I insisted on going to
the Hospice to see her before they put the lid on the
coffin. I was glad I did. She did look 'At Rest'. They'd
done her hair and put make-up and blusher on her so her
cheeks looked quite healthy. And although she was
terribly thin, the white shroud they put on her plumped
her out a bit, even though you could see the bones at her
hips. Up to then, I always 'saw' a shroud like a kind of
flour bag. It's not, it's more like a loose dress. It was
ladylike and I think that's why it suited her so well.
Mammy'd always been a lady.

She'll be praying for you now, the nun held her hand.

She looks like an angel, doesn't she and that's how you'll think of her now.

I closed my eyes and tried to picture Mammy in heaven, smiling and laughing with joy and greeting all the other angels. I asked the nun could I be alone with her for a few minutes.

When the nun was gone I opened my eyes again and whispered Starlight Starbright into Mammy's ear, and then I kissed her on the forehead, the way she used to kiss me. She was cold and smooth but I really do think she was 'At Rest'. I could feel it from her.

I didn't see Patsy at the funeral until we were all outside and waiting for the hearse to move off. I hate that bit at funerals, no one seems to know what to say to the bereaved and they all talk to one another very loudly about the races and the weather or it won't be long until Christmas. Anything at all except what they're thinking about, like, thank God it's not me this time or, I wonder who's next. The forecourt of the church was absolutely enormous, like the tarmac in front of an airport where they park the planes, and it looked even bigger that day with the tiny little crowd in the middle of it clustered around the hearse. I got angry on Mammy's behalf. I didn't want people thinking that the death notice was a lie, that she didn't have a wide circle of friends.

Since she never practised her own religion I had decided that we wouldn't bother trying to get the Protestants interested in her at this stage and I had her brought to our local Catholic church. The Vincent and the social workers helped with this and I have to say that the priest who said the Mass that day was very nice. I wouldn't have any readings or anything like that, I don't like hypocrisy, but he asked me a few things about her so he could include them in his sermon.

Some of it worked, some of it didn't. I wasn't all that

keen on his enthusiasm about God showing that he loved Mammy very specially because he gave her so much suffering to bear, and how she was very lucky to be now enjoying her extra special reward. But he meant well. The best bit was him talking about her gentleness, and about how her children loved her. That was certainly the truest thing anyone ever said about anyone.

When I saw Patsy, I went over to her and shook her hand. I know it's usually the other way around but she was sort of hanging back and I suppose I was being a bit belligerent on Mammy's behalf. I was certainly not going to show anyone I was ashamed of the smallness of the crowd.

She had her mother with her and that was a bit of a shock. I remembered her as a dowdy little woman with a hairnet and here she was with streaks and a miniskirt and black opaque tights. Like a model, well, a small model. It was weird, I can tell you, when I thought of the way Mammy was just before she died because they had to have been within a few years of one another in age.

Although, as I told you, Mammy was only thirty-eight, she looked about sixty. It was the bad teeth, I suppose, and the way her hair had got so thin. She smoked a lot too and that gives you dreadful lines.

I thought you wouldn't know me, Patsy says.

She was older, of course, we all were, but I would have recognized those eyes and that hair anywhere. She still wore it long. She was already in fifth year in secondary school, just a year before the Leaving Cert. She was always brainy. But at least I was still as tall as her. That was something. And I wasn't ashamed of my clothes either. New everything. My social worker had come up trumps.

The hearse was moving off and we had to go. Sorry,

Patsy, I said to her, but thanks for coming, I really appreciate it. I did too. She promised to stay in touch but I thought to myself, That's the end of it. You know the way people just say these things.

But to my astonishment, Mammy wasn't gone three days when there was a knock on the door and there stood Patsy. I said I'd come, she goes, handing me a bunch of flowers.

Now this happens to be the first bunch of flowers I've ever got in my life. They're pink carnations, the kind you see everywhere nowadays outside newsagents' shops but, that time, you'd have had to go to a flower shop or to Moore Street.

I'm overwhelmed. Thanks a million, I say, come on in.

The place is a mess, because I'm in the middle of giving it a good cleaning. James is asleep for his nap so we have a bit of time.

There'd been nearly a problem with leaving just me and James in the flat, it was supposed to be for a much bigger family, but thank God they didn't insist on us moving out straight away. My social worker was able to argue that it would have been too disruptive for me and James to have to leave what had been our family home. And at that time she thought it was a good idea to have the access visits there. Big mistake. I'll tell you why later.

Sorry about the mess, I say to Patsy, as I pick up the scrubbing brush and the basin, don't fall, will you, it's very slippy . . .

We smile at each other and she sits down, and honest to God it was like we'd seen each other only yesterday. I place the flowers in a jug of water and make her a cup of tea and we sit down and have a right old natter. And that's the start of it. Friends again for ever. Or so I thought.

On the way up to the Maddens in Drumcondra, I think to myself that I will be able to tell Patsy about James. She'd be better hearing it from me, anyway, rather than from some other source, like the newspapers. It's just that I find it very hard to admit it to anyone at all.

→ Eight ←

They lived in a nice place, the Maddens. It was end-of-terrace, on a corner, with a lovely glassed-in balcony over the front door, probably coming out from the master bedroom. I love sun porches and balconies. All that light.

I was quaking and it took me ages to get up the courage to open the gate. If they'd been looking out, which they weren't, they'd have probably had me sussed as a suspicious character — although there was a bus stop in front of them and I'd spent ages pretending I was waiting for a bus while I spied out the territory, so to speak.

They had a side entrance, probably for the business. Their front door was shiny green, the brasses done to a T. The knocker was one of those fancy ones, like a lion's head, and the car in their driveway was a '94 Toyota Corolla with the plastic still on the seats even though we were nearly half-way through 1996. There wasn't a single daisy on their lawn. But a black mark was, she had put plastic flowers in the window of the sitting-room. They weren't even the good silk ones that you'd have to go really close to know. You could tell a mile away.

Plastic flowers get on my wick. I take after Mammy, she always thought they were common and I agree with her.

You get used to making judgements about people when you're a professional cleaner and I instantly put the Maddens down as the houseproud but fussy type. I'd already pigeonholed Mrs Madden as maybe a bit timid, judging by her hat she'd worn both times at the court, so she probably wouldn't have been the one to decide about the plastic flowers. He couldn't stand pollen and falling petals and all the rest of it, so he laid down the law and she wouldn't stand up to him. I could have been wrong but why else would she put plastic flowers in the window of such a nice, well-cared-for house?

I have to knock a second time. My hand is shaking, and I hold the lion's head with only the tips of two fingers. You'd be afraid to mark the shininess of it.

Oh Jesus oh God. She opens the door herself. The girl. Rosemary.

It has to be her because she's the only daughter. I know that from James.

Words fail me. E-excuse me, I blubber, but it comes out really high, like a squeak, and then I come to a complete stop. She's pretty, in a prim sort of way, short dark hair in an elfin cut, good little figure, with a peachy-coloured blouse belted inside her jeans. She wasn't wearing any shoes and her toenails were freshly painted. A nice pale colour.

Yes? she goes, half surprised, half impatient. Can I help you?

I don't blame her for being brusque. Opening the door to a complete stranger who's squealing like a stuck pig. I'm – I'm sorry, I go, I was expecting someone else.

She stares at me, frowning. Who are you?

Nobody. I'm nobody. I back off. Sorry to bother you. It's the wrong house.

She steps a bit out into the porch. They have these little evergreen bushes stuck in tubs on either side of the door. Phoney, too, although I have to admit that with these you'd have to be right up against them to know. Which I was, of course.

Who are you? she goes again. And she's staring at me now, really staring. Piercing.

I'm sorry, I go, and I flee down the driveway, just managing not to run. I don't dare to look back but I'm absolutely sure she's watching me. I bet she knows now exactly who I am. I've blown it.

What an idiot. What a complete and utter prat. I can't believe I've made such a fool of myself. I think I see everyone in the road, every single blessed person, busmen, milkmen, oul' ones walking their dogs, looking at me and jeering. I think I see a huge big finger pointing at me from the sky. Look, everyone, look at Angela Devine, the bloody eejit.

Talking about being an eejit, it was I broke off the engagement with Tom Bennett.

And I didn't even have to, that was the really stupid part. He was definitely in love with me, I can see that now. And he was a decent bloke, he really was.

For years I'd considered, on and off, looking him up, just out of curiosity, to find out what happened to him. Then, the minute I'd think of it, I'd lose heart. Where to start? Like, we had no mutual friends. I had no friends anyway, except Patsy, of course, and she was busy at the time with her Leaving Cert and then her job and her own fella, and when we met for a jar or something I didn't want any man tagging along. You can't talk properly when there are fellas there, can you?

Anyway, I hate that group thing or even couples thing. You know, let's all do this or that and aren't we having fun, when you're really gritting your teeth because you can't stand at least fifty per cent of the people you're supposed to be having fun with. Maybe I'm eccentric but

I really only enjoy people one at a time. How can you sincerely talk otherwise?

So during the whole time Tom Bennett and I saw each other, the guts of a year and a half, we were very private. He didn't seem to mind and we didn't seem to need anyone else.

I suppose I could trace his present whereabouts through his orphanage or through the Salvation Army. But he's probably married with a squad of kids. He always said he wanted kids. You can see why. Remember, we're talking here about someone who invented the Finglas Waltons. The last thing he'd need is someone from his past landing in on top of them all. Especially someone who'd jilted him.

What happened was he came home drunk. We weren't exactly living together — you couldn't, the welfare officers have eyes in the back of their heads and I wasn't going to jeopardize my entitlements. And of course there were those so-called good neighbours of ours who'd have been only too delighted to spill the beans. (Although, to be fair, some of them were very good during Mammy's last illness, I have to say that for them. That's Irish people for you. They're the best in the world when you're down. They love you then.)

He used to sneak in after dark and stay some of the night and then sneak out again. It was quite hard to do, it was at the time when the vigilante movements against the pushers were just beginning, nothing as organized as the Concerned Parents or COCAD but pretty effective all the same. They were watching the courtyard and the landings like hawks but luckily our place was at the end of a row, near the entrance to the whole complex. And instead of going down the steps into the yard, Tom Bennett was able to drop soundlessly over the balcony and scarper before anyone knew what was happening.

The first time he came in drunk I was shocked, completely shocked. He never drank much, or so I'd thought. I was nearly too shocked to give out to him but I did, naturally. I had to let him know it wasn't on.

And of course the next morning he couldn't remember a word of what I'd said so I might as well have saved my breath. He was dying, vomiting, the whole works. And naturally full of remorse. He told me what had happened. Apparently that Jason and that Sharon were getting married. (Shotgun, of course.) He'd been at Jason's stag.

Why didn't you tell me? I go. I'd have been prepared.

I didn't want you to worry and I didn't think it'd get out of hand the way it did, he's really humble, and as contrite as Peter after the Agony in the Garden. I keep silent, let him grovel. I mean, I've seen enough at this stage of my life to know what drink does to families. There is no way, *no way*, I'm going to let any fiancé of mine behave like that. And once you start down that slippery slope you're gone. It's only a short step to beatings.

He's sitting there with his head in his hands and he can't even touch the cup of tea in front of him and I'm looking at him, at the tousled top of his head – his hair had grown a lot and he had a pony tail now – and, of course, I start feeling sorry for him. I put my arms around him and he immediately snuggles in tight and says sorry, Ange, sorry, sorry, sorry. He'll never do it again. It's a once-off.

Not even at any other stags?

Definitely not.

Even your own?

Definitely. Definitely. It's finished. No more drink. Cidona from now on.

Strangely enough, we had sex then. It wasn't great, naturally – the smell off of him would knock down an elephant at twenty paces – but he was very tender and loving and I suppose it gave me a certain satisfaction to be forgiving.

That happened to be one of the access days. The five of us saw each other every fortnight. The social workers would collect the other three from their foster homes – Justine and Nicola were together in Darndale but Francesca was in Stillorgan on the southside. They couldn't get anyone on the northside to take her at the time they all went into care and she settled in well so they didn't want to move her when a place became available near the other two. Her foster parents were even considering adopting her.

It was a bit of a disaster, though, in one way, because she was going to a school in Stillorgan and she had this accent. In fact, there was no getting away from it, she was a snob and she was always fighting with the rest of us as though we weren't good enough for her. (Remember I told you about her kicking up stink when she was brought back to the flat? Well, that's why. We weren't good enough for her any more.)

The social workers were aware of the problem, I have to say that for them, but I could also see that they were on the horns of a dilemma. They were worried about how we were developing as a unit, with her being ashamed of us and being grudging about participating in the access visits, but although their priority is always to keep natural families together as much as possible they could see she was incredibly happy with her foster family and they didn't want to ruin that.

Anyway, we had to meet for access and she'd no option about it. I'd organize James and the whole five of us would do something with one of the social workers, like on a fine day go to Stephen's Green to feed the ducks and then we'd have chips afterwards. God love the social workers, they probably drew straws. We were some handful.

Wet days were miserable. We usually hung around in some place like the lobby of the Gresham Hotel or the Royal Dublin, trying to make our Cokes last until it was time for the chips. We'd very little to talk about, to tell you the truth, and Justine and Nicola were always ganging up on Francesca because of the snobby way she treated them, so the social worker and I spent half the time trying to keep the peace. James inevitably got bored and cranky. None of us wanted to talk about Mammy even though the social workers were always bringing up the subject to try and lead us into it.

A great time was had by all, I don't think.

After the sex that day, I left Tom Bennett in bed with his hangover while I got up to get James ready. He said he'd sleep it off and we'd go out to Howth or some place when I got back. It did occur to me that lately he seemed to have no qualms about missing work. This wasn't the first day he'd spent in our place when he was supposed to be at Cadbury's. But I reckoned I'd done enough giving out for one day and he was so miserable, even despite the sex, that I didn't want to kick him when he was down.

The third time he came in drunk, that was the end.

I forgave him the second time – that was someone at work's twenty-first, he said – but I told him that second time if he ever came in again like that it would be the end. (And that second time there was no sex, although he tried. I wouldn't have it.)

The odd thing is you'd think he would stay away, wouldn't you? I wouldn't have known anything about it then. It was like he *wanted* to be caught. So when the third time happened, I had to keep my word. I'd said it would be the end and it had to be. It was the hardest thing I'd ever had to do in my life up to then.

I had to think not only of myself but of James. He was still only a baby. I couldn't expose him to someone untrustworthy for all of his little life, he'd enough strikes against him as it was.

And once you're married, you're married. That's my philosophy. The divorce legislation that's going through now, I'm not so sure about it. I know all about personal freedom and civil rights but I voted no.

I'm half sorry now, though. If it was held again I'd probably vote yes. I can't stand it that I've cast my lot in with the kind of people who challenged the result of the referendum in the courts. All right, it was a terribly close result, but in my opinion the yes people won fair and square and I hate sore losers. I don't want anyone to think I'm one of them. The majority is the majority, even if it's only one person. That's democracy and if you don't like it you go and live in China.

It was certainly not for religious reasons that I voted no, I don't even go to Mass. I voted that way because I thought that William Binchy had a good argument about changing the nature of marriage – that if you get married in a 'divorce jurisdiction' you're not entering a permanent bond at all.

We had a lecture once at one of the missions in school from a Jesuit. (He was one of the reasons I wanted to send James to Belvedere because he was very impressive.) The lecture was about moral dilemmas now that we were approaching womanhood. One of the things he said always stuck in my mind. It was about mental reservations. According to the Church, you're entitled to say anything you like, even if it's not true, and provided you make a mental reservation at the time it's not a lie. Suppose you're apprehended in Dunne's and you're accused of shoplifting a pair of tights. You can look the dick straight in the eye and say, 'I didn't steal a

⇥ Nine ⇤

G uess what? Our luck changed!
Five hundred pounds!

I couldn't believe it. I bought the scratch card when I got the *Herald*. I try to limit myself to two a week, usually on either a Monday or a Tuesday and then again on a Thursday or Friday. For one thing it makes the week go by a bit faster, but for another I deliberately buy them on the days that there's no Lotto draw. I have a feeling that to buy them on the days of the draws would be greedy. Tempting fate.

And I wouldn't mind but I wasn't even thinking about fate or luck, because this Monday was the fourth remand – Patrice Murphy's told us it's going to be a long haul until the trial because of the book of evidence, the backlog, all that – and I was too worried about what I'd find when I opened the paper. (I can't understand how the papers haven't copped us yet. Or maybe it's one of those things where you think the entire world revolves around you, and what's happening is that your story is not half as important as you think. If that's the case, lucky us and thank God there's so much going on in the world and in the courts to distract them.) I still haven't got up the courage to tell Patsy.

I was thinking so much about all of this, I forgot to

scratch the card until after tea. Just think! It had been sitting there in my bag the whole time with its lovely secret message.

After I scratched – the third five hundred came out only on the very last panel – it was like when something is lost or stolen and you don't believe it. You keep going back and back to the empty space as though it'll be miraculously there again. Well, it was the same with that card. Every time I'd go back to the table where I'd left it I'd be half afraid to look in case I hadn't read it right – that one of the five hundreds was really a five thousand or a fifty, or that the whole card would be just plain gone. No. There it was every time.

I mean, with all my jobs, even if we had gigs every single Sunday plus a wedding on a Saturday, I wouldn't make that much in six weeks. More than a whole month's wages, a month and a half's wages, just for a pound.

The danger is, of course, that you'll go out again straight away and buy a hundred more.

Immediately, though, I began to see the downside. Typical.

Was that it, the apogee of it? Was that the best it was going to be, ever? So now I'd never get to spin the wheel for the quarter of a million on *Winning Streak*? Only a measly five hundred in the whole of a lifetime?

I couldn't believe how ridiculous I was being, looking a gift horse in the mouth like this. Five minutes ago I had a couple of quid in my purse. Now I have five hundred and I'm miserable? Get a grip, Ange . . .

That five hundred is only the first instalment. *Winning Streak*, here we come!

That win gave me shivers up my spine for another reason too. When I was a child, about seven or eight, I think – Francesca was already out in Stillorgan and

Mammy was pregnant with Justine – didn't she win five hundred pounds on the Golden Goose. That was a competition that you entered when you bought your groceries. It made hardly any difference to us as it happened, because one of the boyfriends, I can't remember which, took it off of her to 'mind it' for her. Mind it, my eye. All we got out of it was a new Hoover (when she was well she was a demon for cleaning) which, in due course, made the trip down to my uncle's in Marlborough Street. But she was so excited about it for the short while she had it. I still remember the evening the man from the Golden Goose shop came to tell us.

We could be a lucky family, you know . . . I don't think it's a coincidence that we both won *exactly* five hundred. There's more going on here than coincidence. Do you think it was an accident that I won five hundred when that was the *exact* amount I was in hock for? (Plus interest but that wouldn't be all that much since the stuff had been in only a few weeks.) I rest my case.

So the five hundred thing is serendipity in our family. That's a favourite word of Pat Kenny's on his radio show. I was delighted when I heard him use it the first time because it's one of my favourites, too. It has a wonderful fairy ring to it, you can almost see its little wings beating with delight. It was a word I originally learnt from Mammy. She didn't have a great vocabulary, now, not brilliant, but certainly streets ahead of the people in the flats. She encouraged me.

I associate the word serendipity with forget-me-nots, I'm not quite sure why, other than that the sounds are quite similar, light. Maybe it's because forget-me-nots were her favourite flowers, they're country flowers. She had a tablecloth, hand-embroidered with them, and she kept it until the very, very last. Maybe she explained serendipity to me when the tablecloth was on display and that's why I make the association but, unfortunately, I can't remember. With the exception of her jewellery and her christening spoon, it was the last of her good things to go and I think this was what finally broke her heart.

So was I to use the five hundred to get her stuff back out of hock or not? I couldn't make up my mind. On the one hand it was her precious jewellery and winning the exact money seemed like a message that I should. On the other hand, we could have done with a few little things around the house and I knew she would want me to have the place nice.

Or was I meant to use it to help James? Sort of a fighting fund, like all the unions have. I decided to sleep on it.

I didn't tell him although I was bursting to. It didn't seem right to be so joyful when he was in such awful trouble.

I couldn't keep it to myself, though, so I went out to ring Patsy to tell her but she was out. Her youngest, Darren, answered the phone. He's a bit of a pup, but I'd never say that to her. He never says hello on the telephone, just yes, or what do you want, or who's that. If we had a telephone, my fella'd know his telephone manners, I'm telling you.

At least I had an English class that night so I didn't have to sit in all night, hugging the great news to myself like a security blanket. My insides felt like a swelling air bubble that I was afraid would pop so I just had to tell someone. I told Mr Elliott while I was helping him distribute the sheets of notes. He's very good that way, he writes out commentaries and notes for us and makes enough copies to go round.

Congratulations, he goes, that's great. It seemed mechanical, though, like saying happy birthday to someone else's friend. So it kind of deflated me. Here was I thinking it was the best thing that ever happened to me, the first rung on the stairway to heaven, and all he can say is congratulations, that's great, in the same tone of voice as if I'd gone back to Unislim and had lost a couple of pounds.

I was determined, though, not to let the lovely feelings go. All through the class I sat there and daydreamed. Suppose I went for the option of keeping the money and not redeeming the jewellery . . . Another part of my brain would kick in then – *tut, tut!* I knew how Christ felt in the desert. Get thee behind me, Satan.

I've always wanted a decent hearthrug for in front the fireplace, Reddy's idea of good taste is a half-moon rug with a cat on it in that kind of fluffy synthetic bathroom-mat material.

A Black and Decker, definitely. Hammer action so you can drill through walls. It would give me a great feeling of independence. And maybe a little tumble drier. I hate hanging out washing, and a tumble drier would be just the height of luxury. Although I've heard they use an awful lot of electricity.

If I did keep it, I should give something to Concern, God love those poor people out in the Third World. Or to Sister Stan for the homeless. I like Trust too, I saw Alice Leahy once on a chat show, and she struck me as doing the most charitable work of all. I mean, could you do the things she does for those poor old men? Like cutting their toenails and treating their poor scabby scalps? Ugh!

I got a great insight into being homeless the night I had to sleep rough down at the Irish Life Centre. Please God neither of us will ever, *ever* have to go through that. I couldn't bear to think of James sleeping rough. It's hard to describe how you feel. Lonely, of course, that goes without saying, but it's a special kind of loneliness. Like you don't belong to anyone and no one belongs to you and you're floating away from the world into some terribly cold, disconnected place and no one would ever come to look for you. That's very scary.

Thank God I had to go through it only that one night. Despite being so worried about what was going on back at the flats, the most irrelevant pictures kept waltzing into my mind. Her special toothbrush that she got from the dental hospital so she wouldn't hurt her gums. The half tin of yellow paint she got from a neighbour to do up the door again where one of the boyfriends had kicked it.

It's funny what adds up to a home, isn't it?

Talking about lonely, I bet Lady Macbeth must have been one of the loneliest people on the planet. I know she was a bad egg but I still felt sorry for her. I mean, deep down, I'd say she only wanted the best for her man and it just all got out of control.

Mr Elliott is getting us to act out bits of both plays to make them come alive for us and to help us remember them. I'm always petrified he'll ask me. He never has, yet, so no doubt my number will be up soon. It must have been terrible for the poor children long ago who had to learn every single famous speech in the plays off by heart for the exams and then get slapped if they didn't know it. What am I talking about, sure didn't it happen to me when I was doing the Inter. I was an execrable pupil, I freely admit that. But I didn't deserve to be slapped. Nobody did.

Thank God the education system is a lot more enlightened now. James doesn't know what it's like to be afraid of a teacher. And if one of them had once lifted a finger to him I'd have been on top of him like a ton of bricks.

Mr Elliott keeps hammering into our heads that we should be able to quote verbatim a few key speeches but nowadays, he says, the examiners go for the sense and the context and the analysis more than the actual words of the play or the poem. All the others in the class ooh and aah over the big, grand speeches, but for entertainment I go for the offbeat bits, like in *Macbeth* when Ross comes in with the Old Man.

> *Threescore and ten I can remember well;*
> *Within the volume of which time I have seen*
> *Hours dreadful and things strange; but this sore night*
> *Hath trifled former knowings.*

Can't you just see them? Nothing's changed in four hundred years, has it? I hear them every day over there on the benches in Mountjoy Park across the road. Coats on and collars turned up even though the sun might be splitting the stones. Giving out the pay about the youth of today and the Government and the price of a pint. Keeping the footballs or the basketballs that roll over towards them from the playground, just out of badness. Falling over each other with horror stories. Everything's always dire, according to them, God love them, with their waddly, ancient Jack Russells on ratty-looking leads that must be as old as the flood. I wonder do they start with big dogs and then move downwards as they get older . . .

We've a mixed bag in our class, including a woman of seventy-four who has three great-grandchildren. There's a carpenter, Ken, who is very nice, I've struck up quite a friendship with him. A rock musician (at least, he says he's a rock musician, I have my doubts) and a couple of other men in cardigans who sit at the back looking furtive. I wouldn't blame them, it's nearly all women and the majority seem to be housewives. We're all doing it to better ourselves. Some of them even say they're going to go on for a degree.

I don't think I will. At least here we're all in the same boat. We missed out first time round and we feel sympathetic towards one another.

But maybe that's not strictly true. I think it's a bit of a waiting and watching game so far and I think I can see the beginnings of rivalry in a couple of the women. In my experience, women are desperately competitive, far more so than men. And very much so with each other. Men seem to be invisible when women are competing for whatever's going. It's like the Tour de France. The women are the peloton always and they let the men off in front while they watch each other. Amn't I very knowledgeable, now, about the cycling? (You have to admit that peloton sounds much better than 'the main bunch'! Everyone in Ireland is able to toss off those cycling terms since Stephen Roche's three great victories in 1987. Not many little countries can boast the Tour de France, the World Championship *and* the Giro d'Italia all in the same year – eh?)

That was a great year. Will you ever forget Stephen coming down the Champs Elysées with his hands in the air and Charlie Haughey up there on the platform to meet him. Leave it to Charlie. I like him. I think deep down, all Dubs do think he was the best Taoiseach we ever had. You wouldn't be ashamed of him, like, in foreign company. He knows about wines and he can talk about the French Revolution with the best of them.

So far there have been no As at all in the class. And, so far at least, I didn't detect any change in any of them towards me after my B. I suppose it was such a rare bird – because I get mostly Cs and Ds – that no one felt threatened. But I'm watching and waiting. In a university it must be much worse. I think I'd feel like a fish out of water. We'll see. Maybe I'll feel more positive about it when (and if) I get the Leaving. Sometime in the next millennium!

At one stage I did have great hopes of James going to university. Wouldn't Mammy have been proud then, and it would certainly have been one in the eye for the folks down in Birr. Her revenge. I knew it was out of the question for him to be a vet, but maybe zoology or agriculture, something that would really interest him. I could just see him as a student. I see them streeling around town all the time, with their black clothes and their clumpy Docs. They're endearing, in a way, they always look as though they're going on a mission of deadly importance. I suppose at that age everything is important. I don't remember much of that myself, my entire energy was consumed by just looking after James and minding the two of us.

He's very down in himself at the moment. And, to tell you the truth, I can't think of a single thing to say to cheer him up. The solicitor's too busy for me to be bothering him but I must say I think free legal aid is a wonderful invention. I don't know what we'd do without it and I can't think what the poor people must have had to go through in the old days.

The day I went to Drumcondra, which would be a couple of weeks ago now, he questioned me when I got back to make sure I hadn't. I lied. I told him I'd changed my mind. I'd calmed down enough by the time I got home to able to make it convincing.

Her face haunts me.

I can't sleep that night after I've seen her, my imagination is running away with me. I keep seeing him and her together in the Furry Glen. Did she scream? Did he hit her? I can't stand it any longer.

It's about three o'clock in the morning and I hear him

still mooching about in the bedroom, even with all the staying in bed he's not a great sleeper at night, particularly recently.

I go in. Did she scream?

What are you talking about?

You know what I'm talking about. Did she scream?

Shut up. Get out of my room.

I won't get out of your room until you tell me what happened that night. You owe me that much, I'm in hock for you—

I didn't ask you to go in hock for me – all you think about is money—

Tell me what happened or I'll—

Or you'll what?

We glare at each other. He always gets me that way. He knows damn well I won't throw him out. Tough love, they call it. I'm not sure I could ever face tough love. I love him too much. And each other is all we have.

But this time I'm not going to go meekly. There's a lot at stake here, I have to try to understand. I sit down on his bed. I'm not going until you talk to me properly.

It's three o'clock in the bloody morning, he goes. Exactly, I say back to him. So you can see how serious I am.

We start a silence match. He sits down too, he has an old car seat he found in a skip somewhere up on the North Circular Road. One thing about these old houses that people like Reddy have converted, there's plenty of space for you to spread out. He puts on his Walkman and all I hear is the g-dhunk g-dhunk from the little earphones. He'll deafen himself but they all do it. I'm getting irritated although I'm not going to show him that. I'm trying to demonstrate that on this one I'm impervious. So I just sit there, like Mount Rushmore.

His walls are decorated with posters I wouldn't be

caught dead looking at, Black Grape and Oasis, his Kung Fu stuff and Eddie Irvine. He's mad into racing cars. And The Cure and Megadeth, although up to recently I thought The Cure was yesterday's news. Apparently not. Apparently they're making a comeback and they're even coming to Dublin.

The silence match stretches on. He's not going to open his mouth and I'm not going to leave this room until he does.

I stare at those posters as though I'm in a museum. They all come to Dublin now, from Springsteen to Take That and Tina Turner. Even Pavarotti and Placido Domingo and Barry Manilow. Dublin's huge on the international circuit.

They all love coming here because of how warm we are as an audience. I heard Garth Brooks couldn't *believe* that everyone in the audience knew the words of every one of his songs, even the new ones on his new album that was only just being released. I've never been to see any of them myself but I'll tell you one thing, if Barbra Streisand ever comes I'll hock more than my possessions to be in the front row. Although I believe I'll be killed in the homosexual rush. I don't care who else likes her or who doesn't, as far as I'm concerned she's fabulous. I went to see *The Way We Were* three times. Cried buckets. *The Owl and the Pussycat* twice. And don't talk to me about *Funny Girl*. She can do anything, sing, act, direct, anything. (I didn't go to *Yentl* out of loyalty.)

The minutes tick by, as they say – although he has no clock in his room.

I'm starting to shiver, because I've only my nightdress on. He's grand, of course, because he sleeps in his clothes. I hate that, I've tried to teach him to be hygienic at all costs but since he was about sixteen, I've been wasting my breath. If he's tired, he just gets into bed and pulls the duvet up over his ears and that's the end of it. I suppose I should be grateful he takes off his boots.

So you're not going to tell me? The shivering is getting to me.

Of course he doesn't react. His head is bopping to the g-dhunk g-dhunk, and he has his eyes closed like he was receiving the stigmata. So I go over and lift one of the earphones and I bawl at him, Turn that damn thing off. He gets such a fright he actually does.

Right, I go. I'm too cold and tired now to pursue this tonight but I'm warning you, I want to know what went on and that's the end of it. So don't think you can weasel out of it. I march out of the room.

When I'm back in the bed-settee the doubts start to creep in. Am I just being a voyeur? But her face is there every time I close my eyes. I won't lower myself to ask did she lead him on. Sex is a very complicated matter.

→ Ten ←

Less than two weeks to the Leaving. Yet I'm glad PA System has that wedding on Sunday. I don't think I could stick hanging around the house. His mood becomes very black on Sundays, which, of course, is understandable since he has to face the remands on the Mondays.

I suppose you're surprised I can even *think* of something as ordinary as the Leaving or gigs. To tell the truth, I'm so uptight I've amazed myself that I'm able to concentrate on the books at all – but I am. The human mind never ceases to astonish me.

You can't be wound up to high doh all the time, can you? I don't think your brain would take it. (When I was a child I never associated high doh with singing, I always pictured it as *dough*. Bread dough. I could never understand why everyone thought 'being up to High Dough' was so awful.)

Weddings with us – it's a straight cash deal, nice and clean. We charge eighty quid for the church, forty each. Handy money for an hour's work. It's word-of-mouth and we have a fair reputation now. The only drawback about them, when you compare them to pub gigs, is that you have to dress as if you're a guest and that's a bit of a pain. But we're in the background – we don't do the afters because they usually want to dance and anyway those afters get pretty messy with drink — so we don't have to put on too much of the ritz.

Actually, it's as easy as pie, we have the songs down. Pie Jesu. Panis Angelicus. From A Distance. Barcarolle sometimes, if the priest doesn't object. And usually the happy couple wants something that means something to them. Once we were asked to do King Of The Road because the groom was a truck driver but the priest drew the line there.

The classroom that Thursday was hot, and I don't mean just because of all the tension. It was real summer heat — I started this summer thinking we were going to have fabulous weather all season long.

I got a bit dreamy, to tell you the truth. I love the way the setting sun lights up the top panes of the glass in these windows so it doesn't even look like glass, more like delicate polished copper. They're sash windows. Georgian. I think I've already told you that this is one advantage we have, living in Dublin. Our Georgian heritage. There is a Georgian Society in Dublin, very active. They advise you how to go about restoring your house. In different circumstances, if I owned our couple of rooms, I'd certainly be a member, although I don't know if they'd have me. You might have to own a whole house. But there's a lovely plaster ceiling rose in James's bedroom and some of the coving in the living room is intact. It's carved in that classical shape, I think it might be Greek, you know, sort of like continuous open swastikas. It'd be nice to know what to do with it to stop it flaking off on to your shoulders so anyone who spends any time in our place looks like they have a bad case of dandruff. I'd even paint it myself if I knew what were the correct colours.

But with Reddy, you might as well be talking to the wall. The fanlight over the front door has had two bits of cardboard in it covering the broken glass since we moved in and that was nearly ten years ago. If he won't even fix that there wouldn't be much hope of him fiddling around with bits of plaster. There's new legislation now, which I think will force him to upgrade the place. He has to register as a landlord with the Government, I think, and they send inspectors. The sooner the better. I'll give them an earful, I will.

All the houses around our square are Georgian, even Discount Electrical. I don't know for sure but they probably have a preservation order on them so that's why Discount Electrical and DID can't put up huge horrible signs.

Proper order, too. To appreciate why, you'd need to see our square on a very early summer morning. Sometimes I try to go out there a few minutes before the minibus calls to collect me for work, just to look at it with all the litter cleaned away. The Corporation is good like that, they're up at the crack of dawn with their sweepers and their little pushcarts. I certainly appreciate them anyway, one professional to another!

Those mornings, you just wouldn't believe the peace and the beauty. Especially if it's a sunny day. No people, no cars. The blackbirds singing their hearts out, the dew on the trees glistening like marcasite. In those early summer mornings it's easy to imagine the people who lived in this square before us. I don't mean this century but years before, when the dresses were huge and made of fabric like cambric or sprigged muslin and everyone wore corsets and they had people handing them down from horse carriages at our front door. I'd have loved that (except for all the manure, of course, but then you'd have servants to clean up that). And strolling in the park with your gentleman friend. Totally safe. That was the time when there were no gurriers, only urchins.

This classroom we're sitting in was probably part of the drawing room in this place. It's an awful pity to see the plywood partitions cutting up all the lovely rooms and the folding doors permanently sealed up. But no blame for the partitions and so on to the people who run this school. They're just entrepreneurs, good entrepreneurs.

In my opinion it's well worth what they charge. I know you can do your Leaving Cert in the state VECs for half nothing but here they get terrific teachers who deserve every penny they make. I'm all for entrepreneurs being rewarded, provided they don't earn it by doing something hookey.

I'm not sure these people even own this building.

Oh, God, he's looking at me. Look away, Ange, don't catch his eye. Anyway, with only two weeks to go we should be concentrating on our notes, not still acting out the bloody thing.

Angela, did you hear me? Are you with us at all this evening?

Sorry, Mr Elliott.

Would you read Ophelia's speech for us. I don't know how you've escaped so far – Ken, you're Hamlet, Mrs B, you be the Gentlewoman. Yes, come on, stand up, the three of you. Start with you, Hamlet—

I go beetroot. *Beetroot*. But I have to stand up.

I'm quite taken aback when Ken starts. God, he's actually quite good. And I never noticed before that he has such a nice voice.

Your woman's useless, but! I wonder does Ken sing— Angela?

Sorry, sorry, Mr Elliott, I'm nervous, I got a bit distracted.

Try to concentrate, Angela! Please?

Can we start from the beginning again?

No. Start where you come in.

I start. And do you know what? After I get over the initial embarrassment, I find I quite enjoy reading in public. Maybe I'm a secret exhibitionist! I can tell everyone's listening . . .

And Ken is looking over at me, quite surprised too. Bet he didn't think old mousy-boots had it in her . . .

That was very good, Angela, Mr Elliott says, when I come to the end of the speech – you were all very good. Now, ladies and gentlemen, who can tell me why Hamlet reacts the way he does to Ophelia – yes, Dwayne?

I don't listen to Dwayne, I bet Dwayne isn't his real name at all. Rock star, my foot!

I wish we could do it again, dammit, I'd certainly do it much better second time around. Now I'm quite sorry this is the last time we'll be formally acting out the play. *Hamlet* isn't nearly as good as *Macbeth*, though – it's like they're all behind a set of net curtains in that palace.

Poor old Lady Macbeth, what an end. I wonder if she really went to hell? I'm terrified of fire. Don't laugh but until I went to my first cremation I had this incredible vision of what it was. Hell had nothing on it and I was petrified at the thought of going up to Glasnevin to attend it. It was the mother of one of the women at work who was for the flames. I thought that you'd see the remains being taken out of the coffin and shovelled into the fire and the poor face being consumed, the hair on fire and so on. I couldn't sleep a wink the night before.

No hell any more, or so they say. Hell is other people now. I can relate to that, you'd want to walk down O'Connell Street sometimes late on a Saturday night and see what's going on there. It's like one of those intense films from South America you get late night on Channel Four. I wouldn't walk there at times like that, certainly not without James to accompany me. It's a whole other world. Menacing. Not something you could put your finger on, it's just to do with the way the gangs and crowds of young people hang around together and look at you. (And remember where I came from! If they make me afraid, what would it be like to be someone from the suburbs or the country.)

And the things you read these days about poor inoffensive shop assistants being terrorized with syringes full of HIV and gougers beating up old people in rural Ireland and throwing them down wells and shovelling a load of sand on top of them.

Still, I suppose it's not quite as bad as some other parts of the world, or so we're told anyway.

So was there a cut-off point at some stage where those who were infallibly sent to hell were just unfortunate to be born during the time that hell existed? I don't believe a word of Papal Infallibility. Never did. As soon as it was explained to me at school I knew it was a lie. Probably to stop people asking awkward questions. Put your hand down, Angela Devine, you just have to believe it, it's an article of faith. They always said that if you pursued them. Or, You're not supposed to understand it, it's a mystery. That was a great one.

Don't ask me how I knew about infallibility, I just knew. I mean, if the Pope is infallible he's God, isn't he? Isn't it only God who's perfect? (I know the old argument about them being only infallible when they're speaking *ex cathedra*, but it seems to me they insist on being infallible all the time if you challenge anything they say.)

The last time I prayed, really prayed, was the night I sent Tom Bennett packing. I don't know what I was praying for. I meant it when I banished him and I was certainly not going to renege but I was sick to my stomach. I didn't regret it exactly, it was more like, *what have you done?* It was the exact opposite of the giant air bubble feeling after I won the five hundred pounds on the scratch card. This was like my whole body was a crater as big as Australia.

I'm ashamed to say I prayed like a baby, to Saint Jude, would you believe, although up to then he never did anything for me. He's the patron of hopeless cases. I was a hopeless case, all right. I'd made the decision and I had to stick with it but you wouldn't know by my behaviour that night, blubbering and carrying on.

He's pretty far gone when he comes to the door, swaying on his feet and bouncing off the uprights when I open up to his knock. I take one look at him and order him out. What? His eyes are bleary. He's blinking very, very slowly.

You heard me, I go, out. And this is the end of it, we're finished. I warned you and I meant it.

What?

He can't understand words of one syllable. He's bobbing in the doorway there like he's in one of those baby bouncers. I'm so angry that at this stage there isn't a chance I'll weaken. Although he does look pretty pathetic with his mouth hanging open and drool running down his chin. His fly is open too. You'd never think by looking at him that he's usually a sharp dresser. I give him a little shove and he looks shocked. What? he goes again.

Have you a one-word vocabulary or what? I say. I want to shout, the noise is forcing its way up my throat, but I don't want to wake James. You and I are no longer engaged, I go as calmly as I can. It is over. Capeesh?

Well eff off, so, he says it quite quietly and he's still looking surprised. He backs off and I close the door and that's that.

It doesn't really dawn on me what's happened until

about twenty minutes later and that's when I begin to cry. And then the praying starts. Like I've been brainwashed from a baby. Cry – pray – cry – pray. Or like a spy, who has this 'pray' microchip buried in her which is only activated by tears.

Stupid. Because I don't believe people should pray for things in a fair-weather way. It's like being married, you're in it for better for worse, for richer for poorer, not just for worse or for poorer, which was the way I seemed to be acting. In the club or out of it. And I was out. I couldn't cherrypick just because I needed it.

Lately, though, I find myself envying people who can get comfort from religion. I see them hurrying into Gardiner Street church just down the road from here, that's a Jesuit place, and when they're going in, they look as though they feel, well, here's at least one place where we really belong.

On the other hand, if it was really a religion the way Jesus Christ founded it, wouldn't one of the local clergy have called around to James and me to ask if there was any way he could be of assistance? Isn't that what they're supposed to do – after all, we are parishioners even if we are lapsed. They're not supposed to make judgements, are they? They're supposed to rush to help souls in trouble, no matter how sinful.

And don't tell me they don't know. Of course they know. They bloody know everything. In the olden days how come they seemed to know girls were pregnant nearly before they knew it themselves.

The tension of this thing is obviously getting to me. The last thing James and I need at this moment in time is a Jesuit on the doorstep.

It's eating me up, the thought of him raping a girl in the Furry Glen. If it was really rape, of course.

I wish I'd already told Patsy, then I'd have someone to

discuss it with. I've tried to analyse why I haven't told her, she is my best friend after all and I see her regularly. Something's stopping me.

There's something on her mind too and I bet it's Martin. She rarely mentions him voluntarily these days. When I ask her how he is, or how he's doing, she becomes animated. Jaunty. Everything's always hunky-dory.

Too hunky-dory.

He's got the prize for selling the most cars for two months in a row, the partnership (he's in with another fella in a fast-food place somewhere on the South Circular Road) is going a bomb, he's had this great idea where he and another pal are going to start importing some bits of a computer which are terribly expensive in Ireland. They'll do it through the North, all above board and legal, pay all the import duties and they'll still make a fortune.

If it's true that he's doing so well, I sometimes wonder why she does the gigs and the weddings. Forty pounds, even into her hand, shouldn't make that much difference to her. I did ask her once but she dismissed it airily. It's her fun money, she says.

Somehow that doesn't wash with me. You just know by the way she's talking that there's something going on underneath. And then there's the constant moan about the children being at such an expensive stage.

Yet I don't want to pry into her business. If she wants to tell me, she'll tell me. Like me. If I really wanted to tell her I'd tell her.

In a funny way, I think what's holding me back is that I've been confiding all my troubles in her for years now and she's never confided any back. Not real ones. She appears to go tit-for-tat, telling me when her kids fail their Christmas exams or whatever.

But I know she has real troubles, she has to, everyone has. So we've become unequal. If I tell her about James, that will tip the balance. We'll be so unequal then as to be out of sight of one another. And I don't want to be unequal to anyone, even my best friend. It's a conundrum, I know, but it's what I feel. And the older I get the more I trust my feelings. She'll probably be hurt if she finds it out from the papers before I tell her but that's a bridge I'll have to cross when I come to it.

To give her her due, she was thrilled for me about the scratch card. Genuinely. And she's going, oh, Angela, you should take a holiday. We should both go, we'll go to Minorca, Martin has a contact in a travel agency, he'll get us a discount.

Of course, then I was up against another conundrum. I couldn't tell her about my problem as to whether to use the money to redeem Mammy's stuff because she'd want to know why I hocked it in the first place.

What about James, I say to her, I can't leave him. Pish tosh, she says back, what age is that boy? You're going to have to cut those apron strings sooner or later.

She hasn't a clue. It's all right for her, with her nice family with a mammy and a daddy and a real semi-detached house on the Navan Road.

I mumble something and she lets it be but she warns me it's only for now. She's going to insist that I knock some enjoyment out of my winnings because we'll all be dead long enough.

I hated not telling her the truth. We were losing intimacy.

Anyway, I didn't have the money yet. Would you believe, two weeks on and I still hadn't brought in the scratch card to the GPO to cash it in. I sort of felt that when I did that the die was cast. It's like cutting a round birthday cake with flawless royal icing as white as diamonds. As soon as you make the first cut with the knife it's ruined and you'll never get that perfection back. That scratch card with those three beautiful five hundreds was perfect the way it was. I loved it. If I was to give it over to get the money, it wouldn't be perfect any more, even if they gave me lovely new crisp notes.

Because then I'd be up against all the decisions. In a funny way, as long as that card was there, uncashed, I saw it as sort of protecting me from my problems. A talisman. Every time I looked at it, it grew into my chest like a warm ball of wool.

Crazy, really, when you think of it, because every week that went by the interest was mounting up at the pawnbroker's.

All right, I say to James, when I get home from the class, we still haven't got a trial date and you still haven't told me.

He goes to leave the room but I block his bedroom door. Please, James, I'm standing by you. You see I am. Why don't you trust me?

That does it. He bursts into tears.

Oh, God, when I think of it the tears come back into my own eyes. I mean, he acts so tough. And here he is, crying like he's four and the playground bully has just thumped him. He's heartbroken.

What can I do. I stand there. I want to throw my arms around him and squeeze all the tears out of him and take them into myself for him. But I can't. He's too big for that, he'd die. I'd give anything in the world, everything I owned, to make it all go away but I can't do that either. So I just wait. Don't cry, I go, don't cry, James. And I'm still having a desperate job trying to keep from crying myself. He's saying something through the crying, how did I get into this mess, but he's saying it with his mouth open wide, so it's hard to understand. How did I get into this mess, how, how, how.

It'll be all right, I go, it'll be right, James. Sit down and we'll talk about it, we'll talk about our strategy.

He's snivelling and naturally he doesn't have a tissue so I go to get some. Luckily I've just done the shopping so we have a whole box. I hand him a wad of them. Here you go, come on now, blow your nose. It's going to be all right.

He takes the tissues and blows and then there's another storm of crying and then it dies away.

Would you like a cup of tea? I go. And a chocolate Kimberley? I'd splashed out a bit that week, what with the five hundred snug in its hidey-hole down by the side of the bed-settee.

He nods miserably.

I go to make the tea and take a bit of time about it to let him compose himself and when I come back he's sitting just staring at the floor. But at least he's calm again. Because it's midsummer, there's still light in the sky even though it's well after half past ten. And our windows are so huge we haven't had to turn on the lights yet. He's sitting in shadow, with his face turned to the outside world, like a silhouette against the brightness. As you've probably gathered, the backs of their necks always gets to me. I don't know why. It always looks so tender and vulnerable on boys. Not exactly weak but naked. Like it's been made ready for the guillotine.

Which James's was in a way.

He hasn't had a haircut for a good while (thank God, because he favours the skinhead look, number-one blade) and a bit of his hair is flopping down over his forehead like a kid's. Hair grows a lot faster in summer.

He takes the tea and the Kimberley but he's afraid to

look up at me. I know him so well I can tell. I wait again while he unwraps the biscuit and takes the first bite. And then the first slug of tea.

Tell me about it now, I say.

→ Eleven ←

The following night, I went back to Patsy's house for a cup of coffee after one of the gigs. A huge twenty-first birthday bash. I was surprised when she told me about the booking. I wouldn't have thought our kind of music would have been suitable. But apparently the father had heard us during some Sunday-morning pub gig when he was in curing a hangover from the night before. Probably he was in the doghouse and we were handy. You know, sort of as a peace-offering to the wife – look, I do care, I've made these arrangements . . .

It turned out to be a very rich family from Castle-knock. And I needn't have worried about how our music was going to be received, they had *two* marquees, one for the birthday girl and her pals, one for themselves and the parents and their own friends. We were in theirs. Imagine! A garden big enough to take two marquees with enough space between them so the loudness of the disco didn't interfere with us. Caterers. Professional barmen, balloons, flowers, even special buses for after the party so people could drink themselves silly and not be caught driving by the Guards. All for a twenty-one-year-old!

And the presents! None of your travelling alarm clocks or your cheapo cassette tapes from O'Connell Bridge.

Real gold jewellery, vouchers for a hundred pounds from Brown Thomas, stuff for the girl's pony. There was a special table for the presents in the hallway of the house and I sneaked a look.

We don't know the half of the money in this country.

But they still only paid us the going rate. Ah well, that's how they keep it, I suppose.

When we let ourselves in Patsy's house was quiet and dark. I'm usually tired and looking for my bed on Friday nights after the week – and I had the Saturday job to think about – but you do get fired up after singing, so when she suggested going back to her place I agreed right away. Her mother was staying with her for a few days and I didn't want to run into her because the tension between her and Patsy is terrible. But I figured it was late enough for her to be in bed and I was right.

Would you prefer a drink? Patsy asks, as she switches on the lights in the kitchen. No thanks, I go, coffee will be fine. Then I ooh and aah over her new kitchen. They had it done by a designer from one of those places that specializes in kitchens and bathrooms and this is the first time I've seen it. It's gorgeous, all pine, with dark red tiles on the wall and a white tiled floor. Two sinks, all the appliances built in.

She has one of those new tumble driers where you don't have to put a hole in the wall, it condenses the steam and puts it in a bottle. It's been on the tip of my tongue for weeks to ask her about her old one – don't get me wrong, I'd buy it from her – but I don't want to put her under any obligation. She might have given it away to a charity and then she'd feel awful about not thinking of me. My plan is to find an excuse at some stage to go into their garage. It might be stored there – and then I could bring up the subject by-the-way. Do you really like the kitchen? she asks.

It's beautiful, I say, and I'm being sincere. It's like something out of a magazine.

She doesn't seem to care one way or the other what I think about the kitchen. She seems distracted as she measures coffee beans into a grinder and plugs in the coffeemaker. You'd think you were in a restaurant.

Neither of us says anything as we wait for the coffee to be ready. She stares at the machine and I'm so tired I just sit there at the table drinking in the peace. The sound of the percolator plunking away to itself is soothing.

We're sipping the stuff, still saying nothing, when suddenly, without warning, the tears start to slide down her face.

I'm absolutely poleaxed. I've never, ever seen Patsy crying before, at least not since we hooked up together again after Mammy's funeral. Of course I saw her crying as a child. We were both always crying when we were in Sister Concepta's class. She used to slap us with this leather belt that she kept around her waist with one long end hanging down. I often wondered later on what she thought about when she put it on every morning. I mean, she had to put it on for no other reason but to slap us, it certainly wasn't necessary for keeping up her habit! Was she saying her matins when she fastened it? Did she see us all out on the line and her going down it, slapping us one by one? Did she look forward to it? (I wonder is that the origin of the sayings 'give him a belt' or 'hit her a belt'. I never thought of that before.) She used to shove the tip of her tongue out through her lips as she concentrated on lining up our hands just right for maximum impact.

What's the matter? I go. Please, Patsy, what's the matter? I get up and go around the table and put my arms round her. (It's weird that I was able to do that with her and not with James.) She shakes her head, it seems she can't say anything.

Talk about feeling helpless.

There has to be something the matter, I'm nearly in tears myself, tell me, please. Go on, no matter how bad it is it can't be that bad. I'm thinking cancer. You know the way you do. But she looks fine.

Then I'm thinking, Martin's left her. Is it Martin? I say it very gently, I don't want to make things worse.

It seems I've hit the nail on the head. She has a box of tissues on the counter top near where we're sitting – she has this island unit in the middle of the new kitchen – and she takes a handful and blows her nose. She's nodding while she's blowing and the tears are really pouring now.

Oh, God, another woman, is it?

I think so, she goes, and you can barely hear her.

I wait. These days, I seem to spend half my life waiting. I'm half sorry I didn't accept her offer of a real drink although I've given up drink for the duration. Not that I drink much, hardly at all as a matter of fact, but at the moment it's a combination of wanting to keep a clear head and some sort of instinct that I have to make sacrifices if this thing with James is going to turn out all right. Superstition, I suppose. But it gives me a feeling that I'm doing *something* rather than just hanging around waiting for things to happen to us. One good thing – I'm losing weight. Patsy had remarked on it earlier that evening, looked keenly and then asked if I'd gone back to Unislim on the sly.

The whole thing comes spilling out. She found condoms in the pocket of one of his suits.

I stare at her. I'm on tricky ground here, I don't quite know what their marital arrangements are in that department. Women are funny about sex. They either tell you everything – you should hear some of the stuff that goes on after a few jars at our Christmas party at the cleaning job – or they go all coy. Patsy is somewhere in between. Over the years I've got hints that their sex is pretty volatile, great one time, useless the next, but I never initiate the conversations. I have nothing to offer in return, the Tom Bennett situation is such history now that it's antique and I wouldn't want the confidences to be a one-way street.

It turns out that those condoms are a dead giveaway because she had her tubes tied after Darren.

Now this is the first I've heard of this but I try not to show how surprised I am. She doesn't notice. She's looking into her cup of coffee. She's barely touched it yet. You remember I went off that time for a few days, she says, supposedly to a hotel in the country to learn to play bridge?

I remember, I say. Well, I didn't go to play bridge, she goes, I went to a clinic and had it done.

I see, I say. I'm trying to sound matter-of-fact. Patsy goes to Mass and even confession. Having your tubes tied is definitely out as far as the Catholic Church is concerned, but now is not the time to go into that.

I keep my voice quiet. I'd been wondering about that, I say, because you never seemed to want to play bridge again—

Well, that's when I had it done.

We both sit staring into our coffee.

So did you ask him about the condoms? This is awful. Nobody thanks you for interfering in a marriage. They might be going through just a temporary thing and then she'll be embarrassed that she told me.

She shakes her head.

Why not?

Because there'll be a huge row and he'll leave me. She bursts into tears again, real heavy sobbing.

Through the noise she manages to get a few things out. The main problem seems to be not just Martin leaving, but that if he does she thinks she'll be destitute. That if he skips she won't be able to find him. And as she's told me so often before, the three kids are just coming into the expensive stage. Darren is still only six but Maeve is due to start secondary school in September and Pauline has a Confirmation coming up next year.

I have to be sure. Is that what'd really bother you? I ask when I'm pretty sure she can hear me. The money? Not him leaving?

She puts her hands over her face. I don't know, I don't know.

I think as fast as I can. Now I see why she's doing the gigs. It wasn't just for fun money.

I try to disregard what James told me about seeing Martin in that club. Look, I go, just finding a handful of condoms doesn't mean a damn thing. Maybe he was minding them for a friend who's married and having an affair. Maybe it was for a stag and they were going to play a trick on the fella – had he any stags coming up?

She's just sitting there with her hands over her face and shaking her head and crying and saying, I don't know, all the time.

I have to let her cry. I realize I don't remember seeing his car in the driveway. He drives an Audi, she has a little Toyota Starlet. She was as proud as punch when he got it for her for their anniversary two years ago. (I know all about cars. You couldn't live with James Devine and not know about cars.)

I see another opportunity to get in. Where is he now? I ask.

I don't know, I don't know, she goes, wailing, and then she hushes up, afraid her mother will hear and come down to see what's up. She's beginning to sound like a stuck record.

I realize that's unkind and I try desperately to think of

some positive input. We wear a lot of make-up for the gigs and hers is now all over her face, mascara and kohl spreading black spiderwebs through her blusher. She looks her age too, whatever way the light is shining on her neck you can see those horrible crinkles, like unironed washing. I hated seeing her like that. She's usually so chic. The situation isn't helped by the fact that our working dresses are black — we copied them from the backing singers in *The Commitments*. Black is all right when you're on stage but it's dreadful under fluorescent light.

All right, I go with as much confidence as I can inject into my voice. Let's look at this clearly. What we have here is just a suspicion, isn't that right? This could be just a bad patch. You've no idea that he's playing around. Not really. What we have to decide is whether to face him with it or not. There are pluses and minuses in each way of doing things. You could scare him into sense or you could push him into running, it depends what he's feeling at the moment. He might want to be caught or he might want to be given an excuse to go. And don't forget there might be a perfectly innocent explanation.

But where is he now? she goes. It's two o'clock in the morning and he's not here—

That's a fair point, I have to admit that.

But, I go then, we have to decide what you want and what's the best course to take, taking the kids into account. And the principal thing, if we do find out he's messing, we have to decide how much you can put up with and what you really want deep down in your heart. It's your life, Patsy, you have to think of yourself. This is not a rehearsal.

I'm ashamed of this. This isn't me, it's Gay Byrne on the radio. I'm obviously listening to too much of him. The money factor is not to be discounted, I say quickly, and you know and I know what happens when marriages break up. It's the women and kids that have to take the drop.

Now I don't really believe that, not deep in my heart. What I really believe is that some women – most women actually – are far better at coping than they want men to think. But Patsy's in no condition to go into the niceties and I know that this is probably what she wants to hear.

For whatever reason, something clicks and she stops crying. She scrubs at her eyes: I must look a fright. She gives this pathetic little laugh.

This is breaking my heart, this is the woman who's always holding the reins. You do, I say like a teacher. Now go and wash your face and we'll talk this over rationally.

Thanks, Ange, she says, and goes to repair the damage. They have a downstairs loo.

I drink my coffee – cold as rainwater now – while I think things over. How I've missed the depths of poor Patsy's problem I can't imagine because it didn't just happen overnight. I'd had my little niggles, like I've told you before, but I never dreamt they were anything more than that. Thought I was just being cynical. I'm kicking myself now for not being more aware.

I suppose I've been so wrapped up in our own troubles. Where they're concerned by the way, I have to tell you that at least I know now exactly what we're dealing with there.

It turns out to be a very simple, very small, tawdry little story.

The whole episode had started the previous night. They were at a party in a house somewhere up in the Strawberry Beds, some friend of this Rosemary's. Another twenty-first – I seemed to be haunted by twenty-firsts, these days. Anyway, they were all drinking, cider, beer, vodka. And a few of them also had marijuana and E. James did *not* take the drugs. He swears he didn't and I believe him. Maybe I'm being gullible but I believe him.

I asked him where the parents were during all this. They were away, apparently, it was a free house.

Anyway, they're all drinking and dancing and having a good time and a few of them are availing themselves of the bedrooms. Rosemary and James are dancing and he gets the signal that she's giving him the come-on. They go outside into the garden but it's freezing that night and it's starting to rain. There and then they make a date to meet the following day. And she kisses him and she says, You bring the condoms.

He's telling me all of this and he can't look at me. I don't blame him.

Next day they meet as arranged and he's all excited. He can't sleep the night before, thinking about what's going to happen. He says he's never gone the full, whole way with anyone before. (And here we all are, thinking young people today are at it like rabbits from the age of twelve!) They go up to the Park and on the way they have a few little spats, he's going too fast on the bike, that sort of thing. In hindsight I can see that she was being very tense. And to be fair to her, maybe she was already regretting her invitation. But if she was, that was the time to say it, wasn't it?

So they get to the park and he stashes the bike in some bushes and they go down into the Furry Glen. Because it's a weekday and the weather is still a bit cold, there's nobody about, only two girls on horses who don't give them even a look.

There's a particular place down by the bridge over the little lake where the forest is very thick. She wants to stop to look at the baby ducks swimming about under the bridge and he's trying to drag at her to come in under the trees, come on, come on. She pulls her hand away, no, there's plenty of time. She thinks the little ducks are beautiful, wishes she'd brought bread to throw at them. He's kissing her everywhere he can and she's half responding, half not. Then she starts to give out to him. Tells him to have some patience.

Then some old lady comes along, dawdling, picking up bits of twigs and dead leaves and putting them in a bag she's carrying. James gets embarrassed, thinking she may have seen him kissing Rosemary, and then he looks closely at her and sees she's not paying a blind bit of attention. In fact, he thinks she's a bit of a head case. Come on, he drags at Rosemary again, I haven't got all day, I've got to get back to work. He tells me he's dying of frustration at this point, that he's like a kettle that can't boil.

Because she insists, they wait until the old lady passes and then they go into the forest and lie down. He's all set to do it straight away but she wants to take her time. It's her first time, too, to go all the way and she wants it to last. She doesn't want him to take off any of her clothes. She'll do it herself in her own good time. He's going mad now.

She puts her arms around him and starts kissing him and he takes that as the signal. He starts getting really excited and shaking and kissing her back wildly and she tells him to take it easy or the whole thing's cancelled. He tries, he tells me he really *tries* to stop himself, to take it easy like she said, but some demon takes hold of him and he starts pulling at her clothes. Her underclothes. He mumbles this as he's telling me, he obviously can't say the word knickers. I've brought him up better than that.

She slaps his hand away and when he sulks, she laughs. Now will you take it easy, she says. She kisses him some more. He's going mad now. He thinks he's going to burst. He rolls on top of her. First she lets him and keeps kissing him and stroking his back and then she stops. Stop it, she tells him, stop it . . . He admits she says that.

But, according to him, he can't stop it then, it's too late. And he rips off her knickers and goes into her. He can't remember the next couple of seconds but he hears her scream, not a loud scream into the sky, just a scream into his ear, where she calls him a terrible name. He won't say what it is in front of me. I can well imagine.

And now, according to him, he immediately stops and pulls out. He insists he did not have an orgasm. He now has a pain down there which is so bad it's worse than when he had to get his appendix out.

As proof he didn't go the whole way to orgasm, he tells me he had forgotten to put his condom on and she didn't get pregnant. It seems James's grasp of the facts of life and of virginity and conception is less than perfect. Well, I did my best.

They lie there, not exactly side by side, more with their backs to each other. The pain he has eases off a bit. He feels and hears her getting her clothes to rights again. She stands up and he does himself up and stands up too.

She tells him she's very annoyed at what he did to her knickers, the elastic at the waist has snapped and she can't wear them now. But he can tell by the way she stuffs them into the pocket of her anorak and won't look him straight in the face that she's ashamed about the whole thing. He is too, now. He's mortified, actually, feels like a right prat.

They go back to the bike and neither of them says a word. He takes her to Drumcondra and lets her off. She says goodbye to him and he thinks she's calmed down. But he hasn't the nerve to make another date. Not just yet.

Instead, he just says, See ya around. Yeah, she says, see ya.

Now this is his version and I accept it is one of the areas which is in dispute. According to her statement, I haven't seen it but the solicitor told me, she does not say see ya or anything like it. According to her statement, she's so traumatized and agitated about what happened earlier she runs away as fast as she can go to get away from him. Without saying anything at all.

He *insists* she said see ya and that she walked. And that, as far as he was concerned, they were both just a bit embarrassed.

I think this is crucial. I mean, if she did talk to him and say see ya – well, you can work it out for yourself. It opens up a host of possibilities. And she did take the lift home from him on the back of the bike. She would have had to hold on to him. Would she have accepted such intimate contact if she'd been so traumatized by a man who'd just raped her?

Whatever about who's in the right in that regard, he's very upset for the next couple of days, doesn't know quite what to do next and that's why he buys the Cadbury's Roses to bring up to her. Cadbury's Cadbury's Cadbury's . . .

I don't know what to make of the whole incident, to tell you the truth, I've told you as he told me and as honestly as I can. Is that rape or is it not?

Patsy comes back from the loo. She's taken off all her make-up and her face is red and greasy from the remover. You'd know she'd been crying, you couldn't miss it, you can hardly see her eyes. My heart goes out to her.

We bat the problem of Martin to and fro but we come to no conclusions. We decide to sleep on it and that she'll do nothing, say nothing, for the short term anyway. If he brings up the matter of his whereabouts tonight – and we think this is unlikely – she'll just pretend she came in and went to bed and she was so tired she didn't even notice he wasn't there.

It's so late now I decide not to embark on telling her about James, although with the balance between us redressed, I know I'm going to be able to tell her after all. It's not that I'm glad she's having problems too – far from it – but it does make me feel that James and I aren't alone.

✦ Twelve ✦

Another remand. The weeks are flying by. Half of me is dreading the awful day getting closer, the other half welcomes the way Mondays keep coming up so quickly. Because the sooner we get this trial over with and know the worst, or the best, the better.

He certainly didn't mean to rape her. I'll go to my grave believing that much.

I've tried to be fair and to look at it from her side. She definitely told him to stop. He definitely didn't stop.

On the other hand, she's there by appointment to do it. It was she who told him to bring the condoms. She willingly went in with him to that wood to do it. All right, she changed her mind and of course I accept that she had every right to change her mind.

At that stage, though, he was too far gone, he mightn't even have heard her telling him to stop at the beginning when there was still time for it to stop short of – you know . . . He certainly believes he didn't hear her.

Like, didn't he stop the minute she screamed into his ear? As soon as he understood she really meant it? Shouldn't that count on his side?

She just got scared is my interpretation of it. Probably it was only when it was really happening did she realize what she was getting into. Probably worried that her parents would find out. Who knows.

I remember in my own early days, long before I met Tom Bennett, there was an oul' fella in the flats, oul' Mooney, who used to flash at me and not only at me, at anything in a skirt. One day he caught me when I was taking a short-cut through the back alley between the street and the flats. He got me up against a wall – I must have been only about thirteen at the time – and shoved his manky dirty thing in under my skirt. Yuck. It felt like a horrible dry worm. I never reported him. I suppose I should have.

But it didn't blight my whole life.

Neither did the episode with the boy I met at one of the discos run by some outfit or other – I can't remember the name of it now – which was trying to provide amenities for young people in the inner city. I was fourteen and a half then. He was a nice-looking boy, tall, fair-haired, the kind I always go for. We danced a bit and at a certain stage, we sneaked out around the back. There were loads of couples hard at it up against the wall.

We started to snog and things began to get out of hand. I could feel him getting too excited for his own good. I started to say, No, stop it, no, and he wouldn't. He just kept on. He might have gone the whole way with me, he had my knickers half-down and his own fly open – he was much bigger and stronger than I was – if it hadn't been for the girl keeping nix on the corner who spotted the chaperone coming so we all had to scatter.

That episode didn't blight my life either but I suppose nowadays I could claim it did. If it happened now I could probably bring him to court for sexual assault. But it never occurred to you in those days, you just put it down to experience and got on with it. The statistics say that more than one in ten Irish children have suffered sexual assault. Well, I definitely did, with oul' Mooney, but I would definitely not count the time with the boy out the back at the disco because I was half to blame as far as I was concerned. God knows, we were warned enough about boys.

And as far as I'm aware, I'm not psychologically scarred. Or am I? If I went to a psychiatrist, would he find that I am?

And does Patsy's experience count? We did have a discussion about this once. The only time she could remember anything like that happening to her was the day she was on the top of a number 54 bus on the way out to visit her auntie in Terenure and an oul' fella (they're always oul' fellas) sat in beside her and slid his hand up under her skirt. We were always told just to get up straight away if that happened and tell the conductor. She did that and that was the end of it. She didn't even tell her auntie because loads of us knew people to whom it had happened. And she had thought no more about it until we were both racking our brains that day to find out did we fit into the statistics on child sexual abuse.

We decided we were both marginal, but I suppose nowadays not many of the experts in the field would agree. And if you were to ask me objectively, I'd say that if it had happened twenty years ago, James's episode with Rosemary would have been on the marginal side too. Unfortunately for us, it's not twenty years ago.

Do you know what I think? I think she got in a row at home about where she was that afternoon – maybe they started getting on her case about mitching from her bookkeeping course. Or the mother found grass stains on her – or even the torn knickers. Yes, that would have been it. She had no way to explain the state of those knickers without implicating herself. So to defend herself she cried rape.

It wouldn't be the first time that's happened.

It's nearly time for this morning's proceedings to start. He's fidgety this morning, and it took me ages to get him out of bed. I think he's still not sleeping.

I'm not looking at Mrs Madden, nor she at me. We're both sitting in the same places each time. At least she is, she must be first in the queue every Monday. The courtroom is so crowded at the beginning of the sessions that sometimes I can't find a seat but I tend to hang around in roughly the same area. It's a funny thing but familiarity always makes you feel a little less uncomfortable, doesn't it?

We're lucky so far that the girl from RTE, who's the only reporter I've recognized here from the beginning, is still showing no interest in us. Bigger fish to fry, I suppose, with the trial that's coming up after all us remands. I think it's about fraud. Money anyway, you'd know by the number of senior counsel. And today there are two other girls and a man I haven't see before on the press bench so there must be something big.

I hope to God one of them's not from the *Herald*. Rape is meat and drink to that paper and everyone I know reads it.

If I closed my eyes, I could draw this courtroom from memory now. We're all getting to know each other, especially the other groups of remand people. Some of the defendants are in custody, my heart goes out to them, the weather is gorgeous at the moment and they come up looking like E.T.

Actually, it's amazing how quickly you get acclimatized to who everyone is and what everyone does in a courtroom. If I wasn't so worried I'd be blasé about it, it's that familiarity again. For instance, I'm not all that pushed any more about people looking at us. We can look straight back at them – I mean, why are *they* here? What do *they* have to hide? And we're all innocent until proven guilty, aren't we? Solicitors seem to be the only ones in the whole system who look completely at ease and in control of things. In fact, most of the time they look quite bored.

And as for the barristers, God love some of them, they look as if they've just got out of nappies.

And now that I've settled in a bit, I can see details I missed the first few times like, I can't get over how shabby some of the older barristers look. I mean, they're supposed to be earning a fortune, you'd think they'd get their gowns cleaned, wouldn't you? At least brush the dandruff off the shoulders and get someone to sew on a few buttons. The young women are a bit better, I have to admit, but even they could smarten up a bit, shoe polish must be going out of fashion. And I have a thing about scuffed heels, nobody need have scuffed heels in this day and age, not with all the heel bars in this city. I insist that James is turned out as shiny as a soldier. I believe it will pay off in the long run.

I can still feel him shaking beside me. Familiarity is certainly not helping him much.

We haven't seen any juries yet because we're always gone before the jury is called for whatever case is on that day but the court clerk must be the most miserable-looking individual I have ever seen in my life. Talk about being unhappy in his work. He seems to have a tic.

Now that we're on barristers, ours is a bit too nonchalant about the whole thing for my liking. St John Markey (would you believe!) looks about thirteen. I exaggerate, he looks about seventeen. They don't have to wear the wigs any more but most of them still do, and St John's looks as though it's just come out of its tissue paper. I suppose it makes them feel more grown-up. The state side has a much older man. I wish we could get an older man, I think I'd feel more confident.

All rise.

I remember *Rowan and Martin's Laugh-in* when I was a little girl. 'Here comes the judge' was one of the catchphrases on it.

Oh, God, is it my imagination or did she nod down at us? She certainly looked down at us. Kind of speculatively. I definitely wasn't imagining that – there was a look on her face for an instant. What does that mean? Does it mean she's thinking about James's case? In her mind is James already guilty? Dammit, I wish we'd drawn a man judge . . .

I'm just being ridiculous. There's been no evidence yet. And they're required to be impartial.

Our solicitor Patrice Murphy thinks she'll be very straight with us. He has a small reservation, though, she's quite new and nobody knows yet what her track record is going to be. And nobody knows what she feels about rape, because when she was a barrister she was never involved in either prosecuting or defending one. Or, not any notorious one that anyone heard about.

I wonder; do women barristers try not to take on rape cases on grounds they might be prejudiced? It's a very emotive area.

Jesus, St John Markey has one foot up on the bench while he's talking to the judge. I bet she won't like that. Put your foot down, you eejit, you . . .

I often wonder how much of Mammy is in me. To be more accurate, I worry about it. It's one of the reasons I'm very strict with myself. Even when I have a whole day off, such as Sundays with no gigs, I get up and dress myself properly, ironed blouse, polished shoes, the lot. Some of the women at work come in in track suits and runners. I despise track suits and runners. I know they're comfortable – or so they say – but I think they're the lazy option. They say, Who cares, who'll see us at five o'clock in the morning, but that's not the point. We see ourselves, don't we? I'm meticulous about keeping my nails clean and although it costs a fair bit, I have my hair cut every six weeks and I go to the dentist at least once a year.

Maybe all of this make me a bit of an obsessive but I'd be afraid that if I let myself go at all I'd start down the slippery slope. You have to be careful of your genes.

I'll never know for sure but I'd say what happened to Mammy was that she'd had nobody to set her an example, even though, reading between the lines, her own mother seems to have been a bit of a tartar. (Her father was apparently more easygoing.)

Unfortunately I gather that even when those children were small, neither of their parents had much to do with them. They were in business in Birr and they were always, literally, minding the shop. Shops, plural – they had two, a hardware shop and a clothes shop. Their children were looked after by maids and housekeepers all the time but, from what Mammy said, the staff turnover was pretty high. They were always being fired for nicking, or on suspicion of nicking, or they couldn't take the sharp end of Mammy's mother's tongue and they left in high dudgeon.

Imagine, though! Our family once had servants!

Although her father's stock was probably Irish, Devine is quite an Irish name, my grandmother's maiden name was de Vere. That part of Ireland, Laois and Offaly, are the two counties which were the first to be planted by the English. One day, just out of the blue, the King of

England granted our land to some of his English pals and
cleared us off them. In fact, Offaly was called King's
County and Laois was Queen's County. (To the day she
died Mammy referred to Portlaoise and Tullamore as
Williamstown and Maryboro – they were named after
King William and Queen Mary.) It was weird for me to
be learning about this in history class in school and to
know that my own family were probably planters. I kept
quiet about it, of course.

You'd know, right up to the end, that she had blue
blood in her. There was something about her, a sort of
delicacy, and she had small, elegant hands which were
very expressive, they reminded me of little cabbage
moths. So you can see how ill-fitted she was for life in
the flats. It's no wonder what happened to her actually
did.

On her behalf it makes my blood boil when I read
articles in the papers going on and on about single
mothers with five or six children sponging off the state.
What did they expect her to do? Put us all in the bin? I'm
not saying she shouldn't have toed the line a bit more but
she tried, she really did. She just had a fatal flaw and she
couldn't manage in the real, cruel world. She had no
training for it. Her mother apparently wouldn't let her
open her mouth to her and the maids and housekeepers
didn't give a damn. She had no role model.

Why don't they write their brilliant articles about
those people who used her, used our place as a squat and
a party venue and then dumped her and left her to fend
for herself when the authorities intervened. Every time
the going got a bit rough they bunked off and left her to
try to pick up the pieces herself. Even Joey, the one I
think was Francesca's father and whom, as you know, I
liked.

I hate them.

If it hadn't been for my stubbornness (and, I must acknowledge again, the pretty enlightened social worker I had at the time) she'd have had nobody to look after her and she would probably have died a lot sooner than she did.

After that awful night when they took James from her and I ran away and slept rough and she'd vanished when I got home after the zoo the next day, I searched for her all over the city, all the hospitals. Although I hated doing it, I went down into the really rough places, derelict sites down by Jervis Street and down along the Quays, even the docks.

I went through quite a see-saw in feelings that couple of days, the awful low of the night living rough, followed by the surprising high of meeting Tom Bennett at the zoo, followed again by the trek around the dives and most awful secret places of Dublin while at the same time fighting for the right to mind James. I was wrecked at the end of it.

On one of my returns to the flats, I can't remember now which day it was, my social worker had put a note in our door to contact her.

It was she who told me they'd found Mammy and she was now in hospital. There'd been a disturbance at a squat on the Richmond Road and the police were called. That's how she was found.

She'd gone there with that filthy, horrible man, the last guy she was with, I can't remember his name, I'd pollute my brain. He was by far the worst, he was a dealer and a junkie and a drunk as well. Those days there were only a few of them around and the cops knew exactly who they were so this fella only came out after dark, like the rat he was. He took advantage of her sweetness. Mammy rarely drank, she didn't like the taste. I hope he's dead and rotting in hell.

The social worker warned me not to get a shock when I went up to see her. So I prepared myself, or so I thought.

I was devastated when they brought me in to her bedside. Her face was all purple. Half of it was bruising, half of it was just discoloration. She never came out of hospital again, only to go over to Harold's Cross to the Hospice. To die.

They were absolutely lovely to her there. They washed her properly every day and you could really feel their love. It's a great consolation to know she died peacefully and 'At Rest'. But every single day of my life I live with the guilt of not having been able to look after her.

So you can see why, although I'm a much tougher proposition, I still feel I have to watch myself. Her blood is my blood and you're always your mother's daughter, aren't you? Of course, there is my father to take into account too. I sincerely hope he was made of sterner stuff than she was. Because now and then, under the strain of all of this with James, I do feel myself wilting.

I suppose looking after James is my way of making it up to her. I would have done it anyway, it's just that I hope that, wherever she is, she knows I'm doing it.

Although as it turns out, of course, I obviously didn't look after him well enough.

He's getting worried about keeping up the pretence at work, says he's running out of excuses as to where he is every Monday morning. I can't keep saying I'm going to a clinic, he goes, they'll think I have Aids.

Well, let them fire you, I go back, as confidently as I can. We'll manage.

Speaking of managing, I eventually cashed my precious, beautiful scratch card. It nearly broke my heart to see it go, having all that money just wasn't the same. I've decided not to redeem Mammy's stuff just yet. He might lose his job and we'll need every penny we can get. I've tried to follow the consider the lilies in the field concept but it just doesn't wash with us, somehow.

One of Mammy's sisters was called Lily, the other was Adeline. The brother was called Jeremy. Is called Jeremy. They're probably still alive. James is their nephew. It would be lovely to be able to go and talk to my aunties and uncle and have a family around me at a time like this, but I could just see their reaction if I arrived in their lives and announced why I'd decided to contact them after all these years.

Excuse me, hello, are you the Devines? The de Vere Devines? How do you do, I'm your long-lost niece and this is your long-lost nephew, we're the ones belonging to the derelict. There are three more of us . . . And, by the way, he's being charged with rape at the moment. Any chance of a bit of solidarity?

Can you imagine?

The last time the whole five of us met for an access visit, Francesca left after ten minutes. She told the social worker that she'd had it and she didn't want anything more to do with any of us. There was a big argument, I was really annoyed with her and I could tell the social worker was too, no matter how valiantly she tried to be professional and hide it. But Francesca was coming up to sixteen and there was not much anyone could do. At sixteen she was free to live her own life.

Thinking about it, what was probably bothering her was that after all the promises, her foster family hadn't adopted her yet (and they never did). I've never been able to find out whether there was some technical hitch or whether they changed their minds. All of that kind of stuff is very confidential and you might as well be trying to break into the Vatican as winkling information out of the Eastern Health Board or the Adoption Board.

I suppose I didn't help the situation. I was just twenty-one and I was probably inclined to play the mammy a bit too much, lording it over the others. Well, I was feeling pretty much like a mammy, with some justification, it has to be said. James was five and I hadn't killed him yet.

We were in the lobby of the Gresham – all of us except James were fed up with the feeding-the-ducks lark. Anyway, the Gresham was handy, it's in O'Connell Street and easily accessible to us all. It was summer and the place was crammed with people having afternoon tea and drinks, a lot of them tourists. I don't know what they thought of our happy little group. (I don't think! They couldn't have missed what was going on.)

Our Cokes haven't even arrived yet when Francesca's on her feet, reacting to something Nicola said. A silly mimicking of how she pronounces her Os now that she's living on the Riviera. You see, it was the beginning of Dalkey being called the Irish Riviera because of all the rock stars et cetera who were moving in there. Nicola was being jealous, the family she and Justine were with were lovely but they were struggling a bit to make ends meet. Anyway, she was wrong. Francesca became part of the poppyseed rail syndrome long before she moved to Dalkey from Foxrock.

With my usual tact, I make the insult worse by laughing. My guard was a bit down that day.

This ribbing is all the excuse Francesca needs. She jumps up and starts to march out of the hotel. The social worker jumps up and runs after her and then I jump up and run after her. Like three of the bloody Marx Brothers.

The social worker and I are arguing with Francesca just in front of the swing doors, with the porter holding one of them open for us and looking at us like, are yiz going out or are yiz not. I'm holding on to Francesca's arm and she's tugging and tugging and the social worker is talking to her in a quiet, intense voice, asking her to reconsider.

She's adamant. She's going back to Dalkey and that's the end of it. And she's coming on no more access visits.

The social worker goes with her to see her to the bus – she's allowed to travel on her own at this stage – and I go back to the other three. They're just sitting there, staring. I arrive at the same time as the Coke and the buns. James immediately takes his up and forgets everything else. Go on, I say to the others, we'll see her next time, you know how she is, and we all tuck in while we wait for the social worker to come back.

But there was no next time.

It's funny how people can just slip out of your life. You'd think you'd have some clue. In a film you'd have all the music, telling you it was significant. It's always a humbling experience to know that something terrifically important to you is of no importance whatsoever to the world at large.

Like when I went down to cash my scratch card. I had to queue at the hatch. That was the first disillusionment, I'd thought I'd be the only one. Special.

Nevertheless, when my turn came, my heart was thumping as I pushed it under the bars protecting the clerk.

I don't know what I was expecting but I would have liked it marked in some way. Bells ringing? Hooters? Even something negative – if he was to challenge me to produce evidence that I hadn't stolen it, or look for proof of identity.

Something. Anything to say that this was not an ordinary transaction.

The guy was bored out of his trolley. He never even looked up at me. Not one word passed between us, not one. That'll teach me. Talk about Macbeth's hubris.

Thirteen

I answer the door on the Monday evening and it's Patsy. Now this is odd – for her to come to the flat unannounced. She usually calls only to pick me up in her car for a gig, or on the rare occasion we're going to the pictures. And she looks weird, her face is scrunched.

Come on in, I go, this is a surprise. I'm even more surprised because she knows the first English paper in the Leaving is coming up, and I should be studying. It'd be unlike her to cut across that.

The way she looks I'm immediately thinking of Martin. Is everything OK at home?

She doesn't answer, just comes in. The hallway in our place is a kip, holey lino on the floor, the original wallpaper painted over so many times it's flaking off so the skirting boards look like they're covered with shavings of mouldy chocolate.

Don't mind this place, it's getting worse by the day, I say, trying to be cheerful as we go up the stairs. These could be nice if he'd put a bit of carpet on them, or even lino. The banisters could be beautiful as a matter of fact, I've always loved how at the bottom they curl into themselves like a periwinkle's shell.

We go through the door of our flat. Thank God James

is not home from work yet – he usually goes for a pint with some of the lads – and the place is decent. When he's sprawled in front of the telly you can hardly see him for half-full cups and empty crisp bags. Cup of tea? I ask, going towards the kettle.

No, thanks. It's the first time she's said anything.

I leave the kettle. That bad? I say sympathetically. Sit down and tell me all about it.

Instead she comes across to me and holds out the cutting. A nineteen-year-old courier from Mountjoy Square in Dublin was remanded on continuing bail in the Dublin District Court today. He is accused of raping a twenty-year-old woman in the Phoenix Park.

One of those little stories in boxes down the side of a page. The exact words are engraved in my brain.

Wouldn't you know it, the one Monday I don't buy the *Herald*.

Patsy says nothing, she's obviously waiting for me. There's no point in protesting or telling fibs, she knows James is a courier. She knows he's nineteeen. She knows we live in Mountjoy Square. Doesn't take Remington Steele to figure it out.

It's a surreal moment. I'd been watching an Eddie Murphy film and it's still running. Patsy and I looking at one another, me holding the cutting, her as grim as death and Eddie Murphy going ha ha ha! in that manic way of his. I go over and I switch him off. I'm sorry I didn't tell you, I say to Patsy, I was going to but I couldn't get up the nerve.

She's still standing there. Still looking at me.

Did he do it? she asks in a peculiar voice.

That's what the trial is going to be about, I retort. He says it was consensual and I believe him. I'm looking straight into her eyes. I love Patsy but I'm not going to be intimidated by anyone on this. I can't get a handle on what she's thinking or why she's behaving like this, this is not a Patsy I've seen very often.

You've picked up the jargon very quickly, she says.

I don't know what to say next. Let's sit down, I go, are you sure you won't have a cup of tea or coffee?

No, thank you, she says very quietly.

I stare at her and she stares back. If we had a ticking clock it'd be ticking very loudly at this point. She's the one who breaks it. Look, she goes, I'm sure you're going through a terrible time and I'm very sorry for you but, you see, I have a couple of daughters . . .

I'm shattered. Her meaning is perfectly clear. My best friend is making judgements without even hearing the story.

It's out before I can stop it. Why did you come here, so, if you're so afraid you and your precious daughters might be contaminated by us?

She doesn't answer, just looks at me with an expression that I can only say borders on the pitying. I'm sorry, Patsy, I say humbly, I didn't mean that, you know I didn't—

I know you didn't, Ange, she goes. I just wanted to come and tell you that I've found out about it and to reassure you that, in case you're worried, it won't make any difference to our professional relationship. She's tight but sad.

I beg your pardon—

Looking back at it now, I think that at this point I must have sat down. It was still too new to take in.

Why would I be worried about our professional relationship? I was being genuine here, it had never occurred to me that James's unfortunate situation could have anything to do with PA System.

Before I can say anything else, she puts the cutting down on the coffee table in front of the bed-settee. I'll pick you up next Sunday morning, all right? She says this very gently. I'll be praying for you. Oh, and good luck on Wednesday in the exam, I'll send you a good-luck card. She tries to smile but you never saw a less successful smile in your life.

She turns and goes. Leaves me with my mouth hanging open. The whole scene had taken only about two minutes.

To this day I've never fully worked out why she came that evening – unless it was to rub my nose in it and I wouldn't want to believe that of her.

I guess she did me a favour. At least she showed me exactly what we were facing in the wider world. There ended my half-baked, no, *quarter*-baked, idea of going to the Rape Crisis Centre and looking for counselling or some kind of help for us.

It was a beautiful evening – no pathetic fallacy tonight – and the walls of the flat were suddenly very close to each other. I felt I couldn't breathe.

I should have gone back to the studying but instead I grabbed my keys and hightailed it out, across the road and into Mountjoy Park. In the summertime it doesn't close officially until half past eight.

It's full of people who seem to have no worries, groups of young ones with their buggies, the usual old jossers and their dogs who never seem to leave the place, kids playing football and basketball. Even a girl swaying around the place using a hula-hoop. Now there's a blast from the past. I manage to find a bench and make myself relax, letting the sunshine soothe the back of my neck and my shoulders.

I start to feel a bit better. A small blue butterfly flutters past my foot and lands on a wallflower in one of the beds nearby and then takes off again. I wouldn't have known this until recently, but did you know that butterflies can't

fly when there is no sunshine? One of the men in one of
the offices we clean was in early one morning, just after
seven. He dumped an *Irish Times* in a bin beside his desk
and on a whim, when I was doing the bins in his section,
I took it out and saved it. I learned about the butterflies
in it – that paper is full of this kind of information.
Apparently butterflies are solar-powered. They have to
have energy from the sun to be able to lift themselves.
On cloudy days, or even when clouds pass over on sunny
days, they immediately rest, clinging on to grass or a
bush or something.

At the risk of sounding like someone from the PR
department of Dublin Corporation, once again, I have to
give fair dues to the people who run the parks. They
won't be bested. They plant little baby trees in this park
and the gurriers come up and break them. They
immediately replace them and along come the gurriers
again. They plant them again. And so on and so on until
they wear the gurriers down. God knows how many
little trees it takes but so far this year the parks people
are winning and there are three new flowering cherries
here now that haven't been touched for at least a week
and which will maybe survive.

The last time I was in here I saw a young fella
systematically using a bicycle chain to swipe the head off
every tulip in the place, hundreds of them. Unfortunately, I didn't interfere. I'm sorry I didn't now, chain
or no chain. I'll tell you, if I catch any little thicko at
those little trees this evening, or anyone deliberately
trampling the flowerbeds, the way I'm feeling right now
I don't think I'd be responsible for my actions. This
evening I'd welcome an opportunity to have a go.

I find myself watching a man playing with a small dog
at the far side. It's an uplifting thing to watch a man and

a dog, if you throw a stick or a ball, the dog always behaves as though it's the first time you've ever done it. He's always thrilled skinny with you even if you've left him locked up for days. Dogs are the tsars of forgiveness in this world.

So, anyway, I'm sitting there and I'm half watching this man and his dog, and half watching the little sun-fuelled butterfly going about its business. But all the time I'm going over and over in my mind what happened between me and Patsy. It was bizarre. One paragraph. The word rape. That's it, that's enough, no more questions. She's my best friend and she doesn't give me a chance to present our side. Not even remotely interested.

But why? All I could see was that odd look in her eyes. Pity definitely, but there was something else. A sort of triumph? Glee? Surely not.

Well, tough. We've managed on our own before and we'll manage again. I believe in him. If I don't, who will?

There and then I make up my mind to go and have a proper talk with the solicitor, find out what the worst-case scenario is. I know we're only free legal aid but there's a lot at stake here and the state will pay him for his time.

I'm feeling much more optimistic already. I look away from the butterfly and across the park to the man and his dog again and find they're much closer. And what do you know, it's Ken, the guy from my class. He happens to be looking this way and I've waved before I knew what I was doing.

Why did I do that? What kind of a stupo am I? Now (a) he'll think I'm forward and (b) I don't want company, I'm not in the mood for chitchat.

Too late. He picks up the dog and come towards me, a

big smile all over his face. Hi, he goes. Isn't it a lovely evening? I couldn't look at those English notes for one more minute. Are you nervous about Wednesday?

Hi, I answer, yes, it is a lovely evening. And if we don't know the stuff now we never will. Do you live around here?

I'm in the Custom Hall complex down the road. The two of us are. He looks at the dog under his arm. And you?

Over there – I wave my arm vaguely in the direction of DID Electrical.

Well, you haven't far to go for your electrical appliances anyhow! He blushes. I see for the first time that he's quite shy, we haven't talked all that much in the classroom.

I look away from him to give him a chance to compose himself. You're sort of in the trade, aren't you? A carpenter? I didn't know you were allowed keep dogs in apartments?

You're dead right, he says, you're not allowed keep any pets. But we're very careful.

When I look back he's stroking the dog's head. This dog has no tail but his rear is crazy with wagging. He's panting, his tongue fluttering as fast as a bird's wing. Sure he's only small, Ken says, and I've trained him to be quiet. He's in the van with me all day and I smuggle him in and out of the block in my rucksack.

I never would have put this chap down as a dog lover. Don't know why – not that I gave it much thought! He's lovely, I go, what's his name?

Sam.

Sam. I reach up and stroke the dog's head myself and he gives me a lick. Obviously this is one of those dogs who love everyone. That's a nice name for a dog, I say, is he a purebred?

Ken takes this as an invitation to sit down beside me and does so. Not at all, he says, letting the dog jump out of his arms on to the ground, I got him in the pound. It'd break your heart to go up there, Angela, you'd want to take them all. I had to be choosy, though, I wouldn't have been able to keep a big dog in my place, it wouldn't have been fair. And anyway, I'd have been caught! He grins.

He has a lovely grin, something else I hadn't noticed before.

We chat a bit and he gets a bit easier with me. When he was looking for a dog, he had to go to the pound up beyond Finglas. Apparently the cats' and dogs' home, which used to be very handy, just off the Quays there, near where the gasometer was, has moved out to the sticks, Rathfarnham or some place.

The dog is lying across his shoes now. He bends down and strokes it again. Can you believe it, Angela, this fella was rescued off of a Hallowe'en bonfire. They'd tied his legs together so he couldn't run and they'd tied his tail to a tyre so he'd be sure to burn.

Who rescued him?

The Guards rescued him, he says. They always patrol the bonfires in certain parts of the city. They were just in time. His tail is gone, you can see that, and look . . . He picks the dog up again and shows me a place on the belly where there's no hair and the skin is like crazy paving. The dog licks him again. Gratitude never-ending.

Who'd do that to a dog, I go, I don't know what this country's coming to. That was good of the Guards, though.

Yeah, Ken agrees, the man who rescued him had to go to hospital to get dressings on the burns on his hands.

He lets the dog jump down again. How are things with you in general?

Uh-oh! I go to myself, wondering if there's anything behind this question. It's occurred to me this guy might have seen the *Herald*.

Grand, grand, I go. Cautiously.

We run out of conversation. But although the silence is a bit awkward, I realize it's normal-social-awkward, not embarrassed-awkward. It had been just an ordinary question.

You read very well the other night, he says then, looking across the park. You could probably be an actress if you put your mind to it.

Rubbish, I go, but I'm pleased. You're not bad yourself, I say then. You have a lovely voice. I sing a bit and I can tell you would be a singer too.

Not in the slightest, he goes. The bath. That's about the height of it. A singer, eh? I was always trying to guess what you did. He brings his eyes back from the far end of the park. You're really a singer? Professionally?

You could say that, I go.

Then I can't resist it. So when you were guessing, what did you think I might do?

I thought something in an office, maybe, a solicitor's office or a bank. He looks down at Sam who seems to have fallen asleep. Since you're only now doing the Leaving, I thought maybe you might be one of those yellow pack workers. An alarmed look across his face and he looks back at me. Sorry, I don't mean to insult you.

You're not insulting me, I say. I'm chuffed that he thinks I'm an office worker – even a yellow pack. I see nothing wrong with being a yellow pack, by the way, even though, according to the unions, they're being totally exploited, doing the same work as fully paid workers under the pretence of being trained. My attitude is, it's work, isn't it? Would they prefer the poor kids to leave school and have to go straight on the dole? Or emigrate? All right, it isn't great pay but it can lead to something. At the very least it's experience to put on your CV. If James had the opportunity I'd make him jump at it.

Suddenly it's important that this Ken thinks the best of me. Don't get me wrong, I'm not ashamed of being a cleaner and I don't want to fudge what I do, but something makes me leave it ambivalent. I'm not quite an office worker, I say, although my main work does involve visiting offices.

I hope I'm looking serious.

I knew, I knew you had something to do with an office, Ken goes. You always look so neat.

M-mmm, I go. Piling on the mystery. I hope he never attends an occasion where he sees me in a French maid's outfit! (I'd been thinking of giving up the kissogram business anyway. Maybe now's the time. Especially with that extra injection of cash.)

So where do you sing? he asks, maybe I could come to one of your shows sometime.

Maybe. I'll let you know if I'm doing one I'd consider suitable.

I can't believe it, I'm being flippant with this guy, it could almost be called flirting.

We smile again at each other. He picks up Sam, I'd better be getting back, this fella needs his beauty sleep. And anyway, I still have to do a bit of revision. Good luck with the work, see you in the salt mines.

I return the wish, he says goodbye and off he goes.

That was the holy all of it but it left me with a nice feeling. Which, of course, I instantly dismissed. I'd no right to be having any nice feelings about men. Not at this point in my life. Not until we get certain things sorted out one way or the other in my real life. And I've managed perfectly well without a man since Tom Bennett.

I look for the butterfly and it's gone, even though the sun is still out. Probably heading to its roost. Do butterflies roost?

At least I know he's not married. Who'd be married and live in one of those piffling little apartments and have to smuggle in a dog for company?

One of the girls, I think it was Justine, found a kitten in the laneway behind the flats one day. The poor little thing, it couldn't have been more than a couple of weeks old, hardly any hair and no teeth to speak of. I fed it with my finger, dipping it in milk and it latched on – it was a very strange sensation. I couldn't give it enough that way, though, and it died within twenty-four hours. Justine couldn't have cared less. She'd forgotten about it. She was only two and a half, something like that, I know that because she was taken into care just before her third birthday.

That was one of the times I was taken, too. They never learned. I was back out in less than twenty-four hours. Into care again, back out again, in, out, like a yo-yo. At one stage they were going to commit me into Madonna House – residential. There was no way I was having that. Although they couldn't control me, they couldn't say I was out of control or a danger to society or to myself. Because all I was doing was coming back to my home. And I was doing nothing illegal. Just illegal by their rules for children at risk. In my opinion I was at risk of nothing I couldn't handle. Mammy had to have someone responsible with her.

By the way, I don't mean to imply, just because I keep going on about our problems, and social workers, and my siblings being put into foster homes, that I had a completely rotten childhood. I emphatically did not. The bad times were gruesome all right, but there were good times too. Take school. Apart from my being pretty much a dunce – because I didn't care about the lessons and never did my homework – school was good fun, especially after the monster Concepta skedaddled out of our lives.

Also, the social workers cared a lot and did the best they could for us. We had help from a lot of good people in the Vincent, and when Mammy was well, she was the sweetest, most gentle mother you could imagine.

It's probably a difficult concept for you to take in, that a woman who according to the authorities was unable to look after her children, who could never name the fathers of any of them and who was a substance abuser, could be the sweetest and most gentle of mothers and be really loved by us all. Well, all I can tell you is I loved her to bits and I wanted more than anything in the world to protect her.

It was hardly her fault she wasn't ready for the world when she came to Dublin and found herself in the flats, was it? I blame her parents. What about their responsibilities in the matter?

And I do have good times to look back on with her, very good times. For instance one day she and myself and Nicola, who was just a baby then, went to see Santa Claus in Clery's. It was a memorable Christmas, the best ever, because for once there were no boyfriends around and she was clean.

God knows where she got the money but off the three of us went, walking down to O'Connell Street as though we hadn't a care in the world. We moved slowly because she was quite frail but she was in great spirits. When she was up to it, Mammy was a chatter, about anything and everything. And very charitable about people who were not in the least charitable about her.

It's dry, not half as cold as it should be for December, and the streets are jammed with cheerfulness. The Christmas lights are on, it's half past three and already getting dark and I hold her arm tightly so we won't bump into people. We stop at RTV Rentals at the intersection of Talbot Street and North Earl Street and isn't *Sesame Street* on all the tellies in the window! My happiness is complete. Big Bird in full glorious colour – it's the first time I've seen that he's yellow. At home he's only in black and white. Colour is a complete novelty at this stage for most people.

She waits there with me while I watch through the glass – which has a big Santa drawn on it in artificial snow – all the way to the end of the segment. Everyone around is saying happy Christmas and hawking huge happy parcels and the woman with the barrow on Marlborough Street just around the corner is shouting five for two bob the Christmas tangerines. I'm leaning against Mammy, warm and quiet, and happiness spreads all through me like a virus.

I adore Christmas ever since that time. If it was up to me and I had unlimited resources, James and I would be up to our necks in artificial snow with Rudolf blow-ups in every corner of the flat and the ceiling invisible under the weight of paper chains. Every present would be in luxurious gift boxes, like they do them up in America, where people just lift the lids to see what's in the tissue paper inside. And I'd get a piano and we'd drink mulled claret and sing carols.

It's funny, I remember hardly anything about the actual Santa that day with Mammy and Nicola, but I remember every step of that walk, every second of the feel of her thin arm in mine.

I wish James could have known her like I did. It's a terrible gap in our relationship. I've tried to keep her memory alive for him but I haven't even a photograph to show him because we never had any.

I'm going to brave it down to Birr, I think, while I'm sitting on that bench in Mountjoy Park after Ken has gone home. I'll find her family and ask for a photograph, they must have something, her Confirmation or something – Protestants have Confirmations, don't they? We deserve at least that much.

I'm half afraid, though. Afraid that they will have exorcized her so completely that they'd have nothing at all. That would kill me. In my imagination I see her mother making a bonfire and throwing everything to do with Mammy on it after casting her out.

And to think that that woman is James's and my grandmother. Talk about the witches in *Macbeth*!

→ Fourteen ←

On the subject of genes, I wish we knew who James's father is. A boy needs a father at a time like this. But the chances of finding him are non-existent, the birth cert has a blank space under where the father's name should be and not one of us has a clue about his identity. Given the type they all were, there's a fair chance he'd be dead anyway.

I did my best to start the tracing during that court business a few years ago, I got in touch with my old social worker to ask for help. She'd given up the job, too stressful, but she had kindly left me her address in case I ever wanted to have a chat.

Unfortunately, even with all her experience, we had no luck. When she came back to me in the end, she explained that nineteen years ago, they would have kept records of boyfriends only if they were abusers. Or if they had acknowledged themselves as fathers at some point and someone was alleging serious neglect.

Even substance abuse wasn't all that a big deal then amongst the authorities, although I think probably there was a fair bit of it going on, not as much as now, obviously, but a fair bit nonetheless. (The difference is, now it's been discovered by the politicians and the whole country, and we're all 'concerned'.) I know for a fact that nowadays the social workers tally every spittle of everyone who comes within an ass's roar of one of the kids on their books. They have to be so careful now, situations can blow up so quickly into public uproar and then they're held responsible.

At least being illegitimate is not the stigma it used to be, I have to hand it to the Catholic Church, even they don't use the word any more. One of the women I work with got an annulment last year. She worried herself half to death about it. Like, if no marriage ever existed, ever, it meant her kids were illegitimate, didn't it? She was a religious kind of woman and she didn't want that.

Then one morning, at our tea-break, her eyes are out on stalks. Ah, no, they told her in a letter she got from them. Not any more. Nowadays the children stay legitimate.

When you think about it they're a howl, aren't they? I am the rock, my eye. More like, I am the quicksand. What about all the poor kids they made bastards of in the past thousands of years? Floating around in the now non-existent limbo I expect.

He's at home when I get back from Mountjoy Park. The best way to describe him is to say that he's stricken. He's sitting with his head in his hands. The telly isn't even on.

What's the matter? I ask him.

He doesn't tell me to eff off, he just jerks the top of his head towards the table where the cutting is lying as Patsy left it.

Oh, God, I say, I shouldn't have left it there for you to find like that, I'm sorry.

He mutters that it didn't make any difference. That he'd seen it already, they showed it to him.

Who showed it to you?

At work. He keeps his head in his hands.

There's nothing I can think of to say other than would you like a cup of something? Or if you like I'll go down to the chipper and get us each a one and one.

He shakes his head again.

I sit down. What did they say to you? How bad was it?

Apparently it was pretty bad, the word spread like wildfire amongst the lads and he got funny looks all morning. The boss called him in at dinner-time and asked him was it true. He had to admit it.

Now I get horrified and I yell at him how could he be so stupid. I hadn't meant to sound harsh, it just came out that way, like I'm his judge and jury too. I need a chastity belt for my tongue sometimes. But then I find out that he didn't admit the actual rape, just that he's been charged.

The holy all of it is, he's been put on suspension. He was told not to come back to work until it's all over. And if he's cleared in the trial his job is still open to him.

Big if.

That happened at dinner-time. Where was he until now?

At last he takes his hands down from his head and looks at me. I'm expecting him to eff and blind me, and tell me to mind my own effin' business, that it's his own affair where he effin' was. But no. Instead, he looks at me like he's one of those baby seals in the Arctic that they're just about to bludgeon to death. I was just riding around, he says.

That image is going to haunt me. James, big, macho James, in all his leathers and on his big thundering bike, just riding around. Maybe even with tears in his eyes. I think it must be worse with boys. Girls roar crying and let it out. Boys keep it all inside where it rumbles around and gets to volcano proportions. Or suicide proportions.

would have liked to hear that they lived in a place like South Fork. Else what's the point of being famous?

Ken hadn't worked for any of Ireland's celebrities and the height of his mate's achievement was the Byrnes so that's the end of that conversation. He points across the water. That's the Bull Wall over there, he says, it's the northside equivalent of where we're walking, and you probably know Dollymount Beach behind it.

We're talking quite easily now. Sam's zigzagging from side to side of the South Bull, giving me heart attacks. There are no fences or barriers along the edges and I'm terrified he'll fall in. I'm not the only one having seizures, he's cutting in and out between all the other walkers, nearly tripping them up.

I do, indeed, know Dollymount. A few times, one of the social workers took us out there on fine access days and to give her her due, she went the whole hog, buckets, spades, even a beachball. I suppose she got pretty fed up with all the fighting and the squabbling in the hotel lobbies and in Stephen's Green when we were supposed to be feeding the ducks. Maybe, God love her, she thought the wide open spaces would help Francesca's disposition. (Boy, was she wrong there . . .)

I wasn't all that pushed about the place, it's miles and miles of sand and dunes with the sea so shallow you can't even swim. And with the family dynamics the way they were, it was never a successful outing. None of us seemed able to find much to do. Sandcastles? Our family? Give us a break.

Right now, though, it's hardly appropriate to launch immediately into our dysfunctional history so I ask Ken why is he doing the Leaving Cert, why does he need to when he seems to have a nice little business going for himself.

He's not quite sure why, it turns out. It was something to do in the evenings and he always feels a bit inadequate admitting to people that he never got it.

And you? He turns the tables.

The same. I smile and leave it at that. By this time we're at a half-way point on the South Bull where there's a bench seat in front of a little building marked 'Half Moon S.C. founded 1898'. It doesn't take a genius to work out what the S.C. stands for, because there are two men swimming just off it, not really swimming, puddling around, enjoying themselves and talking to each other. I wouldn't swim there if you paid me, Ken goes, looking at them and wrinkling up his nose.

Although I take his meaning, I don't get any bad smells at the moment. In fact the only smell I can detect right now is quite sweetish – seaweed maybe, or the day's heat coming back off the warm rocks. (I have to admit, though, that because of the sewage pumping station beside it, the smell up closer to the Pigeon House did leave a lot to be desired.)

The seat in front of the Half Moon S.C. is vacant and we sit down. Sam jumps up on Ken's lap and snuggles down like a cat. Now we're directly facing the city and God, is it a lovely sight . . .

See that big building with the red roof? Ken says after a bit, pointing towards Dollymount and an enormous house in the shape of a Swiss chalet. Its roof is more than plain red, it's like fire under the sinking sun. That's Royal Dublin golf club, he goes, I'm a member.

He says this as though it's the most natural thing in Ireland that a manual worker who doesn't have his Leaving Cert could be a member of a golf club.

I see, I say back. Then, what's your last name by the way?

Sheils.

Mine's Devine.

We go silent again. But because there isn't a breath of wind, we can make out individual words and sentences as other walkers chat to each other as they pass.

In the city you never really notice sunsets. Or even the sky, much. When you look up, even in a park, all you see is a square and not this quiet, infinite space that makes all the buildings of Dublin, plus the mountains on the southside, look like toys.

And it's hard to describe properly that huge setting sun in front of us, red as the inside of a volcano. *Huge*. A magnificent, spectacular rosy ball descending through fluffed-out jet trails and letting its colour seep out over the blackening spires and cranes and spiny docks. We can see that one of the ferries is getting ready to leave. There's wispy smoke coming from it, lifting straight upwards.

Soon we hear a sound like a deep drumming and another ship, this one stacked with containers, glides past us. The sea on either side of it is like satin smoothly rippling. And because of the sunset, the colours on these ripples are graduated from dark pink near the ship to a delicate dove grey by the time they reach our side of the water.

All this calm and beauty. I could be the *Starship Enterprise*, floating along.

The mood is broken when a brown mongrel-type dog comes up and sniffs at Sam and Sam puts the run on him sharpish. I start worrying again about James.

Ken picks up the shift. Are you ready to head back, or do you want to walk all the way out to the lighthouse?

I'd better not, I say, and I use the cuban heels as an excuse. They're murder on these big blocks, I tell him. I can't appreciate all this lovely scenery because I have to have my head down all the time watching out for the cracks.

He stands up, letting Sam jump off his lap. Here, let me help you, hold my arm, he says. I stand up and take his arm and we set off.

Immediately I feel very odd. He links me quite loosely, but a bit too loosely, if you know what I mean and we both become self-conscious about it. I know this is crazy but I haven't walked linked to a man for years and years and I've obviously lost the knack. I feel, and I'm sure he feels, that we have blinking signs all over us. Look At Us! We're An Item!

It's ludicrous, here we are, walking through the completest, most wonderful sunset, and all I can think of is trying to make sure the pressure along my arm is uniform and that I'm not transmitting any signal. The more I try to relax, the stiffer my arm gets and the stiffer his gets in return until – I'm sure he feels the exact same – our arms feel like two of those enormous cement drainage pipes welded together for all eternity. We're just a pair of walking arms.

It seems to take three hours to get back to the Pigeon House where he's parked the van. And when we separate to go to our respective doors, the feeling of release is so great that I feel shaky. He keeps his head down as he gets into the driver's seat.

We stop for chips at a place in Ringsend that he knows. He brings them out to the car and bit by bit, as we're eating, we start to be able to talk again. He tells me a little about himself. He's originally from Fairview, but when he was about fourteen, his parents, through one thing and another, found themselves thrown on to the Corporation's lists and they all had to move out to Ballymun, to one of the towers. I see him looking at me sort of sideways to see how I'll react. He's as much of a snob as me!

Ballymun? I go, I've loads of friends in Ballymun.

Which is a lie. But I see by him that it was the right thing to say. I believe those flats are lovely inside, I start to embroider. Don't they have free heat? And all the hot water you can use? I believe it's boiling in the wintertime?

Yeah, he says, the problem is not the flats, the problem is some of the scumbags outside the flats.

I decide not to pursue the flats issue in case he asks me my so-called friends' names. What happened that you all had to move? I ask him. But tell me to mind my own business if you like.

They had a shop that failed.

Closedown.

This is a man who obviously hasn't talked to anyone for a long time. But in a little while he does thaw. He tells me quite wistfully that until they moved to Ballymun he was in Sutton Park school. No fault to Ballymun Comprehensive, he goes, they did their best in pretty tough circumstances, it was just that I wasn't tough enough myself . . .

So after the Inter Cert, he decides to chuck it in. He'd always been good with his hands and he starts work right away, mowing people's lawns, clipping hedges, that kind of thing.

And when I'd be mowing their lawns I'd see doors about to come off their hinges – I'd offer to fix them. Gradually it built up. Women recommended me to their friends. He chats on, quite easy again, I suppose it helps that we're both eating the chips.

The big news comes then. He's twenty-nine years old and four years ago he separated from his wife, Diandra. They'd no kids.

Is it Michael Douglas's wife who's called Diandra, I ask him.

He looks across at me, surprised. I didn't know that,

he goes. I thought it was just one of those makey-uppey names. Come to think of it, he goes then, I've never seen her birth cert. I bet she couldn't have been christened that. How long has Michael Douglas been married?

I shouldn't have said anything about Michael Douglas.

I start to draw him out further about himself. It turns out he's neither a carpenter nor an electrician, not formally, he has no training. He just continued on with what he had started after the Inter Cert. I'm one of those people who are good with their hands, he says. He never has any problem getting work and makes quite a good living. He'll do anything that comes along, a bit of gardening, plumbing, building a wall, repairing a roof, anything. He also uses the van – to shift furniture for people who are moving or to carry stuff to one of the tip heads. There are apparently thousands of people in this city – and not just rich people – who can't be bothered to take the time even to mow their own lawns. Or who don't know how to change a washer in a tap and are not interested in learning. He shakes his head in wonderment. Imagine . . .

One woman got him out specially just to fix a Dustbuster to a wall.

Another one hired him to do a few bits and bobs, wallpaper a hall, cut a few trees, trim bushes, change plugs. He looks at me. Now you won't believe this. This woman had a husband and three sons.

I widen my eyes, marvelling. (I don't think! He hasn't met James Devine!)

And then there are all the elderly widows living on their own, Ken goes on. He always feels very sorry for them. He's done a deal with another mate of his who goes to the North every so often to bring back stuff. This guy brings him job lots of items like burglar alarms and security lights and window-locks. He gives the materials to the widows at cost, charges them only for the labour. This is the Climate of Fear we're all living in these days. He shakes his head again.

He's gone up several notches in my estimation. It's nice of him not to overcharge widows, myself having been on the receiving end of shysters who salivate when they see a woman on her own in need of someone to screw a shelf to a wall.

How does he get the work? I open my mouth and stuff in the last handful of chips — the ones from the bottom of the bag encrusted with salt, I love those.

Usually word-of-mouth, he tells me. He leaflets as well. Leafleting is huge in Dublin. You can't open the front door of our place without tripping over a mountain of them, everything from double glazing to undertakers to Toymasters, all offering deals of a lifetime.

A wasp flies into the car and it takes us ages to get rid of it.

Then Ken uses the H word. It's following me around. He advertises in the *Herald* Useful Services small ads column. Handyman available with van. Honest, reliable and hard-working. He puts the ad in when the word-of-mouth falls off a bit and always gets enough work out of it to tide him over. Again, it seems to be mostly women, he says. He's half apologetic — I'm not implying women are helpless, far from it.

I know you're not, I say. I've always meant to buy myself a Black and Decker. I just never had the spare cash — or when I did there was always something more urgent to spend it on.

You can borrow mine any time. He grins. Now, changing the subject, what about yourself? We've been talking about me all the time. Tell me about you. Where's your office?

I ball up the chip bag so it fits in the palm of my hand.

There doesn't seem to be a bin bag in the van and he's put his under his seat. I couldn't litter if you paid me, littering is one thing Mammy had great principles about, at least when she was well. I'll have slime in my hands from carrying an apple core all the way home if I can't find a bin.

We'll leave me for next time, I say, presumptuous enough. I should be getting back – I promised myself I'd do at least two hours of revision tonight. And I've an early start in the morning.

Right-oh, he goes and reaches for the key in the ignition. Before he turns it he darts a look at me. I enjoyed it, he says.

I smile at him. Me, too. Good luck tomorrow.

Good luck.

We move off.

Just my luck, of course. Separated. Nothing is ever simple in my life.

✦ Fifteen ✦

The two English papers traditionally take up the whole first day in the Leaving Cert and I should imagine this enrages the jumper brigade because Irish is supposed to be our official first language.

Although the exam room was spacious enough and all the windows were open, the place felt like the inside of an oven. Outside, the sun was raising the tar on the roads – it's always glorious weather during the weeks of the state exams, and I always feel sorry for the poor kids who are going to be cooped up inside for the whole two or three weeks it takes to do the whole panoply. Today, though, I feel sorry for myself. Talk about ask me sister, I'm sweatin'!

The butterflies in my tummy went wild (maybe it was all the sunshine, ha ha!) when I saw the pink Honours paper lying there in front of me. I tried to calm myself down by being chuffed that I was here at all. Who'd have thought. Angela Devine from the flats. Leaving Cert English. Honours.

We were taking the exam in a boys' school with a whole load of fellas, who were very well behaved, contrary to my expectations.

And then the moment came when the supervisor told us we could turn over the paper. Did you ever hear a shower of hailstones?

When I read it, I couldn't believe my eyes, I nearly cheered out loud. Someone up there loves me, I thought, because there were two of the essays I could have done standing on my head. A Farewell to Adolescence. A City of Dreams.

Here I'd been, dreading the choices would all be philosophical – they can be terribly abstract in the Leaving Cert – or something to do with the Peace Process or the EU, neither of which would be my strong point. But, A Farewell to Adolescence? A City of Dreams? And me a Dublin woman? And Guardian of the Adolescent of the Year?

I raced through the Unprescribed Prose section of the paper then pounced on A City of Dreams. I let my imagination run riot, threw caution to the winds regarding Mr Elliott's warnings about structures and what you have to start with in your opening paragraph and how you have to develop your themes and summarize at the end. Out the window. I've long thought, anyway, that the people who correct these exam papers must long for a bit of relief from that sort of stuff.

This was me and my city – the South Bull and its sunsets, a Dublin, I wrote, dressed in cloth of gold. You get the flavour . . .

I wrote until the last possible minute, but towards the end the heat was getting to me and I was finding it hard to keep a grip on the biro, my right hand was covered in ink and the plastic was so slippy with sweat it kept sliding. I find that Bics tend to crack under extreme pressure. Mind you, as Tom Bennett used to say, what do you expect for tuppence, Moby Dick?

But when the supervisor called time up, I felt it had all been worth it and I floated out of that exam hall on a high.

Mr Elliott was waiting for us when we got out. He

went through the prescribed passages with us – I hadn't done too badly at all, I found – and then he asked us all one by one which essay we had done. When my turn came, he gave me a rather peculiar look when I told him.

What's the matter? I ask. He's frightening me now.

Nothing, nothing, he says, but you know you and your essays, Angela, that imagination of yours and your big words. I hope you kept your feet on the ground with this one. Did you remember the structures I taught you?

I'm looking at him and I'm remembering the argument one of the other women in the class had with him about surely it's better to be creative. Him saying back to her that we should keep the creativity for the writing classes and groups he was sure we'd all belong to sooner or later. That what they were looking for in the Leaving Cert was structure and summary and intelligent, well-ordered argument. That's definite, he'd said, trust me on this one.

Now I feel about one inch tall. There I'd been thinking C1 or even a B2 if I was lucky enough to get the right fella marking me. (You have to be a genius to get an A in English.) That old hubris again.

I reassure Mr Elliott that I had, of course, remembered everything he'd taught me but I'm talking out of a burst balloon. Far from a C1 or a B2, now I'm thinking, Ah, well, all I want really is to pass the damned thing . . .

Ken is listening and he obviously sees that I'm upset because when Mr Elliott turns away to the woman beside me, he asks me if I'd like to go for a drink later, after the second paper. We deserve it, he goes, especially if you did as well as I think you did.

I'll be eternally grateful to him for that.

So I agree to go for a drink. With the adrenalin still pumping I convince myself that I *deserve* a bit of an outing. Anyhow, I just couldn't face the flat right now, not with poor old James moping around and MTV blaring – although I've learned to block it out. I can usually read or study as if I'm in a forest glade.

It's only when I'm half-way through the poetry section of the second paper that afternoon that I remember Patsy didn't send me a good-luck card like she'd promised. I try to shrug it off but I'm afraid that for a little while it comes between me and my Patrick Kavanagh.

Our exam room is in one of those old-fashioned assembly halls made from a bunch of classrooms between which you can open a series of partition doors. Today, these tall doors are folded back all along the wall, like Beefeaters standing to attention. Even still, the atmosphere is stifling, worse than the morning. And the place is so venerable that, no matter how much you clean it, it'll always be dusty. Old plaster, old wood. (Trust me, I know about these things!) The windows are set high – I suppose to stop pupils daydreaming out of them – and you can see this dust floating in the light slanting from them. Motes. Millions of motes.

Not that I'm watching dances of dust. Even though it might well be fairy dust. Because the good news is that, to my absolute amazement, once again I have it cracked. I could have answered nearly every single question in every section of this English paper.

And would you believe that in the play section we've been asked to 'consider the qualities of *Hamlet* which account for its popularity as a play throughout the ages'. Which gives yours truly a chance to compare the inhuman pressures on the human mind of Hamlet versus the even worse pressures on Macbeth and to discuss why Hamlet is more popular. (Wrongly, in my opinion, as you know.) This paper could have been set by yours truly's guardian angel. What a doddle. Thank you, Mr Elliott. Thank you, angel . . .

It's odd that I'm thinking pressure here, because wait till you hear what happened next.

For a short while all I can hear in the room is sighing and the odd rustle of paper or small scrape of a chair. I'm writing furiously – the old Bic slipping and sliding again in my hand – when from behind me I hear this sound, like a little scream, but not quite. I'm not the only one who heard something, everyone else did too. We all turn around.

There's a kid freaking out in the second last row. At first I think he might be having a fit or something, his head is back and his shoulders are shaking but then I see the tears pouring down his face and I realize he's having some sort of emotional breakdown.

The supervisor goes down to him and puts a hand on his shoulder to see what's the matter but it turns out to be the wrong thing to do because I'll never forget as long as I live what happened next. The kid shoots to his feet and overturns the desk – no, 'overturns' is too mild a word, he throws it over so violently that he catapults it into two other desks and chairs and the whole lot, boys and all, take a tumble. Desks, chairs, papers, pens, answer books, rulers, arms, legs, all flying.

Then he starts on a rampage around the room, flailing with his arms, kicking out at people. There's pandemonium. The rest of us are jumping up to get out of his way. More chairs get overturned. The supervisor is running around the room after him.

Now the kid picks up one of the chairs and flings it at a window, breaking the glass. We all duck. The glass comes back in and flies all over the room because there's a wire security grille on the outside. Now he's kicking, throwing over everything in his path.

One strange thing – you'd think he'd be roaring. No. All you can hear is the furniture and the glass and the rest of us making little whimpery noises while we're scurrying out of his way.

He picks up a second chair and the supervisor dashes to the door and yells at the boy who's on duty outside to go quick and get the head teacher and to tell him to fetch the Guards and a doctor.

You might ask what are the rest of us doing. Absolutely nothing is the answer. We're all like we're in shock. Paralysed. All we're doing is looking. There's a sort of exclusion zone around him.

The kid throws his second chair at the window just as the head teacher comes running in the door. The head teacher is yelling, Gary! Gary! but the kid completely ignores him and throws a third chair, bang! What's left of the glass shatters.

The head teacher rushes forward and something clicks with the kid. He runs away from the window and into a corner. He turns around to face the opposition. Now the head teacher and the supervisor do a pincer movement, coming at him from two sides. The head, fair dues to him, is not making any jerky moves and has both of his arms outstretched, hands open, like a gunfighter showing the other dude that he's unarmed. Come on, Gary, he's saying, come on, no one's going to hurt you. He's talking like you'd talk to a wild animal. And that's exactly how the kid is behaving now, he has his back shoved tight into the corner with his legs splayed in front of him and arms out on both sides against the walls as though he's supporting the whole building. His head is up and sort of sideways, like a stag who's going to be shot in the neck.

As it happens, I'm one of the people nearest to him, so near that I can see the veins, like little red threads, in his eyes. My heart goes out to him. I've never seen a more terrified expression on anyone. Even James when the cops came.

Now there's near silence in the room. After all the crashing and banging it's eerie to hear nothing except the head teacher going softly, Come on, Gary, come on outside. We're going to get someone to look after you, everything's going to be all right, you're not going to get into any trouble, come on, Gary . . .

The kid makes a strangled noise, high in his nose, 'mmmffff,' as though he's frightened to death, which for sure he is.

I step forward, hear myself saying to the head teacher, Excuse me, let me help, I have a fella at home, I can probably handle this. I don't wait for permission, instead, I walk up in front of the kid and look him straight in the eye. Look, I go, as quietly as I can speak, I give you my word that I won't let anyone do anything to you. Come on out with us. Don't worry about the damage to the bloody windows, it's only a bit of glass, it's easily cleaned up.

Isn't that right? I say, over my shoulder to the head teacher but without taking my eyes off Gary.

That's right, goes the head teacher.

There's this pause and then the kid peels his arms off the two walls he's plastered against.

The head teacher and I take him one arm each and the three of us walk out through the door. The face on the attendant boy outside is a study. He couldn't be more than sixteen, glasses, pimples, half of him thinks all his birthdays have come at once with all this drama, half of him is scared to death. He's probably thinking he'll be blamed for something.

Gary is broken. Apart from anything else, he'll fail English and if you've to have any hope of getting into third level, you can't really afford to fail English. He goes off with the head teacher towards his office because I have to get back inside to finish the exam.

And that's the end of it from my end. You might well ask why I'm going to the bother of telling you this, like, Gary is not my problem, is he? It's just that the incident brought it home to me – where it hurts – how vulnerable boys of that age are. I'm sure I don't have to spell it out for you any more than that.

Back inside the exam hall, the supervisor is standing wiping his forehead with a hanky – he's the jumper type, they always have real hankies – and when he sees me arrive back and now it's all over he galvanizes. It's only then I realize what I've done. 'I can handle this'? I can't even handle my own brother. But somehow it worked. It was quite a valuable lesson, if you act as though you're in charge, you probably are.

The supervisor springs up on to the dais at the top of the room and makes a little speech. This incident is unprecedented, *unprecedented* in all his experience. And the best thing to do now is to get all the desks and so forth to rights again and to continue. And we're all to calm down and he hopes we're not too upset to continue our examination.

One of the men in our group speaks up and asks if we can have a short recess to collect our thoughts.

Out of the question. The supervisor is recovering his status now and he tells us, sternly, that he hopes no one has taken advantage of the situation.

We all laugh, nervously, because we know what he's talking about – cogging – but we don't really know whether he means it as a joke or not.

He doesn't. Because he tells us that he's going to stay up there watching our every move until we put the room together again and all get back to work. He'll make allowances for what happened. We can have an extra fifteen minutes at the end of the time to make up for the upset.

Big deal.

As it happened, it didn't take me all that long to get back into discussing the pressures on Ophelia. I'm about to compare them to the pressures of Lady Macbeth when I decide not to go overboard. There's a difference between displaying knowledge and showing off. I suppose knowing these differences is what being a mature student is all about. So for what remains of the time I've allocated to the play question, I concentrate on poor old lily-faced Ophelia.

And eventually, when the man on the dais calls time up, I'm happy enough. I'd put in the work, the questions fell my way and I've done my best.

Ken and I decide to go the the Gravediggers, which is a pub he knows at the back wall of Glasnevin cemetery. It isn't too far away and it's very famous because of its association with James Joyce and Bloomsday. We think it might be appropriate for people who'd just finished Leaving Cert English. But wouldn't you know it, as we're just about to leave, we hear Mr Elliott suggesting the same outing to others of the group.

Ken and I look at each other and then, without saying anything, we know we want to be on our own. I find this disturbing, for want of a better word.

Are you sure you won't come with us for a drink, Angela? Mr Elliott is put out. I think he likes the feeling of running the modern equivalent of a hedge school and doesn't want to let any of us go. No thanks, I say, Ken here has kindly offered me a lift. I hear my own voice saying this too brightly, as though I've something to conceal.

Get a grip, Angela Devine.

As we walk towards the van, Ken stares straight ahead and suggests another pub he knows, the Brian Boru, which is not all that far from the Gravediggers.

Anyway, he says as he starts the engine, it's much of a muchness, the Brian Boru is in *Ulysses* as well.

I'm impressed. You've read it then?

Have you?

We laugh.

The pub is one of those refurbished jobs, darke woode and olde worlde jugs and Gold Flake mirrors on the shelves in amongst the bottles. It's nice, though. Because this is now tea-time, the place is buzzy with office workers, mostly young.

We have three drinks in quick succession and I'm having a great time. In fact, by the time I'm finishing the third I'm quite giddy and I think he is too. But all of a sudden I'm thinking urgently of James, I'm probably spooked by the incident with the berserk kid.

I tell Ken I have to go. Now he looks off into the middle distance. Is this the end then? I mean, I'd like to see you again. He's beetroot and I realize I'm being offered a proper date. It's donkey's years since anyone asked me on a date.

Well, that's not strictly accurate. Men have asked me. To be precise it's donkey's years since I had either the time or the inclination to consider going on one.

The drink makes me reckless. Are you asking me out? I mean *out*?

If it was possible for him to go any redder he would have. What a good idea. He tries to laugh. Dismal failure. Yes, as a matter of fact. As a matter of fact I am. Asking you out.

Then the answer is yes.

When so? We could go to a film?

Sure. It's ages since I've been to a film.

We arrange to meet the following evening to go to see *Sense and Sensibility*. At my suggestion, we make it the six o'clock show rather than the night-time one. If there's any suggestion in his mind that we might become an item, I want to slide gradually towards it, see how it hangs with me. He agrees. He's so embarrassed I can see the pulse throbbing in his forehead. I don't know how this man ever got around to getting married.

It's quite late, well after tea-time, when I get home. Even before I open the door of the flat I can hear the cacophony of the rock music. I despise MTV. I tried and tried to be flexible and modern and understanding about the needs of the young and so forth but now I've decided that its co-called music is just noise. You can't hear the words of the songs and the singers are nearly always out of tune.

There are a few exceptions, I suppose. I definitely like Bono's voice, it has a haunting, lyrical quality to it and he does sing in tune. It makes me wince, though, because he's strained it with not minding it so now he's hoarse even when he talks in interviews on the radio. In my humble opinion, if he goes on the way he is he won't have any of it left by the time he's fifty. (Not that he needs my opinion, from what I hear he's enough fortunes made at this stage never to have to open his mouth again.)

Their backing has some discernible pattern to it too, The Edge's guitar work is quite exciting. In fact, I have to confess that if I had the money I'd go to a U2 concert. I believe they're brilliant live.

We're very proud of all our world-class singers and bands from Ireland, you know. For a small country, I think we're great, for instance who'd have thought only twenty-five years ago that we'd keep winning the Euro-vision Song Contest? Or Nobel Prizes? And, of course, in other fields – no pun intended – we have Ronnie Delaney

and Sonia O'Sullivan and Michelle Smith and Eamonn
Coughlan. Not to speak of Paul McGrath and George
Best and all the golfers and writers and cyclists.

When you consider that we have half the population of
Haiti. When is the last time you heard of a world
superstar from Haiti? Papa Doc and that's it.

I steel myself to open the door and go in. Hi, I say to
James. The music is so loud I see his lips saying, Hi, back
but I can't hear him. He's lolling on the bed-settee with
both legs over one of the armrests and he has three plates
– *three* – on the floor in front of him with two empty
glasses and two cups. Plus he's pouring crisps into his
mouth, using the bag like a funnel, and he has a can of
Coke in the other hand.

Something snaps in me – maybe I'm a bit reckless
because of the few gins I've had with Ken in the Brian
Boru. I march over to the telly and I turn it off.

I turn around. Get your great big spawgs down off the
arms of that settee and clean up this room.

He opens his mouth to say something back and then a
miracle happens. He closes it again without saying
anything, he takes the legs down and stands up. He
gathers together all the plates and cups and glasses and
takes them over to the sink. He runs the water. I'm left
with my mouth hanging open.

Then I go and ruin it. I start in on him about how hard
I work for the two of us and how I don't want to have to
come home to see chaos around me when all he has to do
is to put in a modicum of effort . . . That it's not fair . . .
I hear my own voice rasping on and on like a rusty needle
on a cracked record.

He throws one of the glasses at the back of the sink and
it breaks.

Eff off, he says. (Except he doesn't say 'eff'.) And he
storms out of the flat.

My instinct is to run after him but I don't. I could kill myself. Here he hands me a golden opportunity for progress in the relationship between us and I blow it.

All right, in one respect I have right on my side, he should have a bit more consideration and try to make more of an effort, domestically speaking, but in his defence, he has to be absolutely miserable. In turmoil. He was probably comfort eating. And it hasn't been easy for him, no siblings, no father or mother, just one much older sister. A pretty bossy sister at that. Now he has all of this rape stuff to contend with. And in all fairness to him, he has been indulged a great deal – I have to take some of the blame for his self-centredness.

I stand there in the silence. The flat seems desperately empty. I realize that this is probably what it's going to be like when he goes to gaol.

I mean if, of course . . .

I notice a dinge in the armrest of the settee where his legs were and I go over to smooth it out. It's still warm. I get upset. It's that bloody gin, no wonder they call it mother's ruin. Now who knows what'll happen. Talk about selfish.

→ Sixteen ←

Two pieces of good news.

I forgot the next day's hangover when I read the letter from Patrice Murphy. It was addressed to James, of course, and although normally I wouldn't dream of opening up his post – not that he gets much! – in this instance I felt justified.

Number one, James's boss had agreed to go into court as a character witness. Number two, even better, the psychiatric evaluation of him had come in and thank God it was quite favourably disposed. The psychiatrist was of the opinion that the incident with Rosemary Madden was most likely aberrant and was unlikely to reoccur.

I didn't get a chance to tell James until quite late that evening. He didn't come in until nearly half past ten.

When I did tell him I could see, although he was trying to hide it, that he was thunderstruck about his boss. After all, this guy was the same one who had suspended him.

Unfortunately, when he arrived in, I was on my way out the door, kissogramming, so I couldn't hang around to discuss the implications. With him bringing in no money I had to earn every penny I could so I had had to abandon (temporarily, I hope) my plans to give up those gigs. I'm sorry, I say to James, I have to go now but I won't be long.

Wha'? He looked at me as if I had two heads.

I didn't engage. I was having to force myself to go out to work that night and I didn't want any extra hassle. Apart from all the trauma that was going on in our lives, this particular night I was acutely aware of what a wally I looked in the outfit. It'd still be daylight up to eleven o'clock and you'd want to see the looks I get in the street!

I started this work about six years ago, up to then I couldn't go out much at night because babysitters cost too much and it didn't make economic sense. But when James came to be about thirteen, going on fourteen, I spotted the ad in one of those free newspapers they deliver through your door, and I figured he was old enough to be left alone a couple of nights a week. 'Top wages for suitable candidates. Sense of humour essential.'

How hard could it be? I'd always believed I've a sense of humour (although lately I'm not so sure!).

The interview went grand. I'd been afraid they'd ask me to strip in front of them but they didn't. Maybe it helped that I made sure I wore a short skirt that day. The chap interviewed me just as if it was for a real job although a lot more informal, of course. He asked me what my attitude would be to kissing fellas, or putting them across my knee and spanking them. I said, Whatever turns them on is fine by me, provided it's all play and it doesn't get out of hand. I could see him watching me carefully while I talked.

And how would I feel about going in a novelty costume, like a stripping banana or a wicked chicken.

No problem, I said, looking at a point on the wall behind his head so that I wouldn't burst out laughing. He gave me a gig on a trial basis for that very night.

It went OK – he obviously checked back with the client – so he gave me another one and put me on the books. So that was that.

The only difficulty was that I didn't have a telephone so I had to make sure to ring them to tell them when I was available. Just as well, as it turned out, because it left me more in control. If I didn't want to work, I just didn't ring in. And on our side, if we were short urgently – say, if the Hoover broke down or if we had to get a new kettle or a toaster – then I knew I had an avenue to raise instant cash for it.

Within a couple of months I was an old hand. Once you get the hang of it, you can be anything. It's just a matter of not being too inhibited and of focusing on the client. It's half acting, half yourself. All eyes are usually on the victim anyway, not on you. And if you concentrate on him – ninety-nine per cent it'll be a him – then it's actually quite easy.

When I got better acquainted with the boss he told me that he knows within two minutes of meeting a girl or a fella whether they're going to be able to do the job well. He says he finds that the work is an extension of a person's own personality. Well, whatever it says about me I started even to enjoy it. (For a while.) It seems I may have a genuine talent for entertaining people.

I definitely found that the more of the kissogram work I did the more confident I became. For instance it certainly helped with PA System. Patsy and I didn't start those gigs until I was well into my stride with the kissograms and I found that when I stood in front of an audience I wasn't half as nervous as I should have been. I was able to concentrate on their enjoyment rather than on what they were going to think of me. You start with an advantage in these circumstances, they're on your side, at least at the beginning. After all, they paid their money so they could have a good time, not to be critical.

At the beginning, I kept this side of my life very quiet

— they still don't know at the cleaning job, although the clock is ticking and very soon I'm sure I'll run into one of my cleaning colleagues at some gig or other. Dublin *is* a village, everyone who lives here says it all the time, you can't walk down O'Connell Street without meeting at least one person you know.

I didn't tell even Patsy until I'd been doing it for the best part of two years. I must say she took it well. But I often wonder what Mammy would think. She was such a lady, I doubt she would approve of all the innuendo. She certainly would have hated the pair work, like when two of us go as a priest and a nun.

The money was a godsend, of course, it was because of the extra cash that James and I were able to move out of the flats and into the private rented sector.

So anyway, this particular gig this night, I'm requested as a French maid. I tippy-tap into the pub, feathers and fur flying, so to speak.

The first person I see is St John Markey.

Talk about shock. I don't know which of us was the more taken aback. Yet why should I have been so surprised to see this baby barrister in a pub in Dorset Street? Somehow you don't associate Dorset Street with lawyers. They'd be more Grafton Street or the Shelbourne, southside anyway . . .

Whatever. I'm absolutely mortified. Of course I pretend I don't recognize him and I go and do my job. But I'm tickling the victim with my feather duster and I'm ooh-la-laahing and telling him he's a naughty boy and making a holy show of the poor guy but all the time all I can think of is St John Markey's eyes boring into the back of my head. Or into some other place on my anatomy. These French maid's outfits are pretty skimpy.

Would this go hard for James? I mean, when this kid is

arguing James's case in front of a judge will he be seeing me in my Wonderbra and my frilly knickers under my lace apron?

I was never more glad to get out of a place. And luckily that gig was the only one I'd accepted for that night, so I was true to my word about getting home early.

It turns out that this is a lucky break. Because James is in bits when I get in. I mean in *bits*. He's in his bedroom, face down on his bed. No telly on, no music, no lights. He's rigid.

What's the matter? I go, did something happen?

What did I think was the matter. He says it to the wall and he doesn't move a single muscle.

I say nothing more at that stage, I feel totally helpless. That's one of the worst aspects of this entire situation. There is nothing I can do about it. It's rolling towards us like an avalanche. We see it, we hear it, it's above us, but we've nowhere to go to get out of its path. We just have to stand there, staring up at it over our heads. Waiting for it to bury us.

Correction. Waiting for the main weight of it to bury us. It keeps dropping little mini-avalanches on us as warnings of what is to come.

I make two cups of tea and I bring them into his room. Listen, James, I say, here's a cup of tea for you. Drink it. Come on—

I don't want it. Still to the wall.

I know you don't want it but please. Drink it for me—

I don't effin' want it.

Sit up, then. I want to talk to you.

Eff off and leave me alone.

I stand my ground, it's my turn now. I won't eff off, I say quietly. I'm staying here until you sit up. I didn't get us into this problem but I'm staying with you. I'm not abandoning you.

Whether it was me swearing or what – he's certainly not used to that – he slowly sits up. I hold out his cup of tea and he takes it, still without looking at me.

We sit there, both of us sipping at the tea. I'm trying to tell myself that what I'm doing is just being there for him. I don't care if on the surface he seems not to want me. I'm the adult here. I have to trust what I believe is right for him.

There's some kind of disturbance out in the street, a couple of drunks probably, man and woman. Shouting and roaring. Lots of bad langauge. To me, it makes the two of us inside, in that quiet room, seem unreal. It's not real behaviour to be sitting here with the lights out, sipping tea and not saying anything.

You know how that happens? How you recede from where you're sitting and look down on yourself and at what you're doing as if you're watching yourself in a play? James and I are sitting on this bed, he's as hollow as a ghost and I'm in a French maid's outfit and we're barely visible amongst the heaps of his clothes all over the place.

We're not real people. We're the Macbeths.

It's funny that *Macbeth* should come into my mind at this point. It's the exchanges between the Doctor and Macbeth. She's completely mad now but he's still asking the doctor what's wrong with her. The doctor tells him that she's not physically sick at all but troubled with thick-coming fancies that keep her from her rest.

Exactly. The fancies and fears are always worse than the actuality. Shakespeare's brilliant. Even if I fail the bloody English exam, at least I'll have had the privilege of having read Shakespeare for once in my life.

One quibble I do have about the Shakespeare curriculum, though. Whereas I admit you need to be taught how to understand it because of the archaic language and so forth, I have a gut feeling that all the analysis and questioning and notes that you have to study ruins the actual play for you. I wonder if Shakespeare, when he wrote *Hamlet*, or any of the other plays, really meant people to be comparing and contrasting or discussing it? To go back to *Macbeth*. That's a gut-feeling play. You just know in your gut what's going on when you hear it acted out.

Mr Elliott told us that the people in the Globe Theatre used to munch their lunch while they were watching the plays and shout across to each other and heckle the actors. That sounds like they were having fun. I don't know how many Leaving Cert students would think Shakespeare was fun.

Do you think I'm a rapist? His voice is small and light and scared.

Of course not, I go.

I'm glad it's nearly dark.

I'm sure you'll appreciate that, in the circumstances, *Sense and Sensibility* was not exactly a barrel of laughs for me. I tried to put a good face on it on the way up to the Omniplex where the picture was playing. (That's another good thing about Dublin, by the way, I think we must have about a hundred cinemas at this stage and there are more promised.)

Ken Sheils and I speculate about the Leaving and what marks other people in the class might get. We exhaust this topic by Whitehall church.

Tell me a little bit about Diandra, I go then, do you see

her often? Immediately he looks across as me as though I've hit him.

I try to laugh it off. This is not a trick question, I say, I'm just making conversation but if you'd rather not—

No, no, he says quickly. Of course I don't mind talking about her.

He has to brake quickly, because he nearly forgot to turn off the dual carriageway into Santry, and Sam shoots forward against the dashboard. He has a habit of standing upright, with his hind legs on the floor of the van and his front ones on the base of the gear lever between the two front seats.

We sort Sam out then Ken starts to tell me about Diandra and him. She was only seventeen when they got married. Everyone was naturally dead set against it and wanted her to wait at least until she was eighteen. But then she broke down and admitted she was pregnant. There was murder, of course, but what could anyone do?

They got a flat in Ballymun, which is where her folks lived, and after they were safely married, she had this really quick miscarriage – which, according to Ken, didn't take a feather out of her. He says this without a hint of bitterness. According to him, at the beginning, he genuinely tried to make the best of it, but it wasn't long before they started having serious rows.

And no, he doesn't see much of her now. Hasn't seen her for about six months. She doesn't care as long as the cheques keep coming in the door. Now he's sounding a bit sour.

It turned out that Diandra was using him to get away from home. Her mother was living with some deadbeat – the father was long gone – and Diandra couldn't stick the guy. Hands all over the place, she told Ken. She had two brothers who couldn't stick the situation either and spent half their lives in Diandra and Ken's flat rather than in their own. Then they started bringing their friends in. It became like Father McVerry's hostel for the homeless.

I'm not sure I'm liking the sound of all of this, I mean, this was Ken's home too. Where was he while all this squatting and mayhem was going on in his house? Up in Mars?

I ask him why he didn't put his foot down. We're just turning into the car park of the Omniplex now. The place is hopping. These shopping centres with their cinemas are breeding – I don't know if Dublin can handle many more of them, but so far there seems to be no limit to the number of people who throng them, day and night.

I reckoned that she was very young and that things would get better, he says. Anyway, I was out working all the time. I had to. She liked going out, nice clothes.

I think about that for a minute or two. This Diandra is some tulip, as far as I can see, but then I wasn't there at the time, was I?

I know he has a father and a mother, both still *in situ*. And four siblings – two brothers, two sisters. They were all living at home, together, until recently when Ken got his own place at the Custom Hall and then, within months, one sister and one brother got married. How did his own folks feel about the way he was treated by Diandra and her family?

Sam has to brace himself between us now because Ken's swinging the van around the little roundabout in front of the cinemas. I can see he's using the manoeuvre to fob me off. He straightens up the car again and starts to travel down between the rows of parked cars. My folks? he says then. My folks didn't know.

He finds a space and puts the van into it. He turns off the engine and gives Sam a Bonio.

When we're getting out and he's locking the van, he

says casually, I never told them why we got separated. I'm not close to my parents. The way he says it closes the conversation. I'm beginning to see that, with this guy, there's a complicated area down there he doesn't want to open up.

This news about him and his folks and them not being able to talk to each other comes as a real shock to me. To me, up to now, Ken Shiels's early life had sounded like *The Little House on the Prairie* – real mother and father and sisters and brothers all living together.

What is it about me and families, do I jinx them just by knowing them? Take Tom Bennett's so-called family, I was over the moon about that one and look what happened there. And now here's Ken's.

Or maybe I just don't know what goes on inside real families because my own experience is so lacking. I'm probably trying too hard to latch on. Seems to me like I'm a homing pigeon who keeps bumping into walls. Maybe all the ordinary families are only on the telly! (Or down the country.)

I cried all the way through *Sense and Sensibility*. I didn't look, but I have a feeling Ken wasn't too chirpy either. It was exactly the wrong picture to go to if you come from a dysfunctional background. All that hominess and people being concerned about each other. All that hugging.

So, as you can see, the evening was not a success although we did make plans to meet again the following Saturday night to go for a meal. Apart from my birthday last year, when Patsy took me to a lovely little Italian pizza place just off Chatham Street, I have been in a restaurant approximately three times in ten years. You probably don't believe me but it's the truth. When I told Ken this, he perked up. Well, in that case I'll have to take you to somewhere very special.

I tried to perk up too and nearly managed it. But not for long.

Because when I open the door to the flat, I find James is not alone. Patrice Murphy is there with him.

He stands up when I get in. Hello, Ms Devine, I hope you don't mind the intrusion. You have no telephone, you see, and I was passing here, I was working late. I thought I'd pop in rather than wait until I saw you on Monday. You got my letter, I see – he points to where it's lying on the table.

James is avoiding my eye.

No problem, I say, thanks. I was delighted to hear the news.

Neither James nor he looks even the remotest bit delighted.

What's up? I go, everything's going all right, isn't it?

The answer, when it eventually comes, is yes and no. Certainly no from my point of view.

Everything is proceeding, as they say, but Patrice Murphy is here to try to persuade James to plead guilty to sexual assault. He says that if James does this, the case will be likely to go well for him because sexual assault is a lesser offence than rape. From the state's point of view, it would help ease the backlog and save legal expenses and the cost of a jury trial. From our point of view, apart from pleading to a lesser charge, psychologically, it would also mean that we wouldn't have this awful prospect hanging over us for ever and ever. But, most importantly, the victim won't have to be put through the ordeal of giving evidence. Judges apparently like that and they take it into account when they're handing down sentences. And I think that any judge would see that James's remorse at what happened that day is genuine. That would be very helpful.

Patrice Murphy bounces – did I tell you he has this

habit of doing little bounces on the balls of his feet when he's concentrating? When I talk about a backlog, he says, the courts are completely bogged down. It's not unusual to have to wait a year or more for a jury trial. We could get character witnesses to bolster the psychiatrist's opinion that what James did that day was uncharacteristic and that he would be extremely unlikely to reoffend.

He's bouncing away, I'm standing there, looking between him and James, whose head is nearly on the floor by now. I'm dumbstruck.

But he's not guilty, I say, when I can get a word in edgeways. You know his side of the story as well as I do. That's not rape or sexual assault, is it? They were there to do it— Remorse – are you remorseful, James?

I take a couple of steps towards James. James, say something.

James looks at the floor.

I start in then and go on and on about the condoms and all the rest of it. Patrice Murphy listens patiently. When I wind down, he says again that his professional, legal advice, solicitor to client, is that James should plead guilty to sexual assault. His tone of voice is exactly the same as it was before I started. It's like I haven't said one thing.

I turn to James. I'm desperate. What do you think? I ask him, say something, for God's sake. It's your life. You're the one who has to decide. What do you want to do?

He mutters something to his toes.

What? I go, I can't hear you.

He looks at me full frontal. I want to get this over with, one way or the other, I'm sick to death of it.

I panic. You're going to plead guilty to something you didn't do just because you're sick to death of hanging around? Land yourself in gaol for sure? Where's your courage? I'm so het up I don't give a damn, normally I wouldn't dream of having a family row in front of a stranger.

I'm going to gaol anyway, James looks at his toes again. You know I am.

He's really annoying me now. I don't know anything of the sort, I say. Who says you're going to gaol? People are acquitted in courts as well as being convicted. Have you never heard of the word justice?

He looks up at me then. A pitying look. It stops me in my tracks because there's a world there in his eyes that I don't know. I recognize it, though. I'm bang up against a generation gap but also, much worse than that, I see what kids of his generation expect for themselves. Nothing. In James's eyes I see a life with no expectations.

This kills me. All his life I've tried to convince him to expect that miracles do happen. That if you pay your dues and are decent, that decent things will happen back. I can see in one instant that I've been wasting my time.

I sit down. You're going to plead guilty, aren't you?

The solicitor puts his oar back in now. Don't be too upset, Ms Devine.

Please don't call me Ms. I'm a Miss.

Petty, I know, but I had to show some spark of life. And I do hate Ms. And I don't care whether or not married men should change their titles. That's nothing to do with me. I'm not a married woman and that's the end of it. I'm a Miss.

Your man doesn't bat an eyelid. I'm sorry, Miss Devine, he says, you never know nowadays, do you? To get back to what we were talking about, the substantive issue, as it were, I've had the opportunity to review the case with St John Markey and he agrees with me. Our strong advice is that James here should plead guilty.

Now what's in my head is the look on St John Markey's face when he recognized the French maid who came into the pub in Dorset Street.

St John Markey's junior, isn't he? Not a senior? I'm

playing for time now because I have to think of some other arguments.

Patrice Murphy lowers his voice as though he's in a church. Yes, St John is a junior but in my opinion he's very fine. He'll certainly be a senior before long.

All right. Supposing, just supposing we agree. What sentence could James get?

He shrugs a little shrug. I can't guarantee anything, of course, but our strong guess is that when the judge hears all the facts in the case, the sentence will be minimal. He will ask for a victim impact report—

I interrupt him. What's minimal? How long?

Two years? Maybe eighteen months if we're lucky?

Eighteen months if we're lucky? Does this guy have any idea how long eighteen months in Mountjoy Gaol would seem to someone like James Devine?

Somehow I manage to keep my voice steady. And if we're not? Or if we don't take your advice and let it go to trial?

It's possible to get a life sentence for rape.

If you're found guilty.

If you're found guilty.

Which is a big if . . .

He doesn't answer.

What this guy's telling us is that one way or the other we're going to gaol. Our own solicitor. Even though he knows exactly what happened. So much for fair play and justice.

James is still just sitting there and I turn to speak. Speak for yourself, James.

He screws up his face like he used to do when he was a child and was going to cry. He's whispering, I can't stand it any more. I just want to get this over with.

Seventeen

Needless to remark, with the trial hanging over us, I couldn't think of going out for a meal with Ken Sheils that Saturday night so I put a note in through his letterbox cancelling it. He wasn't too hard to find, I was lucky, found his letterbox on only the second block I tried in his apartments complex. (I'd been worried that he mightn't be using his real name – some people don't put their real names on their letterboxes because of security or to keep former wives and girfriends away.) I was very apologetic in the note but I said something had come up in my personal life.

Coincidentally, that Saturday was my birthday. James hadn't remembered – he never does so I hadn't expected anything from him – but for the first year ever since we were kids, Patsy hadn't remembered either. Ah, well, I suppose oblivion comes to us all!

I couldn't have celebrated anyway, in the circumstances. For some reason, I kept thinking back to James as a baby, as though it was his birthday and not mine.

He was a gorgeous child, genuinely beautiful. I thought I was the bee's knees wheeling him up and down our street with oul' wans googling at him and admiring him. And you know, nowadays, even since all this trouble, I still don't see him as this surly leathered 'youth' with his

earring and his big spawgs hanging over the arm of my
bed-settee. I still see this little lad in his go-car, soother
in his mouth and a battered denim baseball cap on his
head with his curls peeping out from under it. Or him
crying his heart out over a baby deer that's being eaten
by a cheetah on one of his wildlife programmes.

He's very good-looking, you know. By far the best-
looking of all five of us, I'd say – although since I haven't
met them for so long I'm not quite sure how the other
three are looking lately. His only drawback at present is
his skin, which is a bit spotty – I assume from all the
crisps. He's around six feet or six feet one and although
he's thin, I'm sure when he fills out a bit he'll have a
brilliant body. Also, when he gives his hair a chance to
grow, like right now, it's real film-star hair, dark and
crisp.

And considering all the pints and the smokes and the
late nights, not to speak of his work taking him through
the traffic fumes of Dublin, his eyes are pretty clear.
Actually, I don't mind boasting for once, his eyes are
amazing, large and pale grey with a paler, honey-
coloured fleck through them. Those eyes kill you if he
looks straight at you, as I know to my cost. It's probably
one of the reasons he was able to get away with murder
when he was small. Whoever his father was, he had to
have been a stunner.

At first, when I took him out of Temple Street hospital
that time, the social workers and public health nurses
were all over me, checking up on whether I was looking
after him properly or not. I can just imagine the case
conferences! They rode me very tightly. The nurse went
mad when she found out I'd flavour his milk with Ribena
– what about his teeth? All that sugar. They were only
his baby teeth, I said back to her. I promised her I'd go
easy but I made a mental reservation. Like hell I'd stop

giving him something that he really liked. Anyway, it was full of vitamin C. I hid the Ribena bottle when she was due to visit.

(Anyway, who's had the last laugh? James has fantastic teeth.)

I found early on that there's no mystery about caring for a baby. Feed him, change him, love him, feed him again. Their stomachs are perfectly designed. If you give them too much, or the wrong stuff, they'll sick it up again. If in doubt, feed, that was my motto.

Yet because for those first few weeks I was so desperately anxious about Mammy, I was probably not as good at being a mother to him as I should have been. I do worry about this, they say that the first few months of mothering are crucial to babies, to how their characters and personalities turn out. It could be all my fault that he's in this trouble now – but you'd drive yourself mad if you thought too deeply about everything you've done, or failed to do in your life, wouldn't you?

Once Mammy was put into hospital it was plain she was not going to survive, even though no one would come right out and say it. Apart from being malnourished and all the rest of it, she had pneumonia. And as I told you, now I reckon she could have been HIV. I must check sometime when exactly HIV came to Dublin. She could easily have been one of the first. Once again demonstrating the Devines' great good fortune.

The hospital was old and every crack in the paintwork on the wall of her ward is as clear to me today as it was that first visiting hour. When I walked in I immediately resented that she was in a bed surrounded by those of geriatrics. My mammy was *young* . . . These people were all on their last legs, coughing up phlegm and making disgusting noises. Some were obviously senile, roaring all the time for the nurses.

And the smell! Urine, of course, but another smell, too, which I can only describe as being like rotting fruit.

I definitely want to die young. I made up my mind that night and have never changed it.

When I calmed down a bit, I had to admit that in some respects she did look every bit as decrepit as the others. She'd cut her hair, or what was left of it, and there were bald patches showing through the clumps. As well as the purpling on her face, bruising and discoloration and so forth, she had her eyes closed and under the neon light, the sockets were so dark they were nearly black. She had a big cut on one of her cheekbones and a crusty cold sore on her lip. She was on two drips and she had an oxygen mask covering half her face. It gurgled.

It took me all my courage not to turn tail and rush out of there. I could have too, she was so out of it she'd never have known. Hello, Mammy, I said.

She opened her eyes and looked at me with this milky look. I realized she didn't know who I was. And then the strangest thing happened to me. I got so angry I wanted to kick her. Hard.

Can you believe that? Here's my mother, the person who means more to me than anyone else in the whole world. She's probably in desperate pain, probably dying, she's probably frightened and lonely, and here am I, furious with her. It's like I'm hit by a huge red wave of rage that scoops me up and throws me towards the ceiling. I want to hit and kick and roar. I want to overturn the bed and beat her around the place with my fists.

Yet at the same time I'm feeling all this, I'm also dying with sorrow.

Can you understand any of that? I didn't at the time. In fact, I remember I became so guilty about my reaction that it took me years to get over it.

Funnily enough, studying *Macbeth* brought it all back, not literally, of course, because it's all ancient history now, but I certainly identified with some of the blacker emotions unleashed by the witches in that play. It's something to do with control. You think you're in control but you're not. As a matter of fact, you're in control of nothing at all in this world, not even your own feelings. No wonder people have to believe in some sort of a god. Someone has to be in charge of this chaos.

Anyway, I did the best I could that night. I forced down the rage and I gave her the pathetic little bunch of flowers I'd brought in. Her eyes filled with tears, although she said nothing – she wouldn't have been able to anyway with the oxygen mask – and I could see she still thought I was some stranger. I didn't stay long. I couldn't.

That night, when I got back to the flat, I did something of which I remain so ashamed that I cannot possibly tell you what it is. Perhaps some other time. All I'll say now about that horrible wheeling merry-go-round period of my life is that the memory of what I did still frightens me.

To get back to James as a baby. He, of course, had no idea what big events were going on in his little life. All he cared about was his bottle and his soother and me. This was a bit of a boost for me. Despite everything else, I felt loved and important and necessary in someone's life.

The other three? Forget it. Francesca, as I've explained already, even at that age, wished us all off the planet so she could get on with her real life. For an eleven-year-old she was as poised as a model. Justine and Nicola, who were eight and six at the time, were doing all right in their foster homes. The fact that they had a big sister and a little brother didn't really impinge. They were happy to come to the access visits because of the Coke and the chips. They would have been just as happy to go to a circus or a pantomime. Probably happier.

No, the real family now was James and me.

When it was clear Mammy was not going to get any better, she was moved to the hospice in Harold's Cross. I cried buckets when they told me. It was so final. Everyone knew that once you went in there you would never leave it again except in a wooden box. Nowadays no one is afraid of the hospice – all our Irish stars are involved in fund-raising for it, I suppose it's sort of insurance for them, they know there's a good chance they'll need it themselves some day. Then, though, Dubliners *whispered* the word 'hospice' because it's full name was the Hospice for the Dying.

I shouldn't have cried because everything improved that day, including my ability to cope with what was happening. As soon as she was settled in, the entire world calmed down, so much so that I didn't dread going to see her any more. All that anger which had surged up in me each time I'd seen in her in the hospital? Gone.

Her whole appearance changed straight away, she sort of smoothed out, if you can imagine that. And although she lasted only six weeks longer and never did come to terms properly with who James and I were, every time I think back to Mammy's very last days on this earth, thanks to the hospice, I see her surrounded by light and warm golden air.

I have to say that Tom Bennett was a brick during this time. One of the things that kept me going was the laughs we were able to have despite everything. He put up with me when I was in the dumps, or inclined to feel sorry for myself, or when I cancelled one of our dates because James was poorly. He even used to come out to Harold's Cross with me during those last few weeks. He didn't accompany me into the building, just waited outside and minded James so I could be uninterrupted with Mammy. The more I think of it now, the more I admire him for all of that.

All ancient history now.

Getting back to the story, on the Sunday morning after Patrice Murphy's visit, I found it hard to act naturally with Patsy on the way to the PA gig. She, on the other hand, was all over me. (Still hadn't remembered my birthday, though!) She cracked jokes, told me this long, endless saga about a plumber who didn't come to put in a dishwasher for her, gave me all her plans about their holidays in August. They were going to Minorca. Why don't you come, Ange? she goes, spend that money you won, for God's sake, you deserve a break.

She doesn't look at me while she's saying this. She knows damn well I can't come. And she knows why. All the time she's prattling on, James's predicament lies between us like a big black slug. And I don't like to tell her that there's already quite a dent in that money. What's more I'm damned if I'm going to tell her he's pleading guilty.

How's Martin? I ask, when I can get a word in edgeways, I'm a bit surprised you're going on holidays with him after what happened.

This is mean of me, I know, but I can't stand what's going on between her and me. I don't think that fundamentally I'm a bitchy person but the minute I saw her that morning I started to resent her. I certainly can't behave as if there's *nothing* going on. How dare she behave like that about James?

Martin? she goes, like she's surprised. Oh, Martin's fine, busy as all get out. And then she's off again on a story about him and his partner meeting some suspicious characters in the bar of their hotel in Belfast when they were up there on business the day before last. According to her, she wouldn't be surprised if they were even Provos. I worry about him going up there all the time, she says, with the ceasefire so shaky and all, you never know what's going to happen . . .

This is the same Patsy who's been so upset recently about finding a condom in Martin's pocket. I give up on human nature.

The gig is in one of those huge pubs, as big as haybarns, which have about as much soul as boxing arenas. They serve Sunday lunch and live music and you sure are left in no doubt about which is the real attraction. We're on from two o'clock till three which in theory is supposed to mean they get their food out of the way first. In practice, it always means that we're performing to the backs of people's heads and trying to drown out the sound of kids whinging that they don't like what's on their plates.

This morning bears out my worst fears. I see immediately we walk in that we're in trouble.

The place is packed with a mixed bag of punters, men in twos and threes who probably have nowhere else to hide out from the wives going demented at home, families with squads of kids running riot and throwing stuff, gaggles of women who are already well on and shrieking even though the pub is open less than half an hour. It's so thick with smoke that my mascara starts to sting straight away.

Patsy throws her eyes to heaven and for that one quick moment, we're best friends and it's like nothing has happened. We roll up and roll on and give the punters what they've paid for and in the end they give us quite a decent round of applause. I defy anyone to notice anything awry in our behaviour towards each other during that show. This is where experience counts.

After the gig, on the way home, she's off again with the stories, bright and brittle as a new tack.

I can't stand it one minute longer. Look, I say, I want to talk about what we're not talking about. I'm cleaning off my make-up at the time, using the little mirror behind the passenger sun visor. I deliberately scrub and scrape so I won't have to look at her. I feel I should give her a chance.

Oh? she goes.

I stop with the cotton wool. Please, Patsy, I say, this is me, Angela. We both know what I mean.

She looks injured. I'm damned if I do—

James. I cut her off before she gets too far down that road.

That shuts her up.

James? I say again, can we talk about James?

Oh, that.

Yes, I go, that. It's the single biggest thing in my life at the moment, Patsy, and I need to talk to someone about it. Correction. I'd like to talk to you about it.

She's now gripping the steering wheel as though she's afraid it'll turn into a flying saucer and get away from her. Angela, it's none of my business.

I know that strictly speaking it's none of your business, I say as gently as I can, but you're my friend and I'm your friend and I'm in trouble here. James and I are in trouble, Patsy. Please. I could do with a bit of help. Support . . .

That last bit was quite a shock. You know me, I can't bear to ask anyone for anything. Talk about swallowing your pride.

It turned out to have been wasted effort.

As far as Patsy was concerned she was sympathetic towards me, fair enough, but as for James, he had got himself into this situation and he shouldn't expect anyone else but himself to get him out of it. She sounds so weird suddenly that I look hard at her. What's the problem, Patsy, I ask her, did someone you know get raped?

Of course not. Of *course* not. She's outraged. In fact, she's so over the top about this that I feel it would be prudent to let it go. I'm right, though, there is something more to it. Her face is white.

I say nothing for a while and we drive on. There's a tape on of Barbra Streisand playing at some live concert where she's linking the songs by talking about all the psychoanalysis she's had and how it made her into a truer, better person. We could do with a few shrinks in this car right now.

Patsy turns to me. Please, Ange, don't let this thing affect our relationship.

Of course not, I go.

The two of us are beginning to sound like parrots.

When she lets me out at my grotty front door, we don't part as enemies, but to say that the customary ease between us is diminished is an understatement.

When I got in James wasn't in the flat and there was nothing on the telly that interested me so, after I'd changed my clothes and cleaned myself up, I went for a walk to clear my head. (Ken Shiels has a lot to answer for. Another walk? This was becoming a habit!)

Although it did have a few little incidents, this walk won't count for much when the history of Great Walks is written. I came out of our place, turned right down Gardiner Street, walked as far as Tops in Pops. Didn't see the potato skins outside, skidded, nearly killed myself. I could have developed instant back trouble or whiplash, but he's a nice guy and James and I always get our spuds there. I picked myself up, no real damage except a ladder in my tights and a rip along the seam in the armhole of my anorak. Walked on, turned right into Parnell Street, then left into O'Connell Street. Got to

O'Connell Bridge, couldn't think where to go next so I just turned round for home. At least I took a different route, along the Quays. Thrill a minute, that's me.

Maybe it's because I live in the area but it doesn't cost me a thought to walk by myself along the roughest streets in Dublin. Like everyone else, I know what's going on, syringe robberies, muggings, handbag snatches, all the rest of it. (In fact Handbag Corner is only a hundred yards from our place. Nowadays it's not a quarter as bad as it used to be, and there's even another new block of yuppie apartments going up on that corner. But the inside lane of the roadway continues to be empty when the lights are red. Old fears die hard.) Is any other city any better?

Anyhow, here I am, Miss Streetwise 1996, strolling home along the Quays, when I feel this thump on my back and at the same time someone tugging at the strap of my shoulder bag.

Thank God my reflexes are good. I manage to hold on to the bag as I whirl around and here are these two young fellas behind me, couldn't have been more than nine or ten years old. I let this roar out of me and before I know it I'm laying into them with the bag like it's a weapon. I don't know what comes over me, suddenly I'm Don Quixote. I frighten the wits out of them and they scarper.

An old wino, who's been hanging over the Liffey getting sick, has seen the whole thing. He turns his head round to me, are you all right, missus?

I am, of course, but then the reaction sets in and I get a bit shaky. So I go and stand beside him looking into the Liffey until the shakiness passes.

Now the funny bit. He starts a conversation with me about how Dublin's going to the dogs lately. This is a wino. A derelict.

Here's me with a ladder in my tights, in my cheap Dunne's anorak, which has the armpit ripped. Here's him without a tooth in his head and his face invisible under a hundred layers of dirt and hair. We're both standing there, looking down at the greeny-brown skin of the Liffey with his sick still floating on it and we're talking like philosophers about lack of political will, poverty traps and gaps, misplaced resources, judges having always to moan that there's nowhere for them to send juvenile delinquents.

Goodbye so, I say eventually, when we run out of anything more to say, I'd better be getting home. I start to open my bag to give him a quid for his trouble.

He holds up his hand. Ah no, missus, he says, no, you wouldn't insult me now, would you?

He tips his forehead in a sort of military salute and then shuffles off up the Quays towards O'Connell Bridge. I'm so flabbergasted I can do nothing except stand there with my hand still stuck inside my bag and my eyes out on stalks looking after him. You think you know people and then something like this happens and you realize you haven't a bull's notion.

Maybe it's the wino, maybe it's the mood I'm in, but on the way home I review my life. It's not something I normally do, I'm too busy just getting by.

Now, though, whichever way I look at it, I can't come up with much to cheer about. Leaving poor James out of it altogether, I'm up to my neck in manure.

An abbreviated summary. I'm in my middle thirties and not getting any younger. Financially I'm in that no man's land between poverty and making do. I've no relatives, fewer friends and what friendship I've had – i.e. Patsy – is going down the tubes. Also, based on our performance at *Sense and Sensibility* (we hardly talked at all on the way home and I hadn't heard from him since

I'd cancelled our Saturday meal) my burgeoning relationship with Ken Shiels is unburgeoning fast. Most of my
work is of the pits variety and being realistic, Leaving
Cert qualifications notwithstanding, there's little prospect of the situation getting any better in that area.

Little prospect? *No* prospect, with the unemployment
figures rising every month and five hundred young fellas
with honours Leaving Certs and even degrees applying
for jobs as messenger boys in one of the semi-state
companies. Unprecedented response, the guy said to
Marian Finucane on *Liveline* – I think he was the
personnel manager of the company that advertised.
Someone else rang in then and said he had a Ph.D in
English and all he could get by way of employment was
pumping petrol.

I think you will agree that at that point my lifestyle and
future looked pretty. Not.

And the day after I'm drawing up that little list James
is due to plead guilty to raping a girl and no doubt is
going to go to gaol.

✦ Eighteen ✦

The trial. Without further ado.

I absolutely hate this part of the story so I'll be as factual and as clinical as I can. Considering the circumstances and what happened.

I didn't ask for the day off work, I just didn't show up that morning. I heard the minibus beeping outside but I pulled the covers over my head and tried to ignore it. It's the first time I've ever done that, but I knew if I was asked why I wanted time off – which I would have been – I'd start to stammer and stutter. And anyway, I thought it would be bad luck to lie. If I'm fired, I'm fired. So be it.

I didn't sleep that night and neither did James. He went to the bathroom about six times. Once or twice I felt him looking over at me but I pretended to be asleep. There was nothing of comfort I could think of to say.

He was ready to leave forty-five minutes before we'd said we'd go. When he emerged from his room, and I saw behind him that he'd made his bed—

Should I take a sheet? He tries to make a joke of it, tries to laugh. He's shaking.

I can't write any more of this section.

We got to the Four Courts early. We were to see St John Markey and Patrice Murphy at half past nine, we were there at a quarter past. We knew our way around by then so we waited for them in the circular entrance area. This is massive, with a marble floor and a huge dome above it, which I heard on a radio programme is a hundred and fifty feet high – no wonder it's such an intimidating place when you first see it. I suppose that's the idea. You wouldn't want justice dispensed in a shed. You're not supposed to feel comfortable.

It probably should have made us feel better to see so many people in the same boat as us but it didn't at all. There was a sort of collective fear in the air. You could sense it buzzing. Within five minutes of us arriving, I don't know who was shaking more, me or James.

By far the saddest people in that whole place were the defendants, you could easily pick them out – their eyes kept shifting around as if they didn't know where to look. They shuffled cheap shoes and pulled at badly knotted ties. On the other hand, it was a hard call who looked worse, them or the relatives. The mothers and fathers and wives. Trying to look brave and hopeful at the same time, to be loyal to their defendant because they loved him (it was nearly always a him) while at the same time trying to show that of course they didn't condone what he'd done. And all the time you could see they were hoping no one they knew would see them in this awful place and in this terrible situation. I recognized the phenomenon. With feeling.

Those where the relatives who had bothered to turn up. There were an unfortunate few defendants who had no one with them. God. Can you imagine?

Patrice Murphy came up to us at about twenty-five to ten and brought us to meet St John Markey in an interview room. His wig was on crooked and he had to do a lot of flittering through files to find our case. He got more and more flustered, maybe he was embarrassed that he couldn't find it straight off. Maybe he was remembering the Wonderbra.

Personally I didn't give a sugar what his problem was. I had more deadly business on my mind. Like if this guy was competent to handle such a delicate case. Patrice Murphy seemed calm enough, though, and seeing this made me feel a tiny bit better.

James wouldn't look any of us in the eye.

Mr Elliott always pointed out in our prose selections how the good writers always furnish the room, i.e. help the readers to visualise where the action is taking place.

Right.

The little interview room where we meet our lawyers is bare and functional. Table. Chairs. Windowpane streaked with dirt, sun pouring through. Too hot even at that hour of the morning. Lino on the floor. A creased copy of last night's *Herald* on one of the chairs. The dominant colour pale brown. Rumble, like the constant roar of the sea, of lorries and cars outside on the Quays.

Markey eventually finds our file but it's Patrice Murphy who takes us through what's going to happen. He reassures us that our character witness – James's employer – and our psychiatrist, the one who had written that this incident was aberrant, will definitely be there.

I had volunteered to go on the stand to vouch for James so I ask them about it, but neither of the lawyers think now that this will make much difference. We won't close it off as an option just yet, Patrice Murphy goes, but I think it's highly unlikely we'll call you.

I'm ashamed to say that I'm relieved. Very. Poor James.

Patrice Murphy wishes us luck and then he and St John Markey go on to their next clients. Markey has a very busy day today, he's told us. Much good that'll do us.

As soon as they leave, James gets another attack of diarrhoea and has to go to the cloakroom. That leaves me sitting there by myself. I'm not feeling so terrific while I'm waiting for him to come back. It isn't nausea, precisely, just that churning feeling at the base of your stomach where you feel it's full of water rather than your insides. Every time I look at my watch, this lake of water sloshes around.

The next bit I remember absolutely.

James comes back at a quarter to ten. I ask him if he's all right and he nods. His face is as white as a plate. He looks at me with those amazing eyes of his. She's out there, I saw her, he says.

He doesn't have to tell me who he means. I'm flabbergasted she's here. Because with James pleading guilty, there was no need for her to come. She's only a witness in this case in any event and now she won't be called.

She can be here for only one thing, to see her revenge being exacted. What does she want? Blood? No point in asking myself that question, I know the answer. Revenge is not a beneficial emotion.

James goes to the window and rubs at one of the streaks on it with the corner of his jacket. Don't, I go, automatically, you'll ruin it . . . Then I stop. In the scheme of things does it really matter if the sleeve of a defendant's jacket is a bit grubby when he gets sent to gaol?

When we get into that courtroom, try not to look at her, I say.

Easy for you, he whispers. Then he turns round from the window and stares at me again.

What? I go — what is it?

Look, he goes, whatever happens today, thanks for everything. He turns around to the window again.

I can't speak. I leave it to you to imagine what I feel.

Next thing, we're in. First, there are the remand cases to be dealt with.

Don't I just wish . . . Aren't human beings hilarious? There was I, bitching to myself all through James's remands, wishing we could just get to trial and get the bloody thing over with and now here I've been granted my fondest desire and I want to unwish it. My heart is tattering in my chest and I can't breathe properly.

I can't even begin to imagine what James is feeling.

It goes on and on.

We get to a few trials where people are pleading guilty.

Larceny, judge.

Wishes for fifty-seven other charges to be taken into account, judge.

Breach of the peace, judge.

The goods taken amounted to a total value of twenty-nine pounds forty-one pence, judge.

I want to run. How many more do we have to endure before we get to it?

Oh, God – it's happening. His name is being called. Jesus. It's not only the bottom of my stomach, everything inside my whole body is water, even my brain. Here's St John Markey saying his client has decided on a certain course of action . . .

The next hour? I find it virtually impossible to remember it in sequence. I know the way it *had* to have happened, the start of the case, James's barrister, character witnesses, the psychiatrist, judge, et cetera. But it's a series of impressions, expressions, sounds, feelings, physical sensations rather than a logical progression of events.

To start at the end, you wouldn't believe it. Just over

ninety minutes after his case started, James and I found ourselves shaking hands with Patrice Murphy on the footpath outside the Four Courts.

If anything, the lake in my insides was more wave-ridden, if there's such a word, than before. It's like I was pushed through a time machine. I, Angela Rose Devine, was ninety minutes advanced but what had happened in the rest of the world during that time hadn't caught up with me yet.

The huge bright fact. James was convicted and sentenced to five years, suspended for one year. If he's of good behaviour during that year, the judge will review the sentence. Which probably means, according to Patrice Murphy, that he won't go to gaol. Congratulations, he says.

As I'm telling you this, I'm rolling the words, the whole scene, around and around at the top of my brain but they still won't percolate down any further. The judge recommended counselling for James, she told him he could consider himself a fortunate young man, gave out to him a bit, said his remorse seemed genuine, spoke directly to Rosemary Madden in the body of the court, sympathized, hoped she could put this distressing event behind her as quickly as possible. Next case.

I'm standing out on those Quays. I don't remember how I got here. I'm looking stupidly from Patrice Murphy to James and back again. I can't believe it. He's out. He's not in a cell.

James can't believe it. He's sweating, even though the wind whipping off the Liffey would cut the socks off an alligator.

Rosemary Madden certainly couldn't believe it. She rushed out of the courtroom at the end of the judge's words. The tears were pouring down her face. The mother bombed out after her, but not before glaring daggers in our direction. As for the woman from the Rape Crisis Centre, I leave it to your imagination. Daggers? Scimitars. Slash hooks. *The Pit and the Pendulum*.

I have a feeling Patrice Murphy can't believe it either, despite all his assurances to us earlier. He has to rush back in – his next case is already in progress – and he just keeps saying to us that he wishes us well and that we'll be in touch in due course. He has to shout because of the articulated trucks that are revving in the line of traffic on the Quays. That was a good decision, he yells. I felt all along it was going to go in our favour.

My eye. He felt no such thing. Why was he talking eighteen months?

He claps James on the shoulder and James doesn't react, just looks back at him, dazed. Goodbye now, says Patrice Murphy. Now he shakes hands with me. His hands are sweaty.

I look around me. I don't know what to do next, to tell you the truth. The lorries inching past seem as unreal as everything else in this scene, like they belong to another planet or at least a part of someone else's life. I can't feel relieved, I can't feel anything at all. I'm free-drifting.

At this moment I can't even completely remember what I had been expecting that morning before we got here.

Now, some time later, I'm ashamed to reveal that when I'd got up that morning I'd packed a little goody bag for him. Comics and snack bars and crisps. What did that say about my faith in my brother? In my defence, I was terrified. Mountjoy Gaol is hell, especially for newcomers. They're always doing reports on it on the radio, young men and boys have hanged themselves there and it's so crowded they have to sleep on the floor sometimes when they're remanded in custody. It's also a hotbed of drug abuse.

I'm so moithered I can't remember much about what our side's psychiatrist said in that courtroom. He was impressive, that I do know. Quiet. Matter-of-fact. He seemed to think that James and I together constituted a stable background for him – which at first I thought was a laugh, considering the true circumstances.

But then, when you think about the definition of the word 'stable' maybe the guy had a point. All right, it wasn't ideal, but James has only lived in two places in his life and he has been living with the same person since he was two months old. In one way maybe that could be defined as stability.

Fair dues to him, James's courier boss came up trumps too. He wasn't exactly heaping praise on James but he did say he was conscientious and honest. And, best news of all, he told the judge that he would give James his job back.

As I say, this is all episodic in my mind, I was taking too much in all at once, dividing my attention between Rosemary Madden, the judge, and the witnesses.

Rosemary Madden's expression was so intense it was frightening. She was dressed like a widow or a nun. Severe. Black high-necked dress with a white Peter Pan collar, black tights, black shoes. No make-up. A thin gold cross and chain hanging from under the collar. Her hair gelled back behind her ears so that her eyes looked enormous in her face. I have to confess that while on one level I felt awful about her being in the situation she was in, on another I was enraged. If I ever saw anyone dressed to fulfil a role, she was that person.

On the other hand, fair's fair, I suppose. We were dressed to impress as well, James's hair was shiny, his shoes were polished, his tie was silk – I blew some of the scratch card money on it in Marks and Spencers – £19.99 for one tie! – and I'd kept the new suit well pressed and clean. He hadn't been allowed to wear it anywhere except in court.

He would have looked fantastic if it wasn't for the terrified expression on his face. Yet now I can see how this may well have worked to his advantage with the judge. I can imagine how she would not have dealt quite so kindly with someone who seemed cocky and impudent.

I can recollect more of what the judge said to Rosemary Madden than what she said to us. It was sort of like a public speech. Even though she was talking directly to the victim – she was quoting from the victim-impact report, obviously for the benefit of us all. And, from our point of view, it did sound pretty horrendous – it talked about psychological scarring. It also said that while the victim was a strong, brave young woman who, in the opinion of the psychologist who wrote the report, would make a good recovery over a period of time, the event had been extremely traumatic for her.

While the judge was still talking, I remember that I zeroed in on that psychological scarring. Why wasn't I psychologically scarred by oul' Mooney and the boy who'd tried it on with me?

But then I'm on the other side in this case so I would think like this, wouldn't I?

She told James to stand up and she started to talk to him. Scold him, really. Her voice sounded to me as though it was coming from the bottom of a well, I couldn't make out the words although I recognized the scolding tone. I did hear her say 'five years' and then she stopped. Then all I could see was the top of her head as she started to write.

I couldn't get enough breath. Five years. Far worse than what Patrice Murphy had said, five years was like getting a thump in the breastbone. So much for it going well for him if he pleaded guilty, thanks a whole heap, Patrice Murphy . . . Five years, in a way it was a relief to know the worst. Not really . . . And then I started trying to look on the bright side. Maybe we could appeal. And no matter what, he'd be out in a couple of years and the way prison releases are going now, because of the overcrowding, he might even serve a lot less.

This all raced through my mind in a tenth of a second, you know the way it does.

I composed my expression to look over at James.

Something was awry. James was looking stunned, no one was making a move to take James down, St John Markey was shuffling his papers.

I looked up at the judge. She was still writing.

Across the courtroom at the detectives. They were muttering to each other.

I heard Rosemary Madden's reaction and I looked around. The door to the courtroom was to one side and her path to it was quite long so I was able to see her face as she raced out. I caught the expressions of her mother and her counsellor.

I didn't understand.

James was now looking round towards me. St John Markey was still messing with files. James was coming towards me with Patrice Murphy. Patrice Murphy was smiling.

Smiling.

Then we were outside and he was explaining to me what had happened.

So now he's gone back inside and I'm still standing there on these Quays with all this noxious traffic, trying to make sense of everything. It's starting to rain. That's real. Cold drops on my face. My cheeks are so hot I'm expecting the drops to sizzle. I always go beetroot when I'm stressed. It's like I've been hypnotized by Paul Goldin or Tony Sadar and I think I'm a statue.

Are we going or what? James says. Or are we going to stand here all day? He's looking around, nervous.

Yeah, I go, come on.

I ask him if he's hungry. That's automatic. Safe. I'm still at it – if in doubt, feed. Neither of us was able to eat anything this morning and this is a boy who would have got out of the lifeboats and back on to the *Titanic* if he saw a cheese sandwich sliding down the deck.

We decide to go to McDonald's. We start to walk up towards O'Connell Street.

We hear James's name being called. We turn around. Rosemary Madden's mother and the woman from the Rape Crisis Centre are standing on the steps of the Four Courts.

It's the mother who comes forward. You . . . she says. That's all. It's enough. There's enough venom in that word to fill an encyclopaedia of insults. I cringe inside. Something comes out of my mouth. I'm sorry. My heart starts banging again and beside me I feel, rather than see, James getting frantic.

Naturally I'm not going to show them that we're intimidated. Come on, James, I go. I grab his arm and haul him away. We're walking fast up the Quays when Rosemary Madden herself catches up with us. She runs in front of us, blocking us so we can't pass her.

Her language is unprintable. Her face distorts. It's like I'm looking at a film and the camera moves in and all I can see is this big mouth saying these things. The two front teeth, I see, have something, maybe a sliver of a cornflake or something, stuck between them. It's horrible to hear this, see this . . .

Leave us alone, eff off, James says back, but his heart isn't in it. He's still pretty shook. We try to get around her but she's still mouthing off, blocking us. She's certainly belying her demure appearance. She's roaring like a fishwife.

By this time there's quite a little crowd gathered. The mother and a man – who I figure has to be the father – have caught up with her and they're standing beside her. Staring at us. Now they're joined by two others, obviously her brothers, one thickset, a bit like the father, the other just a teenager. They're all just staring, like they're trying to knock us down with their eyes. A few passers-by stop to see what's going on. You know the way people stand a little sideways with their arms folded, or clutching their shopping, just watching the entertainment. It's a big dreadful scene. I want to die. Come *on*, James says again, and he drags at me.

Somehow we manage to get past them all.

When we get to McDonald's, the breakfasts are finished so I settle just for an apple turnover and coffee. I expect James to go the whole hog, Big Mac meal, but all he wants is a small fries. That's how upset he is.

We both sit there and neither of us can think of anything to say. We just eat.

When will you go back to work? I ask him.

He looks at me as though I'm from another planet. I'll see you at home, he goes, getting up and leaving. I have barely enough money to pay.

Then a brilliant thought occurs to me. No need for the bail money any more. As soon as my new bonds arrive from the post office, I can apply straight away to have them turned back into cash. I can redeem Mammy's jewellery. And he can have his video back.

Nineteen

You would think that would be the end of it, or at least the beginning of the end. That James would have gone back to work and so would I and we would have started to put the whole thing behind us.

Unfortunately no.

The first couple of days were all right, considering. James did go back to work, no problem, or none that he would tell me anyway. All the newspapers published a fairly factual account of what had happened. It was not as bad as it could have been. There were no photographs.

And there wasn't really much trouble about me not showing up for work on the Monday. Old Furry Slippers made me pay for it on the Tuesday, of course, she was all pursed lips and well-don't-let-it-happen-again. Then she made me do the toilets. I didn't really mind. I was still half shocked from the events of the day before and I wanted to be by myself as much as possible.

Over the first few days, I did get a few sideways looks from some of the women in work but that didn't bother me in the slightest because it could have been so much worse. They could have been coming up sympathizing with me — and you know what kind of sympathy that would have been.

Four days passed and I was just beginning to settle

down, in that I was not mentally looking over my shoulder a hundred per cent of the time. I decided to get my act together. I rang up and asked for as many kissogram gigs as they could let me have. Was I punishing myself? – you know I want to give up those gigs – I don't know. Anyway, he gave me four gigs, one on the Wednesday, three on the Thursday night. I managed them well because I knew I was pretty safe – no one would look beyond the outfits.

Then the bombshell hit.

It was Friday. I was getting ready to go out for a drive with Ken Sheils. He had called up to the flat on the Wednesday evening about tea-time and had asked me if I'd like to go for a spin in the Dublin mountains that weekend. Saturday was out of the question because of the deli and shopping and so forth and PA System had an event in Navan on the Sunday so we settled on the Friday afternoon, he'd take it off.

Feck it, he goes, I'm self-employed. What's the use of being self-employed if you don't get to treat yourself to a day off now and then in the summer?

You obviously got my note?

Sure. He shrugs. No big deal.

I watch him carefully but he gives no sign at all that he knows something untoward has happened. Some people don't read papers, thank God. I'm also waiting for him to ask me how I'll be able to get the time off from the office but he doesn't. I guess he's not naturally a curious person.

At about twenty past two on the Friday, I was putting on a bit of make-up. I'd washed my hair, I had on a new pair of white cotton jeans and a nice navy T-shirt. The sun was shining and the weather forecast was good, James was at work – which was great because I wasn't quite ready yet to introduce him to Ken — and as far as possible, all was fair enough with my world.

The radio was on. *Liveline* with Marian Finucane, except it wasn't her, it's never her in the summer, they all get very long holidays out there in RTE. This was someone called Breege-óg. (I'm just taking a stab at how to spell the name, that's how it sounds.)

Liveline is a programme I like a lot, largely because of Marian. She's a warm person, who's sympathetic and fair to everyone. Mind you, I do switch it off occasionally when the whinging and whining gets too much for me. That's not Marian's fault, it's not her who's doing the giving out.

It's a howl, actually. We're always hearing from some quarters about the little people of Ireland having no voice and no one to represent them because of the media all being liberal and the anti-Catholic bias of the opinion-makers, et cetera. But in my opinion, if a Martian came to Ireland and wanted to know what the little people were thinking about, all he would have to do would be to switch on the radio or the television. The little people voiceless? You have to be kidding me.

So I'm listening to *Liveline* while I'm trying out a new blusher I bought in the pound shop in O'Connell Street to cheer myself up. Breege-óg says our next caller doesn't want to be identifed so we'll call her Paula. You're really upset and angry, Paula, she goes. Tell us what happened.

This Paula starts in and I'm transfixed. Immediately I know who it is. It's Rosemary Madden's mother.

She's on about how her daughter was denied justice in the courts. How she was brutally raped. How the rapist has walked free with the connivance of psychiatrists and do-gooders. How the judge was a disgrace . . .

Breege-óg cuts in there. Steady on, Paula, she says, we don't know all the factors the judge took into account in the case and the judge isn't here to defend himself—

Mrs Madden goes ballistic. The judge wasn't a him it was a her, that's what makes it so horrendous. She's screeching and roaring now, and Breege-óg can't get a word in edgeways although she does her best to soothe her and quieten her down. I know how you must be feeling, Paula, she says. Do you have anyone you can talk to?

Mrs Madden breaks down completely. There's one of those horrible, dreadful hiatuses where all you can hear is sobbing. It's so bad that Breege-óg seems upset and stuck for words. She asks Mrs Madden if she's all right.

More sobbing.

I'm sure everyone can really sympathize, Paula . . .

Click. Beep beep. Mrs Madden has hung up the phone.

Breege-óg says that these things happen on live radio and she's so sorry that Paula is so upset and that she hopes she can get some help. There is help out there for you, Paula, she says. If you get back on to us we can put you in touch with someone who can help you.

She changes her voice, goes on to the next caller, Marie, who wants to talk about her son who has Down's syndrome. Marie, she says, is at the end of her tether because her son can't get a proper education in the system we have. There aren't enough resources being put in. Tell us about your son, Marie . . .

That is what I wanted to talk about when I rang up, Breege-óg, this Marie says back, but I was holding on for a while there and after listening to that poor lady and what she's after going through . . . I can't tell you how angry I am. I'm enraged. I know if it was my daughter . . .

She's off. She's forgotten all about her Down's

syndrome son. There's now a rapist walking free in Dublin while Paula's poor daughter, and poor Paula herself and all her family, are the ones serving life sentences. While that rapist is probably going to rape again. Statistics prove this. Once a sex offender, Breege-óg, always a sex offender. It's a disgrace, Breege-óg. And the politicians don't care. Marie hopes Paula and her unfortunate daughter are going to appeal. There should be checks and balances on these judges. There should be a committee of citizens . . .

All this time I'm standing there with the blusher brush in my hand. It feels like a boulder of ice. I can't even make myself turn off the radio.

I know *Liveline*, it's one of the most popular programmes. I know what's going to happen now. This is going to run on to all the other programmes. All the papers. Even the English tabloids. Everyone in Ireland will be wanting to call in to every radio show with their own opinion. I relaxed too soon.

Somehow I reach out and manage to turn it off but, of course, it's still there. I can still hear all their voices. Marie's and Paula's and Breege-óg's and God knows who's on now. I'm terrified. They're going to get James, after all.

I sit down on the bed-settee. I've made the flat pristine because it will be the first time Ken Sheils sees it. But I don't see the bunch of carnations in the nice jug, the polished surfaces, the unnatural tidiness. I'm staring at an ashtray with 'A Present from Tramore' on it in the middle of the table. I can't take my eyes off it.

I don't know how long I sit there.

Our doorbell rings. I jump. Literally. It sounds like a fire alarm. I look at my watch, five to three, Ken Sheils is five minutes early. I try to stand up but I'm a jelly.

I get hold of myself and plaster what I hope is a bright

smile on my face as I go to open the door. Wouldn't you
know it, on the landing I meet one of my neighbours.
We all keep ourselves to ourselves in this house but
obviously you can't avoid people completely and we all
know a modicum about each other. This man is one of
my least favourites. God forgive me, I've never liked him
– but if I'm honest, I probably never gave him a chance.
You know the way you just take against people without
knowing why. Maybe it's because of the poor man's
unfortunate appearance, all nose and chin. His name is
Dwyer, he's a civil servant, something in the Department
of Defence, I believe. He wears woolly cardis.

As we're both going towards the door there's no
avoiding him so I nod hello to him and say something
crappy about it being a lovely day.

It is indeed a lovely day, Miss Devine, he goes, and he
looks at me. Sidelong.

Now there are looks and looks. Am I just being
paranoid or is this look one of those meaningful ones?
For instance, did he hear *Liveline* and did he read the
papers on Tuesday and has he put two and two together?

What's he doing at home in the middle of a Friday
afternoon, anyway? Shouldn't he be at work?

We get to the door together, and just as he reaches for
the snib, our doorbell rings again. That's for me, I go –
as if it's any of his business. That's what paranoia does to
you. It makes you explain your next breath.

I open the door. It's not Ken Sheils, it's two men. One
of them has a camera. I just have time to see this before
the flash goes off in my face. At the same time I hear one
of them shouting James's name. That's all I hear before I
slam the door shut.

In the hall, Dwyer blinks. But he doesn't look all that
surprised and I see now that I wasn't being paranoid. He
does know exactly what has been going on and without a

shadow of a doubt he had heard *Liveline*. The doorbell rings again.

I become calm. If you wouldn't mind, I say, I'm going back to our flat. I'd appreciate it if you wouldn't open the door until I'm well inside.

He nods. (Thinking about it now I suppose this was the most drama that ever happened in his whole life. I can imagine the subsequent tea breaks in the Department of Defence.) Thank you, I say, and with as much dignity as I can find, I go back to our flat. The doorbell rings again.

I sit down inside our place and I start to shake. What am I going to do? What are we going to do? We can't just stay here passively and let this happen to us.

The doorbell rings.

But we can't leave the jurisdiction either because James has to go through his counselling sessions. Although it wasn't made a condition of the suspension of the sentence, Patrice Murphy tells us that it would be in James's best interests to attend them religiously. So it will look good when the sentence comes up for review.

Still, who'd find us if we just went down to the North Wall or out to Dun Laoghaire and got on the boat. We buy the tickets at the ferry port and just walk on with the rest of the punters, walk off in Holyhead and that could be the end of us. We wouldn't be the first Irish people to vanish in England. They don't check identification and you don't need passports between here and the UK. And since we're both able-bodied we wouldn't be registering for any social-welfare payments or official help of any kind . . .

The more I think about it the better it all sounds.

Next thing, there's a knock on our own door. I can't believe it. That stupid so-and-so Dwyer let them in after all. Go away, I yell. Just go away.

There's silence for a few moments. Then Ken Sheils says, It's me, Angela. It's Ken. Is everything all right?

I'm so upset I've temporarily forgotten about him.

I open the door. What's going on? he says. What are those two thugs doing on the doorstep? They're looking for you, they tried to come in with me . . .

Again I get calm. I don't know what it is with me. I get calm in the most stressful situations and I turn to blancmange as soon as everything is all right. Come in, Ken, I say, I've something to tell you.

I'd like to say he was great about it. He was in a way but then again he wasn't. He didn't run out, or throw up his hands in horror. On the other hand he didn't come right out and say, I'm really sorry for your trouble and is there anything I can do. Which is, of course, what I wanted him to say.

Instead, he just kept saying, I see.

I left nothing out. I didn't spare James but I didn't spare your woman either. I told Ken exactly what had happened, how she'd wanted to have sex and then didn't but how it was too late for James to stop. How she was the one who initiated the whole thing by telling him to bring the condom. About *Liveline* and the papers and how we were now going to be crucified.

I see, he says.

Look, I go, I'll understand if you don't want anything to do with us.

I see.

But he's my brother and he's all I have and I'm all he has and that's the end of it. He has to come first. So I'll understand.

I see.

Christ, I'm thinking, if he says that one more time I'll kick him. This is the first time I've noticed this annoying habit of his. I'm all over the shop now, I'm trying to hold on to my temper. So do you? I ask him.

Do I what?

Do you want to let it go?

Do you mean do I want not to see you again?

That's what I mean, yes. I'll understand.

I see.

Has he gone on like this before? I don't remember. Now I have to wait for his decision. By this time I don't care. To be frank I'd just as soon he'd leave right now and take his van and his wretched little mongrel with him. I've never cared much about the Dublin mountains anyway. There's nothing much there and even if there is you can't see it because it's always cloudy and raining.

You can keep the Dublin mountains.

The doorbell rings again and Ken and I look at each other. Well, we can't stay here, he says. Let's go anyway, we can talk more about it.

This sounds ominous. I've told him everything already. What he means is he needs time to work out his own attitude. But I can't stay here, so I agree.

What about the two on the doorstep? I say then, I don't fancy having that camera shoved in my face again.

Ken asks if there's a back entrance.

There isn't, but there is a fire escape. To get to it you have to get out through the window of our facilities. I'm not even embarrassed telling him this. This is oul' Reddy's fault, not ours.

I scribble a note to James, telling him to be careful, that he might be ambushed either here or at work. Of course, he might be caught as he's coming in before he gets the note but there's not a lot I can do about that.

Then we leave the flat, feet first, through the window and on to the fire escape. I feel absolutely stupid. As I haul myself up on to the hand basin, dislodging hunks of powdery plaster, I'm thinking, This is the future, this is not the last time I'm going to have to do this, or James either.

Ken Sheils starts to sweep the plaster aside with his foot. Leave it, leave it, I go . . . On the positive side, I'm thanking my lucky stars I have jeans on. Can you imagine the indignity of doing this in a skirt?

Because it was a Friday, the traffic was terrible until we got as far as Dundrum and after that it was plain sailing. Ken was very quiet and I just left him to it. I felt fatalistic, to tell you the truth. The next move was not up to me. Thank God for car radios and thank God Ronan Collins was on. His music is pretty good and he has a very easy style. Undemanding, but he can be funny in a gentle sort of way. I couldn't have stood it, I think, if we'd had to listen to any of the pop stations. They're grand if you're feeling young and good about yourself. Which, at that moment, I certainly wasn't.

Do you know what, I have to revise my opinion of the Dublin mountains. Even I have to admit that the Sally Gap is spectacular, just spectacular. I don't say it out loud because Ken Sheils still hasn't opened his mouth.

On the other side of the Sally Gap we stop at the side of the road and get out. Ken stands with his head thrown back. Taste that air, he goes, taste that freshness. I feel a bit of a prat but I copy him anyway, closing my eyes and throwing back my head and taking several deep lungfuls, so deep that I get dizzy. He's got it wrong, I think. In my opinion it isn't the taste of the air, it's the absence of taste that gives you the sensation. Because there's nothing to smell, the air cuts right through the fug in your nose and your throat which, up to that moment, you didn't even know you'd had.

There's no wind at all, which Ken says is unusual for

up here but as a result you can hear this concert of buzzing and humming. Insects. Moths (butterflies?), a lot of bees. There are a couple of little streams nearby, you can hear them running. And the birds! And the little clouds! I'd had no idea it could be like this. James and radio programmes and all our troubles could be a million miles away.

I turn my head and find him looking at me. When I catch his eye he reddens a bit. I took the liberty of bringing a picnic, he says, I hope you don't mind.

Mind? I'm now so hungry I'd eat a rasher off a sore leg. I haven't had anything to eat since our tea-break at work this morning at about quarter past seven. It's now nearly four o'clock.

He takes the picnic out of the back of his van – he's made three different kinds of sandwiches, salad, egg, and ham, and he has tea in a flask with two cups. He's even brought the sugar separately, and a Madeira cake. I'm bowled over. No man has ever made me a picnic before. I'm beginning to feel like I'm in an English novel.

We spread out his anorak on a flat, grassy place a little way in off the road and we sit together on it side by side. We're baking, I'm beginning to wish I'd worn a skirt instead of the jeans. The grass we're sitting on is spongy and he says that's because we're in the heart of a bog. It's hard to imagine that underneath us are thousands, millions of years' worth of squashed trees. The colours all around us are quiet, browns and golds and soft greens. And the contours of the mountains – Ken says they're not real mountains, just hills – are quiet too, curved rather than peaky.

Not one single car.

Now here comes the only human being we've seen since we've sat down. A cyclist. German. (No, I'm not that clever, he has a little German flag flying from the top of his backpack.) He nods 'hello' to us as he comes abreast, then he freewheels down the hill away from us, shiny black bum in the air, like two olives in a jar. I cycle a bit myself, Ken goes shyly. I smile at him. Ice now thoroughly broken.

You can see the city, or most of it, from where we sit. It wears a sort of grey haze. That's the pollution, Ken says, but then tells me it used to be much worse. Some days from here you couldn't even *see* the city, just this huge ball of grey. Especially in winter, before Mary Harney's smokey-coal ban a few years ago. If the Government did nothing else it did that, he says.

I'm surprised he mentions Mary Harney. I wouldn't have put you down as one of her lot, I say to him.

What would you say I am? He grins at me.

I'm on tricky ground here. In this country lifelong feuds can start with simple political discussions. Remember the row with Tom Bennett all those years ago about Patrick Pearse and the Easter Rising?

I do admire Mary Harney, she has great integrity, to me the Progressive Democrats would be mainly southsiders. Ken is not only a northsider, he's a manual worker – definitely not standard PeeDee. That's your own business, I say cautiously.

I'm nothing at all, he says. I'm sick of the lot of them. I don't vote.

There's no answer to that, is there? I grin back at him and take another sandwich.

I look back out over the city while I'm chewing. I feel quite proud. This is my city and it's lovely, curving all the way along the sparkling rim of the sea. I pick out landmarks. The Ballymun towers. The RTE mast. I can follow the course of the Liffey, cutting right through to what I know now is the South Bull – and of course, those are the Pigeon House chimneys, I say, although I shouldn't get a medal for recognizing them, they're the biggest things in the whole city.

Where's the airport? I ask him.

Ken points out a little glint of silver, the sun shining on an aeroplane taking off. He looks away then and I try to figure out what he's thinking. Which is difficult. I don't really know the guy at all. Cycles a bit. Doesn't vote although he seems to like Mary Harney, they're the new items of information. I'm surprised he hasn't mentioned the James situation. Definitely lacking in the curiosity department.

I'm certainly not going to bring it up. Whatever else, I'm not a masochist.

Now that I think of it, here we are, on our third time out, two mature adults. Who haven't even held hands, much less kissed each other. It suits me but I wonder about him. Gay, maybe? But then there's Diandra . . . Although he wouldn't be the first, would he?

That must be Dun Laoghaire Habour, I go, to cover over the awkwardness. And this brings me back full circle to my predicament. Less than two hours ago I was thinking about the boat.

It is, yes, he says back, and look, the new high-speed ferry is coming in, do you see it?

I see it. Teenchy. Minute.

Even though we seem on the surface to be getting along just fine, the James situation is hanging between us, the exact same way it did between Patsy and me.

→ Twenty ←

Next I must report to you on a trip to Birr.

I had asked Ken would he take me, that day we were having the picnic in the Dublin mountains – I suppose I felt I had nothing to lose. I was prepared for him to refuse, given the circumstances, but to my amazement he said yes. I explained that I had an inner demon that would never be satisfied until I went down there.

I start to tell him why – about Mammy and all – but I get stuck straight away. Somehow, no matter what I was going to say about her, it wasn't going to come out right. I wasn't going to be able to explain to someone who never knew her what she was really like. That she wasn't just this social problem or that social worker's case. So I clam up. Sorry, I say, it's something I can't really talk about. I just need to go to Birr, that's all. It's to do with my roots.

He gives me a funny look. You don't have to give me your reasons, Angela, he goes, I'd be happy to take you. We could both do with a day away from Dublin. (Reading between the lines that day, from some of the things he said about Diandra, she was pushing him a bit. Looking for money, for instance. I didn't ask for the details because, to tell you the truth, I didn't want to know. I had enough to worry about.) He hesitates, then, Will you be able to take more time off work?

Oh, yes, I say, there'll be no problem about that.

I still wasn't ready to go into my complicated work life. I'd tell him sometime but not now. And he had no idea how right he was when he said I could do with a day away from Dublin.

It doesn't take a genius to guess why the need to go to Birr suddenly became so urgent. I felt that if I could get down to where Mammy's origins were, maybe it would help James and me. Make things sort of solid. Best-case scenario was finding her relatives and having them talk to me, brilliant-case scenario would be if they came onside and said they'd be our family again. I had this stupid vision where the two of us could nestle into a cat's cradle of relatives.

But even the worst-case scenario — just seeing the place and the family business and her house and all the rest of it — wasn't at all bad. Those places were always going to be there. Immemorial. We'd know at least where I came from and that's important

She had planted certain things in my mind about Birr. The Manchester Martyrs, for instance, Allen, Larkin and O'Brien, who died for Ireland sometime in the last century. Two of them were from around Birr and there was a monument to them in the town. If I could see where she lived, even the monument to the Manchester Martyrs, at least I'd have some framework to picture around her in my mind every time I thought about her. I hated picturing her only in the environment of the flats. Or dying in her hospice bed. In my mind, when I thought of her as a *person*, as opposed to the woman she was forced to be, she was surrounded by soft fabrics and daisies.

I also felt she was prompting me to go. Is that too weird?

We set off for Birr on the Wednesday after our Dublin
mountains excursion. He picked me up at one o'clock – I
went down to the front door when he rang because
James hadn't gone to work that day. In fact he hadn't
been to work for three days. (He said this was OK by his
bosses, and that he had some holiday time due. I didn't
know whether to believe him or not but there wasn't
much I could do about it. I couldn't physically drag him
down there, now, could I?)

Anyway, that Wednesday I didn't want to complicate
matters by having James and Ken Meet. That's how it
was looming in my head at the time, a Meeting, with a
capital letter. If I was being honest with myself, I was
already beginning to see the situation between Ken and
me as something more than friendship.

He wasn't making it easy for me, however, there were
very few hints from his side about how he felt. For
instance, after he left me home from the Dublin
mountains that day, he squeezed my hand when he said
goodbye. Pretty straightforward, you might say, eh? Yet
when I got to remembering it later I couldn't make up
my mind whether it was a romantic squeeze or the kind
of squeeze you give without thinking – like pucking your
friend in the arm when you see something interesting and
want her to see it too before it disappears.

I suppose that we were making progress of a sort.
Although we hadn't discussed the Problem With James
any further during that Friday picnic, at least now he
knew about it and I could feel him thinking about it on
and off during that whole afternoon. It has to be
significant that he hadn't headed for the hills, hasn't it?

I won't go into the precise contents of the Sunday
papers. I got all of them, even though I knew what had to
be facing us. After *Liveline*, it was inevitable that they'd

all have a field day, but I was like a rabbit faced with a snake. A posse of snakes.

I had this glacier in the pit of my stomach when I left the house to go to the newsagent's and it seemed to grow bigger and bigger with every step. I nearly forgot to buy my scratch card, so that will tell you how upset I was.

Don't things happen at the most inappropriate times? Wouldn't you know it, for the very first time I get three stars to enter for the TV game show (with twenty-five million others, of course!). As I'm scribbling my name and address on the back of the card, those newspapers are like fire under my arm and the newsagent's voice is like a grinder. Mike Murphy is gone for the summer, Marty Whelan's the main man now and it's not *Winning Streak* any more, it's *Fame and Fortune*—

Hey, he goes, when I'm scooting out, you forgot your envelope.

Thanks. I rush back. I grab the envelope and run.

I'm not able to wait until I get back home to learn the worst – anyway, I want to protect James. So I divert into the park, sit down on a bench and start to read. The birds are singing. That's a travesty.

The front page of the *Sunday World* has a huge, blurry picture of James leaving the courthouse. They've put a small black rectangle across his eyes. Like a little coffin. Quite appropriate. Anyone who sees that picture and who knows him will be able to recognize him at a hundred yards.

I don't read the article ('Inside, Pages 2, 3, 6 and 7') Instead I look at the *Sunday Independent*. It isn't front-page news, thank God for that, but it's bad enough. Worse than bad. It's one of those little coloured boxes at the top. In this box they've put the same picture of James that the *Sunday World* used, including the little coffin.

And beside it they've advertised what all their biggest writers have to say on the subject.

Eamon Dunphy included.

When I see this I know we're sunk. Eamon Dunphy was a footballer at some stage in his life, with a club in England, but he's now the *Sunday Independent*'s star writer and when he decides to take a scunner against someone he really goes all out. He's absolutely passionate about despising people. Judging by what he writes, he seems to live in a permanent state of apoplexy about other people's opinions and shortcomings.

I'm not sure how many people take him seriously, but for me that doesn't count today. Everyone reads him. The women at work. They all say, 'Isn't he desperate?' but they read him every Sunday for entertainment value, to see who he's having a go at. Ireland's like that. We'll sympathize to your face when someone says something nasty about you. And we'll be rubbing our hands in glee behind your back. We love to see someone pulled down a peg.

I'm no better than anyone else, I read Eamon Dunphy's column, and while from time to time I've felt sorry for the people he's having a go at, I'm ashamed to say never sorry enough to stop me reading the article. It doesn't matter that it was thoughtlessness on my part, I'm disgusted at myself now that I see only too well what the object of his derision must have been going through, not to speak of that person's family. Do those people who write so glibly in those newspapers have any idea about the hurt and damage they cause? If they do, they've a lot to answer for.

I'll be more careful about what I read or believe in future, I'll tell you, because now I realize they couldn't know a lot of the facts behind what they're writing about. For instance, I'd be amazed if any journalist knows *why* James's judge suspended his sentence. She had 'background' reports they wouldn't have seen. Or that they shouldn't have seen. Stuff about the actual incident in the Furry Glen that day that wasn't openly talked about in court. Rosemary Madden's part in all of this is crucial, I believe.

I'm so upset by the thought of what Eamon Dunphy has probably written that I can't look at the front pages of the other newspapers. Instead, I take the whole bundle, leave the park, cross the road, and go round the back of the house where Reddy's left out a few ancient dustbins for his residents' use. I stuff all of those papers as far down inside one of those bins as I can. I'd burn them but that would draw attention to myself. Thank God James isn't up yet.

I leave you to imagine what the atmosphere between Patsy and myself was like on the way to our gig a couple of hours later. Listen, she said immediately, as I got into the car, I've seen the papers and I think that we really shouldn't discuss the situation. Not at all – all right?

All right, I said.

She made conversation, of course, all about Martin and some pal of his who had invited him to go to London. They were at Wimbledon yesterday, Ange, she says gaily.

As though I gave a damn.

Turns out she's always wanted to go to Wimbledon for the tennis. This was news to me.

And they're going to try to get tickets for the European Cup Final this evening, she says, all chirpy. Martin's friend has contacts over there . . .

I'd had to sit through the Germany–England semi-final with James so at least I knew who was in the final. Oh? I go. Germany and Czechoslovakia? Sounds like a thrill a minute to me. (I know it's the Czech Republic now but I keep forgetting. I don't even know where Bosnia is any more. All that part of Europe is as unreliable as the Shifting Whispering Sands.) She looks sharpish at me. Are you being sarcastic?

I put on my innocent look. (Well, I can't be St Teresa of the Roses all the time, can I?)

Thank God none of the customers at the deli knows me except by my first name, because of the badge I wear. Even if I did have the second name on there I doubt they'd twig. I hate the way they say Angela too deiberately. And too much, that's the dead giveaway. You're the hired help and they know it and you know it but they want to show how liberal they are. It's called equality, I don't think. Even the regulars wouldn't recognize me if I met them in some other part of the shopping area. I've served them ten minutes ago, I've been serving them every Saturday for years, yet take the pinny and the name badge off and they've never seen me before.

The day before that Sunday, which was my first appearance at the deli after the court case, I was on full alert during my whole shift but as far as I could detect, they were all just being their ordinary airy selves. I'd had to come clean with the owner – she was going to know everything anyway from the reports of James's trial – but I have to say she was marvellous about it. She isn't a friend of mine but she behaved more like a friend than Patsy is currently doing. If there's anything I can do, she said, and I could tell she meant it.

To get back to the trip to Birr. Ken seemed quite cheerful and ordinary when he came to the door punctually at one minute to one on the Wednesday. I watched him very closely for any signs of conflict but I saw none. So I reckoned (a) he hadn't read the papers,

(b) he'd read them and decided to ignore them, or (c) he was holding fire for a while.

I admire punctuality, I really do.

It must be great to be your own boss, I remark, as we cross the road to where the van is parked.

Sometimes, he says back, sometimes. Like now, when I want to take off for somewhere and I can just go without asking leave of anyone. King of the Road, that's me! He smiles and he looks quite jolly so I reckon the choice is now narrowed down to (a) or (b).

Sam licks me when I get in. I think he believes I'm now part of the fixtures and fittings. I give him a pat but, for myself, I'm nervous about what was facing me. I hadn't slept all that well for obvious reasons and when old Furry Slippers made me redo a long corridor with the polisher that morning I was so tense I snapped at her.

She couldn't believe it. I think that up to then she'd thought I was Miss Meek 1996 or the aforementioned Teresa. The last thing I needed was a row, however, so I buttoned my lip, apologized for being rude, made the excuse that I was very tired, and then pushed that damn polisher away from her like it was a howitzer gun and I was using it to kill enemies lurking in the pattern on the lino.

How are you, Ken goes, as we're heading through the traffic and out of town. You look very pale.

I'm grand, I say, grand. A bit dozy – early mornings, you know how it is.

So far so good, I think, as he chats on about what we can expect to see in Birr. An enormous telescope, apparently. World famous, owned by some lord. And before we go any further, he says then, I'm glad your brother's case turned out well for you. Let's forget about all our troubles today and concentrate on having a good time. I've never been to Birr. It's one of those towns you have to have a reason to go to because it's not on the way from anywhere to anywhere else.

In one way I was delighted with this neat wrapping up of James's case like that. In another, though, I wasn't so sure. Pfft! gone. Just like that. James is a *person*, a human being with feelings. I said nothing, though, I was being done a favour here. Quite a big one. I know what you mean about Birr, I said. That was a fib. I didn't know diddly squat about Birr, as I told you, even though I'd looked it up on a map.

It was a fine day, sort of. One of those days where it's warm all the time but the sun can never quite make it through the clouds. The air in the van was stuffy and I hadn't been lying when I said I was dozy. Even still, my mind was churning.

I'd tried to rehearse what I was going to say if and when I successfully met Mammy's relations, but no matter from what angle I had tried to see it, some other argument they might come up with would instantly occur to me. I was starting in on this circle again, driving myself mad, so I decided to let it go and to enjoy the drive. Just to wait until I got there and to let things happen.

Big mistake.

The omens were not good for that day. The first thing we see as we're leaving the city is this commotion at a big crossroads just beyond the beginning of the Naas dual carriageway. An island of Guards and squad cars, dozens of them, around the traffic lights, lorries and cars backed up in all four directions, being diverted away. The lights were going green, red, orange, green, red, orange, all to themselves with nothing moving around them. There were loads of other cars parked along the grass partition down the middle of the road, drivers and passengers all out on the verges. All staring in the same direction. At a red car.

One of the Guards directed us to keep moving along the shoulder of the road, and as we passed the lights, I saw that the front of the red car, which was pointing in the Dublin direction, was covered in a blanket. That meant there was a body or bodies. I was puzzled, though, because I couldn't see what the red car had hit. No other cars dented or smashed up.

Maybe a heart attack at the wheel? This was Ken, who kept straining over his shoulder to look back at the scene, so much so that, talk about heart attacks, I was afraid *we'd* have an accident!

Maybe, I said back.

Whatever had happened, it had been a long time since I'd seen so much Gárda activity. The nearest was a huge hugger-mugger in the flats between two of the criminal families who were always having wars with each other. That one went on for hours, in the courtyard and the entryways, and by the end there were so many blue lights flashing on the roofs of the squad cars you could read your evening paper by them.

As it turned out, it had been no accident or heart attack that day but very bloody murder. There was indeed a body in that red car. Two thugs had come up on a motorcycle and had shot a reporter whose mission was exposing the crime underworld in Dublin. She had been just sitting there, waiting for the lights to change when bam!

It was a huge thing for days in the city and in the rest of the country. I suppose the reason everyone was going ballistic was that she was a reporter and not just a Joe Soap. I always have mixed feelings about this kind of thing, where the death of a politician or a famous person seems to be presented as far more tragic than the death of someone ordinary. I didn't know this reporter's work, because largely I try to avoid as many horrible stories in the newspapers as I can – I have enough of them at home, ha ha! – but according to everyone I talked to and everything I read, she was very brave. She'd been shot before, in the leg, and had also been sent death threats, but none of it had stopped her writing her stuff and I suppose this accounted for all the hoo-ha.

I have to admit that maybe this bravery is the other side of the coin when you talk about journalists and newspapers. I still wish, though, that the rest of them would take a leaf out of this girl's book and go after the real stories in Ireland and leave people like us alone. We all see events from our own point of view, don't we.

Mind you, the only thing that surprised me when I found out the true story was that people were surprised in the first place. All the politicians were on the telly saying it was a descent into chaos and an attack on the foundations of the state and all the rest of it, but sure do they not know there are fellas being stabbed and shot on a daily basis all over the city? And didn't the same thing happen a couple of weeks previously down the country when a detective was shot the same way as that poor girl!

None of them seem to have the first clue about what it's really like to live day to day in places like the flats where I grew up. Even where I live now. I don't count many politicians or other toffs amongst my neighbours. They should all be forced to live in the inner city for a few weeks. A few days, even – anyone round where I live could bend their ears about what's going on in the real world.

Imagine, though, dinner-time on a summer day. Five bullets. She was a mother too, Lord rest her.

But since we didn't know the story, Ken Sheils and I just blessed ourselves, made cluck clucking noises like you do, isn't it terrible, Lord have mercy on their souls, and carried on down the Naas dual carriageway.

I have to say that even along here, and then a bit later on both sides of the motorway, even though it was so close to the city the countryside was gorgeous. Like a magic carpet. Splurges of bright red poppies, cows up to their armpits in green and yellow fields, hedges and trees drenched with creamy-coloured flowers. Ken said this was hawthorn, and that this year was a great year for it because of the brilliant summer we had in 1995.

We hit our next problem when we turned off the main road and found that the way to Birr was covered in rough stone chips called, apparently, loose chippings. Ken says this is how they do the roads in the country – they just throw down lorry-loads of this stuff and let the passing cars do the work of squashing them into the tar on the surface. He hates it, they do it every single summer, according to him, and it's brutal on the paintwork of your car. Little pieces of the stone fly up from under your tyres and the tyres of everything that passes you, particularly going in the opposite direction. Not to speak of potentially shattering your windows.

He shows me what everyone does – you put one of your fingers up high on the windscreen as if you're pointing out, and this is supposed to stop the glass breaking if it does get hit. He didn't know the principle behind how this works but everyone does it.

It wasn't long before I saw an unexpected side of Ken Shiels.

Twenty-One

The incident started quietly enough. I was admiring the lovely gardens, full of flowers, in the bungalows by the side of the road. It must be lovely to have a garden. We have the park, I know, but it's not the same.

We pass one particularly nice one and I point it out to Ken but he's so afraid of the loose chippings that he's slowed down to the point where we're crawling at about ten miles an hour and he won't look. M-mmm, he goes, m-mmm . . .

At this point, a big lorry comes up behind us. Because the road is narrow he can't pass and he has to crawl behind us. The driver starts leaning on his horn.

The first time he does it, it's so loud, like a ship's siren, I nearly jump out of my skin but Ken just flushes up and white-knuckles the steering wheel. Feck him, he says, who does he think he is?

Pa-a-arp! the horn goes again. The guy is right up behind us, right on our tail. He's so close I look behind and I can see the edges of the tomatoes in his sandwich on the dashboard.

Ken grips the steering wheel even tighter, if that's possible. I'm not going to be bullied, he goes – and would you believe he slows down even more. Now he's going so slowly the needle on the speedometer isn't even moving. The guy behind goes crazy. Pa-a-arp, pa-a-a-aarp, pa-a-a-a-a-a-a-a-a-rp! He's playing a symphony.

Next thing he pulls out and tries to pass us. Ken speeds up and moves out a little, just enough to frustrate the guy because now there's a tractor coming in the other direction. By this time, I'm gripping the sides of my seat. I know no good is going to come of this, I can feel it in my bones. I can also feel waves of heat coming from Ken Shiels. I swear.

The lorry driver waits until the tractor goes past then he pulls out suddenly and attempts to pass us again. Ken speeds up, moves out a little.

Pa-a-a-a-rp! Now the lorry's lights are going as well as the horn. I can see them flashing in the mirror but I'm afraid to look back. I'm also afraid to say anything to Ken – after all, I don't know him that well and I'm a guest in this van.

We come to a bend in the road and on the other side of it we find we're coming towards a bunch of travellers' caravans parked on a wide verge. They have horses pegged out at intervals all along. One of the traveller boys, about twelve or thirteen, is pulling one of these horses on the end of a rope from one side of the road to the other. The horse is pulling and dancing a bit. There's no danger, because we're going so slowly, but Ken jams on the brakes and – you've guessed it.

The lorry runs into the back of us. Not hard but enough to jolt us about a bit. And the sound of the crash! Have you ever been inside a hollow van when it's been hit?

Sam goes crazy, barking up a storm.

Ken turns on the flashers and so does your man and the two of them jump out. I'm afraid to – anyway, it's none of my business – so I just sit tight. I stare straight ahead. I literally don't know where to look because now the travellers, men, women, kids, have started to pour out of their caravans to watch the fun.

I can see the altercation in the side mirror of the van if I turn my eyes a tiny bit to the right. The driver is small and stocky with a beer belly as wide as a door. He has this belly stuck up against Ken and except for it being in the way the two of them are nose to nose. I can hear them with no effort at all but I can't make out what they're saying. They're both roaring so loudly that all the words are swallowed up in the general mayhem. There is quite a lot of effing, that much I can make out.

A traveller woman comes up to me and knocks on my window. I wind it down. Would you like a cup of tea, missus? she asks me. She has a kid on her hip who has the dirtiest nose I've ever seen. Two green waterfalls are rolling into that kid's open mouth and neither the kid nor its mother makes any effort to staunch the flow. You can hear its poor chest rattling.

No thank you, I go. I try to smile.

It's no trouble, missus, the woman says, I've the kettle on. She goes to pull at the handle of the door. She smiles at me, she has terrible teeth.

Until that moment, I never knew I was prejudiced against travellers. But now I panic. I immediately think everything in this van is going to be stolen if I leave it unattended. All Ken's tools and stuff. Sam obviously has the same idea. He's hurling himself against the door across my lap. He thinks he's a Rottweiler.

I grab him and try to hold on to him but it's like grappling with a whirlwind. No, really, thank you, it's all right, I have to shout to make myself heard above the dog, I had tea not half an hour ago at home.

I'm sickening myself with this. The poor woman is only trying to help. I suppose I'm conditioned to believe the worst about people at the moment. Where did these feelings come from? A bigot, me?

Next thing some man comes around and pulls the woman away from the door. He's not gentle about it either. He grunts something at her and she leaves.

Sam gives one last bark. A sort of triumphant 'r-rrufff!' – that's seen *them* off – then he jumps into the back and settles down again on his blanket.

Meantime, all this bedlam is still going on behind me. Now there must be at least thirty people standing back enjoying the show and I can see why they think this is the height of entertainment. I remember Mammy telling us not to act like tinkers. Now here were the tinkers being given an excuse to roar at their children not to be acting like settled people!

There's also a traffic jam, two tractors, one car with a foreign registration plate and another van. Not to speak of the boy and his horse, who are still in the middle of the road.

I continue to look straight ahead. Cows. Low hills. Huge fields. Beautiful colours in the fields and in the garden of a house in the distance – you can see why the Americans think Ireland is so green. I wish I was a cow. I wish I was anything except Angela Devine here in this van, embarrassed out of my brains. Anyone but companion to this man who's going purple in the face and who's roaring and shouting and cursing like a sailor. I sincerely hope these travellers don't think he's my husband. Or even my boyfriend.

There's a lull and Ken comes back to the driver's side of the van to get his insurance papers out of the glove compartment. Now the purple's gone from his face – it's as white as paper. I daren't say anything.

When he goes back to the lorry driver, they scrutinize

each other's documents. Some of the traveller men are wiping the bumpers of the two vehicles with their hands as though they're assessing them, talking amongst themselves. The driver of the foreign-registered car is getting out. He's enormous. About six foot eight. How he fits into a Volkswagen Golf I don't know. He wanders over to the verge and takes a picture of the traveller camp. They don't like it but he seems not to notice. Three teenage boys are standing alongside our van, quite close, staring in at me.

I get twice as paranoid.

What's the matter with you, Angela? You're the one who *beats up* gurriers. *Dublin* gurriers, for God's sake. These boys, they're perfectly respectful, they're just inquisitive, that's all. *Get a grip* . . .

Sorry about that, Ken says, a few minutes after we're finally creeping along again over the loose chippings. He bangs the heel of his hand off the steering wheel. I couldn't let him away with it.

I don't answer, I'm still shook at my own reaction to the travellers. I *know* travellers in Dublin. I have a regular woman who comes in every so often for a chat and a cup of tea. But back there I was like a fish out of water, had no idea of how to behave. This trip is very educational.

Is there much damage to the van?

Just one of the brake lights, Ken says back, but it wasn't that, it was the arrogance of the man. I won't be bullied. Nobody bullies Kenneth Shiels.

That's a bit of a jolt, it's the first time it's occurred to me that he's a Kenneth. But I can see he's getting het up again so I don't say anything more. He glances across at me. I hope it hasn't spoiled your outing for you.

For obvious reasons we arrive at Birr in a quiet mood.

I suppose we might as well buy a guide book, he says,

as we drive into a wide square which seems to be used as the town's main car park. My stomach is fluttering so all I can do is nod.

While he's in the shop, I get out of the van and lean on the warm bonnet. Look around, get my bearings. The real tourist. First thing I see is Dooly's Hotel on the far side of the square. Now my stomach really flips its bananas. This is it, this is really it. Mammy talked about Dooly's. It's where her parents used to go.

Ken comes back. All I could get was this. He shows me a little booklet with flowers on the cover and a picture of two houses. The man behind the counter told me that Birr has the only branch of the Georgian Society outside Dublin, is that any use to you?

I can't speak, I don't give a sugar about Georgian societies, I'm still seeing Mammy's mother and father having their night out in Dooly's. Cups of tea? Sherry? What?

Great, thanks, I go, taking the booklet from him.

She wouldn't give me up for adoption or put me into an orphanage, that's what I reckon. That's probably why she had to flee to Dublin. It must have been so dreadful for her. I've a lot to be grateful for.

Ken and I go for a walk down what seems to be the main street, O'Connell Street. Just like Dublin. I wonder how many O'Connell Streets there are in Ireland. I hate Daniel O'Connell. He was bloody oul' Concepta's favourite patriot. She beat him into us.

It's still warm, still cloudy, but with the sun still struggling to shine. I suppose I'm hypersensitive now but I think I feel her everywhere. Did she go into this drapery shop with the knickers in the window? It certainly looks as though it hasn't changed much. What about that hardware shop across the street? There are people gossiping here and there, all along the street, who would have been about her age if she was still alive. Did they know her?

When I tune in as Ken and I pass them, I hear they're all talking about the reporter murdered on the Naas dual carriageway and this is when Ken and I put two and two together. It's was a very shivery feeling. That poor girl, Lord have mercy on her, was alive and whistling just a few minutes before we came up to her car.

We come to the end of the street and another, smaller square. Here's the famous monument to the Manchester Martyrs. Dear God, one of them, the one from Cork, was only nineteen. James's age. Executed. By gun? Hanged? I can imagine the feeling in his stomach that morning when he woke up. If he slept at all. I hope he didn't write to his mother. It would have killed her if he did. I know if James wrote to me on the eve of his execution I wouldn't be able to read it. I'd probably want to kill myself rather than read it.

What am I thinking about? That drapery shop and that hardware shop could be the very business that belonged to Mammy's family. Neither of them had Devine on them but that didn't matter. Maybe they never had Devine on them. In Dublin, Clery's is still Clery's although as far as I know there hasn't been a Clery for yonks.

That must be the castle – the one with the telescope—

What? Ken's voice has sounded like thunder.

That must be the castle down there. He's pointing to the end of a street where there's a high grey wall and a massive stone building flying a flag.

I couldn't care less about any castle. She mentioned it, I think, but not so it made much of an impression on me. She certainly never mentioned any telescope – I'd have remembered that. (Now that I think about it, it was surprising she didn't talk about the castle, since the

family was Protestant.) Yes, it must, I say, and I turn
away immediately to walk back up O'Connell Street
towards the van. I want him to stop yakking.

Do you not want to see it? He catches up with me.

I want to shout at him. I want him to go away. He's
behaving as though I'm a normal visitor to this town, as
though I just want to see the sights.

I grit my teeth. Remind myself he's the one doing the
favours here. How could he know when I haven't told
him? I try to smile. You must let me buy you some
petrol.

He looks at me as though I have two heads. It's diesel,
he says, very slowly. I must seem demented to him.
Well, I am.

Look, I go, I hope you don't mind or you won't be
insulted or anything, but this is proving to be more
difficult for me than I thought it would.

He frowns and I realize he thinks I mean being here
with him. It's not you, I say quickly. What I mean is, just
being here for the first time is the problem, I'll explain it
all to you some day. Would you mind awfully if we split
up for half an hour or so, so I can wander around by
myself? Would you mind going for a drink – or a cup of
coffee even? I'd spotted a nice coffee-shop-cum-deli
across the road.

Sure, he goes, of course. See you in half an hour then
– back at the van? He walks off and goes into the coffee
shop. Through the window I can see him pointing at a
cake under the glass-topped counter. Professionally,
even from the outside, I would rate this as a pretty good
deli.

I'm still standing on the other side of the street,
pretending to be reading *Birr: Heritage Town* – the little
guide book. Now what do I do? My lack of a definite plan
is glaring. I can hardly go up to some stranger and say,

Did you know Rose Devine and where could I find any of
her family, please? I'm beside the drapery shop so I turn
and look in the windows. Quite nice stuff. Through the
doorway I can see there are no customers, only three
people who look as if they own the place or at least work
there. I stand there, trying to get up the nerve.

Maybe the hardware shop across the road? It's very
busy – everyone would hear the questions, look at me . . .

I walk back slowly towards the van and it's when I get
to it I have this brainwave. The Gárda station is right in
front of where we parked. The Guards know everything,
they'd help. I should ask for the Devines and say I was a
long-lost cousin. I consider putting on an American
accent and then decide this would be stupid.

As you can imagine, in my present circumstances,
Gárda stations are inclined to give me the heebie-jeebies
so it takes all my courage to go in.

A lot of toing and froing in there and telephones
ringing – and the first setback is that the young Guard at
the front desk doesn't know from Adam who the Devines
might be. He's a recent transfer into the town. He goes
off to consult a senior colleague, who comes back with
him. This individual is exactly one of those Guards you
see in old black and white films on the telly, the ones
made in Ireland with Abbey actors. He's roundy, with a
grizzled head and a kind, shrewd face. Good afternoon,
he says, who's asking for the Devines?

I'm a relative from Dublin, I say, I just happen to be
passing through and I thought I'd look them up.

And what's your name?

Angela, I go. Angela Devine.

The slow look the Guard gives me leads me to believe
he knows exactly who I am and my heart starts to thump.
But he couldn't possibly know. He couldn't possibly. I
try to keep my face as blank as I can.

And what branch of the family would you be now? He's still looking . . .

There's nothing for it. I'm Rose's daughter, I say as formally as I can.

Ahh, he goes. I see.

Is this the first year I've noticed or does the whole of Ireland say 'I see' at every available opportunity?

The Guard, who I reckon would be about the same age as Mammy would be now, leans on the counter as though he's haggling for a horse. He shakes his head, puts on a sad expression. Very sad, very sad, he goes. There's only one of them left in the town now, Adeline. You know what happened, of course? His eyes are boring into me. The younger Guard is pretending to be sorting through the entries in a big ledger at a desk. He's all ears. I lower my voice a bit but then he just happens to have to come nearer where I'm standing to search for something on a set of shelves. This gets on my wick but there's nothing I can do about it.

I admit to the older Guard I don't know anything of what occurred and that I've never met any of my relatives.

He makes a clucking sound, shakes his head again, I should probably let Adeline fill you in.

Could you direct me to where Adeline lives?

He leans on the counter again to give me the directions. My aunt Adeline apparently lives about half a mile outside the town on a little byroad – we passed the turnoff to it coming in. You can't miss the house, he goes, she has an old Morris Minor she parks outside it, right into the hedge. He puts his hands on his big hips. Not that she drives it any more. Don't be expecting too much now. She keeps herself to herself a lot. He sticks out his hand. You're welcome to Birr. And I have to say you have the look of your mother. But she was dark.

I'm back outside. No wonder poor Mammy had to flee to Dublin, it's quite clear you can't sneeze here but everyone gets a cold. I look around the square for Ken Sheils. Then I remember it was I who insisted he go for coffee. I have to cool my heels for a bit. Just as well. Steady me up – but now that I'm so near—

Did they have a chauffeur, I wonder.

I saw a picture of Mammy's parents once. That was some lady that was, straight as a pole, formidable chest, dress buttoned right up under her chin. She wasn't someone you'd mess with in her shop, I'd imagine.

He was quite fat and smaller than her, with one of those handlebar moustaches. Maybe it was the moustache, maybe it was Mammy's mother's severe expression and that dress, but they looked more old-fashioned than they should have because they couldn't have been more than their middle thirties in the picture. Early forties at the most. And that had to have been a maximum of only forty years ago. The fifties, for God's sake, not the Middle Ages. Yet somehow those people – my grandparents! – looked Victorian or Edwardian.

I don't know where that snap is now. As I told you before I have practically nothing of my heritage.

Maybe Adeline will have more pictures, better ones. She was the youngest, so she would be only around fifty now. That's young in 1996 so maybe she won't hold a grudge. Maybe she'll welcome me with open arms. At last maybe I'll have a family. I've often wondered do I have cousins. I should have asked that Guard if Adeline is married . . . Suppose Adeline knows who my father is? Was. Is? Oh, my God—

Whoa, whoa. You're going too fast. One thing at a time. You're here to look for your *family*. Mammy's family. Take it easy . . .

→ Twenty-Two ←

We see the Morris Minor when we come around a bend. It's ancient, all right, one of those estate ones with a square wood frame along the back. Paint flaking off, you could see it had once been navy blue. Sweat starts to trickle down between my shoulder blades and it isn't just because the sun has come out at last.

Ken turns off the engine. We get out. The quietness! Nothing but fields and grass and hedges for miles around. Flies buzzing like helicopters all over the dry cow dirt on the tarmac, a car on the main road a half mile away as loud as if it's right beside you. The air here is much heavier than it was on my last country trip, the day we went up the Dublin mountains. That was lofty, this is thick like syrup. You have to wade through it.

We walk towards Adeline's house, which is a concrete cottage – a bungalow, really – set back off the road behind a high hedge that badly needs cutting. No flowers in the garden, just untidy grass full of dandelions. Hens and ducks grubbing around.

Hey! Ken says. What about those! Look at those, aren't they extraordinary? He's pointing at a pair of stone lions, big ones, set on both sides of the front door. They look terribly out of place, they're three-quarters the

height of the door. Who are we visiting anyway? He
looks at me.

I still haven't got around to giving him my complex
family history. This woman should be my aunt, my
mother's sister, I say to him. I've never met her before.
She must have brought those stone lions from her old
home, they were well off in their day. This sounds
terrible. Prissy. So I add quickly that I'll tell him
everything in the very near future. To give him his due,
he doesn't bat an eyelid.

The gate gives a groan when we push it open. As for
the front door behind those lions, Ken knows by looking
at it that it had probably not been opened since the turn
of the century. Never mind painted. Not a shred of paint
left. Neither is there a knocker or a bell.

Maybe there's no one in. Ken looks up at the roof and
this irritates me. Who the hell does he think he's going
to see up there? Maybe the flying nun?

I'm being totally unfair. She's in, all right, I say, that's
her car outside the hedge.

Will we go round the back? he goes, she probably uses
the back door, most people do in the country— Then he
notices me hanging back. Do you want me to wait in the
van? I don't mind, really . . .

No. I'd like you to come round with me, will you?

Sure, he says, come on so. He puts his arm around my
shoulders. Don't worry, he goes, she's not going to take
a bite out of us, is she? She'll probably be delighted to
meet her long-lost niece. He squeezes the shoulder under
his hand.

We see her the minute we come around the side of the
house. Wellington boots, man's trousers, an old raincoat
and a man's pork-pie hat. The back garden is twice as
untidy as the front and she's digging stuff which has to be
manure into a vegetable plot. I call to her but she doesn't

miss a dig. It's only when I get up close to her that I see she's wearing a Walkman. Two little earphones coming down from under the hat.

I walk around her into her line of vision and she looks up at me as though strangers are only to be expected in this vegetable patch on Wednesday afternoons in June. Yes? pulling one of the earphones a little bit away from her ears.

Hello, I say, are you Adeline Devine?

Hold on a second, she says, and plonks the earphone back into her ear. She listens for a few seconds and then makes a sort of grunting sound as though she's fed up. She lifts the hat and pulls off the headset, settles it around her neck. Her hair, as grey as a badger's, looks as though it's been cut with a lawnmower. She puts the hat back. Gazes at me. And who might you be?

I tell her.

I'd like to be able to report that she did something significant, like they do on such occasions in films or in books. Like, she should have let out a long, low whistle or stuck her spade dramatically into the manure. Anything.

Instead, she starts hauling spadefuls of the manure towards her. So? she goes, what do you want? If it's your inheritance, there's nothing, you're wasting your time. I don't own this house. She has a peculiar accent. Not Anglo, exactly, but not Irish either — her Ts are soft, that's Irish, but she doesn't pronounce her Rs and that's Anglo. Her voice is deep and fruity. The stink from the manure is terrible.

She's continuing to dig as though I'm not there. I don't know what to say or to do next. I'd just like to talk, I say to her, I promise you I'm not looking for anything. I just came to visit you—

Now she does shove the spade into the earth. I don't

get visitors. I don't ask for them and they don't come. I can't imagine why you'd want to visit me. That business is all finished. We look at each other and it's touch and go. Out of the blue, I'm not a bit nervous any more. 'That business' is the one involving my mother, Rose. Well, I'm not going to have it. Not from her or from anyone. My friend and I drove all the way down here just to meet you, I say, as though I'm the Queen of England. He took time off work. It wouldn't kill you to be civil.

Behind me, I hear Ken give a little cough. I'm sure he can't believe what he's hearing.

Well, well, well, Adeline goes, taking off her hat again and fanning her face with it. You certainly don't take after your mother. Wouldn't say boo to a goose. Who's your friend, then? She peers around me towards Ken.

I introduce him.

We'd better go inside, she says, but supplies are low. She makes no move and the three of us are left standing there looking at each other.

As matter of fact we do have a flask and a few sandwiches. This is Ken, calm as you please. I'll go and get it.

My aunt Adeline and I wait for him to come back. We say nothing at all to each other. She seems not put out in the least so I'm determined not to be put out either. She's my aunt and I'm her niece and I've every right to be standing here. We listen to flies. A *lot* of flies.

Ken comes back and the three of us go into the house. The kitchen to be precise. More hens. Hens' droppings. Piles of English newspapers, the ones at the bottom as yellow as bananas. Bottled gas cooker and a Super Ser, and the sink is one of those huge porcelain ones that stand on trestles. No electricity, as far as I can see. Looks like the only modern thing in the whole place is the

Walkman now hanging from the belt of Adeline's trousers.

To take you out of your suspense, the story of my relatives after my mother left for Dublin is a short one.

And no, I didn't ask who my father was – or is. Not yet. Somehow it didn't seem appropriate. My aunt Adeline gave me no opening, either. To tell you the truth, her attitude was a puzzle. I mean, how would *you* react if your sister's daughter, whom you've never seen or imagined, arrived on your doorstep? Wouldn't you be at least a *tiny* bit interested?

Neither does it take a feather out of her when I tell her Mammy is dead. Doesn't surprise me, she says. Don't tell me any of the gory details, all water under the bridge now. Poor Rose. Never very bright. But wouldn't listen to anyone, would she?

The story is that after my mother left, my grandfather and grandmother and their three remaining children continued to live in their nice house in the town. My grandparents ran their shops. Eventually Jeremy married a wealthy South African and went to live in Cape Town. Lily married an English captain she met at a hunt ball in Galway and moved with him to Derbyshire.

One night in 1968, when Adeline was out, her parents' house caught fire. My grandfather died in the flames, my grandmother died two days later in hospital. There was no insurance and when the businesses were looked at, it turned out they were in such debt they would have gone under in any case, even without the fire. Creditors had been holding off, apparently out of respect for what the family represented in the town.

Wouldn't happen today, my aunt Adeline says in her strange accent as she's lorrying into Ken's sandwiches and drinking his tea. No respect for tradition these days, any of 'em. (Nevertheless, she's already told us that this house belongs to someone in her church who doesn't ask her for any rent.) She now lives on unemployment assistance. I would have thought this would be humiliating for a person of her background, but not a bit of it. She tells us without a trace of irony that she deserves every penny of it after all she and her family did for this wretched country. As a matter of fact, it should be more.

She knows a bit about horses – I'm quite good on horses, someone should employ me to give tips. And I have my own vegetables and eggs. Here, chuck, chuck, chuck, now she's shaking the crumbs of Ken's sandwiches off her trousers onto the floor. She sells the surplus – free-range eggs are all the rage now, even in Birr. She says Birr like it sticks in her throat.

She was twenty-one at the time of the fire, which would make her now only about forty-nine years old. She looks way over sixty. She hasn't seen either Lily or Jeremy since the funeral of their parents, and as far as she knows from Christmas cards, which is the only communication between them, neither of them had any children. So any hope I had of cousins was out the window. On my mother's side at least.

She tells us all of this in a single burst, like she wants to get it over with as soon as possible. As if maybe she won't get rid of us until she gives us value for our trip.

But at least now I knew who I was and where I came from.

Naturally it didn't sink in properly until much, much later. But a couple of really good things came out of that day. For a start, I now knew it was no insult that none of them came to Mammy's funeral. My grandparents were well dead at the time, Lily and Jeremy were far away and Adeline seemed to read only English newspapers so she wouldn't have seen the death notices.

And she did have some photographs, which she gave me — Keep them, keep them, waving her arms at me as though I'm a plague of locusts, I don't want them, they just clutter up the place.

When we go back to Dublin the events of that day weren't over, not by a long chalk. I was dog-tired, and after Ken dropped me off, I could barely put one foot in front of the other climbing the stairs to the flat. I could already feel the kick of the cup of tea, the smoothness of the pillowcase against my cheek . . .

But when I pushed open the door, I saw a note on the floor. It had been shoved under.

James was in hospital. He'd had an accident.

Please contact such and such a number at the Mater hospital because James has had an accident, that's all it said. I didn't recognize the handwriting and I've never found out who put it in. Dwyer, probably.

Thank God it was the Mater, because it's only up the road from us. I flew. I think I've told you I hate hospitals, and that's true, but my own feelings were furthest from my mind as you can imagine.

He's still in Casualty when I get there. They let me in to see him only on sufferance, because they didn't want visitors getting in the way, they're too busy. But when I explain that I'd just got the message, they give me five minutes.

I hardly recognize him in the cubicle. He's asleep but even if he hadn't been I can't see how he could have opened his eyes. His entire face is bloody, and so swollen on one side that he looks like a man I once saw on TV who'd had a lot of chemotherapy. His lips are split and like two half-collapsed balloons, he's on a drip and one of his arms is strapped into a sort of cradle.

The nurse who comes in with me explains that they'd had to cut off his leather jacket – the remains of it are draped over the end of the bed – because the arm in the cradle is broken and he also has several broken ribs. I'll leave you with him for a minute, she goes, don't be upset by what he looks like, I've had much worse coming through here. He'll be fine after a bit of TLC. We're admitting him as soon as we can get a bed.

I have to warn you, though, she says, we're actually looking for eighteen people to be admitted at the moment and we might have to send him somewhere else. She sees my expression. Don't worry, she goes, we'll send him in a taxi and a nurse will go with him. She looks down at him, tweaks the pillow. He'll be groggy. We've given him something for the pain.

What happened? Did he fall off his bike?

I'd have to go and look at his chart. He's been here a while and the shift has changed. I do know that the ambulance crew picked him up somewhere quite near here.

She reacts to a call from outside. Sorry, she says quickly, five minutes now—

She bustles out. It's then I remember that his bike was parked outside the flat, locked to the railings as usual. In fact, Ken had remarked on it as he left me off. Said it was in very good condition for such an old one.

There's an unexpected atmosphere in this place. It's too quiet, cubicle curtains gently swishing forwards and backwards, low voices from the doctors and nurses, a quiet moan, except it's not really a moan, more a sigh. Pain and suffering changed down to low gear. I'd been in Casualty before, of course, but not for years, so I suppose that subconsciously I was now thinking it would be like *ER* with all that yelling and clacking and racket.

This semi-silence is a bit unnerving. And there's an awful smell — disinfectant, well, you'd expect that, but it's mixed in with another, very strong odour, like fabric Elastoplast. I presume it's the smell of hospital bandages. Or it might be plaster of paris.

I study James. He's lucky to be in a cubicle, there are poor unfortunates out there on trolleys. His head is turned away from me.

It occurs to me I should ring up to say I won't be showing up for the kissogram job tonight. Then I think the hell with it. Let them fire me. Big talk for someone who has only four hundred and thirty odd left of the scratch-card money.

Don't ask.

James, I go in a low voice, James . . .

His head turns and he looks at me. At least, he tries to. It's pathetic. I can barely see any eyes. Two small, roaring red openings in the mass of damage. He tries to say something but nothing comes out.

He tries again. This time I understand him. He didn't have the tenner to give to the office when he was brought in. Would I pay it to them? Imagine! In his condition and all he can think about is a lousy tenner. It's some sort of tax you have to pay to the Government.

Of course I'll pay it, I go. Then, You were in a fight, weren't you?

He doesn't have to answer. I can see by the way he reacts that I'm only too right.

I won't go on about what he said or what I said next as I'm sure that once again you're way ahead of me. The summary of what happened is that he was jumped by four men. In a little laneway off Dorset Street, near the pub he drinks in with his pals. He was on the way to the pub when these guys grabbed him and dragged him down this lane, where they got him up against a wall and beat him senseless with a golf club and baseball bats. And he thinks a hammer.

He didn't recognize the guys. The last thing he remembers when he was lying on the ground in his own blood is that one of them said to him he should make sure to remember them. That they were citizens concerned with justice. And that justice was not being done.

And that he should, for his own safety, get out of Dublin.

He's lucky to be alive. A hammer.

If I tell you I was shocked but not surprised, I hope that doesn't sound too confusing. I suppose now is as good a time as any to give you some flavour of what was happening with the media.

I'm afraid that putting those Sunday papers in the bin didn't make the storm go away. Monday and Tuesday were even worse than Sunday.

It was because Rosemary Madden had allowed herself to be interviewed. She came into the *The Gay Byrne Show* for the Monday morning, two days before my trip to Birr.

It was actually Joe Duffy that day, not Gay, and he interviewed her in that special hushed way they all have for when something really sensational has happened. I was sitting listening to it as though I was somebody else, not me. There was no stir from James's bedroom, although he does have his ghetto-blaster in there with him and for all I know he could have been listening too. (He wouldn't get up that morning when I called him after I got home from work.)

I turned down the radio and sat really close to it. I felt paralysed. I couldn't believe the way she was talking about James. She called him a beast. Her life was over, she said. All in the quiet murmur on the turned-low radio.

Her photograph was on the front page of the *Herald* on the Monday evening, Alongside the usual one of James with the coffin over his eyes.

Tuesday morning, front page, *all* the papers. And inside. (This time I read them.) And all that day she was being interviewed again on radio.

The gist of all these interviews and articles was the same. Rosemary's home was inundated with messages of support, people were sending her bouquets of flowers and cuddly toys. People were inviting her to their houses in the country to have a holiday. One travel agent offered her two weeks in Majorca. Politicians and prominent people were ringing up to express their concern. All the reports described her as 'tearful but determined'. She hadn't decided yet, they said, whether or not to appeal the leniency of the sentence.

The interviews got bigger. Women's groups were outraged. Everyone was queuing to be interviewed to say how sickened they were. People were asking for the resignation of the Minister for Justice, saying that judges had to be brought under some kind of control.

The message was clear. James would have to pay.

Sprinkled here and there were snippets with one or two people saying we had to be careful about civil rights and that we shouldn't be overreacting to a single judgement but I was so upset that to me those people's views didn't count. I'd never heard of any of them and they were drowned in the tidal wave of general opinion.

The morning of the day Ken and I went to Birr, the *Irish Times* ran a section in the letters page under the heading Rape Sentencing. In it, one woman wrote that she would be willing to start a public collection so that

Rosemary could get the best lawyers in the country to appeal the sentence all the way to Europe. Another argued that because of her courage in going public, Rosemary Madden should be given the freedom of the city.

The letter that got to me most said James should be castrated. The man who wrote that one said he would be willing to perform the operation himself.

Twenty-Three

Listen, James, I say to him in his bed in Casualty, don't let them get you down. Rest now and get some sleep. I'll check to see where you end up and I'll come in and see you first thing tomorrow morning no matter where you are. I don't care about visiting hours, they'll let me in. I'm going to get us some help, some real help. Whoever did this can't get away with it, I won't let them.

I had no idea what I was talking about but I knew I had to do something.

Don't, he goes, don't, just leave it, you'll only make things worse.

I stand up. Nothing more's going to happen to you, I say, I promise you that. Now try and get some sleep.

I lean over and kiss him on the forehead. I haven't done that since he was about seven but he doesn't pull away. I turn quickly and leave the place. I'm too far gone for tears.

There's a public telephone under one of those hood affairs outside the doors to the Casualty room, but wouldn't you know it, there's a woman talking on it. I wait. My brain is racing. I'm putrid with anger. James and I have paid for what he has done, over and over again. We've paid for it in spades. Look at us, we're basket cases. Look at his ruined face.

I'm a completely different person from the one who thought, up there in the Dublin mountains — was it only four or five days ago? — that we might take the boat to England. The hell we will. We're going to fight this.

The woman on the phone is making complex arrangements to be picked up. The person she's talking to apparently hasn't a clue where the Mater hospital is, let alone the Casualty entrance. She's making a dog's dinner of giving the directions . . . No . . . let me see . . . After you cross O'Connell Bridge and come up O'Connell Street, the best way to come would be up the North Circular Road . . . No . . . Wait a minute . . . It might be better to come at it from Eccles Street . . . do you know Eccles Street? . . . Well, do you know Dorset Street . . . Do you know where the Plaza Cinerama used to be? It's now the Wax Museum . . .

I feel like kicking the crutch from under her.

At last she hangs up and I dial Patrice Murphy's number. Needless to remark, I know it off by heart at this stage.

I get an answering machine. I've forgotten what time it is, of course, everyone's left his office by now. I briefly consider ringing him at home but decide against it. I leave a message that I'll ring again first thing in the morning. That it's very urgent.

I go to pay the bloody tenner into the office. Find I only have seven pounds and a few odd bits of change. They're nice about it. Sort of. Take it or leave it, says the new Angela Devine. I stalk off.

When I let myself in, the flat is more empty than I've ever known it — the note about James is still where I left it on the little table beside the door. I remember once listening to Gay when some woman was on giving out about her children's untidiness and he says back to her that some day you'll tidy up and it's going to stay tidy, missus, because they'll all be gone. Make the most of them while you have them, missus. For the first time, I know what he means, really know. I want James to be there, with his big spawgs over the arm of my settee and his crisp bags. I even wish MTV was on. And that I'm swimming in cigarette smoke.

I walk around the flat, which doesn't take long. I strip James's bed. Might as well take advantage of his absence to bring his bedclothes to the launderette. When the room is as neat as I can make it, without getting myself into trouble for disturbing some of his precious rubbish, I go back out into the living room. Adeline's folder of snaps is still where I left it too, on top of the telly.

I pick them up, look at them again. Still nothing, no emotion. Just like the first time I went through them. I'd expected to go all teary. Maybe they're not affecting me because they're such standard fare – Mammy and her sisters and brother as children on holiday in Bangor, Co. Down. Mammy riding a seaside donkey. Mammy and Adeline in their Sunday school clothes. It was lovely to have them but it's hard to see your mother in a child's face. This is what history is, dead and gone.

I did ask Adeline had she no more up-to-date photographs but we were standing at the back door at this stage and it was clear she couldn't wait for us to go. She was dangling the earphones of the Walkman, swinging them to and fro, dying to put them back where they belonged, in her ears.

No, she shook her head, that's the lot. Mother threw everything else concerned with Rose on the compost heap after she left.

I got such a shock, and it wasn't only because it

confirmed my own vision of her throwing things on a bonfire. It was largely because that kind of action is so *unmotherly*. Even if she'd burned stuff, you could put it down to a passionate fit of anger at how her daughter betrayed their principles. But a compost heap, where everything would take months to rot. That was some coldness. Adeline looked closely at me, shrugged. You really don't know much about Rose, do you?

I know a lot about her from the time I was born, I said back to her, tartly enough, I lived with her for the guts of seventeen years, after all. I waited. To see if she showed any curiosity.

Not a bit of it. She looked at her watch, put one of the earphones to her ear.

It's extraordinary, isn't it? Could you imagine wiping your own sister completely off your slate? As for the way she was treating me, I've never been so thoroughly dismissed in my life. We weren't on the same planet, Adeline was now living in whatever was coming through her ear. She was muttering. Come on, come on . . . Obviously some horse-race.

Ken gave me a quick little grin and took my arm. And that's how we left. I don't think my new-found auntie even noticed us going. I looked back before we went around the corner of the house and she was marching back towards the vegetable plot. That grizzly-haired Guard was right to warn me not to have high expectations. To be charitable about it, maybe she was so used to living on her own she'd become a bit eccentric.

A *bit*?

The Guard. It's as we were walking back past the stone lions it occurred to me he's the one I could ask about my father. He knew my mother, didn't he? He seemed to know everything about the others in the

Devine family — chances were he knew everything that breathed within ten miles of Birr over the past three or four decades.

I didn't want to ask Ken to drive me back to the station right then, though, some tasks are too private. Anyway I had trespassed enough on his generosity for one day. So I filed the Guard away for the future. (I have to admit I got a bit excited. It was the first time I felt I had a genuine chance. A teeny one, but real . . .)

I have to say that Ken Sheils was brilliant throughout this whole episode. He didn't open his mouth except to say how do you do when I introduced him to Adeline. But all the time we were there he kept this expression on his face, interested but detached, if you can get the picture. Like someone who doesn't want to be impolite but doesn't want to intrude either. He smiled when either Adeline or I smiled, nodded and looked interested if one of us looked at him. He even had the manners not to make any comment about her when we finally got away and were alone again in the van.

I don't know what I feel about this man. I've so much on my mind and in my heart at the moment that I suppose I haven't had much time to decide.

When we pull up outside my flat a couple of hours later we sit in the van for a little while. Sam jumps into my lap, turns around once, flops down and goes to sleep. It's flattering when a cat or a dog does that, isn't it? It means that it's accepted you as its friend. Or, at the very least, that you're no threat to its master. Makes you feel very peaceful.

I'd ask you in for a cup of coffee, I say to Ken, but I'm dropping on my feet.

Next time? He gives that grin of his.

For sure. Look, I say then, it's about time for you to

know all about me and my circumstances, *all* about me. I'm sure you're dying to know after today – I owe you an explanation.

Not at all, he goes, not at all. You'll tell me in your own good time.

I stroke Sam's ears, they feel like chenille. It's not a pretty story, I say quietly.

You mean James? Now he's stroking Sam's ears too. We're being very careful that our hands don't touch. We take an ear each. As for Sam – if Sam was a cat he'd be purring.

Not only James, I say. You know nothing about our background. Or even where I work—

No hurry. He stops stroking Sam, who looks hurt, leans over, gives him a little lick. We've plenty of time, Angela, he goes softly. Haven't we?

Whether it's the tiredness or the continual emotional up-and-down I don't know but I experience a genuine feeling of happiness. Small, but real. Right in the middle of everything that was going on. We have, Ken, I say.

There's another one of those moments, a pause where anything could happen. And before he does it I know exactly what's going to happen next. He's going to lean over and kiss me.

He does. It's the slightest of kisses, just a peck on the cheek. But it's nice. Our first.

Call down to me if you need anything, he says, now you know which apartment I'm in.

I will, I say, thanks. I peck him back. Thanks for everything, today and everything.

You're very welcome, he goes. We smile at each other. He takes Sam off my lap and I get out. He's still watching me when I get to the door, so I turn and wave before letting myself in.

And then, of course, I find the note about James, and have to rush to the Mater.

After I've tidied the tidy flat until I'm ready to scream, I can't stay in it another minute. I have to get out. And I'm not tired any more, at least not so that I'd go asleep.

Then as soon as I'm out on the street I remember I've nowhere really to go. I remember the kissogram gig and decide that, despite my bolshie attitude earlier, in all fairness I should ring them, even at this late stage. Let them fire me, as I said, but I have to give them the opportunity to get in a replacement for tonight – what's happening in my life isn't the poor client's fault, after all.

So I ring. The boss isn't there. I leave a message with one of the other girls. Cowardly, but I don't care. After I hang up I'm standing indecisively in the phone box. Now what? I haven't been to a film by myself for a million years and I don't want to start now. I could go for one of my famous walks but the way I'm feeling I'd probably do some criminal damage to something on the way.

I ring the Mater, find that James has been admitted to a ward there and hadn't been taxied anywhere else. That's good news, he could have been sent up to Beaumont or even across to St James's and there you're talking hours on the bus. Before I know what I'm doing I find myself ringing Patsy.

Hello? It's Martin who answers.

Hello, this is Angela, is Patsy there?

Hold on a minute – he sounds teed off. But that's nothing new, Martin always sounds teed off so I don't take it personally.

Hi, Ange, Patsy's on the line, she doesn't sound great either, they must be having a row. However, there's no point in beating around the bush. I need to talk to you, Patsy, could we meet?

Instantly the blinds come down, I can actually hear them, gdhunk! Ohh-hhh? Long drawn out. When?

Right now. Immediately. Can we, please? I don't care if I sound as though I'm desperate. I am desperate.

It's a bit difficult at the moment, she goes. There's a pause. Then, Maeve and Pauline have to be picked up from gymnastics in twenty minutes and I have to help Darren with his homework. Would it do tomorrow?

I have the feeling that she's just making this up, that she just doesn't want to come out, but I go for broke. Patsy, you're my friend. You're my only real friend in the world. I need you, I really do.

Pause.

I see . . . Cautiously.

I'm sorry to do this to you. Could Martin pick up the girls?

Pause. Then, Well, if it's that important, hang on till I ask him. The sound goes muffled, she's obviously put her hand over the receiver. I can't hear what she's saying.

A motorbike roars along the street outside the phone box, one not unlike James's. If only it were James's. When he gets better, when we come through this somehow, I'll never give out about motorbikes again. I'll never again give out about anything—

Patsy comes back on the line. All right, she goes, I'll come straight away. Where are you? Do you want me to come to the flat?

I couldn't stand the thought of going back into that clean, empty flat. No, I say, could we meet somewhere? A café or something? She agrees, and we make arrangements to meet in twenty minutes' time in a fast-food place on Dorset Street. Thank you, Patsy, I go, I really appreciate it.

See you soon, she says.

I try to kill time on the way to the café, but it's only a

few hundred yards from the flat and no matter how much I dawdle I'm there early.

An immediate blast of heat from the grill when I go in. That lovely smell, hot fat, frying onions, salt-and-vinegar. I know I shouldn't admit this, but I've always liked the atmosphere in fast-food joints. No one's better than anyone else when you're in there, particularly late at night when a lot of the customers have a few pints on board. Greasy chips are the common denominator of Irish people. I'm a kissogram girl and a cleaner but when I'm in Some Like It Hot or the Nite Bite or any of the others I'm every bit as good or bad as the solicitor or the wino or the bookie or even the higher civil servant sitting beside me. Could even be a judge.

Don't mention judges.

This particular evening is quiet. A woman, probably homeless – she has one of those drag-along shopping trolleys packed with plastic bags. A couple in their late teens or early twenties who've obviously had a row, they're staring in opposite directions. A taxi driver studying racing form in the *Daily Mirror* – I recognize him, I'd been in his cab a couple of times, we nod to each other. A young fella with a fancy collarless shirt, a waistcoat, a linen jacket and a mobile phone. Drug dealer, probably. He has that sort of plump, alert look. Gelled hair.

I take a seat facing out so I can watch the street. I don't want to think. I've been thinking too much for my own good. Yet I can't avoid it. The overwhelming thought is that, after all my hopes and dreams for us, how come we've ended up like this? I feel hunted. As far as I can see I've done nothing wrong and yet here I am feeling like a criminal.

I realize I'm just acting sorry for myself. Fat lot of use that's going to be to James, or to myself either.

I pick up the menu, one of those plasticized jobs. I pay close attention to it, like it's Holy Writ. Bunburger and Chips, Beans and Chips, Egg and Chips, Sausages and Chips, Deep Fried Plaice and Chips. I wouldn't touch a bunburger these days, not with Mad Cow Disease.

That self-pity stuff keeps pressing in in front of the print. BEVERAGES. Tea, Coffee, Milk, Coca-Cola, Fanta.

To my horror I feel tears coming into my eyes. Stop it, Angela, stop it this instant. Concentrate. SIDE ORDERS. Chips, Mushrooms, Beans, Garlic Bread — I hate garlic bread, I just hate it . . .

> For thou art with me here upon the banks
> Of this fair river; thou my dearest Friend,
> My dear, dear Friend; and in thy voice I catch
> The language of my former heart, and read
> My former pleasures in the shooting lights
> Of thy wild eyes.

Now where did that come from all of a sudden? 'Tintern Abbey', we did it *ad nauseam* because Mr Elliott tipped it to come up in the English paper. It did, too, and when it did I surprised myself with how much of it I knew off by heart.

Probably the reason it came into my mind right now is because it's Wordsworth talking about his sister Dorothy. It's exactly James and me. That had never occurred to me before. (It's odd I don't like poetry, I should like it because I certainly don't have a tin ear — I am a singer, after all.)

I see Patsy passing by the window of the café — she's driving very slowly, obviously looking for a place to park. I haven't thought out what I'm going to say. I haven't even thought what approach I'll take with her. All I know is I need to talk to someone. To my friend.

Hello. Patsy arrives with her breath in her fist. Sorry, are you here long?

Not long. What do you want? This is on me.

She wants nothing, only a cup of coffee.

Are you sure?

Sure. She looks terribly uneasy. The waitress comes over and we order. I've eaten nothing at all since lunch-time so I order sausages and chips and tea for myself.

Before you start, Patsy says as the waitress goes off, I've something to tell you too. As a matter of fact, I'm delighted you rang. I have to talk to someone, we were in the middle of a row – you might have noticed he sounded a bit peculiar on the telephone?

It takes me a second to jerk myself out of my own misery. I did notice, I go, yes?

Do you remember the condom episode with Martin? she says back. Well, I confronted him with it.

She's off. What can I say? We'll get around to me in due course, I suppose.

Immediately I feel like a heel for entertaining such a thought. Patsy is jigging around in her seat, she's obviously as upset about her problems as I am about mine. And although we're at a table with a notice which says thank you for not smoking, she's lit up and is dragging on her cigarette as though her life depends on it. It doesn't matter all that much here, I suspect. It's not the kind of place where people are going to be sniffy about no-smoking areas.

✦ Twenty-Four ✦

It turns out that this particular row between Patsy and Martin was the mother and father of all rows. She still hasn't got to the bottom of the situation but she is now convinced, absolutely convinced, that he's having an affair. And not just a one-night stand either, she goes.

At last I can get a word in – How do you know?

It's the *way* he's denying it. It's too important to him. If it was just a one-night stand or a fling, he'd have admitted it once I showed him the condom. Instead he acted all offended as though it was all my fault. He says I'm making the whole thing up and that I planted the damn thing just looking for a row. He asked me if I was suffering from PMT, if you don't mind. Then he asked me if I was going through the change.

She's nearly weeping now. I can see that the hand holding the cigarette is trembling. I feel desperately sorry for her – she looks shrivelled up. A lot older. She shuts up when the waitress comes back with our order.

I give her a bit of time to compose herself while I shake vinegar over my chips. The salt is all congealed in the shaker so I have to take the top off to dig it out. I can't wait for her to finish so I can tell her my own horrendous situation. Duelling problems!

I do my best to talk the thing through with her. Or,

rather, I let her talk and smoke while I work my way through my meal. The sausages aren't great — after a couple of bites I push them aside. The chips are grand. When you're in trouble yourself it's almost soothing, I suppose, eating chips and listening to someone else's troubles.

There were Signs, apparently, and she's kicking herself that she didn't cop on a lot earlier. It wasn't only the old cliché about the late nights when he was 'meeting clients'. He alternated between bringing her lavish presents one day and the next day being irritated if she just said hello to him. She noticed he was standing on the bathroom scales a lot, talking about joining a gym, leaving his tie off even when he was wearing a suit, pulling his belly in every time they were out shopping together and passing a plate-glass window. He asked her to buy muesli.

I can't offer any solutions, I can see that very clearly. I have to admit that I was never very comfortable with Martin. He always seemed a bit dodgy to me. I wouldn't dream of saying it, though, even now when Patsy's spilling her guts out about how awful he is. You never know, they could be billing and cooing next week and I'd be the worst in the world then.

I know I talked to you about this before, Ange, she goes, stubbing out her butt in her saucer. But having suspicions about someone and finding out you were right are two different things. Very different. You always think you'll be better off if you know . . . That's before you know . . .

She bends her head. Lights up another cigarette. I signal the waitress that I need more salt.

Ironclad confirmation that all the time I thought Patsy was using the dough from the PA System gigs as fluff money or to buy fancy gadgets for her new kitchen, she was doing nothing of the sort. Like me, she was stashing

it away in the post office. That's how jittery she was
about him.

Now, of course, all's changed. She's going to take him
for every penny he has. Pauperize him. He's not going to
get away with it.

She's through the second cigarette and she's stopped
being so miserable. She's bulling. Enough about that
bastard, she goes, sorry for going on about it but you're
one of the few people I can talk to. I'm not asking you
for advice, Ange, this is something I have to decide for
myself. She takes a tissue out of her handbag, blows her
nose. I'm sorry you got me tonight right in the middle of
it. I bet you're sorry you rang, eh?

M-mmm, I go through a mouthful of chips. Then I say,
Of course I'm not sorry I rang. I'm not sure whether I'm
being absolutely truthful here. It doesn't seem to matter,
because her question was rhetorical. She pulls her saucer
close to her and stubs out the second cigarette in it as
viciously as though it's Martin's face. I don't know how
you can eat all that grease, she says.

She folds her arms, sits back against the leatherette
seat. Then, So what did you want to talk to me about? I
suppose it's about James? Has something happened?
Something else, I mean?

She listens quietly while I tell her. But she's wearing
that peculiar, closed-in expression I'd been half expecting
but hoping wouldn't be there. I rattle on, however — it
does feel good to get it off my chest.

She waits until I've run out of steam. How long will he
be in hospital?

When I tell her I don't know she lights her third
cigarette. Thinking. Then she launches into a long list of
things I should do. Have I been to the police yet, I should
go first thing tomorrow morning, actually, I should go
right now, the minute I leave this restaurant. What I

should tell them when I go. How I should get someone
to advise me on security for the flat . . .

How James has a definite case against whomever
assaulted him, who I should get as a solicitor, a paid one,
not one from free legal aid — I could easily do a deal with
one on a no foal no fee basis so it wouldn't cost me
anything in the long run. The free legal aid people are
very good but they're rushed off their feet.

All of her suggestions are good, helpful, practical,
there is nothing I can fault. And yet all the time I have
this nagging suspicion that it's all too pat, *too* helpful.

Too much on the surface. She might as well be talking
about two people in a show she saw on the television.

Can you tell me what's really going on, Patsy? I say,
interrupting her when she's talking about electronic door
alarms. I can get all this stuff from brochures or from the
police. I want to talk to you as my friend.

She looks at me. Exaggerated surprise. I'm just trying
to be helpful.

I know you are. And everything you said is indeed very
helpful. Brilliant. But I haven't heard one word of
sympathy for either me or James. Just answer me one
question. Do you think he deserved that hiding he got? Is
that it?

Talk about a pause. This one feels as long as the
Shannon. You know when your whole body goes still,
inside. It's like your blood stops. Well, that's what this
pause does to me. I'm in space, everything's slowed
down. The fellow who's doing the cooking behind the
counter throws a couple of hamburger patties on the grill
and the hissing and spitting seems as loud as Hurricane
Charlie.

I just can't, Patsy goes at last. Please don't ask me to
go against what I really feel. I can't pretend. But I am
your friend, I truly am. I'll do anything I can to help you,

anything. I'll lend you – I'll *give* you money, you must be hurting by now, all those extra expenses and with James not working any more—

I stand up. If I had a million years I couldn't explain how bad I feel at this moment. It's like I'm standing by myself on a rock in the middle of the sea and I can't see anything in any direction except miles and miles of grey water. There's nothing more to be said, Patsy, I go, but I appreciate your advice and your offer. Thanks.

I take a fiver out of my bag and leave it on the table. I'm really sorry for your trouble with Martin, I really am. I hope everything works out for you.

She looks as upset as I feel. What's wrong? she says, don't go, let's talk about it—

I leave the caff. I can't say anything more.

I walk towards home. I genuinely understand how she feels, that's always my problem, I can always see the other person's point of view. She thinks James is a rapist and that's it. Black and white.

How can I blame her? Rape is a terrible crime, no doubt about it. Her feelings are her feelings and I can't ask her to go against them. And she is, no doubt, reacting exactly like everyone else in Ireland. Certainly judging by the letters' pages and the phone-in programmes. As I told you, I don't count the handful of people who are going on the programmes saying that we should all step back and be cautious about asking for draconian changes in the law or in the judiciary. They're just acting out of their text books.

Real people all feel exactly like Patsy.

I find I can't go into the flat. I pass it without even hesitating. Next thing I find myself ringing Ken Shiels's doorbell.

Sam is delighted to see me. It's nice to have someone loving me, even if it's only a mongrel. Ken's surprised, but in a nice way, he was just about to go to bed, but of course I should come in—

Then he sees my face. What's happened?

I can't answer, my throat seizes up. He takes my hand. Come in, love, come in . . .

The apartment is neat but with hardly any furniture. A bit like a monk's cell. Or what I've imagined a monk's cell must be like. A modern monk. White walls. No pictures. Beige carpet, one beige easy chair, a table and two dining-room chairs. A telephone table with only a telephone and a little stack of his leaflets, squared off. A stand with a telly. The only splashes of colour in the room are from the cover of the *RTE Guide* and from the red blanket in Sam's basket in a corner of the room.

I'm surprised, with him being a carpenter and a handyman. I suppose I'd been expecting lots of nice shelves, coffee tables, lovely pine kitchen units that he'd made himself. His units are white, completely anonymous.

Would you like a drop of brandy? he goes, after he sits me down in the easy chair.

No thanks, I say, but a cup of coffee, if you're making it . . .

All I was looking for, or so I thought, was a bit of company. But to make a long story short, we went to bed together. I suppose you'll find that hard to believe, given the circumstances. I would myself. Particularly since you're talking about someone who hadn't been to bed with anyone since Tom Bennett.

It happened as easily as one two three. When he came in with the coffee, he gave me a cuddle. You poor old thing, he said.

That did it. In one long swoop I told him about finding the note and about James, about Patsy's attitude. Then I told him I wasn't an office worker, that I was a cleaner.

I told him I had been a kissogram girl but I'd given that up. I told him about the deli on Saturday mornings. I haven't exactly mis-led you about letting you go on thinking I work in an office, I said at the end, but I wouldn't blame you if you don't want anything to do with me.

Drink your coffee, he said gently. Are you sure you don't want a real drink?

I felt that if I took a drink right then I would probably not be able to stop drinking, I'd probably drink for the rest of my life. I'd probably become a complete alky.

He came over and put his arms around me. It was a bit awkward for him because I was sitting and he had to kneel on the floor. I mean it, Ken, I said, I wouldn't blame you in the slightest.

He pulled my head down to him and kissed me. Properly this time. It made me feel as though I'd been holding my breath for days and I was allowed to let it out.

When the kiss finished he gave me another hug and said I was a silly moo to worry about what anyone thought about me being a cleaner. You do a helluva lot more useful work in offices than most of the people there. He kissed me again. It was lovely.

At least he had a four foot six bed, but the bedroom was as bare as the rest of the apartment. Except for his bicycle against the wall. A surprising bright blue. He must take it up in the lift with him.

I was behaving in a really odd manner – odd for me, that is. I wasn't thinking of what he might think of me, or whether he was thinking I was a tart for presenting myself to him on a plate like this. Or even if he thought I was fat. I wasn't thinking of a single consequence, I didn't care what he thought, actually, I was for once saying what was on my mind, doing what was in my desire.

As we were getting into the bed I told him how long it had been for me and that I was nervous. All he said in response was, Oh, goody, you've a lot of time to make up, then, haven't you?

Sex was different with Ken, much slower, more tender. More definite, too, if you understand what I mean. Maybe it was because he was married and was used to it. He had a nice body, as good as Tom Bennett's (older, of course) but it was smooth and hard, with terrific muscles. I suppose it's all the physical work he does.

He wanted me to stay the rest of the night in his apartment but I felt I needed to be in the flat. In some way I couldn't explain right then, I felt I would be betraying James if I stayed the whole night with a lover and anyway, I had no right to be out on the tiles when there was a chance I could be needed at home. (Although even as the thought occurred to me, I knew it was absurd, James couldn't possibly need me, he was no doubt fast asleep. But there you are. Your instincts are your instincts.)

Ken accepted this and walked me home. It was nice, I felt like I was part of the real world, where normal people in normal situations do normal things. Like get kissed goodnight at their front doors while gurriers whistle and jeer and shout obscenities as they pass by. I loved it.

After I kissed him back, he started telling me to lock my door and not to open it to anyone. He'd call around first thing in the morning to see me to make sure I was all right.

But I get up very early, I say, I told you I'm a—

He puts a finger on my lips to shut me up. I know, he goes, but you're not the only one in the world with an early start. I get up early too and I'll see you at about five. I'll ring the doorbell four times so you'll know it's me.

Him talking to me like this gives me the weirdest sensation, I'd never had a feeling like it before. Yes, Ken, I say humbly, thank you . . . I twig. He's minding me! It's like he's my daddy. This must be what it's like.

Be sure you get some proper sleep now, he goes, and kisses me again.

Once I get into bed, I can't sleep. I'm wrecked physically and mentally, but at the same time I'm exhilarated. That had to be the sex, I think for a while, but then I start wondering if it isn't more the novelty of someone fussing over me. Like I belong somewhere.

I certainly like it. For the moment at least.

The next thing I'm picturing my daddy like I used to when I was a child. I'd never indulged in it that much because it always felt to me as though I was being disloyal to Mammy. Even now, even with her dead so long, I still feel slightly guilty about it.

How old is he now? Does he still have his fair, Viking hair? Does he live around Birr? (If Birr is where he came from. He could have been a traveling salesman or an itinerant actor or a casual farm labourer. I have to root him somewhere, though, don't I?)

Is he a farmer? Does he have a degree from university? Is he rich? Famous, even? Could he be something really terrific like a brain surgeon, who'd given up a great career to go to the Third World or Bosnia? Or is he a quiet married man with six kids in a Corporation house in Finglas whom his family adore? So much so they're saving up to give him and their mother the trip of a lifetime to Australia.

Does he ever think about me? Does he even know about me?

I suppose it was the sex that did it but that night

brought down an avalanche of the most amazing feelings. And memories.

Tom Bennett. Poor Tom, I wonder where he is now. It's very odd how you can be so close to someone for so long, how you can be nearly married to him, how you see two heads in front of the sunset at the end of your life – and then something happens and it's as though you never met him. He disappears so completely out of your world that sometimes you have to work really hard to remember even what his touch felt like.

If you remember, way, way back I told you about the night I first saw Mammy in hospital. About doing something of which I was so ashamed that I could never bear to think about it, much less tell anyone. What triggered it was the stew of rage and sorrow I was in after seeing Mammy in the hospital with her discoloured face encrusted with scabs and her wretched, hacked hair. I think it was the first time reality hit me. For the first time I saw that there was no hope. This was the end of the road for us. She was going to die. I was slap bang up against those words. Die. Death. Dead.

And this made me really furious with her. How dare she leave us when we hadn't even got started? I know that when you look at it now this sounds really stupid. But honest to God, deep down, even through the worst days, when she was black and blue or comatose, or worst of all, when she brought home some new guttersnipe, I believed that, somehow, everything was going to turn out all right. Sometime.

In some future rainbow.

That if only we could get over this bad patch or that bad patch, if I was strong enough, or loving enough, or good enough, everything would get better and she'd settle down with us. That because we deserved it, somehow it'd happen. Something to do with justice.

Having seen her that night, though, all my hopes and long-term plans for us lay in smithereens. And for the first time I could see it wasn't anything to do with fate. The rage bubbled up when I started blaming her. Why couldn't she just stand up to them, all those people who used her? No, who *abused* her. How could she be so *weak*?

At the same time I was devastated at the loss that was going to happen to us.

All this preamble is not by way of excuse – there can be no excuse for what I did. It's only by way of explanation.

When I got back from seeing her and picked up the baby from the neighbour who was minding him, I let us into our flat. I walked round and round with him in my arms but the rage wouldn't settle. 'Walking' doesn't cover it, I was behaving like a madwoman. Every time I came to a clear space on a wall, I'd bang my back against it. Hard. I probably would have been smashing my head if I hadn't been holding James. But then he would have got hit too.

At first he thought it was a game we were playing – at least, I think he did because he didn't show that he was upset in any way. He just looked surprised every time he got the jolt. But then he started to whinge.

That nearly finished me altogether. I felt I was going to explode.

He got louder and louder and more upset, and wouldn't stop, no matter how much I shushed or rocked him. As you know by now I'm not a violent person but after a few minutes of this, I didn't trust myself not to hit him just to shut him up. Or to do something much worse. Like throwing him out through the window. So I dumped him in his cot and left him there. Screaming his head off.

Still I couldn't stick the noise so I went out onto our

balcony to get as far away from it as I could. It wasn't even the noise, it was what it represented. Need. Total dependence. Total demand. Me, me, *me*. I want, I need, *you owe*.

I didn't want this. From the bottom of my heart I didn't want it. I was still a teenager. Never mind that I asked for it, fought for it, went the full distance with the Eastern Health Board to get it.

I shut the front door. I could still hear him. Screaming.

I'm lying there on my bed-settee after coming home from Ken Sheils's apartment, and I'm in this bizarre state where I can't sleep but I don't feel in the least bit tired. My body's prickling from the sex but my mind is humming with guilt, round and round like a car on a Scalextric track.

I ran out of the flats. I left James there. On his own. Hysterical. A little baby.

While I went looking for Tom Bennett.

Twenty-Five

I find Tom Bennett in a pub on the Quays. He's surprised to see me, naturally. He's not looking the best. The copper hair I admire so much is greasy and all over the place, he hasn't shaved for maybe a couple of days and the stubble is horrible. Gingery.

What gives? he goes when I walk up to him and ask him to buy me a drink.

Nothing gives, I go back, I've just had it, that's all.

Oh, is that all, he goes. Welcome to the club. He buys me a Bacardi and Coke and we find a place to sit down.

I tell him Mammy's going to die.

That's terrible, just terrible, he says. Are you sure?

I'm sure.

Drink up, he says, I'll get you another.

I protest, feebly, but the first drink is already hitting the spot. It doesn't take much to persuade me to have the second one. Bacardi and Coke goes down very easily, especially for someone who's not used to spirits at all. It's like Coke on its own, really, only sweeter. It's only when I'm finished the second one and I'm feeling no pain, that he tells me it was a double. I'm too far gone to argue.

James's screaming is filling up my head.

Tom Bennett is very sweet to me. He doesn't get

embarrassed when I start to cry and when people around us start to stare. Instead he puts an arm around me, scowls at them, yells, Eff off, you've little to think about . . . This works, they put their eyes back in their sockets.

Let's get out of here, he says.

We leave and when the fresh air hits me I feel sick. I want to vomit, but somewhere in my mind I realize that would be the last straw for Tom and I manage to control it. Let me take you home, he says.

All I'm thinking about now is that James is dead in the cot. And it's all my fault. And even if he's not dead, someone in the flats will have been only too delighted to ring the Guards or the Eastern Health Board and get him taken away from me for neglect. It serves me right. I'm going to be prosecuted one way or the other. How am I going to tell Mammy?

Suddenly I have to get back there as quickly as possible. On my own. I don't want Tom Bennett to see what I've done.

I make up some cock-and-bull story about endangering my guardianship of James (in my condition I can just imagine the way my tongue got around that one!) if I brought a man anywhere near the flat that night. Tom seems to accept that although, to tell you the truth, everything from this moment to the time I get back home is more than a little fuzzy.

He comes with me as far as the entryway and then leaves me. Like a perfect gentleman.

If only Tom Bennett hadn't been a drinker the way he was shaping up to be, James could even have had a father. But I still think I made the right decision in the end. To be married to an alcoholic must be the real pits. I've seen enough of it in my time – you should hear some of the women at work.

Anyway, I insist Tom goes away and leaves me alone.

There's the usual messing and commotion going on in the entryway and in the courtyard but our flat is just overhead, and if James was still screaming, I should have been able to hear him.

I don't.

I'm afraid to go up. He's either dead or the Eastern Health Board has already taken him away. I'm as sober as Matt Talbot now. I'm in one of those states where my mind is clicking as cleanly as ice in a glass.

He's definitely dead. Because if the Eastern Health Board had been here there'd be plenty of people around to give me the bad news.

Well, I'm sure you've guessed by now that he wasn't dead.

He was lying in the cot with his blankets all twisted around his little legs. Asleep but hiccuping silently. You know the way they do when they've cried themselves to sleep and they're disconsolate.

I'm sure you can see how I find this very difficult to tell you. Talk about guilt! But maybe now that I've admitted it, the guilt will ease off a little. It's never left me since the night it happened. It's one of those episodes that wakes you up at four o'clock in the morning and you sweat and curl your toes and then put your head under the pillow so no one will hear you groan.

I picked him up and changed his clothes, they were all damp from perspiration and tears. I kissed him and kissed him. I gave him his bottle and concentrated really hard on telling him I loved him. Which I did. I love you, James. I love you. He kept gazing at me over the bottle with those enormous, beautiful eyes of his. Such trust. They're so forgiving, aren't they? It makes you feel even worse.

I didn't put him back in his cot, I took him into bed with me. I sang to him, all the songs I remembered from

Mammy's days with us. Rockaby Baby and We're Poor Little Lambs, and All In The April Evening. Then I whispered nursery rhymes, Ding Dong Dell, and Round And Round The Garden and Jack and Jill. And of course, Starbright, counting it out on his fingers. He loved it. I was concentrating so hard that I'm absolutely sure he understood how sorry I was and how much I adored him. I kept loving him until he fell asleep.

I swore that night as I looked at his little face that I'd never, ever leave him alone again, even for a minute. In a way, now that I think about it, the need to go home after sex with Ken Sheils in his apartment could well be linked, subconsciously, with that promise I made James that night after I'd left him. Because this really is his hour of need.

It occurs to me that he and I have never talked about anything that really matters. Is this what people mean by the generation gap? Like, we live together, so why is it we can't talk to one another person to person, like I do with Patsy – or like I assume he does with his pals?

Or maybe not. Do young fellas talk to each other? Does any woman know?

I've looked at him of an evening, when he's absorbed in something on the telly. He's so lovely, and so vulnerable. And sometimes seems so lonely I've wanted to throw my arms around him and say, Listen, whatever it is, don't worry about it. I'm here and you're all right with me. I love you no matter what.

Something always stops me, though. It's not just that I know he'd push me away – he'd certainly do that – it's something more. Like every word we speak to each other has a history of grievance. Each syllable reeking. As a result, being careful is second nature to me now, how's he going to react to this, what's the best way to say that to him . . . On his side, he's clammed up, not going to risk any response at all. Down to self-protective grunts and monosyllables. There's a word wall between us.

If I'm being truthful, I have to admit it's probably of my doing, each wordbrick formed from shoulds and shouldn'ts – why did you do this, James, you should have done that. You should get up earlier, you shouldn't drink so much, you shouldn't watch so much telly. You shouldn't talk to me like that, you should pull your socks up, look what's happened now, I told you should have done X . . .

I can see, too late probably, that I was trying to live up to some notion about what was 'good' for him. Discipline. Work ethic. Politeness. Work ethic again. Oh, I was a great one for the work ethic. I forgot about the lilies in the field. (All right, it's a theory that's hard to take when you're out working and he's in lazing. On the other hand, why do you think nature ordained some bees to be queens and some to be drones?)

From the time he could think for himself, James quite understandably resisted all my nagging, and after a while it became automatic for him to oppose everything I said or asked, good or bad. If it came from me it was to be fought at all costs. Now that I understand this a little, I don't blame him. I'd like to see the way I'd react if someone was permanently telling me what I should and must do. I find it hard enough to take instructions from Furry Slippers and she's responsible for my bread and butter.

It was so much easier when he was a baby, all I had to do was to hold him and rock him and make baby noises at him. Love him. I look at his school snaps and his eyes are full of bright, merry light. Up to about age eight or nine maybe. Then it died. Since then we've locked together in a war neither of us understands but that we can't get out of. I think it would be a great relief to both of us if we could start again as strangers. If we could get to know each other from the outside in.

Sadly, it's unlikely to happen now, unless I can find a way where both of us can gain free access to the enormous reservoir of love, the one hidden behind the wall of grievance wordbricks we've erected.

Correction again, the wall *I*'ve erected. Babies don't come supplied with bricks.

Well, it was up to me to do the work. At some stage, during what was left of that long, fraught night, I came to another decision. I firmly made up my mind that I was going to find a father for us. His or mine, either would be great.

On balance, going by the events so far in Birr, I recognized that finding mine was going to be the easier option since I had somewhere to start. If that old Guard couldn't help I would go back to Adeline, and I wouldn't care how iffy she'd be about it. Or to the local teacher, or to the clergy – Protestant, Catholic, whichever. The clergy are hard on the heels of the Guards when it comes to knowing what's what in their catchment areas.

It was hard to predict how my father would react. After all, he would be only a distant blood relative to James (I'd tried to work it out – half-half-son?). I didn't care, fundamentally, because he owed *me*. Therefore, if I asked him, he'd be *obliged* to help James, wouldn't he? Out of guilt, if for no other reason. I had no qualms about putting this kind of pressure on him, none whatsoever.

What's more, in the dead of that night I didn't give a sugar if my father turned out to be one of those people who believed that James should be castrated or put to gaol for the rest of his life or flogged until he couldn't stand. Tough. His beliefs were irrelevant here. We needed him and that was that. (Anyway, he might hold those views initially but we were going to change his mind.)

I managed to doze for a couple of hours but by the time Ken's four rings came to the door, I'd been dressed and waiting for the guts of half an hour. He's shaved and shining, wearing a pressed denim shirt and jeans. He could be in an ad for Old Spice. Good morning, he says, keeping his voice low.

Come in, I whisper back to him.

Talk about Old Spice – he comes in on a gust of aftershave, which one I don't know. James's Lynx is the only one I can recognize instantly. He sits down on the bed-settee, as easy in himself as King Farouk.

I have to rush him a bit, we don't have all that much time before the minibus comes for me. I'd the kettle already boiled and toast made. I've something to ask you, I say to him, when I'm pouring water on the coffee.

Fire ahead, he goes. But before you say anything, he says in a rush, that was wonderful last night. I hope it's the first of many such nights. It's obviously a little speech he's prepared.

I enjoyed it too, I say. I hand him the coffee and toast. It's time for my own speech.

I know it's a bit early in the morning, I start off, and I'm sorry to be serious, but I have to get one thing straight. I've told you about James, I haven't held anything back, but at this point I need to know what you really feel about the situation. About him.

I sit down, take a bite out of my own toast and wait.

He sips his coffee and he looks at me over the top of the cup. I've no opinion one way or the other, he goes, I just want to help you as much as I can.

I keep looking at him, continue to wait.

He gets it. Very quietly, he puts down his cup. But that's not enough, is it?

I'm afraid no.

Well, if you want me to be completely honest—

That's the general idea.

I can see him choosing his words. He's studying the faded pattern on the upholstery of the bed-settee. I hate rape, he says. I can't stand the thought of it. He hesitates again, still picking words. But the way you describe what happened, I would feel quite sympathetic.

I take a mouthful of my coffee. Don't taste anything.

The only thing is, Ken says, I'm sorry, but you've asked me to be honest, the only thing is, I haven't heard the other side of the story. He's now looking at the floor. I'm sorry, Angela, he goes again, but that's the way I feel. Until I would know what the girl's side is, I can't be objective. Or say what I really feel.

It's a quarter past five in the morning. It's a great day, sunny, the birds are having a jamboree over there in the park, there's hardly any traffic so the street outside is as quiet as Adeline's. I had sex last night for the first time in nearly twenty years and I'm sitting on my own bed-settee with the man who had sex with me. And what he's just said is killing me.

He's looking at me at last but he's terribly uncomfortable. Is that OK? Do you understand?

He's asking my permission to reject us. *He's* asking *me* do *I* understand! Angela, he goes, leaning forward and taking my hand, Angela, don't let this come between us. I look at my hand and his together. They don't fit.

I manage to get something out. So long as we know where we stand—

Angela, please, he goes. After what happened last night, after the way we were—

Don't worry about it, I go. I take my hand out of his and stand up. It's no big deal. Honestly! I bring my cup over to the sink although it's still full of coffee. I throw the coffee down the drain and turn on the tap.

He comes over behind me. Please, Angela. I thought we were—

Of course we are, I say, as cheerfully as I can. Give us your cup there, are you finished?

I run water into his cup and rinse it as though my life depends on it.

He puts his arms around me from behind. Angela—

Oops! I go, I think I hear the minibus outside. I turn off the tap and wipe my hands, rush towards where I've put my bag on top of the telly, Sorry, I'm not throwing you out or anything but they don't wait long. I've got to dash—

Will you kiss me goodbye?

Of course I will. (Who is this person with the bright, cheery, *false* voice?)

I kiss him, he kisses me back. His is passionate. I can tell he feels he's off the hook. Whoa, I go, it's a bit early in the morning, isn't it? I kiss him once more. Peck. I feel like Judas. But at present I haven't the energy to tell Ken Sheils I don't want to see him again.

I have to save all my energy. No Ken. No Patsy. Just us.

Work was the pits that morning as you might expect. I screwed up, forgot to do one of the stalls in the men's toilets.

Furry Slippers was delighted at the chance to have a real go at me. The peaked-cap syndrome. When you give people who are only one jump up from you a bit of authority, it goes to their heads completely. I have to say she was a queen in this area. Peaked cap? Tiara! She called me aside, making sure as many people as possible saw this, and put on her sad-but-sorrowful face. You seem distracted lately, Angela. Now I know you've had your family troubles, and we've been tolerant of that, but when it gets to the stage where your colleagues have to be carrying you—

I let her at it. I'd read that the way these drug barons and tough guys, who are the bosses of organized crime in Dublin, deal with police interrogations is by picking a small spot on the wall and concentrating on it. That's what I did. There was a little screw hole in the door just behind her head and I watched it as though it was a microdot. My task was to decode it with my X-ray eyes – *your work has not been up to scratch lately, Angela, I'm sure even you can see that* – I imagined little woodworms wriggling in and out of the screwhole, generations of them. Too gross.

So I imagined that this hole was Stargate, like in the movie. A doorway to another dimension in time. I'd make myself small with a magic machine and I'd slip through it into the future. Or the past. Or anywhere better than here where she was still droning.

You don't seem to be *listening*, Angela, I don't seem to be getting *through* to you . . .

Sorry, I'm a bit tired this morning.

She sighs. She's Vanessa Redgrave. You're tired every morning, Angela, but I'm going to give you another chance, *yet* another chance, mark you, so please go back into that toilet and clean it properly. *All* of it. Right?

By the time I get to the Mater, thank God I've been able to scour my brain clean of toilets, Furry Slippers, everything to do with that bloody job. Oh, God, if only I could win the Lotto. (I wonder how many people are saying the exact same thing at this moment. The dignity of work, my eye . . .)

I march straight past the porter in the front hall as

though I'm bringing in something vital to someone very high up. I've hidden the grapes I'm bringing to James in my handbag. By the way, why does everyone bring grapes into a hospital? They used to be exotic, a great treat, but not now. I suppose it's a tradition, like Lucozade. The hospital smell this morning isn't totally bandages and disinfectant, it's mixed in with rashers.

I can tell he was watching for me because the instant I arrive at the door of the ward he hooshes himself up on the pillow, as much as he can with all the strapping and bandaging and so forth.

The consultants are doing their rounds and in a public ward they're supreme. In my mood, do I care? Pope John Paul could be doing his rounds or the Shah of Iran. I'm never intimidated by these guys in any case. They put their trousers on, one leg at a time, just like the rest of us. If I sound bitchy this morning it's because I'm feeling bitchy.

James had already been seen in any case – the Great Man with his entourage was already two beds down the row from him. Hello, I say, how are you feeling this morning?

Not the Mae, he says back.

I'm not surprised, I say, as I put the grapes on his locker. You don't look the Mae. You look the exact opposite of the Mae, as a matter of fact, you look terrible.

The bruising was not only black and blue this morning, but yellow and green as well.

Well, thanks a whole lot, he says. That makes me feel really much better, that does. He tries to glower at me but the effect is spoiled by the fact that both his eyes are still mostly shut.

I look down at him. Actually I regard him. After the sleepless night I've just had, not to speak of the situation with Ken Sheils and the row with Furry Slippers, I'm not inclined to put up with any lip from James Devine.

Then I remember that this was the old Angela. What about the darkest part of last night and my internal discussions about the relationship between him and me, brick walls and so forth? I take a deep breath and exhale slowly through my nose like you're supposed to do in yoga. I went to a yoga class once but the more I tried to relax my muscles one at a time, twenty others got rigid to compensate, but this time something works and I calm down a bit. I pull up a chair and sit. James, I say, could we talk?

What? He goes on full alert, looks as though I've threatened him with a machete. We are talking, he says.

I mean really talk. Without either of us having an attitude.

What do you mean, attitude? I don't have any attitude.

I wait. I can see he doesn't know what's got into me. He shifts around in the bed, then he winces. Is it very bad? I go, with as much sympathy as I can inject into my voice. I'm not acting, I'm digging deep into my real feelings. In normal circumstances I'd be giving out yards to him for getting us into this pickle. What kind of night did you have? I ask.

Immediately I understand something else – I have to stop asking him questions. When was the last time you had a conversation with a friend which was solely a question and answer session, with one party asking all the questions? You wouldn't remain friends for long, would you? I only ask, I correct myself quickly, because I had a terrible night myself. I couldn't sleep.

He's looking at me sideways. He doesn't know what the hell is going on. I slept all right, he mutters, they gave me a tablet.

Did it knock you ou— er, I mean that's what they

usually do in hospitals. Those pills are great for knocking you out. I remember Patsy gave me a couple of hers once when I was nervous about something. I forget what it was now. I think I slept solidly for three days — I missed work. God, I'll never forget it — did I tell you I've started walking? It's great exercise. And the fresh air! I went out to the South Bull the other night. Oh, James, it was gorgeous . . .

I'm chattering like a budgie. The expression on his poor bashed face would make a cat laugh, it's like he was expecting *The Sound of Music* and here I am with *The Texas Chainsaw Massacre*. Or vice versa, given his point of view on films.

I carry on. I'm on to my visit to the town of Birr and the Manchester Martyrs—

He pulls himself up and interrupts me. What's going on? Lookit, I don't give a fiddler's about the South Bull or whoever it is from Manchester— He makes a face and lies down again. He's done something to himself that has hurt him.

You must be in agony, I chirrup. Listen, I'm not staying long, I just came in to see how you're doing, this isn't my real visit. I've to make a few telephone calls, to the solicitor and so on. I'll come in again at the proper visiting time.

Before he could stop me, I'd stood up and leaned over and kissed him on the forehead. 'Bye, I say.

I leave. I don't look back. I consider it a personal triumph that I didn't even ask him what he might want me to bring in for him.

Twenty-Six

Patrice Murphy was in to take my call. Slow down, Angela, he says, slow down. I'm taking notes as you talk. Have you been to the Gárdaí?

I don't recall asking him to call me Angela but I let it pass. When I tell him I haven't gone to the Guards, he says I should go immediately and report the assault. He asks if there were any witnesses and when I tell him not so far as I know, he starts in on am I sure? Can James remember much of what was going on? Would he recognize these men?

All these questions. It's like now I've recognized what I've been doing to James, God's decided to have a go back at me!

Fitzgibbon Street must be one of the most rundown police stations in Dublin. Don't get me wrong, the Guard I speak to couldn't have been nicer. He's from the country – Kerry, maybe, or Cork. God love him, coming from those lovely airy places into what he faces in the inner city. He remains friendly even when I tell him who James is and why we think he's been beaten up. Don't worry, missus, he says. No matter what the lad's done or not done, he still has rights. Just one thing, he didn't provoke this by any chance?

No, I told you what happened, he was jumped.

Don't upset yourself, mam, I have to ask these things. Come in here.

He brings me inside the counter and sits me down, takes down all the details I know and says they'll be going up to the Mater to interview James. He'll have to file a complaint, he says.

I can't see it myself. If I know James, he'll want to take his hiding and then have nothing to do with it any more. The problem is, this Guard tells me, if he doesn't stand up to these bullies now there'll probably be more of the same in store for him.

I'm rightly depressed when I get out of there.

I know we've hardly any groceries in the house and that I should do a bit of shopping but I'm abruptly so tired that I have to go straight home. I don't even have the energy to pull out the bed-settee, so I lie down on the seat of it without even taking off my shoes. I barely have enough energy to reset the alarm clock for lunch-time.

But, wouldn't you know it, immediately I lie down, my brain revs up again, not least because I can see the two coffee cups on the draining board, the ones Ken and I used this morning.

At present I'm amazed to find I don't feel anything about Ken and me breaking up. I suppose that'll come later. I'm not looking forward to telling him. Mind you it was hardly *Romeo and Juliet*, now, was it? Our so-called romance hadn't got off the ground.

I'm probably immune to love at this stage. All the stores have been used up on James.

Thank God I didn't see the beating because I've seen enough of them in my time. When they're talking on the radio about women getting hammered by their husbands or boyfriends and I hear them asking, Why doesn't she just leave? it's clear to me they've never been in the situation. It's too close to home, at any rate. Where was our Mammy to go? And that was only her. What about the rest of us?

It used to kill me, though, it really used to. Seeing her cover her head as best she could while she took it used to make me so angry with her.

Having got a few cracks myself when I tried to intervene, I learned early on there was no point in trying to protect her. A lot of the time she'd be doped up and wouldn't co-operate anyway, so for me the best thing to do was just to get out of there as fast as possible. On more than one occasion, I walked the streets for hours, trying to keep out of sight of any of the authorities, until I reckoned she and whoever it was had passed out. It was easier in the day-time but I developed great coping skills even for after dark.

It became a lot more difficult after James was born because I had to take him with me, but thank God that dilemma occurred in a serous way only once or twice during the couple of months he and Mammy were on this earth together. The crunch on those occasions came when we were sneaking back in and I was terrified he'd make a noise. He was a great little baby, though, as I've told you, hardly ever cried.

My strategy spilled over into the next day. To keep the nosy-parkers at bay I'd make sure that I – and for those couple of occasions during the last months, James and I – would be seen parading around, him well dressed, washed and brushed, both of us cheerful and happy and normal.

Pathetic, I suppose, but it worked.

When I finally nodded off that morning after visiting that hospital, my sleep was boiling with scary snatches of dreams. Incredibly vivid. Giant woodworms with heads like gargoyles slithering towards me. Or I was on a bus and fellas carrying hammers were stalking the aisle, looking for me. Then I was on *Winning Streak*, spinning the wheel, everyone was cheering, but the wheel suddenly turned into a gallows. Then, thank God, the alarm went off, as loud as the Last Day trumpet and I shot up into a sitting position, not having the faintest clue where I was, heart thumping like a kango hammer. For the first few seconds, Mike Murphy was still standing in front of me with his eyes twinkling at me through his dirty hangman's hood . . .

Never did oul' Reddy's wallpaper look so lovely.

I hauled myself to my feet, washed, then changed my clothes and dosed myself with the strongest coffee I could stomach before I set off again for the hospital. I didn't know what I was going to tell James. I'd promised him I was going to sort things out. Hadn't got very far, had I? Only drawn the cops on him. For which he would not thank me. My calf muscles felt like anchors as I dragged myself up Eccles Street.

When I got as far as the steps up to the front door of the Mater, I still had my head down, concentrating on coming up with something positive to say to James. Visiting hour was still five minutes away, so there were a lot of people milling around.

Hello, Angela!

This is so unexpected, I jump. I look up – and who's standing there right in front of me only Ken Sheils. He's carrying a bunch of flowers. Real florist's ones, an arrangement. They're for you, he says, I reckon you could do with a bit of cheering up. Everyone's looking, he has this silly grin on his face, and I feel myself starting to go beetroot. Talk about reversing roles.

How am I supposed to react? My brain won't work. Thanks, I go, taking the flowers. Thanks a lot, that was very good of you. Then, challenging, Are you coming in to see James with me?

Of course. If you want me to, that is.

I can see that in his own mind he's being very brave, very open-minded. Or am I being a cow? I'm too tired to care so I take it at face value. That'd be nice, I go, it'll give James someone different to talk to.

They open the door then and everybody rushes in. Like we're racing each other for the best seats at a concert or something – maybe they don't have enough chairs for visitors in the Mater hospital. Ken and I wait until the rush dies down. I feel calm anyhow, that's a blessing. I'm wavering . . . The flowers are gorgeous.

It crosses my mind that when I get home, maybe I should do Love Like Hate Adore Kiss Court Marry with our names. Childish but so is throwing apple peel over your shoulder. So is hopping three times on one leg around the Metal Man in Tramore. (Mammy did that umpteen times to know a husband within the year. Hah!) We all perform these little rituals.

The way he acts after the introductions, it seems James couldn't care less who Ken is, but I know differently and in my new mood of honesty I'm not letting him away with it. You've never met any of my friends before, James, have you? Except Patsy, of course.

No, he mutters. He glances at the flowers I'm carrying. Ken gave me these, I go, aren't they lovely? I didn't bring you in anything, I didn't know what you wanted.

Actually I had brought something, the photographs of Mammy that Adeline gave me, but even though Ken was in on this I didn't think it would be appropriate now for James and me to be looking at them together. It's all right, James says, I don't need anything. I'll be out of this kip in a day or two, anyway.

I ignore this. Ken's in business for himself, I say. Then

I turn to Ken. And of course, Ken, you already know that James is a courier.

I sit back and let them at it.

I must say, considering the circumstances, Ken is pretty good. He launches into the subject of motorbikes and James perks up immediately. I'm temporarily superfluous to requirements.

The ward is big – sixteen beds, three enormous windows at one end, south-facing. They'd opened the blinds and curtains fully so the sunshine is streaming in. With all the men's flowers and plants lined up on the windowsills – their lockers aren't big enough – the effect is bright and colourful. Thank God times have changed to the extent that you can now bring flowers in to men. I remember when no man would be caught dead near so much as a daisy.

I half tune in to the hum of talk from all the visitors. He said it was the size of a small grapefruit . . . Six injections, *six* . . . But sure it's all over now, thanks be to God . . . Twenty-seven stitches . . . It's hard to kill a bad thing . . . They gave it to me in a jar . . .

Et cetera.

It's so artifical, isn't it, all that? The patient trying to bridge the gap between being self-pitying and giving his visitors just enough of his pain and suffering to *earn* their sympathy. As for the poor old visitors, earnestly listening while trying desperately to think of what next to say that'll sound neutral enough not to draw on themselves yet another saga of blood or pus but that won't be taken as callous.

It's very warm and this, added to the low talk, is almost hypnotic, I find myself fighting drowsiness. To keep myself awake, I try to pay attention to the motorbike chat beside me. Greek to me, of course, but I sit up straighter, concentrate. Engine ccs. Carburettors.

Differentials. It strikes me then that what's happening here is a bit like don't mention the war.

I wait for a pause. Have the Guards been in? I've reported the assault and I've also been on to the solicitor.

Do you want me to leave? Ken half stands to go. I'm sure you'd like to discuss this in private.

It's up to you, I say. I don't mind if you stay. I turn to James. Ken knows all about everything. I've told him the lot.

I can see neither of them is happy with this but frankly, my dear, I don't give a damn.

What's going to happen? James asks uneasily.

They'll come in to interview you, I say, and then it's up to them.

Silence. Ken gives a little cough. Then, Did you ever see one of those Honda Gold Wings, James, he goes, I wouldn't call them motorbikes at all, they're just armchairs with wheels.

So be it, I think, and I tune out.

A little bit later, Ken does leave. I walk him down to the door of the ward. In the corridor outside, I enrol him to drive me again to Birr. No point in beating around the bush, I tell him baldly the reason why and he agrees immediately. James was to be released from hospital on the Monday, provided the results of one last blood test were OK, so Ken and I make an arrangement to go down to Birr on the afternoon of the Saturday beforehand. That way, neither of us would miss work.

Now you might think I was being ruthless, considering this was the guy who only this morning I was never going to see again. Well, you'd be dead right. I was being ruthless. Wouldn't you be? I would have used my granny if I had one.

Anyway, I'm thinking, maybe I shouldn't be too hasty about breaking up – it was quite possible he'd thought things over and had decided his attitude that morning had been unfair. It's highly likely that's why he came to the hospital – at least I should give him the benefit of the doubt. And as I told you, out there on those steps, I started to go soft . . .

By Friday James looked to be well on the mend. Physically, at least, even though the bruising on his face was still as bright as a rainbow.

He seemed down in himself, though, more than I'd seen him since the day he was first brought in. Everything in the hospital was now poxy. The food, the nurses, his fellow patients. The telly, which was mounted too high on the wall at the end of the ward and was turned at the wrong angle to him. Poxy. All of it.

Had I brought the Jaffa cakes? He loves Jaffa cakes, it was all he'd asked for all week.

I give the new packet to him. He tears it open immediately and lays into them. You'll get spots, I go, all that chocolate isn't good for you.

Who effin' cares? He stuffs another one into his mouth.

I sit down. What's new? I ask him, not that I expected any answer – conversation with James is still like pulling hens' teeth. And you may well ask about my good intentions in the matter of instituting a new era of open communication between us. I haven't quite lost sight of that, I'll get back to it soon. It's just too tiring at the moment.

I learn why everything is so poxy all of a sudden. He stops eating long enough to tell me. The Guards have been back in to him with photographs of people they want to eliminate from their inquiries about assaulting him. He hadn't recognized any of them. Worse than that, he's received an anonymous letter.

Show it to me, I say. He looks around the ward before opening his locker.

The letter is on lined blue notepaper, the small size.

Dear Scumbag, That's only a taste you got, you little shit. Get the hell out of this country, and take that lily-livered judge with you, the one who freed you to walk on the earth with decent people. Get out now or it'll be the worse for you and your sister. And next time it won't be just a beating. And don't even think of bringing the police into this. We'll know if you do.

Handwriting slanted heavily backwards. I know that trick, that's to disguise it. It's unsigned, of course.

Did you show this to the police? I ask James. He shakes his head. He's into the Jaffa cakes again but I can see by his eyes that he's terrified. To give me time to think, I pretend to be examining the envelope. This letter has been addressed to him in the correct ward.

They say they'll know if I tell the Guards, and now they'll think I showed it to them, he says. I got that letter before they came in.

As if I haven't made the connection myself. If he is being watched, certain assumptions will have been made. They won't think anything of the sort, I go, but I'm not as confident as I hope I sound. You can't let them get to you like this. Did you agree to file a complaint about the assault?

Yeah, I did – they said I can come to the station when I get out of here. But I can't now – what about that letter? He's so distressed, crumbs from the Jaffa cake he's holding are raining all over the bed.

All right, all right, calm down. I look around the ward. Who could possibly be watching him? Most of the men in the other beds are elderly, no one is looking over at us, they all seem normally preoccupied with their own families and friends.

It's hardly the staff of the hospital. Someone's visitor?

I make myself sound authoritative: The first thing you do is give this to the police, I'll give it to them if you won't.

Don't, don't, he goes, he looks so frightened that my heart goes out to him. All right, I say, but I'm keeping it.

I put the letter in my handbag. These things are poison, James, they're sent to frighten people. You're to put it out of your mind. You're perfectly safe here. You don't think they're going to come in here to your hospital bed, do you?

How did they know which ward I was in?

I wish he hadn't asked that question. I don't know, James, I say. But you're definitely safe here. And by Monday you'll be home and we'll have sorted something out. Patrice Murphy will help. Someone will help, I promise you.

That's when he starts to spew.

I, Angela, don't have the first idea about what it's like out there, I'm so naïve, I still think that most people are all right, and that might be true for people of my generation, but James and his friends really know the score. Out on the streets, you only have to look at someone in the wrong way, or he can think you look at him the wrong way, just one wrong look and you get a dunt and maybe you end up with a black eye . . . And then he gets his friends and comes back after you, and you and your friends find yourselves in a major fight that you never asked for. Sometimes they come at you with knives . . .

He's leaning over towards me now, unloading right into my face, so worked up I believe that if he didn't have a plaster on his arm he'd probably have grabbed my throat. I, Angela, don't have the first clue what's going on, what it's really like. I'm still living in a dream world,

I still think Dublin's all right because no one attacks women for no reason. Like they attack fellas for no reason.

I try to say something but he won't be stopped.

Shut up, shut up, you don't know. It's like effin' Beirut out there. You can't walk down a street any more with any of your friends, you can't have a drink in a pub, and it's not only at night, it can be in the middle of the day, you don't have to do anything to them, you only have to be minding your own business. It's all right for women, they don't get the hassle—

I stand up. James, James, I go, stop, please. Stop this . . . I keep my voice low but I can see that we're beginning to attract curious glances from some of the other patients and their visitors.

He falls back on his pillows and the tears start to roll out of his eyes. That's the problem, he goes. You don't believe me, nobody believes me, nobody knows what it's like. But ask any of my friends, ask any fella at all, they know . . .

He cops himself on, looks around in case anyone's noticed. He catches a couple of looks and puts his good arm over his eyes. He is a person in despair.

It's all right, James, I whisper. Nobody really heard anything.

Yeah, yeah, right, he goes, and he turns his head away from me. You just don't have a bleedin' clue.

How can I answer him? Give him some reassurance? He's wrong to think I don't know what goes on on the streets, I do. But he's shocked me, to tell you the truth. In my ignorance, I'd thought kids like him were street-wise – that what goes on in Dublin was no problem to them. I'd bought the toughie line they all peddled.

I'd worried about him every time he went out, of course – you're seeing the knife going in, or their teeth being knocked out, you can hear the sound of steel-tips breaking cheekbones.

But it's not possible to live with the octane of that a hundred per cent of the time – you'd go mad – so you soften it up and spread it out until the worry becomes flat and vague, with no specific highlights. It's like a permanent smell. You tell yourself you can't be at their sides twenty-four hours a day and anyway they're of age, they're adults, and you can't keep them inside as though they're still babies. So you hope, guiltily, that if it has to happen, it'll happen to someone else's and not to yours and after a time you get used to the slightly fearful way we all live now.

The problem is that the serious fear constantly regenerates itself. You're always only a moment, a telephone call away from bad news. (A note pushed under your door!) Every time it happens to any of them, he's yours. I see a newspaper photograph of some kid's bashed-in face in a hospital bed and my imagination instantly substitutes James's.

I'd managed to calm him down before I left but I was still in two minds whether or not to go to the police about that letter. I was certainly going to show it to Patrice Murphy and get his advice. Although the sum total of his advice in this matter so far – go to the police – hadn't achieved anything great, had it? Except to put even more wind up poor James.

And on that score, it was a bit of a worry to me that he hadn't been able to recognize anyone in the photographs they had brought in to him. That meant that the lowlifes who beat him up were not any of the usual crowd of bully boys the police would know. Amateurs are probably far more dangerous.

→ Twenty-Seven ←

Do you remember when Jane Eyre says, 'Reader, I married him'? That's not exactly what I have to tell you but it's just as dramatic.

Reader, I found him. My father.

Talk about lucky. I couldn't believe how easy it was in the end — maybe I should have done it years ago. (But then again maybe not. I wasn't ready, probably. Anyway, I didn't need him as urgently.)

But wait until you hear!

With the prospect of the trip you can imagine how difficult I found it to keep my patience with the Samanthas and the balsamic-vinegar brigade that Saturday morning. Although I say so myself, I was brilliant — mind you, I had to be, with all the problems facing us I certainly didn't want to lose *that* job.

And then I had to rush across the city to see James. He was morose enough but at least he was calmer and I could see he was pleased I'd come, although perish the thought he should say so.

He wasn't having very many visitors. To put it bluntly he wasn't having any visitors except me and one of his pals, Ferdia, the boy who works for his father's computer business and who has a car. He came in once.

One for the books. Here was I thinking this chap was

to be avoided because of loose morals – you'll remember
he was the one who lent his car to James and Rosemary
Madden so they could mess in it outside the club that
first night they clicked – and here was he the one who
comes up trumps when James needed a pal.

To make things more obvious, as though to underline
how everyone else had headed for the hills, Ferdia had
signed the plaster cast. The slagging you write on casts is
meant to be cheery and jokey but that lonely name, one
boat in an empty sea, nearly made me cry. I had thought
of offering to sign it myself too, to take the bare look off
it, but then realized this might be rubbing it in too much.

James needed cheering up. So I adopt my most
businesslike-yet-optimistic voice. I tell him why I'm in
such a rush and can't stay long.

He's indifferent, of course, couldn't care less if I'm
going to Timbuktu.

Would it not be nice if we had a father in our lives?
Not to live with or anything, just in the background.

I couldn't be arsed.

I ignore the vulgarity. Well, I'd like it, I say, wish me
luck.

Good luck.

Like I told you. Conversation with him isn't easy.

It was cloudy, threatening rain, when Ken and I set off
for Birr that afternoon. Right up to the time we hit the
Naas dual carriageway I was continuing to toy with the
idea of going straight to Adeline to ask her what she
knew of my father. By the time we were passing
Rathcoole, though, I'd decided to hold her in reserve. I
wanted this to be as hassle-free as possible. (I guess I was
pussyfooting a bit – not sure quite how much I could
take. Adeline is nothing if not blunt.)

The Guard's name turned out to be Mick Flanagan. He
wasn't at the station when we got there but I described

him and we were directed by one of the other Guards out to his house. We were told to look out for a dormer bungalow with a field of cabbages to one side of it about three miles outside the town on the main Tullamore Road.

When we get there, I'm nervous, naturally, but he couldn't have been nicer. He comes to the door himself, what can I do for you? Then he recognizes me. Well, hello again.

I tell him immediately why we're here, no point in beating around the bush.

Well, well, well, he goes. Then, unexpectedly, he laughs. He's not wearing a jacket, only a stripy blue and white shirt, frayed around the buttonholes – and when he laughs heartily like this, he wheezes like a heavy smoker. It occurs to me that at his age he should be a sergeant at least. Maybe he's just too easy-going.

Come in for a cup of tea, he goes, wiping his eyes and shaking his head as if he's just heard some secret joke. I'm all by myself, Saturdays are very busy around here, the missus and the daughters are off on the fast track as usual, leaving me to fend for myself. Come in.

I'm reluctant, you know how it is, but I don't want to be rude. So we go in. It's a nice, snug house, I'd love it for James and me. Plenty of windows too, all looking out at the garden which wraps around the whole outside. I'd have to change the décor, though, too many patterns in the wallpapers and carpets and so forth. I like plain.

We follow him into the kitchen. More patterns – on the tiles, lino, cushions and antimacassars, on the millions of gewgaws on every surface. The wife seems to be into patchwork. There are two patchwork tea-cosies on one of the windowsills and a patchwork cloth on the table.

You know, I'm not surprised to see you, I was half expecting you back, Flanagan says as he's plugging in the kettle. I did warn you that Adeline wouldn't have been all that helpful. Would I be right now?

I don't want to let Adeline down – after all, she is my relation. She was grand, I go, she wasn't expecting us, she was out in the garden and I think we caught her on the hop.

His belly rolls jiggle as he laughs again. Oh dear, he goes. He moves a tea towel off the rail of the solid fuel cooker and settles his big behind against it. He folds his arms across his chest. Don't get me wrong now, he goes, we're all fond of her. We're thin on the ground for gentry around here – except for the castle, of course.

Can you help me? I say. I don't want this to take up too much time, although he seems to have centuries of it at his disposal.

He gets serious. I can help you all right, but I'm not sure it would be right just to give you a name straight off. Aren't there procedures that have to be gone through in cases like this?

Yes, I go. And I wouldn't expect you to do anything illegal. But there'd be no law against you telling me what you remember about my dead mother, surely? And that could include who she hung around with before she left here for Dublin. Her pals.

I was handing it to him on a plate. I'd thought it out very carefully because I knew only too well about the formal procedures that you have to go through to trace your parents in, like, adoption situations, where they have to agree to be traced. But this wasn't an adoption situation.

M-mmm, he goes. He doesn't know what he's in for, does he? Then he laughs again at that secret joke.

This laughing is beginning to worry me. What's so funny? Before I can ask, Mick Flanagan has turned towards Ken. Is this your husband?

No, I say quickly, before Ken gets embarrassed. This is Ken Sheils, he's a friend.

And so, Ken, what do you think of this? Flanagan settles himself, crosses his arms over his chest again. Do you not think that sometimes it might be better to let sleeping dogs lie?

I believe Angela knows what's best for her, Ken says quietly.

Your man drops the laughing policeman personality and gives me one of those looks I recognized at our first meeting. He may be jolly but he's nobody's fool.

Just then the kettle boils and he occupies himself making the pot of tea. How come you haven't been down here before, Miss Devine? he asks. His back is to me but I get the weird feeling he can still see me.

That's a question I can't answer, I say truthfully. I did dicky with the idea but I just never got around to it.

I hesitate, he isn't moving. His back is listening hard. I feel he needs me to say more. So I say, Maybe I was afraid of what I'd find out.

He turns quickly to face Ken and me, he's stirring the tea in the pot, round and round, round and round. And how sure are you that your father comes from these parts? The Devines had money, they were a family who went away on their holidays every year. Your mother could have hooked up with a Connemara man, or even a Dub.

I stare at him. Is he going to help me or not? She could have, I say as steadily as I can, and of course I don't know for sure he's from here. I'm starting from here, that's all, it seems to me to be the logical place to begin looking.

Whatever I've said, it seems to be the correct response. He relaxes, brings the teapot over to the table, where there are already cups – patterned, of course –

hanging from a mug tree. His tone changes, he's formal now. If I tell you where to go, he says, I'd appreciate it if you wouldn't say where you got the information. He sits down, looks off into space. It wouldn't be long before he'd find out who sent you anyway, he says, almost to himself. Then, looking me straight in the eye, But so long as you don't confirm it and I don't confirm it, there'll be no real harm done. All right?

Ken and I look at one another. I agree to keep my mouth shut. The Guard pours the tea into three mugs.

I get a cold shiver — as kids we used to say this meant someone has just walked over your grave. I don't think until that moment I had fully realized what I was doing. I had come to Birr instinctively, like a lemming. Now here I was on the very edge of the cliff. Who was it said, don't wish for something you don't really want? Suppose my father turned out to be a criminal? Was that why the Guard found this so amusing?

The palaver with the tea is taking centuries. Pouring milk from a carton into a milk jug, lifting the lid off the sugar bowl to see if there's enough in it. I'm ready to scream.

Right, he says eventually, heaping sugar into his own mug. Derrybride, he goes, it's just beyond Tullamore, you can't miss it. And you're looking for the only detached house in the village. If he's not there, his office is in the next village, he sometimes works on Saturdays, you can't miss that either. It's on the main street. Big place, double-fronted.

And the name? My heart is thumping a Lambeg tattoo.

His eyes sharpen up. Pius Crawford, he says.

Pause.

Then, The name means nothing to you?

I shake my head. I find it an odd question.

Ken puts a hand on my arm. Are you all right, Angela?

I don't blame him. I must look like a corpse. Pius Crawford. My name should be Angela Crawford. I swallow hard. Why would the name mean something to me? I ask this Guard.

Mr Crawford's well known around the midlands, he goes. He's — you're sure you haven't come across the name?

I shake my head. Well, he goes, shall we say Mr Crawford's a bit of a — what do you call it? A zealot, that's it. He's full of zeal when it comes to certain things.

Like what things?

You're familiar, I suppose, with organizations such as No Divorce?

Yes.

Mr Crawford and his wife are founder members of an organization called Catholic Rights. It's a small group, but its views would be broadly similar to those espoused by No Divorce, Youth Defence, groups of that nature. Only more so. In fact, I've heard it said that compared to Catholic Rights, all of those other groups look like Rastafarians.

It's now clear why he had been laughing. I'm not laughing.

Apparently, Pius Crawford, who is an auctioneer by profession and who has seven children, leads rosary rallies outside cinemas where they're showing anything with any sex in it. And as for the Irish Big Three, contraception, divorce, abortion, Pius and his mates, mostly women, have been known to chain themselves to the railings of churches to make their point. He also organizes petitions against everything from the Stay Safe Programme for school kids, to altar girls to women's shelters.

Women's shelters? I'm beginning to get my voice back.

Mick Flanagan raises an eyebrow. They believe these

shelters are anti-family. He's watching me hard. I'm surprised you haven't heard of him, even up in Dublin.

Look, he says carefully, now that you know what you're up against . . . He hesitates. And, to be fair, what poor old Pius'd be up against if you brought this out into the open. Maybe it would be simpler to forget about approaching him. If you change your mind, I promise I won't breathe a word to anyone about your visit.

This kills me. The hell with Pius Crawford's problems. What about our problems? I wasn't going to be diverted. I could see the irony, enigma, difficulty, all the rest of it, I simply wasn't going to be diverted. I had to keep my mind focused. James needs help. Plain as that.

I stare at Guard Flanagan. How do you know it's him?

He sits back in his chair as much as his bulk allows. The whole town knew it at the time, he says quietly. In fact the whole town was agog, I hope you won't take offence at this, Miss Devine, but around here the story was better than *Dallas*. The Crawfords were, are, big farmers and they and your grandparents were the local nobs. Friendly with each other too, in kind of a distant way. This was before ecumenism – he says this gently, without a hint of sarcasm.

Her family kicked her out because he was a Catholic, is that it? I was ready to fire up on her behalf.

Your grandparents weren't the worst, he says. They were upset, of course, very upset.

He leans forward again. Here, he goes, you haven't touched your tea. Have a hot drop. He pours – the sound in the still kitchen is as loud as Niagara Falls – then sits back again. Sure God love them, all this happened more than thirty years ago—

Thirty-six.

If you say so. More sugar? Milk? Would you like a biscuit or a scone?

Ken and I both refuse anything to eat. I'm having difficulty raising the tea to my mouth, the cup knocks against my teeth. Ken notices. Reacts.

I put down my cup. Why was the whole town agog?

Not to put a tooth in it, the Guard says, looking at me with those clever eyes, it wasn't only the situation itself. Your poor mother didn't seem to care who knew or what anyone thought.

He fills us in on what happened, as clearly as he can remember. Even more than my grandparents, Crawford's family went into a complete tailspin when they heard the big news. If I tell you, he says, that Pius Crawford has two brothers named Bonaventure and Canice and a sister named Annunciata you might get the picture. Pius was a second son and as you know, second sons in farming families were usually destined for the seminary. So when this happened, no seminary. And in a family like that . . .

He shrugs.

The Crawfords wanted the whole thing hushed up, they wanted my mother to be sent away to England where she could have the child — me! — secretly adopted.

Even if you were to leave me out of this altogether, I'd be finding this story extraordinary — we were talking the seventies here. I'd thought those kinds of attitudes went out with the Eucharistic Congress.

Mammy wouldn't be sent away, however. Both families and the clergy on both sides tried to persuade her but she believed that Pius Crawford and she truly loved one another. She became hysterical — the Guard picks his words delicately here but it's not difficult to read between the lines — and although her own parents tried everything they could think of to restrain her, she haunted the Crawfords' house for weeks on end at all hours of the day and night, calling out and screaming that she'd kill herself if Pius didn't come out to her. (Inside the house, the Crawfords, presumably, were beating him with rosary beads . . .) He never came out.

Flanagan is fuzzy about how she left Birr. All I know about that, he goes, is that one morning it was all over the town that Rose Devine had vanished. There were rumours, of course, that she'd gone to the States, to England, she'd jumped into the river. Well, I knew she'd jumped into no river, a colleague of mine who'd known her here but who had been transferred to Portlaoise definitely saw her getting a lift from a car going towards Dublin just outside Abbeyleix. God love the Devines, he shakes his big head, but it wasn't long before the next nine days' wonder came along and the town switched its attention away from poor Rose.

I know he's watching for my reaction. I feel not in the least emotional. As cold as the Arctic Ocean — isn't that odd?

Don't think badly of her, he says slowly. She was very young. I'd often wondered what happened to her afterwards, but when I saw your picture and your name in the paper . . .

What picture? What paper?

It was in one of the tabloids, the Star, maybe, or the Irish Sun. You didn't see it?

I shake my head. Then I remember the day I opened the door and the flash went off in my face. I hadn't looked at any of those papers. Now I understand how word had got around so fast right at the very beginning. It wasn't only those reports in the Herald.

For a couple of minutes, we're all three of us sitting there like the three blind mice. It had been almost too easy. An anticlimax, if you can believe that.

You see, deep in my heart I hadn't expected to get the name first go. Maybe it's because I'm a city woman, and hadn't fully realized how closely people live in each other's pockets in the rest of Ireland.

This is balderdash. I'm making excuses for myself. How many times have I been astounded at the extent to which Dublin itself is a village?

It's as clear as morning that if I'd come here ten years ago, fifteen years ago when I should have, I would have saved myself years of wishing and wondering. So why didn't I come here before? Because I knew, probably subconsciously, that I'd be afraid.

I was dead right. I am afraid. My phantom dad was grand and now here I've ruined him.

I have to face the fact that this sudden drive to find my father was just that, a *drive* to find him because I was feeling helpless. Unable properly to help James.

Even on the way down here I'd been seeing this Guard saying something like, Oh, yes, we never saw him after he went off that time to join the RAF. Broken-hearted he was. (For the RAF substitute the Foreign Legion. Or the Missions.) And then Ken would drive me to Adeline, and she'd rack her brains and give me a bit more information. Yes, we always wondered, he never came back, you know, not even for a visit . . .

I could continue then on my safe quest, writing to the Ministry of War, or the French Foreign Office or whoever I had to write to. And at the end of it, somewhere Out There in the woolly future, my dad, all square-jawed and clean-cut, was going to be waiting for his little girl, Kenneth More in *Reach for the Sky*. Rueful about his single indiscretion but delighted now to be offered this golden opportunity to make amends.

Well, the joke was surely on me – in more ways than one. I wanted clean-cut? I sure got clean-cut. And now I had to go to confront it.

I can't get over how much you're the image of your mother, the Guard says into the silence.

I stand up suddenly. Thanks, Guard, I say, I really appreciate it.

Take your time about this, he lumbers to his feet. Crawford's not going to go away, he'll still be here tomorrow and next week – next year. Think carefully about what you're at. He drops his eyes, almost shyly. Remember, he goes, he probably loved her as much as she loved him. Things were handled differently, those days.

This guy's likeable, But I don't want to hear any more. Not just now.

We leave and get into the van. Sam, who normally gives me a lick when he meets me, even after a short absence, stays well away. Dogs have a sixth sense, or so they say.

Drive quickly, I say to Ken.

He obeys without argument. Derrybride? he asks. I tell him yes and he starts the van and heads it in the Tullamore direction. I think in some ways he's as stunned as me.

Although he couldn't be. No one could be. From the beginning of the universe, no one ever has been as stunned as me. And still, for some reason I can't explain, I have to face it. Even if my father is Genghis Khan.

So much for driving quickly. Once again we hit the dreaded loose chippings and we're crawling at about ten miles an hour. I'm so tense I think I'm going to go into orbit. I'm drumming. All we need now is a lorry to come along and start beeping at us. You'll see some Angela Devine then so you will . . .

Why did you think that Guard never got promotion? I ask Ken, when we're a few minutes into the journey. He looks sideways at me. What do you mean?

Don't you find that irritating? When someone says, What do you mean?, when you've just said what you mean. I hold on to my temper. He sounds and acts too intelligent to be only a Guard, I say. At his age he should be at least a sergeant.

Who knows? says Ken, nodding his head like a wise old man. Maybe he stepped on the wrong toes. This is a small town.

At least I think that's what he said. I wasn't listening. I couldn't care less about Mick Flanagan and whether he made commissioner.

What am I going to say to this Pius Crawford?

Twenty-Eight

I hope you don't mind my asking, Ken breaks the silence between us as we're driving along, but are you and James all right for money?

That brings me up short, I can tell you. I hope I'm not giving off poverty vibes. We're grand, I go, thanks.

We weren't grand at all. By this time, you see, not only was my poor scratch-card hoard disappearing fast, but our budget was beginning to miss the few bob from the kissogram gigs. We'd be all right in the short term but it was the long term that worried me. The pay in the cleaning job was miserable, plus, my future in PA System was looking iffy to say the least. With Patsy preoccupied elsewhere – and she's the one who organizes the business side of our engagements – not to speak of her recent attitude to me, I wasn't all that hopeful we'd survive. We had no gig the following morning. As a matter of fact, I hadn't heard from her at all since that disastrous scene in the café.

Added to which, because of his injuries, James was going to be off work for the foreseeable future so he was not going to be able to take care of his monthly loan payment on his bike.

You might well ask why I didn't break into the money I had saved in the post office. After all, there was nearly three thousand there.

I don't know if you'll understand this but I felt if I broke up the wholeness of that money we'd be lost. In a way, I didn't see the total sum represented by those bonds and certs as real money, not like the pounds and coins you'd have in your purse. When I thought about it I saw the stash as a tight little ball, a perfect entity in itself. Sacred. Don't laugh now, but the nearest analogy I can give you is that this is the way I used to see the Holy Trinity when I was a child, the Three Persons all wound in together in a ball, so tightly packed you didn't know which Person's Arms and Legs and Feet fitted which Head.

The money was just as indivisible. It was an all or nothing wholeness – to be used for a house or a major operation. Or bail. But not for rent or bread.

We really will be fine, I say again.

You'd ask if you needed a dig-out?

(Never in a million years.)

You're very good, I go.

Right at this moment, anyway, I couldn't give a sugar about money. I'm like a hen on a hot griddle. We're still crawling. How much further, do you think? I try not to sound like a harpy.

We should be there in less than five minutes, Ken says.

I knew a Pius in the flats when I was young, and a bigger creep you never met. A flasher by the age of fourteen. (Could have given oul' Mooney, King of the Flashers, a run for his money.) I have this theory that if you've hated someone when you were a child, everyone you meet with the same name afterwards is automatically suspect. They really have to be honeys to get over the handicap of the name. I sure hope this particular Pius is the one who's going to disprove my thesis. I am *not* hopeful.

Ken slows down even more as we meet a tractor coming the other way on the road. It's another brilliant day, really hot and bright, and the dust this tractor is throwing up along with the loose chippings is quite a cloud. After we get past safely, Ken looks over at me, his lips are twisted in a grin against himself. Bet you thought I was going to hit him, didn't you?

I smile back. It breaks the tension a bit, but not much.

I can see you're very nervous, Ken goes, are you sure you want to go through with this? We can come back another day – I don't mind driving you, I really don't. You've a terrible lot on your plate at the moment.

I hadn't even told him about the letter.

We're here now, I say back. We might as well get it over with. I just want to see him, I'm not looking for any great confrontation.

Have you planned out how you're going to introduce yourself? he goes.

I hadn't. I tell him now that I'm just going to play it by ear. But don't worry, I say to him, you can drop me off, you needn't be involved in the slightest. I'm thinking to myself, I hope to God he's here, I couldn't bear another drive to his office. Then I'm thinking in the same second, Please, God, don't let him be here, don't let him be anywhere!

I want to be involved, Ken goes, please, Angela, I want to be. He puts his hand on my knee.

Just in time, I stop myself from jumping away. That wouldn't be fair. But I don't want his hand there, it feels enormous. Oppressive. The best I can manage without shoving it off is to put my own hand over it and to give it a squeeze. Thanks, I go. You're very good.

I hate myself for this. What a hypocrite. Only a few days ago I enjoyed the feeling of that hand. But now there's a sort of presumption about it I can't stand. Like, we've done it so we're intimates.

But I can't take my hand away without making it seem like a big deal. The crux is that I think he's the hypocrite. He wants to be involved in this – in me – and yet he can't really bring himself fully to be on James's side. Flowers and hospital visits can't paper over those cracks.

I guess I'm not a passionate person. Maybe where sex is concerned it's just that I haven't had the practice – a twenty-year gap is quite a gap.

On the other hand, my reaction mightn't have anything to do with sex or passion. It's more likely to be one of my character flaws rearing its ugly head again. I don't know what it is about me, any time anyone expects me to do something or to be something, I instantly want to do and be the exact opposite.

Oh, stop with the psychoanalysis again, Angela! Do something.

Both our hands are still lying there on my leg, like a pair of heavy puddings. I cross my legs so he's forced to take his away, but not before I squeeze his a second time to take the harm out of it.

We come to Derrybride – petrol pump, Marian shrine, pub and six terraced cottages, festooned with hanging baskets, a grassy triangle edged with flowers on one side of the crossroads. A big rock with lettering on it, Tidy Towns Special Commendation. One big house, detached.

We find we can't pull up directly outside the detached house because there are too many cars parked along the kerb so we pass it and park in the first space we can find, thirty or forty yards further on, past the crossroads.

I roll down the van window, look back at my father's house. It's long and low, a ranch-style bungalow set well back on a large site bounded by a low hedge, which is tidy to within an inch of its life. Rosebeds all along the short driveway, kid's mountain bike lying in the middle of the lawn beside — wouldn't you know it — a small grotto made of real rocks. I think this one is Our Lady of Lourdes, but I've forgotten which of the Our Ladys has her hands held out and which has them folded. Six arches running all along the front of the house, two cars parked in a tarmacadamed area to the side. The front door is open.

When Ken turns off the engine I can hear laughing and talk. It's coming from the back garden of the house. They must be having a party.

It's then I get the first inkling of how to do this. My father is an auctioneer. That's going to be the key — no pun intended, ha, ha! — to how I can manage to approach him so his family won't get suspicious. I'm thinking of the seven children here, I wouldn't want to upset them.

I go very calm. There's never a happy medium with me, is there? It's either panic or ice.

Still time to leave, Ken says quietly. They seem to have visitors.

There'll never be a perfect time, I say back to him. Anyway, we're here.

Are you sure you don't want me to come in with you?

No thanks, I go, this is something I have to do by myself. I give his hand a squeeze, a heartfelt one this time because he is genuinely being an all-round good egg. I get out.

As I walk towards the house, the laughing and the buzz of conversation gets louder. It seems to be quite a party. I see a young child, maybe three years old, run through the open front doorway and out into the garden. The child is gorgeous, blondie curls, dressed in a lovely pair of bright pink dungarees. Benetton? Before she can get too far, a woman in a yellow summer dress appears, catches her up in both her arms, and carries her back inside. On the way back in she nuzzles the child's tummy

and says something which makes the child giggle. Like
wind chimes. I can just imagine what she said – C'mere
to me, you little rascal. Something like that. They look
like a pair of happy squirrels.

I'm just at the gates now – wrought iron, wide open –
and I hesitate. Was that my father's wife? If it is, she
looks nice. The poor woman doesn't know what's going
to hit her. My feet itch to run but I've come this far.

I go in and walk up the driveway.

It's cool along the front of the house, under the arches,
the ground beneath them is flagged with stone. Niches on
both sides of the front door – God almighty, I've only
noticed now, two more shrines, statues of the Sacred
Heart and St Martin of Porres! Through the doorway, I
can see two women gossiping in a kitchen at the end of
the hall. They're side by side with their backs leaned up
against a kitchen counter, they've wine glasses in their
hands.

One of them sees me and comes out – Hello? She's
friendly, looks about fifty or so.

Could I have a word with Mr Crawford? He's the
auctioneer? My voice sounds steady enough except I'm
conscious of my Dublin accent. The woman doesn't act
in the least surprised. Sure, she goes, come through.
They're all in the back garden.

I wouldn't like to interrupt the party.

Not at all, she says back. You obviously don't know
Pius! Saturday's normally a working day for him in any
case but our Pius wouldn't be the one to turn away
business on any day of the week, or at any time, day or
night. She laughs.

In different circumstances I'd like this woman to be
my friend. She has uncomplicated written all over her.

I hope *she's* not the wife.

I've no choice but to follow her through the house. I

suppose it's because I know who Pius Crawford is and what he stands for that I can see nothing but religion everywhere. Mind you, you couldn't miss it, more pictures of Our Lady and the Sacred Heart, two Papal Blessings, another statue of St Joseph.

Isn't it funny but here I am under this incredible strain and I still have time to notice this kind of thing? I must be in a state of heightened awareness. I even register the kitchen. It's gorgeous. Like something you'd seen in *Hello!* where the owners have dedicated their lives to making a home for themselves and their lovely children. Peachy-coloured walls, a shiny red range, built-in units, honey pine presses, black and white tiles on the floor in a chequerboard pattern. A woman is rinsing dishes at the double sink while another is taking them from her and loading them into a large open dishwasher. Both these women, plus my guide's companion, smile at me as I pass through.

We go out through a set of French doors on to a patio. The garden is beyond.

It's a First Communion party. A little girl is racing around, veil flying out behind her. Like a lively seagull. She's playing football with two men. Her ankle-length crinolined dress is swaying like a bell, her tiny satin handbag dangles from her wrist, she hasn't taken off her lace gloves. But she has removed her shoes, her ankle socks are green with grass stains. In another part of the garden, a little boy, his white Communion suit already beyond redemption, is one of a swarm of children hanging upside down from a climbing frame.

Aren't they dotes? says the friendly woman, stopping for a moment on the patio and fondly indicating both children. The two of them are cousins and the two families combined for the celebration. Pius has by far the biggest garden of anyone in the family. Naturally. She laughs again. Ah, sure I shouldn't be giving out about him, he's not the worst.

I feel like Attila the Hun.

Please let me wait here by the door, I say, I don't want to disturb everyone.

All right, she says, I'll go and get him. What name shall I say?

Sheils, I go immediately.

I hadn't known I was going to say that.

She goes off towards the far side of the garden. Immaculate grass, not a weed in sight. A large glasshouse and a shed at one side, the play equipment – climbing frame, swings, sandpit – at the other, and at the far end, facing where I'm standing, a little summerhouse with a canvas awning, in the shade of which sits a group of six or seven elderly people, most of them wearing sun hats. A little table near them under a white beach umbrella supports two tiered cakes with white icing, nearly as big as wedding cakes.

The main tables have been set in a long row all along one side of the grass. Salmon, turkey, beef, salads, tarts, pies and about ten bowls of desserts. The meal is over, but people are still picking away at the remains. That was some spread – and as for the drink! The bar is as well stocked as a pub – there's even a steel barrel with a tap, beer or stout.

If I tell you there must have been forty or forty-five adults at this party, and maybe as many children, all scattered in loose little groups with loads of space in between, it might give you some idea of how big this garden is. I suppose space isn't at a premium in the country.

I watch my guide walk across the lawn and towards a group of adults who are sitting on deck chairs about twenty feet from the old people's summerhouse. She leans down and speaks to one of the men who has his back to me. He turns round and looks in my direction.

He's still too far away for me to see his features clearly. But I do see he has fair hair.

I'm so sensitized that, despite what the woman said, I can see he's pissed off at being interrupted at his party. His shoulders sort of slump in an irritated way. But he gets up, takes his jacket off where it's been hanging on the rail of his deck chair, comes towards me. A couple of people in his group who had turned round to look towards me too, turn back. My woman guide joins them.

Pius Crawford is shrugging on the jacket of his suit, he's refastening his tie as he starts towards me. He's quite big, about six feet. The hair, I see now, is receding a bit. He has freckles. I wasn't prepared for freckles. Freckles are friendly. I've always gone for freckles in men, as I think I've told you. Maybe this is why.

He's actually quite nice-looking – oh, God, I don't know how I feel about that. This man doesn't seem to be the whited sepulchre or creeping Jesus I was expecting. This man has 'Dad' written all over him. *Little House on the Prairie* dad. It'd be easier for me to be brave if he was repulsive. Or would it? He's arranging his face into a smile. He's holding out his hand. Good afternoon, Mrs Sheils, he says. What can I do for you? His hand is big, warm.

Could we talk somewhere? I say.

Sure, he goes. Come on into the house. We'll be able to find somewhere out of the mayhem, I hope.

He hasn't a clue. All he's seen is a prospective client.

We go in through the kitchen – the women smile at me again – and then into a little den place off the hall. Wood panelling on the walls, a real healthy Busy Lizzie blooming from a china bowl on the windowsill, family

pictures, including two wedding pictures and a graduation picture of a lovely-looking girl with long straight
blonde hair. An older couple – who could be my
grandparents! – yet another Papal Blessing. And on top
of his computer terminal is a statue of St Francis of Assisi.
I know this saint for sure because of the robes and the
little bird he has on his hand.

Pius Crawford closes the door. I work from here as
well as from the office, he says, we can be private here.
He points to a chair. Sit down, Mrs Sheils.

I sit. He does, too. He opens a big hardbound
notebook and turns the pages until he finds a blank one.
Now, he goes, taking a pen from a glass stand beside the
computer, then swivelling his chair to face me. You have
a property you want to sell, maybe? You're looking to
buy in our area?

No, I say. Look, Mr Crawford, this is nothing to do
with property.

Oh?

I've something to tell you that's not going to be easy
for either of us.

Now he sort of straightens in his chair. Oh? he goes
again. Still he hasn't copped.

My name isn't Sheils, I go, it's Devine. I know I'm fair
like you but people say I'm very like my mother.

Twenty-Nine

He cops.
    The freckles on his face and on the places where his hair had receded seem to get darker as the skin underneath goes white. I'd feel sorry for him if I didn't feel so peculiar myself. Kind of dizzy, as though there's an electric wheel buzzing in my blood. Weirdly disappointed, too – what had I been expecting, us to fall into each other's arms?

What's your first name? He's hoarse. Whispering. As if I'm his worst nightmare, which I probably am.

Angela.

This seems to kill him altogether. He looks at the door as if we're in some kind of hostage siege and he wants someone to come and break it down to rescue him. Then he looks back at me. It can't be, he says, I already have a daughter called Angela. He glances at the girl in the graduation picture.

I'm so uptight, I nearly laugh – you know, the way you do at the most awkward times – but the situation is too serious and I manage to control myself. Is that her? I look at the picture too. He nods. His eyes are as huge as those you see on those little desert creatures – what are they? Meerkats? The ones that stand up straight on their little hind legs, peering around for danger, that send sentries to the tops of tall trees?

What are the odds? (Although Angela isn't all that uncommon a name.) Well, you've two now, I say. You can call us Angela One and Angela Two.

He stares at me. Blinks. Stares at me again. Next thing I lose it and start to jabber, I hear myself rabbiting on like a madwoman. I'm sorry to disturb his Communion party, I'm not here to disrupt his life, yakkity yak . . .

I manage to roll to a halt by telling him why I needed to intrude on him just at the moment. Because we're in a bit of trouble at the moment, I go, James and I.

Silence from his side.

I'm beginning to feel a bit more in control. I really *don't* want to cause trouble, I say again—

James? Who's James? he's whispering.

James is not your problem, I tell him, he's my problem, but as I told you, we need help. I came here because you're my last resort. I've no other relatives. Well, none in Ireland anyway. Except Mammy's sister, Adeline. I met her last week. But I don't think she could help. Anyway, she's only an aunt.

His colour is beginning to come back. I see, he says slowly. He looks out through his window at his normality. I knew something like this would happen some day, he says, to no one in particular. Now that you're here, it's almost a relief, do you know that – er – Angela?

He doesn't look like it's a relief. He looks like he's standing on the parapet of a bridge and I'm behind him with a gun.

I say nothing, I've said enough. He glances outside, then around the room, like a forest animal who's smelt guns. He gets up, crosses the room and locks the door. Just in case, he says. But don't worry, we won't be disturbed, no one comes in here when I'm working or with a client.

This increases my confidence. I'm not worried about being disturbed. He is.

He comes and sits down again in front of me. I've been praying for your mother for so many years.

Fat lot of good that did poor Mammy, I'm thinking.

His eyes fix on me. How did you find me?

I remember my promise to Mick Flanagan. Your affair with my mother was very public knowledge in Birr, I say firmly. Once I came to the town and started asking questions, finding you was easy.

He starts to bluster. So it was Birr, at least we've now established that much. Thank you. Who in Birr? *Who* in Birr gave you my name? I have a right to know—

It's an old tactic, divert down a side road to buy time, but I'm wise to it, James does it all the time. It could be any number of people I talked to, I say to him. For instance, wasn't my aunt Adeline around at the time it was all happening?

He stops dead. Recovers a little. Was it she who told you?

I told you I'm not saying.

Well, here's another thing – why now, may I ask? It's a bit peculiar, isn't it – after all this time?

Mr Crawford, we both have a lot of explaining to do, we can talk about this again – I know you're anxious to get back to your party. Believe me, if I'd tried to find you ten, even twenty years ago, I can assure you I would have found you just as easily. I just didn't try, that's all. The timing wasn't right, I wasn't ready, I was too busy with more crucial things, I didn't *need* to find you *enough* until now . . . All kind of reasons, I guess.

Anyway, I return his gaze, can you know why you

yourself did or didn't do everything, every moment of your life?

His eyes hunt the room then come back to me. How many other people know about this?

The person who told me, as far as I'm concerned – no two. I'd temporarily forgotten Ken Sheils, out there in the van. Privately I'm remembering what Mick Flanagan said, that it was the talk of the town at the time. Poor Pius, leave him his delusions.

Who are these people? Are they local?

Look, Mr Crawford, I gave my word that I wouldn't tell anyone who gave me your name. The second person who knows about me and you isn't going to open his mouth. He's a friend of mine, drove me here. He's out there now waiting for me – he's from Dublin, so it's unlikely—

How much do you need?

It takes a second. Then I'm furious. How dare he think I'm a gold-digger? We're not looking for money, I say haughtily.

Then what? I'm sorry, he goes, what kind of help? This James, he's your son?

Although the implication is clear and I should probably take further offence (like mother, like daughter!) I don't. He's made me slightly uncertain. He's not playing the script I wrote for him on the way over here after talking to Mick Flanagan.

And although he hasn't exactly rolled out the welcome wagon, the oddest emotions are billowing around inside me. I'm having to fight not to like him. On the contrary, despite his bombast, I discover I very much *want* to like him. I'd been prepared for a super-Catholic version of Uriah Heep, who would fight me or throw boiling oil all over me, or try to repel me with a silver crucifix. To be fair to him, I'd say this man is only reacting normally to an abnormal demand.

James is not my son, I go, he's my brother. He's Rose's son. Sorry, he's actually my *half*-brother. (In case he starts to think that maybe Mammy had twins!) I've looked after him since he was a baby. He's in a little trouble with the law.

I can see his brain is working overtime.

By the way, I go, in case you think it's his father I should be looking for, you're probably right. The problem is, I have no idea where to start looking. Unfortunately for you — I manage a smile which I hope will break a bit of ice between us — you're the first in the firing line. I can hear my voice going lame.

All this time he's had his big notebook open in front of him on the desk and his pen in his hand. It's a fountain pen and he's gripping it so tightly there's ink leaking down his fingers. He puts it down very slowly and then closes the book.

Tell me about Rose.

He said this with such softness in his voice — this wasn't in the script either — that it really gets to me. Now I start worrying about the way he's feeling. About his emotions. Typical. I storm in here full of determination and courage and now I'm probably going to start behaving like his counsellor.

I try to harden up again. She's dead, I say firmly.

He makes the Sign of the Cross, Lord have mercy on her. How did she die? How long ago?

Stupid twit that I am, I decide to spare him the more sordid side of Mammy's life in Dublin. I tell him that she fell into poor circumstances when she first left Birr and she found it difficult to manage. Then I skip to the end. She died peacefully, I tell him. In the hospice. Nearly twenty years ago.

How difficult in Dublin? Was she poor?

Yes. Very poor. We were very poor.

He looks off towards the wall behind my head. Was it cancer? he goes. Did she go to the hospice because she was dying of cancer?

I stare at him. If Flanagan was even half-way correct about him, this man probably wouldn't have the remotest clue about a quarter of the problems which afflicted poor Mammy towards the end. We think it was, I say.

He peels his gaze off the wall. And did she get married in Dublin? Or is your half-brother illegitimate too?

Talk about insulted. I think of that happy little girl wheeling around in her beautiful, expensive Communion frock. Of the manicured lawns and the roses and the beautiful kitchen and all those warm, secure women who can smile at strangers. Yes, he is illegitimate, I say. I shoot at him with my eyes. And so are Francesca and Justine and Nicola.

Rose had *five* children? The horror in his face could even be comical.

Yep. By five different fathers.

Shattered, he gazes back at me. Probably there was he thinking all his life that his Rose went celibate through the rest of hers because she was still broken-hearted about him.

I've inflicted such damage that I'm finding it hard to hang tough. I don't know, do I, what pressures his own family put on him not to come out to see her when she was calling hysterically from under his window? Flanagan said he was so young—

Up and down, up and down, this has to be near the top of the see-saw conversation league. Stop it, Angela, you have to keep your mind on why you're here.

Through the open window, the sounds from the party

outside, the high-pitched voices of children, a woman calling to one of them in cross tones, seem to be coming from another universe. To help me stay strong, I conjure up a picture of James's battered face. I keep this picture in my mind while I sit there in the quiet, giving my father (my *father*!) a chance to digest this walking catastrophe sitting in front of him.

A quick wail from a child, and a man holding out his arms is crossing from right to left across the slice of garden I can see from where I'm sitting. The old people at the summerhouse are hardly talking to each other, just enjoying being there, like old people do. It occurs to me that a few of those old people could be related to me. Grand-aunts or grand-uncles. Even my paternal grand-parents. And which of those shiny people out there are my aunts and uncles by blood and marriage? I remember one of the names now – Bonaventure. I have an uncle Bonaventure. I wonder would he let me call him Bono, ha, ha!

You might think I'm treating this whole thing facetiously. Definitely not, it's just the way my mind works. I'm having to keep tight rein on myself, I'm afraid I'll start jabbering again and blow it. Let him off the hook.

The silence continues. I can feel his presence now. It's very strong, very male. I'm glad my father isn't some awful puny person. I think that, given other circum-stances, I could definitely like him.

He's fiddling with a paperweight on the desk beside him. It has a bunch of forget-me-nots inside it. His colour has improved. You say you've raised James, he's still living with you?

Yes.

If Rose is gone twenty years he must be—

I said nearly twenty. James was two months old when she died. He's still nineteen.

Where are they, the other three?

I tell him the truth — including the fact that we don't communicate much — and when I've finished, his demeanour is almost back to what it was when we first shook hands. Poor Rose. He shakes his head.

Then he blows it. But we're taught, aren't we, that repentance can take place between the saddle and the ground?

Repentance! For what? For her being her? He's making it easy for me. Prayers won't help her now, I go, she's dead.

He shafts me a look.

*I'*ll pray for her, Angela, he goes. As I told you, hardly a day goes by since she disappeared that I haven't.

Piffle, I think to myself. His prayers were really a terrific help when she was having her skull split by some junkie. But facing an enemy he can recognize, i.e. an unbeliever, has put spunk into him. He folds his arms. Now, Angela, level with me. Tell me, what do you really want?

My mind goes strange. I don't quite know what I want. To see him? To touch him? To have him embrace us into his family? To have him fall on his knees and beg forgiveness?

He's watching me carefully. If it's not money, what is it? Could you be specific?

Before I can answer, there's a rat-tat on the window. It's the little girl in the Communion dress. Her veil is falling down on the side of her head and she's trying to straighten it with one hand while rat-tatting on the window with the other. Are you coming *out*, Daddy? We're going to cut the *cakes* . . .

A woman appears behind the little girl and takes her hand. She's tall, tanned and bottle blonde – the expensive, ashy kind – slim as bamboo, wearing a straight white dress with a red belt. Sorry, Daddy, she calls through the window, don't mind her, she'll have to learn a bit of patience. Take your time. She smiles at me.

Your wife? I say when both have vanished from view.

Yes. He glances over his shoulder towards the garden. Dorothy. She's English. She converted so we could get married.

Bully for her, I go, and instantly regret it. She's nice, I say. Really. (It does cut a bit, though, to think Mammy could have become this lovely, polished person.)

Are you going to ruin all this for me, Angela? He says it very, very softly.

I engage his eyes, dredging up my strongest reserves. I've no desire to ruin anyone's life, I say just as softly. I'm not going to blackmail you, if that's what you mean. I've rarely asked anyone for anything, it's a point of principle with me not to be obligated to anyone, ever. You can take it that I'm asking you now to help me and my brother only because you're a last resort. And I'm sorry to say this so bluntly, but it's my opinion that you owe us.

He goes very still.

I sit up as straight as I can, like I'm Queen Nefertiti or someone. Are you going to help us or not?

He seems to cave in. It's extraordinary, his chest actually becomes concave. You still haven't told me how can I help.

I remember I read somewhere that Tony O'Reilly from Heinz once said he hates people to pussyfoot when they have bad news. That facts are friendly.

So I don't put a tooth in it. I tell Pius Crawford about

my brother's trial and conviction – erroneous conviction – but that my opinion doesn't count. That he's out on a suspended sentence. That because of this he's been beaten up and threatened with worse. That he's getting anonymous letters in his hospital bed. That the papers are in full cry after him—

Then I wing it. We need somewhere safe to live outside Dublin, I say as solidly as I can. A place where we'll attract no attention. And it has to be arranged quickly. Like early next week, the earlier the better. I thought with you being an auctioneer . . .

He seems to catch my mood and to see there's no point in arguing. Nowhere near Tullamore or Birr, he goes, all right? He sits up, he's brisk, we're in barter mode. I can see that this is what this man's good at. You can hear the confidence returning with every syllable.

For the time being, I ignore the bit about staying as far away from him as possible. As well as helping us find a place, maybe you could help us get jobs – auctioneers know a lot of people, right? Business people? We'd be all right for money at least for a while. I've saved a couple of thousand towards a place of our own and now is clearly the time to use it.

I'm getting warmed up, now I'm seeing a cottage with roses around the door and me growing turnips in the back, like Adeline. A whole new life, straight out of Thomas Hardy. (I stop short at the picture of James as an honest labourer.) We might even be able to buy a place if the price was right, I go, as if I've thought this out, which I haven't, but with house prices shooting up every week the way they are maybe what I have wouldn't cover deposits and legal fees and all the rest of it. Could you go guarantor for us?

I'm impressing myself with my jargon.

As soon as we're settled and we're earning, I continue, if it has cost you anything to help us, we'd pay back every single penny it cost. Even if it takes years.

Now I know I'm getting carried away so again I stop. I'd been about to promise that if he helped us, in return we wouldn't bother him or his family. I'm not going to let us down that far. Let him think what he likes about us. We're people, human beings. He can't wish us away, and while we're not going to go out of our way to make trouble for him and his nice family, now that we're out in the open, we're not going back underground. I remind myself that this is quite reasonable. That he owes us.

His chair, one of those high-backed executive leather jobs, is a bit higher than mine and he's looking down at me like he's a judge. If I understand it correctly, you want me to help someone who's *raped* a girl?

He's my brother. And it's a matter of opinion whether he raped that girl or not. He's not in gaol, is he? He's free. And it wasn't rape he was convicted of, it was sexual assault—

He interrupts. That doesn't take away from the fact that he was convicted—

He's also a blood relative of yours, by the way.

What?

Yep. Through me. Think about it.

I never saw anyone before of whom it could truly be said that his jaw dropped. Well, I see someone on this occasion. His mouth hangs open and you'd think his face had just fallen into a mincer. I couldn't care less, I'm fighting for James's life here.

He looks out towards the window. An older boy is playing Donkey with the Communion girl and two other little girls. The old people are still sitting in their same positions, like in a painting. Angela, my father says eventually, without looking around at me, will you give me a little time? My whole world—

He shrugs.

We don't have time, Mr Crawford, I say quietly. We really don't. You're our only hope. Since Mammy – Rose – is not here to look after James, I have to. He comes first.

You're asking me to help a *rapist*, Angela. Look out there at Esther – he gives this helpless little wave towards the outside – just *look* at her.

Esther's your little girl who made her First Communion?

Yes, he whispers.

The child is racing after the ball with which they've been playing Donkey. She's holding on to her veil with one hand. Mr Crawford, I say, maybe you'll understand this. I'm asking you to be a Christian. Forgiveness. Charity. I promise you, if you let me tell you James's side of the story—

Please! He holds up his hand. I couldn't bear it.

Well, it's not only James, then, is it? It's me. I'm asking you to help me. That anonymous letter – I told you I'm warned in that too. I'm your daughter, Mr Crawford. If you like, we'll do blood tests.

There's no need. I believe you. At last he looks away from the window. You've no need to prove to me you're Rose's daughter. I have eyes, don't I? He spreads his hands and examines the nails. They're big and square with not a scintilla of dirt under them. I've never forgotten her, you know, he says. Not for one day.

Why didn't you come out and see her when she was crying for you? Despite my best intentions, my voice is rising. She was *pregnant*, you owed her—

Don't you think I know she was pregnant? He looks

away again. It's a long story. It's too dreary. You wouldn't want to hear it.

There's something so private in the way he says this that it would take a person with a really black heart to insist on intruding. I file it away, though. I'll be bringing it up again. Through the window, we see Esther stop playing and look towards us. She puts her hands on her hips and her head to one side, frowning in at us like an irritated little housewife.

Her father reacts instinctively. With pleasure. Then he remembers my presence and checks himself.

I know you have to go, I say. I stand up. Look, Mr Crawford, I'm sorry for the shock I've given you but, as I hope I've impressed on you, the problems we have are very urgent.

You shouldn't have to call me Mr Crawford, should you? He stands up too.

It doesn't matter what we call each other, I say. I can hardly rush up to you and start calling you Daddy.

He frowns. Can you at least give me one day to think about this? To get used to it?

Yes. Of course.

Give me your telephone number?

When I tell him we don't have one, it seems to throw him almost as much as finding out I was his daughter. We make arrangements for me to telephone him at his office first thing on Monday morning. I give him my address. And then, as an afterthought, I give him the only telephone number at which I can be contacted. It's for emergencies only, I said, and it's on Saturday mornings. (Not that I could see for a second what emergency could arise — but in this day and age you have to have some sort of telephone number, don't you?)

Now we're both left standing, not knowing from Adam how to get out of this room. There's this terrible moment when we both take a step forward at exactly the same time and nearly bump into one another. Then we stop and have to take a step back again. He makes this gesture with one arm towards the door. I'm to go first, like he's the host and I'm the honoured guest.

We're standing very close so I'm very conscious of how tall he is. And there's a faint smell of fresh sweat off him, and grass. It's nice.

Before I go, I ask him suddenly if he really says rosaries outside cinemas.

He blinks. Does this matter to you?

It does, I go.

He looks down at his feet. I believe this earth is sinful, he says softly, we're all sinners. The evidence of my own sinfulness is standing right in front of me at this moment. He hesitates. I wanted to be a priest when I was a boy. He sounds sincere and convinced but to me there's something not quite right about the sound of this. It doesn't match somehow . . . And now that I think of it, I didn't altogether go along with his commitment to the between-the-saddle-and-the-ground stuff either. (This was something I well remembered from school. The notion that even Stalin and Hitler could be in heaven always sounded a bit off to me. Stalin and Hitler could go to heaven but the poor unbaptized babies had to go to limbo?)

It'll be a while, though, before I can work out why Pius Crawford is saying one thing and my instincts are telling me another, but I've done enough here for one day.

I'll get out of your hair now, I say.

You're sure only the two people know? Can you vouch for both of them that they won't spread this around?

I'm about to get angry again, say that I'm a human being, not merely a Problem but then I think, what's the

point? I can vouch for one of them, I tell him. And if it
will put your mind at rest, given who the other person
is, I doubt if – if the other person will be shouting it from
the rooftops.

I'd nearly said 'he'.

He shows me out as far as the front door. He can't get
rid of me fast enough. I can feel the panic in him in case
someone from his lovely family at his lovely party sees
us. I can feel him already out in that lovely back garden,
making up stories, shrugging about having to get business
wherever and whenever he can find it. Always on duty,
that's me, smiling, grabbing his little girl and throwing
her up in the air. Maybe even hugging her. Calling to his
other Angela – she's probably out there too, isn't she?

The poor guy. As it turns out, I'm glad Mick Flanagan
prepared me for worse because in my opinion Pius
Crawford's not *too* bad. Although it's too early to say
what his character is really like, at least he's manly
looking and at his age a lot of his inner character has to
be already written on his face – you know the way that
happens.

He could have been a weed.

→ Thirty ←

By chance, I met one of my kissogram colleagues on the Sunday morning. I was on my way to Bewley's in Westmoreland Street to treat myself to a proper cup of coffee and I met her in Marlborough Street, just as I was passing Carthy's the pawnbrokers. It was desperate to think of Mammy's jewellery lying abandoned in there behind the steel shutters. I should have used the scratch-card money to get it back straight away. The minute those bonds came in the post I was going to cash them and redeem everything. I'd have to come up with an extra hundred or so if I was going to get the video as well – I suppose I owed that to James.

Hello there! She tips me on the shoulder from behind.

I spin around. Oh, hello! I'd never liked this particular girl, she always behaved as if the work was beneath her. On the other hand she could afford to be like that. For a start she was young. And gorgeous, with a little face that would remind you of Demi Moore – come to think of it, her looks weren't a million miles away from Rosemary Madden's. And like Rosemary Madden, she was from somewhere nice, like Drumcondra or Glasnevin. Passing through the lower orders while she waited for something better to come along or, more probably, for Mr Right.

She was coming from Mass in the Pro-cathedral. After

we shoot the breeze about it being a lovely morning, she tells me the boss went mad when I didn't turn up that first night – and continued not to turn up. If any of them saw me, this girl says, they were under orders to tell me not to show my face around his office again.

Well, you've told me now, I say, thanks. I make a move to go.

How's your brother? she asks, in a neutral sort of voice but I'm on permanent guard and I've no intention of falling into any traps.

Brilliant, never better, I say, as sweetly as I can. Well, I must be off. Tell our mutual friend you gave me his message and that I miss him too, ha, ha! I walk off. Devil-may-care, that's me.

I continued on to Bewley's as planned, but I didn't enjoy it. I couldn't settle. All that normal noise, clattering crockery, chat. All those normal people, boys and girls with contact rashes on their faces, who'd obviously spent the night together and who couldn't bear to let go of one another's hands across the table, men with the Sunday papers, tourists with maps and bum bags and little purses from which they carefully counted out their coins. Not one of these folk, as far as I could see, had a care in the world. Even the young waiters and waitresses, who frequently look stressed in Bewley's, seemed cheerful to me this morning.

It seemed so long since the situation had been anywhere near normal for me, I'd forgotten what it felt like. On the other hand, I guess I had become so used to this churning, knife-edge feeling I live with now, maybe I'd find it difficult to recognize any more what normal felt like.

Poor Ken Sheils had got the brunt of this edginess on the way home from Tullamore the evening before. (He certainly hadn't known what he was taking on when he

met me!) As you can imagine, I was in no mood for
confiding, or even for talking. I felt I owed it to him to
say something, however.

Look, I say when I get into the van after I leave my
father, before you ask, the past half-hour was difficult, as
you can imagine, very, very difficult, although he's quite
a nice man, much nicer than that Guard led us to believe.
But I can't tell you what's going to happen next or what
any of us is going to do. Because I don't know.
Everything's up in the air. Do you mind if we don't talk
about it any more than that? Is that enough to tell you?

He looks wounded. You don't have to tell me anything
at all, Angela, I didn't ask—

I know you didn't and I appreciate it. But I feel I owe
you an explanation. I'm not being awkward, it's just I
can't say any more than I've just said. Do you
understand?

The poor guy's game, I have to admit that. He doesn't
push, doesn't argue. And the only thing he says during
the whole journey home comes when we're passing the
spot beyond Newlands Cross where the journalist was
murdered. There are little mounds of flowers there now,
browned by the heat and sun and the dust of passing
traffic. And a plain wooden cross with her name on it.

Scumbags, is all he says.

I apologize to him for my mood as he drops me outside
our door but he tells me there's no need to. When this is
all sorted out, he says, you can buy me a pint.

I'll buy you more than a pint, I say, and I give him a
puck in the shoulder. When I win the Lotto I'll buy you
a Rolls-Royce so you can get rid of this old banger.

He laughs and cuffs me back.

As I'm looking around at all this normality in Bewley's,
I remember that, in all the excitement, I never posted
my three-star scratch card. I don't even know where it is

now. I'm also thinking that maybe I should have called for Ken and offered to buy him a cup of coffee. But would it be fair to ruin his day? No matter how hard I'd try, I know I wouldn't be able to talk to him about anything even half-way everyday. James. My father. James again.

What an obsessive bore I've become. Some day, I vow to myself, we will have a cup of coffee here – and we'll be normal too. This from the woman who not four days ago decided she never wanted to see this man again. Irrational or what?

As it turned out it was just as well I was on my own this morning because my father was everywhere, through all my thoughts. No matter how hard I tried I couldn't shake him off. Everywhere I saw a man with a build even vaguely like his, I'd compare them. I'd look into my coffee. Did he like coffee or tea? I'd see a man reading the *Sunday Tribune*. Did he buy the *Sunday Tribune* or the *Sunday Independent*? Maybe both. Was he searching all the papers this morning for articles about his half-half-son? When he was making pillow-talk last night with his convert wife, did she ask him, just in idle conversation, who I was and what I wanted – and how did he get out of that one?

An American girl near me was wittering on about her star sign. She was a Pisces. For what it's worth, I'm a Cancer, on the cusp of Gemini. I haven't a clue what goes best with either, but at least with two sun signs to choose from, Pius Crawford and I have two chances to be compatible.

There's something nagging away at me underneath the more obvious stuff. I bring it up and examine it.

It's the religiosity. There's definitely something odd about it. Even making allowances for my own prejudices, in the short time I was talking to him, Pius Crawford's holiness didn't altogether wash with me. All right, so he does his rosary crusades and he writes outraged letters and all the rest of it but, in the flesh, the holy things he said did not seem to strike quite the right note. Like a bell that has a crack in it.

I got back to the flat at about twelve. It was as hot as a launderette even though I'd waited until the last minute before I went out to close the windows. For the previous few days, we'd seemed to be going through a mini-heatwave, although according to the weather forecast, this was supposed to break today.

In general, the weather isn't great this year. We'd all been hoping for another Mediterranean summer like we'd had in 1995 – I'd even heard a few dingbats saying that the fantastic weather we had last year was a reward from God because of the ceasefires in the North! If that's the case, maybe we're being punished this year because of the Canary Wharf bombing in London.

Actually, I was shocked about that bombing. Everyone was. We'd got used to peace and to just ordinary giving out about the politicians – they're all a shower, what Peace Process! et cetera. Before that bombing some of the customers in the deli even confided that they were going to try out the North for their holidays this year. (Shop assistants are like hairdressers. Holidays are *the* hot topic of conversation.)

They say that Canary Wharf is going to be the equivalent for Irish people of where-were-you-when-President-Kennedy-was-shot. We'll all remember exactly where we were when we heard about it – and typically, I was probably the last person in the country to hear about it. I hadn't seen the news the night before – James had been at home in charge of the remote control as usual – so I didn't hear until the next day, when it was the sole topic of conversation amongst the women in the minibus.

Tick-tock.

There are still nearly two hours to go before I leave for the hospital.

There isn't much to see out through the open window of the flat. The square is peaceful. I notice that all the yuppies in the new 'Georgian' apartments at the far side have their windows open like me. People are strolling alongside the railings around the square, pushing baby buggies and carrying newspapers under their oxters. I seem to remember reading somewhere that each city has a different heartbeat and every resident and visitor subconsciously responds to it. Like if you're in Manhattan or Tokyo you'll automatically walk faster than you would, say, in Thurles or Sligo. Dublin's Sunday beat is completely different from the rest of the week. Even the cars are driven more slowly. Maybe it's because a lot of them have grannies in the back, out for a Sunday drive.

Wouldn't that be blissful? To have a granny to take for a Sunday drive . . .

Before I know it, I've started fantasizing again. Me, my new father, James, one of our uncles or our auntie driving us all, including our aged relatives, out to the seaside for a breath of fresh air.

Stop it, Ange. I look at my alarm clock by the bed-settee. Only a few minutes gone. The whole place is as clean as a mortuary so it's pointless looking for something to polish. I've nothing to read – you might think I have a lot of books but I've already read every single one of them, many of them twice – and because I couldn't bear to read any more articles about James I hadn't bought a paper. I'm not hungry, Bewley's milky coffee has filled me up.

This must be what real loneliness is about. Forget the Old Woman of the Roads and her little house and stool and all. Loneliness is not only having no one to talk to, it's having nothing to do on a bright Sunday morning when everyone else has.

I get up and turn on the radio. Big mistake. There's a barney going on, people shouting at each other and Andy O'Mahony, who's the presenter of this programme, going, 'One voice, please, one voice.' They're squabbling about James. Two or three women, as far as I could make out.

I'm stuck to the floor, staring at our transistor radio. Annoyed women on the radio lose it. Their voices go up towards a screech.

Or maybe it's just the subject matter that's making me so critical. I should turn it off but I can't. Part of me wants to hear just how bad this is going to be.

Andy O'Mahony succeeds in intervening, gives one woman the floor. She's so furious, her voice is wobbling. At least she's lowered it. Listen, she goes, you have a male-dominated society and a male-dominated judiciary – well-educated, middle-class judges all out of the same mould. Private schools, golf clubs, Fitzwilliam Tennis Club, the Royal George Yacht Club, all the rest of it. Mighty massed ranks against the courage of one little girl—

Hold on a minute, hold on a minute, a man, not Andy O'Mahony, interrupts.

Andy says the name but I don't recognize it. The woman tries to shout him down but Andy shushes her, tells the man to go ahead. This judge wasn't part of the male establishment, this man says. Correct me if I'm wrong but this was a woman judge, wasn't it?

Same difference, says the woman in a disgusted tone of voice. It's the ethos I'm talking about, the environment in which our whole judicial system operates. Do you think, does anyone here think, that little Rosemary Madden will ever get over what she's been through? Does any woman ever get over an outrageous attack like this? This girl is a modern-day Joan of Arc. It's because of her bravery in coming forward, in being identified—

I turn it off.

The silence roars back at me. Rosemary Madden, Rosemary Madden.

I lie down on the bed-settee. I try to force my imagination into Rosemary Madden's mind. I have to. I can't go through the rest of my life not seeing the other side of this story.

But my imagination won't do it right off. It keeps sliding away, to my father, to money, to Mammy, to what time it is, to the washing I promised myself I'd do later, to Patsy and Martin and their problems, to what's happening outside in the square. Even poor old Tom Bennett gets a look-in. But I lead my brain back and back and back. Eventually it gives in and concentrates. The outline of Rosemary's story I know from James, the detail of it I fill in.

My name is Rosemary, I am a young woman of twenty. I have everything going for me. I'm pretty and I have a good family, a great address. My mother is very quiet but she makes our house nice for us. In an old-fashioned way. The family printing business is doing OK although I don't have much to do with it. My older brother works with my dad, in a set of prefabs at the back of our house, and one or both of them come in for their dinner in the middle of the day when they're not out calling on clients. My other brother, two years younger than me, has just done his Leaving Cert. He's a pain in the you-know-what but all teenage boys are and he's not the worst, really. We fight but not seriously. I like clothes, especially ones which show off my body. I'd like to be a bit taller, like Claudia Schiffer, but I'm still proud of my body. I paint my toenails pink. I'm thinking of putting a blonde streak in the front of my hair. Maybe magenta.

I'm not a genius but I'm not stupid either. I might even have gone on to Third Level – not university, of course, but I did scrape enough points in the Leaving to be offered a course in Waterford RTC. I wasn't all that pushed about leaving home, however, and I'd had enough of school. My parents didn't object when I didn't take the offer.

But then I found it quite hard to get work I liked. I wasn't going to work in McDonald's, no way. Daddy offered to find something for me to do in his own business. A telephonist or receptionist or something. No fear of that either. You wouldn't meet many people in the prefabs at the back of our house. Working with your family is not my idea of independence. I want to spread my wings.

It got a bit tense after a year or so – my dad was getting a bit irritated at having to hand out money all the time – and I had to do something.

So now I'm on a Youth Employment Scheme, which at first I thought was going to be a disaster because a lot of people think these schemes are all a con job to keep people off the official dole. But to tell you the truth, secretly I have to admit that what was really bothering me is that I knew there would be kids on the scheme with whom I wouldn't normally dream of associating. And indeed there are. They have dreadfully common accents and they're all named after people in Coronation Street or the Pope. If I'm honest I was a bit afraid of them. That I'd be attacked or ripped off or robbed. I found out, would you believe, that they were as afraid of

me as I was of them. We sorted it out after a while and
now we have quite good fun.

The work turned out to be OK. Under a Community
Initiative Scheme, we're helping to set up a computer
database to link together a set of small businesses in an
unemployment blackspot in the North City. That's what
they tell us anyway. Actually, though, it's quite interesting with very little really hard work involved. We're
bookkeeping and they're letting me loose on the computer side of it. I'm quite good at computers.

I was at a club in town one night where I met a
motorcycle courier, a really good-looking guy with
amazing eyes, although his skin could do with a bit of
Clearasil. But he's a massive dancer and I really fancied
him right from the word go. He fancied me, too. In fact,
I was sure he couldn't believe his luck – only scrubbers
would normally be interested in motorcycle couriers
from the inner city. (To me Mountjoy Square is the inner
city.) But he has a great body. Great kisser, too.

This is where I, Angela, started having difficulty. It was
hard for me to keep myself in Rosemary Madden's eyes
as soon as I got near the physical stuff. I suppose most
mother figures have difficulty picturing their boys kissing
and so on. This isn't to say you don't accept it, you do.
You can see it out there, but the actions involved are sort
of gauzy. It's when you come right close up, to see the
lips, that the problem arises.

I skirt away from it but when you come right down to
it, I can't, can I? It's the nub of this whole problem.

I don't make myself go all through the dating and the
parties and so forth. I make myself skip to the nitty-
gritty. The afternoon in question and the Furry Glen.
Like most Dubliners, I know the Furry Glen in a vague
sort of way. The Phoenix Park is the biggest park in
Europe, blah blah, and we're all very proud of it. But the

Furry Glen is at the far side from me. There's no bus service straight through, and most times I've ever been to that park it was to the zoo side because that's where the 10 bus terminus is. I remember the Furry Glen for the trees and the lake and the very steep hills. But the night James told me about the rape, I could see the scene vividly, even the little bridge and the ducks. So I must have been there more often that I'd thought.

I force myself to walk down that path with James and Rosemary. I see the sun coming through the trees (although he didn't tell me whether or not it was a sunny day), I hear birds singing. I see the horse riders he told me about and the old lady they were afraid would see them vanish into the bushes.

I see the two of them going in under the trees.

I'm Rosemary Madden again. It's dark in here, well, more gloomy than dark. And it's colder than I expected. The ground is damp. I'm afraid my clothes will get ruined, stained.

But I lie down and James lies down too. He's panting, all over me. His kisses are very hard. I'm getting frightened. What will I tell my parents about my clothes? I'm sure they're getting stained – we're lying on earth and pine needles and grass. And will they guess I've lost my virginity? Can you tell by a person's face?

But I'm the one who brought him here. The condoms are burning a hole towards me through his pocket. I can't feel them physically, of course, but I can in another way. I want to get out of it now but I don't know how.

Stop it, James, stop it—

He pulls away. What's wrong with you? You wanted this as much as I did. Are you just a tease or something?

Of course I want it.

I let him kiss me again. I want it and I don't want it all at the same time. It's going too fast for me, my knickers are tearing, he's too rough, I'm getting scared now — I can feel him—

I, Angela, jump up from the bed-settee. I can't do any more of this. It would drive me into Grangegorman. I can't split myself.

Anyway I don't want to. I don't *have* to because we have justice on our side. I'm gone way over the top, way beyond what James told me happened. Even way beyond what she said happened and the feelings she said she had in her statement. Me and my imagination — Mr Elliott always said it would get me into trouble.

I'm sweating and it's not from the heat of the day.

James and I have to find somewhere safe and quiet until the ruckus dies down. My father will help us. I'm James's sister and I'm on his side and that's that. No ifs, ands or buts. I'm James's *sister*. I'm standing by him. I believe James's side of the story. She asked him to bring the condoms. No way was it all one-sided. The judge is on our side. The judge judged everything. She thought he was worth giving a chance to. So do I. I'm sorry for Rosemary Madden's problems — or I would have been if she hadn't blown it. She's Joan of Arc now. To herself. To all her supporters.

Well, to me she's not. To me she's just a girl scared of her parents and of what she's done. So she has to cover up and blame James. She told her parents a story and she's sticking with it because she can't back down now. And now she doesn't have to because she's a heroine.

Joan of Arc?

Not.

Not to me. I have to believe Rosemary Madden's just a girl who's in love with all the attention. If I couldn't convince myself of that, I'd probably have to give up.

Thirty-One

Daddy, she called him. That's what clicks it for me.

The penny drops while I'm sitting in Mountjoy Park, killing time until I had to walk up to the hospital. For the second time in less than four hours, I wasn't able to stay in that silent flat a minute longer. I've now to add another worry to the list. How am I going to handle telling James about Pius Crawford?

At least the weather's holding, it's like a real summer's day, the kind you used to see in the illustrations in your school primer — you know, with the blue sky and the one little fluffy cloud and Máire agus Seán in their summer T-shirts bouncing their striped liathróid. (That reminds me — I have to make a decision fairly soon about whether I'm going to register for Irish for the next year's Leaving. Ugh!)

The wife calling him Daddy was the key to what rang wrongly about my father's religious zeal. Don't ask me to explain why I think the two things are connected, they just are. Call it instinct. I couldn't be sure, but I'd have been prepared to bet that it was she who was running the show. He was playing along with her, it wasn't coming from inside himself.

You see she's a convert and they're always the most fervent and scrupulous when it comes to their adopted religion — you just watch the behaviour from now on of the Duchess of Whatever across the water who came over to us recently. Converts are far more strait-laced than the people who are born into it. We take it for granted. We know it's always there for us if and when we decide to flop back after taking a walk on the wild side, but they're so fervent they won't put a toe out of line. It's all so new and exciting for them they take it terribly seriously.

I hope, by the way, you don't think I'm totally anti-religion. I'm not. It's just not for me, that's all. I'm the first to admit that there are some terrific priests – Father McVerry with his homeless boys, for instance, or the Franciscans on Merchants Quay with their Aids patients. All those other quiet men who work out of the public eye and who genuinely see their God in the poor and the destitute and the prisoners. My beef is with the rest of them who are always watching out for someone else's sin and trying to protect the whole of Ireland from it.

The clincher for me in my father's case comes when you add Dorothy's conversion to the way he was brought up by the kind of people who'd call a kid Bonaventure. (In the matter of his own family, though, I have to say that Esther isn't at all bad – and, of course, neither is Angela. I wonder what the rest of their children are called. One huge plus in this whole affair – it's only now it's dawning on me. *Seven* half-siblings. An entire tribe all at one go! If I ever get to meet them . . .)

Look at it this way – even if you didn't *want* to be standing outside cinemas waving rosary beads you'd have found it very difficult to stand up to them all, wouldn't you? Especially if you were someone with a guilty con-science, like him.

Or am I just making excuses for him? Is this just another of my stupid fantasies?

It was a good idea to come outside – I can feel myself calming down. Mountjoy Park is a hive of slow Sunday activity. The usual knot of geezers watching the world. The breeze waving through the leaves on the trees, kids tumbling, parents reading the papers. A knot of backpackers unrolling everything out of enormous rucksacks on to the grass as if they're setting up house. There's a youth hostel in the square and we get a lot of foreign kids around here. God love them, they haven't a clue that they're taking their lives in their hands walking down Gardiner Street. They're so sweet and blond and vulnerable, with their little padlocks which swing and bob around on the straps of their packs like neon invitations flashing, me, me, mug me! Sure they're not even a challenge to the gurriers around here.

One of them, a kid of about seventeen or eighteen, maybe, would remind you of Tom Bennett from the back. The same coppery hair colour.

You know, I've never lost a yen to find out whatever happened to him afterwards – I suppose you always feel that about your first love. Whatever, I'm dying for this backpacker to turn around so I can see if it's only the hair. I'm sitting there and I'm willing him to turn and then I cop myself on. Here I go, slithering back to the past again. Is this some sort of protective thing? That when the present gets unbearable you slip away to things you can control in your imagination? No wonder there are so many happy people in lunatic asylums.

Out of the blue, I start to daydream about one fantastic evening Tom Bennett and I spent together just before the end.

It was the time we went to the airport.

Now, on the surface that might not appear to be a very romantic date, but wait until you hear.

He'd warned me to wear my best clothes, so I put on one of Mammy's linen dresses, the cream one, and a black velvet bolero the babysitter lent me for the occasion.

That was one thing about the flats. We all mucked in, any of us who were on friendly terms. She'd agreed to babysit James for the whole evening, from tea-time on. She was the eldest in the flat next door so there was no problem about her walking home. We didn't have to be back until midnight.

When he turns up to collect me, I see he wasn't joking about us wearing good gear. He has on the famous crocodile jacket and the tight black jeans. And again his contacts in instead of his glasses.

Where are we going? I ask him, as we walk through the entryway.

Just wait and see, he goes, with this mysterious smile.

This dream date didn't begin very well. For a start, we had to wait nearly forty-five minutes for the 41 out to the airport, and even when it came, the journey took for ever. By the time we got out there, I can tell you I was pretty cranky. I just couldn't see the point, I kept telling him, of getting dressed up just to go out and look at a lot of aeroplanes. And having to spend half the evening on a bus, to boot!

He didn't lose his good humour for a single minute, though, and when we eventually got there, even though I was still grumbling – for God's sake, why can't we just go to the pictures like normal people, that kind of thing – he whisked me up the escalator.

Then he turns me and steers me into the restaurant. Not the self-service, the real one, the Silver Lining, with white tablecloths and cloth serviettes and a thick carpet on the floor.

But that isn't the end of the surprise. The second we arrive, we're welcomed like we're royalty and led over to a table by the window where we could look out at the planes. There's a bottle of wine in a silver bucket (on legs) already cooling beside that table, and at the place where

I'm put sitting, a little posy of flowers tied up in a white ribbon.

I'm struck dumb. Especially since I'd given him such a hard time about the whole thing. I've never been in a restaurant like this in all my life. The nearest I'd come to it was the lobby of the Gresham.

It's so peaceful. After the mayhem outside in the airport proper, in here is sort of an expensive hush. A murmur. You can barely hear even the engines of the aeroplanes you could see outside the wall of glass windows, which run all along one side. Is this all right for you, madam, sir? The man – small, dicky bow, dress suit – who's shown us to our table has this delighted smile on his face, like he's in on some great secret. He is, too. Turns out one of the fellows Tom Bennett plays football with is a trainee chef in this restaurant and the whole thing has been arranged in advance.

We sit down. Luckily I know how to behave – the benefit of listening to Mammy's stories again. I know about letting the waiter put my serviette on my lap and about using cutlery from the outside in and crumbling your bread instead of cutting it and so forth, although this is the first time I'd ever had to do it. Tom Bennett is watching me and learning from me. I always knew you were a lady, deep down, he whispers. His eyes are shining. Do you like it?

Like it? I go – I love it! It's brilliant.

We deserve a bit of a treat. Stick with me, kid, he goes, the sky's the limit. No pun intended!

The whole thing is almost too good – you know the way that can sometimes happen? How you can get overwhelmed so you can't react properly and it's only the next day or even the next week that you realize what's really happened.

The food is great. He lets me order, although to tell

you the truth I'm taking a wild stab at some things. Like
paté, for instance — a first. Then lovely thick soup — the
soup spoons are *enormous* — then fresh salmon, another
first, with some kind of sauce. We finish with ice cream
and then coffee out of tiny cups. Espresso. I have to
pretend I like it although I feel it's like licking tarmaca-
dam. The wine was difficult for me too, those days, I was
a Bacardi and Coke person.

After the meal he takes me into the bar. *Hopping!* The
counter is like a river, because the barmen are so rushed
off their feet they have barely time to fill out pints never
mind clean off the slops. Within minutes, my eyes are
sore from the smoke — people apparently smoke like
crazy before they get on planes. We have to shout to be
heard but it's a great buzz.

We can't find seats or a table so he puts me in a position
by the wall near the bank of windows where we can watch
all the action. Then he goes off to order — a small brandy
each.

He comes back with the drinks and we sip them and
I'm smelling the flowers in my posy and I'm feeling
terribly sophisticated and happy. I'm on such a high —
thrilled skinny that Tom Bennett would go to all this
trouble for me. He puts an arm around my shoulders.
Enjoying yourself?

Fantastic, I go.

He puts on an accent, like W. C. Fields. I brought you
here, m'dear, because some day all of this will be yours.
Then, right into my ear, Next time we're in here
together, we won't be in here just looking. We'll maybe
be going on our honeymoon, what?

You can imagine what that did to my equilibrium. It
was certainly one of the happiest evenings of my life.

And then, of course, not too long after, I give him

his walking papers. Ah, well, some things are just not to be.

The backpacker with the coppery hair has lain down on the grass now and put an open book over his face as though he's going to have a snooze. So I won't get to see if he does or does not resemble Tom Bennett. I'd still love to meet him again, just for a natter, see how he turned out.

There's still some time to kill so I decide to start walking up to the hospital. I take the long way around, Dorset Street, Whitworth Road and Phibsboro Road. It's hotter than I reckoned, though, and by the time I get to the Mater, I'm in a lather. It's not only the heat. I still haven't figured out the correct approach in telling James about Father Pius.

But James pre-empts me. He's sitting on the side of bed, waiting. He's dressed. He's being released.

This is not entirely a welcome development. For a start, I haven't a thing in the house to feed him with. Oh, I go, how come? What about that last test?

He's been told Casualty's jammed, the nurses are under strength, they need the bed. He's to contact his family doctor about the test. It's not essential that he be here for the results. Anyone who's able to put two feet under him is being sent home today.

Right, I go. Now I'm thinking, We'll have to take a taxi – more money! – because he isn't well enough to walk. And those poor old photographs of Mammy are taking another trip home unseen. I'll show them to him when we get home, it'll be something for us to do.

No chance – because when the taxi pulls up in front of the flat, who's sitting on the steps?

Patsy.

Her hair is stringy, her Goldie Hawn face is scrunched

up and woebegone like a monkey's. Ominously, she has a big black rubbish bag with her, it's bulging full but she's clutching the top of it as though she's afraid it'll blow away.

I'm astonished at the rush of savagery I feel looking at her. Normally I'd be barging over to console her, to ask her what's wrong, but the minute I see her I develop this hard ball of angry air in the middle of my chest that's puffing up and wants to explode. I'm *delighted* she's going to be confronted with the sight of James.

I help James out of the taxi – he's still wearing the splint and the sling on his arm and he's finding it difficult to move the rest of his body with the pain in his ribs. But then, of course, with her sitting there, he won't let me help him up the steps.

Hello, Patsy, I say, as civilly as I can when we get up next to her, what brings you here?

She doesn't answer me. Instead she bursts into tears. Not ordinary crying, big crying. Sobbing. As if she doesn't care a hoot who sees her making a show of herself. God, I hate scenes. Come in, I say quickly, come on in.

We all go up the stairs – the stink of cats' urine is particularly bad today, or maybe I'm just noticing it more. James is pulling himself up with his good arm via the banisters, Patsy is still wailing. You get the picture. I can't wait to get into the flat and close the door behind us, I can hear the neighbours listening. As if we weren't notorious enough! I discover I'm not being paranoid about this because as I reach our flat, I hear a small click. I look just in time to see the handle on Dwyer's door coming back to its normal position.

I get us all in. Patsy collapses on to the bed-settee, buries her head, storms away. James looks as though he wants to run back to the hospital as fast as he can. I don't think he's ever before seen a grown person go on like this. She'll be all right, I say to him above the hullabaloo, you go on into your room, I'll bring you in something to drink in a few minutes. Lie down and take a rest, all right?

He looks at her again, then goes into the room and closes the door after him. Patsy hears the slam and glances up. Her face is covered in bright red blotches. She looks terrible. At least she's trying to control herself now. I'm soh-ho-horry, she goes, hiccuping, I'm re-he-heally so-ho—

I sit down at the table and look at her, as though she's an interesting species. Seeing someone upset like this, I'd usually be in bits weeping along with them but I don't feel a thing.

I'm a bit shocked, this new me is as hard as concrete. I know exactly how I should be behaving. I should be asking her gently to tell me what's wrong, even putting my arms around her. I think about doing that, I even see myself doing it, but I don't move from my chair. It wouldn't be honest.

Because right now I feel no friendship towards her at all. If anything, as well as this huge anger in the middle of my chest, I'm more than a little irritated that she's turned up like this when I've so much on my plate already. It hits me that I have something in common with Rosemary Madden after all, this hard, hot sensation is what revenge must feel like.

At last Patsy twigs something's unusual and that she's not getting the reception she obviously expected. Stops crying. Gazes at me with bloodshot, streaming eyes.

I know I shouldn't have turned up without warning like this—

Don't worry about it, I say.

She sits back on the settee and looks at her two hands in her lap. I've left him, she says, I've left the bastard.

Is that your luggage? I go, looking at the black plastic

bag. And what about the children? Does Martin know you've come here?

I'll sort all that out when I get fixed up. She looks at me sort of sideways. Are you all right? You seem a bit peculiar.

Tell me about Martin, I say back. I have no intention of getting into any personal discussions with her about myself. I stand up. Will I make you a cup of tea? I'm afraid we're out of biscuits.

She blows her nose. I'm sorry, Ange, I'm putting you out – and I know my timing couldn't be worse.

Not at all. Tea?

Yes, please, tea would be nice. Her voice is all quavery.

She sits staring through the window while I go through the motions. It would be in my nature to fill this silence, to chatter and yammer and try to cover up for any embarrassment there might be between us. But this new hard Angela does no such thing. I rinse out the teapot with hot water and get great satisfaction out of every little ping and clang. I don't say one word. I don't even look over my shoulder to see how she is now. I don't give a sugar actually. In a way it's a lovely clean feeling, very uncomplicated. Like a clear blue flame. And very calming.

I'm thinking the two of them deserve each other, her and Martin.

Are you very angry with me? Is that it?

Damn. I start to weaken. It's the smallness of the voice that does it. Patsy's usual voice would get on your nerves half the time, it's so cheerful and bubbly. This voice is like an orphan's.

After all, she was a good friend all these years. And she turned up to Mammy's funeral when she didn't have to. And she gave me flowers afterwards and came to see me in her lunch hours, to help me get through the grief. And it was her got all the gigs for PA System – she didn't have to have me on board, since singing talent is ten a penny in this city, she could have taken on someone much more dynamic. She took me because of our friendship.

Like hell I'm going to cave in completely, though. I turn towards her, swishing the hot water round and round in the teapot while behind me the noise of the kettle starts that roaring it gives off prior to boiling. You're right, Patsy, I say, I'm very angry with you. And I think you know why. I'm sorry for your present trouble but make no mistake about it, I'm very angry.

She looks back at me. If you could imagine one of those tiny dogs. The kind you can fit into a teacup – a chihuaha, is it? All eyes and scrawny faces.

It's James. Are you angry with me about James?

I swish the water out of the teapot into the sink. Bingo, I say. Right first time.

There's something you don't know, she says.

Try me. I put a spoonful of tea into the hot teapot.

She tells me then that an uncle of hers sexually assaulted her when she was eleven. Wouldn't you think she would have told me that before? When we were racking our brains about sexual assault statistics? So much for us being best friends! I look back at her. I'm imagining a little eleven-year-old body, real straight, without breasts, with lovely smooth skin. And a big hairy man.

But nothing happens. Instead, I receive an image of James and his Technicolored face and his poor battered body.

The kettle snaps off.

That's terrible, Patsy, I say. That's really terrible, an awful thing to have happened. I can imagine how you must have suffered. But it has nothing to do with James and me. I pour the boiling water onto the tea-leaves in the teapot.

✦ Thirty-Two ✦

Naturally I said she could stay.

Funny, I stopped being angry as soon as I started to lay down the ground rules. Yes, I was sorry that she'd been sexually assaulted, but it could have no bearing on what I was worrying about right now. My opinion on James was clear and just as she didn't want to discuss that situation, I didn't want to discuss hers of twenty-five years ago. I'd discuss her and Martin, of course, if that was her wish.

And this was James's home. It's not a castle, Patsy, I said, but it's the only home he has. He's not to be made feel uncomfortable in it.

Then, when I saw the way she looked after all this, I couldn't continue. Here was Patsy, my leader, meekly saying, Yes, Ange, and No, Ange, like I was the mother superior and she the new postulant. To stay angry at this beaten person would have been like taking a pickaxe to Bambi.

Why did you come here? I ask her, when we've settled down to have our cups of tea. Why didn't you go to your ma's house? Patsy's mother lives only a mile or so away from her, in Old Cabra.

I couldn't face her, Patsy says back. Anyway, she wouldn't be interested.

She's still snuffling a bit. She blows her nose hard.

Sorry, she goes, I'm whining, aren't I. She blows her nose a second time and then her voice comes back on with some of its usual zip. We'd get on each other's nerves after two minutes, she says. Oh, Ma'd love the drama of it all but she wouldn't be interested in the problem as such. She wouldn't be interested in me myself personally and how I felt.

As always, I find this kind of thing hard to believe, the woman was a mother, wasn't she? But I know of old that the relationship between these two is not brilliant. Privately, I've always believed the fault was more Patsy's than the ma's.

Patsy seems to resent that her mother doesn't want to play the little old granny. Remember I told you about the miniskirt and the dyed hair at Mammy's funeral? Well, the skirts are a bit longer now but the hair is still dyed and the face is still thick with make-up. According to Patsy, her mother spends most of her time playing golf or going to race meetings with her pals. It drives Patsy mad. She thinks her mother's get-up and lifestyle are completely inappropriate for a woman of her age and although she's never come right out with it, I believe that she wants her ma to be baking scones and planting herbaceous borders. We've had millions of arguments about it. It's illogical to me that while she herself always wanted the freedom to do her own thing – the gigs and driving her own car and having continental holidays and all the rest of it – she resents the older woman having the same desires. Or, more specifically, fulfilling those desires. Shove over, Patsy seems to be saying to her mother, it's my turn now.

But maybe I think that only because I would be so grateful at present to have any kind of a mother. Anyhow, it's between the two of them and I'm not going to help by interfering.

Whoever said that hot tea was the best drink for cooling you down was suffering from delusions, because drinking this one is making me feel hotter than ever. It's become so stifling in the flat that even the bluebottle crashing about against the windowpane is half-hearted about it. It wouldn't surprise me if we were about to have a thunderstorm. The sky outside the window is that dirty chrome colour, which is always ominous.

If you're staying, I say, you'll have to sleep with me, unless one of us sleeps on the floor.

Lucky the settee's a double, so, isn't it? She tries to smile but it doesn't work.

It occurs to me then that in all the years we'd known one another Patsy and I had never spent a night together. Kids nowadays have sleepovers and pyjama parties but who do you think I could have invited to the flats? To see what was going on in our place?

In other circumstances, for her to stay the night might have even been fun for Patsy and me. You know, sitting up all night, giggling and doing each other's hair and nails. That's what I hear from the women at work that their daughters do.

So tell me, I say.

The story is pretty pathetic. The row they were having on the night she came down to meet me in the fast-food place continued to rumble on until in the end it seems they weren't even sure what they were fighting about. Then, today, Martin tells Patsy he's going for a drink in the pub at lunch-time. She tells him he's to be home for his dinner at one. He says he won't, that he'll be back at closing time. She says if he isn't home at one o'clock she won't be here when he does come home . . .

Et cetera.

I hope I'm not making too little of the trauma she's

going through but I'm starting to feel impatient again. In
some ways, bad and all as he is, James inside there in the
bedroom is more mature than these two. As I'm listening
to the saga (and then he said . . . and then I said . . .), I
feel like yelling that the pair of them should just grow
up. So who cares if you have your dinner at one o'clock
or two o'clock or ten o'clock at night. I know infidelity's
awful, I know it is. But, from what she tells me, with
Martin it's only sex he's after with the others. Marriage
is more than sex, isn't it? But then I curb myself. Who
am I to talk about marriage? I'm the hurler on the ditch.

She has to get it out of her system, I know – but as I
listen on and on, as she goes through every little detail of
every awful thing he's ever done to her, my attention
starts to wander . . .

I think I told you I never liked Martin, didn't I? I
probably didn't tell you one of the main reasons for it,
though, because up to now I wouldn't have wanted to let
Patsy down.

The so-and-so once tried to grope me. Imagine! At
their Christmas drinks party. In Patsy's own house. With
Patsy herself inside in the sitting room.

I was in the kitchen breaking ice out of the ice trays to
put into this joke ice bucket they have in the shape of a
top hat. It's a devil of a job getting ice out, isn't it? I was
effing and blinding under my breath – I don't swear out
loud but when I'm giving out to myself it's a different
matter – because I'd just broken off two of the false nails
Patsy had given me as a present.

I've half of it out when your man comes up behind me.
I don't hear him until I feel these arms going around me
from behind and these hands nuzzling my breasts. Oh,
Angela, he whispers into my ear, you've got the most
gorgeous knockers, I've always wanted to do this—

He didn't get a chance to do any more because I back-kicked him in the shins. Little get. No, I never liked Martin.

It was nice of Patsy to invite me to go to Minorca with them but, to tell you the truth, my idea of hell would be to be cooped up with Martin. Anyway, they'll hardly be going to Minorca now . . . I'm lucky in some ways that James is the central relationship of my life and that I don't have a husband to worry about. How would you divide your loyalties? It must be very stressful to have more than one person to put first.

Patsy's still talking, I try to tune in. She's now beginning to worry about how Pauline and Maeve and Darren are getting on. About time she thought about her children, but I'm really wondering if it will ever be the same between us. I'm cast in the role of constantly listening to her and her problems – and boy, have I listened! – but now, when I need help with the biggest problem I've ever had, she can't hack it.

I know friendship is not about tit-for-tat, and I don't want it to be, but a bit of two-way would be nice occasionally.

She stops talking. Abruptly. Glances sideways at me. I know what you're thinking, she says. You're still thinking I haven't been sympathetic enough about yours and James's predicament.

Each time this happens, when she picks up what I'm thinking, it does give me a land. As a matter of fact, yes, I say, I was thinking something along those lines.

I'm very sorry, she goes. My attitude was probably wrong. Can you forgive me?

I stare back at her. I think of the innocent days, all the long years of innocence we had together. Of course I forgive you, I say. Slowly. Trying to sound as warm and sincere as I should be about this. Because there's no point in continuing this resentment against her, she just wouldn't understand.

It was that 'probably' that did it. She thinks she was 'probably' wrong. I know for certain now that we'll never get back to where we were. It's a real tragedy.

Patsy sees what she wants to see. Great, she says. Old friends are best, eh, Ange? I'm really grateful to you for all you're doing for me. I know it's hard for you to understand how hurt you can get within a marriage.

Patronising or *what*?

She's off and all I have to do again is nod and look grave. But she has triggered something. Old friends? What old friends? She's the only old friend I have. Actually the only friend I ever had. I was so busy with James and with just plain surviving that I never had time to develop friendships. Or (might as well be honest) I'd kept such a tight wall around myself and James that I'd kept any possible friends out. Maybe lack of friends runs in our family, I don't remember Mammy having any friends, besides the 'friends' that she brought home to the flat. And as for James's so-called friends, they aren't so hot in the loyalty and support department, are they?

I realize Patsy's looking at me, waiting for an answer to some question. What? I go, sorry, Patsy, I wasn't paying attention.

She sighs. She's coming back a little towards the old bossy Patsy. I was asking you what are the cops doing about the assault?

I don't know. I shrug. Probably what they do about all assaults. Very little. James didn't recognize any of the photographs they showed him. But since you ask . . .

Might as well go the whole hog, I think, as I get up and go over to my handbag, extract the Dear Scumbag letter from it. What do you think I should do with this?

She glances down at it, reads it, but it doesn't seem to

have the effect on her that it had on me. It's horrible, of course, she says, but I wouldn't get too upset about it. It's just par for the course. Look, she says then, do you mind if I say something?

Depends what it is, I say. (Uh-oh! I don't think I want to hear this—)

It's about James.

What about James? I tense up.

She gets all earnest. Despite what you think, she says, I do understand how you feel. You're probably not going to like what I'm going to say next but I've honestly been wanting to say it to you for a long time.

Go ahead, I say. But I don't want her to go ahead. Not now or in the future. This is not going to be helpful.

She doesn't notice anything in my tone of voice or if she does she ignores it. There comes a time, she says, when kids have to own up to their own failures. He got into trouble with a girl and the law, he should be punished for it. It's only right. It'll make a man of him, Angela.

I'm transfixed. Cold feet are marching up and down my spine. I can't identify yet whether it's from anger, outrage, panic, shame — what . . .

It's something to do with that word punish. The humiliation, the submission of it. I can't stand it. It's a word I *hate*. Along with retribution. I could never cope with reading anything in the papers or books about something as cold-blooded as official retribution. I've never been able to understand how Nazi-hunters can keep that flame burning for fifty years and for one second I can't contemplate the death penalty, even arguments about it. It's far too cold-blooded. I dream frequently about being hanged, I may have told you. It's my recurring nightmare.

I'm the type who could be mugged and then when I'd

see the guy who's mugged me in court, I'd immediately drop the charges. I'd see how nervous he is, I'd start thinking about what's facing him in gaol, his sorrow and loneliness, the pain of his mother, and that'd be me gone. I guess that makes me a very weak person. I'm certainly aware there's no logic to the way I think, particularly when I'm the person who so recently liked the taste of what I perceived as revenge. As human beings go, I'm quite a conundrum to myself. But, quite definitely, where James is concerned I'd rather die than see him 'punished'. I find it difficult even to say the word.

For once, Patsy doesn't pick up what's going through my head. She's looking at me but not seeing me, she's off on a crusade to convince me. James is a big boy now – what age is he? Nineteen? You'll have to let go, Ange, let him make his mistakes and pay for them himself. If dreadful things happen to him, well, they happen to us all and we all have to fend for ourselves eventually.

She stops as though she's waiting for an answer. I can't give one.

Amn't I right? Patsy says. You do too much for that boy. What'd he do if you were hit by a bus in the morning?

You're absolutely right, I say. But what I'm thinking is, what do you know? It's easy for you, I'm thinking, you smug little bitch, with your two point ten children and their ballet and swimming lessons and gymnastics and horse-riding and car pools. And your husband with his contacts and his cash economy. And your family holidays to Minorca and your terrific kitchen and your 'doing things as a family' and your bloody top-hat ice bucket. Bad and all as Martin is, he's your children's father and he does love them. That much I do know. There's two of you sharing the burden. Doesn't he bring them to football matches? Even the girls? Doesn't he help with the car pools when he's at home?

You're absolutely right, I say again.

It gives me no pleasure saying this, she shakes her head sorrowfully, and I'm not going to preach to you. I've said my say and, of course, it's up to you what you do.

She stands up. Look, I'm going to go outside to the phone box to ring home. You're right, I'm being selfish. The kids'll be worrying.

I hadn't heard myself saying anything about her being selfish.

Now she's shaking her head again, vigorously this time. But I'm not going home. Hell'll freeze over before I go back to that bastard. She leaves the flat.

She'll go home. Probably the minute she comes back in.

She hasn't left the flat ten seconds when *crack!* a huge clap of thunder rocks the place. It's followed by an instant deluge, so loud it drowns out the sound of the bus engine which has been revving outside at the traffic lights. Good. She'll be soaked. Good enough for her.

I rush over to the window to close it. It's already too late, the curtains are wet. I don't care, the wetter the better. How dare she? How dare she invade the private relationship between James and me?

But then I have to admit that it's not entirely Patsy's fault. At some very deep level I'm furious because something I've been maybe thinking about in tiny little dribs and drabs has been brought out in the open like this. What she said has impinged and it's shame-making.

Before I know it, I'm in James's room. The rain is just as loud in here, even though his window is shut tight. The air is so humid, you'd feel you'd nearly need windscreen wipers to see through it.

Did the cops ever get back to you about that assault?
Have you done anything about it yourself?

He's lying on his bed with his hands behind his head.
He has his Walkman on. He sees me come in and takes
off the headset. Is she gone?

Temporarily, I say. Answer the question. Did they
come back to you?

Did who come back to me?

The cops. Did they come back to you about the
assault?

No. He turns away from me and lies with his face to
the wall. Look, leave me alone. I don't care whether
they come back to me or not. I don't care about any of
it.

I look at his thin back. I notice that the cast on his arm
is getting grubby. I'm testing out what Patsy said to me.
I'm trying to be objective and to see this person as a
young man who has to take care of his own problems.
I'm trying not to see him as James. Trying very hard.

I hear myself saying, All right, James, I will leave you
alone.

Good, he goes.

In a minute, after we've talked—

I don't feel like talking.

I can feel my top teeth grinding into my bottom ones.
I insist, I say. I'm not leaving until you turn around.
Please turn around and look at me.

Go away.

How many times do I have to tell you? I won't go
away. Turn around.

All right! *What?* He spins in the bed and glares at me.
But for once he isn't intimidating me. I just want to talk,
I say as calmly as I can, that's all.

Well, go ahead, talk. Hurry up. What do you want to
talk about?

This isn't easy, James. Please don't make it harder. What have I ever done to you that you should be as hostile as this to me?

For Christ's sake, he says, if you've something to say to me, say it. Why is everything always about *you*?

Now it comes pouring out. That's just it, I say. This is about me and it's about time I talked about me. Your days of hanging out of me are numbered, James. I'm a person. I'm a human being. I'm not just an anonymous robot who's here to support you and to pick up the pieces after you mess up. It's time you stood on your own two feet. You're nineteen and I'm tired of supporting you. I'm not your mother, you know, I'm only your sister — and I'm a woman. I'm tired of being taken for granted, I want my own life.

This is a jolt to my system. I didn't know I felt like this. But I find I mean it. Saying it has made me discover that I mean it.

Most of it, anyhow. What about the bit about not being his mother? I suppose, technically speaking, I mean that too, but it's sort of splitting hairs, isn't it? He didn't come out of my womb and that does give you an extra special bond. Maybe it's because I wasn't ever a mother that I can't imagine how a mother could feel any more love for a son than I feel for James. (Being a mother of a criminal must be torture.)

Someone in the street lets out a scream. They must be getting caught in the rain, which seems to be lashing down louder and louder.

Looking at James's expression, I'm in danger of starting to feel sorry for him as usual. I've never spoken to him this way in my life. I've lashed out, yelled, said things I didn't mean, called him names. But this is different, this has the ring of absolute truth. He knows it. The shock on his face is genuine.

Before I can weaken, I carry on. You've had a raw deal in your life, I know that, I say firmly. I'm sorry about it, but I've done the best I can. I'm exhausted, James.

His bruised eyes are wide. I know you're not my mother, Angela, he says. He hardly ever uses my name.

I read somewhere about the best way to deal with situations like this. When you have an advantage, don't use it.

Right, I say, I think I've made my point. Would you like a cup of tea or something?

Yeah, he whispers. He's still looking at me.

I go out into the kitchen. I start to shake as I'm filling the kettle. And I still have to tell him about Pius.

Damn Patsy.

→ Thirty-Three ←

Monday morning. Still haven't told James, but my father has come up with a plan. When I hear it I'm in two minds about it. To put it mildly.

At first I rejected it outright. It seemed so outlandish. I'll give him this much, he's nothing if not a lateral thinker!

I ring him from a phone box outside an office block I've just helped to clean. This booth is along the Grand Canal, near Mount Street Bridge. The rain is bashing hell out of the metal roof — we've had nearly eighteen hours of it at this stage — and the road is clogged with rush-hour traffic. He's whispering at his end, but even if he'd been shouting I'd be finding it hard to hear him.

After due consideration, he's saying, his best advice would be that James should go down to the monks in the abbey at Mount Melleray. That he would arrange it. It would give you and James breathing space, he says. It'd take him out of the fray for a while until things calm down a bit.

I'm sorry, Mr Crawford, I say, it's very noisy here, you'll have to speak up a bit. Did I hear you right? Did you say something about monks?

Instead of speaking louder he slows down. I . . . know . . . the . . . Abbot, I . . . know . . . him . . . personally

. . . and . . . I've . . . taken . . . him . . . into . . . my
. . . confidence . . .

Monks? Abbots?

Can I think about it? I say.

Take all the time in the world, he says back. His voice
has got stronger – I can hear the relief. I haven't hit the
roof. I'm going to agree to us being nicely packaged away
from his nice life. James will wear sackcloth and ashes in
a monastery until all the publicity blows over. And, of
course, the main beauty of this great plan is that the two
of us, particularly me, can be safely kept away from
Tullamore. You have my office number now, he says. All
it'll take is a telephone call and we're all set.

Mr Crawford, I say quickly, I'm not sure about—

A motorcyclist – it'd have to be a courier, of course –
zooms past the line of traffic on the inside. Right through
the lake which extends six feet out from the kerb where
I'm standing. I'm soaked up to the chest.

Sorry, I say. Look, can I ring you back? There's too
much noise here—

I can hear he's put the receiver very close to his mouth
now. Would it be possible, Angela, that we could keep
this between the three of us? For the time being, that is.

If it wasn't James and me involved here it would be
almost endearing. I don't find it endearing. Does
Dorothy know? I ask him. Up to this summer I'd had no
idea I could be so bitchy.

Bull's-eye.

Dorothy? he goes, and I can hear the fright. Er –
not yet. Then, in a rush, But of course I'm going to tell
her.

Of course, I say. I'll telephone you back sometime
later on today. I smash down the telephone. Lucky for
me this phone is one of the vandal-proof ones.

A monastery – the very idea!

I call into the Fitzgibbon Street Guards on my way home. No developments in the assault case.

I wasn't really expecting any, was I? When what they're looking for is someone, or a group of someones, giving just deserts to a rapist. I'm getting bitter now? So be it.

It occurs to me to ask this Guard I'm talking to if there would be any difficulty about James going to a monastery – not that I'm agreeing he should go to any monastery, far from it, but just in case . . .

Could it go hard on him next year with the judge if we started cancelling his counselling sessions? (From the little he's said about the first one, I'd be afraid his counsellor will just cement his prejudices about women having it every way, these days. Reading between the lines, she struck me as a feminist first and a counsellor second, more interested in making sure he accepts that men are scum and women are saints. Mind you, that's James talking and I haven't met the woman.)

This Guard can't see what objection there could be to him going to Mount Melleray, apparently once the court case is over, the cops, technically speaking, have no more to do with it. And if we need the lad to identify anyone, he goes, we'll know where he is.

I get home and I broach the subject of the monastery with James. You think my reaction was anti? I leave his to your imagination. Ballistic doesn't cover it. Very little of it is printable.

I'm to forget it, he's not for a second going to go to any bleedin' bog-arsed monastery, no way José, forget it, *forget* it! That's just a small flavour.

Would you believe I find myself arguing with him, as if I'm in love with this notion? Could he at least think about it? Like, has he any better ideas?

I'll think about it all right, he says, in your dreams. It's my life, you know. At least it was when I looked the last time. *I*'ll decide what I'll do and when I'll do it. Whose bleedin' looper idea was this?

Mine.

I've funked it again.

Bleedin' airhead, he yells. I'll decide, right? Not you or anyone else. He storms off into his room.

I go about the place like a dervish, tidying up. I should be the one to go to Mount Melleray, get a bit of peace for myself, leave him to his own devices, the pup. Does he not realize the pickle he's in, that everyone's only trying to help? I wasn't joking when I asked if he had any better ideas. I certainly can't come up with any. What are we going to do? Wait for the knock on the door? The next ambush in another laneway? I see now it was pie in the sky that the two of us should go and live in a cosy cottage someplace, with me in a new job. What am I qualified for? How many contract cleaning companies are there in rural Ireland?

I'm like a mad thing, pulling all the books off the shelves to dust them, squirting Jif over everything in sight. I throw the cushions off the bed-settee to clean underneath them – and there's one of Patsy's earrings.

I stop, calm down. In a way I'm glad I've found this, in a way I'm not. It means I'll have to contact her again to let her know I found it.

I want to see her because I can't bear to have bad blood between us, I don't want to see her because we'll never be friends again. At least, not like we were. I suppose I could post it to her in a Jiffy-bag . . .

I stand there looking at the golden circlet in the palm of my hand. It's in the shape of a dolphin, chasing its tail. Patsy has a thing about dolphins and Martin bought her these earrings for their tenth anniversary.

Yesterday afternoon when she comes back from the

phone box after ringing home, she's like a drowning
kitten, her mascara is running down her face and her
bouffant hairdo is as flat as straw. She's frantic. It rang
and rang, she says, but there was no answer. Where are
they all? I have to go home and see where they all are.

This is the person who was never going back, never,
no way, who didn't care what they did, any of them.
She'd even got the operator to try to make sure it was
really ringing and that it wasn't out of order.

Hang on a sec, I say, you're soaked. I give her a towel
to scrub her hair – this is obviously when the earring
came off. She's scrubbing away and she's half crying.
They should be there, we weren't going anywhere today
– I have to go home right away. Sorry, Ange – I guess
you think I'm really off the wall.

Not at all, Patsy, I say.

She's racing out of the flat. The front doorbell rings.
She gallops down the stairs, me after her.

Yep. You're right. It's Martin. Half hangdog, half
aggressive. Hey, Pats, he goes, I knew you'd be here. I
have the kids in the car.

Splat! She gives him a box. Right in the face. Then she
throws herself at him, arms around the neck, sobbing, all
that, with the front door open and the rain creasing the
pavement outside and me standing there like a third leg.
If this is marriage you can have it.

I'm still looking down at this earring, I can't make up
my mind. So I put it in one of the presses, safely inside a
broken cup that we don't use.

Where is this place anyway? It's James, the door has
opened without me hearing it. I have my back to him and
I turn around. He's standing in the doorway with a
belligerent face on him. I haven't a clue, I go, I'd have to
buy a map.

Forget it. Don't bother. Slam! He's gone back into his room.

We're obviously making progress of sorts. If that's what I really want. Dammit, a monastery? Angela Devine? James Devine? How come I find myself on Pius Crawford's side? It's because I'm desperate, that's why.

I still hadn't rung him back by eight o'clock that evening and neither James nor I had brought up the subject of Mount Melleray again. Then the decision was made for us.

First, a brick came through the window. A half brick to be precise. I suppose because we're on the first floor a whole brick would have been too difficult to aim properly. We were watching television and things were fairly frosty between us. We were letting the telly do the talking.

I was getting fed up of it and as usual, I decided to make the first move in the ice-breaking department. I was walking across the room to fetch Adeline's photographs to show him when the window shattered. It seems he's destined never to see those bloody snaps.

The noise of a brick coming through your window is shocking, absolutely shocking. I wouldn't wish it on my worst enemy. It's like a bomb going off inside your head. This huge explosion and then all this glass crashing onto hard surfaces.

We both duck.

Then – I suppose this shows our different personalities – I run to the window in an effort to see who threw it, while James curses and swears and then barrels out the door and down the stairs.

To me, everything outside looks normal. People standing under umbrellas at the bus stop. Cars swishing by. Trees dripping dark green in the park across the street. No one legging it as far as I can see . . . And it's a cliché, I know, but where are the Guards when you need them? I wouldn't mind but lately, particularly since that journalist was murdered, they're foot-patrolling much more than they used to around here.

I can't see James. Whoever it was must have run the other way, towards Dorset Street. Immediately I find myself worried sick that whoever James might be chasing could have a knife. Even a gun. Guns are ten a penny in Dublin these days. Any gurrier with a twenty-pound note seems to be able to hire one for the night.

Have you ever noticed that if you drop even a small drinking glass how much of it there seems to be when it breaks? Huge chunks of the stuff had come in on top of the sink, slivers of it have stuck into the soles of my shoes, I can't see them but each step produces tiny crunches.

Bits of brick had scraped off against the sides of the sink, crumbs caught in the ruching of the curtains. I realize the rain is squalling in through the jagged glass, what's left of it, in the window, and I start looking around for something temporary to patch into it.

James comes back without any further damage to himself, thank God. Did he see anyone?

No.

He helps me clean up. With his good hand he fixes a piece of a cornflake packet over the hole in the window with Sellotape. Not that it's going to do much good in this rain.

That was item one on the menu for the evening. It wasn't long before we got to item two.

Guess who drops by unexpectedly, about forty minutes later. Our dear landlord, Mr Reddy, that's who. May I come in? He has on his grave face and he has his rent book in his hand. I know we're paid up to date so

I've no worries on that score. Behind me, James turns up the telly, an ad. That terrific one for Peugeot cars, search for the hero inside yourself. You'd have to laugh.

I'm not laughing, though. It's not convenient at the moment, I say, as firmly as I can. Reddy flushes up. Well, then, I'll say what I have to say out here, he says. I'm afraid I'm going to ask you to leave.

Leave?

Yes, leave. He has this naturally quavery voice and it's even more quavery than usual. I've had a number of complaints, he goes. And although I didn't know it until now – he's looking over my shoulder – I see you've broken a window . . .

Who were these so-called complaints from?

Never mind who they were from. I run a respectable establishment here.

Now why is that our Dwyer down the landing pops into my mind? He who just happens always to be on site when there's any trouble.

I know who the complaints were from, I say to Reddy, and however many there were, correct me if I'm wrong, I could take a wild guess that they were all from the same party. And all unjustified. Now, if you'll excuse me, I know my rights. I slam the door. Lean against it.

He's knocking again. I can feel the knocking against the middle of my back. I should have anticipated this, one of the other neighbours confided in me once on rent day that Reddy is a member of one of those super-Catholic outfits who lean to the right of the Ku Klux Klan. Maybe it's Pius Crawford's Catholic rights, ha ha!

Some Christianity he's showing at the moment, wouldn't you say?

I try to ignore the knocking. Stare at the telly. The Peugeot ad is over and here's one now for a programme coming up later in the week. It's for *Davis*. I don't watch

Davis often, even if I have charge of the television, but I wouldn't be too keen on it in any case because it's one of those panel discussion programmes about serious issues. At that time of night my brain is usually scrambled and I'm looking for something really naff where I don't have to think. Preferably with a few laughs.

Miss Devine, Miss Devine. I can hear Reddy's voice squeaking outside over Derek Davis's.

Derek Davis is staring at the camera from under his eyebrows. Date rape, he says, in a voice from the mummy's crypt. In the wake of the release on to the streets of James Devine—

James zaps the telly. He's sitting in his chair like it's Oul' Sparky and he's waiting for that switch to be thrown. Reddy is still knocking into my back. Miss Devine, I've every right – open this door. I've *every* right—

Shut up! I scream at the door, I hammer on it with both my fists, banging back at Reddy.

I'm going now but I'll be back tomorrow, he shouts through the door. Then he seems to wait. I hold my breath. The silence in the flat is deafening.

Next thing I can hear him walking away, going down the stairs. Our door thwacks a little as he slams the outside one.

I turn around and look at James. For all my big brave words, I know we're on a lost cause. I also know James knows – neither of us can stomach much more of this. He's trembling.

We can certainly fight being thrown out of our home if we have the guts for it. Tony Gregory is our local TD, he'd help us, he'd easily handle Reddy. And even though we haven't signed any contract, we've been here so long we have definite rights. Rights to proper notice, for instance.

What is the point, though, of staying in a place where

you're not wanted, where your neighbours want you out? It was different when I thought he might want to throw us all out in order to develop the place into yuppie apartments. That'd be easy to fight. But now we're pariahs. Now I know what it must feel like to be a drug dealer in the middle of the Concerned Parents' territory.

Will you get the hell down to that monastery, for God's sake? I say. Just for a while at least. (So much for principles . . .)

Eff off, he goes, I'm going near no monastery.

Leaving the time not exactly ripe for intimate discussions on the finding of fathers.

How I went to work the next morning, how I pushed that polisher around, I don't know. But, anyway, I did. I suppose when everything is crashing down around you it helps to keep to some kind of a routine. I did find myself going into daydreams, though. Like I didn't recognize my own hand at one stage. I gazed at it, this white, unfamiliar thing splayed against a yellow duster. Starfish?

To my astonishment, James is up and dressed when I get home. It's a different story this morning, every inch of bravado seems to have been sucked out of him. The telly isn't on and he isn't eating. He's sitting at the table staring into space.

What is it, James? Did something else happen?

Nothing happened.

What's up, then? Why are you just sitting there?

It's a free country, isn't it? But his heart isn't in it, he's as cowed as a whipped pup.

I put my bag down and glance with longing at the bed-settee. I'm so tired my eyes can't focus. I force myself to stay standing. James, I say gently, look at me.

He shakes his head. Gazes at his fists, balled on his knees.

I'm as sceptical about monks and monasteries as you

are, I say, but one thing I do know, they're lovely tranquil places. I'm positive you won't have to do the Catholic bit if you don't want to, they take everyone in – Muslims, Hindus, Jews, atheists – anyone who asks. They don't even ask you why. Think about it, James. You need a break from all this hassle. It won't be for long.

(If I'd thought last May, when this all started, that Angela Devine would be urging her brother to go to a monastery!) James doesn't respond or move. It's terrible to see him like this.

Slowly, he nods.

It's then I finally tell him about Pius. He listens quietly.

What do you think? I ask him at the end.

He's your da, he's nothing to do with me, is he? The hopeless expression in his eyes'd kill you.

By lunch-time that Tuesday a sort of recklessness has taken me over. I've pushed my tiredness into the background, I'm determined we're going to be well on our way out of Reddy's kip before he comes knocking again on our door.

Thank God it has at last stopped raining when I go down to the phone box to ring Pius Crawford. It'll have to be immediately, I tell him, tomorrow. There have been developments this end, and we have to leave our flat.

What kind of developments?

It'd take too long to tell you.

He'll be happy to make the arrangements. (I'll bet!) What time shall I tell them he'll arrive?

I'll have to find out about the buses, I say. Tell them sometime tomorrow afternoon or evening, that should cover it. Then I have to ask him where the blasted monastery is . . .

Angela, he goes, after he's finished telling me, please feel free to telephone me any time. His voice is hushed. We'll make arrangements to meet sometime soon, all right?

That'd be nice, I say.

He changes completely. Yes, thank you, I'll be in touch in the near future. Everything goes muffled, his hand has gone over the mouthpiece. He's talking to someone—

Here he is back, Thanks for everything, see you soon, God bless now, goodbye.

And, surprise surprise, I'm left with a dead telephone in my hand. This must be what it's like to be a married man's mistress.

✦ Thirty-Four ✦

The odd thing is, I find I'm not even upset about my father's reaction. Funny, isn't it? You spend half a lifetime wondering, and then when you galvanize yourself and get lucky enough to find him, it's like – well, what is it like?

I find I'm too exhausted to analyse my present feelings about Pius Crawford. I'm confused, certainly, but it's all too new. It took thirty-six years to get to this place, nothing is going to happen overnight and in all fairness he has to be given a bit of breathing space. On the other hand, he's not getting off the hook in the matter of my half-siblings. Sometime in the future I definitely want to meet my brothers and sisters. Definitely. That other Angela looked nice.

I decide I might as well take advantage of being in the telephone box. I ring Patsy and tell her she'll have to come and get her earring if she wants it, that I'd be afraid it'd get lost when we move.

She sounds shocked, as well she might. Move? What do you mean, move?

What I said. Move. You know, pantechnicons, packing.

Don't be like that. Why are you moving? Have you a place?

When I tell her no, to give her her due, she offers that James and I could stay with them until we get sorted out. Martin and I would love to have you.

I thank her for her offer but say we'll be fine. Hah! I'm thinking, Martin and I . . . Who was right? They're all lovey-dovey again. Until the next time.

I know what you're thinking, Angela, she says. You're thinking, what's going on with Martin and me – that there we were only yesterday—

I interrupt her. It's your business, Patsy. Look, I have to go, I've a lot of phone calls to make and I've to start packing. I'll be in touch. We'll be in tonight if you want to come for your earring.

I hang up.

For the rest of that day I couldn't shake off the feeling that James and I were making parcels of our lives. Putting everything in compartments and sealing them up, maybe even for ever.

Yet somehow, far from being momentous or tragic, the packing became gay. I should have been sad to leave, James and I had spent a long time in this place – James the greater part of his life. Bad and all as it was, it was home to us. Yet, despite all our problems and traumas, I was finding it a little exhilarating to think we were going to someplace new. I had got into a rut here.

I have to say that James did Trojan work, considering the plaster on his arm. And for the first time in ages we were working together as a team, the two of us having fun. We were consulting each other. What about this? (A raggedy cushion.) Nah! Out. Bam! The candlewick bedspreads? Uh-huh – gone! We became sort of feverish. Tearing papers, sweeping up drawersful of junk. This? (The Present from Tramore ashtray.) Out! Ornaments? All out. Why we ever needed ornaments – why anyone needs ornaments – I don't know.

When we'd cleared the bookshelves and stacked all the books in the middle of the floor, guess what fell out of *Macbeth*? My three-star scratch card in its envelope. I put it safely in my handbag.

I'd bought several packets of the jumbo-sized black rubbish bags. Leaving our clothes and toiletries until later – and my books because I'd have to get boxes for those – we reserved one pack to hold what we wanted to keep.

As it turned out, we didn't need the pack because everything we wanted to save fitted into two of the bags – yes, that's all, two! We divided our crockery and cutlery into what we needed to eat and drink and what were just spares. We kept four sets of sheets and four towels, a frying pan, our electric kettle and iron, our tin opener and a few spatulas, kitchen knives and serving spoons. James kept his precious CDs, his tapes and his ghetto-blaster. (And, would you believe, his baby toys. A rattle and a set of alphabet blocks I hadn't even known he had because they were buried so deep under the jumble of clothes in his wardrobe.) My lacquered tray, because wherever we end up, I don't want to give up my Saturday-afternoon deli snacks.

The whole process was most instructive. Two lives. Two whole lives totalling nearly fifty-six years and if you discount our clothes, the sum total of the possessions we really needed – or wanted – could fit into two jumbo-sized plastic bags. (Plus my books and it's arguable whether you need books. Certainly not at subsistence level – ask Mammy or any of her 'friends'.)

I look around. Are we sure we want nothing else?

I briefly consider Patsy's ruched curtains. No. A Present to Reddy.

The two of us do one last search but can find nothing more. What about the TV? All of a sudden, James is looking sad. What'll we do without a telly? And what about my bike?

The TV is Reddy's. If our new place, wherever it is, doesn't come with one we'll have to rent. Anyway, I tell him, you won't be looking at telly for a while where you're going!

All gaiety collapses. I could have bitten out my tongue. What about the bike? he's demanding now. I need that bike.

Look, you can get another one when your arm is better and when things settle down, I tell him. We can't keep it, you've got to see that. I'll ring the place you bought it from first thing tomorrow, tell them we can't keep up the payments. They'll take it back – thank God it's still in good condition.

He becomes really upset about that bike but what option did we have? I couldn't exactly bring a motorbike with me, neither could he, and it wasn't doing either of us much good chained up and attracting penalty interest on the payments.

Speaking of options, I'm in no position to have scruples about asking for help with the move – so who could I ask?

Guess.

James and I took turns that evening sitting by the window to watch for any bricks.

I finally gave him the photographs. He spread them out and looked at them but, as far as I could judge, they had little effect on him.

I'd been reading too much into what his reaction might be. He didn't know Mammy at all – I keep forgetting that and these were snaps of a long-ago little girl. Why don't you keep them, I suggest to him, bring them with you to Mount Melleray?

I'm thinking that maybe in the peace and quiet he'll be able to study them better and then they might begin to mean something to him. He simply shrugs, turns his attention back to the television. But I notice he bundles them as neatly together as a pack of cards.

At about ten o'clock, just before it got dark, I slipped out to go down to Ken Sheils's place. I wanted to ask him about moving us, I had a note ready to put in his mailbox in case he wasn't in.

I hadn't seen him since Birr and so much had happened in between that it felt like weeks and not just a couple of days – I mean, that trip had been on the Saturday and this was only the Tuesday evening . . .

I could see his window was open – it looks out on to the street. He was at home.

Hi, he says, after he buzzes me in. He's on the landing, hanging over the stairs. His voice is echoing in the stairwell even though he's talking just above a whisper so as not to draw the attention of the other residents.

Hi, I whisper back.

I'm breathless when I get up to his landing. (I don't like lifts. What if there's a fire?) I know it's late, I go, and I'm sorry to disturb you, but I was wondering if you would do me a favour tomorrow?

He hesitates. Birr again, is it? It'll have to be tomorrow night I'm afraid because I've a job.

No, it's not Birr. And tomorrow night would be perfect. We're moving out of our flat and I have a few bits and pieces that I'll need help with. I thought if you and your van were free . . .

I can't read the expression on his face, it's closed in. I assume he thinks this is a bit much to ask. I get embarrassed. Look, it doesn't matter, don't worry about it. I can get at taxi, it's not furniture or anything, we only have a few plastic bags, and books, they'll easily fit.

Of course don't get a taxi, he goes. Come in — would you like a cup of coffee?

It's on the tip of my tongue to refuse but then it flashes through my mind that I can't just keep asking this guy to do things for me while keeping him at arm's length.

Sam immediately jumps up on my lap when I'm in and sitting down. I stroke his silky little body. Ken goes into the kitchen section of the room, begins quietly to make the coffee. I'm really sorry about this, I go, I don't mean to keep using you like this just because you own a van—

I don't think you're using me at all.

It's just that, when I asked you, the expression on your face—

I was admiring how you looked. He doesn't turn around. He might as well have being telling me the price of coffee beans in Colombia.

I concentrate on Sam.

This guy invented silence. He feels no need to chatter when he has nothing to say. Whereas before, I guess, I found this to be rather an odd, even intimidating habit, now I find it restful. The quiet sort of radiates out from him.

All you can hear is the odd clink as he takes cups out, places spoons on the saucers. When he's silent like this, you don't feel you have to talk either. So I don't. (Quite a novelty for the Gabber Angela!) Inside, though, I'm giving myself a stern scolding. I'm telling myself I'll have to sort out the situation between Ken and me once and for all. All right, we're never going to be *Gone With The Wind*. But then, at my age, am I likely to find *Gone With The Wind*? I read stories all the time in *Hello!* about fifty- and sixty-year-olds who are head over heels about each other, *Romeo and Juliet* ('this one is for keeps'), so why not me?

Do I even want *Gone With The Wind*? I suppose

everyone does, to a degree – but we all know that it doesn't last and couldn't I settle for what seems to be on offer here? Good old-fashioned reliability, steadiness, companionship. And sex too. The sex was all right, wasn't it?

I can't see straight about this guy. I'm starting to depend on him too much and that's complicating things to the extent that I'm putting reins on myself – as you know, I hate being one tittle dependent on anyone. Yet every time I've hit a crisis lately, who was the first person I ran to? And it wasn't just because he had transport. Patsy has transport and I didn't run to her, did I? To and fro, pro and con, my brain starts to hurt from all this ruminating.

He brings the coffee over, pulls up one of the dining-room chairs to sit in front of me, takes Sam from me. You'll have to write down my telephone number, he goes, save you all this running down Gardiner Street in the middle of the night. This move is a bit sudden, isn't it? Where are you moving to?

I tell him about the brick and Reddy and Dwyer.

I'll say one thing for you, Angela, he goes, no one can say you lead a dull life. He sips his coffee. Have you considered that maybe that brick was unconnected with your troubles – could it be just a casual passer-by? Some little thug?

No, I say. It has to be connected. It's too much of a coincidence.

M-mm, he goes, as if he doesn't believe me.

I sip my coffee, which is lovely and mild. I saw the jar – he uses the Cap Colombie, it's very expensive. Maybe you have a point, he says then, in his slow way. Maybe you and James should move. These media hypes always die down after a little while but now, with these books—

What books?

He stares at me. You don't know? It was in the papers last Sunday.

What books?

His face creases, he's desperately uncomfortable. I sit up on the edge of the chair. Tell me, I go, please, Ken. What books?

He tells me. Apparently there are two journalists racing each other to see who'll be the first to get books out on the subject of date rape in Ireland. Star centre-piece (surprise, surprise), Rosemary Madden's case.

That'll teach me. I was getting too quiet, too relaxed. Thinking I have things under control. I put the coffee cup down on the floor beside me. Carefully, because my hand seems to have lost a lot of its strength. Did it say when these books are likely to come out?

No — I'm sorry, Angela, I've upset you now. I shouldn't have said anything about it but I thought you knew. Look, he puts his own cup down beside mine and takes my hands in his, try not to worry about it. Tell your solicitor. You might be able to take out an injunction.

I think about going through that whole rigmarole, widening all those wounds. And I have no idea whether or not free legal aid would handle injunctions to stop people publishing books.

I might, I say, I'll see. (I don't know what I'm saying here. I'm on automatic. But I do know one thing, I'm certainly not going to allow the two of us to be sitting ducks. Books take a while to come out, don't they? But if they're racing each other—)

Ken lets go of my hands, sits back again in his chair. Where are the two of you moving to? I tell him about James going to Mount Melleray. As for me, I say, I don't know where I'm going yet, but during the day tomorrow I'll find somewhere temporary, just for a few nights while I look around for a flat. I'll get one easy. The *Herald* is full of them.

Where temporary? he asks. You mean a hotel or something? Or have you a friend you could stay with, that friend, Patsy?

Something like that, I say back. I realize for the first time that I've got so carried away with the packing – and am so relieved about James being sorted out, temporarily at least – that I haven't thought through the question of where to go myself.

We don't actually have to go tomorrow, we have until Friday at the very least before the next rent money is due. But you know how once you make a decision to do something like that you have to do it right now. Then I remember that Gardiner Street, right here where we're sitting now, is full of hostels and bed-and-breakfasts further down towards the Liffey. I'll be fine, I say to Ken, I'll probably move into one of the bed-and-breakfasts down the road.

Why don't you move in here for the few days?

I know by his face that this popped out.

Ken! I go as if I'm totally taken aback – which, of course, I am – but my brain surges like a rocket. I have to be very careful here.

Sorry, he goes, that was a bit previous of me.

It would be so easy just to say yes. To have the decision made, to have someone look after me. But he has only one bedroom. One bed. And yet I don't want to hurt him.

Not at all, I say, don't be sorry, I just don't know how to react. You're a very generous man and I appreciate the offer very much—

But you're afraid I'll want to sleep with you again.

I stare at him. Thank God it's out in the open. Well, won't you?

Of course I'll want to, he says. He's being brave although it's obvious he's still mortally embarrassed. But only if you want to, too, Angela. I'm not a— He bites it off.

Rapist. He was going to say, I'm not a rapist.

For once I'm not offended, I'm really not. I could see he didn't mean any offence and he wasn't referring to James, it's just one of those things that people say.

It's all right, I say. But I'm glad you brought it up, we do have to talk about this. Even if this business of me staying here hadn't come up. You must think I'm a horrible person. After all, we have gone to bed together already and now here I am going all prissy. You must be asking yourself what the hell is wrong with me, was I just leading you on . . .

You are not a horrible person, Angela, he says slowly. And I know full well you were not leading me on. As a matter of fact, I've been asking myself if I've been the one who's been forcing myself on you.

Now we're both stuck for words. We're tiptoeing around each other, like a pair of little children meeting each other in the playground for the first time. We should be honest with each other, I say eventually.

Yes, we should. He shifts a little in the chair as though he's getting ready for some really big attack.

It's he who breaks it. So what do you want from me?

This is useless, of course. Gets us nowhere. Before I can answer it, he leans forward in his chair again. I'd do anything for you, Angela, he says, but the question I want answered is what I just asked you. What do you really want from me?

We're still tiptoeing. We're both afraid of our lives to do or say anything that could be used in evidence against us later. The first one to declare loses. It's time to be blunt. Look, Ken, I say, this isn't going to be helpful, but

I don't know what I want in the long term. I'm sorry but I don't. I do know what I want right now — a bit of peace. I can't keep up with what's happening to me or to James.

It's my turn to lean forward now, our heads are only inches apart although I don't really notice. I'm thinking so fast that my tongue can barely keep up. I'm blurting.

Look what's just happened to me this summer, for a start there's the James situation and what that has taken out of me — out of both of us, with everyone hounding us, the press, everyone. To tell you the truth, I feel absolutely cornered. But I'm the only one he has, Ken.

I'm so worked up I put both my hands to the sides of my head, because I feel if I don't it might explode. He's gazing at me like I'm some kind of lunatic, which is exactly what I must look and sound like. I can feel the little veins jumping in my temples.

Do you know what that must feel like? I ask him. To have no family at all, only one person? At least at one stage of my life I knew what it was like to have more than one person. You know, too. The fact that James and I don't get along all that well on the surface doesn't really matter. How could we? There's no one else for him to have a go at. He's had a raw deal in his life, he really has, and he has to be very angry inside.

What's more, there's the small detail of me meeting my father for the first time ever. How do you think I feel about that little development after all these years? And do you know what? I can't make up my mind whether I'm pleased or sorry we found him last Saturday . . . Maybe I should have left well enough alone. But it's too bloody late now, isn't it? Then there're my money troubles, not helped by the fact that I've dropped out of at least one, probably two of my four part-time jobs.

Also I'm being thrown out of the place we've lived in for years—

I run out of steam. To me, the chronicle of my life this summer reads like I should just go and jump off the nearest bridge as quickly as possible and stop wasting everyone's time.

Maybe now you can see how mixed up I am, I say in a quieter tone of voice. How I can't concentrate on whether or not we should sleep together. To tell you the truth, Ken, that's about the furthest thing from my mind. Sex, even the mention of it, seems irrelevant to me. It's absolutely nothing personal.

I understand. Ken's face is deadly serious now. I really do, Angela. But I do take issue with you. Sex can be very comforting—

I'm opening my mouth again when he shushes it with one finger. On the matter of beds, on staying here, my offer stands. That chair you're sitting on opens out into a bed. No problem.

I look back at him as though he had two heads. I don't understand you, I say. Are you St Francis of Assisi or what?

Thirty-Five

Ken Sheils flashes me a grin. I'm far from St anybody, he goes. You haven't a clue about me, you should meet the lovely Diandra – she'd fill you in sharpish. He looks sad all of a sudden.

I couldn't stay here, it wouldn't be fair.

What's not fair about it? I'll admit I would love for us to develop something together, but if it's not to be it's not to be. Listen, Angela, you've been through a very rough time and if it's peace you want, you couldn't be in a better place than here. Think of it as your personal Mount Melleray. I'll be out working. Sam'll be out with me. You'll have the place to yourself all day. You wouldn't believe how quiet these apartments are, all of us solitary worker bees in the little solitary cells of our hive. We're all dead scared even to say hello to each other in case we'd be thought to be minding the other fella's business. There's plenty of room as you can see. He waves an arm around the apartment. There's a whole empty wardrobe in there in the bedroom. My clothing requirements, as you can gather, are modest. He looks at his feet. And I think I wouldn't mind at all knowing you were here to come home to – even for just a few days and even if there was nothing more to it than a bowl of soup in the evenings. He holds up his hand like a lollipop lady — stop, stop! Don't get all panicky. I'm not presuming anything. We could simply play house for a few days, couldn't we, Angela?

He's niced me to death. I think of the peace, the cleanliness of the place. No Dwyer, no Reddy. All right, I say. For a couple of days. If you're really sure.

Am I sure? I'm obviously not the orator I think I am.

We smile at one another. I won't take up much space, I say, I haven't much stuff, my clothes and a few black plastic bags.

Great. Ken gets to his feet. Look forward to it — I'll get you the spare keys. And by the way, I won't hear a word of argument, the guest gets the bedroom. I sleep out here.

But—

I *said* — not a word of argument. He puts a finger on my lips to shut me up.

Thanks. I say it humbly because I mean it humbly. Being me, though, I'm still worried that this won't run as smoothly as is being offered. The nights are long and we'll be only a few feet away from each other. Still, it is only for a couple of days and I do get up very early in the mornings.

He's not finished. There is one condition, he goes. And that is that you start behaving like the gorgeous person you are. Do you look at yourself in mirrors at all? You're a beautiful woman, Angela.

I gape at him. No one in my life, not even Tom Bennett, has ever said that to me and I haven't a clue how to react. Mirrors? I don't have time to examine myself in mirrors. And when I do look into one, when I'm washing my teeth, all I see is a mole under the hairline on the left-hand side. I'm certainly not beautiful. No way. How — how do I behave? I stammer it. I — I need my hair cut . . .

Your hair's perfect, he says back quietly. Cut it if you like but it's perfect. And so is your face. He grins. And so is your body and so are your legs – as I so well remember.

Well, there was no answer to that, was there?

He insists on walking me home. But he doesn't kiss me like he did before. It's like he's now put an exclusion zone around me.

I was still half shocked as I climbed the stairs and then let myself back into our place, so out of it that I actually got a surprise when I saw the state it was in – the books piled in the middle of the floor, the bare look of the shelves above the sink, the scored surface of Reddy's table. During the time I was out, I'd semi-forgotten the clearout James and I had given it.

I noticed that Adeline's photographs were no longer where he had put them, on the draining board.

And here's James himself, not sitting by the window as he's supposed to, to watch for potential thugs. James has the attention span of a one-day-old kitten. Instead, he's hunched in the middle of it all, plastic bags to the right of him plastic bags to the left. Staring at Reddy's telly for the last time.

No point in recriminations. Any problems? I say to him.

Uh-uh! he goes. I flop onto the settee. James, we mightn't see each other for a while.

He doesn't remove his gaze from grand-prix racing. The noise is frightful. Look, I go, would you turn that down a bit? I want us to talk.

He gives this big exaggerated sigh and zaps the television off. Same old belligerent James. It's like the brick, the brief intimacy of us packing together, his genuine fear and misery of only a few hours ago have never happened. I'm tempted just to go to bed – after all, I have to get up again in six hours' time, but I meant what I said to Ken Sheils on James's behalf. It must be awful to have just one person in your life.

It's in my mind to talk to him about everything important that I haven't said to him, all our lives together. But now that he's staring at me, I can't think of any of it. I'm as inane as ever. Are you all set for Mount Melleray?

He picks up the zapper again but before he can use it, Look, I go quickly, what I really want to say is that I'm going to miss you, James. I'm going to miss you terribly.

He's going to fall off his chair with surprise and confusion. Then he stands up, I'll miss you too, muttered so quickly and quietly that I would have missed it if the place hadn't been so deathly quiet. Then he's gone into his room.

It isn't much, I know, but to me it's unbearably moving.

In bed that night, I can't sleep. It's my last night here, his too. Our last night as a family, such as it is. I have the deepest, strongest instinct that this night is like a guillotine. We are about to be chopped apart. Even if he stays in that monastery for only one day, for half a day, this is the end of whatever chance we've been given to develop a particular relationship. No more working on that one. We were given nineteen years and our time is up. From now on it has to be something else.

I always knew this night would come, I even wished for it, for James's sake — and, to a lesser extent, for mine, so that I could have a life too. But it's something I never truthfully confronted before and now that it's so unexpectedly here, the moment has struck with terrible ferocity. Too soon, too soon, I'm screaming inside. Give me another chance. One more month — one week? All right, just one more day . . .

This hurricane is narrowed to this pinprick. James is leaving me.

Pictures. James in a blue babygro with a matching soother and hair like feathers. James terrified by the dark and unfamiliar surroundings and coming into my bed on the first night we slept in this flat – he was five, nearly six. All those long treks to the school principal when he was late, or forged sick notes, smoked, didn't have this that or the other homework done. All that MTV. His leathers everywhere. Coke cans. Crisps. Sodden towels. Lynx aftershave. Him arriving home with bunches of motorway daffodils, throwing them on the table without meeting my eye. My heart in my mouth every time I heard him vroom off on the bike. The whiteness of his face the day those two cops came in. His smile. His rare and dazzling smile.

I'm lying there just after four o'clock, looking at the ceiling and waiting for the time to get up. Through James's closed door I hear him sobbing.

I'm paralysed. I should go in, take him in my arms. But I know he'd reject the gesture. The moment passes. I don't hear him any more.

Next morning, when I come home to this flat after work for the last time, he's up again. Businesslike, as much as a boy with a mottled face can look businesslike. His bruising has faded quite a lot, though, and to be fair he doesn't look at all bad. If it wasn't for the cast on his arm he could even pass for someone who'd just had a small argument with a lamp-post or a door.

He certainly seems calm, resigned. Even friendly, which is not a disposition I readily associate with James. Given what I heard from his room last night, I would have expected him to be a bit more cut up. Maybe the upset is too deep to show on the surface. Get this thing over, that seems to be the mood for today. He's shaved. He's packed his gear. The facilities look bereft, you know the way they do, without all the cans and accoutrements.

What about money? I sigh, exaggerate, slip back for safety into my old ways. You'll need money.

I'd been worrying about this. I had no way of raising instant cash – certainly nothing left to hock – and the bonds take more than a week to come through for encashment. I hadn't even received the latest ones yet.

There are moneylenders, of course, but I'd sooner eat earwigs. One of the women at work is in desperate straits because of moneylenders. Would you believe, it all started with Communion outfits for her twins, she didn't want her kids to be outshone. The Vincent is trying to help her out but she just seems to be getting deeper and deeper in. Once those Shylocks get a hold of you they never let go.

The post office savings office is opposite Trinity College. Utilitarian. We got there at just after ten o'clock but even so, there was a big queue ahead of us. You had to take a number. The next number available was 39 and they were only on number 11 at this stage. We didn't have that kind of time.

Stay here, I go to James. He sits down on one of the chairs in the waiting area.

I'm so deep down distraught I don't care who thinks what of me. I march up to the counter and butt in on a transaction. Excuse me, I say to the woman customer (who's not amused), I'm terribly sorry, but this is very urgent.

I ask the clerk if I could see a supervisor immediately.

The customer sighs heavily and drums her fingers on the counter. I ignore her as the clerk rings someone. He puts down the phone, tells me to wait over at the side, by a glass door. I don't even look at James, I'm sure he's mortified at my snotty behaviour.

To make a long story short, the supervisor takes on board what dire straits we're in and says he'll do what he can. I'm not looking for the moon, I say firmly, in case he hasn't got the message. Just nine hundred pounds. And it's my money, after all. He gives me a funny look. He looks at the bonds I've brought in. You're lucky, the bonds are now computerized, he goes, come back in forty-five minutes.

James and I use the time by going across the river to BusÁrus to check the timetables. Maybe the crying last night took away some of the poison. He's so docile it's killing me. I want him to yell at me, balk at what I'm asking him to do. BusÁrus is an extraordinary place. I know it's for transients − it's where you get all the country buses and the ones to take you to the airport − but that's not why it feels so lonely. After all, the airport is for transients too but it feels solid, exciting, outwards-looking. BusÁrus feels as though the structure itself is temporary, a bit hopeless, like nothing belongs there, nor ever did, not the staff, the kiosks and shops, not even the big tiles on the floor.

Today the place seems sadder than ever, although there are young backpackers everywhere and busy knots of sailors clustered around the area where you book the tour buses. Town is hopping with sailors, especially O'Connell Street and Grafton Street and, I believe, Temple Bar.

We stop in front of the big timetable boards. The time James and I have left together is now measurable.

Last week a big American aircraft carrier came in for the Fourth of July celebrations. It was too big to anchor in Dublin, had to stay a couple of miles out to sea. The whole of Dublin was agog. Teenage girls were behaving as if the sailors were Oasis but it wasn't only them. Would you believe 175,000 people (out of our tiny population) entered a competition run by the National Lottery for people to be able to go out and visit the ship? All the women at work, for instance. I meant to, I just didn't get around to it. Wouldn't it be lovely to have a life so uncomplicated that you could go bananas about the visit of five thousand American sailors to your city?

We find there's a bus he can get at twenty past one.

My stomach fills with that watery feeling. Now we know. One hundred and twenty minutes. You might think I'm cracked, thinking about sailors and the National Lottery at a time like this. That's me – busy busy busy!

According to Pius Crawford's directions, he has to go to Dungarvan and then take another bus to Cappoquin and then hitch or walk. Will you take that one? I ask him, as if what we're discussing is whether or not he'll have ice cream after his dinner.

He shrugs. Fine, it doesn't matter which one I take.

Well, they'll be expecting you.

Twenty past one is fine, fine . . .

What about the bike? I'm all biz. Will you be able to take it back to them if I ring them? You won't be able to wheel it with your bad arm, will you? Let me see now, if we took it down between us, one on each side? It's only a few hundred yards to the shop.

He fires up. Stop fussing, for God's sake. I'll be able to manage it perfectly.

You won't, James. How will you be able to manage with your—

Shut up. I will. You saw how I managed with the packing. Some of those bags with the crockery are heavy. He stops. Sees I'm not arguing any more. He looks at me with what could be compassion. It'll be grand, Angela.

I turn back to the timetables as if I haven't memorized the Dungarvan one enough.

There are phones in BusÁrus and I ring the shop while he heads home to finish his packing. The time is leaking away, I can't stop it.

There's aggro at first, from the fellow who answers the phone. But eventually he puts the owner on to me. He asks for further payment. I say no. We to and fro on it a bit while I have to feed in more coins. Then I say, Well, if you won't take it back, you'll have to sue us for the balance of the money because we're not paying any more.

There must have been something about the tone of my voice. He agrees to take the bike, provided it's in good condition and provided James signs X, Y and Z. He'll sign anything, I say, provided there's no more money involved. You'll get the bike back sometime this morning.

By the time I get back to the bonds office, they have the money organized. It's a draft, though, which means I then have to go and get it cashed 'in any post office, mam'.

For me that's the GPO. So I find myself running back across the bridge. And, wouldn't you know it, another queue. Jesus, come on, come on, time, time, how many minutes left now?

The way I'm carrying on, you'd think he was emigrating to Australia and not temporarily to another part of Ireland.

This is the first time either of us has ever gone away from the other. As I told you, he blew his one and only chance, that time when he wasn't able to go to the Gaeltacht, and I don't count the night he spent in the cells, or the all-nighters he pulled earlier this year at parties and suchlike.

I hear myself keening on and on like this, like Lady Macbeth. For Christ's sake, Angela. I force myself to get a grip. I march out of the GPO with more than a thousand pounds in my handbag. Nine hundred plus interest.

I arrange my face before I go into our flat. His luggage – a rucksack and a duffel bag – is piled by the door. The television isn't on. He's leaning against the draining board.

Oh, God, I wish he had the television on. You're ready?

He nods.

I mustn't give in to what I'm feeling. My throat feels like it's filling with ice. I look at the two bags by the door. Is that all you're taking? Very matter-of-fact. And is this what you want me to keep for you? Indicating a loose pile of stuff by the naked bed-settee.

Yes – very quietly.

Let's see now, it's five past twelve, you'd want to be getting a move on if we're to get that bike back and we're to catch that bus. I can't swallow.

Angela, I don't want you to come with me.

But I want to.

No. Vehemently. He stands off the draining board. No. Quieter. He seems to have matured ten years in the last five minutes. I can't read his mood properly. He's calm – but what else?

James—

No. Listen to me, I don't want you to come with me either to the bike shop or to BusÁrus.

But—

Leave it, Angela.

How's he going to wheel the bike with one arm? I don't ask him any more, I feel I've no permission. I can't look at him, I reach into my bag, grab a handful of twenties, pass them over. Here, take this – I thrust it into his hand.

I don't need all this.

Take it, take it, I go. My heart is frantic. If he doesn't take this money I'm going to crumble away into dust. Consider it your share of my winnings. Anyway, you'll need busfare, and I don't know whether you'll have to pay for your board and lodging at that monastery. I'd better give you the address where I'm going to be staying for a few days.

I root around in my handbag again and find a bus ticket. Then I lean too hard on it with the biro and the top snaps off. I have to find another piece of paper. Quick. Which rubbish bag did I put my notepaper and envelopes into? How is it you can never find *one* piece of paper when you're in a hurry?

Use this. He pulls a Lottery receipt out of the inside pocket of his jacket.

I didn't know you did the Lotto? It was something to say.

I scribble Ken's address on the back of the ticket, add his telephone number. I'm good at remembering numbers, but it's easy for me, I don't have to remember very many.

When I find a flat, I say, I'll let you know. I'll write to you at the monastery.

OK. He doesn't even look at the address, just folds the ticket again and puts it back in his inside pocket.

You'd better get going, James, or you'll miss that bus. I can hear my voice saying this hateful thing. Are you sure you'll be able to manage wheeling the bike by yourself with that arm? Are you sure you don't need any help?

It's cool, stop fussing.

The smell of Lynx is very strong. Let me at least help

you bring down your stuff — you can put it in the panniers while you're wheeling it.

He bends down, using his good arm to pick up the two bags. I rush to help him. Let me carry one down the stairs for you. Are you definitely sure you don't want me to take them down to the bus for you — meet you there? James?

He shakes his head.

Then, Cheerio, Angela. See you soon. As he looks full at me, his eyes, those wonderful eyes, hold something I can't read. I've always been able to read James. What's gone wrong? The feelings are like rockets pushing up inside me.

I crack, seize him and hug hard. He doesn't hug me back because he can't with the plaster cast and the bags but for one instant he does lay his rough cheek against mine. You read that emotional pain is like a knife. It's not, it's more like a slicer or a chainsaw.

Next thing I'm looking at an empty doorway.

I manage to hold back on the crying until he's well gone. I'm standing looking at Reddy's bare boards in the hallway outside our door and telling myself I'm being absurd. For God's sake, Angela, will you give over? It'll be two, three weeks *max* . . .

I cried so hard I slept, woke up, didn't know where I was, realized.

When I got up I smelt him everywhere, Lynx, runners, sweat. All I could do was sit. Draw the flat in around me like a womb.

At about three o'clock I roused myself a bit, enough to find stationery. I wrote to Justine and Nicola and, after a bit of hesitation, to Francesca, via her foster mother. I told all three of them the bare bones of the story — and that if they cared to know, their brother could be contacted at Mount Melleray.

I washed my face, walked down to the GPO to buy stamps and to post the letters. I couldn't tell you whether it was raining, dry, the Sahara, what. Yet I suppose it did me good because by the time Ken Sheils arrived, just after tea-time, I felt quiet.

I was still worrying, though, about how he managed with that bike . . .

Thirty-Six

A ll set? Ken looks down at the black bin bags, which I'd stacked neatly just inside the door. Is this all?

Yep. My landlord can have all the rest, bad luck to him. The furniture isn't ours.

And there was I rearranging everything in the apartment to give you space.

Sorry, Ken.

Angela, Angela – he takes my shoulders, gives me a little shake – will you stop all this apologizing? Seriously. You'd apologize for living. Someone soon is going to lose patience with you.

Sorry. It escapes before I can catch it. He sighs, lets me go. What are we going to do with you?

It takes less than quarter of an hour to move me out of the home James and I have lived in for fifteen years. More because I feel I should than because I want to – I'd seen it so often in films and on the television – I walk back in for one last look around. I feel very little. Or at least very little for the place itself. Only that I wish James was there sitting hunched in front of the television. And I'm all cried out on that one.

I decide to keep the keys, let Reddy have the expense of changing the locks. I never want to see him again, even to try to get our security deposit back. It was only twenty quid – a fortune fifteen years ago! Anyway, knowing him, he'd find some reason not to pay it back.

I remember the Daisy Market mirror over James's damage to the wall. I walk over and take it down, revealing the hole in all its glory. At least twenty quid's worth. I win!

When we were going into Ken's apartment with my clothes and belongings, do you know what? Not one person looked out of his or her door to see what all the rustling and kerfuffle was. I'd been defensive about this – after all, I didn't want anyone thinking that I was moving in to live in sin with someone. (Having already been to bed. Talk about inconsistent!)

This is par for the course, Ken says. I did tell you about this – bees, hives? Some weekends you'll hear stereos thumping at various parties but generally we all put feelers out first to make sure the way is clear.

Sam greets me like a long-lost friend, wagging his whole body in the absence of a tail. And Ken himself could not be nicer. When I get into the bedroom, I see he's put a bunch of flowers on a little table beside the bed.

In fact, he's almost too nice. He doesn't put a toe beyond the bedroom door. I'll leave you to get sorted, Angela. I'm making coffee. Come on out whenever you're ready – or don't come out at all. Just do your own thing. This is very important, all right? For as long as you're here, you're to come and go, behave exactly as you would in your own place.

I had pre-sorted the bags while I was packing, so finding what I needed immediately is easy and it takes me less than a quarter of an hour to get settled in. Here's more evidence of Ken's thoughtfulness. He'd told me the previous evening that he'd loads of space in his wardrobe. When I open it? Completely empty except for one anorak.

I go out into the living room. He's reading a newspaper. Where are all your clothes?

He gets up. I've a hall closet — they're in there. Are you ready for your coffee yet?

Sure, thanks. Are you sure I haven't inconvenienced you?

Angela, what did I say to you last night? Will you learn to accept people's good intentions? There's an art to taking as well as giving, you know.

Sorry.

He purses his lips. Grins. There you go again.

I sit down.

He diverts towards me on the way to the kitchen area, Before I forget, here are the keys. And I got another set cut this afternoon, I'd better explain to you how the alarm works.

I'm sitting listening to which key works what lock and what the combination of the alarm is and I don't know how to feel. No man has ever treated me like this before, as though I'm somebody they like, no big deal. I suppose where Tom Bennett was concerned I was a mother-substitute. I've been mother and father and sister and brother to James.

Ken Sheils seems to see me as me.

When we're nearly finished our coffee he looks at his watch. It's only just eight o'clock, he goes, and it's a lovely evening. I'm going for a walk for an hour or so, clear my head. You're welcome to come if you like — but don't feel you have to. You stay in, go out, anything you want.

This guy must have some faults. But apart from a stubborn temper (as seen in the row with the lorry driver

on the way to Birr that first day), so far I can't see any.
What was wrong with that Diandra?

He turns on the telly so we can watch the Lotto draw.
The *Coronation Street* signature tune is playing and the
announcer comes on to remind us that after this week's
Lotto draw we can watch *Touched By An Angel*, then the
Nine O'Clock News, then *Thou Shalt Not Kill*. Here we go,
Ken says, glancing across at me. His eyes are lit up. I do
Multi-draw so I'm in every week.

This reminds me that I have yet to send off my scratch
card.

He gets three numbers. Nearly there, he goes, haven't
had three for a while, I think it's a good omen. I know
I'm going to win soon, I have this feeling . . .

All over the country half the population is saying the
same.

I decide to behave like half the population. My world
had shrunk so much, it was time to unshrink it. I think
I'll come for that walk with you.

You could always buy a Section 23 apartment, you
know, that's what mine is . . . It's half an hour later
and we're moseying along the main drag of the Phoenix
Park under the huge trees. Joggers, strollers, cyclists
whizzing by us in the cycle lane, kids swinging out of
their parents.

I couldn't afford to buy an apartment, I say automatically. Unless my scratch card comes good, the prospect
of me as a homeowner remains as likely as me taking a
hot-air-balloon ride with Richard Branson. (Hunky or
what?)

We're passing the Monument, which Ken informs me
is actually called the obelisk and which is a new one on
me, we always knew it simply as the Monument. The
usual gangs of youngsters racing up and down the wide,
shallow steps, groups of teenagers lying around sipping

beer or Coke. Sam is having a brilliant time, romping and saying hello to fellow dogs.

You probably could afford it, you'd be surprised, he says. All you'd need is about a thousand pounds' cash and with the tax relief and first-time buyers' grant and all the rest of it, you could probably get a one-bed for less than thirty-five pounds a week. And mortgages are so cheap now.

I'll certainly consider that, I say, so as not to seem rude, thanks for the advice. But I make a mental reservation. If and when James and I ever get close to having our own place, it'll be a roses-round-the-door job or nothing. I like Ken's apartment — but in an abstract way. It's clean and fresh but no way is it a home.

I give myself a mental kick. I'm still thinking of James and me together. Stop it. James is gone. I make a huge effort not to see that barren flat.

It's odd to find myself here. In present circumstances the Phoenix Park would be the last place I'd have chosen for a walk. I'm sure, though, that for one moment our connection with it didn't occur to Ken Sheils. I've got to realize that the whole world isn't hanging on the affairs of Angela and James Devine. The sun is still bright, everyone is in summer gear and, without doubt, not one of these hundreds of men, women or children is wasting a single thought on us. In my line of sight, not one person is reading a newspaper or listening to a radio. The Devines? Who? That was last week. What's next?

We walk on as far as the classy white entrance to the American ambassador's house before turning back towards the van. Ken's gift of silence allows all the other senses to operate. If I'd been chatting I doubt if I'd have recognized that lovely summer-evening smell of warm leafy air, or heard the whirr in time to look up at a flight of ducks overhead.

Whatever it is, rosy sun, faraway laughing of the kids, all that spacious greenery, I'm so relaxed now I feel as if it's almost possible to heal.

I got a bit of news today, Ken says, as the van comes in sight. Diandra says she's going for a divorce.

I don't quite know what to say. Although the referendum was passed, at this point no one has got a divorce yet in Ireland.

I try to strike a balance between being sympathetic and being nosy. I hope you won't be killed in the rush!

He picks up a twig off the ground and throws it for Sam. It's no big deal, I suppose. She can have whatever she wants from me, I'm not going to stand in her way. I hate the thought of lawyers and going to court.

Sure what can she get?

He shrugs. Who knows? The apartment. She has her own living arrangements now but who knows, once lawyers and money come into it? She could probably screw me into the ground.

Ah no, I say, she couldn't. It wouldn't be fair.

Well, I'm not going to lose any sleep over it. It's going to be a couple of years anyway, by the looks of things, so I won't have to evict you tomorrow.

It was strange driving past our old gaff, seeing the piece of cornflake-packet cardboard still in place in the broken window. And when we got back inside Ken's apartment I felt stranger still. Awkward.

It's very shadowy in the room because the sky is losing light outside. Do you want to watch a bit of television, he asks, or will you go straight to bed? He's being so correct he's stiff.

I hesitate. It seems rude just to go to bed straight away. I don't mind, I go. I'd need to be in bed by eleven at the latest – I've the usual early start tomorrow.

Fine, he goes. Any preference as to what you want to

watch? He uses the remote control to turn on the television and then excuses himself to go to the bathroom. There's the usual delay while the television warms up, then on comes *Davis*. I'd forgotten about *Davis*. I freeze. Before we go into our discussion, Derek Davis is saying into the camera, I want you to watch this clip of film.

Rosemary Madden's face fills the screen. Of course I'm co-operating with my author, she goes, I want my story to be told. And there's only one authorized version of my story.

From Ken's bathroom comes the sound of the toilet flushing as the camera pulls back from Rosemary Madden's face. Her brother is standing beside her, the older, thickset one. Why shouldn't she make a few shillings out of this? he goes. That scumbag has ruined her life.

Ken is out, sees the screen just as we're back to the studio and Derek Davis. Derek has cards in his hand and he looks up from them. There are a lot of issues surrounding this case—

Ken snatches up the remote control, zaps, up comes Trevor McDonald on *News At Ten*. The American presidential election.

I'm very sorry, Angela, Ken says. I didn't know.

Scumbag, the brother said. A lot of people use the term but to me it's now as clear as day. It was the brother who sent the letter. Probably the brick as well. Probably organized the beating.

I'm numb. I'm tired. I'll care tomorrow.

The next morning I have to leave Ken's apartment extra early because I have to be outside our flat, ex-flat, for the minibus to pick me up. The only iffy moment comes when I'm tiptoeing out through the little lobby towards the front door. Sam, who's in his basket, is awake and watching me and he makes as though to hop out. I shake my head hard and make a face at him. He's obviously a very intelligent little dog because he stays where he is. Ken is snoring lightly in the narrow bed-chair and I make it out without waking him.

Somehow I get through work – thank God none of the women mentions *Davis* – although every bone in my body feels as though it's been through a cement mixer. And when I get back to the apartment, it's empty. Ken has already left for work and the place is spotless. There's a note taped to the kettle.

I'm working in Malahide today and I'll be back at around seven this evening. Help yourself to the contents of the fridge. And here's the juicer, I didn't know whether you knew where to find it. See you this evening – K.

The electric juicer has two oranges beside it.

I'm too tired to eat or drink anything. I do what I haven't done in twenty years. I go back to bed.

I sleep like a zombie and don't wake up again until five past three in the afternoon.

At first I'm still in my dream, a light, airy one, something to do with the Isle of Man, a place I don't know a thing about. But it's a lovely place, sunny, happy, a bit like the Phoenix Park actually, now that I examine it.

But then a weird thing. I realize that it is myself who is light and airy. There's something missing and it's not just fatigue. There's no worry.

I sit up, test this.

The lightness is real. The cloud of agonizing and worrying has lifted. Not altogether, of course, but enough so as I can see out from under it.

I could go so far as to say I feel even a tiny bit happy.

Whoever first said 'out of sight out of mind' was a very clever person. James was not out of mind exactly, but he was certainly not sitting in every brain cell. He's safe down there in his monastery and no one will be calling him a scumbag. There'll be no telly so he won't even hear it from a distance. I see him walking through a lovely old cloister, or through a meadow. Like I always saw Mammy. Daisies et cetera.

I get out of bed, make it to Ken's standards, I hope, and go out into the silent living-room. He certainly told no lies when he said this place was quiet. The living-room window is closed and the noise of the traffic from Gardiner Street below is only a hum. We used to be crucified with road works on this street but Ireland has had the Presidency of Europe since the beginning of June and because Gardiner Street is on the way to and from the airport, there hasn't been a pneumatic drill down there since then. (All we get now are the sirens from the motorcades!)

I don't want to disturb the spotlessness of Ken's kitchen so I decide to go out for something to eat. Yes, I think, Bewley's. Like an ordinary person.

So I do. Everything seems new. Shiny. I love all the tourists. I love the waitresses with their old-fashioned uniforms. I even love the pushing and the shoving at the self-service rail where I queue up for egg and chips. Egg and chips for breakfast at half past three in the afternoon! Mammy'd turn in her grave.

And on the way back, guess what? I go to Carthy's and I redeem her garnet ring and her neck chain. I leave the video for another couple of days because I don't want to be seen hawking it up Gardiner Street. In that area I'd probably be brought straight in to Store Street or Fitzgibbon Street for questioning.

When Ken and Sam come home, I have the kettle on

and the table laid for tea. I've made a salad from what I found in the fridge and from a selection of deli meats I bought on the way home. He wants to play house? I'll give him house.

It really is like playing house, it's like Rock Hudson and Doris Day. He's arrived home exhausted in his work overalls having toiled for us, so my next move is I run over to him and say, Had a bad day, dear? And then I should help him into his steaming bath. And give him his highball. (Although I've never quite understood what exactly a highball is.)

I'm no Doris Day, alas. As he's standing there with his keys still in his hand, looking at all this domesticity, I find it hard to read his face. Being Angela Devine I say, I hope you don't mind? We've ice cream for dessert.

Mind? I love it! He means it too.

After our tea, we go for another walk – across the bridge, down the Quays, towards Alexandra Basin. He knows a lot about the ships docked along there, and the Isle of Man ferry, the container vessels. He explains that the huge steel cakestand on the deck of one of our Irish ships is for helicopters. In turn I can tell him about life on board the *Asgard*, which is also berthed there. It's the Irish sail-training vessel and a friend of Patsy's Martin has something to do with it. (Naturally, because he's a friend of Martin's, he runs it . . .)

I'm glad I can tell him at least something he doesn't know already. There's a certain imbalance in our knowledge of our native city. In the couple of months I've known Ken Sheils I've been more places and learned more about the area within a couple of miles of where I was born than I'd learned all those years of my life living in it.

I'm still testing the airy feeling I woke up with this afternoon. I wonder what James is doing right now, I say to Ken — and would you believe I can say it without choking up.

Probably mitching into the nearest big smoke to have a pint, he says it so easily I can see he's made a lot of progress in accepting James for what he is.

This must be what it's like to be on your holidays.

I test myself some more about James. Should I telephone the monastery? I ask Ken. Just to say hello, make sure he's all right?

It's up to you of course, he goes, but try to think back to when you were his age, flexing your independence. Would you have wanted people checking up on you all the time?

He could be lonely. He's had a very hard time.

He could. But being lonely is part of growing up too. Angela, he hesitates, please tell me to butt out if you want to but maybe he's never had the chance to be independent. Couldn't this be his first real solo flight? And should you trail after him so soon.

Echoes of Patsy.

He takes my hand. Quite casually, no pressure. Why don't you leave it until early next week? He'd welcome a call then. He'd probably see it as genuine concern and friendship rather than as you treating him like a child. He glances sideways at me. The breeze is from behind and his hair is blowing around his face. Tell me to shut up, that this is none of my business. It's just that I can vividly remember back to when I was his age . . . He lapses into his silence.

It's hard to take. He's right, though. Letting go is not physical — it's not them moving out. It's that you have to give them the gift of cutting off worrying about them. The pain kicks in, but I ride with it. I can deal with it. Fairly well.

We've come as far as we can go before we have to

turn in off the river. The East Link Bridge is busy, traffic flowing in both directions. We stand for a minute to look down towards the sea. There are yachts moored in the middle of the river on the far side, a graceful white cruise liner tied up at the quay. Listen, Angela, Ken says, on a related topic, I hope you don't feel you have to be as good as your word and find yourself a flat this week. You're welcome to stay as long as you like. You're a very easy house-guest. Feck it, he says, I'd *like* you to stay. Will you?

I don't look at him but I imagine he's blushing.

There's a show on at the Point on the far side of the river, cars milling around, streams of people converging, the water bus coming alongside. We're too far away to read the posters — it could be ballet or a musical or Christy Moore or some huge international rock act. Why don't I know? There's a whole world happening that I've let slide by.

Now is my opportunity to give my first small gift of freedom to James. Well, as it happens I've done nothing about finding a place so far, I say to Ken. Maybe I'll stay another week, if that's all right with you? (I said the first *small* gift!)

All right? It's more than all right. Ken grins. But be careful, Angela, you might even enjoy yourself. And then where would we be?

→ Thirty-Seven ←

That weekend I wrote a letter to James — I thought this would be a good half-way house between his need to strike out and mine to keep contact. So I was careful, wrote nothing significant, not a word about Rosemary Madden or her brother, or people racing each other to bring out books. Just work and Dublin and events and people I observed. I did tell him I missed him, but in a lighthearted way — I miss you, you clot, I'm suffering from withdrawal symptoms from all that passive smoking. Then I told him a bit about Ken. *He's the friend you met in the hospital and whose address I gave you — remember?* I described Ken's apartment and little Sam.

I finished up by asking him to drop me a line soon, to let me know all the news. That they must have some way of getting letters out of there!

I signed it 'all my love, Angela'.

I posted it on the Saturday evening — remembered to post the famous scratch card too — and then Ken and I went to see *Il Postino*, which I loved, even though I don't normally like subtitles. Afterwards we had ice cream. We chit-chatted about the movie.

Then Ken says, You know what, Angela, you're lovely when you relax. You're lovely anyway, but when you're relaxed you're more beautiful than Princess Di. Did anyone tell you you look a bit like her? He grins.

Go away out of that, I go, you charmer, you! (But who wouldn't be chuffed?)

Are you like your mother? he asks me then. Yes, I say, although I have my father's colouring. The minute I said it, it was like a plug being pulled. I started thinking about Pius Crawford. Uh-oh, Ken says, have I said the wrong thing?

No, not at all. It's just that—

It's just that your father is unfinished business. You find now that it's not enough just to know who he is.

I look across the table at him with new respect. How did he know this? Something like that, I say.

Well, maybe you should finish the business, he says.

No, I say quickly, I haven't the energy. Well, not just at the moment. What I mean is I haven't the courage. I change the subject rapido. What happened with you and Diandra? I ask him.

She couldn't live with me, he says quietly.

I can't believe that, I say. I can't imagine how anyone couldn't live with you. You seem so—

I'm not. I'm not so anything. Don't put me on a pedestal, Angela. That's a very dangerous thing to do.

Well, give me a hint. You know everything about me, after all.

He cocks his head to one side, like Sam does. All right, he goes. It's a pretty tawdry and commonplace little story. Diandra wanted things I couldn't give her. Or, in her opinion, wouldn't give her. She was ambitious for me, for us. For money, really. She wanted the big house, the fancy car. We had row after row about it.

He looks at me very seriously. I'm not ambitious, Angela. If you're looking for a high-flier you'll have to look somewhere else. I'm perfectly happy dandering along doing odd jobs at my own pace and earning whatever I need to live. In Diandra's opinion, I could have done this for a second income, as my nixer. I should have been heading up my own construction company or doing something, anything that would give me more money, or at least status. She used to say she had no intention of being known as the handyman's wife. I tried for a while, I worked for a big building firm, which did have promotional ladders. He grins. Sorry about the pun – but it was pretty good, eh? He becomes serious again, toys with his ice-cream spoon, moving it around the bowl of the sundae dish. Diandra always said I was living as though I was already retired. But, you know, to me that's the perfect way to live. To her I was the under-achiever of the century and in the end she despised me for it. In the end we despised each other, actually. I enjoy what I do, Angela, and I decide when and how I work. He gazes into the middle distance. That may all change now, of course, with the divorce. If she wins more money from me in alimony.

Rubbish, I go. You've no kids. And she can work, can't she? Isn't she able-bodied?

You don't know Diandra, he says quietly. He shuts down. I take the hint. Will we go back?

Speaking of under-achieving or, rather, under-earning, it occurs to me on the Sunday morning as I'm lying in bed, feeling decadent – I don't even want to know what time it is – that if Patsy wanted to find me for a gig or a wedding, she doesn't have this address.

It's not bad, I think, living this placid, mole-like life, where no one except James knows where to find me. (Or my father, in emergencies. And then he has to wait until a Saturday morning, in which case the 'emergency' will presumably have passed!)

I probe to find how I am about missing James this

morning. The all-encompassing hard pain of it has softened out for sure and has become more generalized. I'll love him until the day I die, that's not in doubt. To my surprise, however, because I never contemplated this before, I can certainly live a decent life without seeing him every day. Is that disloyal? I decide not. I decide it's just part of the next phase of both of our lives, I've to step sideways, let him pass me out and go forward. It was what my instinct was telling me the night before he left. Things will never be the same again.

It's not so bad. What's difficult to admit is that it may be better.

One definite improvement – waking up in this bed is like waking up to find you've nestled into a warm cloud. I've been sleeping on a bed-settee for far too long.

I listen for signs of life in the living room, hear none, wiggle my toes, snuggle down for another bit of kip. So if Patsy finds someone else for the act – no difficult task in this town – so be it. Anyhow, given our recent history together, I doubt if we could do a show together now without the cracks showing.

Then I admit that all of the above is just b.s., I'm enjoying myself, end of story. And I don't want the enjoyment to end. Shirley Valentine or *what*!

Ken has big wide breakfast cups. The day stretches ahead and I'm as close to being carefree as I've ever been.

What'll we do today? When we're finished, he collects the cups and brings them from the table over to the sink. Would you like to go for a drive in the country, the seaside, the mountains? But don't let me dictate. Maybe you have plans of your own.

Yeah, right. Plans.

I stretch luxuriously – that's how at home I am –

before I get up to help him. The question is, I say back, what would you be doing if I wasn't here, cluttering up your apartment and your life?

I'd be lonely as hell. I'd tell myself this was a great life, this life of the ascetic, but I'd be lonely as hell.

I'd meant the question facetiously but he has this trick, Ken has, of whipping the ground from under you with his directness. It takes a while to get used to it. James's idea of a long conversation, unless he's in extremis, like he was in the hospital, would be 'There's no food in this place' or 'I'll get the Nite Link' or 'Have you the loan of a few bob?' He doesn't ask many questions that don't relate to his finances or his digestive system.

Ken's still waiting for me to reply. What about it so, have you plans?

I thought I'd take a plane to London, see a show in the West End before I have to be back to clean out a few offices at six o'clock tomorrow morning.

He ignores this. Would you like to spend the day together?

Sure. Why not. What about Mass?

I went this morning. I hope I didn't wake you going out.

Again he takes my breath away. My question had been facetious, it had never occurred to me that he was religious. Hardly anyone I know goes to Mass any more – even amongst the women at work it's usually only the ones over forty.

There's no point in being sarky with this guy.

An hour later we're driving out of Dublin across the M50 toll bridge.

Free*dom*. No California beach babe in her convertible could have felt as free as I did. As well as the giddy notion that no one on earth would be able to find me, before we left I insisted on paying to fill the tank with diesel and he let me. So now I'm not even obligated. This trip is on me.

I roll down the window. Hundreds of feet below us, the cloak of trees and vegetation along the Liffey Valley and the Strawberry Beds is as green as you'd see in a travelogue about the Mekong Delta. It's cloudy, but ahead of us, you wouldn't believe it, the sun is shafting a shining handful of rays on to the Dublin mountains. Real rays. The cover of *My First Missal*.

All this symbolism. What with James in a monastery and Ken here turning out to be a serious Christian, maybe it's time I looked into my own soul!

Where are we going?

I'm not pushed, he says back. I thought we'd just drive, find somewhere to stop, by a river maybe, have a picnic. Drive some more, get back before the rush hour, how's that sound? (Tea-time on Sundays is nearly worse than it is on weekdays. All those Sunday drivers. I suppose it's an indication of all this new affluence we keep hearing about on the radio.)

I settle back, take Sam on my lap and wallow in my new life. I wish we could go back to the city and start again. And again and again, like Groundhog Day. I want this day to last for ever.

We have our picnic by the canal in a village called Rathangan, just off the Curragh in Kildare. It's a lovely place, which has a river as well as the canal. I'm lolling on one elbow, daydreaming at the sky. Then Ken says, Since we're this far, why don't we go on to Derrybride? Beard the lion in his den.

What? That brings me upright quick enough – talk about a douche!

Your father. We'll drop in. Say hello.

We will not. Some other time.

Angela, he says softly, you're putting it off. I'll go with you, I'll support you.

I'm getting angry now. You're damned right I'm putting it off. Look, Ken, I appreciate your inviting me to stay in your apartment and all this – I wave my arm around the general scenery – but I really think––

You really think what, Angela? That I've no right to make suggestions like that? Of course I don't – but it's only a suggestion. He rolls over on his stomach, picks at the short grass. I think you should do this, otherwise you'll never have peace. However, if you don't have the bottle––

That did it, of course.

In order to be fair to Pius Crawford, I insisted on ringing first. We went to the public telephone box in Rathangan and got the home number from Directory Enquiries.

The temptation to hang up became stronger with each ring.

I heard the receiver being lifted, my stomach turned. Click. A child's voice. Well rehearsed. This is Esther Crawford speaking, thank you for calling. Pius, Dorothy, Angela, John, Matthew, Mark, Esther, Luke or Ruth are unable to take your call right now, please leave your name and number. If you wish to ring Pius Crawford about a property, the number is––

I hung up. I already had his office number. I march out of the box, my heart whacking against my ribs.

I got an answering machine. There's no one home. Satisfied now?

He's sitting on the bonnet of the van. He's let Sam out and the dog is nosing around in the gutter beside him. Why are you so angry, Angela?

Look, I say to him, why did you push me on this? What's it to you?

Do you really want an answer to that?

Given what I've discovered about his directness, I suspect maybe I shouldn't pursue this. Try me, I say cautiously.

I want to ask you to marry me, Angela. But not until you're free. And you're not going to be free until you've sorted out all the relationships which preoccupy you twenty-four hours a day. Your father being one of them. He says all of this without a flicker in his voice or in his eyes.

A proposal? Of marriage?

I can't take it in – certainly not when it's delivered like this and when I'm in a lather. And by the way where's Beetroot Man? The guy in front of me is as cool as the Antarctic, he doesn't even get down from the bonnet of the van.

Are you serious? My voice is hoarse.

Deadly.

We drive home in silence. Not the grand, warm, easy silence of before. This silence is so highly charged as to be uncomfortable. On my side, anyway. He doesn't seem to be all that bothered, dammit, he's certainly not behaving as though he's bothered, driving with one elbow relaxed in the open window frame beside him.

Why did what I say make you feel so threatened?

We're back in the apartment and I've just said I'm tired and that I need to get to bed early. I'm hovering near the bedroom door. It's only half past six.

He's leaning against the window-sill of the living room and, with the sky behind him, I can't properly read his expression.

I can't say why, I tell him. It just does, that's all – and, anyway, who's to say I feel threatened?

It can't be because you're afraid of commitment.

You're the queen of commitment. Current decisions about sex aside, I know you're comfortable with me.

Am I?

Yes, you are. He lifts himself off the window-sill. You know you are.

Well, I'm not that comfortable with you at the moment, I can certainly say that for definite. And you talk about when I'm free. You're not free.

I will be – but you're right, it was probably too soon to bring it up.

He walks towards the kitchen. If you don't want me to say what's on my mind, Angela, you shouldn't ask. I believe in telling the truth – you can't develop a relationship on any other basis, can you? Or I can't at any rate. Apart from anything else, truth is easier. Lying is an exhausting business, all that remembering what you said. Are you too tired to have something to eat?

With anyone else I would have huffed off into the bedroom, standing on my dignity, all that. I'd learned to my cost, however, that there was no point in playing the smallest game with Ken. Actually, I say, I'm very hungry. I allow myself a small glare. I didn't get to eat much at our picnic.

I'll make pasta, he goes. Sit down – or would you care to have a nap and I'll call you?

I'll wait, I say. Then, Since we're into truth and being straight, can I ask you something, Ken Sheils? When we met first you were always blushing. That doesn't sit right with the person you're showing me now.

I'm very shy, he says back, as he's organizing saucepans and spoons. I genuinely am. But when I know what I want, no matter what it is, I'm not shy any more. You'll probably find that I'll continue to blush if you introduce me to someone new but I don't think I'll ever blush with you again.

He switches on the cooker, I turn on the telly. I couldn't tell you to this day what came up on the screen.

A second proposal of marriage.

Ten minutes later. There's another thing I've got to ask you, Ken. What about the age difference? Are you not concerned that I'm eight years older than you?

The look he gives me over the counter which divides off the kitchen area is mocking. Come on, Angela, I'm surprised at you.

I'm not deflected. What's more – you asked for honesty – there's your iffiness about James. There can be no question about anything – *anything* – between us of a, well, of a permanent nature, without him.

Do you think I don't know that? He stops sieving tomatoes for a moment. Where James is concerned, I apologize for my initial reaction, I admit it was tactless, but you wouldn't have thanked me in the long run, would you, if I'd pretended it didn't matter? It'd have to have come out at some stage.

Behind him, the pasta boils over and he lowers the heat. As far as I'm concerned, what James has done in the past, no matter what it is, has nothing to do with what he could do or be in the future. From what you tell me the chap really could do with a few lucky breaks. I wish him nothing but happiness.

You've an answer for everything, haven't you?

No, he says quietly, I don't. I've as many questions as I have answers.

This conversation is wearing me out. I raise the volume on the television and pretend to be absorbed in it.

The pasta, when it comes, is very good, angel-hair, with a tomato-based sauce he makes himself once a week and keeps in the freezer part of his fridge. (I told you the man is so perfectly self-sufficient he'd make you sick.)

Am I getting the impression we're seriously considering my proposal? He's pouring the coffee after we've finished.

Unexpectedly, my stupid heart does a small fandango. I don't know, I say. (Am I being as honest as he is?)

Well, I have to say it's better than a no.

With all that had happened – and the coffee too, to be fair – it took me ages to get to sleep that night. At about one o'clock in the morning, I gave up temporarily, stole out to the kitchen and, by the light of the fridge alone, poured myself a glassful of milk. I looked across at the bed-chair as I tiptoed back to the bedroom but it was too dark to know whether or not I'd wakened him. I couldn't hear him either – if he's not awake, he's a very quiet sleeper.

Back in bed, I sipped the milk and reviewed the events of the day. The awayday in the car. Emotional mangles. James, Pius Crawford. Most momentous of all, the proposal.

You do the strangest things in the early hours, don't you? Before I could second guess myself, I took a biro and an old envelope out of my handbag which, the habit of a lifetime, I always keep beside my bed. Poised the pen. Right, I thought, no messing. Do it quickly. And no cheating – no Kenneth Sheils or Angela Rose Devines if it doesn't come out right the first time. It's got to be straight. And only once.

K-E-N-S-H-E-I-L-S.

Underneath, A-N-G-E-L-A-D-E-V-I-N-E.

I look at it. Try to guess the outcome, discover to my horror that now I desperately don't want it to come out wrong.

Now I'm thinking maybe I shouldn't do it at all. The lengths look so unbalanced. Could I just make it Kenneth? After all, that *is* his real name.

No. You promised no cheating.

I started to cross off the common letters, I was back at eleven years old, sixth class. Me and Patsy. He was left with four. Love Like Hate *Adore*. My hand shook as I began my own. Seven. The full shilling.

Love Like Hate Adore Kiss Court *Marry*.

Jesus.

I tore it up. Finished the milk. Turned off the light and lay there.

Jesus.

I was walking along Gardiner Street on my way back to the apartment after work the next morning, and was just approaching the entrance door to the block, when I heard my name being called. I turned around to find two Guards behind me — one of them the nice one from Kerry or Cork to whom I first reported the assault on James, the other talking into the walkie-talkie fixed to the belt across his chest.

Miss Devine — the Kerry one comes up to me. We've been looking for you at the address you gave us on Mountjoy Square. You've moved?

Temporarily, I go. You're out specially looking for me? For how long? Have you got someone for the assault?

He shakes his head, he looks troubled. No, I'm afraid not. And don't get the wrong impression, we're not out this morning specifically looking for you, so don't get alarmed. We're just on our regular foot-patrol. I recognized you because you and I have spoken before. He looks up at the apartment block. Is this where you're living now? Could we come in for a minute? We need to have a word with you.

The keys to the apartment begin to feel sweaty in my hand. Please — is there something wrong?

The Kerry Gárda glances at his colleague, who has finished talking into his little machine. Probably not, he says then. We just need to talk to you. It would really be better if we came in.

I know Ken has to have gone. I'm not sure how he'd feel.

Come in.

They're huge in the little living room, even bigger than the detectives who loomed in Reddy's place. At least there were high ceilings there. What's this about? I look from one to the other.

We found a motorbike registered in your brother's name.

Where? When? I have immediate visions of James and his bike being fished out of the Liffey. Christ, where did you find it, tell me?

Don't be alarmed, please, Miss Devine. It could have been stolen. Where is your brother? He didn't miss it? He glances around the apartment.

You *know* where he is — I asked if it was OK for him to go to Mount Melleray.

Incomprehension on both faces.

Don't you write down these things? I went up and asked would it be OK if he went to a monastery for a while, because of the counselling he was supposed to have. When did you find the bike? Where?

Last Thursday evening.

Oh, God. (And I was out gallivanting . . .)

When did you last see him, mam? the other Guard asks gently.

On the Wednesday, around lunch-time. He was bringing the bike back to the shop where we bought it, or at least that's— He was wheeling it, he still had the cast on his arm — I knew I shouldn't have let him do it on his own. Why didn't you tell me until now? This is Monday morning.

We called to your place both on the Thursday night

and again on the Friday, Miss Devine. No one there seemed to know where you had gone.

I have to sit down. Already the recriminations are crashing around in my brain. Why didn't I mind him? Why didn't I see him to the bus? Why did I let my father talk me into this Mount Melleray thing in the first place? Why didn't I keep him safe by me?

They tell me that the motorbike was found fifty yards from our flat, around the corner outside Belvedere College. It was reported on the Thursday by one of the priests because it was partially blocking one of the entrance gates.

I grab on to this as good news. I'm being silly getting into a tizzy like this. Being James, he abandoned the bike because it was too much trouble to wheel it all the way to the shop. He's more than likely still snug in his bed in the monastery.

The Guards use Ken's telephone to ring Mount Melleray.

James did not show up at the monastery on that Wednesday. He is not there.

✦ Thirty-Eight ✦

You can get used to anything.

That encounter with the two Guards happened on Monday, 15 July. Today is Thursday, 22 August and Ken Sheils and I are entering the school to find out what grades we got in Leaving Cert English. It seems highly irrelevant.

Dwayne, the so-called rock star, is in through the doorway just ahead of Ken and me. Mr Elliott is there, of course, and the other teachers. When he sees me, Éibhear Ó Súilleabháin, the Irish teacher — who, by the way, is *not* wearing a jumper today — comes straight over to me and sympathizes with my plight. Irish people are pretty good that way, I find. They're not embarrassed about genuine tragedy.

Ken gets a B3. I get a B1.

A B1 in English. It's practically unheard of. Mr Elliott is beaming at me and sympathizing with me all at once. Ken doesn't know what to say to me. I'd always thought he was much better than me at English. I'd been telling him that over and over again. But, to be fair, he seems genuinely pleased for me.

The piece of paper you get is a horrible flimsy thing. You can barely read the computer printing on it. All that sweat and worry and work and the outcome is this puny thing.

I can't take it in. B1. There's another B3 but she, Ken and I are the only Bs. The class got mostly Ds with a couple of C2s and one C1. There wasn't a single fail. I'm the star.

Let's go home, I say to Ken.

My first call that first day when we found out James had not turned up at the monastery was to Pius Crawford. He'd heard nothing. He tried to engage me in talk but I cut him off. I said I'd ring again. This time I left Ken's number.

My brain was speeding that morning, as you can imagine, as I was dialling the next number, Patrice Murphy's. An answering machine. It's still only half nine, said the Kerry Guard, these fellas keep bankers' hours, we'll try again in a few minutes.

I have to say that these two could not have been nicer or more helpful. They helped me to trace James's friend, Ferdia, through the computer world in Dublin, which is relatively small. (It helped that the boy's name was unusual.) Then, through Ferdia, I managed to contact all of the other members of their gang who hung around together. Including girls and their girlfriends. Nothing.

Meanwhile, the Guards trawled through all the places they usually trawl on occasions like this. Focus Point, Simon, the Samaritans, the Salvation Army, all the homeless hostels. Bed-and-breakfast registers – after I told them he had a fair amount of money when he left. Nothing. No trace.

They came back and back. Did he have a bank account – no – a credit card – no – anything at all, the use of which could possibly leave some sort of trail, passport? No.

James had vanished.

The holy all of it is that he is nineteen, he's of age. If he wants to disappear he is perfectly entitled to do so.

If the worst hadn't come to pass — and, of course, that was what we were all thinking but not saying — he could be anywhere within the European Union. Almost anywhere. They can still trace you going through borders, apparently. Except from here to the UK. Which made it the most likely.

The tabloids were predictable. SEX ASSAULT YOUTH MISSING. At least I didn't get as upset this time. Maybe I'm becoming immune.

Others aren't. As a sidebar (thank you, O. J. Simpson) guess who turned up at the deli one Saturday morning — I forget whether it was a week or two weeks ago.

I'm serving a Samantha. Over her shoulder I see this grey-faced man in a suit, unusual enough on a Saturday morning. He's neat but he looks wretched, puffy face, as though he's been crying. Which he probably has. It's Pius.

The deli owner lets me go on a break, although we're busy.

We go for a cup of coffee in a fast-food place a few doors down from where I work. Pius doesn't beat about the bush. Immediately we sit down, he shows me a newspaper — one of the local *Eagles* or *Bugles* or whatever it's called. CATHOLIC RIGHTS FOUNDER'S LOVE CHILD. Page One.

I read the first few lines. A bizarre twist to the mysterious tale of the convicted rapist who has now disappeared—

I give it back to him. I couldn't be bothered reading the rest. You ascend into the most extraordinary state when someone goes missing on you in unexplained circumstances, the best way I can describe it is it's like you're permanently dreaming. You don't believe it —

you simply can't believe it. It hasn't happened, he's been there all the time, you just haven't been able to put your finger on him. You wake up, you realize it has happened. Then nothing else matters, nothing else at all.

Pius is waiting for my reaction to his page-one story. I don't give a sugar about Pius. Maybe I will again in the future. After we find James.

That's dreadful for you, I say. I'm sorry that's happened.

You have to tell me who originally told you how to find me so I can go after the effer (he didn't say effer) who sold me out. I notice his accent has broadened.

Why? I ask him. What's the difference? It's not going to change the story – the story's true, isn't it?

He clutches my wrist. Please, Angela, in the name of God, please . . . I have to – I have to do something. I can't just sit at home and let them do this to me, my business, Dorothy.

I don't think I'm a hard-hearted woman but I find this tiresome. Isn't that weird? This guy has had sway over my emotions and my imagination since I began to think for myself. Thirty years or more. Right now, he could be Wallace or Gromit or Homer Simpson. A cartoon.

Nothing matters in my life now except getting from one day to the next and finding James. Or what happened to James. I'm sorry, Mr Crawford, I say, but as you know I gave my word.

It was that effer Mick Flanagan, wasn't it? I've traced it.

No! I told you.

A shred of memory concerning the police station. The younger Guard, all ears.

But maybe that's not fair. My experience with the Guards has been very good. Anyway, whether he did or he didn't is irrelevant. I'm sorry, Mr Crawford, I say firmly, for the last time, I can't tell you who told me. But now that we're talking like this, on neutral territory, so to speak, can you tell me something?

What?

Why did you hide from my mother when she was calling for you outside your house?

He stares at me, this big, handsome man. His eyes protrude slightly, I hadn't noticed that the last time. They're not ugly or anything, or even very remarkable. Just something I observe now. I – I couldn't he goes. My parents, my family—

I gaze back at him. I'm trying to get back those feelings of urgency. My mother. My father. My mother and father together producing me. This is who I am.

It doesn't work. Detachment is a terrible thing. I stand up. We're awfully busy, I'm afraid I'll have to go back.

You're not going to help me?

I can't see what I can do – honestly, I really can't. I won't make things worse for you by going near you again if that'll help. Unless I need to for some reason. And I certainly can't see any reason at the moment.

He stares up at me. He's baffled. Poor Pius.

I repeat it – I have to go now.

I leave the coffee shop. When I look back, he hasn't stood up yet. I realized something I had up to then refused to admit – I'd been holding off on it because letting go of a lifelong fantasy is not easy. What I realized took approximately one brutal second. It wasn't only him, it was her as well. They were the exact wrong pair to fall in love. One was as weak as the other.

It killed me finally to acknowledge what I'd probably known deep in my heart for a long time.

No, that's an exaggeration, I was already going in the door of the coffee shop. I didn't die.

I hope to God he can work things out at home. And

some time in the future I will contact him again. In better circumstances. As I remarked before, there's a whole family down there for me. I'd hate to let them go completely.

I kept going those first few weeks by being busy. Busy with James as a project. I still had a fair bit of money left so I took time off the cleaning job in order to concentrate. I have to say they were very understanding at the company. (Although Furry Slippers' reaction could only be guessed at . . .)

At my suggestion, RTE Radio put out an appeal at the end of their news bulletins for him to contact me – or for anyone who had any information about him to contact me or any Gárda station. Nothing. *Crimeline* will be doing a reconstruction of his last movements when it comes back into the autumn schedules. Isn't it ironic? Now I'm courting the media. Or some of it. The Guards are quite hopeful about the programme producing some results.

The days do turn into weeks. I'm back at work and still living at Ken's place. There's no point in moving now, he said to me, after he came home from work that first day, 15 July. Why don't you wait until things settle down a bit? Anyway, you'll need a base with a telephone. Next afternoon, he went one better, bought me a mobile phone and a spare battery. It hasn't been of much use to me so far but I change the batteries religiously and keep it on at all times, day and night. Stupid. James couldn't possibly ring me on it.

Ken's absolutely convinced James is still alive. I'm hanging on to that. You know how direct and honest Ken is. He wouldn't say it unless he believed it.

I don't know what to believe myself during my more lucid moments. Some days I get very down and think the worst. Horrible pictures lodge in my mind, he's being fished out of the Liffey, there's water spewing out of his nose and mouth. He's washed up on Dollymount Strand, missing fingers and toes, his skull grinning. He's bobbing about, all bloated, in the middle of the Irish Sea — you hear on the news about people going over the sides of ferries. I don't know why I keep seeing him in water. After all, fire is my big bugbear.

He's been murdered. Her brothers and her father were waiting for him that last Wednesday dinnertime. They ambushed him and now he's lying in a shallow grave somewhere in the Dublin mountains.

I mentioned this to the Guards and they said they'd keep it in mind. I gather they showed the anonymous letter to the Maddens — who denied all knowledge. Well, they would, wouldn't they?

I feel sometimes his disappearance is a judgement on me. I wasn't strong enough, good enough, strict enough, loving enough, something enough. God is whipping me back in line. Ken does his best to knock that out of me, sometimes he wins, sometimes he doesn't.

On my good days I see James walking free in London. Maybe working in a pub. (I refuse to contemplate him sleeping in a doorway . . . I utterly refuse. You know how I feel about the appalling vista of homelessness.) Maybe he got on a ship. Maybe he's in South America or Australia.

I rack my brains to try to remember anything he might have been interested in — by now his money would be gone and he'd need a job. Up to now I've been able to think of nothing except motorbikes and television. I tried all the courier firms, then all the motorbike shops in town. I rang RTE. Once I told them who I was and why I was enquiring, they were solicitous. But they'd hired no staff recently and they don't take unskilled people on spec. They recruit through advertising and they hadn't had any competitions that he could possibly have been eligible for. I wanted to ring the BBC but Ken talked me out of it. I mean, where would you start with the BBC?

In case he was lying low and needed simply a subsistence job, I trekked around the security firms (although, given his record, even I knew there was little chance there) and the all-night garages and shops. I spent one whole week walking around department stores and fast-food shops, showing a photograph of him that Ferdia gave me and asking the staff if they'd seen him.

For a while — and I still half harbour this notion — I believed that he'd won the Lotto and was going around the world in high style. Remember the receipt he pulled out of his inside pocket? The one on which he wrote Ken's address?

Well, why not?

I went into the National Lottery office in Abbey Street. Like everyone else I approached, they went out of their way to help, but no, there had been no anonymous winners fitting James's description.

I pray, sort of. It's probably just superstition. Mammy told me once (I think Francesca was there too) that a lot of people in all kinds of different religions believe that each star in the sky is a different guardian angel. So I've started praying to James's guardian angel and to my own, asking them to talk to each other, bring him home to me. Angel of God, my guardian dear, to whom God's love commits me here, ever this day be at my side, to light and guard to rule and guide.

Silly childish stuff, but it does help, particularly when I can't sleep. I concentrate on Mammy's face, ask her to look after him, to find him, make him safe. Starlight, starbright, Mammy, you didn't do much for him in life, please help him now . . .

Et cetera.

In the middle of it all, everyone else's life goes on, you

have to try to fit in. You have to go to work, you have to look at television and eat and talk about other things. You can't live on the edge twenty-four hours a day, not after the first few weeks anyway, it's just not possible.

I even went out to welcome home Michelle Smith and our Olympic team at the beginning of this month. One of the reasons I went was because, weather-wise, the day was probably the worst of this or any other summer, so I felt that very few would turn out for them. You'd hate to let them down.

I was right. Michelle, God love her, was such a game little soul – she's absolutely *tiny*, you know – all you could see was this streaming wet mophead peering out over the edge of the open-topped bus. You had to guess that she was holding up the four medals. Poor girl, she was wetter than she ever was in any swimming pool. And probably frozen. And for all her spunk, all she could see in O'Connell Street below her – at the beginning, anyway, where I was standing – was this row of empty crash barriers and a few hardy souls daring the elements from under a scattering of golf umbrellas.

You do all these ordinary things as if you're a living citizen of the world but you're doing them with the top millionth of your brain. All the rest of you is dead or concerned only with maybe this happened or maybe that happened, suppose we try here, we never thought of that before . . .

And the theories. The bloody endless speculation. Experts. Feature articles and interviews. Psychologists. Retired criminologists. As if you're not speculating enough yourself.

You also get into a state where you're constantly looking for signs, symbols and omens. For instance Ken has an English Usage book and in it, I came across the information that el or il at the end of a name means bright, shining or shining being. Or Angel. I started saying the angel prayers because I'm Angela. That was an omen — see?

Or I'd hear a song on the radio, California Dreamin', say. If I heard something about California on the news within a certain amount of time I'd remember the song, connect the two and be sure it would be a message that James was in California. I became so convinced for one whole day about this that I rang the American Embassy.

You get the picture. Believe it or not, I do find this kind of activity keeps me from going wholly insane.

You might imagine from what I said about the praying that the worst time is the middle of the night, but personally I find the worst time is when you're walking along a street and you see the back of some boy's neck and you're convinced it's James but when you run to catch up with him, there's no resemblance whatsoever. It's a sickening feeling. Or when you remember that we're talking about a boy who couldn't — *can't* — boil an egg for himself.

Some good things always come out of every situation, don't they, no matter how grim. The deep goodness of the people you ask to help. Support from unfortunate families in a similar situation with whom the Guards put me in touch. We all feel the same, you know. One woman's son has been missing for eighteen years — *eighteen years* — and still she waits for him to come home. She has total faith that he will. I hold on to that with her. James will come home.

Another good — or goodish — outcome was that Patsy heard the radio appeal and got back in contact with me.

She and Martin have done their best. He's utilized every contact he has, here, in the North, in Britain, even in Holland and Germany. He has a friend who's a printer — let's hope it's not Mr Madden, I didn't ask! — who printed up leaflets, and Martin and Patsy dropped them in every pub and club and fast-food restaurant in town. They keep inviting Ken and me up to their house for lunch or dinner, or just to drop in.

Patsy and I will never be as close as we were. We'll be friends, we are friends, and that'll never change. But although I've really tried to claw myself back emotionally to the time before the whole thing started so as to be able to pick up the pieces with her, it won't work. I keep seeing her face as she's holding out the original clipping about him and then her putting it on the table.

Eventually, only last week, she did go up to Reddy's house to retrieve her earring – I'd put it in an envelope and left it tucked in at the back of an old radiator in the hallway. I knew no one ever cleaned behind there. (Why didn't I just keep it for her? Remember the state I was in? And I didn't know if we were going to meet again – or even if I *wanted* to see her. Ever again.)

She came back, not only with the earring but with a couple of letters. One made me break down in floods. It was the letter I'd sent to James. Returned. Via Pius Crawford, to whom the Abbot had sent it. My father's note with it said he hoped I was all right and that he was praying for me.

When I managed to pull myself together, I could only stare stupidly at the other one. I nearly laughed, to tell you the truth. I'd been selected to go on *Fame and Fortune* with Marty Whelan. Several weeks ago. I'd forgotten to change Reddy's address to Ken's when I posted the bloody card.

I tore up the letter, which didn't cost me a moment's regret. (Anyhow, could you imagine me on television in my present state, giggling and laughing with Marty Whelan? And who's rooting for you at home, Angela?)

This is the most surprising revelation within a situation

like this. All inessentials fall away. All that stupid old guff
about houses and roses around the door and winning the
quarter of a million? All gone. If I had James back I'd live
with him in a dog kennel. As for taking revenge on the
Maddens? I don't *care* that they sic'd the media on us or if
it was the brother who beat James up. I'd pave their
garden paths with flowers if they could arrange it that I
could see him slouching towards me across Mountjoy
Square.

At least the Maddens had genuine cause for grievance.
I do have difficulty forgiving some others, though – I'm
sure I don't have to spell it out for you who they are.
They just never let go, do they? The latest headline – I
don't read the actual articles because they always
regurgitate the whole story – was about Rosemary
getting engaged. HAPPINESS AT LAST FOR SEX ASSAULT
HEROINE.

Most times, I'm actually too busy to dwell on any
wrongs done to us, real or imagined. If I become bitter,
the biggest loser will be me, isn't that right? The world
will move on and I'll still be stuck.

I still won't totally let go of my Lotto theory. I mean,
if people are anonymous, they're anonymous, aren't
they? The Lotto people might genuinely not know that
he was the one. Ken and I discuss this endlessly. Or,
rather, I talk about it and Ken listens. He points out,
with good reason, that they have to make out the cheque
to a real person. I believe, even though they say they
don't do this, that if someone really insists on anonymity
and demands it, that they can make out the cheque to
cash.

You have to believe in something.

So that's where I stand at the moment. As for Ken and
me? On hold. We did have sex a couple of times and it
was successful enough, I have to say that. I was able to let

go a bit and forget for a few minutes. He was right about one thing, it can be comforting.

But he still has his sleeping arrangements and I have mine. We've developed a routine, very quickly as a matter of fact, but where I'm concerned everything still centres around James. I think it always will – even after we get some definite news one way or the other.

Funnily enough, I think more so than if he was actually here. It's sort of a life sentence.

Ken still thinks that if I can come to terms with whatever has happened or will happen to James, and if I can sort out me and my father – which I intend to sometime in the future (I think) – we should get married. He also says I should go and get some sort of help. Psychological help, counselling or something.

I can't at the moment, I'm too busy.

He says he's prepared to wait a lifetime for me.

Who knows?

Maybe.

The next hurdle is the book – or books. Ken says he'll be there this time to protect me. And maybe, you never know, something good might turn up out of one or both of them in the end. Unlike radio and television programmes, which are nine-day wonders, or newspapers, which end up as pulp for toilet paper, books generally have a long shelf life. I'd imagine they'll use that photograph of James, with or without the little coffin over his eyes. Someone might go into a library some day, somewhere in the world, and recognize him. Such developments do transpire, you know, you read about them every day.

DEIRDRE PURCELL

A Place of Stones

Pan Books   £5.99

*She was rescued from the black, icy Atlantic when she was only a
year old – the sole survivor of a doomed American charter flight.
She grew up in a fisherman's family, among the barren, wind-swept
rocks of Inisheer, on Ireland's stormy coast.*

Molly O'Brien, beautiful Irish actress rose to command the
attention of the world from the stages of Dublin, London and
New York. But behind her glittering success lay a heartache she
could not resolve: and a longing to return to uncover a family's
tragic secret, buried forever in the island place of stones . . .

A Place of Stones
. . . a magnificent portrait of family love and tragedy.

'She writes like a dream . . . this is a real story, told
with simplicity, compassion and a lyrical tenderness. I
read it with joy'
Marie Joseph

'It is as if Deirdre Purcell opened a Pandora's box of
ideas and writing talent, and threw a great amount of
each into her first novel'
Irish Independent

'A big, fat satisfying book . . . all the ingredients of
romantic storytelling are there'
Sunday Independent

'Beautifully crafted . . . a gripping love story'
Sunday Tribune

'A superb first novel'
Annabel

DEIRDRE PURCELL

That Childhood Country

Pan Books   £5.99

They were two young lovers who met by chance on a blazing summer's afternoon near Drumboola in Ireland. The passion which ignited between them that day became an obsession which would dominate their lives . . .

For Rose O'Beirne Moffat, sole inheritor of her father's estate, the cruel parting from her first love brought heartache and a lifelong search for happiness. For John Flynn, forced by poverty to emigrate to Canada, nothing would erase the memory of his forbidden Rose. Across two continents and the long sweep of years, love returns to haunt them from their beautiful childhood country . . .

'Deirdre Purcell . . . scores full marks for compulsion'
She

'. . . tense and racy, it kept this insomniac enthralled till dawn'
Sunday Independent

Praise for Deirdre Purcell's Irish Number 1 bestseller,
A PLACE OF STONES

'An unputdownable story of Irish life and love'
Maeve Binchy

DEIRDRE PURCELL

Falling for a Dancer

Pan Books   £5.99

If the bus hadn't broken down that August afternoon on the road between Dublin and Cork City, Elizabeth would never have met George, the travelling actor who almost destroyed her life . . .

Seduced by the raffish charm of George Gallaher, yet bound by the restrictions of pre-war Ireland, Elizabeth Sullivan is forced to marry another man. Trapped with him in a remote landscape of the Beara peninsula, it is only a matter of time before her sexuality catapults her towards catastrophe, through which, paradoxically, her passion can at last run free.

'An excellent story illuminated with flashes of lyricism and with real insight into female sexuality'
Sunday Times

Now a major BBC television series

DEIRDRE PURCELL

Francey

Pan Books   £5.99

For almost two decades Francey Sullivan has fantasized about his absent actor-father. Having met him only once, he remembers George Gallaher as imposing and exotic. But when he finds him at last, Francey discovers a great deal more than he bargained for . . .

George, still charming and opportunistic, has just buried his rich American wife, Jool. Present at the post-funeral gathering are Francey's half-brother, the watchful, chameleon-like Colin Mannering, and his mysterious wife, Fleur. Francey immediately falls in love with her, but nothing prepares him for the shock that Jool has devised from beyond the grave . . .

Filled with romance, suspense and action, *Francey* is Deirdre Purcell at her storytelling best.

'The rollicking pace of Deirdre Purcell's fourth novel is established without delay . . . and never sags for a second'
Irish Times

'She delivers . . . with panache and warmth'
Madeleine Keane

'Energy, pace and strong storytelling . . . the author's choice of male central characters is a refreshing change'
Elizabeth Buchan
Mail on Sunday